FAR FROM THE MADDING CROWD

Thomas Hardy was born on 2 June 1840 at Higher Bockhampton in Dorset. His father was a stonemason. Hardy attended school in Dorchester and then trained as an architect. In 1868 his work took him to St Juliot's church in Cornwall where he met his wife-to-be, Emma. His first novel, *The Poor Man and the Lady*, was rejected by publishers but *Desperate Remedies* was published in 1871 and this was rapidly followed by *Under the Greenwood Tree* (1872), *A Pair of Blue Eyes* (1873) and *Far from the Madding Crowd* (1874). He also wrote many other novels, poems and short stories. *Tess of the D'Urbervilles* was published in 1891 and he published his final novel, *Jude the Obscure*, in 1895. Hardy was awarded the Order of Merit in 1910 and the gold medal of the Royal Society of Literature in 1912. Emma died in 1912 and Hardy married his second wife, Florence, in 1914. Thomas Hardy died on 11 January 1928.

OTHER NOVELS BY THOMAS HARDY

Desperate Remedies

Under the Greenwood Tree

A Pair of Blue Eyes

The Hand of Ethelberta

The Return of the Native

The Trumpet-Major

A Laodicean

Two on a Tower

The Mayor of Casterbridge

The Woodlanders

The Well-Beloved

Tess of the D'Urbervilles

Jude the Obscure

THOMAS HARDY

Far From the Madding Crowd

VINTAGE BOOKS
London

Published by Vintage 2010

2 4 6 8 10 9 7 5 3 1

Far From the Madding Crowd was first published in 1874

Vintage
Random House, 20 Vauxhall Bridge Road,
London SW1V 2SA

www.vintage-classics.info

Addresses for companies within The Random House Group Limited
can be found at: www.randomhouse.co.uk/offices.htm

The Random House Group Limited Reg. No. 954009

A CIP catalogue record for this book
is available from the British Library

ISBN 9780099518976

The Random House Group Limited supports The Forest
Stewardship Council (FSC), the leading international forest
certification organisation. All our titles that are printed on
Greenpeace approved FSC certified paper carry the FSC logo.
Our paper procurement policy can be found at:
www.rbooks.co.uk/environment

Printed and bound in Great Britain by
CPI Cox & Wyman, Reading RG1 8EX

PREFACE

In reprinting this story for a new edition I am reminded that it was in the chapters of 'Far From the Madding Crowd', as they appeared month by month in a popular magazine, that I first ventured to adopt the word 'Wessex' from the pages of early English history, and give it a fictitious significance as the existing name of the district once included in that extinct kingdom. The series of novels I projected being mainly of the kind called local, they seemed to require a territorial definition of some sort to lend unity to their scene. Finding that the area of a single county did not afford a canvas large enough for this purpose, and that there were objections to an invented name, I disinterred the old one. The region designated was known but vaguely, and I was often asked even by educated people where it lay. However, the press and the public were kind enough to welcome the fanciful plan, and willingly joined me in the anachronism of imagining a Wessex population living under Queen Victoria; – a modern Wessex of railways, the penny post, mowing and reaping machines, union work-houses, lucifer matches, labourers who could read and write, and National school children. But I believe I am correct in stating that, until the existence of this contemporaneous Wessex in place of the usual counties was announced in the present story, in 1874, it had never been heard of in fiction and current speech, if at all, and that the expression, 'a Wessex peasant', or 'a Wessex custom', would theretofore have been taken to refer to nothing later in date than the Norman Conquest.

I did not anticipate that this application of the word to modern story would extend outside the chapters of these particular chronicles. But it was soon taken up elsewhere, the first to adopt it being the now defunct *Examiner*, which, in the impression bearing date July 15, 1876, entitled one of its articles 'The Wessex Labourer', the article turning out to be no dissertation on farming during the Heptarchy, but on the modern peasant of the southwest counties.

Since then the appellation which I had thought to reserve

to the horizons and landscapes of a partly real, partly dream-country, has become more and more popular as a practical provincial definition; and the dream-country has, by degrees, solidified into a utilitarian region which people can go to, take a house in, and write to the papers from. But I ask all good and idealistic readers to forget this, and to refuse steadfastly to believe that there are any inhabitants of a Victorian Wessex outside these volumes in which their lives and conversations are detailed.

Moreover, the village called Weatherbury, wherein the scenes of the present story of the series are for the most part laid, would perhaps be hardly discernible by the explorer, without help, in any existing place nowadays; though at the time, comparatively recent, at which the tale was written, a sufficient reality to meet the descriptions, both of backgrounds and per-sonages, might have been traced easily enough. The church remains, by great good fortune, unrestored and intact* and a few of the old houses; but the ancient malt-house, which was formerly so characteristic of the parish, has been pulled down these twenty years; also most of the thatched and dormered cottages that were once lifeholds. The heroine's fine old Jaco-bean house would be found in the story to have taken a witch's ride of a mile or more from its actual position; though with that difference its features are described as they still show themselves to the sun and moonlight. The game of prisoner's-base, which not so long ago seemed to enjoy a perennial vitality in front of the worn-out stocks, may, so far as I can say, be entirely unknown to the rising generation of schoolboys there. The practice of divination by Bible and key, the regarding of valentines as things of serious import, the shearing-supper, the long smock-frocks, and the harvest-home, have, too, nearly disappeared in the wake of the old houses; and with them has gone, it is said, much of that love of fuddling to which the village at one time was notoriously prone. The change at the root of this has been the recent supplanting of the class of stationary cottagers, who carried on the local traditions and humours, by a population of more or less migratory labourers,

*This is no longer the case (1912).

which has led to a break of continuity in local history, more fatal than any other thing to the preservation of legend, folk-lore, close inter-social relations, and eccentric individualities. For these the indispensable conditions of existence are attachment to the soil of one particular spot by generation after generation.

1895–1902   T.H.

FAR FROM THE MADDING CROWD

CONTENTS

CHAPTER I

DESCRIPTION OF FARMER OAK – AN INCIDENT

WHEN Farmer Oak smiled, the corners of his mouth spread till they were within an unimportant distance of his ears, his eyes were reduced to chinks, and diverging wrinkles appeared round them, extending upon his countenance like the rays in a rudimentary sketch of the rising sun.

His Christian name was Gabriel, and on working days he was a young man of sound judgment, easy motions, proper dress, and general good character. On Sundays he was a man of misty views, rather given to postponing, and hampered by his best clothes and umbrella: upon the whole, one who felt himself to occupy morally that vast middle space of Laodicean neutrality which lay between the Communion people of the parish and the drunken section, – that is, he went to church, but yawned privately by the time the congregation reached the Nicene creed, and thought of what there would be for dinner when he meant to be listening to the sermon. Or, to state his character as it stood in the scale of public opinion, when his friends and critics were in tantrums, he was considered rather a bad man; when they were pleased, he was rather a good man; when they were neither, he was a man whose moral colour was a kind of pepper-and-salt mixture.

Since he lived six times as many working-days as Sundays, Oak's appearance in his old clothes was most peculiarly his own – the mental picture formed by his neighbours in imagining him being always dressed in that way. He wore a low-crowned felt hat, spread out at the base by tight jamming upon the head for security in high winds, and a coat like Dr. Johnson's; his lower extremities being encased in ordinary leather leggings and boots emphatically large, affording to each foot a roomy apartment so constructed that any wearer might stand in a river all day long and know nothing of damp – their maker being a conscientious man who endeavoured to compensate for any weakness in his cut by unstinted dimension and solidity.

Mr. Oak carried about him, by way of watch, what may be called a small silver clock; in other words, it was a watch as to shape and intention, and a small clock as to size. This instrument being several years older than Oak's grandfather, had the peculiarity of going either too fast or not at all. The smaller of its hands, too, occasionally slipped round on the pivot, and thus, though the minutes were told with precision, nobody could be quite certain of the hour they belonged to. The stopping peculiarity of his watch Oak remedied by thumps and shakes, and he escaped any evil consequences from the other two defects by constant comparisons with and observations of the sun and stars, and by pressing his face close to the glass of his neighbours' windows, till he could discern the hour marked by the green-faced time-keepers within. It may be mentioned that Oak's fob being difficult of access, by reason of its somewhat high situation in the waistband of his trousers (which also lay at a remote height under his waistcoat), the watch was as a necessity pulled out by throwing the body to one side, compressing the mouth and face to a mere mass of ruddy flesh on account of the exertion, and drawing up the watch by its chain, like a bucket from a well.

But some thoughtful persons, who had seen him walking across one of his fields on a certain December morning – sunny and exceedingly mild – might have regarded Gabriel Oak in other aspects than these. In his face one might notice that many of the hues and curves of youth had tarried on to manhood: there even remained in his remoter crannies some relics of the boy. His height and breadth would have been sufficient to make his presence imposing, had they been exhibited with due consideration. But there is a way some men have, rural and urban alike, for which the mind is more responsible than flesh and sinew: it is a way of curtailing their dimensions by their manner of showing them. And from a quiet modesty that would have become a vestal, which seemed continually to impress upon him that he had no great claim on the world's room, Oak walked unassumingly, and with a faintly perceptible bend, yet distinct from a bowing of the shoulders. This may be said to be a defect in an individual if he depends for his valuation more upon his appearance than upon his capacity to wear well, which Oak did not.

He had just reached the time of life at which 'young' is ceasing to be the prefix of 'man' in speaking of one. He was at the brightest period of masculine growth, for his intellect and his emotions were clearly separated: he had passed the time during which the influence of youth indiscriminately mingles them in the character of impulse, and he had not yet arrived at the stage wherein they become united again, in the character of prejudice, by the influence of a wife and family. In short, he was twenty-eight, and a bachelor.

The field he was in this morning sloped to a ridge called Norcombe Hill. Through a spur of this hill ran the highway between Emminster and Chalk-Newton. Casually glancing over the hedge, Oak saw coming down the incline before him an ornamental spring waggon, painted yellow and gaily marked, drawn by two horses, a waggoner walking alongside bearing a whip perpendicularly. The waggon was laden with household goods and window plants, and on the apex of the whole sat a woman, young and attractive. Gabriel had not beheld the sight for more than half a minute, when the vehicle was brought to a standstill just beneath his eyes.

'The tailboard of the waggon is gone, Miss,' said the waggoner.

'Then I heard it fall,' said the girl, in a soft, though not particularly low voice. 'I heard a noise I could not account for when we were coming up the hill.'

'I'll run back.'

'Do,' she answered.

The sensible horses stood perfectly still, and the waggoner's steps sank fainter and fainter in the distance.

The girl on the summit of the load sat motionless, surrounded by tables and chairs with their legs upwards, backed by an oak settle, and ornamented in front by pots of geraniums, myrtles, and cactuses, together with a caged canary – all probably from the windows of the house just vacated. There was also a cat in a willow basket, from the partly-opened lid of which she gazed with half-closed eyes, and affectionately surveyed the small birds around.

The handsome girl waited for some time idly in her place, and the only sound heard in the stillness was the hopping of the canary up and down the perches of its prison. Then she looked attentively downwards. It was not at the bird, nor at the cat; it was at an oblong package tied in paper, and lying between them. She turned her head to learn if the waggoner were coming. He was not yet in sight; and her eyes crept back to the package, her thoughts seeming to run upon what was inside it. At length she drew the article into her lap, and untied the paper covering; a small swing looking-glass was disclosed, in which she proceeded to survey herself attentively. She parted her lips and smiled.

It was a fine morning, and the sun lighted up to a scarlet glow the crimson jacket she wore, and painted a soft lustre upon her bright face and dark hair. The myrtles, geraniums, and cactuses packed around her were fresh and green, and at such a leafless season they invested the whole concern of horses, waggon, furniture, and girl with a peculiar vernal charm. What possessed her to indulge in such a performance in the sight of the sparrows, blackbirds, and unperceived farmer who were alone its spectators, – whether the smile began as a factitious one, to test her capacity in that art, – nobody knows; it ended certainly in a real smile. She blushed at herself, and seeing her reflection blush, blushed the more.

The change from the customary spot and necessary

occasion of such an act – from the dressing hour in a bedroom to a time of travelling out of doors – lent to the idle deed a novelty it did not intrinsically possess. The picture was a delicate one. Woman's prescriptive infirmity had stalked into the sunlight, which had clothed it in the freshness of an originality. A cynical inference was irresistible by Gabriel Oak as he regarded the scene, generous though he fain would have been. There was no necessity whatever for her looking in the glass. She did not adjust her hat, or pat her hair, or press a dimple into shape, or do one thing to signify that any such intention had been her motive in taking up the glass. She simply observed herself as a fair product of Nature in the feminine kind, her thoughts seeming to glide into far-off though likely dramas in which men would play a part – vistas of probable triumphs – the smiles being of a phase suggesting that hearts were imagined as lost and won. Still, this was but conjecture, and the whole series of actions was so idly put forth as to make it rash to assert that intention had any part in them at all.

The waggoner's steps were heard returning. She put the glass in the paper, and the whole again into its place.

When the waggon had passed on, Gabriel withdrew from his point of espial, and descending into the road, followed the vehicle to the turnpike-gate some way beyond the bottom of the hill, where the object of his contemplation now halted for the payment of toll. About twenty steps still remained between him and the gate, when he heard a dispute. It was a difference concerning twopence between the persons with the waggon and the man at the toll-bar.

'Mis'ess's niece is upon the top of the things, and she says that's enough that I've offered ye, you great miser, and she won't pay any more.' These were the waggoner's words.

'Very well; then mis'ess's niece can't pass,' said the turnpike-keeper, closing the gate.

Oak looked from one to the other of the disputants, and fell into a reverie. There was something in the tone of twopence remarkably insignificant. Threepence had a definite value as money – it was an appreciable infringement on a day's wages, and, as such, a higgling matter; but twopence — 'Here,' he said, stepping forward and handing twopence to the gate-keeper; 'let the young woman pass.' He looked up at her then; she heard his words, and looked down.

Gabriel's features adhered throughout their form so exactly to the middle line between the beauty of St. John and the ugliness of Judas Iscariot, as represented in a window of the church he attended, that not a single lineament could be selected and called worthy either of distinction or notoriety. The red-jacketed and dark-haired maiden seemed to think so too, for she carelessly glanced over him, and told her man to drive on. She might have looked her thanks to Gabriel on a minute scale, but she did not speak them; more probably she felt none, for in gaining her a passage he had lost her her point, and we know how women take a favour of that kind.

The gatekeeper surveyed the retreating vehicle. 'That's a handsome maid,' he said to Oak.

'But she has her faults,' said Gabriel.

'True, farmer.'

'And the greatest of them is – well, what it is always.'

'Beating people down? ay, 'tis so.'

'O no.'

'What, then?'

Gabriel, perhaps a little piqued by the comely traveller's indifference, glanced back to where he had witnessed her performance over the hedge, and said, 'Vanity.'

CHAPTER II

NIGHT – THE FLOCK – AN INTERIOR –
ANOTHER INTERIOR

IT was nearly midnight on the eve of St. Thomas's, the shortest day in the year. A desolating wind wandered from the north over the hill whereon Oak had watched the yellow waggon and its occupant in the sunshine of a few days earlier.

Norcombe Hill – not far from lonely Toller-Down – was one of the spots which suggest to a passer-by that he is in the presence of a shape approaching the indestructible as nearly as any to be found on earth. It was a featureless convexity of chalk and soil – an ordinary specimen of those smoothly-outlined protuberances of the globe which may remain undisturbed on some great day of confusion, when far grander heights and dizzy granite precipices topple down.

The hill was covered on its northern side by an ancient and decaying plantation of beeches, whose upper verge formed a line over the crest, fringing its arched curve against the sky, like a mane. To-night these trees sheltered the southern slope from the keenest blasts, which smote the wood and floundered through it with a sound as of grumbling, or gushed over its crowning boughs in a weakened moan. The dry leaves in the ditch simmered and boiled in the same breezes, a tongue of air occasionally ferreting out a few, and sending them spinning across the grass. A group or two of the latest in date amongst the dead multitude had remained till this very mid-winter time on the twigs which bore them, and in falling rattled against the trunks with smart taps.

Between this half-wooded half-naked hill, and the vague still horizon that its summit indistinctly commanded, was a

11

mysterious sheet of fathomless shade — the sounds from which suggested that what it concealed bore some reduced resemblance to features here. The thin grasses, more or less coating the hill, were touched by the wind in breezes of differing powers, and almost of differing natures — one rubbing the blades heavily, another raking them piercingly, another brushing them like a soft broom. The instinctive act of humankind was to stand and listen, and learn how the trees on the right and the trees on the left wailed or chaunted to each other in the regular antiphonies of a cathedral choir; how hedges and other shapes to leeward then caught the note, lowering it to the tenderest sob; and how the hurrying gust then plunged into the south, to be heard no more.

The sky was clear — remarkably clear — and the twinkling of all the stars seemed to be but throbs of one body, timed by a common pulse. The North Star was directly in the wind's eye, and since evening the Bear had swung round it outwardly to the east, till he was now at a right angle with the meridian. A difference of colour in the stars — oftener read of than seen in England — was really perceptible here. The sovereign brilliancy of Sirius pierced the eye with a steely glitter, the star called Capella was yellow, Aldebaran and Betelgueux shone with a fiery red.

To persons standing alone on a hill during a clear midnight such as this, the roll of the world eastward is almost a palpable movement. The sensation may be caused by the panoramic glide of the stars past earthly objects, which is perceptible in a few minutes of stillness, or by the better outlook upon space that a hill affords, or by the wind, or by the solitude; but whatever be its origin the impression of riding along is vivid and abiding. The poetry of motion is a phrase much in use, and to enjoy the epic form of that gratification it is necessary to stand on a hill at a small hour of the night, and, having first expanded with a sense of difference from the mass of civilized mankind, who are dreamwrapt and disregardful of all such proceedings at this time, long and quietly watch your stately progress through the stars. After such a nocturnal reconnoitre it is hard to get back to earth, and to believe that the consciousness of such majestic speeding is derived from a tiny human frame.

Suddenly an unexpected series of sounds began to be heard in this place up against the sky. They had a clearness which was to be found nowhere in the wind, and a sequence which was to be found nowhere in nature. They were the notes of Farmer Oak's flute.

The tune was not floating unhindered into the open air: it seemed muffled in some way, and was altogether too curtailed in power to spread high or wide. It came from the direction of a small dark object under the plantation hedge – a shepherd's hut – now presenting an outline to which an uninitiated person might have been puzzled to attach either meaning or use.

The image as a whole was that of a small Noah's Ark on a small Ararat, allowing the traditionary outlines and general form of the Ark which are followed by toy-makers – and by these means are established in men's imaginations among their firmest, because earliest impressions – to pass as an approximate pattern. The hut stood on little wheels, which raised its floor about a foot from the ground. Such shepherds' huts are dragged into the fields when the lambing season comes on, to shelter the shepherd in his enforced nightly attendance.

It was only latterly that people had begun to call Gabriel 'Farmer' Oak. During the twelvemonth preceding this time he had been enabled by sustained efforts of industry and chronic good spirits to lease the small sheep-farm of which Norcombe Hill was a portion, and stock it with two hundred sheep. Previously he had been a bailiff for a short time, and earlier still a shepherd only, having from his childhood assisted his father in tending the flocks of large proprietors, till old Gabriel sank to rest.

This venture, unaided and alone, into the paths of farming as master and not as man, with an advance of sheep not yet paid for, was a critical juncture with Gabriel Oak, and he recognized his position clearly. The first movement in his new progress was the lambing of his ewes, and sheep having been his speciality from his youth, he wisely refrained from deputing the task of tending them at this season to a hireling or a novice.

The wind continued to beat about the corners of the hut, but the flute-playing ceased. A rectangular space of light appeared in the side of the hut, and in the opening the outline of Farmer Oak's figure. He carried a lantern in his hand, and closing the door behind him came forward and busied himself about this nook of the field for nearly twenty minutes, the lantern light appearing and disappearing here and there, and brightening him or darkening him as he stood before or behind it.

Oak's motions, though they had a quiet energy, were slow, and their deliberateness accorded well with his occupation. Fitness being the basis of beauty, nobody could have denied that his steady swings and turns in and about the flock had elements of grace. Yet, although if occasion demanded he could do or think a thing with as mercurial a dash as can the men of towns who are more to the manner born, his special power, morally, physically, and mentally, was static, owing little or nothing to momentum as a rule.

A close examination of the ground hereabout, even by the wan starlight only, revealed how a portion of what would have been casually called a wild slope had been appropriated by Farmer Oak for his great purpose this winter. Detached hurdles thatched with straw were stuck into the ground at various scattered points, amid and under which the whitish forms of his meek ewes moved and rustled. The ring of the sheep-bell, which had been silent during his absence, recommenced, in tones that had more mellowness than clearness, owing to an increasing growth of surrounding wool. This continued till Oak withdrew again from the flock. He returned to the hut, bringing in his arms a new-born lamb, consisting of four legs large enough for a full-grown sheep, united by a seemingly inconsiderable membrane about half the substance of the legs collectively, which constituted the animal's entire body just at present.

The little speck of life he placed on a wisp of hay before the small stove, where a can of milk was simmering. Oak extinguished the lantern by blowing into it and then pinching the snuff, the cot being lighted by a candle suspended by a twisted wire. A rather hard couch, formed of a few corn sacks thrown carelessly down, covered half the floor of this little habitation, and here the young man stretched himself along, loosened his woollen cravat, and closed his eyes. In about the time a person unaccustomed to bodily labour would have decided upon which side to lie, Farmer Oak was asleep.

The inside of the hut, as it now presented itself, was cosy and alluring, and the scarlet handful of fire in addition to the candle, reflecting its own genial colour upon whatever it could reach, flung associations of enjoyment even over utensils and tools. In the corner stood the sheep-crook, and along a shelf at one side were ranged bottles and canisters of the simple preparations pertaining to ovine surgery and physic; spirits of wine, turpentine, tar, magnesia, ginger, and castor-oil being the chief. On a triangular shelf across the corner stood bread, bacon, cheese, and a cup for ale or cider, which was supplied from a flagon beneath. Beside the provisions lay the flute, whose notes had lately been called forth by the lonely watcher to beguile a tedious hour. The house was ventilated by two round holes, like the lights of a ship's cabin, with wood slides.

The lamb, revived by the warmth, began to bleat, and the sound entered Gabriel's ears and brain with an instant meaning, as expected sounds will. Passing from the profoundest sleep to the most alert wakefulness with the same ease that had accompanied the reverse operation, he looked at his watch, found that the hour-hand had shifted again, put on his hat, took the lamb in his arms, and carried it into the darkness. After placing the little creature with its mother he stood and carefully examined the sky, to ascertain the time of night from the altitudes of the stars.

The Dog-star and Aldebaran, pointing to the restless Pleiades, were half-way up the Southern sky, and between them hung Orion, which gorgeous constellation never burnt more vividly than now, as it soared forth above the rim of the landscape. Castor and Pollux with their quiet shine were almost on the meridian: the barren and gloomy Square of Pegasus was creeping round to the north-west; far away through the plantation Vega sparkled like a lamp suspended amid the leafless trees, and Cassiopeia's chair stood daintily poised on the uppermost boughs.

'One o'clock,' said Gabriel.

Being a man not without a frequent consciousness that there was some charm in this life he led, he stood still after looking at the sky as a useful instrument, and regarded it in an appreciative spirit, as a work of art superlatively beautiful. For a moment he seemed impressed with the speaking loneliness of the scene, or rather with the complete abstraction from all its compass of the sights and sounds of man. Human shapes, interferences, troubles, and joys were all as if they were not, and there seemed to be on the shaded hemisphere of the globe no sentient being save himself; he could fancy them all gone round to the sunny side.

Occupied thus, with eyes stretched afar, Oak gradually perceived that what he had previously taken to be a star low down behind the outskirts of the plantation was in reality no such thing. It was an artificial light, almost close at hand.

To find themselves utterly alone at night where company is desirable and expected makes some people fearful; but a case more trying by far to the nerves is to discover some mysterious companionship when intuition, sensation, memory, analogy, testimony, probability, induction – every kind of evidence in the logician's list – have united to persuade consciousness that it is quite in isolation.

Farmer Oak went towards the plantation and pushed

through its lower boughs to the windy side. A dim mass under the slope reminded him that a shed occupied a place here, the site being a cutting into the slope of the hill, so that at its back part the roof was almost level with the ground. In front it was formed of boards nailed to posts and covered with tar as a preservative. Through crevices in the roof and side spread streaks and dots of light, a combination of which made the radiance that had attracted him. Oak stepped up behind, where, leaning down upon the roof and putting his eye close to a hole, he could see into the interior clearly.

The place contained two women and two cows. By the side of the latter a steaming bran-mash stood in a bucket. One of the women was past middle age. Her companion was apparently young and graceful; he could form no decided opinion upon her looks, her position being almost beneath his eye, so that he saw her in a bird's-eye view, as Milton's Satan first saw Paradise. She wore no bonnet or hat, but had enveloped herself in a large cloak, which was carelessly flung over her head as a covering.

'There, now we'll go home,' said the elder of the two, resting her knuckles upon her hips, and looking at their goings-on as a whole. 'I do hope Daisy will fetch round again now. I have never been more frightened in my life, but I don't mind breaking my rest if she recovers.'

The young woman, whose eyelids were apparently inclined to fall together on the smallest provocation of silence, yawned without parting her lips to any inconvenient extent, whereupon Gabriel caught the infection and slightly yawned in sympathy.

'I wish we were rich enough to pay a man to do these things,' she said.

'As we are not, we must do them ourselves,' said the other; 'for you must help me if you stay.'

'Well, my hat is gone, however,' continued the younger. 'It went over the hedge, I think. The idea of such a slight wind catching it.'

The cow standing erect was of the Devon breed, and was encased in a tight warm hide of rich Indian red, as absolutely uniform from eyes to tail as if the animal had been dipped in a dye of that colour, her long back being mathematically level. The other was spotted, grey and white. Beside her Oak now noticed a little calf about a day old, looking idiotically at the two women, which showed that it had not long been accustomed to the phenomenon of eyesight, and often turning to the lantern, which it apparently mistook for the moon, inherited instinct having as yet had little time for correction by experience. Between the sheep and the cows Lucina had been busy on Norcombe Hill lately.

'I think we had better send for some oatmeal,' said the elder woman; 'there's no more bran.'

'Yes, aunt; and I'll ride over for it as soon as it is light.'

'But there's no side-saddle.'

'I can ride on the other: trust me.'

Oak, upon hearing these remarks, became more curious to observe her features, but this prospect being denied him by the hooding effect of the cloak, and by his aërial position, he felt himself drawing upon his fancy for their details. In making even horizontal and clear inspections we colour and mould according to the wants within us whatever our eyes bring in. Had Gabriel been able from the first to get a distinct view of her countenance, his estimate of it as very handsome or slightly so would have been as his soul required a divinity at the moment or was ready supplied with one. Having for some time known the want of a satisfactory form to Wll an increasing void within him, his position moreover affording the widest scope for his fancy, he painted her a beauty.

By one of those whimsical coincidences in which Nature, like a busy mother, seems to spare a moment from her unremitting labours to turn and make her children smile, the girl now dropped the cloak, and forth tumbled ropes of black hair over a red jacket. Oak knew her instantly as the heroine of the yellow waggon, myrtles, and looking-glass: prosily, as the woman who owed him twopence.

They placed the calf beside its mother again, took up the lantern, and went out, the light sinking down the hill till it was no more than a nebula. Gabriel Oak returned to his flock.

CHAPTER III

A GIRL ON HORSEBACK – CONVERSATION

THE sluggish day began to break. Even its position terrestrially is one of the elements of a new interest, and for no particular reason save that the incident of the night had occurred there Oak went again into the plantation. Lingering and musing here he heard the steps of a horse at the foot of the hill, and soon there appeared in view an auburn pony with a girl on its back, ascending by the path leading past the cattle-shed. She was the young woman of the night before. Gabriel instantly thought of the hat she had mentioned as having lost in the wind; possibly she had come to look for it. He hastily scanned the ditch, and after walking about ten yards along it found the hat among the leaves. Gabriel took it in his hand and returned to his hut. Here he ensconced himself, and peeped through the loophole in the direction of the rider's approach.

She came up and looked around – then on the other side of the hedge. Gabriel was about to advance and restore the missing article, when an unexpected performance induced him to suspend the action for the present. The path, after passing the cowshed, bisected the plantation. It was not a bridle-path – merely a pedestrian's track, and the boughs spread horizontally at a height not greater than seven feet above the ground, which made it impossible to ride erect beneath them. The girl, who wore no riding-habit, looked around for a moment, as if to assure herself that all humanity was out of view, then dexterously dropped backwards flat upon the pony's back, her head over its tail, her feet against its shoulders, and her eyes to the sky. The rapidity of her glide into this position was that of a kingfisher – its noiselessness that of a hawk. Gabriel's eyes had scarcely been able to follow her. The tall lank pony seemed used to such doings, and ambled along unconcerned. Thus she passed under the level boughs.

The performer seemed quite at home anywhere between a horse's head and its tail, and the necessity for this abnormal attitude having ceased with the passage of the plantation, she began to adopt another, even more obviously convenient than the first. She had no side-saddle, and it was very apparent that a firm seat upon the smooth leather beneath her was unattainable sideways. Springing to her accustomed perpendicular like a bowed sapling, and satisfying herself that nobody was in sight, she seated herself in the manner demanded by the saddle, though hardly expected of the woman, and trotted off in the direction of Tewnell Mill.

Oak was amused, perhaps a little astonished, and hanging up the hat in his hut went again among his ewes. An hour passed, the girl returned, properly seated now, with a bag of bran in front of her. On nearing the cattle-shed she was met by a boy bringing a milking-pail, who held the reins of the pony whilst she slid off. The boy led away the horse, leaving the pail with the young woman.

Soon soft spirts alternating with loud spirts came in regular succession from within the shed, the obvious sounds of a person milking a cow. Gabriel took the lost hat in his hand, and waited beside the path she would follow in leaving the hill.

She came, the pail in one hand, hanging against her knee. The left arm was extended as a balance, enough of it being shown bare to make Oak wish that the event had happened in the summer, when the whole would have been revealed. There was a bright air and manner about her now, by which she seemed to imply that the desirability of her existence could not be questioned; and this rather saucy assumption failed in being offensive because a beholder felt it to be, upon the whole, true. Like exceptional emphasis in the tone of a genius, that which would have made mediocrity ridiculous was an addition to recognized power. It was with some surprise that she saw Gabriel's face rising like the moon behind the hedge.

The adjustment of the farmer's hazy conceptions of her charms to the portrait of herself she now presented him with was less a diminution than a difference. The starting-point selected by the judgment was her height. She seemed tall, but the pail was a small one, and the hedge diminutive; hence, making allowance for error by comparison with these, she could have been not above the height to be chosen by women as best. All features of consequence were severe and regular. It may have been observed by persons who go about the shires with eyes for beauty that in Englishwomen a classically-formed face is seldom found to be united with a figure of the same pattern, the highly-finished features being generally too large for the remainder of the frame; that a graceful and proportionate figure of eight heads usually goes off into random facial curves. Without throwing a Nymphean tissue over a milkmaid, let it be said that here criticism checked itself as out of place, and looked at her proportions with a long consciousness of pleasure. From the contours of her figure in its upper part she must have had a beautiful neck and shoulders; but since her infancy nobody had ever seen them. Had she been put into a low dress she would have run and thrust her head into a bush. Yet she was not a shy girl by any means; it was merely her instinct to draw the line dividing the seen from the unseen higher than they do it in towns.

That the girl's thoughts hovered about her face and form as soon as she caught Oak's eyes conning the same page was natural, and almost certain. The self-consciousness shown would have been vanity if a little more pronounced, dignity if a little less. Rays of male vision seem to have a tickling effect upon virgin faces in rural districts; she brushed hers with her hand, as if Gabriel had been irritating its pink surface by actual touch, and the free air of her previous movements was reduced at the same time to a chastened phase of itself. Yet it was the man who blushed, the maid not at all.

'I found a hat,' said Oak.

'It is mine,' said she, and, from a sense of proportion, kept down to a small smile an inclination to laugh distinctly: 'it flew away last night.'

'One o'clock this morning?'

'Well – it was.' She was surprised. 'How did you know?' she said.

'I was here.'

'You are Farmer Oak, are you not?'

'That or thereabouts. I'm lately come to this place.'

'A large farm?' she inquired, casting her eyes round, and swinging back her hair, which was black in the shaded hollows of its mass; but it being now an hour past sunrise the rays touched its prominent curves with a colour of their own.

'No; not large. About a hundred.' (In speaking of farms the word 'acres' is omitted by the natives, by analogy to such old expressions as 'a stag of ten.')

'I wanted my hat this morning,' she went on. 'I had to ride to Tewnell Mill.'

'Yes, you had.'

'How do you know?'

'I saw you.'

'Where?' she inquired, a misgiving bringing every muscle of her lineaments and frame to a standstill.

'Here – going through the plantation, and all down the hill,' said Farmer Oak, with an aspect excessively knowing with regard to some matter in his mind, as he gazed at a remote point in the direction named, and then turned back to meet his colloquist's eyes.

A perception caused him to withdraw his own eyes from hers as suddenly as if he had been caught in a theft. Recollection of the strange antics she had indulged in when passing through the trees was succeeded in the girl by a nettled palpitation, and that by a hot face. It was a time to see a woman redden who was not given to reddening as a rule; not a point in the milkmaid but was of the deepest rose-colour. From the

Maiden's Blush, through all varieties of the Provence down to the Crimson Tuscany the countenance of Oak's acquaintance quickly graduated; whereupon he, in considerateness, turned away his head.

The sympathetic man still looked the other way, and wondered when she would recover coolness sufficient to justify him in facing her again. He heard what seemed to be the flitting of a dead leaf upon the breeze, and looked. She had gone away.

With an air between that of Tragedy and Comedy Gabriel returned to his work.

Five mornings and evenings passed. The young woman came regularly to milk the healthy cow or to attend to the sick one, but never allowed her vision to stray in the direction of Oak's person. His want of tact had deeply offended her – not by seeing what he could not help, but by letting her know that he had seen it. For, as without law there is no sin, without eyes there is no indecorum; and she appeared to feel that Gabriel's espial had made her an indecorous woman without her own connivance. It was food for great regret with him; it was also a *contretemps* which touched into life a latent heat he had experienced in that direction.

The acquaintanceship might, however, have ended in a slow forgetting but for an incident which occurred at the end of the same week. One afternoon it began to freeze, and the frost increased with evening, which drew on like a stealthy tightening of bonds. It was a time when in cottages the breath of the sleepers freezes to the sheets; when round the drawing-room fire of a thick-walled mansion the sitters' backs are cold, even whilst their faces are all aglow. Many a small bird went to bed supperless that night among the bare boughs.

As the milking-hour drew near Oak kept his usual watch upon the cowshed. At last he felt cold, and shaking an extra quantity of bedding round the yeaning ewes he entered the hut and heaped more fuel upon the stove. The wind came in at the bottom of the door, and to prevent it Oak laid a sack there and wheeled the cot round a little more to the south. Then the wind spouted in at a ventilating hole – of which there was one on each side of the hut.

Gabriel had always known that when the fire was lighted and the door closed one of these must be kept open – that chosen being always on the side away from the wind. Closing the slide to windward he turned to open the other; on second thoughts the farmer considered that he would first sit down, leaving both closed for a minute or two, till the temperature of the hut was a little raised. He sat down.

His head began to ache in an unwonted manner and, fancying himself weary by reason of the broken rests of the preceding nights, Oak decided to get up, open the slide, and then allow himself to fall asleep. He fell asleep, however, without having performed the necessary preliminary.

How long he remained unconscious Gabriel never knew. During the first stages of his return to perception peculiar deeds seemed to be in course of enactment. His dog was howling, his head was aching fearfully – somebody was pulling him about, hands were loosening his neckerchief.

On opening his eyes he found that evening had sunk to dusk in a strange manner of unexpectedness. The young girl with the remarkably pleasant lips and white teeth was beside him. More than this – astonishingly more – his head was upon her lap, his face and neck were disagreeably wet, and her fingers were unbuttoning his collar.

'Whatever is the matter?' said Oak vacantly.

She seemed to experience mirth, but of too insignificant a kind to start enjoyment.

'Nothing now,' she answered, 'since you are not dead. It is a wonder you were not suffocated in this hut of yours.'

'Ah, the hut!' murmured Gabriel. 'I gave ten pounds for that hut. But I'll sell it, and sit under thatched hurdles as they did in old times, and curl up to sleep in a lock of straw! It played me nearly the same trick the other day!' Gabriel, by way of emphasis, brought down his fist upon the floor.

'It was not exactly the fault of the hut,' she observed in a tone which showed her to be that novelty among women – one who finished a thought before beginning the sentence which was to convey it. 'You should, I think, have considered, and not have been so foolish as to leave the slides closed.'

'Yes, I suppose I should,' said Oak absently. He was endeavouring to catch and appreciate the sensation of being thus with her, his head upon her dress, before the event passed on into the heap of bygone things. He wished she knew his impressions; but he would as soon have thought of carrying an odour in a net as of attempting to convey the intangibilities of his feeling in the coarse meshes of language. So he remained silent.

She made him sit up, and then Oak began wiping his face and shaking himself like a Samson. 'How can I thank 'ee?' he said at last gratefully, some of the natural rusty red having returned to his face.

'Oh, never mind that,' said the girl, smiling, and allowing her smile to hold good for Gabriel's next remark, whatever that might prove to be.

'How did you find me?'

'I heard your dog howling and scratching at the door of the hut when I came to the milking (it was so lucky, Daisy's milking is almost over for the season, and I shall not come here after this week or the next). The dog saw me, and jumped over to me, and laid hold of my skirt. I came across and looked round the hut the very first thing to see if the slides were closed. My uncle has a hut like this one, and I have heard him tell his shepherd not to go to sleep without leaving a slide open. I opened the door, and there you were like dead. I threw the milk over you, as there was no water, forgetting it was warm, and no use.'

'I wonder if I should have died?' Gabriel said in a low voice, which was rather meant to travel back to himself than to her.

'O no!' the girl replied. She seemed to prefer a less tragic probability; to have saved a man from death involved talk that should harmonize with the dignity of such a deed – and she shunned it.

'I believe you saved my life, Miss – I don't know your name. I know your aunt's, but not yours.'

'I would just as soon not tell it – rather not. There is no reason either why I should, as you probably will never have much to do with me.'

'Still I should like to know.'

'You can inquire at my aunt's – she will tell you.'

'My name is Gabriel Oak.'

'And mine isn't. You seem fond of yours in speaking it so decisively, Gabriel Oak.'

'You see, it is the only one I shall ever have, and I must make the most of it.'

'I always think mine sounds odd and disagreeable.'

'I should think you might soon get a new one.'

'Mercy! – how many opinions you keep about you concerning other people, Gabriel Oak.'

'Well, Miss – excuse the words – I thought you would like them. But I can't match you, I know, in mapping out my mind upon my tongue. I never was very clever in my inside. But I thank you. Come, give me your hand.'

She hesitated, somewhat disconcerted at Oak's old-fashioned earnest conclusion to a dialogue lightly carried on. 'Very well,' she said, and gave him her hand, compressing her lips to a demure impassivity. He held it but an instant, and in his fear of being too demonstrative, swerved to the opposite extreme, touching her fingers with the lightness of a small-hearted person.

'I am sorry,' he said the instant after.

'What for?'

'Letting your hand go so quick.'

'You may have it again if you like; there it is.' She gave him her hand again.

Oak held it longer this time – indeed, curiously long. 'How soft it is – being winter time, too – not chapped or rough, or anything!' he said.

'There – that's long enough,' said she, though without

pulling it away. 'But I suppose you are thinking you would like to kiss it? You may if you want to.'

'I wasn't thinking of any such thing,' said Gabriel simply; 'but I will —'

'That you won't!' She snatched back her hand.

Gabriel felt himself guilty of another want of tact.

'Now find out my name,' she said teasingly; and withdrew.

CHAPTER IV

GABRIEL'S RESOLVE – THE VISIT – THE MISTAKE

THE only superiority in women that is tolerable to the rival sex is, as a rule, that of the unconscious kind; but a superiority which recognizes itself may sometimes please by suggesting possibilities of capture to the subordinated man.

This well-favoured and comely girl soon made appreciable inroads upon the emotional constitution of young Farmer Oak.

Love being an extremely exacting usurer (a sense of exorbitant profit, spiritually, by an exchange of hearts, being at the bottom of pure passions, as that of exorbitant profit, bodily or materially, is at the bottom of those of lower atmosphere), every morning Oak's feelings were as sensitive as the money-market in calculations upon his chances. His dog waited for his meals in a way so like that in which Oak waited for the girl's presence that the farmer was quite struck with the resemblance, felt it lowering, and would not look at the dog. However, he continued to watch through the hedge for her regular coming, and thus his sentiments towards her were deepened without any corresponding effect being produced upon herself. Oak had nothing finished and ready to say as yet, and not being able to frame love phrases which end where they begin; passionate tales —

> – Full of sound and fury
> – Signifying nothing –

he said no word at all.

By making inquiries he found that the girl's name was Bathsheba Everdene, and that the cow would go dry in about seven days. He dreaded the eighth day.

At last the eighth day came. The cow had ceased to give

29

milk for that year, and Bathsheba Everdene came up the hill
no more. Gabriel had reached a pitch of existence he never
could have anticipated a short time before. He liked saying
'Bathsheba' as a private enjoyment instead of whistling; turned
over his taste to black hair, though he had sworn by brown ever
since he was a boy, isolated himself till the space he filled in the
public eye was contemptibly small. Love is a possible strength
in an actual weakness. Marriage transforms a distraction into a
support, the power of which should be, and happily often is, in
direct proportion to the degree of imbecility it supplants. Oak
began now to see light in this direction, and said to himself, 'I'll
make her my wife, or upon my soul I shall be good for nothing!'

All this while he was perplexing himself about an errand
on which he might consistently visit the cottage of Bathsheba's
aunt.

He found his opportunity in the death of a ewe, mother of
a living lamb. On a day which had a summer face and a winter
constitution – a fine January morning, where there was just
enough blue sky visible to make cheerfully-disposed people
wish for more, and an occasional gleam of silvery sunshine,
Oak put the lamb into a respectable Sunday basket, and
stalked across the fields to the house of Mrs. Hurst, the aunt –
George, the dog, walking behind, with a countenance of great
concern at the serious turn pastoral affairs seemed to be taking.

Gabriel had watched the blue wood-smoke curling from the
chimney with strange meditation. At evening he had fancifully
traced it down the chimney to the spot of its origin – seen the
hearth and Bathsheba beside it – beside it in her out-door
dress; for the clothes she had worn on the hill were by associ-
ation equally with her person included in the compass of his
affection; they seemed at this early time of his love a necessary
ingredient of the sweet mixture called Bathsheba Everdene.

He had made a toilet of a nicely-adjusted kind – of a nature
between the carefully neat and the carelessly ornate – of a
degree between fine-market-day and wet-Sunday selection. He
thoroughly cleaned his silver watch-chain with whiting, put

new lacing straps to his boots, looked to the brass eyelet-holes, went to the inmost heart of the plantation for a new walking-stick, and trimmed it vigorously on his way back; took a new handkerchief from the bottom of his clothes-box, put on the light waistcoat patterned all over with springs of an elegant flower uniting the beauties of both rose and lily without the defects of either, and used all the hair-oil he possessed upon his usually dry, sandy, and inextricably curly hair, till he had deepened it to a splendidly novel colour, between that of guano and Roman cement, making it stick to his head like mace round a nutmeg, or wet seaweed round a boulder after the ebb.

Nothing disturbed the stillness of the cottage save the chatter of a knot of sparrows on the eaves; one might fancy scandal and rumour to be no less the staple topic of these little coteries on roofs than of those under them. It seemed that the omen was an unpropitious one, for, as the rather untoward commencement of Oak's overtures, just as he arrived by the garden gate he saw a cat inside, going into various arched shapes and fiendish convulsions at the sight of his dog George. The dog took no notice, for he had arrived at an age at which all superfluous barking was cynically avoided as a waste of breath – in fact, he never barked even at the sheep except to order, when it was done with an absolutely neutral countenance, as a sort of Commination-service which, though offensive, had to be gone through once now and then to frighten the flock for their own good.

A voice came from behind some laurel-bushes into which the cat had run:

'Poor dear! Did a nasty brute of a dog want to kill it; – did he, poor dear!'

'I beg yer pardon,' said Oak to the voice, 'but George was walking on behind me with a temper as mild as milk.'

Almost before he had ceased speaking Oak was seized with a misgiving as to whose ear was the recipient of his answer. Nobody appeared, and he heard the person retreat among the bushes.

Gabriel meditated, and so deeply that he brought small furrows into his forehead by sheer force of reverie. Where the issue of an interview is as likely to be a vast change for the worse as for the better, any initial difference from expectation causes nipping sensations of failure. Oak went up to the door a little abashed: his mental rehearsal and the reality had had no common grounds of opening.

Bathsheba's aunt was indoors. 'Will you tell Miss Everdene that somebody would be glad to speak to her?' said Mr. Oak. (Calling one's self merely Somebody, without giving a name, is not to be taken as an example of the ill-breeding of the rural world: it springs from a refined modesty of which townspeople, with their cards and announcements, have no notion whatever.)

Bathsheba was out. The voice had evidently been hers.

'Will you come in, Mr. Oak?'

'Oh, thank 'ee,' said Gabriel, following her to the fireplace. 'I've brought a lamb for Miss Everdene. I thought she might like one to rear; girls do.'

'She might,' said Mrs. Hurst musingly; 'though she's only a visitor here. If you will wait a minute Bathsheba will be in.'

'Yes, I will wait,' said Gabriel, sitting down. 'The lamb isn't really the business I came about, Mrs. Hurst. In short, I was going to ask her if she'd like to be married.'

'And were you indeed?'

'Yes. Because if she would I should be very glad to marry her. D'ye know if she's got any other young man hanging about her at all?'

'Let me think,' said Mrs. Hurst, poking the fire superfluously . . . . 'Yes – bless you, ever so many young men. You see, Farmer Oak, she's so good-looking, and an excellent scholar besides – she was going to be a governess once, you know, only she was too wild. Not that her young men ever come here – but, Lord, in the nature of women, she must have a dozen!'

'That's unfortunate,' said Farmer Oak, contemplating a crack in the stone floor with sorrow. 'I'm only an every-day sort of man, and my only chance was in being the first comer. . . .

Well, there's no use in my waiting, for that was all I came about: so I'll take myself off home-along, Mrs. Hurst.'

When Gabriel had gone about two hundred yards along the down, he heard a 'hoi-hoi!' uttered behind him, in a piping note of more treble quality than that in which the exclamation usually embodies itself when shouted across a field. He looked round, and saw a girl racing after him, waving a white handkerchief.

Oak stood still – and the runner drew nearer. It was Bathsheba Everdene. Gabriel's colour deepened: hers was already deep, not, as it appeared, from emotion, but from running.

'Farmer Oak – I —' she said, pausing for want of breath, pulling up in front of him with a slanted face, and putting her hand to her side.

'I have just called to see you,' said Gabriel pending her further speech.

'Yes – I know that,' she said, panting like a robin, her face red and moist from her exertions, like a peony petal before the sun dries off the dew. 'I didn't know you had come to ask to have me, or I should have come in from the garden instantly. I ran after you to say – that my aunt made a mistake in sending you away from courting me.'

Gabriel expanded. 'I'm sorry to have made you run so fast, my dear,' he said, with a grateful sense of favours to come. 'Wait a bit till you've found your breath.'

'– It was quite a mistake – aunt's telling you I had a young man already,' Bathsheba went on. 'I haven't a sweetheart at all – and I never had one, and I thought that, as times go with women, it was *such* a pity to send you away thinking that I had several.'

'Really and truly I am glad to hear that!' said Farmer Oak, smiling one of his long special smiles, and blushing with gladness. He held out his hand to take hers, which, when she had eased her side by pressing it there, was prettily extended upon her bosom to still her loud-beating heart. Directly he seized it she put it behind her, so that it slipped through his fingers like an eel.

'I have a nice snug little farm,' said Gabriel, with half a degree less assurance than when he had seized her hand.

'Yes; you have.'

'A man has advanced me money to begin with, but still, it will soon be paid off, and though I am only an every-day sort of man I have got on a little since I was a boy.' Gabriel uttered 'a little' in a tone to show her that it was the complacent form of 'a great deal.' He continued: 'When we be married, I am quite sure I can work twice as hard as I do now.'

He went forward and stretched out his arm again. Bathsheba had overtaken him at a point beside which stood a low stunted holly bush, now laden with red berries. Seeing his advance take the form of an attitude threatening a possible enclosure, if not compression, of her person, she edged off round the bush.

'Why, Farmer Oak,' she said over the top, looking at him with rounded eyes, 'I never said I was going to marry you.'

'Well – that *is* a tale!' said Oak with dismay. 'To run after anybody like this, and then say you don't want him!'

'What I meant to tell you was only this,' she said eagerly, and yet half conscious of the absurdity of the position she had made for herself – 'that nobody has got me yet as a sweetheart, instead of my having a dozen, as my aunt said; I *hate* to be thought men's property in that way, though possibly I shall be had some day. Why, if I'd wanted you I shouldn't have run after you like this; 'twould have been the *forwardest* thing! But there was no harm in hurrying to correct a piece of false news that had been told you.'

'Oh, no – no harm at all.' But there is such a thing as being too generous in expressing a judgment impulsively, and Oak added with a more appreciative sense of all the circumstances – 'Well, I am not quite certain it was no harm.'

'Indeed, I hadn't time to think before starting whether I wanted to marry or not, for you'd have been gone over the hill.'

'Come,' said Gabriel, freshening again; 'think a minute or two. I'll wait a while, Miss Everdene. Will you marry me? Do, Bathsheba. I love you far more than common!'

'I'll try to think,' she observed rather more timorously; 'if I can think out of doors; my mind spreads away so.'

'But you can give a guess.'

'Then give me time.' Bathsheba looked thoughtfully into the distance, away from the direction in which Gabriel stood.

'I can make you happy,' said he to the back of her head, across the bush. 'You shall have a piano in a year or two – farmers' wives are getting to have pianos now – and I'll practise up the flute right well to play with you in the evenings.'

'Yes; I should like that.'

'And have one of those little ten-pound gigs for market – and nice flowers, and birds – cocks and hens I mean, because they be useful,' continued Gabriel, feeling balanced between poetry and practicality.

'I should like it very much.'

'And a frame for cucumbers – like a gentleman and lady.'

'Yes.'

'And when the wedding was over, we'd have it put in the newspaper list of marriages.'

'Dearly I should like that!'

'And the babies in the births – every man jack of 'em! And at home by the fire, whenever you look up, there I shall be – and whenever I look up, there will be you.'

'Wait, wait, and don't be improper!'

Her countenance fell, and she was silent awhile. He regarded the red berries between them over and over again, to such an extent that holly seemed in his after life to be a cypher signifying a proposal of marriage. Bathsheba decisively turned to him.

'No; 'tis no use,' she said. 'I don't want to marry you.'

'Try.'

'I've tried hard all the time I've been thinking; for a marriage would be very nice in one sense. People would talk about

me and think I had won my battle, and I should feel triumphant, and all that. But a husband —'

'Well!'

'Why, he'd always be there, as you say; whenever I looked
up, there he'd be.'

'Of course he would — I, that is.'

'Well, what I mean is that I shouldn't mind being a bride at
a wedding, if I could be one without having a husband. But
since a woman can't show off in that way by herself, I shan't
marry — at least yet.'

'That's a terrible wooden story!'

At this criticism of her statement Bathsheba made an addition to her dignity by a slight sweep away from him.

'Upon my heart and soul I don't know what a maid can say
stupider than that,' said Oak. 'But dearest,' he continued in a
palliative voice, 'don't be like it!' Oak sighed a deep honest sigh
— none the less so in that, being like the sigh of a pine plantation, it was rather noticeable as a disturbance of the atmosphere. 'Why won't you have me?' he appealed, creeping round
the holly to reach her side.

'I cannot,' she said, retreating.

'But why?' he persisted, standing still at last in despair of
ever reaching her, and facing over the bush.

'Because I don't love you.'

'Yes, but —'

She contracted a yawn to an inoffensive smallness, so that it
was hardly ill-mannered at all. 'I don't love you,' she said.

'But I love you — and, as for myself, I am content to be
liked.'

'O Mr. Oak — that's very fine! You'd get to despise me.'

'Never,' said Mr. Oak, so earnestly that he seemed to be
coming, by the force of his words, straight through the bush
and into her arms. 'I shall do one thing in this life — one thing
certain — that is, love you, and long for you, and *keep wanting
you* till I die.' His voice had a genuine pathos now, and his large
brown hands perceptibly trembled.

'It seems dreadfully wrong not to have you when you feel so much!' she said with a little distress, and looking hopelessly around for some means of escape from her moral dilemma. 'How I wish I hadn't run after you!' However, she seemed to have a short cut for getting back to cheerfulness and set her face to signify archness. 'It wouldn't do, Mr. Oak. I want somebody to tame me; I am too independent; and you would never be able to, I know.'

Oak cast his eyes down the field in a way implying that it was useless to attempt argument.

'Mr. Oak,' she said, with luminous distinctness and common sense, 'you are better off than I. I have hardly a penny in the world – I am staying with my aunt for my bare sustenance. I am better educated than you – and I don't love you a bit: that's my side of the case. Now yours: you are a farmer just beginning, and you ought in common prudence, if you marry at all (which you should certainly not think of doing at present), to marry a woman with money, who would stock a larger farm for you than you have now.'

Gabriel looked at her with a little surprise and much admiration.

'That's the very thing I had been thinking myself!' he naïvely said.

Farmer Oak had one-and-a-half Christian characteristics too many to succeed with Bathsheba: his humility, and a superfluous moiety of honesty. Bathsheba was decidedly disconcerted.

'Well, then, why did you come and disturb me?' she said, almost angrily, if not quite, an enlarging red spot rising in each cheek.

'I can't do what I think would be – would be —'

'Right?'

'No: wise.'

'You have made an admission *now*, Mr. Oak,' she exclaimed with even more hauteur, and rocking her head disdainfully. 'After that, do you think I could marry you? Not if I know it.'

He broke in passionately: 'But don't mistake me like that! Because I am open enough to own what every man in my shoes would have thought of, you make your colours come up your face and get crabbed with me. That about you not being good enough for me is nonsense. You speak like a lady – all the parish notice it, and your uncle at Weatherbury is, I've heerd, a large farmer – much larger than ever I shall be. May I call in the evening, or will you walk along with me o' Sundays? I don't want you to make up your mind at once, if you'd rather not.'

'No – no – I cannot. Don't press me any more – don't. I don't love you – so 'twould be ridiculous,' she said, with a laugh.

No man likes to see his emotions the sport of a merry-go-round of skittishness. 'Very well,' said Oak firmly, with the bearing of one who was going to give his days and nights to Ecclesiastes for ever. 'Then I'll ask you no more.'

CHAPTER V

DEPARTURE OF BATHSHEBA –
A PASTORAL TRAGEDY

THE news which one day reached Gabriel that Bathsheba
Everdene had left the neighbourhood, had an influence upon
him which might have surprised any who never suspected that
the more emphatic the renunciation the less absolute its character.

It may have been observed that there is no regular path for
getting out of love as there is for getting in. Some people look
upon marriage as a short cut that way, but it has been known
to fail. Separation, which was the means that chance offered to
Gabriel Oak by Bathsheba's disappearance, though effectual
with people of certain humours, is apt to idealize the removed
object with others – notably those whose affection, placid and
regular as it may be, flows deep and long. Oak belonged to the
even-tempered order of humanity, and felt the secret fusion of
himself in Bathsheba to be burning with a finer flame now that
she was gone – that was all.

His incipient friendship with her aunt had been nipped by
the failure of his suit, and all that Oak learnt of Bathsheba's
movements was done indirectly. It appeared that she had gone
to a place called Weatherbury, more than twenty miles off, but
in what capacity – whether as a visitor or permanently, he
could not discover.

Gabriel had two dogs. George, the elder, exhibited an
ebony-tipped nose, surrounded by a narrow margin of pink
flesh, and a coat marked in random splotches approximating
in colour to white and slaty grey; but the grey, after years of
sun and rain, had been scorched and washed out of the more

prominent locks, leaving them of a reddish-brown, as if the blue component of the grey had faded, like the indigo from the same kind of colour in Turner's pictures. In substance it had originally been hair, but long contact with sheep seemed to be turning it by degrees into wool of a poor quality and staple.

This dog had originally belonged to a shepherd of inferior morals and dreadful temper, and the result was that George knew the exact degrees of condemnation signified by cursing and swearing of all descriptions better than the wickedest old man in the neighbourhood. Long experience had so precisely taught the animal the difference between such exclamations as 'Come in!' and 'D— ye, come in!' that he knew to a hair's breadth the rate of trotting back from the ewes' tails that each call involved, if a staggerer with the sheep-crook was to be escaped. Though old, he was clever and trust-worthy still.

The young dog, George's son, might possibly have been the image of his mother, for there was not much resemblance be-tween him and George. He was learning the sheep-keeping business, so as to follow on at the flock when the other should die, but had got no further than the rudiments as yet – still finding an insuperable difficulty in distinguishing between doing a thing well enough and doing it too well. So earnest and yet so wrong-headed was this young dog (he had no name in particular, and answered with perfect readiness to any pleasant interjection) that if sent behind the flock to help them on he did it so thoroughly that he would have chased them across the whole county with the greatest pleasure if not called off, or reminded when to stop by the example of old George.

Thus much for the dogs. On the further side of Nor-combe Hill was a chalk-pit, from which chalk had been drawn for generations, and spread over adjacent farms. Two hedges converged upon it in the form of a V, but without quite meeting. The narrow opening left, which was immediately over the brow of the pit, was protected by a rough railing.

One night, when Farmer Oak had returned to his house, believing there would be no further necessity for his attendance on the down, he called as usual to the dogs, previously to shutting them up in the outhouse till next morning. Only one responded – old George; the other could not be found, either in the house, lane, or garden. Gabriel then remembered that he had left the two dogs on the hill eating a dead lamb (a kind of meat he usually kept from them, except when other food ran short), and concluding that the young one had not finished his meal he went indoors to the luxury of a bed, which latterly he had only enjoyed on Sundays.

It was a still, moist night. Just before dawn he was assisted in waking by the abnormal reverberation of familiar music. To the shepherd, the note of the sheep-bell, like the ticking of the clock to other people, is a chronic sound that only makes itself noticed by ceasing or altering in some unusual manner from the well-known idle tinkle which signifies to the accustomed ear, however distant, that all is well in the fold. In the solemn calm of the awakening morn that note was heard by Gabriel, beating with unusual violence and rapidity. This exceptional ringing may be caused in two ways – by the rapid feeding of the sheep bearing the bell, as when the flock breaks into new pasture, which gives it an intermittent rapidity, or by the sheep starting off in a run, when the sound has a regular palpitation. The experienced ear of Oak knew the sound he now heard to be caused by the running of the flock with great velocity.

He jumped out of bed, dressed, tore down the lane through a foggy dawn, and ascended the hill. The forward ewes were kept apart from those among which the fall of lambs would be later, there being two hundred of the latter class in Gabriel's flock. These two hundred seemed to have absolutely vanished from the hill. There were the fifty with their lambs, enclosed at the other end as he had left them, but the rest, forming the bulk of the flock, were nowhere. Gabriel called at the top of his voice the shepherd's call:

'Ovey, ovey, ovey!'

Not a single bleat. He went to the hedge; a gap had been broken through it, and in the gap were the footprints of the sheep. Rather surprised to find them break fence at this season, yet putting it down instantly to their great fondness for ivy in winter-time, of which a great deal grew in the plantation, he followed through the hedge. They were not in the plantation. He called again: the valleys and furthest hills resounded as when the sailors invoked the lost Hylas on the Mysian shore; but no sheep. He passed through the trees and along the ridge of the hill. On the extreme summit, where the ends of the two converging hedges of which we have spoken were stopped short by meeting the brow of the chalk-pit, he saw the younger dog standing against the sky – dark and motionless as Napoleon at St. Helena.

A horrible conviction darted through Oak. With a sensation of bodily faintness he advanced: at one point the rails were broken through, and there he saw the footprints of his ewes. The dog came up, licked his hand, and made signs implying that he expected some great reward for signal services rendered. Oak looked over the precipice. The ewes lay dead and dying at its foot – a heap of two hundred mangled carcases, representing in their condition just now at least two hundred more.

Oak was an intensely humane man: indeed, his humanity often tore in pieces any politic intentions of his which bordered on strategy, and carried him on as by gravitation. A shadow in his life had always been that his flock ended in mutton – that a day came and found every shepherd an arrant traitor to his defenceless sheep. His first feeling now was one of pity for the untimely fate of these gentle ewes and their unborn lambs.

It was a second to remember another phase of the matter. The sheep were not insured. All the savings of a frugal life had been dispersed at a blow; his hopes of being an independent farmer were laid low – possibly for ever. Gabriel's energies, patience, and industry had been so severely taxed during the years of his life between eighteen and eight-and-twenty, to reach his present stage of progress, that no more seemed to be left in him. He leant down upon a rail, and covered his face with his hands.

Stupors, however, do not last for ever, and Farmer Oak recovered from his. It was as remarkable as it was characteristic that the one sentence he uttered was in thankfulness: –

'Thank God I am not married: what would *she* have done in the poverty now coming upon me!'

Oak raised his head, and wondering what he could do, listlessly surveyed the scene. By the outer margin of the pit was an oval pond, and over it hung the attenuated skeleton of a chrome-yellow moon, which had only a few days to last – the morning star dogging her on the left hand. The pool glittered like a dead man's eye, and as the world awoke a breeze blew, shaking and elongating the reflection of the moon without breaking it, and turning the image of the star to a phosphoric streak upon the water. All this Oak saw and remembered.

As far as could be learnt it appeared that the poor young dog, still under the impression that since he was kept running after sheep, the more he ran after them the better, had at the end of his meal off the dead lamb, which may have given him additional energy and spirits, collected all the ewes into a corner, driven the timid creatures through the hedge, across the upper field, and by main force of worrying had given them momentum enough to break down a portion of the rotten railing, and so hurled them over the edge.

George's son had done his work so thoroughly that he was considered too good a workman to live, and was, in fact, taken and tragically shot at twelve o'clock that same day – another instance of the untoward fate which so often attends dogs and other philosophers who follow out a train of reasoning to its logical conclusion, and attempt perfectly consistent conduct in a world made up so largely of compromise.

Gabriel's farm had been stocked by a dealer – on the strength of Oak's promising look and character – who was receiving a percentage from the farmer till such time as the advance should be cleared off. Oak found that the value of stock, plant, and implements which were really his own would be about sufficient to pay his debts, leaving himself a free man with the clothes he stood up in, and nothing more.

CHAPTER VI

THE FAIR – THE JOURNEY – THE FIRE

Two months passed away. We are brought on to a day in February, on which was held the yearly statute or hiring fair in the county-town of Casterbridge.

At one end of the street stood from two to three hundred blithe and hearty labourers waiting upon Chance – all men of the stamp to whom labour suggests nothing worse than a wrestle with gravitation, and pleasure nothing better than a renunciation of the same. Among these, carters and waggoners were distinguished by having a piece of whip-cord twisted round their hats; thatchers wore a fragment of woven straw; shepherds held their sheep-crooks in their hands; and thus the situation required was known to the hirers at a glance.

In the crowd was an athletic young fellow of somewhat superior appearance to the rest – in fact, his superiority was marked enough to lead several ruddy peasants standing by to speak to him inquiringly, as to a farmer, and to use 'Sir' as a finishing word. His answer always was, —

'I am looking for a place myself – a bailiff's. Do ye know of anybody who wants one?'

Gabriel was paler now. His eyes were more meditative, and his expression was more sad. He had passed through an ordeal of wretchedness which had given him more than it had taken away. He had sunk from his modest elevation as pastoral king into the very slime-pits of Siddim; but there was left to him a dignified calm he had never before known, and that indifference to fate which, though it often makes a villain of a man, is the basis of his sublimity when it does not. And thus the abasement had been exaltation, and the loss gain.

In the morning a regiment of cavalry had left the town, and a sergeant and his party had been beating up for recruits through the four streets. As the end of the day drew on, and he found himself not hired, Gabriel almost wished that he had joined them, and gone off to serve his country. Weary of standing in the market-place, and not much minding the kind of work he turned his hand to, he decided to offer himself in some other capacity than that of bailiff.

All the farmers seemed to be wanting shepherds. Sheeptending was Gabriel's speciality. Turning down an obscure street and entering an obscurer lane, he went up to a smith's shop.

'How long would it take you to make a shepherd's crook?'

'Twenty minutes.'

'How much?'

'Two shillings.'

He sat on a bench and the crook was made, a stem being given him into the bargain.

He then went to a ready-made clothes shop, the owner of which had a large rural connection. As the crook had absorbed most of Gabriel's money, he attempted, and carried out, an exchange of his overcoat for a shepherd's regulation smock-frock.

This transaction having been completed he again hurried off to the centre of the town, and stood on the kerb of the pavement, as a shepherd, crook in hand.

Now that Oak had turned himself into a shepherd it seemed that bailiffs were most in demand. However, two or three farmers noticed him and drew near. Dialogues followed, more or less in the subjoined form: –

'Where do you come from?'

'Norcombe.'

'That's a long way.'

'Fifteen miles.'

'Whose farm were you upon last?'

'My own.'

This reply invariably operated like a rumour of cholera. The inquiring farmer would edge away and shake his head dubiously. Gabriel, like his dog, was too good to be trustworthy, and he never made advance beyond this point.

It is safer to accept any chance that offers itself, and extemporize a procedure to fit it, than to get a good plan matured, and wait for a chance of using it. Gabriel wished he had not nailed up his colours as a shepherd, but had laid himself out for anything in the whole cycle of labour that was required in the fair. It grew dusk. Some merry men were whistling and singing by the corn-exchange. Gabriel's hand, which had lain for some time idle in his smock-frock pocket, touched his flute, which he carried there. Here was an opportunity for putting his dearly bought wisdom into practice.

He drew out his flute and began to play 'Jockey to the Fair' in the style of a man who had never known a moment's sorrow. Oak could pipe with Arcadian sweetness, and the sound of the well-known notes cheered his own heart as well as those of the loungers. He played on with spirit, and in half an hour had earned in pence what was a small fortune to a destitute man.

By making inquiries he learnt that there was another fair at Shottsford the next day.

'How far is Shottsford?'

'Ten miles t'other side of Weatherbury.'

Weatherbury! It was where Bathsheba had gone two months before. This information was like coming from night into noon.

'How far is it to Weatherbury?'

'Five or six miles.'

Bathsheba had probably left Weatherbury long before this time, but the place had enough interest attaching to it to lead Oak to choose Shottsford fair as his next field of inquiry, because it lay in the Weatherbury quarter. Moreover, the Weatherbury folk were by no means uninteresting intrinsically. If report spoke truly they were as hardy, merry, thriving, wicked a set as any in the whole county. Oak resolved to sleep at

Weatherbury that night on his way to Shottsford, and struck out at once into the high road which had been recommended as the direct route to the village in question.

The road stretched through water-meadows traversed by little brooks, whose quivering surfaces were braided along their centres, and folded into creases at the sides; or, where the flow was more rapid, the stream was pied with spots of white froth, which rode on in undisturbed serenity. On the higher levels the dead and dry carcases of leaves tapped the ground as they bowled along helter-skelter upon the shoulders of the wind, and little birds in the hedges were rustling their feathers and tucking themselves in comfortably for the night, retaining their places if Oak kept moving, but flying away if he stopped to look at them. He passed by Yalbury Wood where the game-birds were rising to their roosts, and heard the crack-voiced cock-pheasants' 'cu-uck, cuck,' and the wheezy whistle of the hens.

By the time he had walked three or four miles every shape in the landscape had assumed a uniform hue of blackness. He descended Yalbury Hill and could just discern ahead of him a waggon, drawn up under a great over-hanging tree by the roadside.

On coming close, he found there were no horses attached to it, the spot being apparently quite deserted. The waggon, from its position, seemed to have been left there for the night, for beyond about half a truss of hay which was heaped in the bottom, it was quite empty. Gabriel sat down on the shafts of the vehicle and considered his position. He calculated that he had walked a very fair proportion of the journey; and having been on foot since daybreak, he felt tempted to lie down upon the hay in the waggon instead of pushing on to the village of Weatherbury, and having to pay for a lodging.

Eating his last slices of bread and ham, and drinking from the bottle of cider he had taken the precaution to bring with him, he got into the lonely waggon. Here he spread half of the hay as a bed, and, as well as he could in the darkness, pulled the other half over him by way of bed-clothes, covering himself entirely, and feeling, physically, as comfortable as ever he had been in his life. Inward melancholy it was impossible for a man like Oak, introspective far beyond his neighbours, to banish quite, whilst conning the present untoward page of his history. So, thinking of his misfortunes, amorous and pastoral, he fell asleep, shepherds enjoying, in common with sailors, the privilege of being able to summon the god instead of having to wait for him.

On somewhat suddenly awaking, after a sleep of whose length he had no idea, Oak found that the waggon was in motion. He was being carried along the road at a rate rather considerable for a vehicle without springs, and under circumstances of physical uneasiness, his head being dandled up and down on the bed of the waggon like a kettledrum-stick. He then distinguished voices in conversation, coming from the forepart of the waggon. His concern at this dilemma (which would have been alarm, had he been a thriving man; but misfortune is a fine opiate to personal terror) led him to peer cautiously from the hay, and the first sight he beheld was the stars above him. Charles's Wain was getting towards a right angle with the Pole star, and Gabriel concluded that it must be about nine o'clock – in other words, that he had slept two hours. This small astronomical calculation was made without any positive effort, and whilst he was stealthily turning to discover, if possible, into whose hands he had fallen.

Two figures were dimly visible in front, sitting with their legs outside the waggon, one of whom was driving. Gabriel soon found that this was the waggoner, and it appeared they had come from Casterbridge fair, like himself.

A conversation was in progress, which continued thus: –

'Be as 'twill, she's a fine handsome body as far's looks be concerned. But that's only the skin of the woman, and these dandy cattle be as proud as a lucifer in their insides.'

'Ay – so 'a do seem, Billy Smallbury – so 'a do seem.' This utterance was very shaky by nature, and more so by circumstance, the jolting of the waggon not being without its effect upon the speaker's larynx. It came from the man who held the reins.

'She's a very vain feymell – so 'tis said here and there.'

'Ah, now. If so be 'tis like that, I can't look her in the face. Lord, no: not I – heh-heh-heh! Such a shy man as I be!'

'Yes – she's very vain. 'Tis said that every night at going to bed she looks in the glass to put on her nightcap properly.'

'And not a married woman. Oh, the world!'

'And 'a can play the peanner, so 'tis said. Can play so clever that 'a can make a psalm tune sound as well as the merriest loose song a man can wish for.'

'D'ye tell o't! A happy time for us, and I feel quite a new man! And how do she pay?'

'That I don't know, Master Poorgrass.'

On hearing these and other similar remarks, a wild thought flashed into Gabriel's mind that they might be speaking of Bathsheba. There were, however, no grounds for retaining such a supposition, for the waggon, though going in the direction of Weatherbury, might be going beyond it, and the woman alluded to seemed to be the mistress of some estate. They were now apparently close upon Weatherbury, and not to alarm the speakers unnecessarily Gabriel slipped out of the waggon unseen.

He turned to an opening in the hedge, which he found to be a gate, and mounting thereon he sat meditating whether to seek a cheap lodging in the village, or to ensure a cheaper one by lying under some hay or corn stack. The crunching jangle of the waggon died upon his ear. He was about to walk on, when he noticed on his left hand an unusual light – appearing about half a mile distant. Oak watched it, and the glow increased. Something was on fire.

Gabriel again mounted the gate, and, leaping down on the other side upon what he found to be ploughed soil, made across the field in the exact direction of the fire. The blaze, enlarging in a double ratio by his approach and its own increase, showed him as he drew nearer the outlines of ricks beside it, lighted up to great distinctness. A rick-yard was the source of the fire. His weary face now began to be painted over with a rich orange glow, and the whole front of his smock-frock and gaiters was covered with a dancing shadow pattern of thorn-twigs – the light reaching him through a leafless intervening hedge – and the metallic curve of his sheep-crook shone silver-bright in the same abounding rays. He came up to the boundary fence, and stood to regain breath. It seemed as if the spot was unoccupied by a living soul.

The fire was issuing from a long straw-stack, which was so far gone as to preclude a possibility of saving it. A rick burns differently from a house. As the wind blows the fire inwards, the portion in flames completely disappears like melting sugar, and the outline is lost to the eye. However, a hay or a wheat rick, well put together, will resist combustion for a length of time if it begins on the outside.

This before Gabriel's eyes was a rick of straw, loosely put together, and the flames darted into it with lightning swiftness. It glowed on the windward side, rising and falling in intensity like the coal of a cigar. Then a superincumbent bundle rolled down with a whisking noise; flames elongated, and bent themselves about with a quiet roar, but no crackle. Banks of smoke went off horizontally at the back like passing clouds, and behind these burned hidden pyres, illuminating the semi-transparent sheet of smoke to a lustrous yellow uniformity. Individual straws in the foreground were consumed in a creeping movement of ruddy heat, as if they were knots of red worms, and above shone imaginary fiery faces, tongues hanging from lips, glaring eyes, and other impish forms, from which at intervals sparks flew in clusters like birds from a nest.

Oak suddenly ceased from being a mere spectator by discovering the case to be more serious than he had at first imagined. A scroll of smoke blew aside and revealed to him a wheat-rick in startling juxtaposition with the decaying one, and behind this a series of others, composing the main corn produce of the farm; so that instead of the straw-stack standing, as he had imagined, comparatively isolated, there was a regular connection between it and the remaining stacks of the group.

Gabriel leapt over the hedge, and saw that he was not alone. The first man he came to was running about in a great hurry, as if his thoughts were several yards in advance of his body, which they could never drag on fast enough.

'O, man – fire, fire! A good master and a bad servant is fire, fire! – I mane a bad servant and a good master. O Mark Clark – come! And you, Billy Smallbury – and you, Maryann Money – and you, Jan Coggan, and Matthew there!' Other figures now appeared behind this shouting man and among the smoke, and Gabriel found that, far from being alone, he was in a great company – whose shadows danced merrily up and down, timed by the jigging of the flames, and not at all by their owners' movements. The assemblage – belonging to that class of society which casts its thoughts into the form of feeling, and its feelings into the form of commotion – set to work with a remarkable confusion of purpose.

'Stop the draught under the wheat-rick!' cried Gabriel to those nearest to him. The corn stood on stone staddles, and between these, tongues of yellow hue from the burning straw licked and darted playfully. If the fire once got *under* this stack, all would be lost.

'Get a tarpaulin – quick!' said Gabriel.

A rick-cloth was brought, and they hung it like a curtain across the channel. The flames immediately ceased to go under the bottom of the corn-stack, and stood up vertical.

'Stand here with a bucket of water and keep the cloth wet,' said Gabriel again.

The flames, now driven upwards, began to attack the angles of the huge roof covering the wheat-stack.

'A ladder,' cried Gabriel.

'The ladder was against the straw-rick and is burnt to a cinder,' said a spectre-like form in the smoke.

Oak seized the cut ends of the sheaves, as if he were going to engage in the operation of 'reed-drawing,' and digging in his feet, and occasionally sticking in the stem of his sheep-crook, he clambered up the beetling face. He at once sat astride the very apex, and began with his crook to beat off the fiery fragments which had lodged thereon, shouting to the others to get him a bough and a ladder, and some water.

Billy Smallbury — one of the men who had been on the waggon — by this time had found a ladder, which Mark Clark ascended, holding on beside Oak upon the thatch. The smoke at this corner was stifling, and Clark, a nimble fellow, having been handed a bucket of water, bathed Oak's face and sprinkled him generally, whilst Gabriel, now with a long beech-bough in one hand, in addition to his crook in the other, kept sweeping the stack and dislodging all fiery particles.

On the ground the groups of villagers were still occupied in doing all they could to keep down the conflagration, which was not much. They were all tinged orange, and backed up by shadows of varying pattern. Round the corner of the largest stack, out of the direct rays of the fire, stood a pony, bearing a young woman on its back. By her side was another woman, on foot. These two seemed to keep at a distance from the fire, that the horse might not become restive.

'He's a shepherd,' said the woman on foot. 'Yes — he is. See how his crook shines as he beats the rick with it. And his smock-frock is burnt in two holes, I declare! A fine young shepherd he is too, ma'am.'

'Whose shepherd is he?' said the equestrian in a clear voice.

'Don't know, ma'am.'

'Don't any of the others know?'

'Nobody at all — I've asked 'em. Quite a stranger, they say.'

The young woman on the pony rode out from the shade and looked anxiously around.

'Do you think the barn is safe?' she said.

'D'ye think the barn is safe, Jan Coggan?' said the second woman, passing on the question to the nearest man in that direction.

'Safe now — leastwise I think so. If this rick had gone the

barn would have followed. 'Tis that bold shepherd up there that have done the most good – he sitting on the top o' rick, whizzing his great long arms about like a windmill.'

'He does work hard,' said the young woman on horseback, looking up at Gabriel through her thick woollen veil. 'I wish he was shepherd here. Don't any of you know his name?'

'Never heard the man's name in my life, or seed his form afore.'

The fire began to get worsted, and Gabriel's elevated position being no longer required of him, he made as if to descend.

'Maryann,' said the girl on horseback, 'go to him as he comes down, and say that the farmer wishes to thank him for the great service he has done.'

Maryann stalked off towards the rick and met Oak at the foot of the ladder. She delivered her message.

'Where is your master the farmer?' asked Gabriel, kindling with the idea of getting employment that seemed to strike him now.

' 'Tisn't a master; 'tis a mistress, shepherd.'

'A woman farmer?'

'Ay, 'a b'lieve, and a rich one too!' said a bystander. 'Lately 'a came here from a distance. Took on her uncle's farm, who died suddenly. Used to measure his money in half-pint cups. They say now that she've business in every bank in Caster-bridge, and thinks no more of playing pitch-and-toss sovereign than you and I do pitch-halfpenny – not a bit in the world, shepherd.'

'That's she, back there upon the pony,' said Maryann; 'wi' her face a-covered up in that black cloth with holes in it.'

Oak, his features smudged, grimy, and undiscoverable from the smoke and heat, his smock-frock burnt into holes and drip-ping with water, the ash stem of his sheep-crook charred six inches shorter, advanced with the humility stern adversity had thrust upon him up to the slight female form in the saddle. He lifted his hat with respect, and not without gallantry: stepping close to her hanging feet he said in a hesitating voice, –

'Do you happen to want a shepherd, ma'am?'

She lifted the wool veil tied round her face, and looked all astonishment. Gabriel and his cold-hearted darling, Bathsheba Everdene, were face to face.

Bathsheba did not speak, and he mechanically repeated in an abashed and sad voice, –

'Do you want a shepherd, ma'am?'

CHAPTER VII

RECOGNITION – A TIMID GIRL

BATHSHEBA withdrew into the shade. She scarcely knew whether most to be amused at the singularity of the meeting, or to be concerned at its awkwardness. There was room for a little pity, also for a very little exultation: the former at his position, the latter at her own. Embarrassed she was not, and she remembered Gabriel's declaration of love to her at Norcombe only to think she had nearly forgotten it.

'Yes,' she murmured, putting on an air of dignity, and turning again to him with a little warmth of cheek; 'I do want a shepherd. But —'

'He's the very man, ma'am,' said one of the villagers, quietly.

Conviction breeds conviction. 'Ay, that 'a is,' said a second, decisively.

'The man, truly!' said a third, with heartiness.

'He's all there!' said number four, fervidly.

'Then will you tell him to speak to the bailiff?' said Bathsheba.

All was practical again now. A summer eve and loneliness would have been necessary to give the meeting its proper fulness of romance.

The bailiff was pointed out to Gabriel, who, checking the palpitation within his breast at discovering that this Ashtoreth of strange report was only a modification of Venus the well-known and admired, retired with him to talk over the necessary preliminaries of hiring.

The fire before them wasted away. 'Men,' said Bathsheba, 'you shall take a little refreshment after this extra work. Will you come to the house?'

'We could knock in a bit and a drop a good deal freer, Miss, if so be ye'd send it to Warren's Malthouse,' replied the spokesman.

Bathsheba then rode off into the darkness, and the men straggled on to the village in twos and threes – Oak and the bailiff being left by the rick alone.

'And now,' said the bailiff, finally, 'all is settled, I think, about your coming, and I am going home-along. Good-night to ye, shepherd.'

'Can you get me a lodging?' inquired Gabriel.

'That I can't, indeed,' he said, moving past Oak as a Christian edges past an offertory-plate when he does not mean to contribute. 'If you follow on the road till you come to Warren's Malthouse, where they are all gone to have their snap of victuals, I daresay some of 'em will tell you of a place. Good-night to ye, shepherd.'

The bailiff who showed this nervous dread of loving his neighbour as himself, went up the hill, and Oak walked on to the village, still astonished at the rencounter with Bathsheba, glad of his nearness to her, and perplexed at the rapidity with which the unpractised girl of Norcombe had developed into the supervising and cool woman here. But some women only require an emergency to make them fit for one.

Obliged to some extent to forego dreaming in order to find the way, he reached the churchyard, and passed round it under the wall where several ancient trees grew. There was a wide margin of grass along here, and Gabriel's footsteps were deadened by its softness, even at this indurating period of the year. When abreast of a trunk which appeared to be the oldest of the old, he became aware that a figure was standing behind it. Gabriel did not pause in his walk, and in another moment he accidentally kicked a loose stone. The noise was enough to disturb the motionless stranger, who started and assumed a careless position.

It was a slim girl, rather thinly clad.

'Good-night to you,' said Gabriel heartily.

'Good-night,' said the girl to Gabriel.

The voice was unexpectedly attractive; it was the low and dulcet note suggestive of romance; common in descriptions, rare in experience.

'I'll thank you to tell me if I'm in the way for Warren's Malthouse?' Gabriel resumed, primarily to gain the information, indirectly to get more of the music.

'Quite right. It's at the bottom of the hill. And do you know —' The girl hesitated and then went on again. 'Do you know how late they keep open the Buck's Head Inn?' She seemed to be won by Gabriel's heartiness, as Gabriel had been won by her modulations.

'I don't know where the Buck's Head is, or anything about it. Do you think of going there to-night?'

'Yes —' The woman again paused. There was no necessity for any continuance of speech, and the fact that she did add more seemed to proceed from an unconscious desire to show unconcern by making a remark, which is noticeable in the ingenuous when they are acting by stealth. 'You are not a Weatherbury man?' she said timorously.

'I am not. I am the new shepherd – just arrived.'

'Only a shepherd – and you seem almost a farmer by your ways.'

'Only a shepherd,' Gabriel repeated, in a dull cadence of finality. His thoughts were directed to the past, his eyes to the feet of the girl; and for the first time he saw lying there a bundle of some sort. She may have perceived the direction of his face, for she said coaxingly, —

'You won't say anything in the parish about having seen me here, will you – at least, not for a day or two?'

'I won't if you wish me not to,' said Oak.

'Thank you, indeed,' the other replied. 'I am rather poor, and I don't want people to know anything about me.' Then she was silent and shivered.

'You ought to have a cloak on such a cold night,' Gabriel observed. 'I would advise 'ee to get indoors.'

'O no! Would you mind going on and leaving me? I thank you much for what you have told me.'

'I will go on,' he said; adding hesitatingly, – 'Since you are not very well off, perhaps you would accept this trifle from me. It is only a shilling, but it is all I have to spare.'

'Yes, I will take it,' said the stranger gratefully.

She extended her hand; Gabriel his. In feeling for each other's palm in the gloom before the money could be passed, a minute incident occurred which told much. Gabriel's fingers alighted on the young woman's wrist. It was beating with a throb of tragic intensity. He had frequently felt the same quick, hard beat in the femoral artery of his lambs when overdriven. It suggested a consumption too great of a vitality which, to judge from her figure and stature, was already too little.

'What is the matter?'

'Nothing.'

'But there is?'

'No, no, no! Let your having seen me be a secret!'

'Very well; I will. Good-night, again.'

'Good-night.'

The young girl remained motionless by the tree, and Gabriel descended into the village of Weatherbury, or Lower Longpuddle as it was sometimes called. He fancied that he had felt himself in the penumbra of a very deep sadness when touching that slight and fragile creature. But wisdom lies in moderating mere impressions, and Gabriel endeavoured to think little of this.

CHAPTER VIII

THE MALTHOUSE – THE CHAT – NEWS

WARREN'S Malthouse was enclosed by an old wall inwrapped with ivy, and though not much of the exterior was visible at this hour, the character and purposes of the building were clearly enough shown by its outline upon the sky. From the walls an overhanging thatched roof sloped up to a point in the centre, upon which rose a small wooden lantern, fitted with louvre-boards on all the four sides, and from these openings a mist was dimly perceived to be escaping into the night air. There was no window in front; but a square hole in the door was glazed with a single pane, through which red, comfortable rays now stretched out upon the ivied wall in front. Voices were to be heard inside.

Oak's hand skimmed the surface of the door with fingers extended to an Elymas-the-Sorcerer pattern, till he found a leathern strap, which he pulled. This lifted a wooden latch, and the door swung open.

The room inside was lighted only by the ruddy glow from the kiln mouth, which shone over the floor with the streaming horizontality of the setting sun, and threw upwards the shadows of all facial irregularities in those assembled around. The stone-flag floor was worn into a path from the doorway to the kiln, and into undulations everywhere. A curved settle of unplaned oak stretched along one side, and in a remote corner was a small bed and bedstead, the owner and frequent occupier of which was the maltster.

This aged man was now sitting opposite the fire, his frosty white hair and beard overgrowing his gnarled figure like the grey moss and lichen upon a leafless apple-tree. He wore breeches and the laced-up shoes called ankle-jacks; he kept his eyes fixed upon the fire.

Gabriel's nose was greeted by an atmosphere laden with the sweet smell of new malt. The conversation (which seemed to have been concerning the origin of the fire) immediately ceased, and every one ocularly criticized him to the degree expressed by contracting the flesh of their foreheads and looking at him with narrowed eyelids, as if he had been a light too strong for their sight. Several exclaimed meditatively, after this operation had been completed: –

'Oh, 'tis the new shepherd, 'a b'lieve.'

'We thought we heard a hand pawing about the door for the bobbin, but weren't sure 'twere not a dead leaf blowed across,' said another. 'Come in, shepherd; sure ye be welcome, though we don't know yer name.'

'Gabriel Oak, that's my name, neighbours.'

The ancient maltster sitting in the midst turned at this – his turning being as the turning of a rusty crane.

'That's never Gable Oak's grandson over at Norcombe – never!' he said, as a formula expressive of surprise, which nobody was supposed to take literally.

'My father and my grandfather were old men of the name of Gabriel,' said the shepherd placidly.

'Thought I knowed the man's face as I seed him on the rick! – thought I did! And where be ye trading o't to now, shepherd?'

'I'm thinking of biding here,' said Mr. Oak.

'Knowed yer grandfather for years and years!' continued the maltster, the words coming forth of their own accord as if the momentum previously imparted had been sufficient.

'Ah – and did you!'

'Knowed yer grandmother.'

'And her too!'

'Likewise knowed yer father when he was a child. Why, my boy Jacob there and your father were sworn brothers – that they were sure – weren't ye, Jacob?'

'Ay, sure,' said his son, a young man about sixty-five, with a semi-bald head and one tooth in the left centre of his upper jaw, which made much of itself by standing prominent, like a milestone in a bank. 'But 'twas Joe had most to do with him. However, my son William must have knowed the very man afore us – didn't ye, Billy, afore ye left Norcombe?'

'No, 'twas Andrew,' said Jacob's son Billy, a child of forty, or thereabouts, who manifested the peculiarity of possessing a cheerful soul in a gloomy body, and whose whiskers were assuming a chinchilla shade here and there.

'I can mind Andrew,' said Oak, 'as being a man in the place when I was quite a child.'

'Ay – the other day I and my youngest daughter, Liddy, were over at my grandson's christening,' continued Billy. 'We were talking about this very family, and 'twas only last Purification Day in this very world, when the use-money is gied away to the second-best poor folk, you know, shepherd, and I can mind the day because they all had to traypse up to the vestry – yes, this very man's family.'

'Come, shepherd, and drink. 'Tis gape and swaller with us – a drap of sommit, but not of much account,' said the maltster, removing from the fire his eyes, which were vermilion-red and bleared by gazing into it for so many years. 'Take up the God-forgive-me, Jacob. See if 'tis warm, Jacob.'

Jacob stooped to the God-forgive-me, which was a two-handled tall mug standing in the ashes, cracked and charred with heat: it was rather furred with extraneous matter about the outside, especially in the crevices of the handles, the innermost curves of which may not have seen daylight for several years by reason of this encrustation thereon – formed of ashes accidentally wetted with cider and baked hard; but to the mind of any sensible drinker the cup was no worse for that, being incontestably clean on the inside and about the rim. It may be observed that such a class of mug is called a God-forgive-me in Weatherbury and its vicinity for uncertain reasons; probably because its size makes any given toper feel ashamed of himself when he sees its bottom in drinking it empty.

Jacob, on receiving the order to see if the liquor was warm enough, placidly dipped his forefinger into it by way of thermometer, and having pronounced it nearly of the proper degree, raised the cup and very civilly attempted to dust some of the ashes from the bottom with the skirt of his smock-frock, because Shepherd Oak was a stranger.

'A clane cup for the shepherd,' said the maltster commandingly.

'No – not at all,' said Gabriel, in a reproving tone of considerateness. 'I never fuss about dirt in its pure state, and when I know what sort it is.' Taking the mug he drank an inch or more from the depth of its contents, and duly passed it to the next man. 'I wouldn't think of giving such trouble to neighbours in washing up when there's so much work to be done in the world already,' continued Oak in a moister tone, after recovering from the stoppage of breath which is occasioned by pulls at large mugs.

'A right sensible man,' said Jacob.

'True, true; it can't be gainsaid!' observed a brisk young man – Mark Clark by name, a genial and pleasant gentleman, whom to meet anywhere in your travels was to know, to know was to drink with, and to drink with was, unfortunately, to pay for.

'And here's a mouthful of bread and bacon that mis'ess have sent, shepherd. The cider will go down better with a bit of victuals. Don't ye chaw quite close, shepherd, for I let the bacon fall in the road outside as I was bringing it along, and may be 'tis rather gritty. There, 'tis clane dirt; and we all know what that is, as you say, and you bain't a particular man we see, shepherd.'

'True, true – not at all,' said the friendly Oak.

'Don't let your teeth quite meet, and you won't feel the sandiness at all. Ah! 'tis wonderful what can be done by contrivance!'

'My own mind exactly, neighbour.'

'Ah, he's his grandfer's own grandson! – his grandfer were just such a nice unparticular man!' said the maltster.

'Drink, Henry Fray – drink,' magnanimously said Jan Coggan, a person who held Saint-Simonian notions of share and share alike where liquor was concerned, as the vessel showed signs of approaching him in its gradual revolution among them.

Having at this moment reached the end of a wistful gaze into mid-air, Henry did not refuse. He was a man of more than middle age, with eyebrows high up in his forehead, who laid it down that the law of the world was bad, with a long-suffering look through his listeners at the world alluded to, as it presented itself to his imagination. He always signed his name 'Henery' – strenuously insisting upon that spelling, and if any passing schoolmaster ventured to remark that the second e' was superfluous and old-fashioned, he received the reply that 'H-e-n-e-r-y' was the name he was christened and the name he would stick to – in the tone of one to whom orthographical differences were matters which had a great deal to do with personal character.

Mr. Jan Coggan, who had passed the cup to Henery, was a crimson man with a spacious countenance and private glimmer in his eye, whose name had appeared on the marriage register of Weatherbury and neighbouring parishes as best man and chief witness in countless unions of the previous twenty years; he also very frequently filled the post of head godfather in baptisms of the subtly-jovial kind.

'Come, Mark Clark – come. Ther's plenty more in the barrel,' said Jan.

'Ay – that I will; 'tis my only doctor,' replied Mr. Clark, who, twenty years younger than Jan Coggan, revolved in the same orbit. He secreted mirth on all occasions for special discharge at popular parties.

'Why, Joseph Poorgrass, ye han't had a drop!' said Mr. Coggan to a self-conscious man in the background, thrusting the cup towards him.

'Such a modest man as he is!' said Jacob Smallbury. 'Why, ye've hardly had strength of eye enough to look into our young mis'ess's face, so I hear, Joseph?'

All looked at Joseph Poorgrass with pitying reproach.

'No – I've hardly looked at her at all,' simpered Joseph, reducing his body smaller whilst talking, apparently from a meek sense of undue prominence. 'And when I seed her, 'twas nothing but blushes with me!'

'Poor feller,' said Mr. Clark.

' 'Tis a curious nature for a man,' said Jan Coggan.

'Yes,' continued Joseph Poorgrass – his shyness, which was so painful as a defect, filling him with a mild complacency now that it was regarded as an interesting study. ' 'Twere blush, blush, blush with me every minute of the time, when she was speaking to me.'

'I believe ye, Joseph Poorgrass, for we all know ye to be a very bashful man.'

' 'Tis a' awkward gift for a man, poor soul,' said the maltster. 'And ye have suffered from it a long time, we know.'

'Ay, ever since I was a boy. Yes – mother was concerned to her heart about it – yes. But 'twas all nought.'

'Did ye ever go into the world to try and stop it, Joseph Poorgrass?'

'Oh ay, tried all sorts o' company. They took me to Greenhill Fair, and into a great gay jerry-go-nimble show, where there were women-folk riding round – standing upon horses, with hardly anything on but their smocks; but it didn't cure me a morsel. And then I was put errand-man at the Women's Skittle Alley at the back of the Tailor's Arms in Casterbridge. 'Twas a horrible sinful situation, and a very curious place for a good man. I had to stand and look ba'dy people in the face from morning till night; but 'twas no use – I was just as bad as ever after all. Blushes hev been in the family for generations. There, 'tis a happy providence that I be no worse.'

'True,' said Jacob Smallbury, deepening his thoughts to a profounder view of the subject. ' 'Tis a thought to look at, that ye might have been worse; but even as you be, 'tis a very bad affliction for 'ee, Joseph. For ye see, shepherd, though 'tis very well for a woman, dang it all, 'tis awkward for a man like him, poor feller?'

' 'Tis – 'tis,' said Gabriel, recovering from a meditation. 'Yes, very awkward for the man.'

'Ay, and he's very timid, too,' observed Jan Coggan. 'Once he had been working late at Yalbury Bottom, and had had a drap of drink, and lost his way as he was coming home-along through Yalbury Wood, didn't ye, Master Poorgrass?'

'No, no, no; not that story!' expostulated the modest man, forcing a laugh to bury his concern.

'— And so 'a lost himself quite,' continued Mr. Coggan, with an impassive face, implying that a true narrative, like time and tide, must run its course and would respect no man. 'And as he was coming along in the middle of the night, much afeared, and not able to find his way out of the trees nohow, 'a cried out, "Man-a-lost! man-a-lost!" A owl in a tree happened to be crying "Whoo-whoo-whoo!" as owls do, you know, shepherd' (Gabriel nodded), 'and Joseph, all in a tremble, said, "Joseph Poorgrass, of Weatherbury, sir!" '

'No, no, now – that's too much!' said the timid man, becoming a man of brazen courage all of a sudden. 'I didn't say *sir*. I'll take my oath I didn't say "Joseph Poorgrass o' Weatherbury, sir." No, no; what's right is right, and I never said sir to the bird, knowing very well that no man of a gentleman's rank would be hollering there at that time o' night. "Joseph Poorgrass of Weatherbury," – that's every word I said, and I shouldn't ha' said that if 't hadn't been for Keeper Day's metheglin. . . . There, 'twas a merciful thing it ended where it did.'

The question of which was right being tacitly waived by the company, Jan went on meditatively: –

'And he's the fearfullest man, bain't ye, Joseph? Ay, another time ye were lost by Lambing-Down Gate, weren't ye, Joseph?'

'I was,' replied Poorgrass, as if there were some conditions too serious even for modesty to remember itself under, this being one.

'Yes; that were the middle of the night, too. The gate would not open, try how he would, and knowing there was the Devil's hand in it, he kneeled down.'

'Ay,' said Joseph, acquiring confidence from the warmth of the fire, the cider, and a perception of the narrative capabilities of the experience alluded to. 'My heart died within me, that time; but I kneeled down and said the Lord's Prayer, and then the Belief right through, and then the Ten Commandments, in earnest prayer. But no, the gate wouldn't open; and then I went on with Dearly Beloved Brethren, and, thinks I, this makes four, and 'tis all I know out of book, and if this don't do it nothing will, and I'm a lost man. Well, when I got to Saying After Me, I rose from my knees and found the gate would open – yes, neighbours, the gate opened the same as ever.'

A meditation on the obvious inference was indulged in by all, and during its continuance each directed his vision into the ashpit, which glowed like a desert in the tropics under a vertical sun, shaping their eyes long and liny, partly because of the light, partly from the depth of the subject discussed.

Gabriel broke the silence. 'What sort of a place is this to live at, and what sort of a mis'ess is she to work under?' Gabriel's bosom thrilled gently as he thus slipped under the notice of the assembly the innermost subject of his heart.

'We d' know little of her – nothing. She only showed herself a few days ago. Her uncle was took bad, and the doctor was called with his world-wide skill; but he couldn't save the man. As I take it, she's going to keep on the farm.'

'That's about the shape o't, 'a b'lieve,' said Jan Coggan. 'Ay, 'tis a very good family. I'd as soon be under 'em as under one here and there. Her uncle was a very fair sort of man. Did ye know en, shepherd – a bachelor-man?'

'Not at all.'

'I used to go to his house a-courting my first wife, Charlotte, who was his dairymaid. Well, a very good-hearted man were Farmer Everdene, and I being a respectable young fellow was allowed to call and see her and drink as much ale as I liked, but not to carry away any – outside my skin I mane, of course.'

'Ay, ay, Jan Coggan; we know yer maning.'

'And so you see 'twas beautiful ale, and I wished to value his kindness as much as I could, and not to be so ill-mannered as to drink only a thimbleful, which would have been insulting the man's generosity —'

'True, Master Coggan, 'twould so,' corroborated Mark Clark.

'— And so I used to eat a lot of salt fish afore going, and then by the time I got there I were as dry as a lime-basket – so thorough dry that that ale would slip down – ah, 'twould slip down sweet! Happy times! heavenly times! Such lovely drunks as I used to have at that house! You can mind, Jacob? You used to go wi' me sometimes.'

'I can – I can,' said Jacob. 'That one, too, that we had at Buck's Head on a White Monday was a pretty tipple.'

' 'Twas. But for a wet of the better class, that brought you no nearer to the horned man than you were afore you begun, there was none like those in Farmer Everdene's kitchen. Not a single damn allowed; no, not a bare poor one, even at the most cheerful moment when all were blindest, though the good old word of sin thrown in here and there at such times is a great relief to a merry soul.'

'True,' said the maltster. 'Nater requires her swearing at the regular times, or she's not herself; and unholy exclamations is a necessity of life.'

'But Charlotte,' continued Coggan – 'not a word of the sort would Charlotte allow, nor the smallest item of taking in vain. . . . Ay, poor Charlotte, I wonder if she had the good fortune to get into Heaven when 'a died! But 'a was never much in luck's way, and perhaps 'a went downwards after all, poor soul.'

'And did any of you know Miss Everdene's father and mother?' inquired the shepherd, who found some difficulty in keeping the conversation in the desired channel.

'I knew them a little,' said Jacob Smallbury; 'but they were townsfolk, and didn't live here. They've been dead for years. Father, what sort of people were mis'ess' father and mother?'

'Well,' said the maltster, 'he wasn't much to look at; but she was a lovely woman. He was fond enough of her as his sweetheart.'

'Used to kiss her scores and long-hundreds o' times, so 'twas said,' observed Coggan.

'He was very proud of her, too, when they were married, as I've been told,' said the maltster.

'Ay,' said Coggan. 'He admired her so much that he used to light the candle three times a night to look at her.'

'Boundless love; I shouldn't have supposed it in the universe!' murmured Joseph Poorgrass, who habitually spoke on a large scale in his moral reflections.

'Well, to be sure,' said Gabriel.

'Oh, 'tis true enough. I knowed the man and woman both well. Levi Everdene – that was the man's name, sure. "Man," saith I in my hurry, but he were of a higher circle of life than that – 'a was a gentleman-tailor really, worth scores of pounds And he became a very celebrated bankrupt two or three times.'

'Oh, I thought he was quite a common man!' said Joseph.

'O no, no! That man failed for heaps of money; hundreds in gold and silver.'

The maltster being rather short of breath, Mr. Coggan, after absently scrutinizing a coal which had fallen among the ashes, took up the narrative, with a private twirl of his eye: –

'Well, now, you'd hardly believe it, but that man – our Miss Everdene's father – was one of the ficklest husbands alive, after a while. Understand, 'a didn't want to be fickle, but he couldn't help it. The poor feller were faithful and true enough to her in his wish, but his heart would rove, do what he would. He spoke to me in real tribulation about it once. "Coggan," he said, "I could never wish for a handsomer woman than I've got, but feeling she's ticketed as my lawful wife, I can't help my wicked heart wandering, do what I will." But at last I believe he cured it by making her take off her wedding-ring and calling her by her maiden name as they sat together after the shop was shut, and so 'a would get to fancy she was only his sweetheart, and not married to him at all. And as soon as he could thoroughly fancy he was doing wrong and committing the seventh, 'a got to like her as well as ever, and they lived on a perfect picture of mutel love.'

'Well, 'twas a most ungodly remedy,' murmured Joseph Poorgrass; 'but we ought to feel deep cheerfulness that a happy Providence kept it from being any worse. You see, he might have gone the bad road and given his eyes to unlawfulness entirely – yes, gross unlawfulness, so to say it.'

'You see,' said Billy Smallbury, 'the man's will was to do right, sure enough, but his heart didn't chime in.'

'He got so much better that he was quite godly in his later years, wasn't he, Jan?' said Joseph Poorgrass. 'He got himself confirmed over again in a more serious way, and took to saying "Amen" almost as loud as the clerk, and he liked to copy comforting verses from the tombstones. He used, too, to hold the money-plate at Let Your Light so Shine, and stand godfather to poor little come-by-chance children; and he kept a missionary box upon his table to nab folks unawares when they called; yes, and he would box the charity-boys' ears, if they laughed in church, till they could hardly stand upright, and do other deeds of piety natural to the saintly inclined.'

'Ay, at that time he thought of nothing but high things,' added Billy Smallbury. 'One day Parson Thirdly met him and said, "Good-morning, Mister Everdene; 'tis a fine day!" "Amen," said Everdene, quite absent-like, thinking only of religion when he seed a parson. Yes, he was a very Christian man.'

'Their daughter was not at all a pretty chiel at that time,' said Henery Fray. 'Never should have thought she'd have growed up such a handsome body as she is.'

' 'Tis to be hoped her temper is as good as her face.'

'Well, yes; but the baily will have most to do with the business and ourselves. Ah!' Henery gazed into the ashpit, and smiled volumes of ironical knowledge.

'A queer Christian, like the Devil's head in a cowl,[1] as the saying is,' volunteered Mark Clark.

'He is,' said Henery, implying that irony must cease at a certain point. 'Between we two, man and man, I believe that man would as soon tell a lie Sundays as working-days – that I do so.'

'Good faith, you do talk!' said Gabriel.

'True enough,' said the man of bitter moods, looking round upon the company with the antithetic laughter that comes from a keener appreciation of the miseries of life than ordinary men are capable of. 'Ah, there's people of one sort, and people of another, but that man – bless your souls!'

Gabriel thought fit to change the subject. 'You must be a very aged man, malter, to have sons growed up so old and ancient,' he remarked.

'Father's so old that 'a can't mind his age, can ye, father?' interposed Jacob. 'And he's growed terrible crooked, too, lately,' Jacob continued, surveying his father's figure, which was rather more bowed than his own. 'Really, one may say that father there is three-double.'

'Crooked folk will last a long while,' said the maltster, grimly, and not in the best humour.

'Shepherd would like to hear the pedigree of yer life, father – wouldn't ye, shepherd?'

'Ay, that I should,' said Gabriel, with the heartiness of a man who had longed to hear it for several months. 'What may your age be, malter?'

The maltster cleared his throat in an exaggerated form for emphasis, and elongating his gaze to the remotest point of the ashpit, said, in the slow speech justifiable when the importance of a subject is so generally felt that any mannerism must be tolerated in getting at it, 'Well, I don't mind the year I were born in, but perhaps I can reckon up the places I've lived at, and so get it that way. I bode at Upper Longpuddle across

---

[1] This phrase is a conjectural emendation of the unintelligible expression, 'as the Devil said to the Owl,' used by the natives.

there' (nodding to the north) 'till I were eleven. I bode seven at Kingsbere' (nodding to the east) 'where I took to malting. I went therefrom to Norcombe, and malted there two-and-twenty years, and two-and-twenty years I was there turnip-hoeing and harvesting. Ah, I knowed that old place, Norcombe, years afore you were thought of, Master Oak' (Oak smiled sincere belief in the fact). 'Then I malted at Durnover four year, and four year turnip-hoeing; and I was fourteen times eleven months at Millpond St. Jude's' (nodding north-west-by-north). 'Old Twills wouldn't hire me for more than eleven months at a time, to keep me from being chargeable to the parish if so be I was disabled. Then I was three year at Mellstock, and I've been here one-and-thirty year come Candlemas. How much is that?'

'Hundred and seventeen,' chuckled another old gentleman, given to mental arithmetic and little conversation, who had hitherto sat unobserved in a corner.

'Well, then, that's my age,' said the maltster emphatically.

'O no, father!' said Jacob. 'Your turnip-hoeing were in the summer and your malting in the winter of the same years, and ye don't ought to count both halves, father.'

'Chok' it all! I lived through the summers, didn't I? That's my question. I suppose ye'll say next I be no age at all to speak of?'

'Sure we shan't,' said Gabriel soothingly.

'Ye be a very old aged person, malter,' attested Jan Coggan, also soothingly. 'We all know that, and ye must have a wonderful talented constitution to be able to live so long, mustn't he, neighbours?'

'True, true; ye must, malter, wonderful,' said the meeting unanimously.

The maltster, being now pacified, was even generous enough to voluntarily disparage in a slight degree the virtue of having lived a great many years, by mentioning that the cup they were drinking out of was three years older than he.

While the cup was being examined, the end of Gabriel

Oak's flute became visible over his smock-frock pocket, and Henery Fray exclaimed, 'Surely, shepherd, I seed you blowing into a great flute by now at Casterbridge?'

'You did,' said Gabriel, blushing faintly. 'I've been in great trouble, neighbours, and was driven to it. I used not to be so poor as I be now.'

'Never mind, heart!' said Mark Clark. 'You should take it careless-like, shepherd, and your time will come. But we could thank ye for a tune, if ye bain't too tired?'

'Neither drum nor trumpet have I heard since Christmas,' said Jan Coggan. 'Come, raise a tune, Master Oak!'

'That I will,' said Gabriel, pulling out his flute and putting it together. 'A poor tool, neighbours; but such as I can do ye shall have and welcome.'

Oak then struck up 'Jockey to the Fair,' and played that sparkling melody three times through, accenting the notes in the third round in a most artistic and lively manner by bending his body in small jerks and tapping with his foot to beat time.

'He can blow the flute very well – that 'a can,' said a young married man, who having no individuality worth mentioning was known as 'Susan Tall's husband.' He continued, 'I'd as lief as not be able to blow into a flute as well as that.'

'He's a clever man, and 'tis a true comfort for us to have such a shepherd,' murmured Joseph Poorgrass, in a soft cadence. 'We ought to feel full o' thanksgiving that he's not a player of ba'dy songs instead of these merry tunes; for 'twould have been just as easy for God to have made the shepherd a loose low man – a man of iniquity, so to speak it – as what he is. Yes, for our wives' and daughters' sakes we should feel real thanksgiving.'

'True, true, – real thanksgiving!' dashed in Mark Clark conclusively, not feeling it to be of any consequence to his opinion that he had only heard about a word and three-quarters of what Joseph had said.

'Yes,' added Joseph, beginning to feel like a man in the Bible; 'for evil do thrive so in these times that ye may be as much deceived in the clanest shaved and whitest shirted man as in the raggedest tramp upon the turnpike, if I may term it so.'

'Ay, I can mind yer face now, shepherd,' said Henery Fray, criticizing Gabriel with misty eyes as he entered upon his second tune. 'Yes – now I see 'ee blowing into the flute I know 'ee to be the same man I see play at Casterbridge, for yer mouth were scrimped up and yer eyes a-staring out like a strangled man's – just as they be now.'

' 'Tis a pity that playing the flute should make a man look such a scarecrow,' observed Mr. Mark Clark, with additional criticism of Gabriel's countenance, the latter person jerking out, with the ghastly grimace required by the instrument, the chorus of 'Dame Durden': –

> 'Twas Moll' and Bet', and Doll' and Kate',
> And Dor'-othy Drag'-gle Tail'.

'I hope you don't mind that young man's bad manners in naming your features?' whispered Joseph to Gabriel.

'Not at all,' said Mr. Oak.

'For by nature ye be a very handsome man, shepherd,' continued Joseph Poorgrass with winning suavity.

'Ay, that ye be, shepherd,' said the company.

'Thank you very much,' said Oak, in the modest tone good manners demanded, thinking, however, that he would never let Bathsheba see him playing the flute; in this resolve showing a discretion equal to that related of its sagacious inventress, the divine Minerva herself.

'Ah, when I and my wife were married at Norcombe Church,' said the old maltster, not pleased at finding himself left out of the subject, 'we were called the handsomest couple in the neighbourhood – everybody said so.'

'Danged if ye bain't altered now, malter,' said a voice with the vigour natural to the enunciation of a remarkably evident truism. It came from the old man in the background, whose offensiveness and spiteful ways were barely atoned for by the occasional chuckle he contributed to general laughs.

'O no, no,' said Gabriel.

'Don't ye play no more, shepherd,' said Susan Tall's husband, the young married man who had spoken once before. 'I must be moving, and when there's tunes going on I seem as if hung in wires. If I thought after I'd left that music was still playing, and I not there, I should be quite melancholy-like.'

'What's yer hurry then, Laban?' inquired Coggan. 'You used to bide as late as the latest.'

'Well, ye see, neighbours, I was lately married to a woman, and she's my vocation now, and so ye see —' The young man halted lamely.

'New lords new laws, as the saying is, I suppose,' remarked Coggan.

'Ay, 'a b'lieve – ha, ha!' said Susan Tall's husband, in a tone intended to imply his habitual reception of jokes without minding them at all. The young man then wished them good-night and withdrew.

Henery Fray was the first to follow. Then Gabriel arose and went off with Jan Coggan, who had offered him a lodging. A few minutes later, when the remaining ones were on their legs and about to depart, Fray came back again in a hurry. Flourishing his finger ominously he threw a gaze teeming with tidings just where his eye alighted by accident, which happened to be in Joseph Poorgrass's face.

'O – what's the matter, what's the matter, Henery?' said Joseph, starting back.

'What's a-brewing, Henery?' asked Jacob and Mark Clark.

'Baily Pennyways – Baily Pennyways – I said so; yes, I said so!'

'What, found out stealing anything?'

'Stealing it is. The news is, that after Miss Everdene got home she went out again to see all was safe, as she usually do, and coming in found Baily Pennyways creeping down the granary steps with half a bushel of barley. She fleed at him like a cat – never such a tomboy as she is – of course I speak with closed doors?'

'You do – you do, Henery.'

'She fleed at him, and, to cut a long story short, he owned to having carried off five sack altogether, upon her promising not to persecute him. Well, he's turned out neck and crop, and my question is, who's going to be baily now?'

The question was such a profound one that Henery was obliged to drink there and then from the large cup till the bottom was distinctly visible inside. Before he had replaced it on the table, in came the young man, Susan Tall's husband, in a still greater hurry.

'Have ye heard the news that's all over parish?'

'About Baily Pennyways?'

'But besides that?'

'No – not a morsel of it!' they replied, looking into the very midst of Laban Tall as if to meet his words half-way down his throat.

'What a night of horrors!' murmured Joseph Poorgrass, waving his hands spasmodically. 'I've had the news-bell ringing in my left ear quite bad enough for a murder, and I've seen a magpie all alone!'

'Fanny Robin – Miss Everdene's youngest servant – can't be found. They've been wanting to lock up the door these two hours, but she isn't come in. And they don't know what to do about going to bed for fear of locking her out. They wouldn't be so concerned if she hadn't been noticed in such low spirits these last few days, and Maryann d' think the beginning of a crowner's inquest has happened to the poor girl.'

'O – 'tis burned – 'tis burned!' came from Joseph Poorgrass's dry lips.

'No – 'tis drowned!' said Tall.

'Or 'tis her father's razor!' suggested Billy Smallbury with a vivid sense of detail.

'Well – Miss Everdene wants to speak to one or two of us before we go to bed. What with this trouble about the baily, and now about the girl, mis'ess is almost wild.'

They all hastened up the lane to the farmhouse, excepting

the old maltster, whom neither news, fire, rain, nor thunder could draw from his hole. There, as the others' footsteps died away, he sat down again, and continued gazing as usual into the furnace with his red, bleared eyes.

From the bedroom window above their heads Bathsheba's head and shoulders, robed in mystic white, were dimly seen extended into the air.

'Are any of my men among you?' she said anxiously.

'Yes, ma'am, several,' said Susan Tall's husband.

'To-morrow morning I wish two or three of you to make inquiries in the villages round if they have seen such a person as Fanny Robin. Do it quietly; there is no reason for alarm as yet. She must have left whilst we were all at the fire.'

'I beg yer pardon, but had she any young man courting her in the parish, ma'am?' asked Jacob Smallbury.

'I don't know,' said Bathsheba.

'I've never heard of any such thing, ma'am,' said two or three.

'It is hardly likely, either,' continued Bathsheba. 'For any lover of hers might have come to the house if he had been a respectable lad. The most mysterious matter connected with her absence – indeed, the only thing which gives me serious alarm – is that she was seen to go out of the house by Maryann with only her indoor working gown on – not even a bonnet.'

'And you mean, ma'am, excusing my words, that a young woman would hardly go to see her young man without dressing up,' said Jacob, turning his mental vision upon past experiences. 'That's true – she would not, ma'am.'

'She had, I think, a bundle, though I couldn't see very well,' said a female voice from another window, which seemed that of Maryann. 'But she had no young man about here. Hers lives in Casterbridge, and I believe he's a soldier.'

'Do you know his name?' Bathsheba said.

'No, mistress; she was very close about it.'

'Perhaps I might be able to find out if I went to Casterbridge barracks,' said William Smallbury.

'Very well; if she doesn't return to-morrow, mind you go there and try to discover which man it is, and see him. I feel more responsible than I should if she had had any friends or relations alive. I do hope she has come to no harm through a man of that kind. . . . And then there's this disgraceful affair of the bailiff – but I can't speak of him now.'

Bathsheba had so many reasons for uneasiness that it seemed she did not think it worth while to dwell upon any particular one. 'Do as I told you, then,' she said in conclusion, closing the casement.

'Ay, ay, mistress; we will,' they replied, and moved away.

That night at Coggan's Gabriel Oak, beneath the screen of closed eyelids, was busy with fancies, and full of movement, like a river flowing rapidly under its ice. Night had always been the time at which he saw Bathsheba most vividly, and through the slow hours of shadow he tenderly regarded her image now. It is rarely that the pleasures of the imagination will compensate for the pain of sleeplessness, but they possibly did with Oak to-night, for the delight of merely seeing her effaced for the time his perception of the great difference between seeing and possessing.

He also thought of plans for fetching his few utensils and books from Norcombe. *The Young Man's Best Companion*, *The Farrier's Sure Guide*, *The Veterinary Surgeon*, *Paradise Lost*, *The Pilgrim's Progress*, *Robinson Crusoe*, Ash's *Dictionary*, and Walkingame's *Arithmetic*, constituted his library; and though a limited series, it was one from which he had acquired more sound information by diligent perusal than many a man of opportunities has done from a furlong of laden shelves.

CHAPTER IX

THE HOMESTEAD – A VISITOR –
HALF-CONFIDENCES

BY daylight, the bower of Oak's new-found mistress, Bathsheba
Everdene, presented itself as a hoary building, of the early stage
of Classic Renaissance as regards its architecture, and of a proportion which told at a glance that, as is so frequently the case,
it had once been the manorial hall upon a small estate around
it, now altogether effaced as a distinct property, and merged in
the vast tract of a non-resident landlord, which comprised several such modest demesnes.

Fluted pilasters, worked from the solid stone, decorated its
front, and above the roof the chimneys were panelled or colum-
nar, some coped gables with finials and like features still
retaining traces of their Gothic extraction. Soft brown mosses,
like faded velveteen, formed cushions upon the stone tiling, and
tufts of the houseleek or sengreen sprouted from the eaves of
the low surrounding buildings. A gravel walk leading from the
door to the road in front was encrusted at the sides with
more moss – here it was a silver-green variety, the nut-brown
of the gravel being visible to the width of only a foot or two
in the centre. This circumstance, and the generally sleepy air
of the whole prospect here, together with the animated and
contrasting state of the reverse façade, suggested to the imagination that on the adaptation of the building for farming purposes
the vital principle of the house had turned round inside its body
to face the other way. Reversals of this kind, strange deformities,
tremendous paralyses, are often seen to be inflicted by trade
upon edifices – either individual or in the aggregate as streets
and towns – which were originally planned for pleasure alone.

Lively voices were heard this morning in the upper rooms, the main staircase to which was of hard oak, the balusters, heavy as bed-posts, being turned and moulded in the quaint fashion of their century, the handrail as stout as a parapet-top, and the stairs themselves continually twisting round like a person trying to look over his shoulder. Going up, the floors above were found to have a very irregular surface, rising to ridges, sinking into valleys; and being just then uncarpeted, the face of the boards was seen to be eaten into innumerable vermiculations. Every window replied by a clang to the opening and shutting of every door, a tremble followed every bustling movement, and a creak accompanied a walker about the house, like a spirit, wherever he went.

In the room from which the conversation proceeded Bathsheba and her servant-companion, Liddy Smallbury, were to be discovered sitting upon the floor, and sorting a complication of papers, books, bottles, and rubbish spread out thereon – remnants from the household stores of the late occupier. Liddy, the maltster's great-grand-daughter, was about Bathsheba's equal in age, and her face was a prominent advertisement of the light-hearted English country girl. The beauty her features might have lacked in form was amply made up for by perfection of hue, which at this winter-time was the softened ruddiness on a surface of high rotundity that we meet with in a Terburg or a Gerard Douw; and, like the presentations of those great colourists, it was a face which kept well back from the boundary between comeliness and the ideal. Though elastic in nature she was less daring than Bathsheba, and occasionally showed some earnestness, which consisted half of genuine feeling, and half of mannerliness superadded by way of duty.

Through a partly-opened door the noise of a scrubbing-brush led up to the charwoman, Maryann Money, a person who for a face had a circular disc, furrowed less by age than by long gazes of perplexity at distant objects. To think of her was to get good-humoured; to speak of her was to raise the image of a dried Normandy pippin.

'Stop your scrubbing a moment,' said Bathsheba through the door to her. 'I hear something.'

Maryann suspended the brush.

The tramp of a horse was apparent, approaching the front of the building. The paces slackened, turned in at the wicket, and, what was most unusual, came up the mossy path close to the door. The door was tapped with the end of a crop or stick.

'What impertinence!' said Liddy, in a low voice. 'To ride up the footpath like that! Why didn't he stop at the gate? Lord! 'tis a gentleman! I see the top of his hat.'

'Be quiet!' said Bathsheba.

The further expression of Liddy's concern was continued by aspect instead of narrative.

'Why doesn't Mrs. Coggan go to the door?' Bathsheba continued.

Rat-tat-tat-tat resounded more decisively from Bathsheba's oak.

'Maryann, you go!' said she, fluttering under the onset of a crowd of romantic possibilities.

'O ma'am – see, here's a mess!'

The argument was unanswerable after a glance at Maryann.

'Liddy – you must,' said Bathsheba.

Liddy held up her hands and arms, coated with dust from the rubbish they were sorting, and looked imploringly at her mistress.

'There – Mrs. Coggan is going!' said Bathsheba, exhaling her relief in the form of a long breath which had lain in her bosom a minute or more.

The door opened, and a deep voice said –

'Is Miss Everdene at home?'

'I'll see, sir,' said Mrs. Coggan, and in a minute appeared in the room.

'Dear, what a thirtover place this world is!' continued Mrs. Coggan (a wholesome-looking lady who had a voice for each class of remark according to the emotion involved; who could toss a pancake or twirl a mop with the accuracy of pure mathematics, and who at this moment showed hands shaggy with fragments of dough and arms encrusted with flour). 'I am never up to my elbows, Miss, in making a pudding but one of two things do happen — either my nose must needs begin tickling, and I can't live without scratching it, or somebody knocks at the door. Here's Mr. Boldwood wanting to see you, Miss Everdene.'

A woman's dress being a part of her countenance, and any disorder in the one being of the same nature with a malformation or wound in the other, Bathsheba said at once —

'I can't see him in this state. Whatever shall I do?'

Not-at-homes were hardly naturalized in Weatherbury farmhouses, so Liddy suggested — 'Say you're a fright with dust, and can't come down.'

'Yes — that sounds very well,' said Mrs. Coggan critically.

'Say I can't see him — that will do.'

Mrs. Coggan went downstairs, and returned the answer as requested, adding, however, on her own responsibility, 'Miss is dusting bottles, sir, and is quite a object — that's why 'tis.'

'Oh, very well,' said the deep voice indifferently. 'All I wanted to ask was, if anything had been heard of Fanny Robin?'

'Nothing, sir — but we may know to-night. William Smallbury is gone to Casterbridge, where her young man lives, as is supposed, and the other men be inquiring about everywhere.'

The horse's tramp then recommenced and retreated, and the door closed.

'Who is Mr. Boldwood?' said Bathsheba.

'A gentleman-farmer at Little Weatherbury.'

'Married?'

'No, miss.'

'How old is he?'

'Forty, I should say — very handsome — rather stern-looking — and rich.'

'What a bother this dusting is! I am always in some

unfortunate plight or other,' Bathsheba said complainingly. 'Why should he inquire about Fanny?'

'Oh, because, as she had no friends in her childhood, he took her and put her to school, and got her her place here under your uncle. He's a very kind man that way, but Lord – there!'

'What?'

'Never was such a hopeless man for a woman! He's been courted by sixes and sevens – all the girls, gentle and simple, for miles round, have tried him. Jane Perkins worked at him for two months like a slave, and the two Miss Taylors spent a year upon him, and he cost Farmer Ives's daughter nights of tears and twenty pounds' worth of new clothes; but Lord – the money might as well have been thrown out of the window.'

A little boy came up at this moment and looked in upon them. This child was one of the Coggans, who, with the Small-burys, were as common among the families of this district as the Avons and Derwents among our rivers. He always had a loosened tooth or a cut finger to show to particular friends, which he did with an air of being thereby elevated above the common herd of afflictionless humanity – to which exhibition people were expected to say 'Poor child!' with a dash of con-gratulation as well as pity.

'I've got a pen-nee!' said Master Coggan in a scanning measure.

'Well – who gave it you, Teddy?' said Liddy.

'Mis-terr Bold-wood! He gave it to me for opening the gate.'

'What did he say?'

'He said, "Where are you going, my little man?" and I said, "To Miss Everdene's, please"; and he said, "She is a staid woman, isn't she, my little man?" and I said, "Yes." '

'You naughty child! What did you say that for?'

' 'Cause he gave me the penny!'

'What a pucker everything is in!' said Bathsheba disconten-tedly, when the child had gone. 'Get away, Maryann, or go on with your scrubbing, or do something! You ought to be married by this time, and not here troubling me!'

'Ay, mistress – so I did. But what between the poor men I won't have, and the rich men who won't have me, I stand as a pelican in the wilderness!'

'Did anybody ever want to marry you, miss?' Liddy ventured to ask when they were again alone. 'Lots of 'em, I daresay?'

Bathsheba paused, as if about to refuse a reply, but the temptation to say yes, since it really was in her power, was irresistible by aspiring virginity, in spite of her spleen at having been published as old.

'A man wanted to once,' she said, in a highly experienced tone, and the image of Gabriel Oak, as the farmer, rose before her.

'How nice it must seem!' said Liddy, with the fixed features of mental realization. 'And you wouldn't have him?'

'He wasn't quite good enough for me.'

'How sweet to be able to disdain, when most of us are glad to say, "Thank you!" I seem I hear it. "No, sir – I'm your better," or "Kiss my foot, sir; my face is for mouths of consequence." And did you love him, miss?'

'Oh, no. But I rather liked him.'

'Do you now?'

'Of course not – what footsteps are those I hear?'

Liddy looked from a back window into the courtyard behind, which was now getting low-toned and dim with the earliest films of night. A crooked file of men was approaching the back door. The whole string of trailing individuals advanced in the completest balance of intention, like the remarkable creatures known as Chain Salpæ, which, distinctly organized in other respects, have one will common to a whole family. Some were, as usual, in snow-white smock-frocks of Russia duck, and some in whitey-brown ones of drabbet – marked on the wrists, breasts, backs, and sleeves with honeycomb-work. Two or three women in pattens brought up the rear.

'The Philistines be upon us,' said Liddy, making her nose white against the glass.

'Oh, very well. Maryann, go down and keep them in the kitchen till I am dressed, and then show them in to me in the hall.'

CHAPTER X

MISTRESS AND MEN

HALF-AN-HOUR later Bathsheba, in finished dress, and followed by Liddy, entered the upper end of the old hall to find that her men had all deposited themselves on a long form and a settle at the lower extremity. She sat down at a table and opened the time-book, pen in her hand, with a canvas money-bag beside her. From this she poured a small heap of coin. Liddy chose a position at her elbow and began to sew, sometimes pausing and looking round, or, with the air of a privileged person, taking up one of the half-sovereigns lying before her, and surveying it merely as a work of art, while strictly preventing her countenance from expressing any wish to possess it as money.

'Now, before I begin, men,' said Bathsheba, 'I have two matters to speak of. The first is that the bailiff is dismissed for thieving, and that I have formed a resolution to have no bailiff at all, but to manage everything with my own head and hands.'

The men breathed an audible breath of amazement.

'The next matter is, have you heard anything of Fanny?'

'Nothing, ma'am.'

'Have you done anything?'

'I met Farmer Boldwood,' said Jacob Smallbury, 'and I went with him and two of his men and dragged Newmill Pond, but we found nothing.'

'And the new shepherd have been to Buck's Head, by Yalbury, thinking she had gone there, but nobody had seed her,' said Laban Tall.

'Hasn't William Smallbury been to Casterbridge?'

'Yes, ma'am, but he's not yet come home. He promised to be back by six.'

'It wants a quarter to six at present,' said Bathsheba, looking at her watch. 'I daresay he'll be in directly. Well, now
then' – she looked into the book – 'Joseph Poorgrass, are you
there?'

'Yes, sir – ma'am I mane,' said the person addressed. 'I be
the personal name of Poorgrass.'

'And what are you?'

'Nothing in my own eye. In the eye of other people – well,
I don't say it; though public thought will out.'

'What do you do on the farm?'

'I do do carting things all the year, and in seed time I shoots
the rooks and sparrows, and helps at pig-killing, sir.'

'How much to you?'

'Please nine and ninepence and a good half-penny where
'twas a bad one, sir – ma'am I mane.'

'Quite correct. Now here are ten shillings in addition as a
small present, as I am a new comer.'

Bathsheba blushed slightly at the sense of being generous in
public, and Henery Fray, who had drawn up towards her chair,
lifted his eyebrows and fingers to express amazement on a small
scale.

'How much do I owe you – that man in the corner – what's
your name?' continued Bathsheba.

'Matthew Moon, ma'am,' said a singular framework of
clothes with nothing of any consequence inside them, which
advanced with the toes in no definite direction forwards, but
turned in or out as they chanced to swing.

'Matthew Mark, did you say? – speak out – I shall not hurt
you,' inquired the young farmer kindly.

'Matthew Moon, mem,' said Henery Fray, correctingly,
from behind her chair, to which point he had edged himself.

'Matthew Moon,' murmured Bathsheba, turning her bright
eyes to the book. 'Ten and twopence halfpenny is the sum put
down to you, I see?'

'Yes, mis'ess,' said Matthew, as the rustle of wind among
dead leaves.

'Here it is, and ten shillings. Now the next – Andrew Randle, you are a new man, I hear. How came you to leave your last farm?'

'P-p-p-p-p-pl-pl-pl-pl-l-l-l-l-ease, ma'am, p-p-p-p-pl-pl-pl-pl-please, ma'am-please'm-please'm —'

' 'A's a stammering man, mem,' said Henery Fray in an undertone, 'and they turned him away because the only time he ever did speak plain he said his soul was his own, and other iniquities, to the squire. 'A can cuss, mem, as well as you or I, but 'a can't speak a common speech to save his life.'

'Andrew Randle, here's yours – finish thanking me in a day or two. Temperance Miller – oh, here's another, Soberness – both women, I suppose?'

'Yes'm. Here we be, 'a b'lieve,' was echoed in shrill unison.

'What have you been doing?'

'Tending thrashing-machine, and wimbling hay-bonds, and saying "Hoosh!" to the cocks and hens when they go upon your seeds, and planting Early Flourballs and Thompson's Wonderfuls with a dibble.'

'Yes – I see. Are they satisfactory women?' she inquired softly of Henery Fray.

'O mem – don't ask me! Yielding women – as scarlet a pair as ever was!' groaned Henery under his breath.

'Sit down.'

'Who, mem?'

'Sit down.'

Joseph Poorgrass, in the background, twitched, and his lips became dry with fear of some terrible consequences, as he saw Bathsheba summarily speaking, and Henery slinking off to a corner.

'Now the next. Laban Tall, you'll stay on working for me?'

'For you or anybody that pays me well, ma'am,' replied the young married man.

'True – the man must live!' said a woman in the back quarter, who had just entered with clicking pattens.

'What woman is that?' Bathsheba asked.

'I be his lawful wife!' continued the voice with greater prominence of manner and tone. This lady called herself five-and-
twenty, looked thirty, passed as thirty-five, and was forty. She
was a woman who never, like some newly married, showed
conjugal tenderness in public, perhaps because she had none to
show.

'Oh, you are,' said Bathsheba. 'Well, Laban, will you stay
on?'

'Yes, he'll stay, ma'am!' said again the shrill tongue of
Laban's lawful wife.

'Well, he can speak for himself, I suppose.'

'O Lord, not he, ma'am! A simple tool. Well enough, but a
poor gawkhammer mortal,' the wife replied.

'Heh-heh-heh!' laughed the married man, with a hideous
effort of appreciation, for he was as irrepressibly good-humoured under ghastly snubs as a parliamentary candidate on
the hustings.

The names remaining were called in the same manner.

'Now I think I have done with you,' said Bathsheba, closing
the book and shaking back a stray twine of hair. 'Has William
Smallbury returned?'

'No, ma'am.'

'The new shepherd will want a man under him,' suggested
Henery Fray, trying to make himself official again by a sideway
approach towards her chair.

'Oh – he will. Who can he have?'

'Young Cain Ball is a very good lad,' Henery said, 'and
Shepherd Oak don't mind his youth?' he added, turning with
an apologetic smile to the shepherd, who had just appeared on
the scene, and was now leaning against the doorpost with his
arms folded.

'No, I don't mind that,' said Gabriel.

'How did Cain come by such a name?' asked Bathsheba.

'Oh, you see, mem, his pore mother, not being a Scripture-
read woman, made a mistake at his christening, thinking 'twas
Abel killed Cain, and called en Cain, meaning Abel all the

time. The parson put it right, but 'twas too late, for the name could never be got rid of in the parish. 'Tis very unfortunate for the boy.'

'It is rather unfortunate.'

'Yes. However, we soften it down as much as we can, and call him Cainy. Ah, pore widow-woman! she cried her heart out about it almost. She was brought up by a very heathen father and mother, who never sent her to church or school, and it shows how the sins of the parents are visited upon the children, mem.'

Mr. Fray here drew up his features to the mild degree of melancholy required when the persons involved in the given misfortune do not belong to your own family.

'Very well then, Cainy Ball to be under-shepherd. And you quite understand your duties? – you I mean, Gabriel Oak?'

'Quite well, I thank you, Miss Everdene,' said Shepherd Oak from the doorpost. 'If I don't, I'll inquire.' Gabriel was rather staggered by the remarkable coolness of her manner. Certainly nobody without previous information would have dreamt that Oak and the handsome woman before whom he stood had ever been other than strangers. But perhaps her air was the inevitable result of the social rise which had advanced her from a cottage to a large house and fields. The case is not unexampled in high places. When, in the writings of the later poets, Jove and his family are found to have moved from their cramped quarters on the peak of Olympus into the wide sky above it, their words show a proportionate increase of arrogance and reserve.

Footsteps were heard in the passage, combining in their character the qualities both of weight and measure, rather at the expense of velocity.

(All.) 'Here's Billy Smallbury come from Casterbridge.'

'And what's the news?' said Bathsheba, as William, after marching to the middle of the hall, took a handkerchief from his hat and wiped his forehead from its centre to its remoter boundaries.

'I should have been sooner, miss,' he said, 'if it hadn't been for the weather.' He then stamped with each foot severely, and on looking down his boots were perceived to be clogged with snow.

'Come at last, is it?' said Henery.

'Well, what about Fanny?' said Bathsheba.

'Well, ma'am, in round numbers, she's run away with the soldiers,' said William.

'No; not a steady girl like Fanny!'

'I'll tell ye all particulars. When I got to Casterbridge Barracks, they said, "The Eleventh Dragoon Guards be gone away, and new troops have come." The Eleventh left last week for Melchester and onwards. The Route came from Government like a thief in the night, as is his nature to, and afore the Eleventh knew it almost, they were on the march. They passed near here.'

Gabriel had listened with interest. 'I saw them go,' he said.

'Yes,' continued William, 'they pranced down the street playing "The Girl I Left Behind Me," so 'tis said, in glorious notes of triumph. Every looker-on's inside shook with the blows of the great drum to his deepest vitals, and there was not a dry eye throughout the town among the public-house people and the nameless women!'

'But they're not gone to any war?'

'No, ma'am; but they be gone to take the places of them who may, which is very close connected. And so I said to myself, Fanny's young man was one of the regiment, and she's gone after him. There, ma'am, that's it in black and white.'

'Did you find out his name?'

'No; nobody knew it. I believe he was higher in rank than a private.'

Gabriel remained musing and said nothing, for he was in doubt.

'Well, we are not likely to know more to-night, at any rate,' said Bathsheba. 'But one of you had better run across to Farmer Boldwood's and tell him that much.'

She then rose; but before retiring, addressed a few words to them with a pretty dignity, to which her mourning dress added a soberness that was hardly to be found in the words themselves:

'Now mind, you have a mistress instead of a master. I don't yet know my powers or my talents in farming; but I shall do my best, and if you serve me well, so shall I serve you. Don't any unfair ones among you (if there are any such, but I hope not) suppose that because I'm a woman I don't understand the difference between bad goings-on and good.'

(All.) 'No'm!'

(Liddy.) 'Excellent well said.'

'I shall be up before you are awake; I shall be afield before you are up; and I shall have breakfasted before you are afield. In short, I shall astonish you all.'

(All.) 'Yes'm!'

'And so good-night.'

(All.) 'Good-night, ma'am.'

Then this small thesmothete stepped from the table, and surged out of the hall, her black silk dress licking up a few straws and dragging them along with a scratching noise upon the floor. Liddy, elevating her feelings to the occasion from a sense of grandeur, floated off behind Bathsheba with a milder dignity not entirely free from travesty, and the door was closed.

CHAPTER XI

OUTSIDE THE BARRACKS – SNOW – A MEETING

FOR dreariness nothing could surpass a prospect in the out-skirts of a certain town and military station, many miles north of Weatherbury, at a later hour on this same snowy evening – if that may be called a prospect of which the chief constituent was darkness.

It was a night when sorrow may come to the brightest without causing any great sense of incongruity: when, with impressible persons, love becomes solicitousness, hope sinks to misgiving, and faith to hope: when the exercise of memory does not stir feelings of regret at opportunities for ambition that have been passed by, and anticipation does not prompt to enterprise.

The scene was a public path, bordered on the left hand by a river, behind which rose a high wall. On the right was a tract of land, partly meadow and partly moor, reaching, at its remote verge, to a wide undulating upland.

The changes of the seasons are less obtrusive on spots of this kind than amid woodland scenery. Still, to a close observer, they are just as perceptible; the difference is that their media of manifestation are less trite and familiar than such well-known ones as the bursting of the buds or the fall of the leaf. Many are not so stealthy and gradual as we may be apt to imagine in considering the general torpidity of a moor or waste. Winter, in coming to the country hereabout, advanced in well-marked stages, wherein might have been successively observed the retreat of the snakes, the transformation of the ferns, the filling of the pools, a rising of fogs, the embrowning by frost, the collapse of the fungi, and an obliteration by snow.

This climax of the series had been reached to-night on the

aforesaid moor, and for the first time in the season its irregularities were forms without features; suggestive of anything, proclaiming nothing, and without more character than that of being the limit of something else – the lowest layer of a firmament of snow. From this chaotic skyful of crowding flakes the mead and moor momentarily received additional clothing, only to appear momentarily more naked thereby. The vast arch of cloud above was strangely low, and formed as it were the roof of a large dark cavern, gradually sinking in upon its floor; for the instinctive thought was that the snow lining the heavens and that encrusting the earth would soon unite into one mass without any intervening stratum of air at all.

We turn our attention to the left-hand characteristics; which were flatness in respect of the river, verticality in respect of the wall behind it, and darkness as to both. These features made up the mass. If anything could be darker than the sky, it was the wall, and if anything could be gloomier than the wall it was the river beneath. The indistinct summit of the façade was notched and pronged by chimneys here and there, and upon its face were faintly signified the oblong shapes of windows, though only in the upper part. Below, down to the water's edge, the flat was unbroken by hole or projection.

An indescribable succession of dull blows, perplexing in their regularity, sent their sound with difficulty through the fluffy atmosphere. It was a neighbouring clock striking ten. The bell was in the open air, and being overlaid with several inches of muffling snow, had lost its voice for the time.

About this hour the snow abated: ten flakes fell where twenty had fallen, then one had the room of ten. Not long after a form moved by the brink of the river.

By its outline upon the colourless background a close observer might have seen that it was small. This was all that was positively discoverable, though it seemed human.

The shape went slowly along, but without much exertion, for the snow, though sudden, was not as yet more than two inches deep. At this time some words were spoken aloud: –

'One. Two. Three. Four. Five.'

Between each utterance the little shape advanced about half-a-dozen yards. It was evident now that the windows high in the wall were being counted. The word 'Five' represented the fifth window from the end of the wall.

Here the spot stopped, and dwindled smaller. The figure was stooping. Then a morsel of snow flew across the river towards the fifth window. It smacked against the wall at a point several yards from its mark. The throw was the idea of a man conjoined with the execution of a woman. No man who had ever seen bird, rabbit, or squirrel in his childhood, could possibly have thrown with such utter imbecility as was shown here.

Another attempt, and another; till by degrees the wall must have become pimpled with the adhering lumps of snow. At last one fragment struck the fifth window.

The river would have been seen by day to be of that deep smooth sort which races middle and sides with the same gliding precision, any irregularities of speed being immediately corrected by a small whirlpool. Nothing was heard in reply to the signal but the gurgle and cluck of one of these invisible wheels – together with a few small sounds which a sad man would have called moans, and a happy man laughter – caused by the flapping of the waters against trifling objects in other parts of the stream.

The window was struck again in the same manner.

Then a noise was heard, apparently produced by the opening of the window. This was followed by a voice from the same quarter:

'Who's there?'

The tones were masculine, and not those of surprise. The high wall being that of a barrack, and marriage being looked upon with disfavour in the army, assignations and communications had probably been made across the river before to-night.

'Is it Sergeant Troy?' said the blurred spot in the snow, tremulously.

This person was so much like a mere shade upon the earth,

and the other speaker so much a part of the building, that one would have said the wall was holding a conversation with the snow.

'Yes,' came suspiciously from the shadow. 'What girl are you?'

'O, Frank – don't you know me?' said the spot. 'Your wife, Fanny Robin.'

'Fanny!' said the wall, in utter astonishment.

'Yes,' said the girl, with a half-suppressed gasp of emotion.

There was something in the woman's tone which is not that of the wife, and there was a manner in the man which is rarely a husband's. The dialogue went on:

'How did you come here?'

'I asked which was your window. Forgive me!'

'I did not expect you to-night. Indeed, I did not think you would come at all. It was a wonder you found me here. I am orderly to-morrow.'

'You said I was to come.'

'Well – I said that you might.'

'Yes, I mean that I might. You are glad to see me, Frank?'

'O yes – of course.'

'Can you – come to me?'

'My dear Fan, no! The bugle has sounded, the barrack gates are closed, and I have no leave. We are all of us as good as in the county gaol till to-morrow morning.'

'Then I shan't see you till then!' The words were in a faltering tone of disappointment.

'How did you get here from Weatherbury?'

'I walked – some part of the way – the rest by the carriers.'

'I am surprised.'

'Yes – so am I. And Frank, when will it be?'

'What?'

'That you promised.'

'I don't quite recollect.'

'O you do! Don't speak like that. It weighs me to the earth. It makes me say what ought to be said first by you.'

'Never mind – say it.'

'O, must I? – it is, when shall we be married, Frank?'

'Oh, I see. Well – you have to get proper clothes.'

'I have money. Will it be by banns or license?'

'Banns, I should think.'

'And we live in two parishes.'

'Do we? What then?'

'My lodgings are in St. Mary's, and this is not. So they will have to be published in both.'

'Is that the law?'

'Yes. O Frank – you think me forward, I am afraid! Don't, dear Frank – will you – for I love you so. And you said lots of times you would marry me, and – and – I – I – I —'

'Don't cry, now! It is foolish. If I said so, of course I will.'

'And shall I put up the banns in my parish, and will you in yours?'

'Yes.'

'To-morrow?'

'Not to-morrow. We'll settle in a few days.'

'You have the permission of the officers?'

'No – not yet.'

'O – how is it? You said you almost had before you left Casterbridge.'

'The fact is, I forgot to ask. Your coming like this is so sudden and unexpected.'

'Yes – yes – it is. It was wrong of me to worry you. I'll go away now. Will you come and see me to-morrow, at Mrs. Twills's, in North Street? I don't like to come to the Barracks. There are bad women about, and they think me one.'

'Quite so. I'll come to you, my dear. Good-night.'

'Good-night, Frank – good-night!'

And the noise was again heard of a window closing. The little spot moved away. When she passed the corner a subdued exclamation was heard inside the wall.

'Ho – ho – Sergeant – ho – ho!' An expostulation followed,

but it was indistinct; and it became lost amid a low peal of laughter, which was hardly distinguishable from the gurgle of the tiny whirlpools outside.

CHAPTER XII

FARMERS – A RULE – AN EXCEPTION

THE first public evidence of Bathsheba's decision to be a farmer in her own person and by proxy no more was her appearance the following market-day in the cornmarket at Casterbridge.

The low though extensive hall, supported by beams and pillars, and latterly dignified by the name of Corn Exchange, was thronged with hot men who talked among each other in twos and threes, the speaker of the minute looking sideways into his auditor's face and concentrating his argument by a contraction of one eyelid during delivery. The greater number carried in their hands ground-ash saplings, using them partly as walking-sticks and partly for poking up pigs, sheep, neighbours with their backs turned, and restful things in general, which seemed to require such treatment in the course of their peregrinations. During conversations each subjected his sapling to great varieties of usage – bending it round his back, forming an arch of it between his two hands, overweighting it on the ground till it reached nearly a semicircle; or perhaps it was hastily tucked under the arm whilst the sample-bag was pulled forth and a handful of corn poured into the palm, which, after criticism, was flung upon the floor, an issue of events perfectly well known to half-a-dozen acute town-bred fowls which had as usual crept into the building unobserved, and waited the fulfilment of their anticipations with a high-stretched neck and oblique eye.

Among these heavy yeomen a feminine figure glided, the single one of her sex that the room contained. She was prettily and even daintily dressed. She moved between them as a chaise between carts, was heard after them as a romance after sermons, was felt among them like a breeze among furnaces. It had required a little determination – far more than she had at first imagined – to take up a position here, for at her first entry the lumbering dialogues had ceased, nearly every face had been turned towards her, and those that were already turned rigidly fixed there.

Two or three only of the farmers were personally known to Bathsheba, and to these she had made her way. But if she was to be the practical woman she had intended to show herself, business must be carried on, introductions or none, and she ultimately acquired confidence enough to speak and reply boldly to men merely known to her by hearsay. Bathsheba too had her sample-bags, and by degrees adopted the professional pour into the hand – holding up the grains in her narrow palm for inspection, in perfect Casterbridge manner.

Something in the exact arch of her upper unbroken row of teeth, and in the keenly pointed corners of her red mouth when, with parted lips, she somewhat defiantly turned up her face to argue a point with a tall man, suggested that there was potentiality enough in that lithe slip of humanity for alarming exploits of sex, and daring enough to carry them out. But her eyes had a softness – invariably a softness – which, had they not been dark, would have seemed mistiness; as they were, it lowered an expression that might have been piercing to simple clearness.

Strange to say of a woman in full bloom and vigour, she always allowed her interlocutors to finish their statements before rejoining with hers. In arguing on prices she held to her own firmly, as was natural in a dealer, and reduced theirs persistently, as was inevitable in a woman. But there was an elasticity in her firmness which removed it from obstinacy, as there was a *naïveté* in her cheapening which saved it from meanness.

Those of the farmers with whom she had no dealings (by far the greater part) were continually asking each other, 'Who is she?' The reply would be —

'Farmer Everdene's niece; took on Weatherbury Upper Farm; turned away the baily, and swears she'll do everything herself.'

The other man would then shake his head.

'Yes, 'tis a pity she's so headstrong,' the first would say. 'But we ought to be proud of her here – she lightens up the old place. 'Tis such a shapely maid, however, that she'll soon get picked up.'

It would be ungallant to suggest that the novelty of her engagement in such an occupation had almost as much to do with the magnetism as had the beauty of her face and movements. However, the interest was general, and this Saturday's *début* in the forum, whatever it may have been to Bathsheba as the buying and selling farmer, was unquestionably a triumph to her as the maiden. Indeed, the sensation was so pronounced that her instinct on two or three occasions was to merely walk as a queen among these gods of the fallow, like a little sister of a little Jove, and to neglect closing prices altogether.

The numerous evidences of her power to attract were only thrown into greater relief by a marked exception. Women seem to have eyes in their ribbons for such matters as these. Bathsheba, without looking within a right angle of him, was conscious of a black sheep among the flock.

It perplexed her first. If there had been a respectable minority on either side, the case would have been most natural. If nobody had regarded her, she would have taken the matter indifferently – such cases had occurred. If everybody, this man included, she would have taken it as a matter of course – people had done so before. But the smallness of the exception made the mystery.

She soon knew thus much of the recusant's appearance. He was a gentlemanly man, with full and distinctly outlined Roman features, the prominences of which glowed in the sun with a bronze-like richness of tone. He was erect in attitude, and quiet in demeanour. One characteristic pre-eminently marked him – dignity.

Apparently he had some time ago reached that entrance to middle age at which a man's aspect naturally ceases to alter for the term of a dozen years or so; and, artificially, a woman's does likewise. Thirty-five and fifty were his limits of variation – he might have been either, or anywhere between the two.

It may be said that married men of forty are usually ready and generous enough to fling passing glances at any specimen of moderate beauty they may discern by the way. Probably, as with persons playing whist for love, the consciousness of a certain immunity under any circumstances from that worst possible ultimate, the having to pay, makes them unduly speculative. Bathsheba was convinced that this unmoved person was not a married man.

When marketing was over, she rushed off to Liddy, who was waiting for her beside the yellow gig in which they had driven to town. The horse was put in, and on they trotted – Bathsheba's sugar, tea, and drapery parcels being packed behind, and expressing in some indescribable manner, by their colour, shape, and general lineaments, that they were that young lady-farmer's property, and the grocer's and draper's no more.

'I've been through it, Liddy, and it is over. I shan't mind it again, for they will all have grown accustomed to seeing me there; but this morning it was as bad as being married – eyes everywhere!'

'I knowed it would be,' Liddy said. 'Men be such a terrible class of society to look at a body.'

'But there was one man who had more sense than to waste his time upon me.' The information was put in this form that Liddy might not for a moment suppose her mistress was at all piqued. 'A very good-looking man,' she continued, 'upright; about forty, I should think. Do you know at all who he could be?'

Liddy couldn't think.

'Can't you guess at all?' said Bathsheba with some disappointment.

'I haven't a notion; besides, 'tis no difference, since he took less notice of you than any of the rest. Now, if he'd taken more, it would have mattered a great deal.'

Bathsheba was suffering from the reverse feeling just then, and they bowled along in silence. A low carriage, bowling along still more rapidly behind a horse of unimpeachable breed, overtook and passed them.

'Why, there he is!' she said.

Liddy looked. 'That! That's Farmer Boldwood – of course 'tis – the man you couldn't see the other day when he called.'

'Oh, Farmer Boldwood,' murmured Bathsheba, and looked at him as he outstripped them. The farmer had never turned his head once, but with eyes fixed on the most advanced point along the road, passed as unconsciously and abstractedly as if Bathsheba and her charms were thin air.

'He's an interesting man – don't you think so?' she remarked.

'O yes, very. Everybody owns it,' replied Liddy.

'I wonder why he is so wrapt up and indifferent, and seemingly so far away from all he sees around him.'

'It is said – but not known for certain – that he met with some bitter disappointment when he was a young man and merry. A woman jilted him, they say.'

'People always say that – and we know very well women scarcely ever jilt men; 'tis the men who jilt us. I expect it is simply his nature to be so reserved.'

'Simply his nature – I expect so, miss – nothing else in the world.'

'Still, 'tis more romantic to think he has been served cruelly, poor thing! Perhaps, after all, he has.'

'Depend upon it he has. O yes, miss, he has! I feel he must have.'

'However, we are very apt to think extremes of people. I shouldn't wonder after all if it wasn't a little of both – just between the two – rather cruelly used and rather reserved.'

'O dear no, miss – I can't think it between the two!'

'That's most likely.'

'Well, yes, so it is. I am convinced it is most likely. You may take my word, miss, that that's what's the matter with him.'

CHAPTER XIII

SORTES SANCTORUM – THE VALENTINE

It was Sunday afternoon in the farmhouse, on the thirteenth of February. Dinner being over Bathsheba, for want of a better companion, had asked Liddy to come and sit with her. The mouldy pile was dreary in winter-time before the candles were lighted and the shutters closed; the atmosphere of the place seemed as old as the walls; every nook behind the furniture had a temperature of its own, for the fire was not kindled in this part of the house early in the day; and Bathsheba's new piano, which was an old one in other annals, looked particularly sloping and out of level on the warped floor before night threw a shade over its less prominent angles and hid the unpleasantness. Liddy, like a little brook, though shallow, was always rippling; her presence had not so much weight as to task thought, and yet enough to exercise it.

On the table lay an old quarto Bible, bound in leather. Liddy looking at it said, –

'Did you ever find out, miss, who you are going to marry by means of the Bible and key?'

'Don't be so foolish, Liddy. As if such things could be.'

'Well, there's a good deal in it, all the same.'

'Nonsense, child.'

'And it makes your heart beat fearful. Some believe in it; some don't; I do.'

'Very well, let's try it,' said Bathsheba, bounding from her seat with that total disregard of consistency which can be indulged in towards a dependent, and entering into the spirit of divination at once. 'Go and get the front door key.'

Liddy fetched it. 'I wish it wasn't Sunday,' she said, on returning. 'Perhaps 'tis wrong.'

'What's right week days is right Sundays,' replied her mistress in a tone which was a proof in itself.

The book was opened – the leaves, drab with age, being quite worn away at much-read verses by the forefingers of unpractised readers in former days, where they were moved along under the line as an aid to the vision. The special verse in the Book of Ruth was sought out by Bathsheba, and the sublime words met her eye. They slightly thrilled and abashed her. It was Wisdom in the abstract facing Folly in the concrete. Folly in the concrete blushed, persisted in her intention, and placed the key on the book. A rusty patch immediately upon the verse, caused by previous pressure of an iron substance thereon, told that this was not the first time the old volume had been used for the purpose.

'Now keep steady, and be silent,' said Bathsheba.

The verse was repeated; the book turned round; Bathsheba blushed guiltily.

'Who did you try?' said Liddy curiously.

'I shall not tell you.'

'Did you notice Mr. Boldwood's doings in church this morning, miss?' Liddy continued, adumbrating by the remark the track her thoughts had taken.

'No, indeed,' said Bathsheba, with serene indifference.

'His pew is exactly opposite yours, miss.'

'I know it.'

'And you did not see his goings on!'

'Certainly I did not, I tell you.'

Liddy assumed a smaller physiognomy, and shut her lips decisively.

This move was unexpected, and proportionately disconcerting. 'What did he do?' Bathsheba said perforce.

'Didn't turn his head to look at you once all the service.'

'Why should he?' again demanded her mistress, wearing a nettled look. 'I didn't ask him to.'

'Oh, no. But everybody else was noticing you; and it was odd he didn't. There, 'tis like him. Rich and gentlemanly, what does he care?'

Bathsheba dropped into a silence intended to express that she had opinions on the matter too abstruse for Liddy's comprehension, rather than that she had nothing to say.

'Dear me – I had nearly forgotten the valentine I bought yesterday,' she exclaimed at length.

'Valentine! who for, miss?' said Liddy. 'Farmer Boldwood?'

It was the single name among all possible wrong ones that just at this moment seemed to Bathsheba more pertinent than the right.

'Well, no. It is only for little Teddy Coggan. I have promised him something, and this will be a pretty surprise for him. Liddy, you may as well bring me my desk and I'll direct it at once.'

Bathsheba took from her desk a gorgeously illuminated and embossed design in post-octavo, which had been bought on the previous market-day at the chief stationer's in Casterbridge. In the centre was a small oval enclosure; this was left blank, that the sender might insert tender words more appropriate to the special occasion than any generalities by a printer could possibly be.

'Here's a place for writing,' said Bathsheba. 'What shall I put?'

'Something of this sort, I should think,' returned Liddy promptly: –

> 'The rose is red,
> The violet blue,
> Carnation's sweet,
> And so are you.'

'Yes, that shall be it. It just suits itself to a chubby-faced child like him,' said Bathsheba. She inserted the words in a small though legible handwriting; enclosed the sheet in an envelope, and dipped her pen for the direction.

'What fun it would be to send it to the stupid old Boldwood, and how he would wonder!' said the irrepressible Liddy, lifting her eyebrows, and indulging in an awful mirth on the verge of fear as she thought of the moral and social magnitude of the man contemplated.

Bathsheba paused to regard the idea at full length. Boldwood's had begun to be a troublesome image – a species of Daniel in her kingdom who persisted in kneeling eastward when reason and common sense said that he might just as well follow suit with the rest, and afford her the official glance of admiration which cost nothing at all. She was far from being seriously concerned about his non-conformity. Still, it was faintly depressing that the most dignified and valuable man in the parish should withhold his eyes, and that a girl like Liddy should talk about it. So Liddy's idea was at first rather harassing than piquant.

'No, I won't do that. He wouldn't see any humour in it.'

'He'd worry to death,' said the persistent Liddy.

'Really, I don't care particularly to send it to Teddy,' remarked her mistress. 'He's rather a naughty child sometimes.'

'Yes – that he is.'

'Let's toss, as men do,' said Bathsheba idly. 'Now then, head, Boldwood; tail, Teddy. No, we won't toss money on a Sunday, that would be tempting the devil indeed.'

'Toss this hymn-book; there can't be no sinfulness in that, miss.'

'Very well. Open, Boldwood – shut, Teddy. No; it's more likely to fall open. Open, Teddy – shut, Boldwood.'

The book went fluttering in the air and came down shut.

Bathsheba, a small yawn upon her mouth, took the pen, and with off-hand serenity directed the missive to Boldwood.

'Now light a candle, Liddy. Which seal shall we use? Here's a unicorn's head – there's nothing in that. What's this? – two doves – no. It ought to be something extraordinary, ought it not, Lidd? Here's one with a motto – I remember it is some funny one, but I can't read it. We'll try this, and if it doesn't do we'll have another.'

A large red seal was duly affixed. Bathsheba looked closely at the hot wax to discover the words.

'Capital!' she exclaimed, throwing down the letter

frolicsomely. ' 'Twould upset the solemnity of a parson and clerk too.'

Liddy looked at the words of the seal, and read —

'MARRY ME.'

The same evening the letter was sent, and was duly sorted in Casterbridge post-office that night, to be returned to Weatherbury again in the morning.

So very idly and unreflectingly was this deed done. Of love as a spectacle Bathsheba had a fair knowledge; but of love subjectively she knew nothing.

CHAPTER XIV

EFFECT OF THE LETTER – SUNRISE

At dusk on the evening of St. Valentine's Day Boldwood sat down to supper as usual, by a beaming fire of aged logs. Upon the mantel-shelf before him was a time-piece, surmounted by a spread eagle, and upon the eagle's wings was the letter Bathsheba had sent. Here the bachelor's gaze was continually fastening itself, till the large red seal became as a blot of blood on the retina of his eye; and as he ate and drank he still read in fancy the words thereon, although they were too remote for his sight —

'MARRY ME.'

The pert injunction was like those crystal substances, which, colourless themselves, assume the tone of objects about them. Here, in the quiet of Boldwood's parlour, where everything that was not grave was extraneous, and where the atmosphere was that of a Puritan Sunday lasting all the week, the letter and its dictum changed their tenor from the thoughtlessness of their origin to a deep solemnity, imbibed from their accessories now.

Since the receipt of the missive in the morning, Boldwood had felt the symmetry of his existence to be slowly getting distorted in the direction of an ideal passion. The disturbance was as the first floating weed to Columbus – the contemptibly little suggesting possibilities of the infinitely great.

The letter must have had an origin and a motive. That the latter was of the smallest magnitude compatible with its existence at all, Boldwood, of course, did not know. And such an explanation did not strike him as a possibility even. It is foreign to a mystified condition of mind to realize of the mystifier that the processes of approving a course suggested by circumstance, and of striking out a course from inner impulse, would look the same in the result. The vast difference between starting a train of events, and directing into a particular groove a series already started, is rarely apparent to the person confounded by the issue.

When Boldwood went to bed he placed the valentine in the corner of the looking-glass. He was conscious of its presence, even when his back was turned upon it. It was the first time in Boldwood's life that such an event had occurred. The same fascination that caused him to think it an act which had a deliberate motive prevented him from regarding it as an impertinence. He looked again at the direction. The mysterious influences of night invested the writing with the presence of the unknown writer. Somebody's – some *woman's* – hand had travelled softly over the paper bearing his name; her unrevealed eyes had watched every curve as she formed it; her brain had seen him in imagination the while. Why should she have imagined him? Her mouth – were the lips red or pale, plump or creased? – had curved itself to a certain expression as the pen went on – the corners had moved with all their natural tremulousness: what had been the expression?

The vision of the woman writing, as a supplement to the words written, had no individuality. She was a misty shape, and well she might be, considering that her original was at that moment sound asleep and oblivious of all love and letter-writing under the sky. Whenever Boldwood dozed she took a form, and comparatively ceased to be a vision: when he awoke there was the letter justifying the dream.

The moon shone to-night, and its light was not of a customary kind. His window admitted only a reflection of its rays, and the pale sheen had that reversed direction which snow gives, coming upward and lighting up his ceiling in an unnatural way, casting shadows in strange places, and putting lights where shadows had used to be.

The substance of the epistle had occupied him but little in

comparison with the fact of its arrival. He suddenly wondered if anything more might be found in the envelope than what he had withdrawn. He jumped out of bed in the weird light, took the letter, pulled out the flimsy sheet, shook the envelope – searched it. Nothing more was there. Boldwood looked, as he had a hundred times the preceding day, at the insistent red seal: 'Marry me,' he said aloud.

The solemn and reserved yeoman again closed the letter, and stuck it in the frame of the glass. In doing so he caught sight of his reflected features, wan in expression, and insubstantial in form. He saw how closely compressed was his mouth, and that his eyes were wide-spread and vacant. Feeling uneasy and dissatisfied with himself for this nervous excitability, he returned to bed.

Then the dawn drew on. The full power of the clear heaven was not equal to that of a cloudy sky at noon, when Boldwood arose and dressed himself. He descended the stairs and went out towards the gate of a field to the east, leaning over which he paused and looked around.

It was one of the usual slow sunrises of this time of the year, and the sky, pure violet in the zenith, was leaden to the northward, and murky to the east, where, over the snowy down or ewe-lease on Weatherbury Upper Farm, and apparently resting upon the ridge, the only half of the sun yet visible burnt rayless, like a red and flameless fire shining over a white hearthstone. The whole effect resembled a sunset as childhood resembles age.

In other directions the fields and sky were so much of one colour by the snow that it was difficult in a hasty glance to tell whereabouts the horizon occurred; and in general there was here, too, that before-mentioned preternatural inversion of light and shade which attends the prospect when the garish brightness commonly in the sky is found on the earth, and the shades of earth are in the sky. Over the west hung the wasting moon, now dull and greenish-yellow, like tarnished brass.

Boldwood was listlessly noting how the frost had hardened

and glazed the surface of the snow, till it shone in the red eastern light with the polish of marble; how, in some portions of the slope, withered grass-bents, encased in icicles, bristled through the smooth wan coverlet in the twisted and curved shapes of old Venetian glass; and how the footprints of a few birds, which had hopped over the snow whilst it lay in the state of a soft fleece, were now frozen to a short permanency. A half-muffled noise of light wheels interrupted him. Boldwood turned back into the road. It was the mail-cart – a crazy two-wheeled vehicle, hardly heavy enough to resist a puff of wind. The driver held out a letter. Boldwood seized it and opened it, expecting another anonymous one – so greatly are people's ideas of probability a mere sense that precedent will repeat itself.

'I don't think it is for you, sir,' said the man, when he saw Boldwood's action. 'Though there is no name, I think it is for your shepherd.'

Boldwood looked then at the address –

> To the New Shepherd,
> Weatherbury Farm,
> Near Casterbridge.

'Oh – what a mistake! – it is not mine. Nor it is for my shepherd. It is for Miss Everdene's. You had better take it on to him – Gabriel Oak – and say I opened it in mistake.'

At this moment on the ridge, up against the blazing sky, a figure was visible, like the black snuff in the midst of a candle-flame. Then it moved and began to bustle about vigorously from place to place, carrying square skeleton masses, which were riddled by the same rays. A small figure on all-fours followed behind. The tall form was that of Gabriel Oak; the small one that of George; the articles in course of transit were hurdles.

'Wait,' said Boldwood. 'That's the man on the hill. I'll take the letter to him myself.'

To Boldwood it was now no longer merely a letter to another man. It was an opportunity. Exhibiting a face pregnant with intention, he entered the snowy field.

Gabriel, at that minute, descended the hill towards the right. The glow stretched down in this direction now, and touched the distant roof of Warren's Malthouse – whither the shepherd was apparently bent. Boldwood followed at a distance.

CHAPTER XV

A MORNING MEETING – THE LETTER AGAIN

THE scarlet and orange light outside the malthouse did not penetrate to its interior, which was, as usual, lighted by a rival glow of similar hue, radiating from the hearth.

The maltster, after having lain down in his clothes for a few hours, was now sitting beside a three-legged table, breakfasting off bread and bacon. This was eaten on the plateless system, which is performed by placing a slice of bread upon the table, the meat flat upon the bread, a mustard plaster upon the meat, and a pinch of salt upon the whole, then cutting them vertically downwards with a large pocket-knife till wood is reached, when the severed lump is impaled on the knife, elevated, and sent the proper way of food.

The maltster's lack of teeth appeared not to sensibly diminish his powers as a mill. He had been without them for so many years that toothlessness was felt less to be a defect than hard gums an acquisition. Indeed, he seemed to approach the grave as a hyperbolic curve approaches a straight line – less directly as he got nearer, till it was doubtful if he would ever reach it at all.

In the ashpit was a heap of potatoes roasting, and a boiling pipkin of charred bread, called 'coffee,' for the benefit of whomsoever should call, for Warren's was a sort of clubhouse, used as an alternative to the inn.

'I say, says I, we get a fine day, and then down comes a snapper at night,' was a remark now suddenly heard spreading into the malthouse from the door, which had been opened the previous moment. The form of Henery Fray advanced to the fire, stamping the snow from his boots when about half-way

114

there. The speech and entry had not seemed to be at all an abrupt beginning to the maltster, introductory matter being often omitted in this neighbourhood, both from word and deed, and the maltster having the same latitude allowed him, did not hurry to reply. He picked up a fragment of cheese by pecking upon it with his knife, as a butcher picks up skewers.

Henery appeared in a drab kerseymere greatcoat, buttoned over his smock-frock, the white skirts of the latter being visible to the distance of about a foot below the coat-tails, which, when you got used to the style of dress, looked natural enough, and even ornamental – it certainly was comfortable.

Matthew Moon, Joseph Poorgrass, and other carters and waggoners followed at his heels, with great lanterns dangling from their hands, which showed that they had just come from the cart-horse stables, where they had been busily engaged since four o'clock that morning.

'And how is she getting on without a baily?' the maltster inquired.

Henery shook his head, and smiled one of the bitter smiles, dragging all the flesh of his forehead into a corrugated heap in the centre.

'She'll rue it – surely, surely!' he said. 'Benjy Pennyways were not a true man or an honest baily – as big a betrayer as Joey Iscariot himself. But to think she can carr' on alone!' He allowed his head to swing laterally three or four times in silence. 'Never in all my creeping up – never!'

This was recognized by all as the conclusion of some gloomy speech which had been expressed in thought alone during the shake of the head; Henery meanwhile retained several marks of despair upon his face, to imply that they would be required for use again directly he should go on speaking.

'All will be ruined, and ourselves too, or there's no meat in gentlemen's houses!' said Mark Clark.

'A headstrong maid, that's what she is – and won't listen to no advice at all. Pride and vanity have ruined many a cobbler's dog. Dear, dear, when I think o' it, I sorrows like a man in travel!'

'True, Henery, you do, I've heard ye,' said Joseph Poorgrass, in a voice of thorough attestation, and with a wire-drawn smile of misery.

' 'Twould do a martel man no harm to have what's under her bonnet,' said Billy Smallbury, who had just entered, bearing his one tooth before him. 'She can spaik real language, and must have some sense somewhere. Do ye foller me?'

'I do; but no baily – I deserved that place,' wailed Henery, signifying wasted genius by gazing blankly at visions of a high destiny apparently visible to him on Billy Smallbury's smockfrock. 'There, 'twas to be, I suppose. Your lot is your lot, and Scripture is nothing; for if you do good you don't get rewarded according to your works, but be cheated in some mean way out of your recompense.'

'No, no; I don't agree with'ee there,' said Mark Clark. 'God's a perfect gentleman in that respect.'

'Good works good pay, so to speak it,' attested Joseph Poorgrass.

A short pause ensued, and as a sort of *entr'acte* Henery turned and blew out the lanterns, which the increase of daylight rendered no longer necessary even in the malthouse, with its one pane of glass.

'I wonder what a farmer-woman can want with a harpsichord, dulcimer, pianner, or whatever 'tis they d'call it?' said the maltster. 'Liddy saith she've a new one.'

'Got a pianner?'

'Ay. Seems her old uncle's things were not good enough for her. She've bought all but everything new. There's heavy chairs for the stout, weak and wiry ones for the slender; great watches, getting on to the size of clocks, to stand upon the chimbleypiece.'

'Pictures, for the most part wonderful frames.'

'And long horse-hair settles for the drunk, with horse-hair pillows at each end,' said Mr. Clark. 'Likewise looking-glasses for the pretty, and lying books for the wicked.'

A firm loud tread was now heard stamping outside; the door

was opened about six inches, and somebody on the other side exclaimed —

'Neighbours, have ye got room for a few newborn lambs?'

'Ay, sure, shepherd,' said the conclave.

The door was flung back till it kicked the wall and trembled from top to bottom with the blow. Mr. Oak appeared in the entry with a steaming face, hay-bands wound about his ankles to keep out the snow, a leather strap round his waist outside the smock-frock, and looking altogether an epitome of the world's health and vigour. Four lambs hung in various embarrassing attitudes over his shoulders, and the dog George, whom Gabriel had contrived to fetch from Norcombe, stalked solemnly behind.

'Well, Shepherd Oak, and how's lambing this year, if I mid say it?' inquired Joseph Poorgrass.

'Terrible trying,' said Oak. 'I've been wet through twice a-day, either in snow or rain, this last fortnight. Cainy and I haven't tined our eyes to-night.'

'A good few twins, too, I hear?'

'Too many by half. Yes; 'tis a very queer lambing this year. We shan't have done by Lady Day.'

'And last year 'twer all over by Sexajessamine Sunday,' Joseph remarked.

'Bring on the rest, Cain,' said Gabriel, 'and then run back to the ewes. I'll follow you soon.'

Cainy Ball – a cheery-faced young lad, with a small circular orifice by way of mouth, advanced and deposited two others, and retired as he was bidden. Oak lowered the lambs from their unnatural elevation, wrapped them in hay, and placed them round the fire.

'We've no lambing-hut here, as I used to have at Norcombe,' said Gabriel, 'and 'tis such a plague to bring the weakly ones to a house. If 'twasn't for your place here, malter, I don't know what I should do, this keen weather. And how is it with you to-day, malter?'

'Oh, neither sick nor sorry, shepherd; but no younger.'

'Ay – I understand.'

'Sit down, Shepherd Oak,' continued the ancient man of malt. 'And how was the old place at Norcombe, when ye went for your dog? I should like to see the old familiar spot; but faith, I shouldn't know a soul there now.'

'I suppose you wouldn't. 'Tis altered very much.'

'Is it true that Dicky Hill's wooden cider-house is pulled down?'

'O yes – years ago, and Dicky's cottage just above it.'

'Well, to be sure!'

'Yes; and Tompkins's old apple-tree is rooted that used to bear two hogsheads of cider, and no help from other trees.'

'Rooted? – you don't say it! Ah! stirring times we live in – stirring times.'

'And you can mind the old well that used to be in the middle of the place? That's turned into a solid iron pump with a large stone trough, and all complete.'

'Dear, dear – how the face of nations alter, and what we live to see nowadays! Yes – and 'tis the same here. They've been talking but now of the mis'ess's strange doings.'

'What have you been saying about her?' inquired Oak, sharply turning to the rest, and getting very warm.

'These middle-aged men have been pulling her over the coals for pride and vanity,' said Mark Clark; 'but I say, let her have rope enough. Bless her pretty face – shouldn't I like to do so – upon her cherry lips!' The gallant Mark Clark here made a peculiar and well-known sound with his own.

'Mark,' said Gabriel sternly, 'now you mind this: none of that dalliance-talk – that smack-and-coddle style of yours – about Miss Everdene. I don't allow it. Do you hear?'

'With all my heart, as I've got no chance,' replied Mr. Clark cordially.

'I suppose you've been speaking against her?' said Oak, turning to Joseph Poorgrass with a very grim look.

'No, no – not a word I – 'tis a real joyful thing that she's no worse, that's what I say,' said Joseph, trembling and blushing with terror. 'Matthew just said —'

'Matthew Moon, what have you been saying?' asked Oak.

'I? Why ye know I wouldn't harm a worm – no, not one underground worm?' said Matthew Moon, looking very uneasy.

'Well, somebody has – and look here, neighbours.' Gabriel, though one of the quietest and most gentle men on earth, rose to the occasion, with martial promptness and vigour. 'That's my fist.' Here he placed his fist, rather smaller in size than a common loaf, in the mathematical centre of the maltster's little table, and with it gave a bump or two thereon, as if to ensure that their eyes all thoroughly took in the idea of fistiness before he went further. 'Now – the first man in the parish that I hear prophesying bad of our mistress, why' (here the fist was raised and let fall, as Thor might have done with his hammer in assaying it) – 'he'll smell and taste that – or I'm a Dutchman.'

All earnestly expressed by their features that their minds did not wander to Holland for a moment on account of this statement, but were deploring the difference which gave rise to the figure; and Mark Clark cried 'Hear, hear; just what I should ha' said.' The dog George looked up at the same time after the shepherd's menace, and, though he understood English but imperfectly, began to growl.

'Now, don't ye take on so, shepherd, and sit down!' said Henery, with a deprecating peacefulness equal to anything of the kind in Christianity.

'We hear that ye be a extraordinary good and clever man, shepherd,' said Joseph Poorgrass with considerable anxiety from behind the maltster's bedstead, whither he had retired for safety. ' 'Tis a great thing to be clever, I'm sure,' he added, making movements associated with states of mind rather than body; 'we wish we were, don't we, neighbours?'

'Ay, that we do, sure,' said Matthew Moon, with a small anxious laugh towards Oak, to show how very friendly disposed he was likewise.

'Who's been telling you I'm clever?' said Oak.

' 'Tis blowed about from pillar to post quite common,' said

Matthew. 'We hear that ye can tell the time as well by the stars as we can by the sun and moon, shepherd.'

'Yes, I can do a little that way,' said Gabriel, as a man of medium sentiments on the subject.

'And that ye can make sun-dials, and prent folks' names upon their waggons almost like copper-plate, with beautiful flourishes, and great long tails. A excellent fine thing for ye to be such a clever man, shepherd. Joseph Poorgrass used to prent to Farmer James Everdene's waggons before you came, and 'a could never mind which way to turn the J's and E's — could ye, Joseph?' Joseph shook his head to express how absolute was the fact that he couldn't. 'And so you used to do 'em the wrong way, like this, didn't ye, Joseph?' Matthew marked on the dusty floor with his whip-handle

ᒐAMƎꙄ

'And how Farmer James would cuss, and call thee a fool, wouldn't he, Joseph, when 'a seed his name looking so inside-out-like?' continued Matthew Moon, with feeling.

'Ay — 'a would,' said Joseph meekly. 'But, you see, I wasn't so much to blame, for them J's and E's be such trying sons o' witches for the memory to mind whether they face backward or forward; and I always had such a forgetful memory, too.'

' 'Tis a bad affliction for ye, being such a man of calamities in other ways.'

'Well, 'tis; but a happy Providence ordered that it should be no worse, and I feel my thanks. As to shepherd, there, I'm sure mis'ess ought to have made ye her baily — such a fitting man for't as you be.'

'I don't mind owning that I expected it,' said Oak frankly. 'Indeed, I hoped for the place. At the same time, Miss Everdene has a right to be her own baily if she choose — and to keep me down to be a common shepherd only.' Oak drew a slow breath, looked sadly into the bright ashpit, and seemed lost in thoughts not of the most hopeful hue.

The genial warmth of the fire now began to stimulate the nearly lifeless lambs to bleat and move their limbs briskly upon the hay, and to recognize for the first time the fact that they were born. Their noise increased to a chorus of baas, upon which Oak pulled the milk-can from before the fire, and taking a small tea-pot from the pocket of his smock-frock, filled it with milk, and taught those of the helpless creatures which were not to be restored to their dams how to drink from the spout – a trick they acquired with astonishing aptitude.

'And she don't even let ye have the skins of the dead lambs, I hear?' resumed Joseph Poorgrass, his eyes lingering on the operations of Oak with the necessary melancholy.

'I don't have them,' said Gabriel.

'Ye be very badly used, shepherd,' hazarded Joseph again, in the hope of getting Oak as an ally in lamentation after all. 'I think she's took against ye – that I do.'

'O no – not at all,' replied Gabriel hastily, and a sigh escaped him, which the deprivation of lamb skins could hardly have caused.

Before any further remark had been added a shade darkened the door, and Boldwood entered the malthouse, bestowing upon each a nod of a quality between friendliness and condescension.

'Ah! Oak, I thought you were here,' he said. 'I met the mail-cart ten minutes ago, and a letter was put into my hand, which I opened without reading the address. I believe it is yours. You must excuse the accident, please.'

'O yes – not a bit of difference, Mr. Boldwood – not a bit,' said Gabriel readily. He had not a correspondent on earth, nor was there a possible letter coming to him whose contents the whole parish would not have been welcome to peruse.

Oak stepped aside, and read the following in an unknown hand: –

'DEAR FRIEND – I do not know your name, but I think these few lines will reach you, which I write to thank you for your kindness to me the night I left Weatherbury in a reckless way. I also return the money I owe you, which you will excuse my not keeping as a gift. All has ended well, and I am happy to say I am going to be married to the young man who has courted me for some time – Sergeant Troy of the 11th Dragoon Guards, now quartered in this town. He would, I know, object to my having received anything except as a loan, being a man of great respectability and high honour – indeed, a nobleman by blood.

'I should be much obliged to you if you would keep the contents of this letter a secret for the present, dear friend. We mean to surprise Weatherbury by coming there soon as husband and wife, though I blush to state it to one nearly a stranger. The sergeant grew up in Weatherbury. Thanking you again for your kindness,

I am, your sincere well-wisher,

FANNY ROBIN.'

'Have you read it, Mr. Boldwood?' said Gabriel; 'if not, you had better do so. I know you are interested in Fanny Robin.'

Boldwood read the letter and looked grieved.

'Fanny – poor Fanny! the end she is so confident of has not yet come, she should remember – and may never come. I see she gives no address.'

'What sort of a man is this Sergeant Troy?' said Gabriel.

'H'm – I'm afraid not one to build much hope upon in such a case as this,' the farmer murmured, 'though he's a clever fellow, and up to everything. A slight romance attaches to him, too. His mother was a French governess, and it seems that a secret attachment existed between her and the late Lord Severn. She was married to a poor medical man, and soon after an infant was born; and while money was forthcoming all went on well. Unfortunately for her boy, his best friends died; and he got then a situation as second clerk at a lawyer's in Casterbridge. He stayed there for some time, and might have worked himself into a dignified position of some sort had he not indulged in the wild freak of enlisting. I have much doubt if ever little Fanny will surprise us in the way she mentions – very much doubt. A silly girl – silly girl!'

The door was hurriedly burst open again, and in came running Cainy Ball out of breath, his mouth red and open, like the bell of a penny trumpet, from which he coughed with noisy vigour and great distension of face.

'Now, Cain Ball,' said Oak sternly, 'why will you run so fast and lose your breath so? I'm always telling you of it.'

'Oh – I – a puff of mee breath – went – the wrong way, please, Mister Oak, and made me cough – hok – hok!'

'Well – what have you come for?'

'I've run to tell ye,' said the junior shepherd, supporting his exhausted youthful frame against the doorpost, 'that you must come directly. Two more ewes have twinned – that's what's the matter, Shepherd Oak.'

'Oh, that's it,' said Oak, jumping up, and dismissing for the present his thoughts on poor Fanny. 'You are a good boy to run and tell me, Cain, and you shall smell a large plum pudding some day as a treat. But, before we go, Cainy, bring the tarpot, and we'll mark this lot and have done with 'em.'

Oak took from his illimitable pockets a marking iron, dipped it into the pot, and imprinted on the buttocks of the infant sheep the initials of her he delighted to muse on – 'B.E.,' which signified to all the region round that henceforth the lambs belonged to Farmer Bathsheba Everdene, and to no one else.

'Now, Cainy, shoulder your two, and off. Good morning, Mr. Boldwood.' The shepherd lifted the sixteen large legs and four small bodies he had himself brought, and vanished with them in the direction of the lambing field hard by – their frames being now in a sleek and hopeful state, pleasantly contrasting with their death's-door plight of half an hour before.

Boldwood followed him a little way up the field, hesitated, and turned back. He followed him again with a last resolve, annihilating return. On approaching the nook in which the fold was constructed, the farmer drew out his pocket-book, unfastened it, and allowed it to lie open on his hand. A letter was revealed – Bathsheba's.

'I was going to ask you, Oak,' he said, with unreal carelessness, 'if you know whose writing this is?'

Oak glanced into the book, and replied instantly, with a flushed face, 'Miss Everdene's.'

Oak had coloured simply at the consciousness of sounding her name. He now felt a strangely distressing qualm from a new thought. The letter could of course be no other than anonymous, or the inquiry would not have been necessary.

Boldwood mistook his confusion: sensitive persons are always ready with their 'Is it I?' in preference to objective reasoning.

'The question was perfectly fair,' he returned – and there was something incongruous in the serious earnestness with which he applied himself to an argument on a valentine. 'You know it is always expected that privy inquiries will be made: that's where the – fun lies.' If the word 'fun' had been 'torture,' it could not have been uttered with a more constrained and restless countenance than was Boldwood's then.

Soon parting from Gabriel, the lonely and reserved man returned to his house to breakfast – feeling twinges of shame and regret at having so far exposed his mood by those fevered questions to a stranger. He again placed the letter on the mantelpiece, and sat down to think of the circumstances attending it by the light of Gabriel's information.

CHAPTER XVI

ALL SAINTS' AND ALL SOULS'

ON a week-day morning a small congregation, consisting mainly of women and girls, rose from its knees in the mouldy nave of a church called All Saints', in the distant barrack-town before-mentioned, at the end of a service without a sermon. They were about to disperse, when a smart footstep, entering the porch and coming up the central passage, arrested their attention. The step echoed with a ring unusual in a church; it was the clink of spurs. Everybody looked. A young cavalry soldier in a red uniform, with the three chevrons of a sergeant upon his sleeve, strode up the aisle, with an embarrassment which was only the more marked by the intense vigour of his step, and by the determination upon his face to show none. A slight flush had mounted his cheek by the time he had run the gauntlet between these women; but, passing on through the chancel arch, he never paused till he came close to the altar railing. Here for a moment he stood alone.

The officiating curate, who had not yet doffed his surplice, perceived the new-comer, and followed him to the communion-space. He whispered to the soldier, and then beckoned to the clerk, who in his turn whispered to an elderly woman, apparently his wife, and they also went up the chancel steps.

' 'Tis a wedding!' murmured some of the women, brightening. 'Let's wait!'

The majority again sat down.

There was a creaking of machinery behind, and some of the young ones turned their heads. From the interior face of the west wall of the tower projected a little canopy with a quarter-jack and small bell beneath it, the automaton being driven by the same clock machinery that struck the large bell in the tower. Between the tower and the church was a close screen, the door of which was kept shut during services, hiding this grotesque clockwork from sight. At present, however, the door was open, and the egress of the jack, the blows on the bell, and the mannikin's retreat into the nook again, were visible to many, and audible throughout the church.

The jack had struck half-past eleven.

'Where's the woman?' whispered some of the spectators.

The young sergeant stood still with the abnormal rigidity of the old pillars around. He faced the south-east, and was as silent as he was still.

The silence grew to be a noticeable thing as the minutes went on, and nobody else appeared, and not a soul moved. The rattle of the quarter-jack again from its niche, its blows for three-quarters, its fussy retreat, were almost painfully abrupt, and caused many of the congregation to start palpably.

'I wonder where the woman is!' a voice whispered again.

There began now that slight shifting of feet, that artificial coughing among several, which betrays a nervous suspense. At length there was a titter. But the soldier never moved. There he stood, his face to the south-east, upright as a column, his cap in his hand.

The clock ticked on. The women threw off their nervousness, and titters and giggling became more frequent. Then came a dead silence. Every one was waiting for the end. Some persons may have noticed how extraordinarily the striking of quarters seems to quicken the flight of time. It was hardly credible that the jack had not got wrong with the minutes when the rattle began again, the puppet emerged, and the four quarters were struck fitfully as before. One could almost be positive that there was a malicious leer upon the hideous creature's face, and a mischievous delight in its twitchings. Then followed the dull and remote resonance of the twelve heavy strokes in the tower above. The women were impressed, and there was no giggle this time.

The clergyman glided into the vestry, and the clerk vanished. The sergeant had not yet turned; every woman in the church was waiting to see his face, and he appeared to know it. At last he did turn, and stalked resolutely down the nave, braving them all, with a compressed lip. Two bowed and toothless old almsmen then looked at each other and chuckled, innocently enough; but the sound had a strange weird effect in that place.

Opposite to the church was a paved square, around which several overhanging wood buildings of old time cast a picturesque shade. The young man on leaving the door went to cross the square, when, in the middle, he met a little woman. The expression of her face, which had been one of intense anxiety, sank at the sight of his nearly to terror.

'Well?' he said, in a suppressed passion, fixedly looking at her.

'O Frank – I made a mistake! – I thought that church with the spire was All Saints', and I was at the door at half-past eleven to a minute as you said. I waited till a quarter to twelve, and found then that I was in All Souls'. But I wasn't much frightened, for I thought it could be to-morrow as well.'

'You fool, for so fooling me! But say no more.'

'Shall it be to-morrow, Frank?' she asked blankly.

'To-morrow!' and he gave vent to a hoarse laugh. 'I don't go through that experience again for some time, I warrant you!'

'But after all,' she expostulated in a trembling voice, 'the mistake was not such a terrible thing! Now, dear Frank, when shall it be?'

'Ah, when? God knows!' he said, with a light irony, and turning from her walked rapidly away.

CHAPTER XVII

IN THE MARKET-PLACE

ON Saturday Boldwood was in Casterbridge market-house as usual, when the disturber of his dreams entered, and became visible to him. Adam had awakened from his deep sleep, and behold! there was Eve. The farmer took courage, and for the first time really looked at her.

Material causes and emotional effects are not to be arranged in regular equation. The result from capital employed in the production of any movement of a mental nature is sometimes as tremendous as the cause itself is absurdly minute. When women are in a freakish mood their usual intuition, either from carelessness or inherent defect, seemingly fails to teach them this, and hence it was that Bathsheba was fated to be astonished to-day.

Boldwood looked at her – not slily, critically, or understandingly, but blankly at gaze, in the way a reaper looks up at a passing train – as something foreign to his element, and but dimly understood. To Boldwood women had been remote phenomena rather than necessary complements – comets of such uncertain aspect, movement, and permanence, that whether their orbits were as geometrical, unchangeable, and as subject to laws as his own, or as absolutely erratic as they superficially appeared, he had not deemed it his duty to consider.

He saw her black hair, her correct facial curves and profile, and the roundness of her chin and throat. He saw then the side of her eyelids, eyes, and lashes, and the shape of her ear. Next he noticed her figure, her skirt, and the very soles of her shoes.

Boldwood thought her beautiful, but wondered whether he was right in his thought, for it seemed impossible that this

128

romance in the flesh, if so sweet as he imagined, could have been going on long without creating a commotion of delight among men, and provoking more inquiry than Bathsheba had done, even though that was not a little. To the best of his judgment neither nature nor art could improve this perfect one of an imperfect many. His heart began to move within him. Boldwood, it must be remembered, though forty years of age, had never before inspected a woman with the very centre and force of his glance; they had struck upon all his senses at wide angles.

Was she really beautiful? He could not assure himself that his opinion was true even now. He furtively said to a neighbour, 'Is Miss Everdene considered handsome?'

'O yes; she was a good deal noticed the first time she came, if you remember. A very handsome girl indeed.'

A man is never more credulous than in receiving favourable opinions on the beauty of a woman he is half, or quite, in love with; a mere child's word on the point has the weight of an R.A.'s. Boldwood was satisfied now.

And this charming woman had in effect said to him, 'Marry me.' Why should she have done that strange thing? Boldwood's blindness to the difference between approving of what circumstances suggest, and originating what they do not suggest, was well matched by Bathsheba's insensibility to the possibly great issues of little beginnings.

She was at this moment coolly dealing with a dashing young farmer, adding up accounts with him as indifferently as if his face had been the pages of a ledger. It was evident that such a nature as his had no attraction for a woman of Bathsheba's taste. But Boldwood grew hot down to his hands with an incipient jealousy; he trod for the first time the threshold of 'the injured lover's hell.' His first impulse was to go and thrust himself between them. This could be done, but only in one way – by asking to see a sample of her corn. Boldwood renounced the idea. He could not make the request; it was debasing loveliness to ask it to buy and sell, and jarred with his conceptions of her.

All this time Bathsheba was conscious of having broken into that dignified stronghold at last. His eyes, she knew, were following her everywhere. This was a triumph; and had it come naturally, such a triumph would have been the sweeter to her for this piquing delay. But it had been brought about by misdirected ingenuity, and she valued it only as she valued an artificial flower or a wax fruit.

Being a woman with some good sense in reasoning on subjects wherein her heart was not involved, Bathsheba genuinely repented that a freak which had owed its existence as much to Liddy as to herself, should ever have been undertaken, to disturb the placidity of a man she respected too highly to deliberately tease.

She that day nearly formed the intention of begging his pardon on the very next occasion of their meeting. The worst features of this arrangement were that, if he thought she ridiculed him, an apology would increase the offence by being disbelieved; and if he thought she wanted him to woo her, it would read like additional evidence of her forwardness.

CHAPTER XVIII

BOLDWOOD IN MEDITATION – REGRET

BOLDWOOD was tenant of what was called Little Weatherbury Farm, and his person was the nearest approach to aristocracy that this remoter quarter of the parish could boast of. Genteel strangers, whose god was their town, who might happen to be compelled to linger about this nook for a day, heard the sound of light wheels, and prayed to see good society, to the degree of a solitary lord, or squire at the very least, but it was only Mr. Boldwood going out for the day. They heard the sound of wheels yet once more, and were re-animated to expectancy: it was only Mr. Boldwood coming home again.

His house stood recessed from the road, and the stables, which are to a farm what a fireplace is to a room, were behind, their lower portions being lost amid bushes of laurel. Inside the blue door, open half-way down, were to be seen at this time the backs and tails of half-a-dozen warm and contented horses standing in their stalls; and as thus viewed, they presented alternations of roan and bay, in shapes like a Moorish arch, the tail being a streak down the midst of each. Over these, and lost to the eye gazing in from the outer light, the mouths of the same animals could be heard busily sustaining the above-named warmth and plumpness by quantities of oats and hay. The restless and shadowy figure of a colt wandered about a loose-box at the end, whilst the steady grind of all the eaters was occasionally diversified by the rattle of a rope or the stamp of a foot.

Pacing up and down at the heels of the animals was Farmer Boldwood himself. This place was his almonry and cloister in one: here, after looking to the feeding of his four-footed

dependants, the celibate would walk and meditate of an evening till the moon's rays streamed in through the cobwebbed
windows, or total darkness enveloped the scene.

His square-framed perpendicularity showed more fully now
than in the crowd and bustle of the market-house. In this meditative walk his foot met the floor with heel and toe simultaneously, and his fine reddish-fleshed face was bent downwards
just enough to render obscure the still mouth and the well-
rounded though rather prominent and broad chin. A few clear
and thread-like horizontal lines were the only interruption to
the otherwise smooth surface of his large forehead.

The phases of Boldwood's life were ordinary enough, but his
was not an ordinary nature. That stillness, which struck casual
observers more than anything else in his character and habit,
and seemed so precisely like the rest of inanition, may have
been the perfect balance of enormous antagonistic forces –
positives and negatives in fine adjustment. His equilibrium disturbed, he was in extremity at once. If an emotion possessed
him at all, it ruled him; a feeling not mastering him was entirely
latent. Stagnant or rapid, it was never slow. He was always hit
mortally, or he was missed.

He had no light and careless touches in his constitution, either for good or for evil. Stern in the outlines of action,
mild in the details, he was serious throughout all. He saw no
absurd sides to the follies of life, and thus, though not quite
companionable in the eyes of merry men and scoffers,
and those to whom all things show life as a jest, he was not
intolerable to the earnest and those acquainted with grief.
Being a man who read all the dramas of life seriously, if he
failed to please when they were comedies, there was no frivol-
ous treatment to reproach him for when they chanced to end
tragically.

Bathsheba was far from dreaming that the dark and silent
shape upon which she had so carelessly thrown a seed was a
hotbed of tropic intensity. Had she known Boldwood's moods
her blame would have been fearful, and the stain upon her

heart ineradicable. Moreover, had she known her present power for good or evil over this man, she would have trembled at her responsibility. Luckily for her present, unluckily for her future tranquillity, her understanding had not yet told her what Boldwood was. Nobody knew entirely; for though it was possible to form guesses concerning his wild capabilities from old floodmarks faintly visible, he had never been seen at the high tides which caused them.

Farmer Boldwood came to the stable-door and looked forth across the level fields. Beyond the first enclosure was a hedge, and on the other side of this a meadow belonging to Bathsheba's farm.

It was now early spring – the time of going to grass with the sheep, when they have the first feed of the meadows, before these are laid up for mowing. The wind, which had been blowing east for several weeks, had veered to the southward, and the middle of spring had come abruptly – almost without a beginning. It was that period in the vernal quarter when we may suppose the Dryads to be waking for the season. The vegetable world begins to move and swell and the saps to rise, till in the completest silence of lone gardens and trackless plantations, where everything seems helpless and still after the bond and slavery of frost, there are bustlings, strainings, united thrusts, and pulls-all-together, in comparison with which the powerful tugs of cranes and pulleys in a noisy city are but pigmy efforts.

Boldwood, looking into the distant meadows, saw there three figures. They were those of Miss Everdene, Shepherd Oak, and Cainy Ball.

When Bathsheba's figure shone upon the farmer's eyes it lighted him up as the moon lights up a great tower. A man's body is as the shell, or the tablet, of his soul, as he is reserved or ingenuous, overflowing or self-contained. There was a change in Boldwood's exterior from its former impassibleness; and his face showed that he was now living outside his defences for the first time, and with a fearful sense of exposure. It is the usual experience of strong natures when they love.

At last he arrived at a conclusion. It was to go across and inquire boldly of her.

The insulation of his heart by reserve during these many years, without a channel of any kind for disposable emotion, had worked its effect. It has been observed more than once that the causes of love are chiefly subjective, and Boldwood was a living testimony to the truth of the proposition. No mother existed to absorb his devotion, no sister for his tenderness, no idle ties for sense. He became surcharged with the compound, which was genuine lover's love.

He approached the gate of the meadow. Beyond it the ground was melodious with ripples, and the sky with larks; the low bleating of the flock mingling with both. Mistress and man were engaged in the operation of making a lamb 'take,' which is performed whenever a ewe has lost her own offspring, one of the twins of another ewe being given her as a substitute. Gabriel had skinned the dead lamb, and was tying the skin over the body of the live lamb in the customary manner, whilst Bathsheba was holding open a little pen of four hurdles, into which the mother and foisted lamb were driven, where they would remain till the old sheep conceived an affection for the young one.

Bathsheba looked up at the completion of the manœuvre and saw the farmer by the gate, where he was overhung by a willow tree in full bloom. Gabriel, to whom her face was as the uncertain glory of an April day, was ever regardful of its faintest changes, and instantly discerned thereon the mark of some influence from without, in the form of a keenly self-conscious reddening. He also turned and beheld Boldwood.

At once connecting these signs with the letter Boldwood had shown him, Gabriel suspected her of some coquettish procedure begun by that means, and carried on since, he knew not how.

Farmer Boldwood had read the pantomime denoting that they were aware of his presence, and the perception was as too much light turned upon his new sensibility. He was still in the road, and by moving on he hoped that neither would recognize that he had originally intended to enter the field. He passed by with an utter and overwhelming sensation of ignorance, shyness, and doubt. Perhaps in her manner there were signs that she wished to see him – perhaps not – he could not read a woman. The cabala of this erotic philosophy seemed to consist of the subtlest meanings expressed in misleading ways. Every turn, look, word, and accent contained a mystery quite distinct from its obvious import, and not one had ever been pondered by him until now.

As for Bathsheba, she was not deceived into the belief that Farmer Boldwood had walked by on business or in idleness. She collected the probabilities of the case, and concluded that she was herself responsible for Boldwood's appearance there. It troubled her much to see what a great flame a little wildfire was likely to kindle. Bathsheba was no schemer for marriage, nor was she deliberately a trifler with the affections of men, and a censor's experience on seeing an actual flirt after observing her would have been a feeling of surprise that Bathsheba could be so different from such a one, and yet so like what a flirt is supposed to be.

She resolved never again, by look or by sign, to interrupt the steady flow of this man's life. But a resolution to avoid an evil is seldom framed till the evil is so far advanced as to make avoidance impossible.

CHAPTER XIX

THE SHEEP-WASHING – THE OFFER

BOLDWOOD did eventually call upon her. She was not at home. 'Of course not,' he murmured. In contemplating Bathsheba as a woman, he had forgotten the accidents of her position as an agriculturist – that being as much of a farmer, and as extensive a farmer, as himself, her probable whereabouts was out-of-doors at this time of the year. This, and the other oversights Boldwood was guilty of, were natural to the mood, and still more natural to the circumstances. The great aids to idealization in love were present here: occasional observation of her from a distance, and the absence of social intercourse with her – visual familiarity, oral strangeness. The smaller human elements were kept out of sight; the pettinesses that enter so largely into all earthly living and doing were disguised by the accident of lover and loved-one not being on visiting terms; and there was hardly awakened a thought in Boldwood that sorry household realities appertained to her, or that she, like all others, had moments of commonplace, when to be least plainly seen was to be most prettily remembered. Thus a mild sort of apotheosis took place in his fancy, whilst she still lived and breathed within his own horizon, a troubled creature like himself.

It was the end of May when the farmer determined to be no longer repulsed by trivialities or distracted by suspense. He had by this time grown used to being in love; the passion now startled him less even when it tortured him more, and he felt himself adequate to the situation. On inquiring for her at her house they had told him she was at the sheep-washing, and he went off to seek her there.

The sheep-washing pool was a perfectly circular basin of

brickwork in the meadows, full of the clearest water. To birds on the wing its glassy surface, reflecting the light sky, must have been visible for miles around as a glistening Cyclops' eye in a green face. The grass about the margin at this season was a sight to remember long – in a minor sort of way. Its activity in sucking the moisture from the rich damp sod was almost a process observable by the eye. The outskirts of this level water-meadow were diversified by rounded and hollow pastures, where just now every flower that was not a buttercup was a daisy. The river slid along noiselessly as a shade, the swelling reeds and sedge forming a flexible palisade upon its moist brink. To the north of the mead were trees, the leaves of which were new, soft, and moist, not yet having stiffened and dark-ened under summer sun and drought, their colour being yellow beside a green – green beside a yellow. From the recesses of this knot of foliage the loud notes of three cuckoos were re-sounding through the still air.

Boldwood went meditating down the slopes with his eyes on his boots, which the yellow pollen from the buttercups had bronzed in artistic gradations. A tributary of the main stream flowed through the basin of the pool by an inlet and outlet at opposite points of its diameter. Shepherd Oak, Jan Coggan, Moon, Poorgrass, Cain Ball, and several others were assembled here, all dripping wet to the very roots of their hair, and Bath-sheba was standing by in a new riding-habit – the most elegant she had ever worn – the reins of her horse being looped over her arm. Flagons of cider were rolling about upon the green. The meek sheep were pushed into the pool by Coggan and Matthew Moon, who stood by the lower hatch, immersed to their waists; then Gabriel, who stood on the brink, thrust them under as they swam along, with an instrument like a crutch, formed for the purpose, and also for assisting the exhausted animals when the wool became saturated and they began to sink. They were let out against the stream, and through the upper opening, all impurities flowing away below. Cainy Ball and Joseph, who performed this latter operation, were if possible wetter than the rest; they resembled dolphins under a fountain, every protuberance and angle of their clothes dribbling forth a small rill.

Boldwood came close and bade her good morning with such constraint that she could not but think he had stepped across to the washing for its own sake, hoping not to find her there; more, she fancied his brow severe and his eye slighting. Bathsheba immediately contrived to withdraw, and glided along by the river till she was a stone's throw off. She heard footsteps brushing the grass, and had a consciousness that love was encircling her like a perfume. Instead of turning or waiting, Bathsheba went further among the high sedges, but Boldwood seemed determined, and pressed on till they were completely past the bend of the river. Here, without being seen, they could hear the splashing and shouts of the washers above.

'Miss Everdene!' said the farmer.

She trembled, turned, and said 'Good morning.' His tone was so utterly removed from all she had expected as a beginning. It was lowness and quiet accentuated: an emphasis of deep meanings, their form, at the same time, being scarcely expressed. Silence has sometimes a remarkable power of showing itself as the disembodied soul of feeling wandering without its carcase, and it is then more impressive than speech. In the same way, to say a little is often to tell more than to say a great deal. Boldwood told everything in that word.

As the consciousness expands on learning that what was fancied to be the rumble of wheels is the reverberation of thunder, so did Bathsheba's at her intuitive conviction.

'I feel – almost too much – to think,' he said, with a solemn simplicity. 'I have come to speak to you without preface. My life is not my own since I have beheld you clearly, Miss Everdene – I come to make you an offer of marriage.'

Bathsheba tried to preserve an absolutely neutral countenance, and all the motion she made was that of closing lips which had previously been a little parted.

'I am now forty-one years old,' he went on. 'I may have

been called a confirmed bachelor, and I was a confirmed bachelor. I had never any views of myself as a husband in my earlier days, nor have I made any calculation on the subject since I have been older. But we all change, and my change, in this matter, came with seeing you. I have felt lately, more and more, that my present way of living is bad in every respect. Beyond all things, I want you as my wife.'

'I feel, Mr. Boldwood, that though I respect you much, I do not feel – what would justify me to – in accepting your offer,' she stammered.

This giving back of dignity for dignity seemed to open the sluices of feeling that Boldwood had as yet kept closed.

'My life is a burden without you,' he exclaimed, in a low voice. 'I want you – I want you to let me say I love you again and again!'

Bathsheba answered nothing, and the mare upon her arm seemed so impressed that instead of cropping the herbage she looked up.

'I think and hope you care enough for me to listen to what I have to tell!'

Bathsheba's momentary impulse at hearing this was to ask why he thought that, till she remembered that, far from being a conceited assumption on Boldwood's part, it was but the natural conclusion of serious reflection based on deceptive premises of her own offering.

'I wish I could say courteous flatteries to you,' the farmer continued in an easier tone, 'and put my rugged feeling into a graceful shape: but I have neither power nor patience to learn such things. I want you for my wife – so wildly that no other feeling can abide in me; but I should not have spoken out had I not been led to hope.'

'The valentine again! O that valentine!' she said to herself, but not a word to him.

'If you can love me say so, Miss Everdene. If not – don't say no!'

'Mr. Boldwood, it is painful to have to say I am surprised,

so that I don't know how to answer you with propriety and respect – but am only just able to speak out my feeling – I mean my meaning; that I am afraid I can't marry you, much as I respect you. You are too dignified for me to suit you, sir.'

'But, Miss Everdene!'

'I – I didn't – I know I ought never to have dreamt of sending that valentine – forgive me, sir – it was a wanton thing which no woman with any self-respect should have done. If you will only pardon my thoughtlessness, I promise never to —'

'No, no, no. Don't say thoughtlessness! Make me think it was something more – that it was a sort of prophetic instinct – the beginning of a feeling that you would like me. You torture me to say it was done in thoughtlessness – I never thought of it in that light, and I can't endure it. Ah! I wish I knew how to win you! but that I can't do – I can only ask if I have already got you. If I have not, and it is not true that you have come unwittingly to me as I have to you, I can say no more.'

'I have not fallen in love with you, Mr. Boldwood – certainly I must say that.' She allowed a very small smile to creep for the first time over her serious face in saying this, and the white row of upper teeth, and keenly-cut lips already noticed, suggested an idea of heartlessness, which was immediately contradicted by the pleasant eyes.

'But you will just think – in kindness and condescension think – if you cannot bear with me as a husband! I fear I am too old for you, but believe me I will take more care of you than would many a man of your own age. I will protect and cherish you with all my strength – I will indeed! You shall have no cares – be worried by no household affairs, and live quite at ease, Miss Everdene. The dairy superintendence shall be done by a man – I can afford it well – you shall never have so much as to look out of doors at haymaking time, or to think of weather in the harvest. I rather cling to the chaise, because it is the same my poor father and mother drove, but if you don't like it I will sell it, and you shall have a pony-carriage of your own. I cannot say how far above every other idea and object

on earth you seem to me – nobody knows – God only knows
– how much you are to me!'

Bathsheba's heart was young, and it swelled with sympathy
for the deep-natured man who spoke so simply.

'Don't say it: don't! I cannot bear you to feel so much, and
me to feel nothing. And I am afraid they will notice us, Mr.
Boldwood. Will you let the matter rest now? I cannot think
collectedly. I did not know you were going to say this to me.
O, I am wicked to have made you suffer so!' She was frightened
as well as agitated at his vehemence.

'Say then, that you don't absolutely refuse. Do not quite
refuse?'

'I can do nothing. I cannot answer.'

'I may speak to you again on the subject?'

'Yes.'

'I may think of you?'

'Yes, I suppose you may think of me.'

'And hope to obtain you?'

'No – do not hope! Let us go on.'

'I will call upon you again to-morrow.'

'No – please not. Give me time.'

'Yes – I will give you any time,' he said earnestly and gratefully. 'I am happier now.'

'No – I beg you! Don't be happier if happiness only comes
from my agreeing. Be neutral, Mr. Boldwood! I must think.'

'I will wait,' he said.

And then she turned away. Boldwood dropped his gaze to
the ground, and stood long like a man who did not know where
he was. Realities then returned upon him like the pain of a
wound received in an excitement which eclipses it, and he, too,
then went on.

CHAPTER XX

PERPLEXITY – GRINDING THE SHEARS –
A QUARREL

'HE is so disinterested and kind to offer me all that I can desire,' Bathsheba mused.

Yet Farmer Boldwood, whether by nature kind or the reverse to kind, did not exercise kindness here. The rarest offerings of the purest loves are but a self-indulgence, and no generosity at all.

Bathsheba, not being the least in love with him, was eventually able to look calmly at his offer. It was one which many women of her own station in the neighbourhood, and not a few of higher rank, would have been wild to accept and proud to publish. In every point of view, ranging from politic to passionate, it was desirable that she, a lonely girl, should marry, and marry this earnest, well-to-do, and respected man. He was close to her doors: his standing was sufficient: his qualities were even supererogatory. Had she felt, which she did not, any wish whatever for the married state in the abstract, she could not reasonably have rejected him, being a woman who frequently appealed to her understanding for deliverance from her whims. Boldwood as a means to marriage was unexceptionable: she esteemed and liked him, yet she did not want him. It appears that ordinary men take wives because possession is not possible without marriage, and that ordinary women accept husbands because marriage is not possible without possession; with totally differing aims the method is the same on both sides. But the understood incentive on the woman's part was wanting here. Besides, Bathsheba's position as absolute mistress of a farm and house was a novel one, and the novelty had not yet begun to wear off.

But a disquiet filled her which was somewhat to her credit, for it would have affected few. Beyond the mentioned reasons with which she combated her objections, she had a strong feeling that, having been the one who began the game, she ought in honesty to accept the consequences. Still the reluctance remained. She said in the same breath that it would be ungenerous not to marry Boldwood, and that she couldn't do it to save her life.

Bathsheba's was an impulsive nature under a deliberative aspect. An Elizabeth in brain and a Mary Stuart in spirit, she often performed actions of the greatest temerity with a manner of extreme discretion. Many of her thoughts were perfect syllogisms; unluckily they always remained thoughts. Only a few were irrational assumptions; but, unfortunately, they were the ones which most frequently grew into deeds.

The next day to that of the declaration she found Gabriel Oak at the bottom of her garden, grinding his shears for the sheep-shearing. All the surrounding cottages were more or less scenes of the same operation; the scurr of whetting spread into the sky from all parts of the village as from an armoury previous to a campaign. Peace and war kiss each other at their hours of preparation – sickles, scythes, shears, and pruning-hooks ranking with swords, bayonets, and lances, in their common necessity for point and edge.

Cainy Ball turned the handle of Gabriel's grindstone, his head performing a melancholy see-saw up and down with each turn of the wheel. Oak stood somewhat as Eros is represented when in the act of sharpening his arrows: his figure slightly bent, the weight of his body thrown over on the shears, and his head balanced sideways, with a critical compression of the lips and contraction of the eyelids to crown the attitude.

His mistress came up and looked upon them in silence for a minute or two; then she said —

'Cain, go to the lower mead and catch the bay mare. I'll turn the winch of the grindstone. I want to speak to you, Gabriel.'

Cain departed, and Bathsheba took the handle. Gabriel had glanced up in intense surprise, quelled its expression, and looked down again. Bathsheba turned the winch, and Gabriel applied the shears.

The peculiar motion involved in turning a wheel has a wonderful tendency to benumb the mind. It is a sort of attenuated variety of Ixion's punishment, and contributes a dismal chapter to the history of gaols. The brain gets muddled, the head grows heavy, and the body's centre of gravity seems to settle by degrees in a leaden lump somewhere between the eyebrows and the crown. Bathsheba felt the unpleasant symptoms after two or three dozen turns.

'Will you turn, Gabriel, and let me hold the shears?' she said. 'My head is in a whirl, and I can't talk.'

Gabriel turned. Bathsheba then began, with some awkwardness, allowing her thoughts to stray occasionally from her story to attend to the shears, which required a little nicety in sharpening.

'I wanted to ask you if the men made any observations on my going behind the sedge with Mr. Boldwood yesterday?'

'Yes, they did,' said Gabriel. 'You don't hold the shears right, miss – I knew you wouldn't know the way – hold like this.'

He relinquished the winch, and enclosing her two hands completely in his own (taking each as we sometimes clasp a child's hand in teaching him to write), grasped the shears with her. 'Incline the edge so,' he said.

Hands and shears were inclined to suit the words, and held thus for a peculiarly long time by the instructor as he spoke.

'That will do,' exclaimed Bathsheba. 'Loose my hands. I won't have them held! Turn the winch.'

Gabriel freed her hands quietly, retired to his handle, and the grinding went on.

'Did the men think it odd?' she said again.

'Odd was not the idea, miss.'

'What did they say?'

'That Farmer Boldwood's name and your own were likely to be flung over pulpit together before the year was out.'

'I thought so by the look of them! Why, there's nothing in it. A more foolish remark was never made, and I want you to contradict it: that's what I came for.'

Gabriel looked incredulous and sad, but between his moments of incredulity, relieved.

'They must have heard our conversation,' she continued.

'Well, then, Bathsheba!' said Oak, stopping the handle, and gazing into her face with astonishment.

'Miss Everdene, you mean,' she said, with dignity.

'I mean this, that if Mr. Boldwood really spoke of marriage, I bain't going to tell a story and say he didn't to please you. I have already tried to please you too much for my own good!'

Bathsheba regarded him with round-eyed perplexity. She did not know whether to pity him for disappointed love of her, or to be angry with him for having got over it – his tone being ambiguous.

'I said I wanted you just to mention that it was not true I was going to be married to him,' she murmured, with a slight decline in her assurance.

'I can say that to them if you wish, Miss Everdene. And I could likewise give an opinion to 'ee on what you have done.'

'I daresay. But I don't want your opinion.'

'I suppose not,' said Gabriel bitterly, and going on with his turning; his words rising and falling in a regular swell and cadence as he stooped or rose with the winch, which directed them, according to his position, perpendicularly into the earth, or horizontally along the garden, his eyes being fixed on a leaf upon the ground.

With Bathsheba a hastened act was a rash act; but, as does not always happen, time gained was prudence ensured. It must be added, however, that time was very seldom gained. At this period the single opinion in the parish on herself and her doings that she valued as sounder than her own was Gabriel Oak's. And the outspoken honesty of his character was such that on any subject, even that of her love for, or marriage with, another man, the same disinterestedness of opinion might be calculated on, and be had for the asking. Thoroughly convinced of the impossibility of his own suit, a high resolve constrained him not to injure that of another. This is a lover's most stoical virtue, as the lack of it is a lover's most venial sin. Knowing he would reply truly she asked the question, painful as she must have known the subject would be. Such is the selfishness of some charming women. Perhaps it was some excuse for her thus torturing honesty to her own advantage, that she had absolutely no other sound judgment within easy reach.

'Well, what is your opinion of my conduct,' she said quietly.

'That it is unworthy of any thoughtful, and meek, and comely woman.'

In an instant Bathsheba's face coloured with the angry crimson of a Danby sunset. But she forbore to utter this feeling, and the reticence of her tongue only made the loquacity of her face the more noticeable.

The next thing Gabriel did was to make a mistake.

'Perhaps you don't like the rudeness of my reprimanding you, for I know it is rudeness; but I thought it would do good.'

She instantly replied sarcastically —

'On the contrary, my opinion of you is so low, that I see in your abuse the praise of discerning people!'

'I am glad you don't mind it, for I said it honestly and with every serious meaning.'

'I see. But, unfortunately, when you try not to speak in jest you are amusing – just as when you wish to avoid seriousness you sometimes say a sensible word.'

It was a hard hit, but Bathsheba had unmistakably lost her temper, and on that account Gabriel had never in his life kept his own better. He said nothing. She then broke out —

'I may ask, I suppose, where in particular my unworthiness lies? In my not marrying you, perhaps!'

'Not by any means,' said Gabriel quietly. 'I have long given up thinking of that matter.'

'Or wishing it, I suppose,' she said; and it was apparent that she expected an unhesitating denial of this supposition.

Whatever Gabriel felt, he coolly echoed her words —

'Or wishing it either.'

A woman may be treated with a bitterness which is sweet to her, and with a rudeness which is not offensive. Bathsheba would have submitted to an indignant chastisement for her levity had Gabriel protested that he was loving her at the same time; the impetuosity of passion unrequited is bearable, even if it stings and anathematizes — there is a triumph in the humiliation, and a tenderness in the strife. This was what she had been expecting, and what she had not got. To be lectured because the lecturer saw her in the cold morning light of open-shuttered disillusion was exasperating. He had not finished, either. He continued in a more agitated voice: –

'My opinion is (since you ask it) that you are greatly to blame for playing pranks upon a man like Mr. Boldwood, merely as a pastime. Leading on a man you don't care for is not a praiseworthy action. And even, Miss Everdene, if you seriously inclined towards him, you might have let him find it out in some way of true loving-kindness, and not by sending him a valentine's letter.'

Bathsheba laid down the shears.

'I cannot allow any man to – to criticize my private conduct!' she exclaimed. 'Nor will I for a minute. So you'll please leave the farm at the end of the week!'

It may have been a peculiarity – at any rate it was a fact – that when Bathsheba was swayed by an emotion of an earthly sort her lower lip trembled: when by a refined emotion, her upper or heavenward one. Her nether lip quivered now.

'Very well, so I will,' said Gabriel calmly. He had been held to her by a beautiful thread which it pained him to spoil by breaking, rather than by a chain he could not break. 'I should be even better pleased to go at once,' he added.

'Go at once then, in Heaven's name!' said she, her eyes flashing at his, though never meeting them. 'Don't let me see your face any more.'

'Very well, Miss Everdene — so it shall be.'

And he took his shears and went away from her in placid dignity, as Moses left the presence of Pharaoh.

CHAPTER XXI

TROUBLES IN THE FOLD – A MESSAGE

GABRIEL Oak had ceased to feed the Weatherbury flock for about four-and-twenty hours, when on Sunday afternoon the elderly gentleman Joseph Poorgrass, Matthew Moon, Fray, and half-a-dozen others, came running up to the house of the mistress of the Upper Farm.

'Whatever *is* the matter, men?' she said, meeting them at the door just as she was coming out on her way to church, and ceasing in a moment from the close compression of her two red lips, with which she had accompanied the exertion of pulling on a tight glove.

'Sixty!' said Joseph Poorgrass.

'Seventy!' said Moon.

'Fifty-nine!' said Susan Tall's husband.

'– Sheep have broken fence,' said Fray.

'– And got into a field of young clover,' said Tall.

'– Young clover!' said Moon.

'– Clover!' said Joseph Poorgrass.

'And they be getting blasted,' said Henery Fray.

'That they be,' said Joseph.

'And will all die as dead as nits, if they bain't got out and cured!' said Tall.

Joseph's countenance was drawn into lines and puckers by his concern. Fray's forehead was wrinkled both perpendicularly and crosswise, after the pattern of a portcullis, expressive of a double despair. Laban Tall's lips were thin, and his face was rigid. Matthew's jaws sank, and his eyes turned whichever way the strongest muscle happened to pull them.

'Yes,' said Joseph, 'and I was sitting at home looking for Ephesians, and says I to myself, " 'Tis nothing but Corinthians

149

and Thessalonians in this danged Testament," when who should come in but Henery there: "Joseph," he said, "the sheep have blasted theirselves —" '

With Bathsheba it was a moment when thought was speech and speech exclamation. Moreover, she had hardly recovered her equanimity since the disturbance which she had suffered from Oak's remarks.

'That's enough – that's enough! – O you fools!' she cried, throwing the parasol and Prayer-book into the passage, and running out of doors in the direction signified. 'To come to me, and not go and get them out directly! O, the stupid numskulls!'

Her eyes were at their darkest and brightest now. Bathsheba's beauty belonging rather to the demonian than to the angelic school, she never looked so well as when she was angry – and particularly when the effect was heightened by a rather dashing velvet dress, carefully put on before a glass.

All the ancient men ran in a jumbled throng after her to the clover-field, Joseph sinking down in the midst when about half-way, like an individual withering in a world which was more and more insupportable. Having once received the stimulus that her presence always gave them they went round among the sheep with a will. The majority of the afflicted animals were lying down, and could not be stirred. These were bodily lifted out, and the others driven into the adjoining field. Here, after the lapse of a few minutes, several more fell down, and lay helpless and livid as the rest.

Bathsheba, with a sad, bursting heart, looked at these primest specimens of her prime flock as they rolled there –

'Swoln with wind and the rank mist they drew.'

Many of them foamed at the mouth, their breathing being quick and short, whilst the bodies of all were fearfully distended.

'O, what can I do, what can I do!' said Bathsheba, helplessly. 'Sheep are such unfortunate animals! – there's always something happening to them! I never knew a flock pass a year without getting into some scrape or other.'

'There's only one way of saving them,' said Tall.

'What way? Tell me quick!'

'They must be pierced in the side with a thing made on purpose.'

'Can you do it? Can I?'

'No, ma'am. We can't, nor you neither. It must be done in a particular spot. If ye go to the right or left but an inch you stab the ewe and kill her. Not even a shepherd can do it, as a rule.'

'Then they must die,' she said, in a resigned tone.

'Only one man in the neighbourhood knows the way,' said Joseph, now just come up. 'He could cure 'em all if he were here.'

'Who is he? Let's get him!'

'Shepherd Oak,' said Matthew. 'Ah, he's a clever man in talents!'

'Ah, that he is so!' said Joseph Poorgrass.

'True – he's the man,' said Laban Tall.

'How dare you name that man in my presence!' she said excitedly. 'I told you never to allude to him, nor shall you if you stay with me. Ah!' she added, brightening, 'Farmer Boldwood knows!'

'O no, ma'am,' said Matthew. 'Two of his store ewes got into some vetches t'other day, and were just like these. He sent a man on horseback here post-haste for Gable, and Gable went and saved 'em. Farmer Boldwood hev got the thing they do it with. 'Tis a holler pipe, with a sharp pricker inside. Isn't it, Joseph?'

'Ay – a holler pipe,' echoed Joseph. 'That's what 'tis.'

'Ay, sure – that's the machine,' chimed in Henery Fray reflectively, with an Oriental indifference to the flight of time.

'Well,' burst out Bathsheba, 'don't stand there with your "ayes" and your "sures," talking at me! Get somebody to cure the sheep instantly!'

All then stalked off in consternation, to get somebody as directed, without any idea of who it was to be. In a minute they had vanished through the gate, and she stood alone with the dying flock.

'Never will I send for him – never!' she said firmly.

One of the ewes here contracted its muscles horribly, extended itself, and jumped high into the air. The leap was an astonishing one. The ewe fell heavily, and lay still.

Bathsheba went up to it. The sheep was dead.

'O, what shall I do – what shall I do!' she again exclaimed, wringing her hands. 'I won't send for him. No, I won't!'

The most vigorous expression of a resolution does not always coincide with the greatest vigour of the resolution itself. It is often flung out as a sort of prop to support a decaying conviction which, whilst strong, required no enunciation to prove it so. The 'No, I won't' of Bathsheba meant virtually, 'I think I must.'

She followed her assistants through the gate, and lifted her hand to one of them. Laban answered to her signal.

'Where is Oak staying?'

'Across the valley at Nest Cottage.'

'Jump on the bay mare, and ride across, and say he must return instantly – that I say so.'

Tall scrambled off to the field, and in two minutes was on Poll, the bay, bare-backed, and with only a halter by way of rein. He diminished down the hill.

Bathsheba watched. So did all the rest. Tall cantered along the bridle-path through Sixteen Acres, Sheeplands, Middle Field, The Flats, Cappel's Piece, shrank almost to a point, crossed the bridge, and ascended from the valley through Springmead and Whitepits on the other side. The cottage to which Gabriel had retired before taking his final departure from the locality was visible as a white spot on the opposite hill, backed by blue firs. Bathsheba walked up and down. The men entered the field and endeavoured to ease the anguish of the dumb creatures by rubbing them. Nothing availed.

Bathsheba continued walking. The horse was seen descending the hill, and the wearisome series had to be repeated in reverse order: Whitepits, Springmead, Cappel's Piece, The Flats, Middle Field, Sheeplands, Sixteen Acres. She hoped Tall had had presence of mind enough to give the mare up to Gabriel, and return himself on foot. The rider neared them. It was Tall.

'O what folly!' said Bathsheba.

Gabriel was not visible anywhere.

'Perhaps he is already gone!' she said.

Tall came into the inclosure, and leapt off, his face tragic as Morton's after the battle of Shrewsbury.

'Well?' said Bathsheba, unwilling to believe that her verbal *lettre-de-cachet* could possibly have miscarried.

'He says *beggars mustn't be choosers*,' replied Laban.

'What!' said the young farmer, opening her eyes and drawing in her breath for an outburst. Joseph Poorgrass retired a few steps behind a hurdle.

'He says he shall not come onless you request en to come civilly and in a proper manner, as becomes any 'ooman begging a favour.'

'Oh, oh, that's his answer! Where does he get his airs? Who am I, then, to be treated like that? Shall I beg to a man who has begged to me?'

Another of the flock sprang into the air, and fell dead.

The men looked grave, as if they suppressed opinion.

Bathsheba turned aside, her eyes full of tears. The strait she was in through pride and shrewishness could not be disguised longer: she burst out crying bitterly; they all saw it; and she attempted no further concealment.

'I wouldn't cry about it, miss,' said William Smallbury compassionately. 'Why not ask him softer like? I'm sure he'd come then. Gable is a true man in that way.'

Bathsheba checked her grief and wiped her eyes. 'O, it is a wicked cruelty to me – it is – it is!' she murmured. 'And he drives me to do what I wouldn't; yes, he does! – Tall, come indoors.'

After this collapse, not very dignified for the head of an

establishment, she went into the house, Tall at her heels. Here she sat down and hastily scribbled a note between the small convulsive sobs of convalescence which follow a fit of crying as a ground-swell follows a storm. The note was none the less polite for being written in a hurry. She held it at a distance, was about to fold it, then added these words at the bottom: –

'Do not desert me, Gabriel!'

She looked a little redder in refolding it, and closed her lips, as if thereby to suspend till too late the action of conscience in examining whether such strategy were justifiable. The note was despatched as the message had been, and Bathsheba waited indoors for the result.

It was an anxious quarter of an hour that intervened between the messenger's departure and the sound of the horse's tramp again outside. She could not watch this time, but, leaning over the old bureau at which she had written the letter, closed her eyes, as if to keep out both hope and fear.

The case, however, was a promising one. Gabriel was not angry: he was simply neutral, although her first command had been so haughty. Such imperiousness would have damned a little less beauty; and on the other hand, such beauty would have redeemed a little less imperiousness.

She went out when the horse was heard, and looked up. A mounted figure passed between her and the sky, and drew on towards the field of sheep, the rider turning his face in receding. Gabriel looked at her. It was a moment when a woman's eyes and tongue tell distinctly opposite tales. Bathsheba looked full of gratitude, and she said: –

'O, Gabriel, how could you serve me so unkindly!'

Such a tenderly-shaped reproach for his previous delay was the one speech in the language that he could pardon for not being commendation of his readiness now.

Gabriel murmured a confused reply, and hastened on. She knew from the look which sentence in her note had brought him. Bathsheba followed to the field.

Gabriel was already among the turgid, prostrate forms. He had flung off his coat, rolled up his shirt-sleeves, and taken from his pocket the instrument of salvation. It was a small tube or trochar, with a lance passing down the inside; and Gabriel began to use it with a dexterity that would have graced a hospital-surgeon. Passing his hand over the sheep's left flank, and selecting the proper point, he punctured the skin and rumen with the lance as it stood in the tube; then he suddenly withdrew the lance, retaining the tube in its place. A current of air rushed up the tube, forcible enough to have extinguished a candle held at the orifice.

It has been said that mere ease after torment is delight for a time; and the countenances of these poor creatures expressed it now. Forty-nine operations were successfully performed. Owing to the great hurry necessitated by the far-gone state of some of the flock, Gabriel missed his aim in one case, and in one only – striking wide of the mark, and inflicting a mortal blow at once upon the suffering ewe. Four had died; three recovered without an operation. The total number of sheep which had thus strayed and injured themselves so dangerously was fifty-seven.

When the love-led man had ceased from his labours Bathsheba came and looked him in the face.

'Gabriel, will you stay on with me?' she said, smiling winningly, and not troubling to bring her lips quite together again at the end, because there was going to be another smile soon.

'I will,' said Gabriel.

And she smiled on him again.

CHAPTER XXII

THE GREAT BARN AND THE SHEEP-SHEARERS

MEN thin away to insignificance and oblivion quite as often by not making the most of good spirits when they have them as by lacking good spirits when they are indispensable. Gabriel lately, for the first time since his prostration by misfortune, had been independent in thought and vigorous in action to a marked extent – conditions which, powerless without an opportunity as an opportunity without them is barren, would have given him a sure lift upwards when the favourable conjunction should have occurred. But this incurable loitering beside Bathsheba Everdene stole his time ruinously. The spring tides were going by without floating him off, and the neap might soon come which could not.

It was the first day of June, and the sheep-shearing season culminated, the landscape, even to the leanest pasture, being all health and colour. Every green was young, every pore was open, and every stalk was swollen with racing currents of juice. God was palpably present in the country, and the devil had gone with the world to town. Flossy catkins of the later kinds, fern-sprouts like bishops' croziers, the square-headed moschatel, the odd cuckoo-pint, – like an apoplectic saint in a niche of malachite, – snow-white ladies'-smocks, the toothwort, approximating to human flesh, the enchanter's nightshade, and the black-petalled doleful-bells, were among the quainter objects of the vegetable world in and about Weatherbury at this teeming time; and of the animal, the metamorphosed figures of Mr. Jan Coggan, the master-shearer; the second and third shearers, who travelled in the exercise of their calling, and do not require definition by name; Henery Fray the fourth shearer, Susan

Tall's husband the fifth, Joseph Poorgrass the sixth, young Cain Ball as assistant-shearer, and Gabriel Oak as general supervisor. None of these were clothed to any extent worth mentioning, each appearing to have hit in the matter of raiment the decent mean between a high and low caste Hindoo. An angularity of lineament, and a fixity of facial machinery in general, proclaimed that serious work was the order of the day.

They sheared in the great barn, called for the nonce the Shearing-barn, which on ground-plan resembled a church with transepts. It not only emulated the form of the neighbouring church of the parish, but vied with it in antiquity. Whether the barn had ever formed one of a group of conventual buildings nobody seemed to be aware; no trace of such surroundings remained. The vast porches at the sides, lofty enough to admit a waggon laden to its highest with corn in the sheaf, were spanned by heavy-pointed arches of stone, broadly and boldly cut, whose very simplicity was the origin of a grandeur not apparent in erections where more ornament has been attempted. The dusky, filmed, chestnut roof, braced and tied in by huge collars, curves, and diagonals, was far nobler in design, because more wealthy in material, than nine-tenths of those in our modern churches. Along each side wall was a range of striding buttresses, throwing deep shadows on the spaces between them, which were perforated by lancet openings, combining in their proportions the precise requirements both of beauty and ventilation.

One could say about this barn, what could hardly be said of either the church or the castle, akin to it in age and style, that the purpose which had dictated its original erection was the same with that to which it was still applied. Unlike and superior to either of those two typical remnants of mediævalism, the old barn embodied practices which had suffered no mutilation at the hands of time. Here at least the spirit of the ancient builders was at one with the spirit of the modern beholder. Standing before this abraded pile, the eye regarded its present usage, the mind dwelt upon its past history, with a satisfied sense of functional continuity throughout – a feeling almost of gratitude, and quite of pride, at the permanence of the idea which had heaped it up. The fact that four centuries had neither proved it to be founded on a mistake, inspired any hatred of its purpose, nor given rise to any reaction that had battered it down, invested this simple grey effort of old minds with a repose, if not a grandeur, which a too curious reflection was apt to disturb in its ecclesiastical and military compeers. For once mediævalism and modernism had a common standpoint. The lanceolate windows, the time-eaten arch-stones and chamfers, the orientation of the axis, the misty chestnut work of the rafters, referred to no exploded fortifying art or worn-out religious creed. The defence and salvation of the body by daily bread is still a study, a religion, and a desire.

To-day the large side doors were thrown open towards the sun to admit a bountiful light to the immediate spot of the shearers' operations, which was the wood threshing-floor in the centre, formed of thick oak, black with age and polished by the beating of flails for many generations, till it had grown as slippery and as rich in hue as the state room floors of an Elizabethan mansion. Here the shearers knelt, the sun slanting in upon their bleached shirts, tanned arms, and the polished shears they flourished, causing these to bristle with a thousand rays strong enough to blind a weak-eyed man. Beneath them a captive sheep lay panting, quickening its pants as misgiving merged in terror, till it quivered like the hot landscape outside.

This picture of to-day in its frame of four hundred years ago did not produce that marked contrast between ancient and modern which is implied by the contrast of date. In comparison with cities, Weatherbury was immutable. The citizen's *Then* is the rustic's *Now*. In London, twenty or thirty years ago are old times; in Paris ten years, or five; in Weatherbury three or four score years were included in the mere present, and nothing less than a century set a mark on its face or tone. Five decades hardly modified the cut of a gaiter, the embroidery of a smock-frock, by the breadth of a hair. Ten generations failed to alter the turn of a single phrase. In these Wessex nooks the busy outsider's ancient times are only old; his old times are still new; his present is futurity.

So the barn was natural to the shearers, and the shearers were in harmony with the barn.

The spacious ends of the building, answering ecclesiastically to nave and chancel extremities, were fenced off with hurdles, the sheep being all collected in a crowd within these two enclosures; and in one angle a catching-pen was formed, in which three or four sheep were continuously kept ready for the shearers to seize without loss of time. In the background, mellowed by tawny shade, were the three women, Maryann Money, and Temperance and Soberness Miller, gathering up the fleeces and twisting ropes of wool with a wimble for tying them round. They were indifferently well assisted by the old maltster, who, when the malting season from October to April had passed, made himself useful upon any of the bordering farmsteads.

Behind all was Bathsheba, carefully watching the men to see that there was no cutting or wounding through carelessness, and that the animals were shorn close. Gabriel, who flitted and hovered under her bright eyes like a moth, did not shear continuously, half his time being spent in attending to the others and selecting the sheep for them. At the present moment he was engaged in handing round a mug of mild liquor, supplied from a barrel in the corner, and cut pieces of bread and cheese.

Bathsheba, after throwing a glance here, a caution there, and lecturing one of the younger operators who had allowed his last finished sheep to go off among the flock without re-stamping it with her initials, came again to Gabriel, as he put down the luncheon to drag a frightened ewe to his shear-station, flinging it over upon its back with a dexterous twist of the arm. He lopped off the tresses about its head, and opened up the neck and collar, his mistress quietly looking on.

'She blushes at the insult,' murmured Bathsheba, watching the pink flush which arose and overspread the neck and shoulders of the ewe where they were left bare by the clicking shears – a flush which was enviable, for its delicacy, by many queens of coteries, and would have been creditable, for its promptness, to any woman in the world.

Poor Gabriel's soul was fed with a luxury of content by having her over him, her eyes critically regarding his skilful shears, which apparently were going to gather up a piece of the flesh at every close, and yet never did so. Like Guildenstern, Oak was happy in that he was not over happy. He had no wish to converse with her: that his bright lady and himself formed one group, exclusively their own, and containing no others in the world, was enough.

So the chatter was all on her side. There is a loquacity that tells nothing, which was Bathsheba's; and there is a silence which says much: that was Gabriel's. Full of this dim and temperate bliss he went on to fling the ewe over upon her other side, covering her head with his knee, gradually running the shears line after line round her dewlap, thence about her flank and back, and finishing over the tail.

'Well done, and done quickly!' said Bathsheba, looking at her watch as the last snip resounded.

'How long, miss?' said Gabriel, wiping his brow.

'Three-and-twenty minutes and a half since you took the first lock from its forehead. It is the first time that I have ever seen one done in less than half an hour.'

The clean, sleek creature arose from its fleece – how perfectly like Aphrodite rising from the foam should have been seen to be realized – looking startled and shy at the loss of its garment, which lay on the floor in one soft cloud, united throughout, the portion visible being the inner surface only, which, never before exposed, was white as snow, and without flaw or blemish of the minutest kind.

'Cain Ball!'

'Yes, Mister Oak; here I be!'

Cainy now runs forward with the tar-pot. 'B.E.' is newly stamped upon the shorn skin, and away the simple dam leaps, panting, over the board into the shirtless flock outside. Then up comes Maryann; throws the loose locks into the middle of the fleece, rolls it up, and carries it into the background as three-and-a-half pounds of unadulterated warmth for the winter enjoyment of persons unknown and far away, who will, however, never experience the superlative comfort derivable from the wool as it here exists, new and pure – before the unctuousness of its nature whilst in a living state has dried, stiffened, and been washed out – rendering it just now as superior to anything *woollen* as cream is superior to milk-and-water.

But heartless circumstance could not leave entire Gabriel's happiness of this morning. The rams, old ewes, and two-shear ewes had duly undergone their stripping, and the men were proceeding with the shearlings and hogs, when Oak's belief that she was going to stand pleasantly by and time him through another performance was painfully interrupted by Farmer Boldwood's appearance in the extremest corner of the barn. Nobody seemed to have perceived his entry, but there he certainly was. Boldwood always carried with him a social atmosphere of his own, which everybody felt who came near him; and the talk, which Bathsheba's presence had somewhat suppressed, was now totally suspended.

He crossed over towards Bathsheba, who turned to greet him with a carriage of perfect ease. He spoke to her in low tones, and she instinctively modulated her own to the same pitch, and her voice ultimately even caught the inflection of his. She was far from having a wish to appear mysteriously connected with him; but woman at the impressionable age gravitates to the larger body not only in her choice of words, which is apparent every day, but even in her shades of tone and humour when the influence is great.

What they conversed about was not audible to Gabriel, who was too independent to get near, though too concerned to disregard. The issue of their dialogue was the taking of her hand by the courteous farmer to help her over the spreading-board into the bright June sunlight outside. Standing beside the sheep already shorn, they went on talking again. Concerning the flock? Apparently not. Gabriel theorized, not without truth, that in quiet discussion of any matter within reach of the speakers' eyes, these are usually fixed upon it. Bathsheba demurely regarded a contemptible straw lying upon the ground, in a way which suggested less ovine criticism than womanly embarrassment. She became more or less red in the cheek, the blood wavering in uncertain flux and reflux over the sensitive space between ebb and flood. Gabriel sheared on, constrained and sad.

She left Boldwood's side, and he walked up and down alone for nearly a quarter of an hour. Then she reappeared in her new riding-habit of myrtle-green, which fitted her to the waist as a rind fits its fruit; and young Bob Coggan led on her mare, Boldwood fetching his own horse from the tree under which it had been tied.

Oak's eyes could not forsake them; and in endeavouring to continue his shearing at the same time that he watched Boldwood's manner, he snipped the sheep in the groin. The animal plunged; Bathsheba instantly gazed towards it, and saw the blood.

'O Gabriel!' she exclaimed, with severe remonstrance, 'you who are so strict with the other men – see what you are doing yourself!'

To an outsider there was not much to complain of in this remark; but to Oak, who knew Bathsheba to be well aware that she herself was the cause of the poor ewe's wound, because she had wounded the ewe's shearer in a still more vital part, it had a sting which the abiding sense of his inferiority to both herself and Boldwood was not calculated to heal. But a manly resolve to recognize boldly that he had no longer a lover's interest in her, helped him occasionally to conceal a feeling.

'Bottle!' he shouted, in an unmoved voice of routine. Cainy Ball ran up, the wound was anointed, and the shearing continued.

Boldwood gently tossed Bathsheba into the saddle, and before they turned away she again spoke out to Oak with the same dominative and tantalizing graciousness.

'I am going now to see Mr. Boldwood's Leicesters. Take my place in the barn, Gabriel, and keep the men carefully to their work.'

The horses' heads were put about, and they trotted away.

Boldwood's deep attachment was a matter of great interest among all around him; but, after having been pointed out for so many years as the perfect exemplar of thriving bachelorship, his lapse was an anticlimax somewhat resembling that of St. John Long's death by consumption in the midst of his proofs that it was not a fatal disease.

'That means matrimony,' said Temperance Miller, following them out of sight with her eyes.

'I reckon that's the size o't,' said Coggan, working along without looking up.

'Well, better wed over the mixen than over the moor,' said Laban Tall, turning his sheep.

Henery Fray spoke, exhibiting miserable eyes at the same time: 'I don't see why a maid should take a husband when she's bold enough to fight her own battles, and don't want a home; for 'tis keeping another woman out. But let it be, for 'tis a pity he and she should trouble two houses.'

As usual with decided characters, Bathsheba invariably provoked the criticism of individuals like Henery Fray. Her emblazoned fault was to be too pronounced in her objections, and not sufficiently overt in her likings. We learn that it is not the rays which bodies absorb, but those which they reject, that give them the colours they are known by; and in the same way people are specialized by their dislikes and antagonisms, whilst their goodwill is looked upon as no attribute at all.

Henery continued in a more complaisant mood: 'I once hinted my mind to her on a few things, as nearly as a battered frame dared to do so to such a froward piece. You all know, neighbours, what a man I be, and how I come down with my powerful words when my pride is boiling wi' scarn?'

'We do, we do, Henery.'

'So I said, "Mistress Everdene, there's places empty, and

there's gifted men willing; but the spite − no, not the spite − I didn't say spite − "but the villainy of the contrarikind," I said (meaning womankind), "keeps 'em out." That wasn't too strong for her, say?'

'Passably well put.'

'Yes; and I would have said it, had death and salvation overtook me for it. Such is my spirit when I have a mind.'

'A true man, and proud as a lucifer.'

'You see the artfulness? Why, 'twas about being baily really; but I didn't put it so plain that she could understand my meaning, so I could lay it on all the stronger. That was my depth! . . . However, let her marry an she will. Perhaps 'tis high time. I believe Farmer Boldwood kissed her behind the spear-bed at the sheep-washing t'other day − that I do.'

'What a lie!' said Gabriel.

'Ah, neighbour Oak − how'st know?' said Henery mildly.

'Because she told me all that passed,' said Oak, with a pharisaical sense that he was not as other shearers in this matter.

'Ye have a right to believe it,' said Henery, with dudgeon; 'a very true right. But I mid see a little distance into things! To be long-headed enough for a baily's place is a poor mere trifle − yet a trifle more than nothing. However, I look round upon life quite cool. Do you heed me, neighbours? My words, though made as simple as I can, mid be rather deep for some heads.'

'O yes, Henery, we quite heed ye.'

'A strange old piece, goodmen − whirled about from here to yonder, as if I were nothing! A little warped, too. But I have my depths; ha, and even my great depths! I might gird at a certain shepherd, brain to brain. But no − O no!'

'A strange old piece, ye say!' interposed the maltster, in a querulous voice. 'At the same time ye be no old man worth naming − no old man at all. Yer teeth bain't half gone yet; and what's a old man's standing if so be his teeth bain't gone? Weren't I stale in wedlock afore ye were out of arms? 'Tis a poor thing to be sixty, when there's people far past four-score − a boast weak as water.'

It was the unvarying custom in Weatherbury to sink minor differences when the maltster had to be pacified.

'Weak as water! yes,' said Jan Coggan. 'Malter, we feel ye to be a wonderful veteran man, and nobody can gainsay it.'

'Nobody,' said Joseph Poorgrass. 'Ye be a very rare old spectacle, malter, and we all admire ye for that gift.'

'Ay, and as a young man, when my senses were in prosperity, I was likewise liked by a good-few who knowed me,' said the maltster.

' 'Ithout doubt you was – 'ithout doubt.'

The bent and hoary man was satisfied, and so apparently was Henery Fray. That matters should continue pleasant Maryann spoke, who, what with her brown complexion, and the working wrapper of rusty linsey, had at present the mellow hue of an old sketch in oils – notably some of Nicholas Poussin's: –

'Do anybody know of a crooked man, or a lame, or any second-hand fellow at all that would do for poor me?' said Maryann. 'A perfect one I don't expect to get at my time of life. If I could hear of such a thing 'twould do me more good than toast and ale.'

Coggan furnished a suitable reply. Oak went on with his shearing, and said not another word. Pestilent moods had come, and teased away his quiet. Bathsheba had shown indications of anointing him above his fellows by installing him as the bailiff that the farm imperatively required. He did not covet the post relatively to the farm: in relation to herself, as beloved by him and unmarried to another, he had coveted it. His readings of her seemed now to be vapoury and indistinct. His lecture to her was, he thought, one of the absurdest mistakes. Far from coquetting with Boldwood, she had trifled with himself in thus feigning that she had trifled with another. He was inwardly convinced that, in accordance with the anticipations of his easy-going and worse-educated comrades, that day would see Boldwood the accepted husband of Miss Everdene. Gabriel at this time of his life had outgrown the instinctive dislike which every Christian boy has for reading the Bible, perusing it now quite frequently, and he inwardly said, ' "I find more bitter than death the woman whose heart is snares and nets!" ' This was mere exclamation – the froth of the storm. He adored Bathsheba just the same.

'We workfolk shall have some lordly junketing to-night,' said Cainy Ball, casting forth his thoughts in a new direction. 'This morning I see 'em making the great puddens in the milking-pails – lumps of fat as big as yer thumb, Mister Oak! I've never seed such splendid large knobs of fat before in the days of my life – they never used to be bigger than a horse-bean. And there was a great black crock upon the brandise with his legs a-sticking out, but I don't know what was in within.'

'And there's two bushels of biffins for apple-pies,' said Maryann.

'Well, I hope to do my duty by it all,' said Joseph Poorgrass, in a pleasant, masticating manner of anticipation. 'Yes; victuals and drink is a cheerful thing, and gives nerves to the nerveless, if the form of words may be used. 'Tis the gospel of the body, without which we perish, so to speak it.'

CHAPTER XXIII

EVENTIDE – A SECOND DECLARATION

FOR the shearing-supper a long table was placed on the grass-plot beside the house, the end of the table being thrust over the sill of the wide parlour window and a foot or two into the room. Miss Everdene sat inside the window, facing down the table. She was thus at the head without mingling with the men.

This evening Bathsheba was unusually excited, her red cheeks and lips contrasting lustrously with the mazy skeins of her shadowy hair. She seemed to expect assistance, and the seat at the bottom of the table was at her request left vacant until after they had begun the meal. She then asked Gabriel to take the place and the duties appertaining to that end, which he did with great readiness.

At this moment Mr. Boldwood came in at the gate, and crossed the green to Bathsheba at the window. He apologized for his lateness: his arrival was evidently by arrangement.

'Gabriel,' said she, 'will you move again, please, and let Mr. Boldwood come there?'

Oak moved in silence back to his original seat.

The gentleman-farmer was dressed in cheerful style, in a new coat and white waistcoat, quite contrasting with his usual sober suits of grey. Inwardly, too, he was blithe, and consequently chatty to an exceptional degree. So also was Bathsheba now that he had come, though the uninvited presence of Pennyways, the bailiff who had been dismissed for theft, disturbed her equanimity for a while.

Supper being ended, Coggan began on his own private account, without reference to listeners: –

I've lost my love, and I care not,
I've lost my love, and I care not;
I shall soon have another
That's better than t'other;
I've lost my love, and I care not.

This lyric, when concluded, was received with a silently appreciative gaze at the table, implying that the performance, like a work by those established authors who are independent of notices in the papers, was a well-known delight which required no applause.

'Now, Master Poorgrass, your song!' said Coggan.

'I be all but in liquor, and the gift is wanting in me,' said Joseph, diminishing himself.

'Nonsense; wou'st never be so ungrateful, Joseph – never!' said Coggan, expressing hurt feelings by an inflection of voice. 'And mistress is looking hard at ye, as much as to say, "Sing at once, Joseph Poorgrass." '

'Faith, so she is; well, I must suffer it! . . . Just eye my features, and see if the tell-tale blood overheats me much, neighbours?'

'No, yer blushes be quite reasonable,' said Coggan.

'I always tries to keep my colours from rising when a beauty's eyes get fixed on me,' said Joseph diffidently; 'but if so be 'tis willed they do, they must.'

'Now, Joseph, your song, please,' said Bathsheba from the window.

'Well, really, ma'am,' he replied in a yielding tone, 'I don't know what to say. It would be a poor plain ballet of my own composure.'

'Hear, hear!' said the supper-party.

Poorgrass, thus assured, trilled forth a flickering yet commendable piece of sentiment, the tune of which consisted of the key-note and another, the latter being the sound chiefly dwelt upon. This was so successful, that he rashly plunged into a second in the same breath, after a few false starts: –

I sow'-ed th'-e . . . . .
I sow'-ed . . . . .
I sow'-ed the'-e seeds' of ' love',
  I-it was' all' i'-in the'-e spring',
I-in A'-pril', Ma'-ay, a'-nd sun'-ny' June',
  When sma'-all bi'-irds they' do' sing.

'Well put out of hand,' said Coggan, at the end of the verse. ' "They do sing" was a very taking paragraph.'

'Ay; and there was a pretty place at "seeds of love," and 'twas well heaved out. Though "love" is a nasty high corner when a man's voice is getting crazed. Next verse, Master Poorgrass.'

But during this rendering young Bob Coggan exhibited one of those anomalies which will afflict little people when other persons are particularly serious: in trying to check his laughter, he pushed down his throat as much of the tablecloth as he could get hold of, when, after continuing hermetically sealed for a short time, his mirth burst out through his nose. Joseph perceived it, and with hectic cheeks of indignation instantly ceased singing. Coggan boxed Bob's ears immediately.

'Go on, Joseph – go on, and never mind the young scamp,' said Coggan. ''Tis a very catching ballet. Now then again – the next bar; I'll help ye to flourish up the shrill notes where yer wind is rather wheezy: –

O the wi'-il-lo'-ow tree' will' twist',
And the wil'-low' tre'-ee wi'-ill twine'.

But the singer could not be set going again. Bob Coggan was sent home for his ill manners, and tranquillity was restored by Jacob Smallbury, who volunteered a ballad as inclusive and interminable as that with which the worthy toper old Silenus amused on a similar occasion the swains Chromis and Mnasylus, and other jolly dogs of his day.

It was still the beaming time of evening, though night was stealthily making itself visible low down upon the ground, the western lines of light raking the earth without alighting upon it to any extent, or illuminating the dead levels at all. The sun had crept round the tree as a last effort before death, and then began to sink, the shearers' lower parts becoming steeped in embrowning twilight, whilst their heads and shoulders were still enjoying day, touched with a yellow of self-sustained brilliancy that seemed inherent rather than acquired.

The sun went down in an ochreous mist; but they sat, and talked on, and grew as merry as the gods in Homer's heaven. Bathsheba still remained enthroned inside the window, and occupied herself in knitting, from which she sometimes looked up to view the fading scene outside. The slow twilight expanded and enveloped them completely before the signs of moving were shown.

Gabriel suddenly missed Farmer Boldwood from his place at the bottom of the table. How long he had been gone Oak did not know; but he had apparently withdrawn into the encircling dusk. Whilst he was thinking of this Liddy brought candles into the back part of the room overlooking the shearers, and their lively new flames shone down the table and over the men, and dispersed among the green shadows behind. Bathsheba's form, still in its original position, was now again distinct between their eyes and the light, which revealed that Boldwood had gone inside the room, and was sitting near her.

Next came the question of the evening. Would Miss Everdene sing to them the song she always sang so charmingly – 'The Banks of Allan Water' – before they went home?

After a moment's consideration Bathsheba assented, beckoning to Gabriel, who hastened up into the coveted atmosphere.

'Have you brought your flute?' she whispered.

'Yes, miss.'

'Play to my singing, then.'

She stood up in the window-opening, facing the men, the candles behind her, Gabriel on her right hand, immediately outside the sash-frame. Boldwood had drawn up on her left, within the room. Her singing was soft and rather tremulous at first, but it soon swelled to a steady clearness. Subsequent events caused one of the verses to be remembered for many months, and even years, by more than one of those who were gathered there: —

> For his bride a soldier sought her,
> And a winning tongue had he:
> On the banks of Allan Water
> None was gay as she!

In addition to the dulcet piping of Gabriel's flute Boldwood supplied a bass in his customary profound voice, uttering his notes so softly, however, as to abstain entirely from making anything like an ordinary duet of the song; they rather formed a rich unexplored shadow, which threw her tones into relief. The shearers reclined against each other as at suppers in the early ages of the world, and so silent and absorbed were they that her breathing could almost be heard between the bars; and at the end of the ballad, when the last tone loitered on to an inexpressible close, there arose that buzz of pleasure which is the attar of applause.

It is scarcely necessary to state that Gabriel could not avoid noting the farmer's bearing to-night towards their entertainer. Yet there was nothing exceptional in his actions beyond what appertained to his time of performing them. It was when the rest were all looking away that Boldwood observed her; when they regarded her he turned aside; when they thanked or praised he was silent; when they were inattentive he murmured his thanks. The meaning lay in the difference between actions none of which had any meaning of itself; and the necessity of being jealous, which lovers are troubled with, did not lead Oak to underestimate these signs.

Bathsheba then wished them good-night, withdrew from the window, and retired to the back part of the room, Boldwood thereupon closing the sash and the shutters, and remaining inside with her. Oak wandered away under the quiet and scented trees. Recovering from the softer impressions produced by Bathsheba's voice, the shearers rose to leave, Coggan turning to Pennyways as he pushed back the bench to pass out: –

'I like to give praise where praise is due, and the man deserves it – that 'a do so,' he remarked, looking at the worthy thief as if he were the masterpiece of some world-renowned artist.

'I'm sure I should never have believed it if we hadn't proved it, so to allude,' hiccupped Joseph Poorgrass, 'that every cup, every one of the best knives and forks, and every empty bottle be in their place as perfect now as at the beginning, and not one stole at all.'

'I'm sure I don't deserve half the praise you give me,' said the virtuous thief grimly.

'Well, I'll say this for Pennyways,' added Coggan, 'that whenever he do really make up his mind to do a noble thing in the shape of a good action, as I could see by his face he did to-night afore sitting down, he's generally able to carry it out. Yes, I'm proud to say, neighbours, that he's stole nothing at all.'

'Well, 'tis an honest deed, and we thank ye for it, Pennyways,' said Joseph; to which opinion the remainder of the company subscribed unanimously.

At this time of departure, when nothing more was visible of the inside of the parlour than a thin and still chink of light between the shutters, a passionate scene was in course of enactment there.

Miss Everdene and Boldwood were alone. Her cheeks had lost a great deal of their healthful fire from the very seriousness of her position; but her eye was bright with the excitement of a triumph – though it was a triumph which had rather been contemplated than desired.

She was standing behind a low arm-chair, from which she had just risen, and he was kneeling in it – inclining himself over its back towards her, and holding her hand in both his own. His body moved restlessly, and it was with what Keats daintily calls a too happy happiness. This unwonted abstraction by love of all dignity from a man of whom it had ever seemed the chief component, was, in its distressing incongruity, a pain to her which quenched much of the pleasure she derived from the proof that she was idolized.

'I will try to love you,' she was saying, in a trembling voice quite unlike her usual self-confidence. 'And if I can believe in any way that I shall make you a good wife I shall indeed be willing to marry you. But, Mr. Boldwood, hesitation on so high a matter is honourable in any woman, and I don't want to give a solemn promise to-night. I would rather ask you to wait a few weeks till I can see my situation better.'

'But you have every reason to believe that *then* —'

'I have every reason to hope that at the end of the five or six weeks, between this time and harvest, that you say you are going to be away from home, I shall be able to promise to be your wife,' she said firmly. 'But remember this distinctly, I don't promise yet.'

'It is enough; I don't ask more. I can wait on those dear words. And now, Miss Everdene, goodnight!'

'Good-night,' she said graciously — almost tenderly; and Boldwood withdrew with a serene smile.

Bathsheba knew more of him now; he had entirely bared his heart before her, even until he had almost worn in her eyes the sorry look of a grand bird without the feathers that make it grand. She had been awestruck at her past temerity, and was struggling to make amends without thinking whether the sin quite deserved the penalty she was schooling herself to pay. To have brought all this about her ears was terrible; but after a while the situation was not without a fearful joy. The facility with which even the most timid women sometimes acquire a relish for the dreadful when that is amalgamated with a little triumph, is marvellous.

CHAPTER XXIV

THE SAME NIGHT – THE FIR PLANTATION

AMONG the multifarious duties which Bathsheba had voluntarily imposed upon herself by dispensing with the services of a bailiff, was the particular one of looking round the homestead before going to bed, to see that all was right and safe for the night. Gabriel had almost constantly preceded her in this tour every evening, watching her affairs as carefully as any specially appointed officer of surveillance could have done; but this tender devotion was to a great extent unknown to his mistress, and as much as was known was somewhat thanklessly received. Women are never tired of bewailing man's fickleness in love, but they only seem to snub his constancy.

As watching is best done invisibly, she usually carried a dark lantern in her hand, and every now and then turned on the light to examine nooks and corners with the coolness of a metropolitan policeman. This coolness may have owed its existence not so much to her fearlessness of expected danger as to her freedom from the suspicion of any; her worst anticipated discovery being that a horse might not be well bedded, the fowls not all in, or a door not closed.

This night the buildings were inspected as usual, and she went round to the farm paddock. Here the only sounds disturbing the stillness were steady munchings of many mouths, and stentorian breathings from all but invisible noses, ending in snores and puffs like the blowing of bellows slowly. Then the munching would recommence, when the lively imagination might assist the eye to discern a group of pink-white nostrils shaped as caverns, and very clammy and humid on their surfaces, not exactly pleasant to the touch until one got used to them; the mouths beneath having a great partiality for closing upon any loose end of Bathsheba's apparel which came within reach of their tongues. Above each of these a still keener vision suggested a brown forehead and two staring though not unfriendly eyes, and above all a pair of whitish crescent-shaped horns like two particularly new moons, an occasional stolid 'moo!' proclaiming beyond the shade of a doubt that these phenomena were the features and persons of Daisy, Whitefoot, Bonny-lass, Jolly-O, Spot, Twinkle-eye, etc., etc. — the respectable dairy of Devon cows belonging to Bathsheba aforesaid.

Her way back to the house was by a path through a young plantation of tapering firs, which had been planted some years earlier to shelter the premises from the north wind. By reason of the density of the interwoven foliage overhead it was gloomy there at cloudless noontide, twilight in the evening, dark as midnight at dusk, and black as the ninth plague of Egypt at midnight. To describe the spot is to call it a vast, low, naturally formed hall, the plumy ceiling of which was supported by slender pillars of living wood, the floor being covered with a soft dun carpet of dead spikelets and mildewed cones, with a tuft of grass-blades here and there.

This bit of the path was always the crux of the night's ramble, though, before starting, her apprehensions of danger were not vivid enough to lead her to take a companion. Slipping along here covertly as Time, Bathsheba fancied she could hear footsteps entering the track at the opposite end. It was certainly a rustle of footsteps. Her own instantly fell as gently as snowflakes. She reassured herself by a remembrance that the path was public, and that the traveller was probably some villager returning home; regretting, at the same time, that the meeting should be about to occur in the darkest point of her route, even though only just outside her own door.

The noise approached, came close, and a figure was apparently on the point of gliding past her when something tugged at her skirt and pinned it forcibly to the ground. The instantaneous check nearly threw Bathsheba off her balance. In recovering she struck against warm clothes and buttons.

'A rum start, upon my soul!' said a masculine voice, a foot or so above her head. 'Have I hurt you, mate?'

'No,' said Bathsheba, attempting to shrink away.

'We have got hitched together somehow, I think.'

'Yes.'

'Are you a woman?'

'Yes.'

'A lady, I should have said.'

'It doesn't matter.'

'I am a man.'

'Oh!'

Bathsheba softly tugged again, but to no purpose.

'Is that a dark lantern you have? I fancy so,' said the man.

'Yes.'

'If you'll allow me I'll open it, and set you free.'

A hand seized the lantern, the door was opened, the rays burst out from their prison, and Bathsheba beheld her position with astonishment.

The man to whom she was hooked was brilliant in brass and scarlet. He was a soldier. His sudden appearance was to darkness what the sound of a trumpet is to silence. Gloom, the *genius loci* at all times hitherto, was now totally overthrown, less by the lantern-light than by what the lantern lighted. The contrast of this revelation with her anticipations of some sinister figure in sombre garb was so great that it had upon her the effect of a fairy transformation.

It was immediately apparent that the military man's spur had become entangled in the gimp which decorated the skirt of her dress. He caught a view of her face.

'I'll unfasten you in one moment, miss,' he said, with new-born gallantry.

'O no – I can do it, thank you,' she hastily replied, and stooped for the performance.

The unfastening was not such a trifling affair. The rowel of the spur had so wound itself among the gimp cords in those few moments, that separation was likely to be a matter of time.

He too stooped, and the lantern standing on the ground betwixt them threw the gleam from its open side among the fir-tree needles and the blades of long damp grass with the effect of a large glowworm. It radiated upwards into their faces, and sent over half the plantation gigantic shadows of both man and woman, each dusky shape becoming distorted and mangled upon the tree-trunks till it wasted to nothing.

He looked hard into her eyes when she raised them for a moment; Bathsheba looked down again, for his gaze was too strong to be received point-blank with her own. But she had obliquely noticed that he was young and slim, and that he wore three chevrons upon his sleeve.

Bathsheba pulled again.

'You are a prisoner, miss; it is no use blinking the matter,' said the soldier drily. 'I must cut your dress if you are in such a hurry.'

'Yes – please do!' she exclaimed helplessly.

'It wouldn't be necessary if you could wait a moment'; and he unwound a cord from the little wheel. She withdrew her own hand, but, whether by accident or design, he touched it. Bathsheba was vexed; she hardly knew why.

His unravelling went on, but it nevertheless seemed coming to no end. She looked at him again.

'Thank you for the sight of such a beautiful face!' said the young sergeant, without ceremony.

She coloured with embarrassment. ''Twas unwillingly shown,' she replied stiffly, and with as much dignity – which was very little – as she could infuse into a position of captivity.

'I like you the better for that incivility, miss,' he said.

'I should have liked – I wish – you had never shown yourself to me by intruding here!' She pulled again, and the gathers of her dress began to give way like liliputian musketry.

'I deserve the chastisement your words give me. But why should such a fair and dutiful girl have such an aversion to her father's sex?'

'Go on your way, please.'

'What, Beauty, and drag you after me? Do but look; I never saw such a tangle!'

'O, 'tis shameful of you; you have been making it worse on purpose to keep me here – you have!'

'Indeed, I don't think so,' said the sergeant, with a merry twinkle.

'I tell you you have!' she exclaimed, in high temper. 'I insist upon undoing it. Now, allow me!'

'Certainly, miss; I am not of steel.' He added a sigh which had as much archness in it as a sigh could possess without losing its nature altogether. 'I am thankful for beauty, even when 'tis thrown to me like a bone to a dog. These moments will be over too soon!'

She closed her lips in a determined silence.

Bathsheba was revolving in her mind whether by a bold and desperate rush she could free herself at the risk of leaving her skirt bodily behind her. The thought was too dreadful. The dress – which she had put on to appear stately at the supper – was the head and front of her wardrobe; not another in her stock became her so well. What woman in Bathsheba's position, not naturally timid, and within call of her retainers, would have bought escape from a dashing soldier at so dear a price?

'All in good time; it will soon be done, I perceive,' said her cool friend.

'This trifling provokes, and – and —'

'Not too cruel!'

'– Insults me!'

'It is done in order that I may have the pleasure of apologizing to so charming a woman, which I straightway do most humbly, madam,' he said, bowing low.

Bathsheba really knew not what to say.

'I've seen a good many women in my time,' continued the young man in a murmur, and more thoughtfully than hitherto, critically regarding her bent head at the same time; 'but I've never seen a woman so beautiful as you. Take it or leave it – be offended or like it – I don't care.'

'Who are you, then, who can so well afford to despise opinion?'

'No stranger. Sergeant Troy. I am staying in this place. – There! it is undone at last, you see. Your light fingers were more eager than mine. I wish it had been the knot of knots, which there's no untying!'

This was worse and worse. She started up, and so did he. How to decently get away from him – that was her difficulty now. She sidled off inch by inch, the lantern in her hand, till she could see the redness of his coat no longer.

'Ah, Beauty; good-bye!' he said.

She made no reply, and, reaching a distance of twenty or thirty yards, turned about, and ran indoors.

Liddy had just retired to rest. In ascending to her own chamber, Bathsheba opened the girl's door an inch or two, and, panting, said —

'Liddy, is any soldier staying in the village – sergeant somebody – rather gentlemanly for a sergeant, and good looking – a red coat with blue facings?'

'No, miss . . . No, I say; but really it might be Sergeant Troy home on furlough, though I have not seen him. He was here once in that way when the regiment was at Casterbridge.'

'Yes; that's the name. Had he a moustache – no whiskers or beard?'

'He had.'

'What kind of a person is he?'

'O! miss – I blush to name it – a gay man! But I know him to be very quick and trim, who might have made his thousands, like a squire. Such a clever young dand as he is! He's a doctor's son by name, which is a great deal; and he's an earl's son by nature!'

'Which is a great deal more. Fancy! Is it true?'

'Yes. And he was brought up so well, and sent to Casterbridge Grammar School for years and years. Learnt all languages while he was there; and it was said he got on so far that he could take down Chinese in shorthand; but that I don't answer for, as it was only reported. However, he wasted his gifted lot, and listed a soldier; but even then he rose to be a sergeant without trying at all. Ah! such a blessing it is to be high-born; nobility of blood will shine out even in the ranks and files. And is he really come home, miss?'

'I believe so. Good-night, Liddy.'

After all, how could a cheerful wearer of skirts be permanently offended with the man? There are occasions when girls like Bathsheba will put up with a great deal of unconventional behaviour. When they want to be praised, which is often; when they want to be mastered, which is sometimes; and when they want no nonsense, which is seldom. Just now the first feeling was in the ascendant with Bathsheba, with a dash of the second. Moreover, by chance or by devilry, the ministrant was antecedently made interesting by being a handsome stranger who had evidently seen better days.

So she could not clearly decide whether it was her opinion that he had insulted her or not.

'Was ever anything so odd!' she at last exclaimed to herself, in her own room. 'And was ever anything so meanly done as what I did – to skulk away like that from a man who was only civil and kind!' Clearly she did not think his barefaced praise of her person an insult now.

It was a fatal omission of Boldwood's that he had never once told her she was beautiful.

CHAPTER XXV

THE NEW ACQUAINTANCE DESCRIBED

IDIOSYNCRASY and vicissitude had combined to stamp Sergeant Troy as an exceptional being.

He was a man to whom memories were an incumbrance, and anticipations a superfluity. Simply feeling, considering, and caring for what was before his eyes, he was vulnerable only in the present. His outlook upon time was as a transient flash of the eye now and then: that projection of consciousness into days gone by and to come, which makes the past a synonym for the pathetic and the future a word for circumspection, was foreign to Troy. With him the past was yesterday; the future, to-morrow; never, the day after.

On this account he might, in certain lights, have been regarded as one of the most fortunate of his order. For it may be argued with great plausibility that reminiscence is less an endowment than a disease, and that expectation in its only comfortable form – that of absolute faith – is practically an impossibility; whilst in the form of hope and the secondary compounds, patience, impatience, resolve, curiosity, it is a constant fluctuation between pleasure and pain.

Sergeant Troy, being entirely innocent of the practice of expectation, was never disappointed. To set against this negative gain there may have been some positive losses from a certain narrowing of the higher tastes and sensations which it entailed. But limitation of the capacity is never recognized as a loss by the loser therefrom: in this attribute moral or æsthetic poverty contrasts plausibly with material, since those who suffer do not mind it, whilst those who mind it soon cease to suffer. It is not a denial of anything to have been always without it, and what Troy had never enjoyed he did not miss; but, being fully conscious that what sober people missed he enjoyed, his capacity, though really less, seemed greater than theirs.

He was moderately truthful towards men, but to women lied like a Cretan – a system of ethics above all others calculated to win popularity at the first flush of admission into lively society; and the possibility of the favour gained being transitory had reference only to the future.

He never passed the line which divides the spruce vices from the ugly; and hence, though his morals had hardly been applauded, disapproval of them had frequently been tempered with a smile. This treatment had led to his becoming a sort of regrater of other men's gallantries, to his own aggrandizement as a Corinthian, rather than to the moral profit of his hearers.

His reason and his propensities had seldom any reciprocating influence, having separated by mutual consent long ago: thence it sometimes happened that, while his intentions were as honourable as could be wished, any particular deed formed a dark background which threw them into fine relief. The sergeant's vicious phases being the offspring of impulse, and his virtuous phases of cool meditation, the latter had a modest tendency to be oftener heard of than seen.

Troy was full of activity, but his activities were less of a locomotive than a vegetative nature; and, never being based upon any original choice of foundation or direction, they were exercised on whatever object chance might place in their way. Hence, whilst he sometimes reached the brilliant in speech because that was spontaneous, he fell below the commonplace in action, from inability to guide incipient effort. He had a quick comprehension and considerable force of character; but, being without the power to combine them, the comprehension became engaged with trivialities whilst waiting for the will to direct it, and the force wasted itself in useless grooves through unheeding the comprehension.

He was a fairly well-educated man for one of middle class – exceptionally well-educated for a common soldier. He spoke fluently and unceasingly. He could in this way be one thing and seem another; for instance, he could speak of love and think of dinner; call on the husband to look at the wife; be eager to pay and intend to owe.

The wondrous power of flattery in *passados* at woman is a perception so universal as to be remarked upon by many people almost as automatically as they repeat a proverb, or say that they are Christians and the like, without thinking much of the enormous corollaries which spring from the proposition. Still less is it acted upon for the good of the complemental being alluded to. With the majority such an opinion is shelved with all those trite aphorisms which require some catastrophe to bring their tremendous meanings thoroughly home. When expressed with some amount of reflectiveness it seems co-ordinate with a belief that this flattery must be reasonable to be effective. It is to the credit of men that few attempt to settle the question by experiment, and it is for their happiness, perhaps, that accident has never settled it for them. Nevertheless, that a male dissembler who by deluging her with untenable fictions charms the female wisely, may acquire powers reaching to the extremity of perdition, is a truth taught to many by unsought and wringing occurrences. And some profess to have attained to the same knowledge by experiment as aforesaid, and jauntily continue their indulgence in such experiments with terrible effect. Sergeant Troy was one.

He had been known to observe casually that in dealing with womankind the only alternative to flattery was cursing and swearing. There was no third method. 'Treat them fairly, and you are a lost man,' he would say.

This philosopher's public appearance in Weatherbury promptly followed his arrival there. A week or two after the shearing Bathsheba, feeling a nameless relief of spirits on account of Boldwood's absence, approached her hayfields and looked over the hedge towards the haymakers. They consisted in about equal proportions of gnarled and flexuous forms, the former being the men, the latter the women, who wore tilt bonnets covered with nankeen, which hung in a curtain upon their shoulders. Coggan and Mark Clark were mowing in a less forward meadow, Clark humming a tune to the strokes of his scythe, to which Jan made no attempt to keep time with his. In the first mead they were already loading hay, the women raking it into cocks and windrows, and the men tossing it upon the waggon.

From behind the waggon a bright scarlet spot emerged, and went on loading unconcernedly with the rest. It was the gallant sergeant, who had come haymaking for pleasure; and nobody could deny that he was doing the mistress of the farm real knight-service by this voluntary contribution of his labour at a busy time.

As soon as she had entered the field Troy saw her, and sticking his pitchfork into the ground and picking up his crop or cane, he came forward. Bathsheba blushed with half-angry embarrassment, and adjusted her eyes as well as her feet to the direct line of her path.

CHAPTER XXVI

SCENE ON THE VERGE OF THE HAY-MEAD

'AH, Miss Everdene!' said the sergeant, touching his diminutive cap. 'Little did I think it was you I was speaking to the other night. And yet, if I had reflected, the "Queen of the Corn-market" (truth is truth at any hour of the day or night, and I heard you so named in Casterbridge yesterday), the "Queen of the Corn-market," I say, could be no other woman. I step across now to beg your forgiveness a thousand times for having been led by my feelings to express myself too strongly for a stranger. To be sure I am no stranger to the place – I am Sergeant Troy, as I told you, and I have assisted your uncle in these fields no end of times when I was a lad. I have been doing the same for you to-day.'

'I suppose I must thank you for that, Sergeant Troy,' said the Queen of the Corn-market in an indifferently grateful tone.

The sergeant looked hurt and sad. 'Indeed you must not, Miss Everdene,' he said. 'Why could you think such a thing necessary?'

'I am glad it is not.'

'Why? if I may ask without offence.'

'Because I don't much want to thank you for anything.'

'I am afraid I have made a hole with my tongue that my heart will never mend. O these intolerable times: that ill-luck should follow a man for honestly telling a woman she is beautiful! 'Twas the most I said – you must own that; and the least I could say – that I own myself.'

'There is some talk I could do without more easily than money.'

'Indeed. That remark is a sort of digression.'

'No. It means that I would rather have your room than your company.'

'And I would rather have curses from you than kisses from any other woman; so I'll stay here.'

Bathsheba was absolutely speechless. And yet she could not help feeling that the assistance he was rendering forbade a harsh repulse.

'Well,' continued Troy, 'I suppose there is a praise which is rudeness, and that may be mine. At the same time there is a treatment which is injustice, and that may be yours. Because a plain blunt man, who has never been taught concealment, speaks out his mind without exactly intending it, he's to be snapped off like the son of a sinner.'

'Indeed there's no such case between us,' she said, turning away. 'I don't allow strangers to be bold and impudent – even in praise of me.'

'Ah – it is not the fact but the method which offends you,' he said carelessly. 'But I have the sad satisfaction of knowing that my words, whether pleasing or offensive, are unmistakably true. Would you have had me look at you, and tell my acquaintance that you are quite a common-place woman, to save you the embarrassment of being stared at if they come near you? Not I. I couldn't tell any such ridiculous lie about a beauty to encourage a single woman in England in too excessive a modesty.'

'It is all pretence – what you are saying!' exclaimed Bathsheba, laughing in spite of herself at the sergeant's sly method. 'You have a rare invention, Sergeant Troy. Why couldn't you have passed by me that night, and said nothing? – that was all I meant to reproach you for.'

'Because I wasn't going to. Half the pleasure of a feeling lies in being able to express it on the spur of the moment, and I let out mine. It would have been just the same if you had been the reverse person – ugly and old – I should have exclaimed about it in the same way.'

'How long is it since you have been so afflicted with strong feeling, then?'

'Oh, ever since I was big enough to know loveliness from deformity.'

"Tis to be hoped your sense of the difference you speak of doesn't stop at faces, but extends to morals as well.'

'I won't speak of morals or religion – my own or anybody else's. Though perhaps I should have been a very good Christian if you pretty women hadn't made me an idolater.'

Bathsheba moved on to hide the irrepressible dimplings of merriment. Troy followed, whirling his crop.

'But – Miss Everdene – you do forgive me?'

'Hardly.'

'Why?'

'You say such things.'

'I said you were beautiful, and I'll say so still, for, by — so you are! The most beautiful ever I saw, or may I fall dead this instant! Why, upon my —'

'Don't – don't! I won't listen to you – you are so profane!' she said, in a restless state between distress at hearing him and a *penchant* to hear more.

'I again say you are a most fascinating woman. There's nothing remarkable in my saying so, is there? I'm sure the fact is evident enough. Miss Everdene, my opinion may be too forcibly let out to please you, and, for the matter of that, too insignificant to convince you, but surely it is honest, and why can't it be excused?'

'Because it – it isn't a correct one,' she femininely murmured.

'O, fie – fie! Am I any worse for breaking the third of that Terrible Ten than you for breaking the ninth?'

'Well, it doesn't seem *quite* true to me that I am fascinating,' she replied evasively.

'Not so to you: then I say with all respect that, if so, it is owing to your modesty, Miss Everdene. But surely you must have been told by everybody of what everybody notices? And you should take their words for it.'

'They don't say so exactly.'

'O yes, they must!'

'Well, I mean to my face, as you do,' she went on, allowing herself to be further lured into a conversation that intention had rigorously forbidden.

'But you know they think so?'

'No – that is – I certainly have heard Liddy say they do, but —' She paused.

Capitulation – that was the purport of the simple reply, guarded as it was – capitulation, unknown to herself. Never did a fragile tailless sentence convey a more perfect meaning. The careless sergeant smiled within himself, and probably too the devil smiled from a loop-hole in Tophet, for the moment was the turning-point of a career. Her tone and mien signified beyond mistake that the seed which was to lift the foundation had taken root in the chink: the remainder was a mere question of time and natural changes.

'There the truth comes out!' said the soldier, in reply. 'Never tell me that a young lady can live in a buzz of admiration without knowing something about it. Ah, well, Miss Everdene, you are – pardon my blunt way – you are rather an injury to our race than otherwise.'

'How – indeed?' she said, opening her eyes.

'O, it is true enough. I may as well be hung for a sheep as a lamb (an old country saying, not of much account, but it will do for a rough soldier), and so I will speak my mind, regardless of your pleasure, and without hoping or intending to get your pardon. Why, Miss Everdene, it is in this manner that your good looks may do more harm than good in the world.' The sergeant looked down the mead in critical abstraction. 'Probably some one man on an average falls in love with each ordinary woman. She can marry him: he is content, and leads a useful life. Such women as you a hundred men always covet – your eyes will bewitch scores on scores into an unavailing fancy for you – you can only marry one of that many. Out of these say twenty will endeavour to drown the bitterness of despised love in drink; twenty more will mope away their lives without a wish or attempt to make a mark in the world, because they have no ambition apart from their attachment to you; twenty more — the susceptible person myself possibly among them — will be always draggling after you, getting where they may just see you, doing desperate things. Men are such constant fools! The rest may try to get over their passion with more or less success. But all these men will be saddened. And not only those ninety-nine men, but the ninety-nine women they might have married are saddened with them. There's my tale. That's why I say that a woman so charming as yourself, Miss Everdene, is hardly a blessing to her race.'

The handsome sergeant's features were during this speech as rigid and stern as John Knox's in addressing his gay young queen.

Seeing she made no reply, he said, 'Do you read French?'

'No; I began, but when I got to the verbs, father died,' she said simply.

'I do — when I have an opportunity, which latterly has not been often (my mother was a Parisienne) — and there's a proverb they have, *Qui aime bien châtie bien* — "He chastens who loves well." Do you understand me?'

'Ah!' she replied, and there was even a little tremulousness in the usually cool girl's voice; 'if you can only fight half as winningly as you can talk, you are able to make a pleasure of a bayonet wound!' And then poor Bathsheba instantly perceived her slip in making this admission: in hastily trying to retrieve it, she went from bad to worse. 'Don't, however, suppose that *I* derive any pleasure from what you tell me.'

'I know you do not — I know it perfectly,' said Troy, with much hearty conviction on the exterior of his face: and altering the expression to moodiness; 'when a dozen men are ready to speak tenderly to you, and give the admiration you deserve without adding the warning you need, it stands to reason that my poor rough-and-ready mixture of praise and blame cannot convey much pleasure. Fool as I may be, I am not so conceited as to suppose that!' .

'I think you – are conceited, nevertheless,' said Bathsheba, looking askance at a reed she was fitfully pulling with one hand, having lately grown feverish under the soldier's system of procedure – not because the nature of his cajolery was entirely unperceived, but because its vigour was overwhelming.

'I would not own it to anybody else – nor do I exactly to you. Still, there might have been some self-conceit in my foolish supposition the other night. I knew that what I said in admiration might be an opinion too often forced upon you to give any pleasure, but I certainly did think that the kindness of your nature might prevent you judging an uncontrolled tongue harshly – which you have done – and thinking badly of me and wounding me this morning, when I am working hard to save your hay.'

'Well, you need not think more of that: perhaps you did not mean to be rude to me by speaking out your mind: indeed, I believe you did not,' said the shrewd woman, in painfully innocent earnest. 'And I thank you for giving help here. But – but mind you don't speak to me again in that way, or in any other, unless I speak to you.'

'O Miss Bathsheba! That is too hard!'

'No, it isn't. Why is it?'

'You will never speak to me; for I shall not be here long. I am soon going back again to the miserable monotony of drill – and perhaps our regiment will be ordered out soon. And yet you take away the one little ewe-lamb of pleasure that I have in this dull life of mine. Well, perhaps generosity is not a woman's most marked characteristic.'

'When are you going from here?' she asked with some interest.

'In a month.'

'But how can it give you pleasure to speak to me?'

'Can you ask, Miss Everdene – knowing as you do – what my offence is based on?'

'If you do care so much for a silly trifle of that kind, then, I don't mind doing it,' she uncertainly and doubtingly answered.

'But you can't really care for a word from me? you only say so – I think you only say so.'

'That's unjust – but I won't repeat the remark. I am too gratified to get such a mark of your friendship at any price to cavil at the tone. I *do*, Miss Everdene, care for it. You may think a man foolish to want a mere word – just a good morning. Perhaps he is – I don't know. But you have never been a man looking upon a woman, and that woman yourself.'

'Well.'

'Then you know nothing of what such an experience is like – and Heaven forbid that you ever should!'

'Nonsense, flatterer! What is it like? I am interested in knowing.'

'Put shortly, it is not being able to think, hear, or look in any direction except one without wretchedness, nor there without torture.'

'Ah, sergeant, it won't do – you are pretending!' she said, shaking her head. 'Your words are too dashing to be true.'

'I am not, upon the honour of a soldier.'

'But *why* is it so? – Of course I ask for mere pastime.'

'Because you are so distracting – and I am so distracted.'

'You look like it.'

'I am indeed.'

'Why, you only saw me the other night!'

'That makes no difference. The lightning works instantaneously. I loved you then, at once – as I do now.'

Bathsheba surveyed him curiously, from the feet upward, as high as she liked to venture her glance, which was not quite so high as his eyes.

'You cannot and you don't,' she said demurely. 'There is no such sudden feeling in people. I won't listen to you any longer. Dear me, I wish I knew what o'clock it is – I am going – I have wasted too much time here already!'

The sergeant looked at his watch and told her. 'What, haven't you a watch, miss?' he inquired.

'I have not just at present – I am about to get a new one.'

'No. You shall be given one. Yes – you shall. A gift, Miss Everdene – a gift.'

And before she knew what the young man was intending, a heavy gold watch was in her hand.

'It is an unusually good one for a man like me to possess,' he quietly said. 'That watch has a history. Press the spring and open the back.'

She did so.

'What do you see?'

'A crest and a motto.'

'A coronet with five points, and beneath, *Cedit amor rebus* – "Love yields to circumstance." It's the motto of the Earls of Severn. That watch belonged to the last lord, and was given to my mother's husband, a medical man, for his use till I came of age, when it was to be given to me. It was all the fortune that ever I inherited. That watch has regulated imperial interests in its time – the stately ceremonial, the courtly assignation, pompous travels, and lordly sleeps. Now it is yours.'

'But, Sergeant Troy, I cannot take this – I cannot!' she exclaimed with round-eyed wonder. 'A gold watch! What are you doing? Don't be such a dissembler!'

The sergeant retreated to avoid receiving back his gift, which she held out persistently towards him. Bathsheba followed as he retired.

'Keep it – do, Miss Everdene – keep it!' said the erratic child of impulse. 'The fact of your possessing it makes it worth ten times as much to me. A more plebeian one will answer my purpose just as well, and the pleasure of knowing whose heart my old one beats against – well, I won't speak of that. It is in far worthier hands than ever it has been in before.'

'But indeed I can't have it!' she said, in a perfect simmer of distress. 'O, how can you do such a thing; that is, if you really mean it! Give me your dead father's watch, and such a valuable one! You should not be so reckless, indeed, Sergeant Troy!'

'I loved my father: good; but better, I love you more. That's how I can do it,' said the sergeant with an intonation of such exquisite fidelity to nature that it was evidently not all acted now. Her beauty, which, whilst it had been quiescent, he had praised in jest, had in its animated phases moved him to earnest; and though his seriousness was less than she imagined, it was probably more than he imagined himself.

Bathsheba was brimming with agitated bewilderment, and she said, in half-suspicious accents of feeling, 'Can it be! O, how can it be, that you care for me, and so suddenly! You have seen so little of me: I may not be really so – so nice-looking as I seem to you. Please, do take it; O, do! I cannot and will not have it. Believe me, your generosity is too great. I have never done you a single kindness, and why should you be so kind to me?'

A factitious reply had been again upon his lips, but it was again suspended, and he looked at her with an arrested eye. The truth was, that as she now stood – excited, wild, and honest as the day – her alluring beauty bore out so fully the epithets he had bestowed upon it that he was quite startled at his temerity in advancing them as false. He said mechanically, 'Ah, why?' and continued to look at her.

'And my workfolk see me following you about the field, and are wondering. O, this is dreadful!' she went on, unconscious of the transmutation she was effecting.

'I did not quite mean you to accept it at first, for it was my one poor patent of nobility,' he broke out bluntly; 'but, upon my soul, I wish you would now. Without any shamming, come! Don't deny me the happiness of wearing it for my sake. But you are too lovely even to care to be kind as others are.'

'No, no; don't say so! I have reasons for reserve which I cannot explain.'

'Let it be, then, let it be,' he said, receiving back the watch at last; 'I must be leaving you now. And will you speak to me for these few weeks of my stay?'

'Indeed I will. Yet, I don't know if I will! O, why did you come and disturb me so!'

'Perhaps in setting a gin, I have caught myself. Such things have happened. Well, will you let me work in your fields?' he coaxed.

'Yes, I suppose so; if it is any pleasure to you.'

'Miss Everdene, I thank you.'

'No, no.'

'Good-bye!'

The sergeant brought his hand to the cap on the slope of his head, saluted, and returned to the distant group of hay-makers.

Bathsheba could not face the haymakers now. Her heart erratically flitting hither and thither from perplexed excitement, hot, and almost tearful, she retreated homeward, murmuring, 'O, what have I done! What does it mean! I wish I knew how much of it was true!'

CHAPTER XXVII

HIVING THE BEES

THE Weatherbury bees were late in their swarming this year. It was in the latter part of June, and the day after the interview with Troy in the hayfield, that Bathsheba was standing in her garden, watching a swarm in the air and guessing their probable settling place. Not only were they late this year, but unruly. Sometimes throughout a whole season all the swarms would alight on the lowest attainable bough – such as part of a currant-bush or espalier apple-tree; next year they would, with just the same unanimity, make straight off to the uppermost member of some tall, gaunt costard, or quarrenden, and there defy all invaders who did not come armed with ladders and staves to take them.

This was the case at present. Bathsheba's eyes, shaded by one hand, were following the ascending multitude against the unexplorable stretch of blue till they ultimately halted by one of the unwieldy trees spoken of. A process somewhat analogous to that of alleged formations of the universe, time and times ago, was observable. The bustling swarm had swept the sky in a scattered and uniform haze, which now thickened to a nebulous centre: this glided on to a bough and grew still denser, till it formed a solid black spot upon the light.

The men and women being all busily engaged in saving the hay – even Liddy had left the house for the purpose of lending a hand – Bathsheba resolved to hive the bees herself, if possible. She had dressed the hive with herbs and honey, fetched a ladder, brush, and crook, made herself impregnable with armour of leather gloves, straw hat, and large gauze veil – once green but now faded to snuff colour – and ascended a dozen rungs of the ladder. At once she heard, not ten yards off, a voice that was beginning to have a strange power in agitating her.

'Miss Everdene, let me assist you; you should not attempt such a thing alone.'

Troy was just opening the garden gate.

Bathsheba flung down the brush, crook, and empty hive, pulled the skirt of her dress tightly round her ankles in a tremendous flurry, and as well as she could slid down the ladder. By the time she reached the bottom Troy was there also, and he stooped to pick up the hive.

'How fortunate I am to have dropped in at this moment!' exclaimed the sergeant.

She found her voice in a minute. 'What! and will you shake them in for me?' she asked, in what, for a defiant girl, was a faltering way; though, for a timid girl, it would have seemed a brave way enough.

'Will I!' said Troy. 'Why, of course I will. How blooming you are to-day!' Troy flung down his cane and put his foot on the ladder to ascend.

'But you must have on the veil and gloves, or you'll be stung fearfully!'

'Ah, yes. I must put on the veil and gloves. Will you kindly show me how to fix them properly?'

'And you must have the broad-brimmed hat, too; for your cap has no brim to keep the veil off, and they'd reach your face.'

'The broad-brimmed hat, too, by all means.'

So a whimsical fate ordered that her hat should be taken off – veil and all attached – and placed upon his head, Troy tossing his own into a gooseberry bush. Then the veil had to be tied at its lower edge round his collar and the gloves put on him.

He looked such an extraordinary object in this guise that, flurried as she was, she could not avoid laughing outright. It was the removal of yet another stake from the palisade of cold manners which had kept him off.

Bathsheba looked on from the ground whilst he was busy

sweeping and shaking the bees from the tree, holding up the hive with the other hand for them to fall into. She made use of an unobserved minute whilst his attention was absorbed in the operation to arrange her plumes a little. He came down holding the hive at arm's length, behind which trailed a cloud of bees.

'Upon my life,' said Troy, through the veil, 'holding up this hive makes one's arm ache worse than a week of sword-exercise.' When the manœuvre was complete he approached her. 'Would you be good enough to untie me and let me out? I am nearly stifled inside this silk cage.'

To hide her embarrassment during the unwonted process of untying the string about his neck, she said: −

'I have never seen that you spoke of.'

'What?'

'The sword-exercise.'

'Ah! would you like to?' said Troy.

Bathsheba hesitated. She had heard wondrous reports from time to time by dwellers in Weatherbury, who had by chance sojourned awhile in Casterbridge, near the barracks, of this strange and glorious performance, the sword-exercise. Men and boys who had peeped through chinks or over walls into the barrack-yard returned with accounts of its being the most flash-ing affair conceivable; accoutrements and weapons glistening like stars − here, there, around − yet all by rule and compass. So she said mildly what she felt strongly:−

'Yes; I should like to see it very much.'

'And so you shall; you shall see me go through it.'

'No! How?'

'Let me consider.'

'Not with a walking-stick − I don't care to see that. It must be a real sword.'

'Yes, I know; and I have no sword here; but I think I could get one by the evening. Now, will you do this?'

Troy bent over her and murmured some suggestion in a low voice.

'O no, indeed!' said Bathsheba, blushing. 'Thank you very much, but I couldn't on any account.'

'Surely you might? Nobody would know.'

She shook her head, but with a weakened negation. 'If I were to,' she said, 'I must bring Liddy too. Might I not?'

Troy looked far away. 'I don't see why you want to bring her,' he said coldly.

An unconscious look of assent in Bathsheba's eyes betrayed that something more than his coldness had made her also feel that Liddy would be superfluous in the suggested scene. She had felt it, even whilst making the proposal.

'Well, I won't bring Liddy – and I'll come. But only for a very short time,' she added; 'a very short time.'

'It will not take five minutes,' said Troy.

CHAPTER XXVIII

THE HOLLOW AMID THE FERNS

THE hill opposite Bathsheba's dwelling extended, a mile off, into an uncultivated tract of land, dotted at this season with tall thickets of brake fern, plump and diaphanous from recent rapid growth, and radiant in hues of clear and untainted green.

At eight o'clock this midsummer evening, whilst the bristling ball of gold in the west still swept the tips of the ferns with its long, luxuriant rays, a soft brushing-by of garments might have been heard among them, and Bathsheba appeared in their midst, their soft, feathery arms caressing her up to her shoulders. She paused, turned, went back over the hill and half-way to her own door, whence she cast a farewell glance upon the spot she had just left, having resolved not to remain near the place after all.

She saw a dim spot of artificial red moving round the shoulder of the rise. It disappeared on the other side.

She waited one minute – two minutes – thought of Troy's disappointment at her non-fulfilment of a promised engagement, till she again ran along the field, clambered over the bank, and followed the original direction. She was now literally trembling and panting at this her temerity in such an errant undertaking; her breath came and went quickly, and her eyes shone with an infrequent light. Yet go she must. She reached the verge of a pit in the middle of the ferns. Troy stood in the bottom, looking up towards her.

'I heard you rustling through the fern before I saw you,' he said, coming up and giving her his hand to help her down the slope.

The pit was a saucer-shaped concave, naturally formed,

with a top diameter of about thirty feet, and shallow enough to allow the sunshine to reach their heads. Standing in the centre, the sky overhead was met by a circular horizon of fern: this grew nearly to the bottom of the slope and then abruptly ceased. The middle within the belt of verdure was floored with a thick flossy carpet of moss and grass intermingled, so yielding that the foot was half-buried within it.

'Now,' said Troy, producing the sword, which, as he raised it into the sunlight, gleamed a sort of greeting, like a living thing; 'first, we have four right and four left cuts; four right and four left thrusts. Infantry cuts and guards are more interesting than ours, to my mind; but they are not so swashing. They have seven cuts and three thrusts. So much as a preliminary. Well, next, our cut one is as if you were sowing your corn – so.' Bathsheba saw a sort of rainbow, upside down in the air, and Troy's arm was still again. 'Cut two, as if you were hedging – so. Three, as if you were reaping – so. Four, as if you were threshing – in that way. Then the same on the left. The thrusts are these: one, two, three, four, right; one, two, three, four, left.' He repeated them. 'Have 'em again?' he said. 'One, two —'

She hurriedly interrupted: 'I'd rather not; though I don't mind your twos and fours; but your ones and threes are terrible!'

'Very well. I'll let you off the ones and threes. Next, cuts, points and guards altogether.' Troy duly exhibited them. 'Then there's pursuing practice, in this way.' He gave the movements as before. 'There, those are the stereotyped forms. The infantry have two most diabolical upward cuts, which we are too humane to use. Like this – three, four.'

'How murderous and bloodthirsty!'

'They are rather deathy. Now I'll be more interesting, and let you see some loose play – giving all the cuts and points, infantry and cavalry, quicker than lightning, and as promiscuously – with just enough rule to regulate instinct and yet not to fetter it. You are my antagonist, with this difference from real warfare, that I shall miss you every time by one hair's breadth, or perhaps two. Mind you don't flinch, whatever you do.'

'I'll be sure not to!' she said invincibly.

He pointed to about a yard in front of him.

Bathsheba's adventurous spirit was beginning to find some grains of relish in these highly novel proceedings. She took up her position as directed, facing Troy.

'Now just to learn whether you have pluck enough to let me do what I wish, I'll give you a preliminary test.'

He flourished the sword by way of introduction number two, and the next thing of which she was conscious was that the point and blade of the sword were darting with a gleam towards her left side, just above her hip; then of their reappearance on her right side, emerging as it were from between her ribs, having apparently passed through her body. The third item of consciousness was that of seeing the same sword, perfectly clean and free from blood, held vertically in Troy's hand (in the position technically called 'recover swords'). All was as quick as electricity.

'Oh!' she cried out in affright, pressing her hand to her side. 'Have you run me through? – no, you have not! Whatever have you done!'

'I have not touched you,' said Troy quietly. 'It was mere sleight of hand. The sword passed behind you. Now you are not afraid, are you? Because if you are I can't perform. I give my word that I will not only not hurt you, but not once touch you.'

'I don't think I am afraid. You are quite sure you will not hurt me?'

'Quite sure.'

'Is the sword very sharp?'

'O no – only stand as still as a statue. Now!'

In an instant the atmosphere was transformed to Bathsheba's eyes. Beams of light caught from the low sun's rays, above, around, in front of her, well-nigh shut out earth and heaven – all emitted in the marvellous evolutions of Troy's reflecting blade, which seemed everywhere at once, and yet nowhere specially. These circling gleams were accompanied by a keen rush that was almost a whistling – also springing from all sides of her at once. In short, she was enclosed in a firmament of light, and of sharp hisses, resembling a sky-full of meteors close at hand.

Never since the broadsword became the national weapon had there been more dexterity shown in its management than by the hands of Sergeant Troy, and never had he been in such splendid temper for the performance as now in the evening sunshine among the ferns with Bathsheba. It may safely be asserted with respect to the closeness of his cuts, that had it been possible for the edge of the sword to leave in the air a permanent substance wherever it flew past, the space left untouched would have been almost a mould of Bathsheba's figure.

Behind the luminous streams of this *aurora militaris*, she could see the hue of Troy's sword arm, spread in a scarlet haze over the space covered by its motions, like a twanged harpstring, and behind all Troy himself, mostly facing her; sometimes, to show the rear cuts, half turned away, his eye nevertheless always keenly measuring her breadth and outline, and his lips tightly closed in sustained effort. Next, his movements lapsed slower, and she could see them individually. The hissing of the sword had ceased, and he stopped entirely.

'That outer loose lock of hair wants tidying,' he said, before she had moved or spoken. 'Wait: I'll do it for you.'

An arc of silver shone on her right side: the sword had descended. The lock dropped to the ground.

'Bravely borne!' said Troy. 'You didn't flinch a shade's thickness. Wonderful in a woman!'

'It was because I didn't expect it. O, you have spoilt my hair!'

'Only once more.'

'No – no! I am afraid of you – indeed I am!' she cried.

'I won't touch you at all – not even your hair. I am only going to kill that caterpillar settling on you. Now: still!'

It appeared that a caterpillar had come from the fern and chosen the front of her bodice as his resting place. She saw the point glisten towards her bosom, and seemingly enter it. Bathsheba closed her eyes in the full persuasion that she was killed at last. However, feeling just as usual, she opened them again.

'There it is, look,' said the sergeant, holding his sword before her eyes.

The caterpillar was spitted upon its point.

'Why, it is magic!' said Bathsheba, amazed.

'O no – dexterity. I merely gave point to your bosom where the caterpillar was, and instead of running you through checked the extension a thousandth of an inch short of your surface.'

'But how could you chop off a curl of my hair with a sword that has no edge?'

'No edge! This sword will shave like a razor. Look here.'

He touched the palm of his hand with the blade, and then, lifting it, showed her a thin shaving of scarf-skin dangling therefrom.

'But you said before beginning that it was blunt and couldn't cut me!'

'That was to get you to stand still, and so make sure of your safety. The risk of injuring you through your moving was too great not to force me to tell you a fib to escape it.'

She shuddered. 'I have been within an inch of my life, and didn't know it!'

'More precisely speaking, you have been within half an inch of being pared alive two hundred and ninety-five times.'

'Cruel, cruel, 'tis of you!'

'You have been perfectly safe, nevertheless. My sword never errs.' And Troy returned the weapon to the scabbard.

Bathsheba, overcome by a hundred tumultuous feelings resulting from the scene, abstractedly sat down on a tuft of heather.

'I must leave you now,' said Troy softly. 'And I'll venture to take and keep this in remembrance of you.'

She saw him stoop to the grass, pick up the winding lock which he had severed from her manifold tresses, twist it round his fingers, unfasten a button in the breast of his coat, and carefully put it inside. She felt powerless to withstand or deny him. He was altogether too much for her, and Bathsheba seemed as one who, facing a reviving wind, finds it blow so strongly that it stops the breath.

He drew near and said, 'I must be leaving you.' He drew nearer still. A minute later and she saw his scarlet form disappear amid the ferny thicket, almost in a flash, like a brand swiftly waved.

That minute's interval had brought the blood beating into her face, set her stinging as if aflame to the very hollows of her feet, and enlarged emotion to a compass which quite swamped thought. It had brought upon her a stroke resulting, as did that of Moses in Horeb, in a liquid stream – here a stream of tears. She felt like one who has sinned a great sin.

The circumstance had been the gentle dip of Troy's mouth downwards upon her own. He had kissed her.

CHAPTER XXIX

PARTICULARS OF A TWILIGHT WALK

WE now see the element of folly distinctly mingling with the many varying particulars which made up the character of Bathsheba Everdene. It was almost foreign to her intrinsic nature. Introduced as lymph on the dart of Eros it eventually permeated and coloured her whole constitution. Bathsheba, though she had too much understanding to be entirely governed by her womanliness, had too much womanliness to use her understanding to the best advantage. Perhaps in no minor point does woman astonish her helpmate more than in the strange power she possesses of believing cajoleries that she knows to be false – except, indeed, in that of being utterly sceptical on strictures that she knows to be true.

Bathsheba loved Troy in the way that only self-reliant women love when they abandon their self-reliance. When a strong woman recklessly throws away her strength she is worse than a weak woman who has never had any strength to throw away. One source of her inadequacy is the novelty of the occasion. She has never had practice in making the best of such a condition. Weakness is doubly weak by being new.

Bathsheba was not conscious of guile in this matter. Though in one sense a woman of the world, it was, after all, that world of daylight coteries and green carpets wherein cattle form the passing crowd and winds the busy hum; where a quiet family of rabbits or hares lives on the other side of your party-wall, where your neighbour is everybody in the tything, and where calculation is confined to market-days. Of the fabricated tastes of good fashionable society she knew but little, and of the formulated self-indulgence of bad, nothing at all. Had her utmost thoughts in this direction been distinctly worded (and by herself they never were), they would only have amounted to such a matter as that she felt her impulses to be pleasanter guides than her discretion. Her love was entire as a child's, and though warm as summer it was fresh as spring. Her culpability lay in her making no attempt to control feeling by subtle and careful inquiry into consequences. She could show others the steep and thorny way, but 'reck'd not her own rede.'

And Troy's deformities lay deep down from a woman's vision, whilst his embellishments were upon the very surface; thus contrasting with homely Oak, whose defects were patent to the blindest, and whose virtues were as metals in a mine.

The difference between love and respect was markedly shown in her conduct. Bathsheba had spoken of her interest in Boldwood with the greatest freedom to Liddy, but she had only communed with her own heart concerning Troy.

All this infatuation Gabriel saw, and was troubled thereby from the time of his daily journey a-field to the time of his return, and on to the small hours of many a night. That he was not beloved had hitherto been his great sorrow; that Bathsheba was getting into the toils was now a sorrow greater than the first, and one which nearly obscured it. It was a result which paralleled the oft-quoted observation of Hippocrates concerning physical pains.

That is a noble though perhaps an unpromising love which not even the fear of breeding aversion in the bosom of the one beloved can deter from combating his or her errors. Oak determined to speak to his mistress. He would base his appeal on what he considered her unfair treatment of Farmer Boldwood, now absent from home.

An opportunity occurred one evening when she had gone for a short walk by a path through the neighbouring cornfields. It was dusk when Oak, who had not been far a-field that day, took the same path and met her returning, quite pensively, as he thought.

The wheat was now tall, and the path was narrow; thus the

way was quite a sunken groove between the embowing thicket on either side. Two persons could not walk abreast without damaging the crop, and Oak stood aside to let her pass.

'Oh, is it Gabriel?' she said. 'You are taking a walk too. Good-night.'

'I thought I would come to meet you, as it is rather late,' said Oak, turning and following at her heels when she had brushed somewhat quickly by him.

'Thank you, indeed, but I am not very fearful.'

'O no; but there are bad characters about.'

'I never meet them.'

Now Oak, with marvellous ingenuity, had been going to introduce the gallant sergeant through the channel of 'bad characters.' But all at once the scheme broke down, it suddenly occurring to him that this was rather a clumsy way, and too barefaced to begin with. He tried another preamble.

'And as the man who would naturally come to meet you is away from home, too – I mean Farmer Boldwood – why, thinks I, I'll go,' he said.

'Ah, yes.' She walked on without turning her head, and for many steps nothing further was heard from her quarter than the rustle of her dress against the heavy corn-ears. Then she resumed rather tartly —

'I don't quite understand what you meant by saying that Mr. Boldwood would naturally come to meet me.'

'I meant on account of the wedding which they say is likely to take place between you and him, miss. Forgive my speaking plainly.'

'They say what is not true,' she returned quickly. 'No marriage is likely to take place between us.'

Gabriel now put forth his unobscured opinion, for the moment had come. 'Well, Miss Everdene,' he said, 'putting aside what people say, I never in my life saw any courting if his is not a courting of you.'

Bathsheba would probably have terminated the conversation there and then by flatly forbidding the subject, had not her conscious weakness of position allured her to palter and argue in endeavours to better it.

'Since this subject has been mentioned,' she said very emphatically, 'I am glad of the opportunity of clearing up a mistake which is very common and very provoking. I didn't definitely promise Mr. Boldwood anything. I have never cared for him. I respect him, and he has urged me to marry him. But I have given him no distinct answer. As soon as he returns I shall do so; and the answer will be that I cannot think of marrying him.'

'People are full of mistakes, seemingly.'

'They are.'

'The other day they said you were trifling with him, and you almost proved that you were not; lately they have said that you be not, and you straightway begin to show —'

'That I am, I suppose you mean.'

'Well, I hope they speak the truth.'

'They do, but wrongly applied. I don't trifle with him; but then, I have nothing to do with him.'

Oak was unfortunately led on to speak of Boldwood's rival in a wrong tone to her after all. 'I wish you had never met that young Sergeant Troy, miss,' he sighed.

Bathsheba's steps became faintly spasmodic. 'Why?' she asked.

'He is not good enough for 'ee.'

'Did any one tell you to speak to me like this?'

'Nobody at all.'

'Then it appears to me that Sergeant Troy does not concern us here,' she said intractably. 'Yet I must say that Sergeant Troy is an educated man, and quite worthy of any woman. He is well born.'

'His being higher in learning and birth than the ruck o' soldiers is anything but a proof of his worth. It shows his course to be down'ard.'

'I cannot see what this has to do with our conversation. Mr. Troy's course is not by any means downward; and his superiority *is* a proof of his worth!'

'I believe him to have no conscience at all. And I cannot help begging you, miss, to have nothing to do with him. Listen to me this once – only this once! I don't say he's such a bad man as I have fancied – I pray to God he is not. But since we don't exactly know what he is, why not behave as if he *might* be bad, simply for your own safety? Don't trust him, mistress; I ask you not to trust him so.'

'Why, pray?'

'I like soldiers, but this one I do not like,' he said sturdily. 'His cleverness in his calling may have tempted him astray, and what is mirth to the neighbours is ruin to the woman. When he tries to talk to 'ee again, why not turn away with a short "Good day"; and when you see him coming one way, turn the other. When he says anything laughable, fail to see the point and don't smile, and speak of him before those who will report your talk as "that fantastical man," or "that Sergeant What's-his-name." "That man of a family that has come to the dogs." Don't be unmannerly towards en, but harmless-uncivil, and so get rid of the man.'

No Christmas robin detained by a window-pane ever pulsed as did Bathsheba now.

'I say – I say again – that it doesn't become you to talk about him. Why he should be mentioned passes me quite!' she exclaimed desperately. 'I know this, th-th-that he is a thoroughly conscientious man – blunt sometimes even to rudeness – but always speaking his mind about you plain to your face!'

'Oh.'

'He is as good as anybody in this parish! He is very particular, too, about going to church – yes, he is!'

'I am afeard nobody ever saw him there. I never did, certainly.'

'The reason of that is,' she said eagerly, 'that he goes in privately by the old tower door, just when the service commences, and sits at the back of the gallery. He told me so.'

This supreme instance of Troy's goodness fell upon Gabriel's ears like the thirteenth stroke of a crazy clock. It was not only

received with utter incredulity as regarded itself, but threw a
doubt on all the assurances that had preceded it.

Oak was grieved to find how entirely she trusted him. He
brimmed with deep feeling as he replied in a steady voice, the
steadiness of which was spoilt by the palpableness of his great
effort to keep it so: —

'You know, mistress, that I love you, and shall love you
always. I only mention this to bring to your mind that at any
rate I would wish to do you no harm: beyond that I put it aside.
I have lost in the race for money and good things, and I am
not such a fool as to pretend to 'ee now I am poor, and you
have got altogether above me. But Bathsheba, dear mistress,
this I beg you to consider — that, both to keep yourself well
honoured among the workfolk, and in common generosity to
an honourable man who loves you as well as I, you should be
more discreet in your bearing towards this soldier.'

'Don't, don't, don't!' she exclaimed, in a choking voice.

'Are ye not more to me than my own affairs, and even life!'
he went on. 'Come, listen to me! I am six years older than you,
and Mr. Boldwood is ten years older than I, and consider — I
do beg of 'ee to consider before it is too late — how safe you
would be in his hands!'

Oak's allusion to his own love for her lessened, to some
extent, her anger at his interference; but she could not really
forgive him for letting his wish to marry her be eclipsed by his
wish to do her good, any more than for his slighting treatment
of Troy.

'I wish you to go elsewhere,' she commanded, a paleness of
face invisible to the eye being suggested by the trembling
words. 'Do not remain on this farm any longer. I don't want
you — I beg you to go!'

'That's nonsense,' said Oak calmly. 'This is the second time
you have pretended to dismiss me; and what's the use o' it?'

'Pretended! You shall go, sir — your lecturing I will not hear!
I am mistress here.'

'Go, indeed — what folly will you say next? Treating me like

Dick, Tom and Harry when you know that a short time ago my position was as good as yours! Upon my life, Bathsheba, it is too barefaced. You know, too, that I can't go without putting things in such a strait as you wouldn't get out of I can't tell when. Unless, indeed, you'll promise to have an understanding man as bailiff, or manager, or something. I'll go at once if you'll promise that.'

'I shall have no bailiff; I shall continue to be my own manager,' she said decisively.

'Very well, then; you should be thankful to me for biding. How would the farm go on with nobody to mind it but a woman? But mind this, I don't wish 'ee to feel you owe me anything. Not I. What I do, I do. Sometimes I say I should be as glad as a bird to leave the place – for don't suppose I'm content to be a nobody. I was made for better things. However, I don't like to see your concerns going to ruin, as they must if you keep in this mind. . . . I hate taking my own measure so plain, but, upon my life, your provoking ways make a man say what he wouldn't dream of at other times! I own to being rather interfering. But you know well enough how it is, and who she is that I like too well, and feel too much like a fool about to be civil to her!'

It is more than probable that she privately and unconsciously respected him a little for this grim fidelity, which had been shown in his tone even more than in his words. At any rate she murmured something to the effect that he might stay if he wished. She said more distinctly, 'Will you leave me alone now? I don't order it as a mistress – I ask it as a woman, and I expect you not to be so uncourteous as to refuse.'

'Certainly I will, Miss Everdene,' said Gabriel gently. He wondered that the request should have come at this moment, for the strife was over, and they were on a most desolate hill, far from every human habitation, and the hour was getting late. He stood still and allowed her to get far ahead of him till he could only see her form upon the sky.

A distressing explanation of this anxiety to be rid of him at that point now ensued. A figure apparently rose from the earth beside her. The shape beyond all doubt was Troy's. Oak would not be even a possible listener, and at once turned back till a good two hundred yards were between the lovers and himself.

Gabriel went home by way of the churchyard. In passing the tower he thought of what she had said about the sergeant's virtuous habit of entering the church unperceived at the beginning of service. Believing that the little gallery door alluded to was quite disused, he ascended the external flight of steps at the top of which it stood, and examined it. The pale lustre yet hanging in the north-western heaven was sufficient to show that a sprig of ivy had grown from the wall across the door to a length of more than a foot, delicately tying the panel to the stone jamb. It was a decisive proof that the door had not been opened at least since Troy came back to Weatherbury.

CHAPTER XXX

HOT CHEEKS AND TEARFUL EYES

HALF an hour later Bathsheba entered her own house. There burnt upon her face when she met the light of the candles the flush and excitement which were little less than chronic with her now. The farewell words of Troy, who had accompanied her to the very door, still lingered in her ears. He had bidden her adieu for two days, which were, so he stated, to be spent at Bath in visiting some friends. He had also kissed her a second time.

It is only fair to Bathsheba to explain here a little fact which did not come to light till a long time afterwards: that Troy's presentation of himself so aptly at the roadside this evening was not by any distinctly preconcerted arrangement. He had hinted – she had forbidden; and it was only on the chance of his still coming that she had dismissed Oak, fearing a meeting between them just then.

She now sank down into a chair, wild and perturbed by all these new and fevering sequences. Then she jumped up with a manner of decision, and fetched her desk from a side table.

In three minutes, without pause or modification, she had written a letter to Boldwood, at his address beyond Casterbridge, saying mildly but firmly that she had well considered the whole subject he had brought before her and kindly given her time to decide upon; that her final decision was that she could not marry him. She had expressed to Oak an intention to wait till Boldwood came home before communicating to him her conclusive reply. But Bathsheba found that she could not wait.

It was impossible to send this letter till the next day; yet to quell her uneasiness by getting it out of her hands, and so, as it were, setting the act in motion at once, she arose to take it to any one of the women who might be in the kitchen.

She paused in the passage. A dialogue was going on in the kitchen, and Bathsheba and Troy were the subject of it.

'If he marry her, she'll gie up farming.'

''Twill be a gallant life, but may bring some trouble between the mirth – so say I.'

'Well, I wish I had half such a husband.'

Bathsheba had too much sense to mind seriously what her servitors said about her; but too much womanly redundance of speech to leave alone what was said till it died the natural death of unminded things. She burst in upon them.

'Who are you speaking of?' she asked.

There was a pause before anybody replied. At last Liddy said frankly, 'What was passing was a bit of a word about yourself, miss.'

'I thought so! Maryann and Liddy – Temperance – now I forbid you to suppose such things. You know I don't care the least for Mr. Troy – not I. Everybody knows how much I hate him. – Yes,' repeated the froward young person, '*hate* him!'

'We know you do, miss,' said Liddy; 'and so do we all.'

'I hate him too,' said Maryann.

'Maryann – O you perjured woman! How can you speak that wicked story!' said Bathsheba excitedly. 'You admired him from your heart only this morning in the very world, you did. Yes, Maryann, you know it!'

'Yes, miss, but so did you. He is a wild scamp now, and you are right to hate him.'

'He's *not* a wild scamp! How dare you to my face! I have no right to hate him, nor you, nor anybody. But I am a silly woman! What is it to me what he is? You know it is nothing. I don't care for him; I don't mean to defend his good name, not I. Mind this, if any of you say a word against him you'll be dismissed instantly!'

She flung down the letter and surged back into the parlour, with a big heart and tearful eyes, Liddy following her.

'O miss!' said mild Liddy, looking pitifully into Bathsheba's face. 'I am sorry we mistook you so! I did think you cared for him; but I see you don't now.'

'Shut the door, Liddy.'

Liddy closed the door, and went on: 'People always say such foolery, miss. I'll make answer hencefor'ard, "Of course a lady like Miss Everdene can't love him"; I'll say it out in plain black and white.'

Bathsheba burst out: 'O Liddy, are you such a simpleton? Can't you read riddles? Can't you see? Are you a woman yourself?'

Liddy's clear eyes rounded with wonderment.

'Yes; you must be a blind thing, Liddy!' she said in reckless abandonment and grief. 'O, I love him to very distraction and misery and agony! Don't be frightened at me, though perhaps I am enough to frighten any innocent woman. Come closer – closer.' She put her arms round Liddy's neck. 'I must let it out to somebody; it is wearing me away! Don't you yet know enough of me to see through that miserable denial of mine? O God, what a lie it was! Heaven and my Love forgive me. And don't you know that a woman who loves at all thinks nothing of perjury when it is balanced against her love? There, go out of the room; I want to be quite alone.'

Liddy went towards the door.

'Liddy, come here. Solemnly swear to me that he's not a fast man; that it is all lies they say about him!'

'But, miss, how can I say he is not if —'

'You graceless girl! How can you have the cruel heart to repeat what they say? Unfeeling thing that you are. . . . But *I'll* see if you or anybody else in the village, or town either, dare do such a thing!' She started off, pacing from fireplace to door, and back again.

'No, miss. I don't – I know it is not true!' said Liddy, frightened at Bathsheba's unwonted vehemence.

'I suppose you only agree with me like that to please me. But, Liddy, he *cannot be* bad, as is said. Do you hear?'

'Yes, miss, yes.'

'And you don't believe he is?'

'I don't know what to say, miss,' said Liddy, beginning to cry. 'If I say No, you don't believe me; and if I say Yes, you rage at me!'

'Say you don't believe it – say you don't!'

'I don't believe him to be so bad as they make out.'

'He is not bad at all. . . . My poor life and heart, how weak I am!' she moaned, in a relaxed, desultory way, heedless of Liddy's presence. 'O, how I wish I had never seen him! Loving is misery for women always. I shall never forgive God for making me a woman, and dearly am I beginning to pay for the honour of owning a pretty face.' She freshened and turned to Liddy suddenly. 'Mind this, Lydia Smallbury, if you repeat anywhere a single word of what I have said to you inside this closed door, I'll never trust you, or love you, or have you with me a moment longer – not a moment!'

'I don't want to repeat anything,' said Liddy, with womanly dignity of a diminutive order; 'but I don't wish to stay with you. And, if you please, I'll go at the end of the harvest, or this week, or to-day. . . . I don't see that I deserve to be put upon and stormed at for nothing!' concluded the small woman, bigly.

'No, no, Liddy; you must stay!' said Bathsheba, dropping from haughtiness to entreaty with capricious inconsequence. 'You must not notice my being in a taking just now. You are not as a servant – you are a companion to me. Dear, dear – I don't know what I am doing since this miserable ache o' my heart has weighted and worn upon me so! What shall I come to! I suppose I shall get further and further into troubles. I wonder sometimes if I am doomed to die in the Union. I am friendless enough, God knows!'

'I won't notice anything, nor will I leave you!' sobbed Liddy, impulsively putting up her lips to Bathsheba's, and kissing her.

Then Bathsheba kissed Liddy, and all was smooth again.

'I don't often cry, do I, Lidd? but you have made tears come into my eyes,' she said, a smile shining through the moisture. 'Try to think him a good man, won't you, dear Liddy?'

'I will, miss, indeed.'

'He is a sort of steady man in a wild way, you know. That's better than to be as some are, wild in a steady way. I am afraid that's how I am. And promise me to keep my secret – do, Liddy! And do not let them know that I have been crying about him, because it will be dreadful for me, and no good to him, poor thing!'

'Death's head himself shan't wring it from me, mistress, if I've a mind to keep anything; and I'll always be your friend,' replied Liddy emphatically, at the same time bringing a few more tears into her own eyes, not from any particular necessity, but from an artistic sense of making herself in keeping with the remainder of the picture, which seems to influence women at such times. 'I think God likes us to be good friends, don't you?'

'Indeed I do.'

'And, dear miss, you won't harry me and storm at me, will you? because you seem to swell so tall as a lion then, and it frightens me! Do you know, I fancy you would be a match for any man when you are in one o' your takings.'

'Never! do you?' said Bathsheba, slightly laughing, though somewhat seriously alarmed by this Amazonian picture of herself. 'I hope I am not a bold sort of maid – mannish?' she continued with some anxiety.

'O no, not mannish; but so almighty womanish that 'tis getting on that way sometimes. Ah! miss,' she said, after having drawn her breath very sadly in and sent it very sadly out, 'I wish I had half your failing that way. 'Tis a great protection to a poor maid in these illegit'mate days!'

CHAPTER XXXI

BLAME – FURY

THE next evening Bathsheba, with the idea of getting out of
the way of Mr. Boldwood in the event of his returning to
answer her note in person, proceeded to fulfil an engagement
made with Liddy some few hours earlier. Bathsheba's companion, as a gage of their reconciliation, had been granted a week's
holiday to visit her sister, who was married to a thriving hurdler
and cattle-crib-maker living in a delightful labyrinth of hazel
copse not far beyond Yalbury. The arrangement was that Miss
Everdene should honour them by coming there for a day or
two to inspect some ingenious contrivances which this man of
the woods had introduced into his wares.

Leaving her instructions with Gabriel and Maryann, that
they were to see everything carefully locked up for the night,
she went out of the house just at the close of a timely thunder-
shower, which had refined the air, and daintily bathed the coat
of the land, though all beneath was dry as ever. Freshness was
exhaled in an essence from the varied contours of bank and
hollow, as if the earth breathed maiden breath; and the pleased
birds were hymning to the scene. Before her, among the clouds,
there was a contrast in the shape of lairs of fierce light which
showed themselves in the neighbourhood of a hidden sun, lingering on to the farthest north-west corner of the heavens that
this midsummer season allowed.

She had walked nearly two miles of her journey, watching
how the day was retreating, and thinking how the time of deeds
was quietly melting into the time of thought, to give place in
its turn to the time of prayer and sleep, when she beheld
advancing over Yalbury hill the very man she sought so

anxiously to elude. Boldwood was stepping on, not with that quiet tread of reserved strength which was his customary gait, in which he always seemed to be balancing two thoughts. His manner was stunned and sluggish now.

Boldwood had for the first time been awakened to woman's privileges in tergiversation even when it involves another person's possible blight. That Bathsheba was a firm and positive girl, far less inconsequent than her fellows, had been the very lung of his hope; for he had held that these qualities would lead her to adhere to a straight course for consistency's sake, and accept him, though her fancy might not flood him with the iridescent hues of uncritical love. But the argument now came back as sorry gleams from a broken mirror. The discovery was no less a scourge than a surprise.

He came on looking upon the ground, and did not see Bathsheba till they were less than a stone's throw apart. He looked up at the sound of her pit-pat, and his changed appearance sufficiently denoted to her the depth and strength of the feelings paralyzed by her letter.

'Oh; is it you, Mr. Boldwood?' she faltered, a guilty warmth pulsing in her face.

Those who have the power of reproaching in silence may find it a means more effective than words. There are accents in the eye which are not on the tongue, and more tales come from pale lips than can enter an ear. It is both the grandeur and the pain of the remoter moods that they avoid the pathway of sound. Boldwood's look was unanswerable.

Seeing she turned a little aside, he said, 'What, are you afraid of me?'

'Why should you say that?' said Bathsheba.

'I fancied you looked so,' said he. 'And it is most strange, because of its contrast with my feeling for you.'

She regained self-possession, fixed her eyes calmly, and waited.

'You know what that feeling is,' continued Boldwood deliberately. 'A thing strong as death. No dismissal by a hasty letter affects that.'

'I wish you did not feel so strongly about me,' she murmured. 'It is generous of you, and more than I deserve, but I must not hear it now.'

'Hear it? What do you think I have to say, then? I am not to marry you, and that's enough. Your letter was excellently plain. I want you to hear nothing – not I.'

Bathsheba was unable to direct her will into any definite groove for freeing herself from this fearfully awkward position. She confusedly said, 'Good evening,' and was moving on. Boldwood walked up to her heavily and dully.

'Bathsheba – darling – is it final indeed?'

'Indeed it is.'

'O, Bathsheba – have pity upon me!' Boldwood burst out. 'God's sake, yes – I am come to that low, lowest stage – to ask a woman for pity! Still, she is you – she is you.'

Bathsheba commanded herself well. But she could hardly get a clear voice for what came instinctively to her lips: 'There is little honour to the woman in that speech.' It was only whispered, for something unutterably mournful no less than distressing in this spectacle of a man showing himself to be so entirely the vane of a passion enervated the feminine instinct for punctilios.

'I am beyond myself about this, and am mad,' he said. 'I am no stoic at all to be supplicating here; but I do supplicate to you. I wish you knew what is in me of devotion to you; but it is impossible, that. In bare human mercy to a lonely man, don't throw me off now!'

'I don't throw you off – indeed, how can I? I never had you.' In her noon-clear sense that she had never loved him she forgot for a moment her thoughtless angle on that day in February.

'But there was a time when you turned to me, before I thought of you! I don't reproach you, for even now I feel that the ignorant and cold darkness that I should have lived in if you had not attracted me by that letter – valentine you call it – would have been worse than my knowledge of you, though it has brought this misery. But, I say, there was a time when I knew nothing of you, and cared nothing for you, and yet you drew me on. And if you say you gave me no encouragement, I cannot but contradict you.'

'What you call encouragement was the childish game of an idle minute. I have bitterly repented of it – ay, bitterly, and in tears. Can you still go on reminding me?'

'I don't accuse you of it – I deplore it. I took for earnest what you insist was jest, and now this that I pray to be jest you say is awful, wretched earnest. Our moods meet at wrong places. I wish your feeling was more like mine, or my feeling more like yours! O, could I but have foreseen the torture that trifling trick was going to lead me into, how I should have cursed you; but only having been able to see it since, I cannot do that, for I love you too well! But it is weak, idle drivelling to go on like this. . . . Bathsheba, you are the first woman of any shade or nature that I have ever looked at to love, and it is the having been so near claiming you for my own that makes this denial so hard to bear. How nearly you promised me! But I don't speak now to move your heart, and make you grieve because of my pain; it is no use, that. I must bear it; my pain would get no less by paining you.'

'But I do pity you – deeply – O, so deeply!' she earnestly said.

'Do no such thing – do no such thing. Your dear love, Bathsheba, is such a vast thing beside your pity, that the loss of your pity as well as your love is no great addition to my sorrow, nor does the gain of your pity make it sensibly less. O sweet – how dearly you spoke to me behind the spear-bed at the washing-pool, and in the barn at the shearing, and that dearest last time in the evening at your home! Where are your pleasant words all gone – your earnest hope to be able to love me? Where is your firm conviction that you would get to care for me very much? Really forgotten? – really?'

She checked emotion, looked him quietly and clearly in the face, and said in her low, firm voice, 'Mr. Boldwood, I promised you nothing. Would you have had me a woman of clay when you paid me that furthest, highest compliment a man can pay a woman – telling her he loves her? I was bound to show some feeling, if I would not be a graceless shrew. Yet each of those pleasures was just for the day – the day just for the pleasure. How was I to know that what is a pastime to all other men was death to you? Have reason, do, and think more kindly of me!'

'Well, never mind arguing – never mind. One thing is sure: you were all but mine, and now you are not nearly mine. Everything is changed, and that by you alone, remember. You were nothing to me once, and I was contented; you are now nothing to me again, and how different the second nothing is from the first! Would to God you had never taken me up, since it was only to throw me down!'

Bathsheba, in spite of her mettle, began to feel unmistakable signs that she was inherently the weaker vessel. She strove miserably against this femininity which would insist upon supplying unbidden emotions in stronger and stronger current. She had tried to elude agitation by fixing her mind on the trees, sky, any trivial object before her eyes, whilst his reproaches fell, but ingenuity could not save her now.

'I did not take you up – surely I did not!' she answered as heroically as she could. 'But don't be in this mood with me. I can endure being told I am in the wrong, if you will only tell it me gently! O sir, will you not kindly forgive me, and look at it cheerfully?'

'Cheerfully! Can a man fooled to utter heart-burning find a reason for being merry? If I have lost, how can I be as if I had won? Heavens, you must be heartless quite! Had I known what a fearfully bitter sweet this was to be, how I would have avoided you, and never seen you, and been deaf to you. I tell you all this, but what do you care! You don't care.'

She returned silent and weak denials to his charges, and swayed her head desperately, as if to thrust away the words as they came showering about her ears from the lips of the trembling man in the climax of life, with his bronzed Roman face and fine frame.

'Dearest, dearest, I am wavering even now between the two opposites of recklessly renouncing you, and labouring humbly for you again. Forget that you have said No, and let it be as it was! Say, Bathsheba, that you only wrote that refusal to me in fun – come, say it to me!'

'It would be untrue, and painful to both of us. You overrate my capacity for love. I don't possess half the warmth of nature you believe me to have. An unprotected childhood in a cold world has beaten gentleness out of me.'

He immediately said with more resentment: 'That may be true, somewhat; but ah, Miss Everdene, it won't do as a reason! You are not the cold woman you would have me believe. No, no! It isn't because you have no feeling in you that you don't love me. You naturally would have me think so – you would hide from me that you have a burning heart like mine. You have love enough, but it is turned into a new channel. I know where.'

The swift music of her heart became hubbub now, and she throbbed to extremity. He was coming to Troy. He did then know what had occurred! And the name fell from his lips the next moment.

'Why did Troy not leave my treasure alone?' he asked fiercely. 'When I had no thought of injuring him, why did he force himself upon your notice! Before he worried you your inclination was to have me; when next I should have come to you your answer would have been Yes. Can you deny it – I ask, can you deny it?'

She delayed the reply, but was too honest to withhold it. 'I cannot,' she whispered.

'I know you cannot. But he stole in in my absence and robbed me. Why didn't he win you away before, when nobody would have been grieved? – when nobody would have been set tale-bearing? Now the people sneer at me – the very hills and sky seem to laugh at me till I blush shamefully for my folly. I have lost my respect, my good name, my standing – lost it, never to get it again. Go and marry your man – go on!'

'O sir – Mr. Boldwood!'

'You may as well. I have no further claim upon you. As for me, I had better go somewhere alone, and hide – and pray. I loved a woman once. I am now ashamed. When I am dead they'll say, Miserable love-sick man that he was. Heaven – heaven – if I had got jilted secretly, and the dishonour not known, and my position kept! But no matter, it is gone, and the woman not gained. Shame upon him – shame!'

His unreasonable anger terrified her, and she glided from him, without obviously moving, as she said, 'I am only a girl – do not speak to me so!'

'All the time you knew – how very well you knew – that your new freak was my misery. Dazzled by brass and scarlet – O, Bathsheba – this is woman's folly indeed!'

She fired up at once. 'You are taking too much upon yourself!' she said vehemently. 'Everybody is upon me – everybody. It is unmanly to attack a woman so! I have nobody in the world to fight my battles for me; but no mercy is shown. Yet if a thousand of you sneer and say things against me, I *will not* be put down!'

'You'll chatter with him doubtless about me. Say to him, "Boldwood would have died for me." Yes, and you have given way to him, knowing him to be not the man for you. He has kissed you – claimed you as his. Do you hear – he has kissed you. Deny it!'

The most tragic woman is cowed by a tragic man, and although Boldwood was, in vehemence and glow, nearly her own self rendered into another sex, Bathsheba's cheek quivered. She gasped, 'Leave me, sir – leave me! I am nothing to you. Let me go on!'

'Deny that he has kissed you.'

'I shall not.'

'Ha – then he has!' came hoarsely from the farmer.

'He has,' she said slowly, and, in spite of her fear, defiantly. 'I am not ashamed to speak the truth.'

'Then curse him; and curse him!' said Boldwood, breaking into a whispered fury. 'Whilst I would have given worlds to touch your hand, you have let a rake come in without right or ceremony and – kiss you! Heaven's mercy – kiss you! . . . Ah, a time of his life shall come when he will have to repent, and think wretchedly of the pain he has caused another man; and then may he ache, and wish, and curse, and yearn – as I do now!'

'Don't, don't, O, don't pray down evil upon him!' she implored in a miserable cry. 'Anything but that – anything. O, be kind to him, sir, for I love him true!'

Boldwood's ideas had reached that point of fusion at which outline and consistency entirely disappear. The impending night appeared to concentrate in his eye. He did not hear her at all now.

'I'll punish him – by my soul, that will I! I'll meet him, soldier or no, and I'll horsewhip the untimely stripling for this reckless theft of my one delight. If he were a hundred men I'd horsewhip him —' He dropped his voice suddenly and unnaturally. 'Bathsheba, sweet, lost coquette, pardon me! I've been blaming you, threatening you, behaving like a churl to you, when he's the greatest sinner. He stole your dear heart away with his unfathomable lies! . . . It is a fortunate thing for him that he's gone back to his regiment – that he's away up the country, and not here! I hope he may not return here just yet. I pray God he may not come into my sight, for I may be tempted beyond myself. O, Bathsheba, keep him away – yes, keep him away from me!'

For a moment Boldwood stood so inertly after this that his soul seemed to have been entirely exhaled with the breath of his passionate words. He turned his face away, and withdrew, and his form was soon covered over by the twilight as his footsteps mixed in with the low hiss of the leafy trees.

Bathsheba, who had been standing motionless as a model all

this latter time, flung her hands to her face, and wildly attempted to ponder on the exhibition which had just passed away. Such astounding wells of fevered feeling in a still man like Mr. Boldwood were incomprehensible, dreadful. Instead of being a man trained to repression he was – what she had seen him.

The force of the farmer's threats lay in their relation to a circumstance known at present only to herself: her lover was coming back to Weatherbury in the course of the very next day or two. Troy had not returned to his distant barracks as Boldwood and others supposed, but had merely gone to visit some acquaintance in Bath, and had yet a week or more remaining to his furlough.

She felt wretchedly certain that if he revisited her just at this nick of time, and came into contact with Boldwood, a fierce quarrel would be the consequence. She panted with solicitude when she thought of possible injury to Troy. The least spark would kindle the farmer's swift feelings of rage and jealousy; he would lose his self-mastery as he had this evening; Troy's blitheness might become aggressive; it might take the direction of derision, and Boldwood's anger might then take the direction of revenge.

With almost a morbid dread of being thought a gushing girl, this guideless woman too well concealed from the world under a manner of carelessness the warm depths of her strong emotions. But now there was no reserve. In her distraction, instead of advancing further she walked up and down, beating the air with her fingers, pressing her brow, and sobbing brokenly to herself. Then she sat down on a heap of stones by the wayside to think. There she remained long. Above the dark margin of the earth appeared foreshores and promontories of coppery cloud, bounding a green and pellucid expanse in the western sky. Amaranthine glosses came over them then, and the unresting world wheeled her round to a contrasting prospect eastward, in the shape of indecisive and palpitating stars. She gazed upon their silent throes amid the shades of space, but realized none at all. Her troubled spirit was far away with Troy.

CHAPTER XXXII

NIGHT – HORSES TRAMPING

THE village of Weatherbury was quiet as the graveyard in its midst, and the living were lying well-nigh as still as the dead. The church clock struck eleven. The air was so empty of other sounds that the whirr of the clock-work immediately before the strokes was distinct, and so was also the click of the same at their close. The notes flew forth with the usual blind obtuseness of inanimate things – flapping and rebounding among walls, undulating against the scattered clouds, spreading through their interstices into unexplored miles of space.

Bathsheba's crannied and mouldy halls were to-night occupied only by Maryann, Liddy being, as was stated, with her sister, whom Bathsheba had set out to visit. A few minutes after eleven had struck, Maryann turned in her bed with a sense of being disturbed. She was totally unconscious of the nature of the interruption to her sleep. It led to a dream, and the dream to an awakening, with an uneasy sensation that something had happened. She left her bed and looked out of the window. The paddock abutted on this end of the building, and in the paddock she could just discern by the uncertain grey a moving figure approaching the horse that was feeding there. The figure seized the horse by the forelock, and led it to the corner of the field. Here she could see some object which circumstances proved to be a vehicle, for after a few minutes spent apparently in harnessing, she heard the trot of the horse down the road, mingled with the sound of light wheels.

Two varieties only of humanity could have entered the paddock with the ghost-like glide of that mysterious figure. They were a woman and a gipsy man. A woman was out of the

227

question in such an occupation at this hour, and the comer could be no less than a thief, who might probably have known the weakness of the household on this particular night, and have chosen it on that account for his daring attempt. Moreover, to raise suspicion to conviction itself, there were gipsies in Weatherbury Bottom.

Maryann, who had been afraid to shout in the robber's presence, having seen him depart had no fear. She hastily slipped on her clothes, stumped down the disjointed staircase with its hundred creaks, ran to Coggan's, the nearest house, and raised an alarm. Coggan called Gabriel, who now again lodged in his house as at first, and together they went to the paddock. Beyond all doubt the horse was gone.

'Hark!' said Gabriel.

They listened. Distinct upon the stagnant air came the sounds of a trotting horse passing up Longpuddle Lane – just beyond the gipsies' encampment in Weatherbury Bottom.

'That's our Dainty – I'll swear to her step,' said Jan.

'Mighty me! Won't mis'ess storm and call us stupids when she comes back!' moaned Maryann. 'How I wish it had happened when she was at home, and none of us had been answerable!'

'We must ride after,' said Gabriel decisively. 'I'll be responsible to Miss Everdene for what we do. Yes, we'll follow.'

'Faith, I don't see how,' said Coggan. 'All our horses are too heavy for that trick except little Poppet, and what's she between two of us? – If we only had that pair over the hedge we might do something.'

'Which pair?'

'Mr. Boldwood's Tidy and Moll.'

'Then wait here till I come hither again,' said Gabriel. He ran down the hill towards Farmer Boldwood's.

'Farmer Boldwood is not at home,' said Maryann.

'All the better,' said Coggan. 'I know what he's gone for.'

Less than five minutes brought up Oak again, running at the same pace, with two halters dangling from his hand.

'Where did you find 'em?' said Coggan, turning round and leaping upon the hedge without waiting for an answer.

'Under the eaves. I knew where they were kept,' said Gabriel, following him. 'Coggan, you can ride bare-backed? there's no time to look for saddles.'

'Like a hero!' said Jan.

'Maryann, you go to bed,' Gabriel shouted to her from the top of the hedge.

Springing down into Boldwood's pastures, each pocketed his halter to hide it from the horses, who, seeing the men empty-handed, docilely allowed themselves to be seized by the mane, when the halters were dexterously slipped on. Having neither bit nor bridle, Oak and Coggan extemporized the former by passing the rope in each case through the animal's mouth and looping it on the other side. Oak vaulted astride, and Coggan clambered up by aid of the bank, when they ascended to the gate and galloped off in the direction taken by Bathsheba's horse and the robber. Whose vehicle the horse had been harnessed to was a matter of some uncertainty.

Weatherbury Bottom was reached in three or four minutes. They scanned the shady green patch by the roadside. The gipsies were gone.

'The villains!' said Gabriel. 'Which way have they gone, I wonder?'

'Straight on, as sure as God made little apples,' said Jan.

'Very well; we are better mounted, and must overtake 'em,' said Oak. 'Now, on at full speed!'

No sound of a rider in their van could now be discovered. The road-metal grew softer and more clayey as Weatherbury was left behind, and the late rain had wetted its surface to a somewhat plastic, but not muddy state. They came to cross-roads. Coggan suddenly pulled up Moll and slipped off.

'What's the matter?' said Gabriel.

'We must try to track 'em, since we can't hear 'em,' said Jan, fumbling in his pockets. He struck a light, and held the match to the ground. The rain had been heavier here, and all foot and horse tracks made previous to the storm had been abraded and blurred by the drops, and they were now so many little scoops of water, which reflected the flame of the match like eyes. One set of tracks was fresh and had no water in them; one pair of ruts was also empty, and not small canals, like the others. The footprints forming this recent impression were full of information as to pace; they were in equidistant pairs, three or four feet apart, the right and left foot of each pair being exactly opposite one another.

'Straight on!' Jan exclaimed. 'Tracks like that mean a stiff gallop. No wonder we don't hear him. And the horse is harnessed – look at the ruts. Ay, that's our mare, sure enough!'

'How do you know?'

'Old Jimmy Harris only shoed her last week, and I'd swear to his make among ten thousand.'

'The rest of the gipsies must ha' gone on earlier, or some other way,' said Oak. 'You saw there were no other tracks?'

'True.' They rode along silently for a long weary time. Coggan carried an old pinchbeck repeater which he had inherited from some genius in his family; and it now struck one. He lighted another match, and examined the ground again.

''Tis a canter now,' he said, throwing away the light. 'A twisty, rickety pace for a gig. The fact is, they overdrove her at starting; we shall catch 'em yet.'

Again they hastened on, and entered Blackmore Vale. Coggan's watch struck one. When they looked again the hoofmarks were so spaced as to form a sort of zigzag if united, like the lamps along a street.

'That's a trot, I know,' said Gabriel.

'Only a trot now,' said Coggan cheerfully. 'We shall overtake him in time.'

They pushed rapidly on for yet two or three miles. 'Ah! a moment,' said Jan. 'Let's see how she was driven up this hill. 'Twill help us.' A light was promptly struck upon his gaiters as before, and the examination made.

'Hurrah!' said Coggan. 'She walked up here – and well she might. We shall get them in two miles, for a crown.'

They rode three, and listened. No sound was to be heard save a mill-pond trickling hoarsely through a hatch, and suggesting gloomy possibilities of drowning by jumping in. Gabriel dismounted when they came to a turning. The tracks were absolutely the only guide as to the direction that they now had, and great caution was necessary to avoid confusing them with some others which had made their appearance lately.

'What does this mean? – though I guess,' said Gabriel, looking up at Coggan as he moved the match over the ground about the turning. Coggan, who, no less than the panting horses, had latterly shown signs of weariness, again scrutinized the mystic characters. This time only three were of the regular horseshoe shape. Every fourth was a dot.

He screwed up his face, and emitted a long 'whew-w-w!'

'Lame,' said Oak.

'Yes. Dainty is lamed; the near-foot-afore,' said Coggan slowly, staring still at the footprints.

'We'll push on,' said Gabriel, remounting his humid steed.

Although the road along its greater part had been as good as any turnpike-road in the country, it was nominally only a byway. The last turning had brought them into the high road leading to Bath. Coggan recollected himself.

'We shall have him now!' he exclaimed.

'Where?'

'Sherton Turnpike. The keeper of that gate is the sleepiest man between here and London – Dan Randall, that's his name – knowed en for years, when he was at Casterbridge gate. Between the lameness and the gate 'tis a done job.'

They now advanced with extreme caution. Nothing was said until, against a shady background of foliage, five white bars were visible, crossing their route a little way ahead.

'Hush – we are almost close!' said Gabriel.

'Amble on upon the grass,' said Coggan.

The white bars were blotted out in the midst by a dark

shape in front of them. The silence of this lonely time was pierced by an exclamation from that quarter.

'Hoy-a-hoy! Gate!'

It appeared that there had been a previous call which they had not noticed, for on their close approach the door of the turnpike-house opened, and the keeper came out half-dressed, with a candle in his hand. The rays illumined the whole group.

'Keep the gate close!' shouted Gabriel. 'He has stolen the horse!'

'Who?' said the turnpike-man.

Gabriel looked at the driver of the gig, and saw a woman – Bathsheba, his mistress.

On hearing his voice she had turned her face away from the light. Coggan had, however, caught sight of her in the meanwhile.

'Why, 'tis mistress – I'll take my oath!' he said, amazed.

Bathsheba it certainly was, and she had by this time done the trick she could do so well in crises not of love, namely, mask a surprise by coolness of manner.

'Well, Gabriel,' she inquired quietly, 'where are you going?'

'We thought —' began Gabriel.

'I am driving to Bath,' she said, taking for her own use the assurance that Gabriel lacked. 'An important matter made it necessary for me to give up my visit to Liddy, and go off at once. What, then, were you following me?'

'We thought the horse was stole.'

'Well – what a thing! How very foolish of you not to know that I had taken the trap and horse. I could neither wake Maryann nor get into the house, though I hammered for ten minutes against her window-sill. Fortunately, I could get the key of the coach-house, so I troubled no one further. Didn't you think it might be me?'

'Why should we, miss?'

'Perhaps not. Why, those are never Farmer Boldwood's horses! Goodness mercy! what have you been doing – bringing trouble upon me in this way? What! mustn't a lady move an inch from her door without being dogged like a thief?'

'But how was we to know, if you left no account of your doings?' expostulated Coggan, 'and ladies don't drive at these hours, miss, as a jineral rule of society.'

'I did leave an account – and you would have seen it in the morning. I wrote in chalk on the coach-house doors that I had come back for the horse and gig, and driven off; that I could arouse nobody, and should return soon.'

'But you'll consider, ma'am, that we couldn't see that till it got daylight.'

'True,' she said, and though vexed at first she had too much sense to blame them long or seriously for a devotion to her that was as valuable as it was rare. She added with a very pretty grace, 'Well, I really thank you heartily for taking all this trouble; but I wish you had borrowed anybody's horses but Mr. Boldwood's.'

'Dainty is lame, miss,' said Coggan. 'Can ye go on?'

'It was only a stone in her shoe. I got down and pulled it out a hundred yards back. I can manage very well, thank you. I shall be in Bath by daylight. Will you now return, please?'

She turned her head – the gateman's candle shimmering upon her quick, clear eyes as she did so – passed through the gate, and was soon wrapped in the embowering shades of mysterious summer boughs. Coggan and Gabriel put about their horses, and, fanned by the velvety air of this July night, retraced the road by which they had come.

'A strange vagary, this of hers, isn't it, Oak?' said Coggan curiously.

'Yes,' said Gabriel shortly.

'She won't be in Bath by no daylight!'

'Coggan, suppose we keep this night's work as quiet as we can?'

'I am of one and the same mind.'

'Very well. We shall be home by three o'clock or so, and can creep into the parish like lambs.'

Bathsheba's perturbed meditations by the roadside had ultimately evolved a conclusion that there were only two remedies for the present desperate state of affairs. The first was merely to keep Troy away from Weatherbury till Boldwood's indignation had cooled; the second to listen to Oak's entreaties, and Boldwood's denunciations, and give up Troy altogether.

Alas! Could she give up this new love – induce him to renounce her by saying she did not like him – could no more speak to him, and beg him, for her good, to end his furlough in Bath, and see her and Weatherbury no more?

It was a picture full of misery, but for a while she contemplated it firmly, allowing herself, nevertheless, as girls will, to dwell upon the happy life she would have enjoyed had Troy been Boldwood, and the path of love the path of duty – inflicting upon herself gratuitous tortures by imagining him the lover of another woman after forgetting her; for she had penetrated Troy's nature so far as to estimate his tendencies pretty accurately, but unfortunately loved him no less in thinking that he might soon cease to love her – indeed, considerably more.

She jumped to her feet. She would see him at once. Yes, she would implore him by word of mouth to assist her in this dilemma. A letter to keep him away could not reach him in time, even if he should be disposed to listen to it.

Was Bathsheba altogether blind to the obvious fact that the support of a lover's arms is not of a kind best calculated to assist a resolve to renounce him? Or was she sophistically sensible, with a thrill of pleasure, that by adopting this course for getting rid of him she was ensuring a meeting with him, at any rate, once more?

It was now dark, and the hour must have been nearly ten. The only way to accomplish her purpose was to give up her idea of visiting Liddy at Yalbury, return to Weatherbury Farm, put the horse into the gig, and drive at once to Bath. The scheme seemed at first impossible: the journey was a fearfully heavy one, even for a strong horse, at her own estimate; and she much underrated the distance. It was most venturesome for a woman, at night, and alone.

But could she go on to Liddy's and leave things to take their course? No, no; anything but that. Bathsheba was full of a stimulating turbulence, beside which caution vainly prayed for a hearing. She turned back towards the village.

Her walk was slow, for she wished not to enter Weatherbury till the cottagers were in bed, and, particularly, till Boldwood was secure. Her plan was now to drive to Bath during the night, see Sergeant Troy in the morning before he set out to come to her, bid him farewell, and dismiss him: then to rest the horse thoroughly (herself to weep the while, she thought), starting early the next morning on her return journey. By this arrangement she could trot Dainty gently all the day, reach Liddy at Yalbury in the evening, and come home to Weatherbury with her whenever they chose – so nobody would know she had been to Bath at all.

Such was Bathsheba's scheme. But in her topographical ignorance as a late comer to the place, she misreckoned the distance of her journey as not much more than half what it really was. Her idea, however, she proceeded to carry out, with what initial success we have already seen.

CHAPTER XXXIII

IN THE SUN – A HARBINGER

A WEEK passed, and there were no tidings of Bathsheba; nor was there any explanation of her Gilpin's rig.

Then a note came for Maryann, stating that the business which had called her mistress to Bath still detained her there; but that she hoped to return in the course of another week.

Another week passed. The oat-harvest began, and all the men were a-field under a monochromatic Lammas sky, amid the trembling air and short shadows of noon. Indoors nothing was to be heard save the droning of blue-bottle flies; out-of-doors the whetting of scythes and the hiss of tressy oat-ears rubbing together as their perpendicular stalks of amber-yellow fell heavily to each swath. Every drop of moisture not in the men's bottles and flagons in the form of cider was raining as perspiration from their foreheads and cheeks. Drought was everywhere else.

They were about to withdraw for a while into the charitable shade of a tree in the fence, when Coggan saw a figure in a blue coat and brass buttons running to them across the field.

'I wonder who that is?' he said.

'I hope nothing is wrong about mistress,' said Maryann, who with some other women was tying the bundles (oats being always sheafed on this farm), 'but an unlucky token came to me indoors this morning. I went to unlock the door and dropped the key, and it fell upon the stone floor and broke into two pieces. Breaking a key is a dreadful bodement. I wish mis'ess was home.'

"Tis Cain Ball,' said Gabriel, pausing from whetting his reaphook.

Oak was not bound by his agreement to assist in the corn-field; but the harvest month is an anxious time for a farmer, and the corn was Bathsheba's, so he lent a hand.

'He's dressed up in his best clothes,' said Matthew Moon. 'He hev been away from home for a few days, since he's had that felon upon his finger; for 'a said, since I can't work I'll have a hollerday.'

'A good time for one – a' excellent time,' said Joseph Poor-grass, straightening his back; for he, like some of the others, had a way of resting a while from his labour on such hot days for reasons preternaturally small; of which Cain Ball's advent on a week-day in his Sunday-clothes was one of the first magnitude. ''Twas a bad leg allowed me to read the *Pilgrim's Progress*, and Mark Clark learnt All-Fours in a whitlow.'

'Ay, and my father put his arm out of joint to have time to go courting,' said Jan Coggan, in an eclipsing tone, wiping his face with his shirt-sleeve and thrusting back his hat upon the nape of his neck.

By this time Cainy was nearing the group of harvesters, and was perceived to be carrying a large slice of bread and ham in one hand, from which he took mouthfuls as he ran, the other being wrapped in a bandage. When he came close, his mouth assumed the bell shape, and he began to cough violently.

'Now, Cainy!' said Gabriel sternly. 'How many more times must I tell you to keep from running so fast when you be eating? You'll choke yourself some day, that's what you'll do, Cain Ball.'

'Hok-hok-hok!' replied Cain. 'A crumb of my victuals went the wrong way – hok-hok! That's what 'tis, Mister Oak! And I've been visiting to Bath because I had a felon on my thumb; yes, and I've seen – ahok-hok!'

Directly Cain mentioned Bath, they all threw down their hooks and forks and drew round him. Unfortunately the erratic crumb did not improve his narrative powers, and a supplement-ary hindrance was that of a sneeze, jerking from his pocket his rather large watch, which dangled in front of the young man pendulum-wise.

'Yes,' he continued, directing his thoughts to Bath and letting his eyes follow, 'I've seed the world at last – yes – and I've seed our mis'ess – ahok-hok-hok!'

'Bother the boy!' said Gabriel. 'Something is always going the wrong way down your throat, so that you can't tell what's necessary to be told.'

'Ahok! there! Please, Mister Oak, a gnat have just fleed into my stomach and brought the cough on again!'

'Yes, that's just it. Your mouth is always open, you young rascal!'

''Tis terrible bad to have a gnat fly down yer throat, pore boy!' said Matthew Moon.

'Well, at Bath you saw —' prompted Gabriel.

'I saw our mistress,' continued the junior shepherd, 'and a sojer, walking along. And bymeby they got closer and closer, and then they went arm-in-crook, like courting complete – hok-hok! like courting complete – hok! – courting complete —' Losing the thread of his narrative at this point simultaneously with his loss of breath, their informant looked up and down the field apparently for some clue to it. 'Well, I see our mis'ess and a soldier – a-ha-a-wk!'

'Damn the boy!' said Gabriel.

''Tis only my manner, Mister Oak, if ye'll excuse it,' said Cain Ball, looking reproachfully at Oak, with eyes drenched in their own dew.

'Here's some cider for him – that'll cure his throat,' said Jan Coggan, lifting a flagon of cider, pulling out the cork, and applying the hole to Cainy's mouth; Joseph Poorgrass in the meantime beginning to think apprehensively of the serious consequences that would follow Cain Ball's strangulation in his cough, and the history of his Bath adventures dying with him.

'For my poor self, I always say "please God" afore I do anything,' said Joseph, in an unboastful voice; 'and so should you, Cain Ball. 'Tis a great safeguard, and might perhaps save you from being choked to death some day.'

Mr. Coggan poured the liquor with unstinted liberality at

the suffering Cain's circular mouth; half of it running down the side of the flagon, and half of what reached his mouth running down outside his throat, and half of what ran in going the wrong way, and being coughed and sneezed around the persons of the gathered reapers in the form of a cider fog, which for a moment hung in the sunny air like a small exhalation.

'There's a great clumsy sneeze! Why can't ye have better manners, you young dog!' said Coggan, withdrawing the flagon.

'The cider went up my nose!' cried Cainy, as soon as he could speak; 'and now 'tis gone down my neck, and into my poor dumb felon, and over my shiny buttons and all my best cloze!'

'The poor lad's cough is terrible onfortunate,' said Matthew Moon. 'And a great history on hand, too. Bump his back, shepherd.'

''Tis my nater,' mourned Cain. 'Mother says I was always so excitable when my feelings were worked up to a point!'

'True, true,' said Joseph Poorgrass. 'The Balls were always a very excitable family. I knowed the boy's grandfather – a truly nervous and modest man, even to genteel refinery. 'Twas blush, blush with him, almost as much as 'tis with me – not but that 'tis a fault in me!'

'Not at all, Master Poorgrass,' said Coggan. ''Tis a very noble quality in ye.'

'Heh-heh! well, I wish to noise nothing abroad – nothing at all,' murmured Poorgrass diffidently. 'But we be born to things – that's true. Yet I would rather my trifle were hid; though, perhaps, a high nater is a little high, and at my birth all things were possible to my Maker, and he may have begrudged no gifts. . . . But under your bushel, Joseph! under your bushel with 'ee! A strange desire, neighbours, this desire to hide, and no praise due. Yet there is a Sermon on the Mount with a calendar of the blessed at the head, and certain meek men may be named therein.'

'Cainy's grandfather was a very clever man,' said Matthew

Moon. 'Invented a' apple-tree out of his own head, which is called by his name to this day – the Early Ball. You know 'em, Jan? A Quarrenden grafted on a Tom Putt, and a Ratheripe upon top o' that again. 'Tis trew 'a used to bide about in a public-house wi' a 'ooman in a way he had no business to by rights, but there – 'a were a clever man in the sense of the term.'

'Now then,' said Gabriel impatiently, 'what did you see, Cain?'

'I seed our mis'ess go into a sort of a park place, where there's seats, and shrubs and flowers, arm-in-crook with a sojer,' continued Cainy firmly, and with a dim sense that his words were very effective as regarded Gabriel's emotions. 'And I think the sojer was Sergeant Troy. And they sat there together for more than half-an-hour, talking moving things, and she once was crying a'most to death. And when they came out her eyes were shining and she was as white as a lily; and they looked into one another's faces, as far gone friendly as a man and woman can be.'

Gabriel's features seemed to get thinner. 'Well, what did you see besides?'

'Oh, all sorts.'

'White as a lily? You are sure 'twas she?'

'Yes.'

'Well, what besides?'

'Great glass windows to the shops, and great clouds in the sky, full of rain, and old wooden trees in the country round.'

'You stun-poll! What will ye say next?' said Coggan.

'Let en alone,' interposed Joseph Poorgrass. 'The boy's maning is that the sky and the earth in the kingdom of Bath is not altogether different from ours here. 'Tis for our good to gain knowledge of strange cities, and as such the boy's words should be suffered, so to speak it.'

'And the people of Bath,' continued Cain, 'never need to light their fires except as a luxury, for the water springs up out of the earth ready boiled for use.'

"Tis true as the light,' testified Matthew Moon. 'I've heard other navigators say the same thing.'

'They drink nothing else there,' said Cain, 'and seem to enjoy it, to see how they swaller it down.'

'Well, it seems a barbarian practice enough to us, but I daresay the natives think nothing o' it,' said Matthew.

'And don't victuals spring up as well as drink?' asked Coggan, twirling his eye.

'No – I own to a blot there in Bath – a true blot. God didn't provide 'em with victuals as well as drink, and 'twas a drawback I couldn't get over at all.'

'Well, 'tis a curious place, to say the least,' observed Moon; 'and it must be a curious people that live therein.'

'Miss Everdene and the soldier were walking about together, you say?' said Gabriel, returning to the group.

'Ay, and she wore a beautiful gold-colour silk gown, trimmed with black lace, that would have stood alone 'ithout legs inside if required. 'Twas a very winsome sight; and her hair was brushed splendid. And when the sun shone upon the bright gown and his red coat – my! how handsome they looked. You could see 'em all the length of the street.'

'And what then?' murmured Gabriel.

'And then I went into Griffin's to hae my boots hobbed, and then I went to Riggs's batty-cake shop, and asked 'em for a penneth of the cheapest and nicest stales, that were all but blue-mouldy, but not quite. And whilst I was chawing 'em down I walked on and seed a clock with a face as big as a baking trendle —'

'But that's nothing to do with mistress!'

'I'm coming to that, if you'll leave me alone, Mister Oak!' remonstrated Cainy. 'If you excites me, perhaps you'll bring on my cough, and then I shan't be able to tell ye nothing.'

'Yes – let him tell it his own way,' said Coggan.

Gabriel settled into a despairing attitude of patience, and Cainy went on: –

'And there were great large houses, and more people all the

week long than at Weatherbury club-walking on White Tuesdays. And I went to grand churches and chapels. And how the parson would pray! Yes; he would kneel down and put his hands together, and make the holy gold rings on his fingers gleam and twinkle in yer eyes, that he'd earned by praying so excellent well! – Ah yes, I wish I lived there.'

'Our poor Parson Thirdly can't get no money to buy such rings,' said Matthew Moon thoughtfully. 'And as good a man as ever walked. I don't believe poor Thirdly have a single one, even of humblest tin or copper. Such a great ornament as they'd be to him on a dull a'ternoon, when he's up in the pulpit lighted by the wax candles! But 'tis impossible, poor man. Ah, to think how unequal things be.'

'Perhaps he's made of different stuff than to wear 'em,' said Gabriel grimly. 'Well, that's enough of this. Go on, Cainy – quick.'

'Oh – and the new style of pa'sons wear moustaches and long beards,' continued the illustrous traveller, 'and look like Moses and Aaron complete, and make we fokes in the congregation feel all over like the children of Israel.'

'A very right feeling – very,' said Joseph Poorgrass.

'And there's two religions going on in the nation now – High Church and High Chapel. And, thinks I, I'll play fair; so I went to High Church in the morning, and High Chapel in the afternoon.'

'A right and proper boy,' said Joseph Poorgrass.

'Well, at High Church they pray singing, and worship all the colours of the rainbow; and at High Chapel they pray preaching, and worship drab and whitewash only. And then – I didn't see no more of Miss Everdene at all.'

'Why didn't you say so afore, then?' exclaimed Oak, with much disappointment.

'Ah,' said Matthew Moon, 'she'll wish her cake dough if so be she's over intimate with that man.'

'She's not over intimate with him,' said Gabriel indignantly.

'She would know better,' said Coggan. 'Our mis'ess has too

much sense under they knots of black hair to do such a mad thing.'

'You see, he's not a coarse, ignorant man, for he was well brought up,' said Matthew dubiously. "Twas only wildness that made him a soldier, and maids rather like your man of sin.'

'Now, Cain Ball,' said Gabriel restlessly, 'can you swear in the most awful form that the woman you saw was Miss Everdene?'

'Cain Ball, you be no longer a babe and suckling,' said Joseph in the sepulchral tone the circumstances demanded, 'and you know what taking an oath is. 'Tis a horrible testament mind ye, which you say and seal with your blood-stone, and the prophet Matthew tells us that on whomsoever it shall fall it will grind him to powder. Now, before all the work-folk here assembled, can you swear to your words as the shepherd asks ye?'

'Please no, Mister Oak!' said Cainy, looking from one to the other with great uneasiness at the spiritual magnitude of the position. 'I don't mind saying 'tis true, but I don't like to say 'tis damn true, if that's what you mane.'

'Cain, Cain, how can you?' asked Joseph sternly. 'You be asked to swear in a holy manner, and you swear like wicked Shimei, the son of Gera, who cursed as he came. Young man, fie!'

'No, I don't! 'Tis you want to squander a pore boy's soul, Joseph Poorgrass – that's what 'tis!' said Cain, beginning to cry. 'All I mane is that in common truth 'twas Miss Everdene and Sergeant Troy, but in the horrible so-help-me truth that ye want to make of it perhaps 'twas somebody else!'

'There's no getting at the rights of it,' said Gabriel, turning to his work.

'Cain Ball, you'll come to a bit of bread!' groaned Joseph Poorgrass.

Then the reapers' hooks were flourished again, and the old sounds went on. Gabriel, without making any pretence of being lively, did nothing to show that he was particularly dull.

However, Coggan knew pretty nearly how the land lay, and when they were in a nook together he said —

'Don't take on about her, Gabriel. What difference does it make whose sweetheart she is, since she can't be yours?'

'That's the very thing I say to myself,' said Gabriel.

CHAPTER XXXIV

HOME AGAIN – A TRICKSTER

THAT same evening at dusk Gabriel was leaning over Coggan's garden-gate, taking an up-and-down survey before retiring to rest.

A vehicle of some kind was softly creeping along the grassy margin of the lane. From it spread the tones of two women talking. The tones were natural and not at all suppressed. Oak instantly knew the voices to be those of Bathsheba and Liddy.

The carriage came opposite and passed by. It was Miss Everdene's gig, and Liddy and her mistress were the only occupants of the seat. Liddy was asking questions about the city of Bath, and her companion was answering them listlessly and unconcernedly. Both Bathsheba and the horse seemed weary.

The exquisite relief of finding that she was here again, safe and sound, overpowered all reflection, and Oak could only luxuriate in the sense of it. All grave reports were forgotten.

He lingered and lingered on, till there was no difference between the eastern and western expanses of sky, and the timid hares began to limp courageously round the dim hillocks. Gabriel might have been there an additional half-hour when a dark form walked slowly by. 'Good-night, Gabriel,' the passer said.

It was Boldwood. 'Good-night, sir,' said Gabriel.

Boldwood likewise vanished up the road, and Oak shortly afterwards turned indoors to bed.

Farmer Boldwood went on towards Miss Everdene's house. He reached the front, and approaching the entrance, saw a light in the parlour. The blind was not drawn down, and inside the room was Bathsheba, looking over some papers or letters.

Her back was towards Boldwood. He went to the door, knocked, and waited with tense muscles and an aching brow.

Boldwood had not been outside his garden since his meeting with Bathsheba in the road to Yalbury. Silent and alone, he had remained in moody meditation on woman's ways, deeming as essentials of the whole sex the accidents of the single one of their number he had ever closely beheld. By degrees a more charitable temper had pervaded him, and this was the reason of his sally to-night. He had come to apologize and beg forgiveness of Bathsheba with something like a sense of shame at his violence, having but now learnt that she had returned – only from a visit to Liddy, as he supposed, the Bath escapade being quite unknown to him.

He inquired for Miss Everdene. Liddy's manner was odd, but he did not notice it. She went in, leaving him standing there, and in her absence the blind of the room containing Bathsheba was pulled down. Boldwood augured ill from that sign. Liddy came out.

'My mistress cannot see you, sir,' she said.

The farmer instantly went out by the gate. He was unforgiven – that was the issue of it all. He had seen her who was to him simultaneously a delight and a torture, sitting in the room he had shared with her as a peculiarly privileged guest only a little earlier in the summer, and she had denied him an entrance there now.

Boldwood did not hurry homeward. It was ten o'clock at least, when, walking deliberately through the lower part of Weatherbury, he heard the carrier's spring van entering the village. The van ran to and from a town in a northern direction, and it was owned and driven by a Weatherbury man, at the door of whose house it now pulled up. The lamp fixed to the head of the hood illuminated a scarlet and gilded form, who was the first to alight.

'Ah!' said Boldwood to himself, 'come to see her again.'

Troy entered the carrier's house, which had been the place of his lodging on his last visit to his native place. Boldwood was moved by a sudden determination. He hastened home. In ten minutes he was back again, and made as if he were going to call upon Troy at the carrier's. But as he approached, some one opened the door and came out. He heard this person say 'Good-night' to the inmates, and the voice was Troy's. This was strange, coming so immediately after his arrival. Boldwood, however, hastened up to him. Troy had what appeared to be a carpet-bag in his hand – the same that he had brought with him. It seemed as if he were going to leave again this very night.

Troy turned up the hill and quickened his pace. Boldwood stepped forward.

'Sergeant Troy?'

'Yes – I'm Sergeant Troy.'

'Just arrived from up the country, I think?'

'Just arrived from Bath.'

'I am William Boldwood.'

'Indeed.'

The tone in which this word was uttered was all that had been wanted to bring Boldwood to the point.

'I wish to speak a word with you,' he said.

'What about?'

'About her who lives just ahead there – and about a woman you have wronged.'

'I wonder at your impertinence,' said Troy, moving on.

'Now look here,' said Boldwood, standing in front of him, 'wonder or not, you are going to hold a conversation with me.'

Troy heard the dull determination in Boldwood's voice, looked at his stalwart frame, then at the thick cudgel he carried in his hand. He remembered it was past ten o'clock. It seemed worth while to be civil to Boldwood.

'Very well, I'll listen with pleasure,' said Troy, placing his bag on the ground, 'only speak low, for somebody or other may overhear us in the farmhouse there.'

'Well then – I know a good deal concerning your – Fanny Robin's attachment to you. I may say, too, that I believe I am the only person in the village, excepting Gabriel Oak, who does know it. You ought to marry her.'

'I suppose I ought. Indeed, I wish to, but I cannot.'

'Why?'

Troy was about to utter something hastily; he then checked himself and said, 'I am too poor.' His voice was changed. Previously it had had a devil-may-care tone. It was the voice of a trickster now.

Boldwood's present mood was not critical enough to notice tones. He continued, 'I may as well speak plainly; and understand, I don't wish to enter into the questions of right or wrong, woman's honour and shame, or to express any opinion on your conduct. I intend a business transaction with you.'

'I see,' said Troy. 'Suppose we sit down here.'

An old tree trunk lay under the hedge immediately opposite, and they sat down.

'I was engaged to be married to Miss Everdene,' said Boldwood, 'but you came and —'

'Not engaged,' said Troy.

'As good as engaged.'

'If I had not turned up she might have become engaged to you.'

'Hang might!'

'Would, then.'

'If you had not come I should certainly — yes, *certainly* — have been accepted by this time. If you had not seen her you might have been married to Fanny. Well, there's too much difference between Miss Everdene's station and your own for this flirtation with her ever to benefit you by ending in marriage. So all I ask is, don't molest her any more. Marry Fanny. I'll make it worth your while.'

'How will you?'

'I'll pay you well now, I'll settle a sum of money upon her, and I'll see that you don't suffer from poverty in the future. I'll put it clearly. Bathsheba is only playing with you: you are too poor for her as I said; so give up wasting your time about a great match you'll never make for a moderate and rightful match you may make to-morrow; take up your carpet-bag, turn about, leave Weatherbury now, this night, and you shall take fifty pounds with you. Fanny shall have fifty to enable her to prepare for the wedding, when you have told me where she is living, and she shall have five hundred paid down on her wedding-day.'

In making this statement Boldwood's voice revealed only too clearly a consciousness of the weakness of his position, his aims, and his method. His manner had lapsed quite from that of the firm and dignified Boldwood of former times; and such a scheme as he had now engaged in he would have condemned as childishly imbecile only a few months ago. We discern a grand force in the lover which he lacks whilst a free man; but there is a breadth of vision in the free man which in the lover we vainly seek. Where there is much bias there must be some narrowness, and love, though added emotion, is subtracted capacity. Boldwood exemplified this to an abnormal degree: he knew nothing of Fanny Robin's circumstances or whereabouts, he knew nothing of Troy's possibilities, yet that was what he said.

'I like Fanny best,' said Troy; 'and if, as you say, Miss Everdene is out of my reach, why I have all to gain by accepting your money, and marrying Fan. But she's only a servant.'

'Never mind – do you agree to my arrangement?'

'I do.'

'Ah!' said Boldwood, in a more elastic voice. 'O, Troy, if you like her best why then did you step in here and injure my happiness?'

'I love Fanny best now,' said Troy. 'But Bathsh — Miss Everdene inflamed me, and displaced Fanny for a time. It is over now.'

'Why should it be over so soon? And why then did you come here again?'

'There are weighty reasons. Fifty pounds at once, you said!'

'I did,' said Boldwood, 'and here they are – fifty sovereigns.' He handed Troy a small packet.

'You have everything ready – it seems that you calculated on my accepting them,' said the sergeant, taking the packet.

'I thought you might accept them,' said Boldwood.

'You've only my word that the programme shall be adhered to, whilst I at any rate have fifty pounds.'

'I had thought of that, and I have considered that if I can't appeal to your honour I can trust to your – well, shrewdness we'll call it – not to lose five hundred pounds in prospect, and also make a bitter enemy of a man who is willing to be an extremely useful friend.'

'Stop, listen!' said Troy in a whisper.

A light pit-pat was audible upon the road just above them.

'By George – 'tis she,' he continued. 'I must go on and meet her.'

'She – who?'

'Bathsheba.'

'Bathsheba – out alone at this time o' night!' said Boldwood in amazement, and starting up. 'Why must you meet her?'

'She was expecting me to-night – and I must now speak to her, and wish her good-bye, according to your wish.'

'I don't see the necessity of speaking.'

'It can do no harm – and she'll be wandering about looking for me if I don't. You shall hear all I say to her. It will help you in your love-making when I am gone.'

'Your tone is mocking.'

'O no. And remember this, if she does not know what has become of me, she will think more about me than if I tell her flatly I have come to give her up.'

'Will you confine your words to that one point? – Shall I hear every word you say?'

'Every word. Now sit still there, and hold my carpet-bag for me, and mark what you hear.'

The light footstep came closer, halting occasionally, as if the walker listened for a sound. Troy whistled a double note in a soft, fluty tone.

'Come to that, is it!' murmured Boldwood uneasily.

'You promised silence,' said Troy.

'I promise again.'

Troy stepped forward.

'Frank, dearest, is that you?' The tones were Bathsheba's.

'O God!' said Boldwood.

'Yes,' said Troy to her.

'How late you are,' she continued tenderly. 'Did you come by the carrier? I listened and heard his wheels entering the village, but it was some time ago, and I had almost given you up, Frank.'

'I was sure to come,' said Frank. 'You knew I should, did you not?'

'Well, I thought you would,' she said playfully; 'and, Frank, it is so lucky! There's not a soul in my house but me to-night. I've packed them all off, so nobody on earth will know of your visit to your lady's bower. Liddy wanted to go to her grand-father's to tell him about her holiday, and I said she might stay with them till to-morrow – when you'll be gone again.'

'Capital,' said Troy. 'But, dear me, I had better go back for my bag, because my slippers and brush and comb are in it; you run home whilst I fetch it, and I'll promise to be in your par-lour in ten minutes.'

'Yes.' She turned and tripped up the hill again.

During the progress of this dialogue there was a nervous twitching of Boldwood's tightly closed lips, and his face became bathed in a clammy dew. He now started forward towards Troy. Troy turned to him and took up the bag.

'Shall I tell her I have come to give her up and cannot marry her?' said the soldier mockingly.

'No, no; wait a minute. I want to say more to you – more to you!' said Boldwood, in a hoarse whisper.

'Now,' said Troy, 'you see my dilemma. Perhaps I am a bad man – the victim of my impulses – led away to do what I ought to leave undone. I can't, however, marry them both. And I have two reasons for choosing Fanny. First, I like her best upon the whole, and second, you make it worth my while.'

At the same instant Boldwood sprang upon him, and held him by the neck. Troy felt Boldwood's grasp slowly tightening. The move was absolutely unexpected.

'A moment,' he gasped. 'You are injuring her you love!'

'Well, what do you mean?' said the farmer.

'Give me breath,' said Troy.

Boldwood loosened his hand, saying, 'By Heaven, I've a mind to kill you!'

'And ruin her.'

'Save her.'

'Oh, how can she be saved now, unless I marry her?'

Boldwood groaned. He reluctantly released the soldier, and flung him back against the hedge. 'Devil, you torture me!' said he.

Troy rebounded like a ball, and was about to make a dash at the farmer; but he checked himself, saying lightly —

'It is not worth while to measure my strength with you. Indeed it is a barbarous way of settling a quarrel. I shall shortly leave the army because of the same conviction. Now after that revelation of how the land lies with Bathsheba, 'twould be a mistake to kill me, would it not?'

''Twould be a mistake to kill you,' repeated Boldwood, mechanically, with a bowed head.

'Better kill yourself.'

'Far better.'

'I'm glad you see it.'

'Troy, make her your wife, and don't act upon what I arranged just now. The alternative is dreadful, but take Bathsheba; I give her up! She must love you indeed to sell soul and body to you so utterly as she has done. Wretched woman — deluded woman — you are, Bathsheba!'

'But about Fanny?'

'Bathsheba is a woman well to do,' continued Boldwood, in nervous anxiety, 'and, Troy, she will make a good wife; and, indeed, she is worth your hastening on your marriage with her!'

'But she has a will — not to say a temper, and I shall be a mere slave to her. I could do anything with poor Fanny Robin.'

'Troy,' said Boldwood imploringly, 'I'll do anything for you, only don't desert her; pray don't desert her, Troy.'

'Which, poor Fanny?'

'No; Bathsheba Everdene. Love her best! Love her tenderly! How shall I get you to see how advantageous it will be to you to secure her at once?'

'I don't wish to secure her in any new way.'

Boldwood's arm moved spasmodically towards Troy's person again. He repressed the instinct, and his form drooped as with pain.

Troy went on —

'I shall soon purchase my discharge, and then —'

'But I wish you to hasten on this marriage! It will be better for you both. You love each other, and you must let me help you to do it.'

'How?'

'Why, by settling the five hundred on Bathsheba instead of Fanny, to enable you to marry at once. No; she wouldn't have it of me. I'll pay it down to you on the wedding-day.'

Troy paused in secret amazement at Boldwood's wild infatuation. He carelessly said, 'And am I to have anything now?'

'Yes, if you wish to. But I have not much additional money with me. I did not expect this; but all I have is yours.'

Boldwood, more like a somnambulist than a wakeful man, pulled out the large canvas bag he carried by way of a purse, and searched it.

'I have twenty-one pounds more with me,' he said. 'Two notes and a sovereign. But before I leave you I must have a paper signed —'

'Pay me the money, and we'll go straight to her parlour, and make any arrangement you please to secure my compliance with your wishes. But she must know nothing of this cash business.'

'Nothing, nothing,' said Boldwood hastily. 'Here is the sum, and if you'll come to my house we'll write out the agreement for the remainder, and the terms also.'

'First we'll call upon her.'

'But why? Come with me to-night, and go with me to-morrow to the surrogate's.'

'But she must be consulted; at any rate informed.'

'Very well; go on.'

They went up the hill to Bathsheba's house. When they stood at the entrance, Troy said, 'Wait here a moment.' Opening the door, he glided inside, leaving the door ajar.

Boldwood waited. In two minutes a light appeared in the passage. Boldwood then saw that the chain had been fastened across the door. Troy appeared inside carrying a bedroom candlestick.

'What, did you think I should break in?' said Boldwood contemptuously.

'Oh, no; it is merely my humour to secure things. Will you read this a moment? I'll hold the light.'

Troy handed a folded newspaper through the slit between door and door-post, and put the candle close. 'That's the paragraph,' he said, placing his finger on a line.

Boldwood looked and read —

'MARRIAGES.

'On the 17th inst., at St. Ambrose's Church, Bath, by the Rev. G. Mincing, B.A., Francis Troy, only son of the late Edward Troy, Esq., M.D., of Weatherbury, and sergeant 11th Dragoon Guards, to Bathsheba, only surviving daughter of the late Mr. John Everdene, of Casterbridge.'

'This may be called Fort meeting Feeble, hey, Boldwood?' said Troy. A low gurgle of derisive laughter followed the words.

The paper fell from Boldwood's hands. Troy continued —

'Fifty pounds to marry Fanny. Good. Twenty-one pounds not to marry Fanny, but Bathsheba. Good. Finale: already Bathsheba's husband. Now, Boldwood, yours is the ridiculous fate which always attends interference between a man and his wife. And another word. Bad as I am, I am not such a villain as to make the marriage or misery of any woman a matter of huckster and sale. Fanny has long ago left me. I don't know where she is. I have searched everywhere. Another word yet. You say you love Bathsheba; yet on the merest apparent evidence you instantly believe in her dishonour. A fig for such love! Now that I've taught you a lesson, take your money back again.'

'I will not; I will not!' said Boldwood, in a hiss.

'Anyhow I won't have it,' said Troy contemptuously. He wrapped the packet of gold in the notes, and threw the whole into the road.

Boldwood shook his clenched fist at him. 'You juggler of Satan! You black hound! But I'll punish you yet; mark me, I'll punish you yet!'

Another peal of laughter. Troy then closed the door, and locked himself in.

Throughout the whole of that night Boldwood's dark form might have been seen walking about the hills and downs of Weatherbury like an unhappy Shade in the Mournful Fields by Acheron.

CHAPTER XXXV

AT AN UPPER WINDOW

IT was very early the next morning – a time of sun and dew. The confused beginnings of many birds' songs spread into the healthy air, and the wan blue of the heaven was here and there coated with thin webs of incorporeal cloud which were of no effect in obscuring day. All the lights in the scene were yellow as to colour, and all the shadows were attenuated as to form. The creeping plants about the old manor-house were bowed with rows of heavy water drops, which had upon objects behind them the effect of minute lenses of high magnifying power.

Just before the clock struck five Gabriel Oak and Coggan passed the village cross, and went on together to the fields. They were yet barely in view of their mistress's house, when Oak fancied he saw the opening of a casement in one of the upper windows. The two men were at this moment partially screened by an elder bush, now beginning to be enriched with black bunches of fruit, and they paused before emerging from its shade.

A handsome man leaned idly from the lattice. He looked east and then west, in the manner of one who makes a first morning survey. The man was Sergeant Troy. His red jacket was loosely thrown on, but not buttoned, and he had altogether the relaxed bearing of a soldier taking his ease.

Coggan spoke first, looking quietly at the window.

'She has married him!' he said.

Gabriel had previously beheld the sight, and he now stood with his back turned, making no reply.

'I fancied we should know something to-day,' continued Coggan. 'I heard wheels pass my door just after dark – you were out

256

somewhere.' He glanced round upon Gabriel. 'Good heavens above us, Oak, how white your face is; you look like a corpse!'

'Do I?' said Oak, with a faint smile.

'Lean on the gate: I'll wait a bit.'

'All right, all right.'

They stood by the gate awhile, Gabriel listlessly staring at the ground. His mind sped into the future, and saw there enacted in years of leisure the scenes of repentance that would ensue from this work of haste. That they were married he had instantly decided. Why had it been so mysteriously managed? It had become known that she had had a fearful journey to Bath, owing to her miscalculating the distance: that the horse had broken down, and that she had been more than two days getting there. It was not Bathsheba's way to do things furtively. With all her faults she was candour itself. Could she have been entrapped? The union was not only an unutterable grief to him: it amazed him, notwithstanding that he had passed the preceding week in a suspicion that such might be the issue of Troy's meeting her away from home. Her quiet return with Liddy had to some extent dispersed the dread. Just as that imperceptible motion which appears like stillness is infinitely divided in its properties from stillness itself, so had his hope undistinguishable from despair differed from despair indeed.

In a few minutes they moved on again towards the house. The sergeant still looked from the window.

'Morning, comrades!' he shouted, in a cheery voice, when they came up.

Coggan replied to the greeting. 'Bain't ye going to answer the man?' he then said to Gabriel. 'I'd say good morning – you needn't spend a hapeth of meaning upon it, and yet keep the man civil.'

Gabriel soon decided too that, since the deed was done, to put the best face upon the matter would be the greatest kindness to her he loved.

'Good morning, Sergeant Troy,' he returned, in a ghastly voice.

'A rambling, gloomy house this,' said Troy, smiling.

'Why – they *may* not be married!' suggested Coggan. 'Perhaps she's not there.'

Gabriel shook his head. The soldier turned a little towards the east, and the sun kindled his scarlet coat to an orange glow.

'But it is a nice old house,' responded Gabriel.

'Yes – I suppose so; but I feel like new wine in an old bottle here. My notion is that sash-windows should be put throughout, and these old wainscoted walls brightened up a bit; or the oak cleared quite away, and the walls papered.'

'It would be a pity, I think.'

'Well, no. A philosopher once said in my hearing that the old builders, who worked when art was a living thing, had no respect for the work of builders who went before them, but pulled down and altered as they thought fit; and why shouldn't we? "Creation and preservation don't do well together," says he, "and a million of antiquarians can't invent a style." My mind exactly. I am for making this place more modern, that we may be cheerful whilst we can.'

The military man turned and surveyed the interior of the room, to assist his ideas of improvement in this direction. Gabriel and Coggan began to move on.

'Oh, Coggan,' said Troy, as if inspired by a recollection, 'do you know if insanity has ever appeared in Mr. Boldwood's family?'

Jan reflected for a moment.

'I once heard that an uncle of his was queer in his head, but I don't know the rights o't,' he said.

'It is of no importance,' said Troy lightly. 'Well, I shall be down in the fields with you some time this week; but I have a few matters to attend to first. So good-day to you. We shall, of course, keep on just as friendly terms as usual. I'm not a proud man: nobody is ever able to say that of Sergeant Troy. However, what is must be, and here's half-a-crown to drink my health, men.'

Troy threw the coin dexterously across the front plot and

over the fence towards Gabriel, who shunned it in its fall, his face turning to an angry red. Coggan twirled his eye, edged forward, and caught the money in its ricochet upon the road.

'Very well — you keep it, Coggan,' said Gabriel with disdain, and almost fiercely. 'As for me, I'll do without gifts from him!'

'Don't show it too much,' said Coggan musingly. 'For if he's married to her, mark my words, he'll buy his discharge and be our master here. Therefore 'tis well to say "Friend" outwardly, though you say "Troublehouse" within.'

'Well — perhaps it is best to be silent; but I can't go further than that. I can't flatter, and if my place here is only to be kept by smoothing him down, my place must be lost.'

A horseman, whom they had for some time seen in the distance, now appeared close beside them.

'There's Mr. Boldwood,' said Oak. 'I wonder what Troy meant by his question.'

Coggan and Oak nodded respectfully to the farmer, just checked their paces to discover if they were wanted, and finding they were not, stood back to let him pass on.

The only signs of the terrible sorrow Boldwood had been combating through the night, and was combating now, were the want of colour in his well-defined face, the enlarged appearance of the veins in his forehead and temples, and the sharper lines about his mouth. The horse bore him away, and the very step of the animal seemed significant of dogged despair. Gabriel, for a minute, rose above his own grief in noticing Boldwood's. He saw the square figure sitting erect upon the horse, the head turned to neither side, the elbows steady by the hips, the brim of the hat level and undisturbed in its onward glide, until the keen edges of Boldwood's shape sank by degrees over the hill. To one who knew the man and his story there was something more striking in this immobility than in a collapse. The clash of discord between mood and matter here was forced painfully home to the heart; and, as in laughter there are more dreadful phases than in tears, so was there in the steadiness of this agonized man an expression deeper than a cry.

CHAPTER XXXVI

WEALTH IN JEOPARDY – THE REVEL

ONE night, at the end of August, when Bathsheba's experiences as a married woman were still new, and when the weather was yet dry and sultry, a man stood motionless in the stackyard of Weatherbury Upper Farm, looking at the moon and sky.

The night had a sinister aspect. A heated breeze from the south slowly fanned the summits of lofty objects, and in the sky dashes of buoyant cloud were sailing in a course at right angles to that of another stratum, neither of them in the direction of the breeze below. The moon, as seen through these films, had a lurid metallic look. The fields were sallow with the impure light, and all were tinged in monochrome, as if beheld through stained glass. The same evening the sheep had trailed homeward head to tail, the behaviour of the rooks had been confused, and the horses had moved with timidity and caution.

Thunder was imminent, and, taking some secondary appearances into consideration, it was likely to be followed by one of the lengthened rains which mark the close of dry weather for the season. Before twelve hours had passed a harvest atmosphere would be a bygone thing.

Oak gazed with misgiving at eight naked and unprotected ricks, massive and heavy with the rich produce of one-half the farm for that year. He went on to the barn.

This was the night which had been selected by Sergeant Troy – ruling now in the room of his wife – for giving the harvest supper and dance. As Oak approached the building the sound of violins and a tambourine, and the regular jigging of many feet, grew more distinct. He came close to the large doors, one of which stood slightly ajar, and looked in.

The central space, together with the recess at one end, was emptied of all incumbrances, and this area, covering about two-thirds of the whole, was appropriated for the gathering, the remaining end, which was piled to the ceiling with oats, being screened off with sail-cloth. Tufts and garlands of green foliage decorated the walls, beams, and extemporized chandeliers, and immediately opposite to Oak a rostrum had been erected, bearing a table and chairs. Here sat three fiddlers, and beside them stood a frantic man with his hair on end, perspiration streaming down his cheeks, and a tambourine quivering in his hand.

The dance ended, and on the black oak floor in the midst a new row of couples formed for another.

'Now, ma'am, and no offence I hope, I ask what dance you would like next?' said the first violin.

'Really, it makes no difference,' said the clear voice of Bathsheba, who stood at the inner end of the building, observing the scene from behind a table covered with cups and viands. Troy was lolling beside her.

'Then,' said the fiddler, 'I'll venture to name that the right and proper thing is "The Soldier's Joy" – there being a gallant soldier married into the farm – hey, my sonnies, and gentlemen all?'

'It shall be "The Soldier's Joy," ' exclaimed a chorus.

'Thanks for the compliment,' said the sergeant gaily, taking Bathsheba by the hand and leading her to the top of the dance. 'For though I have purchased my discharge from Her Most Gracious Majesty's regiment of cavalry the 11th Dragoon Guards, to attend to the new duties awaiting me here, I shall continue a soldier in spirit and feeling as long as I live.'

So the dance began. As to the merits of 'The Soldier's Joy,' there cannot be, and never were, two opinions. It has been observed in the musical circles of Weatherbury and its vicinity that this melody, at the end of three-quarters of an hour of thunderous footing, still possesses more stimulative properties for the heel and toe than the majority of other dances at their first opening. 'The Soldier's Joy' has, too, an additional charm, in being so admirably adapted to the tambourine aforesaid – no mean instrument in the hands of a performer who understands the proper convulsions, spasms, St. Vitus's dances, and fearful frenzies necessary when exhibiting its tones in their highest perfection.

The immortal tune ended, a fine DD rolling forth from the bass-viol with the sonorousness of a cannonade, and Gabriel delayed his entry no longer. He avoided Bathsheba, and got as near as possible to the platform, where Sergeant Troy was now seated, drinking brandy-and-water, though the others drank without exception cider and ale. Gabriel could not easily thrust himself within speaking distance of the sergeant, and he sent a message, asking him to come down for a moment. The sergeant said he could not attend.

'Will you tell him, then,' said Gabriel, 'that I only stepped ath'art to say that a heavy rain is sure to fall soon, and that something should be done to protect the ricks?'

'Mr. Troy says it will not rain,' returned the messenger, 'and he cannot stop to talk to you about such fidgets.'

In juxtaposition with Troy, Oak had a melancholy tendency to look like a candle beside gas, and ill at ease he went out again, thinking he would go home; for, under the circumstances, he had no heart for the scene in the barn. At the door he paused for a moment: Troy was speaking.

'Friends, it is not only the harvest home that we are celebrating to-night; but this is also a Wedding Feast. A short time ago I had the happiness to lead to the altar this lady, your mistress, and not until now have we been able to give any public flourish to the event in Weatherbury. That it may be thoroughly well done, and that every man may go happy to bed, I have ordered to be brought here some bottles of brandy and kettles of hot water. A treble-strong goblet will be handed round to each guest.'

Bathsheba put her hand upon his arm, and, with upturned pale face, said imploringly, 'No – don't give it to them – pray don't, Frank! It will only do them harm: they have had enough of everything.'

'True – we don't wish for no more, thank ye,' said one or two.

'Pooh!' said the sergeant contemptuously, and raised his voice as if lighted up by a new idea. 'Friends,' he said, 'we'll send the women-folk home! 'Tis time they were in bed. Then we cockbirds will have a jolly carouse to ourselves! If any of the men show the white feather, let them look elsewhere for a winter's work.'

Bathsheba indignantly left the barn, followed by all the women and children. The musicians, not looking upon themselves as 'company,' slipped quietly away to their spring-waggon and put in the horse. Thus Troy and the men on the farm were left sole occupants of the place. Oak, not to appear unnecessarily disagreeable, stayed a little while; then he, too, arose and quietly took his departure, followed by a friendly oath from the sergeant for not staying to a second round of grog.

Gabriel proceeded towards his home. In approaching the door, his toe kicked something which felt and sounded soft, leathery, and distended, like a boxing-glove. It was a large toad humbly travelling across the path. Oak took it up, thinking it might be better to kill the creature to save it from pain; but finding it uninjured, he placed it again among the grass. He knew what this direct message from the Great Mother meant. And soon came another.

When he struck a light indoors there appeared upon the table a thin glistening streak, as if a brush of varnish had been lightly dragged across it. Oak's eyes followed the serpentine sheen to the other side, where it led up to a huge brown garden-slug, which had come indoors to-night for reasons of its own. It was Nature's second way of hinting to him that he was to prepare for foul weather.

Oak sat down meditating for nearly an hour. During this time two black spiders, of the kind common in thatched houses, promenaded the ceiling, ultimately dropping to the floor. This reminded him that if there was one class of manifestation on this matter that he thoroughly understood, it was the instincts of sheep. He left the room, ran across two or three fields towards the flock, got upon a hedge, and looked over among them.

They were crowded close together on the other side around some furze bushes, and the first peculiarity observable was that, on the sudden appearance of Oak's head over the fence, they did not stir or run away. They had now a terror of something greater than their terror of man. But this was not the most noteworthy feature: they were all grouped in such a way that their tails, without a single exception, were towards that half of the horizon from which the storm threatened. There was an inner circle closely huddled, and outside these they radiated wider apart, the pattern formed by the flock as a whole not being unlike a vandyked lace collar, to which the clump of furze bushes stood in the position of a wearer's neck.

This was enough to re-establish him in his original opinion. He knew now that he was right, and that Troy was wrong. Every voice in Nature was unanimous in bespeaking change. But two distinct translations attached to these dumb expressions. Apparently there was to be a thunder-storm, and afterwards a cold continuous rain. The creeping things seemed to know all about the later rain, but little of the interpolated thunder-storm; whilst the sheep knew all about the thunder-storm and nothing of the later rain.

This complication of weathers being uncommon, was all the more to be feared. Oak returned to the stack-yard. All was silent here, and the conical tips of the ricks jutted darkly into the sky. There were five wheat-ricks in this yard, and three stacks of barley. The wheat when threshed would average about thirty quarters to each stack; the barley, at least forty. Their value to Bathsheba, and indeed to anybody, Oak mentally estimated by the following simple calculation: –

$$5 \times 30 = 150 \text{ quarters} = 500l.$$
$$3 \times 40 = 120 \text{ quarters} = 250l.$$

Total ..   750*l*.

Seven hundred and fifty pounds in the divinest form that money can wear — that of necessary food for man and beast: should the risk be run of deteriorating this bulk of corn to less than half its value, because of the instability of a woman? 'Never, if I can prevent it!' said Gabriel.

Such was the argument that Oak set outwardly before him. But man, even to himself, is a palimpsest, having an ostensible writing, and another beneath the lines. It is possible that there was this golden legend under the utilitarian one: 'I will help to my last effort the woman I have loved so dearly.'

He went back to the barn to endeavour to obtain assistance for covering the ricks that very night. All was silent within, and he would have passed on in the belief that the party had broken up, had not a dim light, yellow as saffron by contrast with the greenish whiteness outside, streamed through a knot-hole in the folding doors.

Gabriel looked in. An unusual picture met his eye.

The candles suspended among the evergreens had burnt down to their sockets, and in some cases the leaves tied about them were scorched. Many of the lights had quite gone out, others smoked and stank, grease dropping from them upon the floor. Here, under the table, and leaning against forms and chairs in every conceivable attitude except the perpendicular, were the wretched persons of all the work-folk, the hair of their heads at such low levels being suggestive of mops and brooms. In the midst of these shone red and distinct the figure of Sergeant Troy, leaning back in a chair. Coggan was on his back, with his mouth open, buzzing forth snores, as were several others: the united breathings of the horizontal assemblage forming a subdued roar like London from a distance. Joseph Poorgrass was curled round in the fashion of a hedgehog, apparently in attempts to present the least possible portion of his surface to the air; and behind him was dimly visible an unimportant remnant of William Smallbury. The glasses and cups still stood upon the table, a water-jug being overturned, from which a small rill, after tracing its course with marvellous precision down the centre of the long table, fell into the neck of the unconscious Mark Clark, in a steady, monotonous drip, like the dripping of a stalactite in a cave.

Gabriel glanced hopelessly at the group, which, with one or two exceptions, composed all the able-bodied men upon the farm. He saw at once that if the ricks were to be saved that night, or even the next morning, he must save them with his own hands.

A faint 'ting-ting' resounded from under Coggan's waistcoat. It was Coggan's watch striking the hour of two.

Oak went to the recumbent form of Matthew Moon, who usually undertook the rough thatching of the homestead, and shook him. The shaking was without effect.

Gabriel shouted in his ear, 'Where's your thatching-beetle and rick-stick and spars?'

'Under the staddles,' said Moon mechanically, with the unconscious promptness of a medium.

Gabriel let go his head, and it dropped upon the floor like a bowl. He then went to Susan Tall's husband.

'Where's the key of the granary?'

No answer. The question was repeated, with the same result. To be shouted to at night was evidently less of a novelty to Susan Tall's husband than to Matthew Moon. Oak flung down Tall's head into the corner again and turned away.

To be just, the men were not greatly to blame for this painful and demoralizing termination to the evening's entertainment. Sergeant Troy had so strenuously insisted, glass in hand, that drinking should be the bond of their union, that those who wished to refuse hardly liked to be so unmannerly under the circumstances. Having from their youth up been entirely unaccustomed to any liquor stronger than cider or mild ale, it was no wonder that they had succumbed, one and all, with extra-ordinary uniformity, after the lapse of about an hour.

Gabriel was greatly depressed. This debauch boded ill for that wilful and fascinating mistress whom the faithful man even now felt within him as the embodiment of all that was sweet and bright and hopeless.

He put out the expiring lights, that the barn might not be endangered, closed the door upon the men in their deep and oblivious sleep, and went again into the lone night. A hot breeze, as if breathed from the parted lips of some dragon about to swallow the globe, fanned him from the south, while directly opposite in the north rose a grim misshapen body of cloud, in the very teeth of the wind. So unnaturally did it rise that one could fancy it to be lifted by machinery from below. Meanwhile the faint cloudlets had flown back into the south-east corner of the sky, as if in terror of the large cloud, like a young brood gazed in upon by some monster.

Going on to the village, Oak flung a small stone against the window of Laban Tall's bedroom, expecting Susan to open it; but nobody stirred. He went round to the back door, which had been left unfastened for Laban's entry, and passed in to the foot of the staircase.

'Mrs. Tall, I've come for the key of the granary, to get at the rick-cloths,' said Oak, in a stentorian voice.

'Is that you?' said Mrs. Susan Tall, half awake.

' Yes,' said Gabriel.

'Come along to bed, do, you draw-latching rogue – keeping a body awake like this!'

'It isn't Laban – 'tis Gabriel Oak. I want the key of the granary.'

'Gabriel! What in the name of fortune did you pretend to be Laban for?'

'I didn't. I thought you meant —'

'Yes you did! What do you want here?'

'The key of the granary.'

'Take it then. 'Tis on the nail. People coming disturbing women at this time o' night ought —'

Gabriel took the key without waiting to hear the conclusion of the tirade. Ten minutes later his lonely figure might have been seen dragging four large waterproof coverings across the yard, and soon two of these heaps of treasure in grain were covered snug – two cloths to each. Two hundred pounds were secured. Three wheat-stacks remained open, and there were no more cloths. Oak looked under the staddles and found a fork. He mounted the third pile of wealth and began operating, adopting the plan of sloping the upper sheaves one over the other; and, in addition, filling the interstices with the material of some untied sheaves.

So far all was well. By this hurried contrivance Bathsheba's property in wheat was safe for at any rate a week or two, provided always that there was not much wind.

Next came the barley. This it was only possible to protect by systematic thatching. Time went on, and the moon vanished not to reappear. It was the farewell of the ambassador previous to war. The night had a haggard look, like a sick thing; and there came finally an utter expiration of air from the whole heaven in the form of a slow breeze, which might have been likened to a death. And now nothing was heard in the yard but the dull thuds of the beetle which drove in the spars, and the rustle of thatch in the intervals.

CHAPTER XXXVII

THE STORM – THE TWO TOGETHER

A LIGHT flapped over the scene, as if reflected from phosphorescent wings crossing the sky, and a rumble filled the air. It was the first move of the approaching storm.

The second peal was noisy, with comparatively little visible lightning. Gabriel saw a candle shining in Bathsheba's bedroom, and soon a shadow swept to and fro upon the blind.

Then there came a third flash. Manœuvres of a most extraordinary kind were going on in the vast firmamental hollows overhead. The lightning now was the colour of silver, and gleamed in the heavens like a mailed army. Rumbles became rattles. Gabriel from his elevated position could see over the landscape at least half-a-dozen miles in front. Every hedge, bush, and tree was distinct as in a line engraving. In a paddock in the same direction was a herd of heifers, and the forms of these were visible at this moment in the act of galloping about in the wildest and maddest confusion, flinging their heels and tails high into the air, their heads to earth. A poplar in the immediate foreground was like an ink stroke on burnished tin. Then the picture vanished, leaving the darkness so intense that Gabriel worked entirely by feeling with his hands.

He had stuck his ricking-rod, or poniard, as it was indifferently called – a long iron lance, polished by handling – into the stack, used to support the sheaves instead of the support called a groom used on houses. A blue light appeared in the zenith, and in some indescribable manner flickered down near the top of the rod. It was the fourth of the larger flashes. A moment later and there was a smack – smart, clear, and short. Gabriel felt his position to be anything but a safe one, and he resolved to descend.

269

Not a drop of rain had fallen as yet. He wiped his weary brow, and looked again at the black forms of the unprotected stacks. Was his life so valuable to him after all? What were his prospects that he should be so chary of running risk, when important and urgent labour could not be carried on without such risk? He resolved to stick to the stack. However, he took a precaution. Under the staddles was a long tethering chain, used to prevent the escape of errant horses. This he carried up the ladder, and sticking his rod through the clog at one end, allowed the other end of the chain to trail upon the ground. The spike attached to it he drove in. Under the shadow of this extemporized lightning conductor he felt himself comparatively safe.

Before Oak had laid his hands upon his tools again out leapt the fifth flash, with the spring of a serpent and the shout of a fiend. It was green as an emerald, and the reverberation was stunning. What was this the light revealed to him? In the open ground before him, as he looked over the ridge of the rick, was a dark and apparently female form. Could it be that of the only venturesome woman in the parish – Bathsheba? The form moved on a step: then he could see no more.

'Is that you, ma'am?' said Gabriel to the darkness.

'Who is there?' said the voice of Bathsheba.

'Gabriel. I am on the rick, thatching.'

'O, Gabriel! – and are you? I have come about them. The weather awoke me, and I thought of the corn. I am so distressed about it – can we save it anyhow? I cannot find my husband. Is he with you?'

'He is not here.'

'Do you know where he is?'

'Asleep in the barn.'

'He promised that the stacks should be seen to, and now they are all neglected! Can I do anything to help? Liddy is afraid to come out. Fancy finding you here at such an hour! Surely I can do something?'

'You can bring up some reed-sheaves to me, one by one,

ma'am; if you are not afraid to come up the ladder in the dark,' said Gabriel. 'Every moment is precious now, and that would save a good deal of time. It is not very dark when the lightning has been gone a bit.'

'I'll do anything!' she said resolutely. She instantly took a sheaf upon her shoulder, clambered up close to his heels, placed it behind the rod, and descended for another. At her third ascent the rick suddenly brightened with a brazen glare of shining majolica – every knot in every straw visible. On the slope in front of him appeared two human shapes, black as jet. The rick lost its sheen – the shapes vanished. Gabriel turned his head. It had been the sixth flash which had come from the east behind him, and the two dark forms on the slope had been the shadows of himself and Bathsheba.

Then came the peal. It hardly was credible that such a heavenly light could be the parent of such a diabolical sound.

'How terrible!' she exclaimed, and clutched him by the sleeve. Gabriel turned, and steadied her on her aerial perch by holding her arm. At the same moment, while he was still reversed in his attitude, there was more light, and he saw, as it were, a copy of the tall poplar tree on the hill drawn in black on the wall of the barn. It was the shadow of that tree, thrown across by a secondary flash in the west.

The next flare came. Bathsheba was on the ground now, shouldering another sheaf, and she bore its dazzle without flinching – thunder and all – and again ascended with the load. There was then a silence everywhere for four or five minutes, and the crunch of the spars, as Gabriel hastily drove them in, could again be distinctly heard. He thought the crisis of the storm had passed. But there came a burst of light.

'Hold on!' said Gabriel, taking the sheaf from her shoulder, and grasping her arm again.

Heaven opened then, indeed. The flash was almost too novel for its inexpressibly dangerous nature to be at once realized, and they could only comprehend the magnificence of its beauty. It sprang from east, west, north, south, and was a perfect dance of death. The forms of skeletons appeared in the air, shaped with blue fire for bones – dancing, leaping, striding, racing around, and mingling altogether in unparalleled confusion. With these were intertwined undulating snakes of green, and behind these was a broad mass of lesser light. Simultaneously came from every part of the tumbling sky what may be called a shout; since, though no shout ever came near it, it was more of the nature of a shout than of anything else earthly. In the meantime one of the grisly forms had alighted upon the point of Gabriel's rod, to run invisibly down it, down the chain, and into the earth. Gabriel was almost blinded, and he could feel Bathsheba's warm arm tremble in his hand – a sensation novel and thrilling enough; but love, life, everything human, seemed small and trifling in such close juxtaposition with an infuriated universe.

Oak had hardly time to gather up these impressions into a thought, and to see how strangely the red feather of her hat shone in this light, when the tall tree on the hill before mentioned seemed on fire to a white heat, and a new one among these terrible voices mingled with the last crash of those preceding. It was a stupefying blast, harsh and pitiless, and it fell upon their ears in a dead, flat blow, without that reverberation which lends the tones of a drum to more distant thunder. By the lustre reflected from every part of the earth and from the wide domical scoop above it, he saw that the tree was sliced down the whole length of its tall, straight stem, a huge riband of bark being apparently flung off. The other portion remained erect, and revealed the bared surface as a strip of white down the front. The lightning had struck the tree. A sulphurous smell filled the air; then all was silent, and black as a cave in Hinnom.

'We had a narrow escape!' said Gabriel hurriedly. 'You had better go down.'

Bathsheba said nothing; but he could distinctly hear her rhythmical pants, and the recurrent rustle of the sheaf beside her in response to her frightened pulsations. She descended the ladder, and, on second thoughts, he followed her. The darkness was now impenetrable by the sharpest vision. They both stood still at the bottom, side by side. Bathsheba appeared to think only of the weather – Oak thought only of her just then. At last he said —

'The storm seems to have passed now, at any rate.'

'I think so too,' said Bathsheba. 'Though there are multitudes of gleams, look!'

The sky was now filled with an incessant light, frequent repetition melting into complete continuity, as an unbroken sound results from the successive strokes on a gong.

'Nothing serious,' said he. 'I cannot understand no rain falling. But Heaven be praised, it is all the better for us. I am now going up again.'

'Gabriel, you are kinder than I deserve! I will stay and help you yet. O, why are not some of the others here !'

'They would have been here if they could,' said Oak, in a hesitating way.

'O, I know it all – all,' she said, adding slowly: 'They are all asleep in the barn, in a drunken sleep, and my husband among them. That's it, is it not? Don't think I am a timid woman and can't endure things.'

'I am not certain,' said Gabriel. 'I will go and see.'

He crossed to the barn, leaving her there alone. He looked through the chinks of the door. All was in total darkness, as he had left it, and there still arose, as at the former time, the steady buzz of many snores.

He felt a zephyr curling about his cheek, and turned. It was Bathsheba's breath – she had followed him, and was looking into the same chink.

He endeavoured to put off the immediate and painful subject of their thoughts by remarking gently, 'If you'll come back again, miss – ma'am, and hand up a few more, it would save much time.'

Then Oak went back again, ascended to the top, stepped off the ladder for greater expedition, and went on thatching. She followed, but without a sheaf.

'Gabriel,' she said, in a strange and impressive voice.

Oak looked up at her. She had not spoken since he left the barn. The soft and continual shimmer of the dying lightning showed a marble face high against the black sky of the opposite quarter. Bathsheba was sitting almost on the apex of the stack, her feet gathered up beneath her, and resting on the top round of the ladder.

'Yes, mistress,' he said.

'I suppose you thought that when I galloped away to Bath that night it was on purpose to be married?'

'I did at last – not at first,' he answered, somewhat surprised at the abruptness with which this new subject was broached.

'And others thought so, too!'

'Yes.'

'And you blamed me for it?'

'Well – a little.'

'I thought so. Now, I care a little for your good opinion, and I want to explain something – I have longed to do it ever since I returned, and you looked so gravely at me. For if I were to die – and I may die soon – it would be dreadful that you should always think mistakenly of me. Now, listen.'

Gabriel ceased his rustling.

'I went to Bath that night in the full intention of breaking off my engagement to Mr. Troy. It was owing to circumstances which occurred after I got there that – that we were married. Now, do you see the matter in a new light?'

'I do – somewhat.'

'I must, I suppose, say more, now that I have begun. And perhaps it's no harm, for you are certainly under no delusion that I ever loved you, or that I can have any object in speaking, more than that object I have mentioned. Well, I was alone in a strange city, and the horse was lame. And at last I didn't know what to do. I saw, when it was too late, that scandal might seize hold of me for meeting him alone in that way. But I was coming away, when he suddenly said he had that day seen a woman more beautiful than I, and that his constancy could not be counted on unless I at once became his. . . . And I was grieved and troubled —' She cleared her voice, and waited a moment, as if to gather breath. 'And then, between jealousy and distraction, I married him!' she whispered with desperate impetuosity.

Gabriel made no reply.

'He was not to blame, for it was perfectly true about – about his seeing somebody else,' she quickly added. 'And now I don't wish for a single remark from you upon the subject – indeed, I forbid it. I only wanted you to know that misunderstood bit of my history before a time comes when you could never know it. – You want some more sheaves?'

She went down the ladder, and the work proceeded. Gabriel soon perceived a languor in the movements of his mistress up and down, and he said to her, gently as a mother —

'I think you had better go indoors now, you are tired. I can finish the rest alone. If the wind does not change the rain is likely to keep off.'

'If I am useless I will go,' said Bathsheba, in a flagging cadence. 'But O, if your life should be lost!'

'You are not useless; but I would rather not tire you longer. You have done well.'

'And you better!' she said gratefully. 'Thank you for your devotion, a thousand times, Gabriel! Good-night – I know you are doing your very best for me.'

She diminished in the gloom, and vanished, and he heard the latch of the gate fall as she passed through. He worked in a reverie now, musing upon her story, and upon the contradictoriness of that feminine heart which had caused her to speak more warmly to him to-night than she ever had done whilst unmarried and free to speak as warmly as she chose.

He was disturbed in his meditation by a grating noise from the coach-house. It was the vane on the roof turning round, and this change in the wind was the signal for a disastrous rain.

CHAPTER XXXVIII

RAIN – ONE SOLITARY MEETS ANOTHER

IT was now five o'clock, and the dawn was promising to break in hues of drab and ash.

The air changed its temperature and stirred itself more vigorously. Cool breezes coursed in transparent eddies round Oak's face. The wind shifted yet a point or two and blew stronger. In ten minutes every wind of heaven seemed to be roaming at large. Some of the thatching on the wheat-stacks was now whirled fantastically aloft, and had to be replaced and weighted with some rails that lay near at hand. This done, Oak slaved away again at the barley. A huge drop of rain smote his face, the wind snarled round every corner, the trees rocked to the bases of their trunks, and the twigs clashed in strife. Driving in spars at any point and on any system, inch by inch he covered more and more safely from ruin this distracting impersonation of seven hundred pounds. The rain came on in earnest, and Oak soon felt the water to be tracking cold and clammy routes down his back. Ultimately he was reduced well-nigh to a homogeneous sop, and the dyes of his clothes trickled down and stood in a pool at the foot of the ladder. The rain stretched obliquely through the dull atmosphere in liquid spines, unbroken in continuity between their beginnings in the clouds and their points in him.

Oak suddenly remembered that eight months before this time he had been fighting against fire in the same spot as desperately as he was fighting against water now – and for a futile love of the same woman. As for her — But Oak was generous and true, and dismissed his reflections.

It was about seven o'clock in the dark leaden morning when

Gabriel came down from the last stack, and thankfully exclaimed, 'It is done!' He was drenched, weary, and sad, and yet not so sad as drenched and weary, for he was cheered by a sense of success in a good cause.

Faint sounds came from the barn, and he looked that way. Figures stepped singly and in pairs through the doors – all walking awkwardly, and abashed, save the foremost, who wore a red jacket, and advanced with his hands in his pockets, whistling. The others shambled after with a conscience-stricken air: the whole procession was not unlike Flaxman's group of the suitors tottering on towards the infernal regions under the conduct of Mercury. The gnarled shapes passed into the village, Troy, their leader, entering the farmhouse. Not a single one of them had turned his face to the ricks, or apparently bestowed one thought upon their condition.

Soon Oak too went homeward, by a different route from theirs. In front of him against the wet glazed surface of the lane he saw a person walking yet more slowly than himself under an umbrella. The man turned and plainly started; he was Boldwood.

'How are you this morning, sir?' said Oak.

'Yes, it is a wet day. – Oh, I am well, very well, I thank you; quite well.'

'I am glad to hear it, sir.'

Boldwood seemed to awake to the present by degrees. 'You look tired and ill, Oak,' he said then, desultorily regarding his companion.

'I am tired. You look strangely altered, sir.'

'I? Not a bit of it: I am well enough. What put that into your head?'

'I thought you didn't look quite so topping as you used to, that was all.'

'Indeed, then you are mistaken,' said Boldwood shortly. 'Nothing hurts me. My constitution is an iron one.'

'I've been working hard to get our ricks covered, and was barely in time. Never had such a struggle in my life. . . . Yours of course are safe, sir.'

'O yes.' Boldwood added, after an interval of silence: ' What did you ask, Oak?'

'Your ricks are all covered before this time?'

'No.'

'At any rate, the large ones upon the stone staddles?'

'They are not.'

'Them under the hedge?'

'No. I forgot to tell the thatcher to set about it.'

'Nor the little one by the stile?'

'Nor the little one by the stile. I overlooked the ricks this year.'

'Then not a tenth of your corn will come to measure, sir.'

'Possibly not.'

'Overlooked them,' repeated Gabriel slowly to himself. It is difficult to describe the intensely dramatic effect that announcement had upon Oak at such a moment. All the night he had been feeling that the neglect he was labouring to repair was abnormal and isolated – the only instance of the kind within the circuit of the county. Yet at this very time, within the same parish, a greater waste had been going on, uncomplained of and disregarded. A few months earlier Boldwood's forgetting his husbandry would have been as preposterous an idea as a sailor forgetting he was in a ship. Oak was just thinking that whatever he himself might have suffered from Bathsheba's marriage, here was a man who had suffered more, when Boldwood spoke in a changed voice – that of one who yearned to make a confidence and relieve his heart by an outpouring.

'Oak, you know as well as I that things have gone wrong with me lately. I may as well own it. I was going to get a little settled in life; but in some way my plan has come to nothing.'

'I thought my mistress would have married you,' said Gabriel, not knowing enough of the full depths of Boldwood's love to keep silence on the farmer's account, and determined not to evade discipline by doing so on his own. 'However, it is so sometimes, and nothing happens that we expect,' he added, with the repose of a man whom misfortune had inured rather than subdued.

'I daresay I am a joke about the parish,' said Boldwood, as if the subject came irresistibly to his tongue, and with a miserable lightness meant to express his indifference.

'O no – I don't think that.'

'– But the real truth of the matter is that there was not, as some fancy, any jilting on – her part. No engagement ever existed between me and Miss Everdene. People say so, but it is untrue: she never promised me!' Boldwood stood still now and turned his wild face to Oak. ' O, Gabriel,' he continued, 'I am weak and foolish, and I don't know what, and I can't fend off my miserable grief! . . . I had some faint belief in the mercy of God till I lost that woman. Yes, He prepared a gourd to shade me, and like the prophet I thanked Him and was glad. But the next day He prepared a worm to smite the gourd and wither it; and I feel it is better to die than to live!'

A silence followed. Boldwood aroused himself from the momentary mood of confidence into which he had drifted, and walked on again, resuming his usual reserve.

'No, Gabriel,' he resumed, with a carelessness which was like the smile on the countenance of a skull: 'it was made more of by other people than ever it was by us. I do feel a little regret occasionally, but no woman ever had power over me for any length of time. Well, good morning; I can trust you not to mention to others what has passed between us two here.'

CHAPTER XXXIX

COMING HOME – A CRY

ON the turnpike road, between Casterbridge and Weather-bury, and about three miles from the former place, is Yalbury Hill, one of those steep long ascents which pervade the high-ways of this undulating part of South Wessex. In returning from market it is usual for the farmers and other gig-gentry to alight at the bottom and walk up.

One Saturday evening in the month of October Bathsheba's vehicle was duly creeping up this incline. She was sitting list-lessly in the second seat of the gig, whilst walking beside her in a farmer's marketing suit of unusually fashionable cut was an erect, well-made young man. Though on foot, he held the reins and whip, and occasionally aimed light cuts at the horse's ear with the end of the lash, as a recreation. This man was her husband, formerly Sergeant Troy, who, having bought his dis-charge with Bathsheba's money, was gradually transforming himself into a farmer of a spirited and very modern school. People of unalterable ideas still insisted upon calling him 'Ser-geant' when they met him, which was in some degree owing to his having still retained the well-shaped moustache of his military days, and the soldierly bearing inseparable from his form and training.

'Yes, if it hadn't been for that wretched rain I should have cleared two hundred as easy as looking, my love,' he was saying. 'Don't you see, it altered all the chances? To speak like a book I once read, wet weather is the narrative, and fine days are the episodes, of our country's history; now, isn't that true?'

'But the time of year is come for changeable weather.'

'Well, yes. The fact is, these autumn races are the ruin of

everybody. Never did I see such a day as 'twas! 'Tis a wild open place, just out of Budmouth, and a drab sea rolled in towards us like liquid misery. Wind and rain – good Lord! Dark? Why, 'twas as black as my hat before the last race was run. 'Twas five o'clock, and you couldn't see the horses till they were almost in, leave alone colours. The ground was as heavy as lead, and all judgment from a fellow's experience went for nothing. Horses, riders, people, were all blown about like ships at sea. Three booths were blown over, and the wretched folk inside crawled out upon their hands and knees; and in the next field were as many as a dozen hats at one time. Ay, Pimpernel regularly stuck fast, when about sixty yards off, and when I saw Policy stepping on, it did knock my heart against the lining of my ribs, I assure you, my love!'

'And you mean, Frank,' said Bathsheba sadly – her voice was painfully lowered from the fulness and vivacity of the previous summer – 'that you have lost more than a hundred pounds in a month by this dreadful horse-racing? O, Frank, it is cruel; it is foolish of you to take away my money so. We shall have to leave the farm; that will be the end of it!'

'Humbug about cruel. Now, there 'tis again – turn on the waterworks; that's just like you.'

'But you'll promise me not to go to Budmouth second meeting, won't you?' she implored. Bathsheba was at the full depth for tears, but she maintained a dry eye.

'I don't see why I should; in fact, if it turns out to be a fine day, I was thinking of taking you.'

'Never, never! I'll go a hundred miles the other way first. I hate the sound of the very word!'

'But the question of going to see the race or staying at home has very little to do with the matter. Bets are all booked safely enough before the race begins, you may depend. Whether it is a bad race for me or a good one, will have very little to do with our going there next Monday.'

'But you don't mean to say that you have risked anything on this one too!' she exclaimed, with an agonized look.

' There now, don't you be a little fool. Wait till you are told.

Why, Bathsheba, you have lost all the pluck and sauciness you formerly had, and upon my life if I had known what a chicken-hearted creature you were under all your boldness, I'd never have – I know what.'

A flash of indignation might have been seen in Bathsheba's dark eyes as she looked resolutely ahead after this reply. They moved on without further speech, some early-withered leaves from the trees which hooded the road at this spot occasionally spinning downward across their path to the earth.

A woman appeared on the brow of the hill. The ridge was in a cutting, so that she was very near the husband and wife before she became visible. Troy had turned towards the gig to remount, and whilst putting his foot on the step the woman passed behind him.

Though the overshadowing trees and the approach of even-tide enveloped them in gloom, Bathsheba could see plainly enough to discern the extreme poverty of the woman's garb, and the sadness of her face.

'Please, sir, do you know at what time Casterbridge Union-house closes at night?'

The woman said these words to Troy over his shoulder.

Troy started visibly at the sound of the voice; yet he seemed to recover presence of mind sufficient to prevent himself from giving way to his impulse to suddenly turn and face her. He said, slowly —

'I don't know.'

The woman, on hearing him speak, quickly looked up, examined the side of his face, and recognized the soldier under the yeoman's garb. Her face was drawn into an expression which had gladness and agony both among its elements. She uttered an hysterical cry, and fell down.

'O, poor thing!' exclaimed Bathsheba, instantly preparing to alight.

'Stay where you are, and attend to the horse!' said Troy peremptorily, throwing her the reins and the whip. 'Walk the horse to the top: I'll see to the woman.'

'But I —'

'Do you hear? Clk – Poppet!'

The horse, gig, and Bathsheba moved on.

'How on earth did you come here? I thought you were miles away, or dead! Why didn't you write to me?' said Troy to the woman, in a strangely gentle, yet hurried voice, as he lifted her up.

'I feared to.'

'Have you any money?'

'None.'

'Good Heaven – I wish I had more to give you! Here's – wretched – the merest trifle. It is every farthing I have left. I have none but what my wife gives me, you know, and I can't ask her now.'

The woman made no answer.

'I have only another moment,' continued Troy; 'and now listen. Where are you going to-night? Casterbridge Union?'

'Yes; I thought to go there.'

'You shan't go there; yet, wait. Yes, perhaps for to-night; I can do nothing better – worse luck! Sleep there to-night, and stay there to-morrow. Monday is the first free day I have; and on Monday morning, at ten exactly, meet me on Grey's Bridge, just out of the town. I'll bring all the money I can muster. You shan't want – I'll see that, Fanny; then I'll get you a lodging somewhere. Good-bye till then. I am a brute – but good-bye!'

After advancing the distance which completed the ascent of the hill, Bathsheba turned her head. The woman was upon her feet, and Bathsheba saw her withdrawing from Troy, and going feebly down the hill by the third milestone from Casterbridge. Troy then came on towards his wife, stepped into the gig, took the reins from her hand, and without making any observation whipped the horse into a trot. He was rather agitated.

'Do you know who that woman was?' said Bathsheba, look-ing searchingly into his face.

'I do,' he said, looking boldly back into hers.

'I thought you did,' said she, with angry hauteur, and still regarding him. 'Who is she?'

He suddenly seemed to think that frankness would benefit neither of the women.

'Nothing to either of us,' he said. 'I know her by sight.'

'What is her name?'

'How should I know her name?'

'I think you do.'

'Think if you will, and be —' The sentence was completed by a smart cut of the whip round Poppet's flank, which caused the animal to start forward at a wild pace. No more was said.

CHAPTER XL

ON CASTERBRIDGE HIGHWAY

FOR a considerable time the woman walked on. Her steps became feebler, and she strained her eyes to look afar upon the naked road, now indistinct amid the penumbræ of night. At length her onward walk dwindled to the merest totter, and she opened a gate within which was a haystack. Underneath this she sat down and presently slept.

When the woman awoke it was to find herself in the depths of a moonless and starless night. A heavy unbroken crust of cloud stretched across the sky, shutting out every speck of heaven; and a distant halo which hung over the town of Casterbridge was visible against the black concave, the luminosity appearing the brighter by its great contrast with the circumscribing darkness. Towards this weak, soft glow the woman turned her eyes.

'If I could only get there!' she said. 'Meet him the day after to-morrow: God help me! Perhaps I shall be in my grave before then.'

A manor-house clock from the far depths of shadow struck the hour, one, in a small, attenuated tone. After midnight the voice of a clock seems to lose in breadth as much as in length, and to diminish its sonorousness to a thin falsetto.

Afterwards a light – two lights – arose from the remote shade, and grew larger. A carriage rolled along the road, and passed the gate. It probably contained some late diners-out. The beams from one lamp shone for a moment upon the crouching woman, and threw her face into vivid relief. The face was young in the groundwork, old in the finish; the general contours were flexuous and childlike, but the finer lineaments had begun to be sharp and thin.

The pedestrian stood up, apparently with a revived determination, and looked around. The road appeared to be familiar to her, and she carefully scanned the fence as she slowly walked along. Presently there became visible a dim white shape; it was another milestone. She drew her fingers across its face to feel the marks.

'Two more!' she said.

She leant against the stone as a means of rest for a short interval, then bestirred herself, and again pursued her way. For a slight distance she bore up bravely, afterwards flagging as before. This was beside a lone copsewood, wherein heaps of white chips strewn upon the leafy ground showed that woodmen had been faggoting and making hurdles during the day. Now there was not a rustle, not a breeze, not the faintest clash of twigs to keep her company. The woman looked over the gate, opened it, and went in. Close to the entrance stood a row of faggots, bound and unbound, together with stakes of all sizes.

For a few seconds the wayfarer stood with that tense stillness which signifies itself to be not the end, but merely the suspension, of a previous motion. Her attitude was that of a person who listens, either to the external world of sound, or to the imagined discourse of thought. A close criticism might have detected signs proving that she was intent on the latter alternative. Moreover, as was shown by what followed, she was oddly exercising the faculty of invention upon the speciality of the clever Jacquet Droz, the designer of automatic substitutes for human limbs.

By the aid of the Casterbridge aurora, and by feeling with her hands, the woman selected two sticks from the heaps. These sticks were nearly straight to the height of three or four feet, where each branched into a fork like the letter Y. She sat down, snapped off the small upper twigs, and carried the remainder with her into the road. She placed one of these forks under each arm as a crutch, tested them, timidly threw her whole weight upon them – so little that it was – and swung herself forward. The girl had made for herself a material aid.

The crutches answered well. The pat of her feet, and the tap of her sticks upon the highway, were all the sounds that came from the traveller now. She had passed the last milestone by a good long distance, and began to look wistfully towards the bank as if calculating upon another milestone soon. The crutches, though so very useful, had their limits of power. Mechanism only transfers labour, being powerless to supersede it, and the original amount of exertion was not cleared away; it was thrown into the body and arms. She was exhausted, and each swing forward became fainter. At last she swayed sideways, and fell.

Here she lay, a shapeless heap, for ten minutes and more. The morning wind began to boom dully over the flats, and to move afresh dead leaves which had lain still since yesterday. The woman desperately turned round upon her knees, and next rose to her feet. Steadying herself by the help of one crutch, she essayed a step, then another, then a third, using the crutches now as walking-sticks only. Thus she progressed till descending Mellstock Hill another milestone appeared, and soon the beginning of an iron-railed fence came into view. She staggered across to the first post, clung to it, and looked around.

The Casterbridge lights were now individually visible. It was getting towards morning, and vehicles might be hoped for, if not expected soon. She listened. There was not a sound of life save that acme and sublimation of all dismal sounds, the bark of a fox, its three hollow notes being rendered at intervals of a minute with the precision of a funeral bell.

'Less than a mile!' the woman murmured. 'No; more,' she added, after a pause. 'The mile is to the county-hall, and my resting-place is on the other side Casterbridge. A little over a mile, and there I am!' After an interval she again spoke. 'Five or six steps to a yard – six perhaps. I have to go seventeen hundred yards. A hundred times six, six hundred. Seventeen times that. O pity me, Lord!'

Holding to the rails, she advanced, thrusting one hand

forward upon the rail, then the other, then leaning over it whilst she dragged her feet on beneath.

This woman was not given to soliloquy; but extremity of feeling lessens the individuality of the weak, as it increases that of the strong. She said again in the same tone, 'I'll believe that the end lies five posts forward, and no further, and so get strength to pass them.'

This was a practical application of the principle that a half-feigned and fictitious faith is better than no faith at all.

She passed five posts and held on to the fifth.

'I'll pass five more by believing my longed-for spot is at the next fifth. I can do it.'

She passed five more.

'It lies only five further.'

She passed five more.

'But it is five further.'

She passed them.

'That stone bridge is the end of my journey,' she said, when the bridge over the Froom was in view.

She crawled to the bridge. During the effort each breath of the woman went into the air as if never to return again.

'Now for the truth of the matter,' she said, sitting down. 'The truth is, that I have less than half a mile.' Self-beguilement with what she had known all the time to be false had given her strength to come over half a mile that she would have been powerless to face in the lump. The artifice showed that the woman, by some mysterious intuition, had grasped the paradoxical truth that blindness may operate more vigorously than prescience, and the short-sighted effect more than the far-seeing; that limitation, and not comprehensiveness, is needed for striking a blow.

The half-mile stood now before the sick and weary woman like a stolid Juggernaut. It was an impassive King of her world. The road here ran across Durnover Moor, open to the road on either side. She surveyed the wide space, the lights, herself, sighed, and lay down against a guard-stone of the bridge.

Never was ingenuity exercised so sorely as the traveller here exercised hers. Every conceivable aid, method, stratagem, mechanism, by which these last desperate eight hundred yards could be overpassed by a human being unperceived, was revolved in her busy brain, and dismissed as impracticable. She thought of sticks, wheels, crawling – she even thought of rolling. But the exertion demanded by either of these latter two was greater than to walk erect. The faculty of contrivance was worn out. Hopelessness had come at last.

'No further!' she whispered, and closed her eyes.

From the stripe of shadow on the opposite side of the bridge a portion of shade seemed to detach itself and move into isolation upon the pale white of the road. It glided noiselessly towards the recumbent woman.

She became conscious of something touching her hand; it was softness and it was warmth. She opened her eyes, and the substance touched her face. A dog was licking her cheek.

He was a huge, heavy, and quiet creature, standing darkly against the low horizon, and at least two feet higher than the present position of her eyes. Whether Newfoundland, mastiff, blood-hound, or what not, it was impossible to say. He seemed to be of too strange and mysterious a nature to belong to any variety among those of popular nomenclature. Being thus assignable to no breed, he was the ideal embodiment of canine greatness – a generalization from what was common to all. Night, in its sad, solemn, and benevolent aspect, apart from its stealthy and cruel side, was personified in this form. Darkness endows the small and ordinary ones among mankind with poetical power, and even the suffering woman threw her idea into figure.

In her reclining position she looked up to him just as in earlier times she had, when standing, looked up to a man. The animal, who was as homeless as she, respectfully withdrew a step or two when the woman moved, and, seeing that she did not repulse him, he licked her hand again.

A thought moved within her like lightning. 'Perhaps I can make use of him – I might do it then!'

She pointed in the direction of Casterbridge, and the dog seemed to misunderstand: he trotted on. Then, finding she could not follow, he came back and whined.

The ultimate and saddest singularity of woman's effort and invention was reached when, with a quickened breathing, she rose to a stooping posture, and, resting her two little arms upon the shoulders of the dog, leant firmly thereon, and murmured stimulating words. Whilst she sorrowed in her heart she cheered with her voice, and what was stranger than that the strong should need encouragement from the weak was that cheerfulness should be so well stimulated by such utter dejection. Her friend moved forward slowly, and she with small mincing steps moved forward beside him, half her weight being thrown upon the animal. Sometimes she sank as she had sunk from walking erect, from the crutches, from the rails. The dog, who now thoroughly understood her desire and her incapacity, was frantic in his distress on these occasions; he would tug at her dress and run forward. She always called him back, and it was now to be observed that the woman listened for human sounds only to avoid them. It was evident that she had an object in keeping her presence on the road and her forlorn state unknown.

Their progress was necessarily very slow. They reached the bottom of the town, and the Casterbridge lamps lay before them like fallen Pleiads as they turned to the left into the dense shade of a deserted avenue of chestnuts, and so skirted the borough. Thus the town was passed, and the goal was reached.

On this much-desired spot outside the town rose a picturesque building. Originally it had been a mere case to hold people. The shell had been so thin, so devoid of excrescence, and so closely drawn over the accommodation granted, that the grim character of what was beneath showed through it, as the shape of a body is visible under a winding-sheet.

Then Nature, as if offended, lent a hand. Masses of ivy grew up, completely covering the walls, till the place looked like an abbey; and it was discovered that the view from the front, over the Casterbridge chimneys, was one of the most magnificent in the county. A neighbouring earl once said that he would give up a year's rental to have at his own door the view enjoyed by the inmates from theirs – and very probably the inmates would have given up the view for his year's rental.

This stone edifice consisted of a central mass and two wings, whereon stood as sentinels a few slim chimneys, now gurgling sorrowfully to the slow wind. In the wall was a gate, and by the gate a bell-pull formed of a hanging wire. The woman raised herself as high as possible upon her knees, and could just reach the handle. She moved it and fell forwards in a bowed attitude, her face upon her bosom.

It was getting on towards six o'clock, and sounds of movement were to be heard inside the building which was the haven of rest to this wearied soul. A little door by the large one was opened, and a man appeared inside. He discerned the panting heap of clothes, went back for a light, and came again. He entered a second time, and returned with two women.

These lifted the prostrate figure and assisted her in through the doorway. The man then closed the door.

'How did she get here?' said one of the women.

' The Lord knows,' said the other.

' There is a dog outside,' murmured the overcome traveller. 'Where is he gone? He helped me.'

'I stoned him away,' said the man.

The little procession then moved forward – the man in front bearing the light, the two bony women next, supporting between them the small and supple one. Thus they entered the house and disappeared.

CHAPTER XLI

SUSPICION – FANNY IS SENT FOR

BATHSHEBA said very little to her husband all that evening of their return from market, and he was not disposed to say much to her. He exhibited the unpleasant combination of a restless condition with a silent tongue. The next day, which was Sunday, passed nearly in the same manner as regarded their taciturnity, Bathsheba going to church both morning and afternoon. This was the day before the Budmouth races. In the evening Troy said, suddenly —

'Bathsheba, could you let me have twenty pounds?'

Her countenance instantly sank. 'Twenty pounds?' she said.

'The fact is, I want it badly.' The anxiety upon Troy's face was unusual and very marked. It was a culmination of the mood he had been in all the day.

'Ah! for those races to-morrow.'

Troy for the moment made no reply. Her mistake had its advantages to a man who shrank from having his mind inspected as he did now. 'Well, suppose I do want it for races?' he said, at last.

'O, Frank!' Bathsheba replied, and there was such a volume of entreaty in the words. 'Only such a few weeks ago you said that I was far sweeter than all your other pleasures put together, and that you would give them all up for me; and now, won't you give up this one, which is more a worry than a pleasure? Do, Frank. Come, let me fascinate you by all I can do – by pretty words and pretty looks, and everything I can think of – to stay at home. Say yes to your wife – say yes!'

The tenderest and softest phases of Bathsheba's nature were prominent now – advanced impulsively for his acceptance, without any of the disguises and defences which the wariness of her character when she was cool too frequently threw over them. Few men could have resisted the arch yet dignified entreaty of the beautiful face, thrown a little back and sideways in the well-known attitude that expresses more than the words it accompanies, and which seems to have been designed for these special occasions. Had the woman not been his wife, Troy would have succumbed instantly; as it was, he thought he would not deceive her longer.

'The money is not wanted for racing debts at all,' he said.

'What is it for?' she asked. 'You worry me a great deal by these mysterious responsibilities, Frank.'

Troy hesitated. He did not now love her enough to allow himself to be carried too far by her ways. Yet it was necessary to be civil. 'You wrong me by such a suspicious manner,' he said. 'Such strait-waistcoating as you treat me to is not becoming in you at so early a date.'

'I think that I have a right to grumble a little if I pay,' she said, with features between a smile and a pout.

'Exactly; and, the former being done, suppose we proceed to the latter. Bathsheba, fun is all very well, but don't go too far, or you may have cause to regret something.'

She reddened. 'I do that already,' she said quickly.

'What do you regret?'

'That my romance has come to an end.'

'All romances end at marriage.'

'I wish you wouldn't talk like that. You grieve me to my soul by being smart at my expense.'

'You are dull enough at mine. I believe you hate me.'

'Not you – only your faults. I do hate them.'

' 'Twould be much more becoming if you set yourself to cure them. Come, let's strike a balance with the twenty pounds, and be friends.'

She gave a sigh of resignation. 'I have about that sum here for household expenses. If you must have it, take it.'

'Very good. Thank you. I expect I shall have gone away before you are in to breakfast to-morrow.'

'And must you go? Ah! there was a time, Frank, when it would have taken a good many promises to other people to drag you away from me. You used to call me darling, then. But it doesn't matter to you how my days are passed now.'

'I must go, in spite of sentiment.' Troy, as he spoke, looked at his watch, and, apparently actuated by *non lucendo* principles, opened the case at the back, revealing, snugly stowed within it, a small coil of hair.

Bathsheba's eyes had been accidentally lifted at that moment, and she saw the action and saw the hair. She flushed in pain and surprise, and some words escaped her before she had thought whether or not it was wise to utter them. 'A woman's curl of hair!' she said. 'O, Frank, whose is that?'

Troy had instantly closed his watch. He carelessly replied, as one who cloaked some feelings that the sight had stirred: 'Why, yours, of course. Whose should it be? I had quite forgotten that I had it.'

'What a dreadful fib, Frank!'

'I tell you I had forgotten it!' he said loudly.

'I don't mean that – it was yellow hair.'

'Nonsense.'

'That's insulting me. I know it was yellow. Now whose was it? I want to know.'

'Very well – I'll tell you, so make no more ado. It is the hair of a young woman I was going to marry before I knew you.'

'You ought to tell me her name, then.'

'I cannot do that.'

'Is she married yet?'

'No.'

'Is she alive?'

'Yes.'

'Is she pretty?'

'Yes.'

'It is wonderful how she can be, poor thing, under such an awful affliction!'

'Affliction – what affliction?' he inquired quickly.

'Having hair of that dreadful colour.'

'Oh – ho – I like that!' said Troy, recovering himself. 'Why, her hair has been admired by everybody who has seen her since she has worn it loose, which has not been long. It is beautiful hair. People used to turn their heads to look at it, poor girl!'

'Pooh! that's nothing – that's nothing!' she exclaimed, in incipient accents of pique. 'If I cared for your love as much as I used to I could say people had turned to look at mine.'

'Bathsheba, don't be so fitful and jealous. You knew what married life would be like, and shouldn't have entered it if you feared these contingencies.'

Troy had by this time driven her to bitterness: her heart was big in her throat, and the ducts to her eyes were painfully full. Ashamed as she was to show emotion, at last she burst out: –

'This is all I get for loving you so well! Ah! when I married you your life was dearer to me than my own. I would have died for you – how truly I can say that I would have died for you! And now you sneer at my foolishness in marrying you. O! is it kind to me to throw my mistake in my face? Whatever opinion you may have of my wisdom, you should not tell me of it so mercilessly, now that I am in your power.'

'I can't help how things fall out,' said Troy; 'upon my heart, women will be the death of me!'

'Well, you shouldn't keep people's hair. You'll burn it, won't you, Frank?'

Frank went on as if he had not heard her. 'There are considerations even before my consideration for you; reparations to be made – ties you know nothing of. If you repent of marrying, so do I.'

Trembling now, she put her hand upon his arm, saying, in mingled tones of wretchedness and coaxing, 'I only repent it if you don't love me better than any woman in the world! I don't otherwise, Frank. You don't repent because you already love somebody better than you love me, do you?'

'I don't know. Why do you say that?'

'You won't burn that curl. You like the woman who owns that pretty hair – yes; it is pretty – more beautiful than my miserable black mane! Well, it is no use; I can't help being ugly. You must like her best, if you will!'

'Until to-day, when I took it from a drawer, I have never looked upon that bit of hair for several months – that I am ready to swear.'

'But just now you said "ties"; and then – that woman we met?'

''Twas the meeting with her that reminded me of the hair.'

'Is it hers, then?'

'Yes. There, now that you have wormed it out of me, I hope you are content.'

'And what are the ties?'

'Oh! that meant nothing – a mere jest.'

'A mere jest!' she said, in mournful astonishment. 'Can you jest when I am so wretchedly in earnest? Tell me the truth, Frank. I am not a fool, you know, although I am a woman, and have my woman's moments. Come! treat me fairly,' she said, looking honestly and fearlessly into his face. 'I don't want much; bare justice – that's all! Ah! once I felt I could be content with nothing less than the highest homage from the husband I should choose. Now, anything short of cruelty will content me. Yes! the independent and spirited Bathsheba is come to this!'

'For Heaven's sake don't be so desperate!' Troy said snappishly, rising as he did so, and leaving the room.

Directly he had gone, Bathsheba burst into great sobs – dry-eyed sobs, which cut as they came, without any softening by tears. But she determined to repress all evidences of feeling. She was conquered; but she would never own it as long as she lived. Her pride was indeed brought low by despairing discoveries of her spoliation by marriage with a less pure nature than her own. She chafed to and fro in rebelliousness, like a caged leopard; her whole soul was in arms, and the blood fired her face. Until she had met Troy, Bathsheba had been proud of her position as a woman; it had been a glory to her to know that her lips had been touched by no man's on earth – that her waist had never been encircled by a lover's arm. She hated herself now. In those earlier days she had always nourished a secret contempt for girls who were the slaves of the first good-looking young fellow who should choose to salute them. She had never taken kindly to the idea of marriage in the abstract as did the majority of women she saw about her. In the turmoil of her anxiety for her lover she had agreed to marry him; but the perception that had accompanied her happiest hours on this account was rather that of self-sacrifice than of promotion and honour. Although she scarcely knew the divinity's name, Diana was the goddess whom Bathsheba instinctively adored. That she had never, by look, word, or sign, encouraged a man to approach her – that she had felt herself sufficient to herself, and had in the independence of her girlish heart fancied there was a certain degradation in renouncing the simplicity of a maiden existence to become the humbler half of an indifferent matrimonial whole – were facts now bitterly remembered. O, if she had never stooped to folly of this kind, respectable as it was, and could only stand again, as she had stood on the hill at Norcombe, and dare Troy or any other man to pollute a hair of her head by his interference!

The next morning she rose earlier than usual, and had the horse saddled for her ride round the farm in the customary way. When she came in at half-past eight – their usual hour for breakfasting – she was informed that her husband had risen, taken his breakfast, and driven off to Casterbridge with the gig and Poppet.

After breakfast she was cool and collected – quite herself in fact – and she rambled to the gate, intending to walk to another quarter of the farm, which she still personally superintended as well as her duties in the house would permit, continually, however, finding herself preceded in forethought by Gabriel Oak, for whom she began to entertain the genuine friendship of a sister. Of course, she sometimes thought of him in the light of an old lover, and had momentary imaginings of what life with him as a husband would have been like; also of life with Boldwood under the same conditions. But Bathsheba, though she could feel, was not much given to futile dreaming, and her musings under this head were short and entirely confined to the times when Troy's neglect was more than ordinarily evident.

She saw coming up the road a man like Mr. Boldwood. It was Mr. Boldwood. Bathsheba blushed painfully, and watched. The farmer stopped when still a long way off, and held up his hand to Gabriel Oak, who was in a footpath across the field. The two men then approached each other and seemed to engage in earnest conversation.

Thus they continued for a long time. Joseph Poorgrass now passed near them, wheeling a barrow of apples up the hill to Bathsheba's residence. Boldwood and Gabriel called to him, spoke to him for a few minutes, and then all three parted, Joseph immediately coming up the hill with his barrow.

Bathsheba, who had seen this pantomime with some surprise, experienced great relief when Boldwood turned back again. 'Well, what's the message, Joseph?' she said.

He set down his barrow, and, putting upon himself the refined aspect that a conversation with a lady required, spoke to Bathsheba over the gate.

'You'll never see Fanny Robin no more – use nor principal – ma'am.'

'Why?'

'Because she's dead in the Union.'

'Fanny dead – never!'

'Yes, ma'am.'

'What did she die from?'

'I don't know for certain; but I should be inclined to think it was from general neshness of constitution. She was such a limber maid that 'a could stand no hardship, even when I knowed her, and 'a went like a candle-snoff, so 'tis said. She

was took bad in the morning, and, being quite feeble and worn
out, she died in the evening. She belongs by law to our parish;
and Mr. Boldwood is going to send a waggon at three this
afternoon to fetch her home here and bury her.'

'Indeed I shall not let Mr. Boldwood do any such thing – I
shall do it! Fanny was my uncle's servant, and, although I only
knew her for a couple of days, she belongs to me. How very,
very sad this is! – the idea of Fanny being in a workhouse.'
Bathsheba had begun to know what suffering was, and she
spoke with real feeling. . . . 'Send across to Mr. Boldwood's,
and say that Mrs. Troy will take upon herself the duty of fetching an old servant of the family. . . . We ought not to put her in
a waggon; we'll get a hearse.'

'There will hardly be time, ma'am, will there?'

'Perhaps not,' she said, musingly. 'When did you say we
must be at the door – three o'clock?'

'Three o'clock this afternoon, ma'am, so to speak it.'

'Very well – you go with it. A pretty waggon is better than
an ugly hearse, after all. Joseph, have the new spring waggon
with the blue body and red wheels, and wash it very clean.
And, Joseph —'

'Yes, ma'am.'

'Carry with you some evergreens and flowers to put upon
her coffin – indeed, gather a great many, and completely bury
her in them. Get some boughs of laurustinus, and variegated
box, and yew, and boy's-love; ay, and some bunches of chry-
santhemum. And let old Pleasant draw her, because she knew
him so well.'

'I will, ma'am. I ought to have said that the Union, in the
form of four labouring men, will meet me when I gets to our
churchyard gate, and take her and bury her according to the
rites of the Board of Guardians, as by law ordained.'

'Dear me – Casterbridge Union – and is Fanny come to
this?' said Bathsheba, musing. 'I wish I had known of it sooner.
I thought she was far away. How long has she lived there?'

'On'y been there a day or two.'

'Oh! – then she has not been staying there as a regular inmate?'

'No. She first went to live in a garrison-town t'other side o' Wessex, and since then she's been picking up a living at seampstering in Melchester for several months, at the house of a very respectable widow-woman who takes in work of that sort. She only got handy the Union-house on Sunday morning 'a b'lieve, and 'tis supposed here and there that she had traipsed every step of the way from Melchester. Why she left her place I can't say, for I don't know; and as to a lie, why, I wouldn't tell it. That's the short of the story, ma'am.'

'Ah-h!'

No gem ever flashed from a rosy ray to a white one more rapidly than changed the young wife's countenance whilst this word came from her in a long-drawn breath. 'Did she walk along our turnpike-road?' she said, in a suddenly restless and eager voice.

'I believe she did. . . . Ma'am, shall I call Liddy? You bain't well, ma'am, surely? You look like a lily – so pale and fainty!'

'No; don't call her; it is nothing. When did she pass Weatherbury?'

'Last Saturday night.'

'That will do, Joseph; now you may go.'

'Certainly, ma'am.'

'Joseph, come hither a moment. What was the colour of Fanny Robin's hair?'

'Really, mistress, now that 'tis put to me so judge-and-jury like, I can't call to mind, if ye'll believe me!'

'Never mind; go on and do what I told you. Stop – well no, go on.'

She turned herself away from him, that he might no longer notice the mood which had set its sign so visibly upon her, and went indoors with a distressing sense of faintness and a beating brow. About an hour after, she heard the noise of the waggon and went out, still with a painful consciousness of her bewildered and troubled look. Joseph, dressed in his best suit of clothes, was putting in the horse to start. The shrubs and flowers were all piled in the waggon, as she had directed. Bathsheba hardly saw them now.

'Whose sweetheart did you say, Joseph?'

'I don't know, ma'am.'

'Are you quite sure?'

'Yes, ma'am, quite sure.'

'Sure of what?'

'I'm sure that all I know is that she arrived in the morning and died in the evening without further parley. What Oak and Mr. Boldwood told me was only these few words. "Little Fanny Robin is dead, Joseph," Gabriel said, looking in my face in his steady old way. I was very sorry, and I said, "Ah! – and how did she come to die?" "Well, she's dead in Casterbridge Union," he said; "and perhaps 'tisn't much matter about how she came to die. She reached the Union early Sunday morning, and died in the afternoon – that's clear enough." Then I asked what she'd been doing lately, and Mr. Boldwood turned round to me then, and left off spitting a thistle with the end of his stick. He told me about her having lived by seampstering in Melchester, as I mentioned to you, and that she walked there-from at the end of last week, passing near here Saturday night in the dusk. They then said I had better just name a hent of her death to you, and away they went. Her death might have been brought on by biding in the night wind, you know, ma'am; for people used to say she'd go off in a decline: she used to cough a good deal in winter time. However, 'tisn't much odds to us about that now, for 'tis all over.'

'Have you heard a different story at all?' She looked at him so intently that Joseph's eyes quailed.

'Not a word, mistress, I assure 'ee!' he said. 'Hardly anybody in the parish knows the news yet.'

'I wonder why Gabriel didn't bring the message to me himself. He mostly makes a point of seeing me upon the most trifling errand.' These words were merely murmured, and she was looking upon the ground.

'Perhaps he was busy, ma'am,' Joseph suggested. 'And sometimes he seems to suffer from things upon his mind, connected with the time when he was better off than 'a is now. 'A's rather a curious item, but a very understanding shepherd, and learned in books.'

'Did anything seem upon his mind whilst he was speaking to you about this?'

'I cannot but say that there did, ma'am. He was terrible down, and so was Farmer Boldwood.'

'Thank you, Joseph. That will do. Go on now, or you'll be late.'

Bathsheba, still unhappy, went indoors again. In the course of the afternoon she said to Liddy, who had been informed of the occurrence, 'What was the colour of poor Fanny Robin's hair? Do you know? I cannot recollect — I only saw her for a day or two.'

'It was light, ma'am; but she wore it rather short, and packed away under her cap, so that you would hardly notice it. But I have seen her let it down when she was going to bed, and it looked beautiful then. Real golden hair.'

'Her young man was a soldier, was he not?'

'Yes. In the same regiment as Mr. Troy. He says he knew him very well.'

'What, Mr. Troy says so? How came he to say that?'

'One day I just named it to him, and asked him if he knew Fanny's young man. He said, "O yes, he knew the young man as well as he knew himself, and that there wasn't a man in the regiment he liked better." '

'Ah! Said that, did he?'

'Yes; and he said there was a strong likeness between himself and the other young man, so that sometimes people mistook them —'

'Liddy, for Heaven's sake stop your talking!' said Bathsheba, with the nervous petulance that comes from worrying perceptions.

CHAPTER XLII

JOSEPH AND HIS BURDEN – BUCK'S HEAD

A WALL bounded the site of Casterbridge Union-house, except along a portion of the end. Here a high gable stood prominent, and it was covered like the front with a mat of ivy. In this gable was no window, chimney, ornament, or protuberance of any kind. The single feature appertaining to it, beyond the expanse of dark green leaves, was a small door.

The situation of the door was peculiar. The sill was three or four feet above the ground, and for a moment one was at a loss for an explanation of this exceptional altitude, till ruts immediately beneath suggested that the door was used solely for the passage of articles and persons to and from the level of a vehicle standing on the outside. Upon the whole, the door seemed to advertise itself as a species of Traitor's Gate translated to another sphere. That entry and exit hereby was only at rare intervals became apparent on noting that tufts of grass were allowed to flourish undisturbed in the chinks of the sill.

As the clock over the South-street Alms-house pointed to five minutes to three, a blue spring waggon, picked out with red, and containing boughs and flowers, passed the end of the street, and up towards this side of the building. Whilst the chimes were yet stammering out a shattered form of 'Malbrook,' Joseph Poorgrass rang the bell, and received directions to back his waggon against the high door under the gable. The door then opened, and a plain elm coffin was slowly thrust forth, and laid by two men in fustian along the middle of the vehicle.

One of the men then stepped up beside it, took from his pocket a lump of chalk, and wrote upon the cover the name and a few other words in a large scrawling hand. (We believe that they do these things more tenderly now, and provide a plate.) He covered the whole with a black cloth, threadbare, but decent, the tail-board of the waggon was returned to its place, one of the men handed a certificate of registry to Poorgrass, and both entered the door, closing it behind them. Their connection with her, short as it had been, was over for ever.

Joseph then placed the flowers as enjoined, and the evergreens around the flowers, till it was difficult to divine what the waggon contained; he smacked his whip, and the rather pleasing funeral car crept down the hill, and along the road to Weatherbury.

The afternoon drew on apace, and, looking to the right towards the sea as he walked beside the horse, Poorgrass saw strange clouds and scrolls of mist rolling over the long ridges which girt the landscape in that quarter. They came in yet greater volumes, and indolently crept across the intervening valleys, and around the withered papery flags of the moor and river brinks. Then their dank spongy forms closed in upon the sky. It was a sudden overgrowth of atmospheric fungi which had their roots in the neighbouring sea, and by the time that horse, man, and corpse entered Yalbury Great Wood, these silent workings of an invisible hand had reached them, and they were completely enveloped, this being the first arrival of the autumn fogs, and the first fog of the series.

The air was as an eye suddenly struck blind. The waggon and its load rolled no longer on the horizontal division between clearness and opacity, but were imbedded in an elastic body of a monotonous pallor throughout. There was no perceptible motion in the air, not a visible drop of water fell upon a leaf of the beeches, birches, and firs composing the wood on either side. The trees stood in an attitude of intentness, as if they waited longingly for a wind to come and rock them. A startling quiet overhung all surrounding things – so completely, that the crunching of the waggon-wheels was as a great noise, and small rustles, which had never obtained a hearing except by night, were distinctly individualized.

Joseph Poorgrass looked round upon his sad burden as it loomed faintly through the flowering laurustinus, then at the unfathomable gloom amid the high trees on each hand, indistinct, shadowless, and spectre-like in their monochrome of grey. He felt anything but cheerful, and wished he had the company even of a child or dog. Stopping the horse he listened. Not a footstep or wheel was audible anywhere around, and the dead silence was broken only by a heavy particle falling from a tree through the evergreens and alighting with a smart rap upon the coffin of poor Fanny. The fog had by this time saturated the trees, and this was the first dropping of water from the over-brimming leaves. The hollow echo of its fall reminded the waggoner painfully of the grim Leveller. Then hard by came down another drop, then two or three. Presently there was a continual tapping of these heavy drops upon the dead leaves, the road, and the travellers. The nearer boughs were beaded with the mist to the greyness of aged men, and the rusty-red leaves of the beeches were hung with similar drops, like diamonds on auburn hair.

At the roadside hamlet called Roy-Town, just beyond this wood, was the old inn Buck's Head. It was about a mile and a half from Weatherbury, and in the meridian times of stage-coach travelling had been the place where many coaches changed and kept their relays of horses. All the old stabling was now pulled down, and little remained besides the habitable inn itself, which, standing a little way back from the road, signified its existence to people far up and down the highway by a sign hanging from the horizontal bough of an elm on the opposite side of the way.

Travellers – for the variety *tourist* had hardly developed into a distinct species at this date – sometimes said in passing, when they cast their eyes up to the sign-bearing tree, that artists were fond of representing the signboard hanging thus, but that they themselves had never before noticed so perfect an instance in actual working order. It was near this tree that the waggon was standing into which Gabriel Oak crept on his first journey to

Weatherbury; but, owing to the darkness, the sign and the inn had been unobserved.

The manners of the inn were of the old-established type. Indeed, in the minds of its frequenters they existed as unalterable formulæ: *e.g.* –

> Rap with the bottom of your pint for more liquor.
> For tobacco, shout.
> In calling for the girl in waiting, say, 'Maid!'
> Ditto for the landlady, 'Old Soul!' etc., etc.

It was a relief to Joseph's heart when the friendly signboard came in view, and, stopping his horse immediately beneath it, he proceeded to fulfil an intention made a long time before. His spirits were oozing out of him quite. He turned the horse's head to the green bank, and entered the hostel for a mug of ale.

Going down into the kitchen of the inn, the floor of which was a step below the passage, which in its turn was a step below the road outside, what should Joseph see to gladden his eyes but two copper-coloured discs, in the form of the countenances of Mr. Jan Coggan and Mr. Mark Clark. These owners of the two most appreciative throats in the neighbourhood, within the pale of respectability, were now sitting face to face over a three-legged circular table, having an iron rim to keep cups and pots from being accidentally elbowed off; they might have been said to resemble the setting sun and the full moon shining *vis-à-vis* across the globe.

'Why, 'tis neighbour Poorgrass!' said Mark Clark. 'I'm sure your face don't praise your mistress's table, Joseph.'

'I've had a very pale companion for the last four miles,' said Joseph, indulging in a shudder toned down by resignation. 'And to speak the truth, 'twas beginning to tell upon me. I assure ye, I ha'n't seed the colour of victuals or drink since breakfast time this morning, and that was no more than a dew-bit afield.'

'Then drink, Joseph, and don't restrain yourself!' said Coggan, handing him a hooped mug three-quarters full.

Joseph drank for a moderately long time, then for a longer

time, saying, as he lowered the jug, "Tis pretty drinking – very pretty drinking, and is more than cheerful on my melancholy errand, so to speak it.'

'True, drink is a pleasant delight,' said Jan, as one who repeated a truism so familiar to his brain that he hardly noticed its passage over his tongue; and, lifting the cup, Coggan tilted his head gradually backwards, with closed eyes, that his expectant soul might not be diverted for one instant from its bliss by irrelevant surroundings.

'Well, I must be on again,' said Poorgrass. 'Not but that I should like another nip with ye; but the parish might lose confidence in me if I was seed here.'

'Where be ye trading o't to to-day, then, Joseph?'

'Back to Weatherbury. I've got poor little Fanny Robin in my waggon outside, and I must be at the churchyard gates at a quarter to five with her.'

'Ay – I've heard of it. And so she's nailed up in parish boards after all, and nobody to pay the bell shilling and the grave half-crown.'

'The parish pays the grave half-crown, but not the bell shilling, because the bell's a luxery: but 'a can hardly do without the grave, poor body. However, I expect our mistress will pay all.'

'A pretty maid as ever I see! But what's yer hurry, Joseph? The poor woman's dead, and you can't bring her to life, and you may as well sit down comfortable, and finish another with us.'

'I don't mind taking just the least thimbleful ye can dream of more with ye, sonnies. But only a few minutes, because 'tis as 'tis.'

'Of course, you'll have another drop. A man's twice the man afterwards. You feel so warm and glorious, and you whop and slap at your work without any trouble, and everything goes on like sticks a-breaking. Too much liquor is bad, and leads us to that horned man in the smoky house; but after all, many people haven't the gift of enjoying a wet, and since we be highly favoured with a power that way, we should make the most o't.'

'True,' said Mark Clark. ''Tis a talent the Lord has mercifully bestowed upon us, and we ought not to neglect it. But, what with the parsons and clerks and school-people and serious tea-parties, the merry old ways of good life have gone to the dogs – upon my carcase, they have!'

'Well, really, I must be onward again now,' said Joseph.

'Now, now, Joseph; nonsense! The poor woman is dead, isn't she, and what's your hurry?'

'Well, I hope Providence won't be in a way with me for my doings,' said Joseph, again sitting down. 'I've been troubled with weak moments lately, 'tis true. I've been drinky once this month already, and I did not go to church a-Sunday, and I dropped a curse or two yesterday; so I don't want to go too far for my safety. Your next world is your next world, and not to be squandered offhand.'

'I believe ye to be a chapel-member, Joseph. That I do.'

'Oh, no, no! I don't go so far as that.'

'For my part,' said Coggan, 'I'm staunch Church of England.'

'Ay, and faith, so be I,' said Mark Clark.

'I won't say much for myself; I don't wish to,' Coggan continued, with that tendency to talk on principles which is characteristic of the barley-corn. 'But I've never changed a single doctrine: I've stuck like a plaster to the old faith I was born in. Yes; there's this to be said for the Church, a man can belong to the Church and bide in his cheerful old inn, and never trouble or worry his mind about doctrines at all. But to be a meetinger, you must go to chapel in all winds and weathers, and make yerself as frantic as a skit. Not but that chapel-members be clever chaps enough in their way. They can lift up beautiful prayers out of their own heads, all about their families and shipwrecks in the newspaper.'

'They can – they can,' said Mark Clark, with corroborative feeling; 'but we Churchmen, you see, must have it all printed aforehand, or, dang it all, we should no more know what to say to a great gaffer like the Lord than babes unborn.'

'Chapel-folk be more hand-in-glove with them above than we,' said Joseph thoughtfully.

'Yes,' said Coggan. 'We know very well that if anybody do go to heaven, they will. They've worked hard for it, and they deserve to have it, such as 'tis. I bain't such a fool as to pretend that we who stick to the Church have the same chance as they, because we know we have not. But I hate a feller who'll change his old ancient doctrines for the sake of getting to heaven. I'd as soon turn king's-evidence for the few pounds you get. Why, neighbours, when every one of my taties were frosted, our Pa'son Thirdly were the man who gave me a sack for seed, though he hardly had one for his own use, and no money to buy 'em. If it hadn't been for him, I shouldn't hae had a tatie to put in my garden. D'ye think I'd turn after that? No, I'll stick to my side; and if we be in the wrong, so be it: I'll fall with the fallen!'

'Well said — very well said,' observed Joseph. — 'However, folks, I must be moving now: upon my life I must. Pa'son Thirdly will be waiting at the church gates, and there's the woman a-biding outside in the waggon.'

'Joseph Poorgrass, don't be so miserable! Pa'son Thirdly won't mind. He's a generous man; he's found me in tracts for years, and I've consumed a good many in the course of a long and shady life; but he's never been the man to cry out at the expense. Sit down.'

The longer Joseph Poorgrass remained, the less his spirit was troubled by the duties which devolved upon him this afternoon. The minutes glided by uncounted, until the evening shades began perceptibly to deepen, and the eyes of the three were but sparkling points on the surface of darkness. Coggan's repeater struck six from his pocket in the usual still small tones.

At that moment hasty steps were heard in the entry, and the door opened to admit the figure of Gabriel Oak, followed by the maid of the inn bearing a candle. He stared sternly at the one lengthy and two round faces of the sitters, which confronted him with the expressions of a fiddle and a couple of warming-pans. Joseph Poorgrass blinked, and shrank several inches into the background.

'Upon my soul, I'm ashamed of you; 'tis disgraceful, Joseph, disgraceful!' said Gabriel indignantly. 'Coggan, you call yourself a man, and don't know better than this.'

Coggan looked up indefinitely at Oak, one or other of his eyes occasionally opening and closing of its own accord, as if it were not a member, but a dozy individual with a distinct personality.

'Don't take on so, shepherd!' said Mark Clark, looking reproachfully at the candle, which appeared to possess special features of interest for his eyes.

'Nobody can hurt a dead woman,' at length said Coggan, with the precision of a machine. 'All that could be done for her is done – she's beyond us: and why should a man put himself in a tearing hurry for lifeless clay that can neither feel nor see, and don't know what you do with her at all? If she'd been alive, I would have been the first to help her. If she now wanted victuals and drink, I'd pay for it, money down. But she's dead, and no speed of ours will bring her to life. The woman's past us – time spent upon her is throwed away: why should we hurry to do what's not required? Drink, shepherd, and be friends, for to-morrow we may be like her.'

'We may,' added Mark Clark emphatically, at once drinking himself, to run no further risk of losing his chance by the event alluded to, Jan meanwhile merging his additional thoughts of to-morrow in a song: –

'To-mor-row, to-mor-row!

And while peace and plen-ty I find at my board,
    With a heart free from sick-ness and sor-row,
With my friends will I share what to-day may af-ford,
    And let them spread the ta-ble to-mor-row.

To-mor-row, to-mor —'

'Do hold thy horning, Jan!' said Oak; and turning upon Poorgrass, 'as for you, Joseph, who do your wicked deeds in such confoundedly holy ways, you are as drunk as you can stand.'

'No, Shepherd Oak, no! Listen to reason, shepherd. All that's the matter with me is the affliction called a multiplying eye, and that's how it is I look double to you – I mean, you look double to me.'

'A multiplying eye is a very bad thing,' said Mark Clark.

'It always comes on when I have been in a public-house a little time,' said Joseph Poorgrass meekly. 'Yes; I see two of every sort, as if I were some holy man living in the times of King Noah and entering into the ark. . . . Y-y-y-yes,' he added, becoming much affected by the picture of himself as a person thrown away, and shedding tears; 'I feel too good for England: I ought to have lived in Genesis by rights, like the other men of sacrifice, and then I shouldn't have b-b-been called a d-d-drunkard in such a way!'

'I wish you'd show yourself a man of spirit, and not sit whining there!'

'Show myself a man of spirit? . . . Ah, well! let me take the name of drunkard humbly – let me be a man of contrite knees – let it be! I know that I always do say "Please God" afore I do anything, from my getting up to my going down of the same, and I be willing to take as much disgrace as there is in that holy act. Hah, yes! . . . But not a man of spirit? Have I ever allowed the toe of pride to be lifted against my hinder parts without groaning manfully that I question the right to do so? I inquire that query boldly?'

'We can't say that you have, Hero Poorgrass,' admitted Jan.

'Never have I allowed such treatment to pass unquestioned! Yet the shepherd says in the face of that rich testimony that I be not a man of spirit! Well, let it pass by, and death is a kind friend!'

Gabriel, seeing that neither of the three was in a fit state to take charge of the waggon for the remainder of the journey, made no reply, but, closing the door again upon them, went across to where the vehicle stood, now getting indistinct in the fog and gloom of this mildewy time. He pulled the horse's head from the large patch of turf it had eaten bare, readjusted the boughs over the coffin, and drove along through the unwholesome night.

It had gradually become rumoured in the village that the body to be brought and buried that day was all that was left of the unfortunate Fanny Robin who had followed the Eleventh from Casterbridge through Melchester and onwards. But, thanks to Boldwood's reticence and Oak's generosity, the lover she had followed had never been individualized as Troy. Gabriel hoped that the whole truth of the matter might not be published till at any rate the girl had been in her grave for a few days, when the interposing barriers of earth and time, and a sense that the events had been somewhat shut into oblivion, would deaden the sting that revelation and invidious remark would have for Bathsheba just now.

By the time that Gabriel reached the old manor-house, her residence, which lay in his way to the church, it was quite dark. A man came from the gate and said through the fog, which hung between them like blown flour —

'Is that Poorgrass with the corpse?'

Gabriel recognized the voice as that of the parson.

'The corpse is here, sir,' said Gabriel.

'I have just been to inquire of Mrs. Troy if she could tell me the reason of the delay. I am afraid it is too late now for the funeral to be performed with proper decency. Have you the registrar's certificate?'

'No,' said Gabriel. 'I expect Poorgrass has that: and he's at the Buck's Head. I forgot to ask him for it.'

'Then that settles the matter. We'll put off the funeral till tomorrow morning. The body may be brought on to the church, or it may be left here at the farm and fetched by the bearers in the morning. They waited more than an hour, and have now gone home.'

Gabriel had his reasons for thinking the latter a most objectionable plan, notwithstanding that Fanny had been an inmate of the farm-house for several years in the lifetime of Bathsheba's uncle. Visions of several unhappy contingencies which might arise from this delay flitted before him. But his will was not law, and he went indoors to inquire of his mistress what were her wishes on the subject. He found her in an unusual mood: her eyes as she looked up to him were suspicious and perplexed as with some antecedent thought. Troy had not yet returned. At first Bathsheba assented with a mien of indifference to his proposition that they should go on to the church at once with their burden; but immediately afterwards, following Gabriel to the gate, she swerved to the extreme of solicitousness on Fanny's account, and desired that the girl might be brought into the house. Oak argued upon the convenience of leaving her in the waggon, just as she lay now, with her flowers and green leaves about her, merely wheeling the vehicle into the coach-house till the morning, but to no purpose. 'It is unkind and unchristian,' she said, 'to leave the poor thing in a coach-house all night.'

'Very well, then,' said the parson. 'And I will arrange that the funeral shall take place early tomorrow. Perhaps Mrs. Troy is right in feeling that we cannot treat a dead fellow-creature too thoughtfully. We must remember that though she may have erred grievously in leaving her home, she is still our sister; and it is to be believed that God's uncovenanted mercies are extended towards her, and that she is a member of the flock of Christ.'

The parson's words spread into the heavy air with a sad yet unperturbed cadence, and Gabriel shed an honest tear. Bathsheba seemed unmoved. Mr. Thirdly then left them, and Gabriel lighted a lantern. Fetching three other men to assist him, they bore the unconscious truant indoors, placing the coffin on two benches in the middle of a little sitting-room next the hall, as Bathsheba directed.

Every one except Gabriel Oak then left the room. He still indecisively lingered beside the body. He was deeply troubled at the wretchedly ironical aspect that circumstances were putting on with regard to Troy's wife, and at his own power-lessness to counteract them. In spite of his careful manœuvring all this day, the very worst event that could in any way have happened in connection with the burial had happened now. Oak imagined a terrible discovery resulting from this after-noon's work that might cast over Bathsheba's life a shade which the interposition of many lapsing years might but indifferently lighten, and which nothing at all might altogether remove.

Suddenly, as in a last attempt to save Bathsheba from, at any rate, immediate anguish, he looked again, as he had looked before, at the chalk writing upon the coffin-lid. The scrawl was this simple one, '*Fanny Robin and child.*' Gabriel took his hand-kerchief and carefully rubbed out the two latter words, leaving visible the inscription '*Fanny Robin*' only. He then left the room, and went out quietly by the front door.

CHAPTER XLIII

FANNY'S REVENGE

'Do you want me any longer, ma'am?' inquired Liddy, at a later hour the same evening, standing by the door with a chamber candlestick in her hand, and addressing Bathsheba, who sat cheerless and alone in the large parlour beside the first fire of the season.

'No more to-night, Liddy.'

'I'll sit up for master if you like, ma'am. I am not at all afraid of Fanny, if I may sit in my own room and have a candle. She was such a childlike, nesh young thing that her spirit couldn't appear to anybody if it tried, I'm quite sure.'

'O no, no! You go to bed. I'll sit up for him myself till twelve o'clock, and if he has not arrived by that time, I shall give him up and go to bed too.'

'It is half-past ten now.'

'Oh: is it?'

'Why don't you sit upstairs, ma'am?'

'Why don't I?' said Bathsheba desultorily. 'It isn't worth while – there's a fire here, Liddy.' She suddenly exclaimed in an impulsive and excited whisper, 'Have you heard anything strange said of Fanny?' The words had no sooner escaped her than an expression of unutterable regret crossed her face, and she burst into tears.

'No – not a word!' said Liddy, looking at the weeping woman with astonishment. 'What is it makes you cry so, ma'am; has anything hurt you?' She came to Bathsheba's side with a face full of sympathy.

'No, Liddy – I don't want you any more. I can hardly say why I have taken so to crying lately: I never used to cry. Good-night.'

Liddy then left the parlour and closed the door.

Bathsheba was lonely and miserable now; not lonelier actually than she had been before her marriage; but her loneliness then was to that of the present time as the solitude of a mountain is to the solitude of a cave. And within the last day or two had come these disquieting thoughts about her husband's past. Her wayward sentiment that evening concerning Fanny's temporary resting-place had been the result of a strange complication of impulses in Bathsheba's bosom. Perhaps it would be more accurately described as a determined rebellion against her prejudices, a revulsion from a lower instinct of uncharitableness, which would have withheld all sympathy from the dead woman, because in life she had preceded Bathsheba in the attentions of a man whom Bathsheba had by no means ceased from loving, though her love was sick to death just now with the gravity of a further misgiving.

In five or ten minutes there was another tap at the door. Liddy reappeared, and coming in a little way stood hesitating, until at length she said, 'Maryann has just heard something very strange, but I know it isn't true. And we shall be sure to know the rights of it in a day or two.'

'What is it?'

'Oh, nothing connected with you or us, ma'am. It is about Fanny. That same thing you have heard.'

'I have heard nothing.'

'I mean that a wicked story is got to Weatherbury within this last hour – that —' Liddy came close to her mistress and whispered the remainder of the sentence slowly into her ear, inclining her head as she spoke in the direction of the room where Fanny lay.

Bathsheba trembled from head to foot.

'I don't believe it!' she said excitedly. 'And there's only one name written on the coffin-cover.'

'Nor I, ma'am. And a good many others don't; for we should surely have been told more about it if it had been true – don't you think so, ma'am?'

'We might or we might not.'

Bathsheba turned and looked into the fire, that Liddy might not see her face. Finding that her mistress was going to say no more, Liddy glided out, closed the door softly, and went to bed.

Bathsheba's face, as she continued looking into the fire that evening, might have excited solicitousness on her account even among those who loved her least. The sadness of Fanny Robin's fate did not make Bathsheba's glorious, although she was the Esther to this poor Vashti, and their fates might be supposed to stand in some respects as contrasts to each other. When Liddy came into the room a second time the beautiful eyes which met hers had worn a listless, weary look. When she went out after telling the story they had expressed wretchedness in full activity. Her simple country nature, fed on old-fashioned principles, was troubled by that which would have troubled a woman of the world very little, both Fanny and her child, if she had one, being dead.

Bathsheba had grounds for conjecturing a connection between her own history and the dimly suspected tragedy of Fanny's end which Oak and Boldwood never for a moment credited her with possessing. The meeting with the lonely woman on the previous Saturday night had been unwitnessed and unspoken of. Oak may have had the best of intentions in withholding for as many days as possible the details of what had happened to Fanny; but had he known that Bathsheba's perceptions had already been exercised in the matter, he would have done nothing to lengthen the minutes of suspense she was now undergoing, when the certainty which must terminate it would be the worst fact suspected after all.

She suddenly felt a longing desire to speak to some one stronger than herself, and so get strength to sustain her surmised position with dignity and her carking doubts with stoicism. Where could she find such a friend? nowhere in the house. She was by far the coolest of the women under her roof. Patience and suspension of judgment for a few hours were what she wanted to learn, and there was nobody to teach her. Might she but go to Gabriel Oak! – but that could not be. What a way Oak had, she thought, of enduring things. Boldwood, who seemed so much deeper and higher and stronger in feeling than Gabriel, had not yet learnt, any more than she herself, the simple lesson which Oak showed a mastery of by every turn and look he gave – that among the multitude of interests by which he was surrounded, those which affected his personal well-being were not the most absorbing and important in his eyes. Oak meditatively looked upon the horizon of circumstances without any special regard to his own standpoint in the midst. That was how she would wish to be. But then Oak was not racked by incertitude upon the inmost matter of his bosom, as she was at this moment. Oak knew all about Fanny that she wished to know – she felt convinced of that. If she were to go to him now at once and say no more than these few words, 'What is the truth of the story?' he would feel bound in honour to tell her. It would be an inexpressible relief. No further speech would need to be uttered. He knew her so well that no eccentricity of behaviour in her would alarm him.

She flung a cloak round her, went to the door and opened it. Every blade, every twig was still. The air was yet thick with moisture, though somewhat less dense than during the afternoon, and a steady smack of drops upon the fallen leaves under the boughs was almost musical in its soothing regularity. It seemed better to be out of the house than within it, and Bathsheba closed the door, and walked slowly down the lane till she came opposite to Gabriel's cottage, where he now lived alone, having left Coggan's house through being pinched for room. There was a light in one window only, and that was downstairs. The shutters were not closed, nor was any blind or curtain drawn over the window, neither robbery nor observation being a contingency which could do much injury to the occupant of the domicile. Yes, it was Gabriel himself who was sitting up: he was reading. From her standing-place in the road she could see him plainly, sitting quite still, his light curly head upon his hand, and only occasionally looking up to snuff the candle which stood beside him. At length he looked at the clock, seemed surprised at the lateness of the hour, closed his book, and arose. He was going to bed, she knew, and if she tapped it must be done at once.

Alas for her resolve! She felt she could not do it. Not for worlds now could she give a hint about her misery to him, much less ask him plainly for information on the cause of Fanny's death. She must suspect, and guess, and chafe, and bear it all alone.

Like a homeless wanderer she lingered by the bank, as if lulled and fascinated by the atmosphere of content which seemed to spread from that little dwelling, and was so sadly lacking in her own. Gabriel appeared in an upper room, placed his light in the window-bench, and then – knelt down to pray. The contrast of the picture with her rebellious and agitated existence at this same time was too much for her to bear to look upon longer. It was not for her to make a truce with trouble by any such means. She must tread her giddy distracting measure to its last note, as she had begun it. With a swollen heart she went again up the lane, and entered her own door.

More fevered now by a reaction from the first feelings which Oak's example had raised in her, she paused in the hall, looking at the door of the room wherein Fanny lay. She locked her fingers, threw back her head, and strained her hot hands rigidly across her forehead, saying, with a hysterical sob, 'Would to God you would speak and tell me your secret, Fanny! . . . O, I hope, hope it is not true that there are two of you! . . . If I could only look in upon you for one little minute, I should know all!'

A few moments passed, and she added, slowly, '*And I will.*'

Bathsheba in after times could never gauge the mood which carried her through the actions following this murmured resolution on this memorable evening of her life. She went to the lumber-closet for a screw-driver. At the end of a short though undefined time she found herself in the small room, quivering with emotion, a mist before her eyes, and an excruciating pulsation in her brain, standing beside the uncovered coffin of the girl whose conjectured end had so entirely engrossed her, and saying to herself in a husky voice as she gazed within —

'It was best to know the worst, and I know it now!'

She was conscious of having brought about this situation by a series of actions done as by one in an extravagant dream; of following that idea as to method, which had burst upon her in the hall with glaring obviousness, by gliding to the top of the stairs, assuring herself by listening to the heavy breathing of her maids that they were asleep, gliding down again, turning the handle of the door within which the young girl lay, and deliberately setting herself to do what, if she had anticipated any such undertaking at night and alone, would have horrified her, but which, when done, was not so dreadful as was the conclusive proof of her husband's conduct which came with knowing beyond doubt the last chapter of Fanny's story.

Bathsheba's head sank upon her bosom, and the breath which had been bated in suspense, curiosity, and interest, was exhaled now in the form of a whispered wail: 'Oh-h-h!' she said, and the silent room added length to her moan.

Her tears fell fast beside the unconscious pair in the coffin: tears of a complicated origin, of a nature indescribable, almost indefinable except as other than those of simple sorrow. Assuredly their wonted fires must have lived in Fanny's ashes when events were so shaped as to chariot her hither in this natural, unobtrusive, yet effectual manner. The one feat alone – that of dying – by which a mean condition could be resolved into a grand one, Fanny had achieved. And to that had destiny subjoined this rencounter to-night, which had, in Bathsheba's wild imagining, turned her companion's failure to success, her humiliation to triumph, her lucklessness to ascendancy; it had thrown over herself a garish light of mockery, and set upon all things about her an ironical smile.

Fanny's face was framed in by that yellow hair of hers; and there was no longer much room for doubt as to the origin of the curl owned by Troy. In Bathsheba's heated fancy the innocent white countenance expressed a dim triumphant consciousness of the pain she was retaliating for her pain with all the merciless rigour of the Mosaic law: 'Burning for burning; wound for wound; strife for strife.'

Bathsheba indulged in contemplations of escape from her position by immediate death, which, thought she, though it was an inconvenient and awful way, had limits to its inconvenience and awfulness that could not be overpassed; whilst the shames of life were measureless. Yet even this scheme of extinction by death was but tamely copying her rival's method without the reasons which had glorified it in her rival's case. She glided rapidly up and down the room, as was mostly her habit when excited, her hands hanging clasped in front of her, as she thought and in part expressed in broken words: 'O, I hate her, yet I don't mean that I hate her, for it is grievous and wicked; and yet I hate her a little! Yes, my flesh insists upon hating her, whether my spirit is willing or no! . . . If she had only lived, I could have been angry and cruel towards her with some justification; but to be vindictive towards a poor dead woman recoils upon myself. O God, have mercy! I am miserable at all this!'

Bathsheba became at this moment so terrified at her own state of mind that she looked around for some sort of refuge from herself. The vision of Oak kneeling down that night recurred to her, and with the imitative instinct which animates women she seized upon the idea, resolved to kneel, and, if possible, pray. Gabriel had prayed; so would she.

She knelt beside the coffin, covered her face with her hands, and for a time the room was silent as a tomb. Whether from a purely mechanical, or from any other cause, when Bathsheba arose it was with a quieted spirit, and a regret for the antagonistic instincts which had seized upon her just before.

In her desire to make atonement she took flowers from a vase by the window, and began laying them around the dead girl's head. Bathsheba knew no other way of showing kindness to persons departed than by giving them flowers. She knew not how long she remained engaged thus. She forgot time, life, where she was, what she was doing. A slamming together of the coach-house doors in the yard brought her to herself again. An instant after, the front door opened and closed, steps crossed the hall, and her husband appeared at the entrance to the room, looking in upon her.

He beheld it all by degrees, stared in stupefaction at the scene, as if he thought it an illusion raised by some fiendish incantation. Bathsheba, pallid as a corpse on end, gazed back at him in the same wild way.

So little are instinctive guesses the fruit of a legitimate induction that, at this moment, as he stood with the door in his hand, Troy never once thought of Fanny in connection with what he saw. His first confused idea was that somebody in the house had died.

'Well – what?' said Troy blankly.

'I must go! I must go!' said Bathsheba, to herself more than to him. She came with a dilated eye towards the door, to push past him.

'What's the matter, in God's name? who's dead?' said Troy.

'I cannot say; let me go out. I want air!' she continued.

'But no; stay, I insist!' He seized her hand, and then volition seemed to leave her, and she went off into a state of passivity. He, still holding her, came up the room, and thus, hand in hand, Troy and Bathsheba approached the coffin's side.

The candle was standing on a bureau close by them, and the light slanted down, distinctly enkindling the cold features of both mother and babe. Troy looked in, dropped his wife's hand, knowledge of it all came over him in a lurid sheen, and he stood still.

So still he remained that he could be imagined to have left in him no motive power whatever. The clashes of feeling in all directions confounded one another, produced a neutrality, and there was motion in none.

'Do you know her?' said Bathsheba, in a small enclosed echo, as from the interior of a cell.

'I do,' said Troy.

'Is it she?'

'It is.'

He had originally stood perfectly erect. And now, in the well-nigh congealed immobility of his frame could be discerned an incipient movement, as in the darkest night may be discerned light after a while. He was gradually sinking forwards. The lines of his features softened, and dismay modulated to illimitable sadness. Bathsheba was regarding him from the other side, still with parted lips and distracted eyes. Capacity for intense feeling is proportionate to the general intensity of the nature, and perhaps in all Fanny's sufferings, much greater relatively to her strength, there never was a time when she suffered in an absolute sense what Bathsheba suffered now.

What Troy did was to sink upon his knees with an indefinable union of remorse and reverence upon his face, and, bending over Fanny Robin, gently kissed her, as one would kiss an infant asleep to avoid awakening it.

At the sight and sound of that, to her, unendurable act, Bathsheba sprang towards him. All the strong feelings which had been scattered over her existence since she knew what feeling was, seemed gathered together into one pulsation now. The revulsion from her indignant mood a little earlier, when she had meditated upon compromised honour, forestalment, eclipse in maternity by another, was violent and entire. All that was forgotten in the simple and still strong attachment of wife to husband. She had sighed for her self-completeness then, and now she cried aloud against the severance of the union she had deplored. She flung her arms round Troy's neck, exclaiming wildly from the deepest deep of her heart —

'Don't – don't kiss them! O, Frank, I can't bear it – I can't! I love you better than she did: kiss me too, Frank – kiss me! *You will, Frank, kiss me too!*'

There was something so abnormal and startling in the childlike pain and simplicity of this appeal from a woman of Bathsheba's calibre and independence, that Troy, loosening her tightly clasped arms from his neck, looked at her in bewilderment. It was such an unexpected revelation of all women being alike at heart, even those so different in their accessories as Fanny and this one beside him, that Troy could hardly seem to believe her to be his proud wife Bathsheba. Fanny's own spirit seemed to be animating her frame. But this was the mood of a few instants only. When the momentary surprise had passed, his expression changed to a silencing imperious gaze.

'I will not kiss you!' he said, pushing her away.

Had the wife now but gone no further. Yet, perhaps, under the harrowing circumstances, to speak out was the one wrong act which can be better understood, if not forgiven in her, than the right and politic one, her rival being now but a corpse. All the feeling she had been betrayed into showing she drew back to herself again by a strenuous effort of self-command.

'What have you to say as your reason?' she asked, her bitter voice being strangely low – quite that of another woman now.

'I have to say that I have been a bad, black-hearted man,' he answered.

'And that this woman is your victim; and I not less than she.'

'Ah! don't taunt me, madam. This woman is more to me, dead as she is, than ever you were, or are, or can be. If Satan had not tempted me with that face of yours, and those cursed coquetries, I should have married her. I never had another thought till you came in my way. Would to God that I had; but it is all too late! I deserve to live in torment for this!' He turned to Fanny then. 'But never mind, darling,' he said; 'in the sight of Heaven you are my very, very wife!'

At these words there arose from Bathsheba's lips a long, low cry of measureless despair and indignation, such a wail of anguish as had never before been heard within those old-inhabited walls. It was the Τετέλεσται of her union with Troy.

'If she's – that, – what – am I?' she added, as a continuation of the same cry, and sobbing pitifully: and the rarity with her of such abandonment only made the condition more dire.

'You are nothing to me – nothing,' said Troy heartlessly. 'A ceremony before a priest doesn't make a marriage. I am not morally yours.'

A vehement impulse to flee from him, to run from this place, hide, and escape his words at any price, not stopping short of death itself, mastered Bathsheba now. She waited not an instant, but turned to the door and ran out.

CHAPTER XLIV

UNDER A TREE – REACTION

BATHSHEBA went along the dark road, neither knowing nor caring about the direction or issue of her flight. The first time that she definitely noticed her position was when she reached a gate leading into a thicket overhung by some large oak and beech trees. On looking into the place, it occurred to her that she had seen it by daylight on some previous occasion, and that what appeared like an impassable thicket was in reality a brake of fern now withering fast. She could think of nothing better to do with her palpitating self than to go in here and hide; and entering, she lighted on a spot sheltered from the damp fog by a reclining trunk, where she sank down upon a tangled couch of fronds and stems. She mechanically pulled some armfuls round her to keep off the breezes, and closed her eyes.

Whether she slept or not that night Bathsheba was not clearly aware. But it was with a freshened existence and a cooler brain that, a long time afterwards, she became conscious of some interesting proceedings which were going on in the trees above her head and around.

A coarse-throated chatter was the first sound.

It was a sparrow just waking.

Next: 'Chee-weeze-weeze-weeze!' from another retreat.

It was a finch.

Third: 'Tink-tink-tink-tink-a-chink!' from the hedge.

It was a robin.

'Chuck-chuck-chuck!' overhead.

A squirrel.

Then, from the road, 'With my ra-ta-ta, and my rum-tum-tum!'

326

It was a ploughboy. Presently he came opposite, and she believed from his voice that he was one of the boys on her own farm. He was followed by a shambling tramp of heavy feet, and looking through the ferns Bathsheba could just discern in the wan light of daybreak a team of her own horses. They stopped to drink at a pond on the other side of the way. She watched them flouncing into the pool, drinking, tossing up their heads, drinking again, the water dribbling from their lips in silver threads. There was another flounce, and they came out of the pond, and turned back again towards the farm.

She looked further around. Day was just dawning, and beside its cool air and colours her heated actions and resolves of the night stood out in lurid contrast. She perceived that in her lap, and clinging to her hair, were red and yellow leaves which had come down from the tree and settled silently upon her during her partial sleep. Bathsheba shook her dress to get rid of them, when multitudes of the same family lying round about her rose and fluttered away in the breeze thus created, 'like ghosts from an enchanter fleeing.'

There was an opening towards the east, and the glow from the as yet unrisen sun attracted her eyes thither. From her feet, and between the beautiful yellowing ferns with their feathery arms, the ground sloped downwards to a hollow, in which was a species of swamp, dotted with fungi. A morning mist hung over it now – a fulsome yet magnificent silvery veil, full of light from the sun, yet semi-opaque – the hedge behind it being in some measure hidden by its hazy luminousness. Up the sides of this depression grew sheaves of the common rush, and here and there a peculiar species of flag, the blades of which glistened in the emerging sun, like scythes. But the general aspect of the swamp was malignant. From its moist and poisonous coat seemed to be exhaled the essences of evil things in the earth, and in the waters under the earth. The fungi grew in all manner of positions from rotting leaves and tree stumps, some exhibiting to her listless gaze their clammy tops, others their oozing gills. Some were marked with great splotches, red as arterial blood, others were saffron yellow, and others tall and attenuated, with stems like macaroni. Some were leathery and of richest browns. The hollow seemed a nursery of pestilences small and great, in the immediate neighbourhood of comfort and health, and Bathsheba arose with a tremor at the thought of having passed the night on the brink of so dismal a place.

There were now other footsteps to be heard along the road. Bathsheba's nerves were still unstrung: she crouched down out of sight again, and the pedestrian came into view. He was a schoolboy, with a bag slung over his shoulder containing his dinner, and a book in his hand. He paused by the gate, and, without looking up, continued murmuring words in tones quite loud enough to reach her ears.

' "O Lord, O Lord, O Lord, O Lord, O Lord": – that I know out o'book. "Give us, give us, give us, give us, give us": – that I know. "Grace that, grace that, grace that, grace that": – that I know.' Other words followed to the same effect. The boy was of the dunce class apparently ; the book was a psalter, and this was his way of learning the collect. In the worst attacks of trouble there appears to be always a superficial film of consciousness which is left disengaged and open to the notice of trifles, and Bathsheba was faintly amused at the boy's method, till he too passed on.

By this time stupor had given place to anxiety, and anxiety began to make room for hunger and thirst. A form now appeared upon the rise on the other side of the swamp, half-hidden by the mist, and came towards Bathsheba. The woman – for it was a woman – approached with her face askance, as if looking earnestly on all sides of her. When she got a little further round to the left, and drew nearer, Bathsheba could see the newcomer's profile against the sunny sky, and knew the wavy sweep from forehead to chin, with neither angle nor decisive line anywhere about it, to be the familiar contour of Liddy Smallbury.

Bathsheba's heart bounded with gratitude in the thought that she was not altogether deserted, and she jumped up. 'O,

Liddy!' she said, or attempted to say; but the words had only been framed by her lips; there came no sound. She had lost her voice by exposure to the clogged atmosphere all these hours of night.

'O, ma'am! I am so glad I have found you,' said the girl, as soon as she saw Bathsheba.

'You can't come across,' Bathsheba said in a whisper, which she vainly endeavoured to make loud enough to reach Liddy's ears. Liddy, not knowing this, stepped down upon the swamp, saying, as she did so, 'It will bear me up, I think.'

Bathsheba never forgot that transient little picture of Liddy crossing the swamp to her there in the morning light. Iridescent bubbles of dank subterranean breath rose from the sweating sod beside the waiting-maid's feet as she trod, hissing as they burst and expanded away to join the vapoury firmament above. Liddy did not sink, as Bathsheba had anticipated.

She landed safely on the other side, and looked up at the beautiful though pale and weary face of her young mistress.

'Poor thing!' said Liddy, with tears in her eyes. 'Do hearten yourself up a little, ma'am. However did —'

'I can't speak above a whisper – my voice is gone for the present,' said Bathsheba hurriedly. 'I suppose the damp air from that hollow has taken it away. Liddy, don't question me, mind. Who sent you – anybody?'

'Nobody. I thought, when I found you were not at home, that something cruel had happened. I fancy I heard his voice late last night; and so, knowing something was wrong —'

'Is he at home?'

'No; he left just before I came out.'

'Is Fanny taken away?'

'Not yet. She will soon be – at nine o'clock.'

'We won't go home at present, then. Suppose we walk about in this wood?'

Liddy, without exactly understanding everything, or any thing, in this episode, assented, and they walked together further among the trees.

'But you had better come in, ma'am, and have something to eat. You will die of a chill!'

'I shall not come indoors yet – perhaps never.'

'Shall I get you something to eat, and something else to put over your head besides that little shawl?'

'If you will, Liddy.'

Liddy vanished, and at the end of twenty minutes returned with a cloak, hat, some slices of bread and butter, a tea-cup, and some hot tea in a little china jug.

'Is Fanny gone?' said Bathsheba.

'No,' said her companion, pouring out the tea.

Bathsheba wrapped herself up and ate and drank sparingly. Her voice was then a little clearer, and a trifling colour returned to her face. 'Now we'll walk about again,' she said.

They wandered about the wood for nearly two hours, Bathsheba replying in monosyllables to Liddy's prattle, for her mind ran on one subject, and one only. She interrupted with –

'I wonder if Fanny is gone by this time?'

'I will go and see.'

She came back with the information that the men were just taking away the corpse; that Bathsheba had been inquired for; that she had replied to the effect that her mistress was unwell and could not be seen.

'Then they think I am in my bedroom?'

'Yes.' Liddy then ventured to add: 'You said when I first found you that you might never go home again – you didn't mean it, ma'am?'

'No; I've altered my mind. It is only women with no pride in them who run away from their husbands. There is one position worse than that of being found dead in your husband's house from his ill-usage, and that is, to be found alive through having gone away to the house of somebody else. I've thought of it all this morning, and I've chosen my course. A runaway wife is an encumbrance to everybody, a burden to herself and a byword – all of which make up a heap of misery greater than any that comes by staying at home – though this may include the trifling items of insult, beating, and starvation. Liddy, if ever you marry – God forbid that you ever should! – you'll find yourself in a fearful situation; but mind this, don't you flinch. Stand your ground, and be cut to pieces. That's what I'm going to do.'

'O, mistress, don't talk so!' said Liddy, taking her hand, 'but I knew you had too much sense to bide away. May I ask what dreadful thing it is that has happened between you and him?'

' You may ask; but I may not tell.'

In about ten minutes they returned to the house by a circuit-ous route, entering at the rear. Bathsheba glided up the back stairs to a disused attic, and her companion followed.

'Liddy,' she said, with a lighter heart, for youth and hope had begun to reassert themselves; 'you are to be my confidante for the present – somebody must be – and I choose you. Well, I shall take up my abode here for a while. Will you get a fire lighted, put down a piece of carpet, and help me to make the place comfortable? Afterwards, I want you and Maryann to bring up that little stump bedstead in the small room, and the bed belonging to it, and a table, and some other things. . . . What shall I do to pass the heavy time away?'

'Hemming handkerchiefs is a very good thing,' said Liddy.

'O no, no! I hate needlework – I always did.'

'Knitting?'

'And that, too.'

'You might finish your sampler. Only the carnations and peacocks want filling in; and then it could be framed and glazed, and hung beside your aunt's, ma'am.'

'Samplers are out of date – horribly countrified. No, Liddy, I'll read. Bring up some books – not new ones. I haven't heart to read anything new.'

'Some of your uncle's old ones, ma'am?'

'Yes. Some of those we stowed away in boxes.' A faint gleam of humour passed over her face as she said: 'Bring Beaumont and Fletcher's *Maid's Tragedy*; and the *Mourning Bride*; and – let me see – *Night Thoughts*, and the *Vanity of Human Wishes*.'

'And that story of the black man, who murdered his wife Desdemona? It is a nice dismal one that would suit you excellent just now.'

'Now, Lidd, you've been looking into my books, without telling me; and I said you were not to! How do you know it would suit me? It wouldn't suit me at all.'

'But if the others do —'

'No, they don't; and I won't read dismal books. Why should I read dismal books, indeed? Bring me *Love in a Village*, and the *Maid of the Mill*, and *Doctor Syntax*, and some volumes of the *Spectator*.'

All that day Bathsheba and Liddy lived in the attic in a state of barricade; a precaution which proved to be needless as against Troy, for he did not appear in the neighbourhood or trouble them at all. Bathsheba sat at the window till sunset, sometimes attempting to read, at other times watching every movement outside without much purpose, and listening without much interest to every sound.

The sun went down almost blood-red that night, and a livid cloud received its rays in the east. Up against this dark background the west front of the church tower – the only part of the edifice visible from the farm-house windows – rose distinct and lustrous, the vane upon the summit bristling with rays. Hereabouts, at six o'clock, the young men of the village gathered, as was their custom, for a game of Prisoners' base. The spot had been consecrated to this ancient diversion from time immemorial, the old stocks conveniently forming a base facing the boundary of the churchyard, in front of which the ground was trodden hard and bare as a pavement by the players. She could see the brown and black heads of the young lads darting about right and left, their white shirt-sleeves gleaming in the sun; whilst occasionally a shout and a peal of hearty laughter varied the stillness of the evening air. They continued playing for a quarter of an hour or so, when the game concluded abruptly, and the players leapt over the wall and vanished round to the other side behind a yew-tree, which was also half behind a beech, now spreading in one mass of golden foliage, on which the branches traced black lines.

'Why did the base-players finish their game so suddenly?' Bathsheba inquired, the next time that Liddy entered the room.

'I think 'twas because two men came just then from Caster-bridge and began putting up a grand carved tombstone,' said Liddy. 'The lads went to see whose it was.'

'Do you know?' Bathsheba asked.

'I don't,' said Liddy.

CHAPTER XLV

TROY'S ROMANTICISM

WHEN Troy's wife had left the house at the previous midnight his first act was to cover the dead from sight. This done he ascended the stairs, and throwing himself down upon the bed dressed as he was, he waited miserably for the morning.

Fate had dealt grimly with him through the last four-and-twenty hours. His day had been spent in a way which varied very materially from his intentions regarding it. There is always an inertia to be overcome in striking out a new line of conduct – not more in ourselves, it seems, than in circumscribing events, which appear as if leagued together to allow no novelties in the way of amelioration.

Twenty pounds having been secured from Bathsheba, he had managed to add to the sum every farthing he could muster on his own account, which had been seven pounds ten. With this money, twenty-seven pounds ten in all, he had hastily driven from the gate that morning to keep his appointment with Fanny Robin.

On reaching Casterbridge he left the horse and trap at an inn, and at five minutes before ten came back to the bridge at the lower end of the town, and sat himself upon the parapet. The clocks struck the hour, and no Fanny appeared. In fact, at that moment she was being robed in her grave-clothes by two attendants at the Union poorhouse – the first and last tiring-women the gentle creature had ever been honoured with. The quarter went, the half hour. A rush of recollection came upon Troy as he waited: this was the second time she had broken a serious engagement with him. In anger he vowed it should be the last, and at eleven o'clock, when he had lingered and watched the stones of the bridge till he knew every lichen upon their faces, and heard the chink of the ripples underneath till they oppressed him, he jumped from his seat, went to the inn for his gig, and in a bitter mood of indifference concerning the past, and recklessness about the future, drove on to Budmouth races.

He reached the race-course at two o'clock, and remained either there or in the town till nine. But Fanny's image, as it had appeared to him in the sombre shadows of that Saturday evening, returned to his mind, backed up by Bathsheba's reproaches. He vowed he would not bet, and he kept his vow, for on leaving the town at nine o'clock in the evening he had diminished his cash only to the extent of a few shillings.

He trotted slowly homeward, and it was now that he was struck for the first time with a thought that Fanny had been really prevented by illness from keeping her promise. This time she could have made no mistake. He regretted that he had not remained in Casterbridge and made inquiries. Reaching home he quietly unharnessed the horse and came indoors, as we have seen, to the fearful shock that awaited him.

As soon as it grew light enough to distinguish objects, Troy arose from the coverlet of the bed, and in a mood of absolute indifference to Bathsheba's whereabouts, and almost oblivious of her existence, he stalked downstairs and left the house by the back door. His walk was towards the churchyard, entering which he searched around till he found a newly dug unoccupied grave – the grave dug the day before for Fanny. The position of this having been marked, he hastened on to Casterbridge, only pausing and musing for a while at the hill whereon he had last seen Fanny alive.

Reaching the town, Troy descended into a side street and entered a pair of gates surmounted by a board bearing the words, 'Lester, stone and marble mason.' Within were laying about stones of all sizes and designs, inscribed as being sacred to the memory of unnamed persons who had not yet died.

Troy was so unlike himself now in look, word, and deed,

that the want of likeness was perceptible even to his own consciousness. His method of engaging himself in this business of
purchasing a tomb was that of an absolutely unpractised man.
He could not bring himself to consider, calculate, or eco-
nomize. He waywardly wished for something, and he set about
obtaining it like a child in a nursery. 'I want a good tomb,' he
said to the man who stood in a little office within the yard.
'I want as good a one as you can give me for twenty-seven
pounds.'

It was all the money he possessed.

'That sum to include everything?'

'Everything. Cutting the name, carriage to Weatherbury,
and erection. And I want it now, at once.'

'We could not get anything special worked this week.'

'I must have it now.'

'If you would like one of these in stock it could be got ready
immediately.'

'Very well,' said Troy, impatiently. 'Let's see what you have.'

'The best I have in stock is this one,' said the stone-cut-
ter, going into a shed. 'Here's a marble headstone beautifully
crocketed, with medallions beneath of typical subjects; here's
the footstone after the same pattern, and here's the coping to
enclose the grave. The polishing alone of the set cost me
eleven pounds – the slabs are the best of their kind, and I can
warrant them to resist rain and frost for a hundred years without flying.'

'And how much?'

'Well, I could add the name, and put it up at Weatherbury
for the sum you mention.'

'Get it done to-day, and I'll pay the money now.'

The man agreed, and wondered at such a mood in a visitor
who wore not a shred of mourning. Troy then wrote the words
which were to form the inscription, settled the account and
went away. In the afternoon he came back again, and found
that the lettering was almost done. He waited in the yard till
the tomb was packed, and saw it placed in the cart and starting

on its way to Weatherbury, giving directions to the two men who were to accompany it to inquire of the sexton for the grave of the person named in the inscription.

It was quite dark when Troy came out of Casterbridge. He carried rather a heavy basket upon his arm, with which he strode moodily along the road, resting occasionally at bridges and gates, whereon he deposited his burden for a time. Midway on his journey he met, returning in the darkness, the men and the waggon which had conveyed the tomb. He merely inquired if the work was done, and, on being assured that it was, passed on again.

Troy entered Weatherbury churchyard about ten o'clock, and went immediately to the corner where he had marked the vacant grave early in the morning. It was on the obscure side of the tower, screened to a great extent from the view of passers along the road − a spot which until lately had been abandoned to heaps of stones and bushes of alder, but now it was cleared and made orderly for interments, by reason of the rapid filling of the ground elsewhere.

Here now stood the tomb as the men had stated, snow-white and shapely in the gloom, consisting of head and foot stone, and enclosing border of marble-work uniting them. In the midst was mould, suitable for plants.

Troy deposited his basket beside the tomb, and vanished for a few minutes. When he returned he carried a spade and a lantern, the light of which he directed for a few moments upon the marble, whilst he read the inscription. He hung his lantern on the lowest bough of the yew-tree, and took from his basket flower-roots of several varieties. There were bundles of snow-drop, hyacinth and crocus bulbs, violets and double daisies, which were to bloom in early spring, and of carnations, pinks, picotees, lilies of the valley, forget-me-not, summer's farewell, meadow-saffron and others, for the later seasons of the year.

Troy laid these out upon the grass, and with an impassive face set to work to plant them. The snowdrops were arranged in a line on the outside of the coping, the remainder within the enclosure of the grave. The crocuses and hyacinths were to grow in rows; some of the summer flowers he placed over her head and feet, the lilies and forget-me-nots over her heart. The remainder were dispersed in the spaces between these.

Troy, in his prostration at this time, had no perception that in the futility of these romantic doings, dictated by a remorseful reaction from previous indifference, there was any element of absurdity. Deriving his idiosyncrasies from both sides of the Channel, he showed at such junctures as the present the inelasticity of the Englishman, together with that blindness to the line where sentiment verges on mawkishness, characteristic of the French.

It was a cloudy, muggy, and very dark night, and the rays from Troy's lantern spread into the two old yews with a strange illuminating power, flickering, as it seemed, up to the black ceiling of cloud above. He felt a large drop of rain upon the back of his hand, and presently one came and entered one of the holes of the lantern, whereupon the candle sputtered and went out. Troy was weary, and it being now not far from midnight, and the rain threatening to increase, he resolved to leave the finishing touches of his labour until the day should break. He groped along the wall and over the graves in the dark till he found himself round at the north side. Here he entered the porch, and, reclining upon the bench within, fell asleep.

CHAPTER XLVI

THE GURGOYLE: ITS DOINGS

THE tower of Weatherbury Church was a square erection of fourteenth-century date, having two stone gurgoyles on each of the four faces of its parapet. Of these eight carved protuberances only two at this time continued to serve the purpose of their erection – that of spouting the water from the lead roof within. One mouth in each front had been closed by bygone church-wardens as superfluous, and two others were broken away and choked – a matter not of much consequence to the well-being of the tower, for the two mouths which still remained open and active were gaping enough to do all the work.

It has been sometimes argued that there is no truer criterion of the vitality of any given art-period than the power of the master-spirits of that time in grotesque; and certainly in the instance of Gothic art there is no disputing the proposition. Weatherbury tower was a somewhat early instance of the use of an ornamental parapet in parish as distinct from cathedral churches, and the gurgoyles, which are the necessary correlatives of a parapet, were exceptionally prominent – of the boldest cut that the hand could shape, and of the most original design that a human brain could conceive. There was, so to speak, that symmetry in their distortion which is less the characteristic of British than of Continental grotesques of the period. All the eight were different from each other. A beholder was convinced that nothing on earth could be more hideous than those he saw on the north side until he went round to the south. Of the two on this latter face, only that at the south-eastern corner concerns the story. It was too human to be called like a dragon, too impish to be like a man, too animal to be like a fiend, and not enough like a bird to be called a griffin. This horrible stone entity was fashioned as if covered with a wrinkled hide; it had short, erect ears, eyes starting from their sockets, and its fingers and hands were seizing the corners of its mouth, which they thus seemed to pull open to give free passage to the water it vomited. The lower row of teeth was quite washed away, though the upper still remained. Here and thus, jutting a couple of feet from the wall against which its feet rested as a support, the creature had for four hundred years laughed at the surrounding landscape, voicelessly in dry weather, and in wet with a gurgling and snorting sound.

Troy slept on in the porch, and the rain increased outside. Presently the gurgoyle spat. In due time a small stream began to trickle through the seventy feet of aerial space between its mouth and the ground, which the water-drops smote like duckshot in their accelerated velocity. The stream thickened in substance, and increased in power, gradually spouting further and yet further from the side of the tower. When the rain fell in a steady and ceaseless torrent the stream dashed downward in volumes.

We follow its course to the ground at this point of time. The end of the liquid parabola has come forward from the wall, has advanced over the plinth mouldings, over a heap of stones, over the marble border, into the midst of Fanny Robin's grave.

The force of the stream had, until very lately, been received upon some loose stones spread thereabout, which had acted as a shield to the soil under the onset. These during the summer had been cleared from the ground, and there was now nothing to resist the downfall but the bare earth. For several years the stream had not spouted so far from the tower as it was doing on this night, and such a contingency had been overlooked. Sometimes this obscure corner received no inhabitant for the space of two or three years, and then it was usually but a pauper, a poacher, or other sinner of undignified sins.

The persistent torrent from the gurgoyle's jaws directed all its vengeance into the grave. The rich tawny mould was stirred into motion, and boiled like chocolate. The water accumulated and washed deeper down, and the roar of the pool thus formed spread into the night as the head and chief among other noises of the kind created by the deluging rain. The flowers so carefully planted by Fanny's repentant lover began to move and writhe in their bed. The winter-violets turned slowly upside down, and became a mere mat of mud. Soon the snowdrop and other bulbs danced in the boiling mass like ingredients in a cauldron. Plants of the tufted species were loosened, rose to the surface, and floated off.

Troy did not awake from his comfortless sleep till it was broad day. Not having been in bed for two nights his shoulders felt stiff, his feet tender, and his head heavy. He remembered his position, arose, shivered, took the spade, and again went out.

The rain had quite ceased, and the sun was shining through the green, brown, and yellow leaves, now sparkling and varnished by the raindrops to the brightness of similar effects in the landscapes of Ruysdael and Hobbema, and full of all those infinite beauties that arise from the union of water and colour with high lights. The air was rendered so transparent by the heavy fall of rain that the autumn hues of the middle distance were as rich as those near at hand, and the remote fields intercepted by the angle of the tower appeared in the same plane as the tower itself.

He entered the gravel path which would take him behind the tower. The path, instead of being stony as it had been the night before, was browned over with a thin coating of mud. At one place in the path he saw a tuft of stringy roots washed white and clean as a bundle of tendons. He picked it up – surely it could not be one of the primroses he had planted? He saw a bulb, another, and another as he advanced. Beyond doubt they were the crocuses. With a face of perplexed dismay Troy turned the corner and then beheld the wreck the stream had made.

The pool upon the grave had soaked away into the ground, and in its place was a hollow. The disturbed earth was washed over the grass and pathway in the guise of the brown mud he had already seen, and it spotted the marble tombstone with the same stains. Nearly all the flowers were washed clean out of the ground, and they lay, roots upwards, on the spots whither they had been splashed by the stream.

Troy's brow became heavily contracted. He set his teeth closely, and his compressed lips moved as those of one in great pain. This singular accident, by a strange confluence of emotions in him, was felt as the sharpest sting of all. Troy's face was very expressive, and any observer who had seen him now would hardly have believed him to be a man who had laughed, and sung, and poured love-trifles into a woman's ear. To curse his miserable lot was at first his impulse, but even that lowest stage of rebellion needed an activity whose absence was necessarily antecedent to the existence of the morbid misery which wrung him. The sight, coming as it did, superimposed upon the other dark scenery of the previous days, formed a sort of climax to the whole panorama, and it was more than he could endure. Sanguine by nature, Troy had a power of eluding grief by simply adjourning it. He could put off the consideration of any particular spectre till the matter had become old and softened by time. The planting of flowers on Fanny's grave had been perhaps but a species of elusion of the primary grief, and now it was as if his intention had been known and circumvented.

Almost for the first time in his life Troy, as he stood by this dismantled grave, wished himself another man. It is seldom that a person with much animal spirit does not feel that the fact of his life being his own is the one qualification which singles it out as a more hopeful life than that of others who may actually resemble him in every particular. Troy had felt, in his transient way, hundreds of times, that he could not envy other people their condition, because the possession of that condition would have necessitated a different personality, when he desired no other than his own. He had not minded the peculiarities of his birth, the vicissitudes of his life, the meteor-like uncertainty of all that related to him, because these appertained to the hero

of his story, without whom there would have been no story at
all for him; and it seemed to be only in the nature of things
that matters would right themselves at some proper date and
wind up well. This very morning the illusion completed its
disappearance, and, as it were, all of a sudden, Troy hated
himself. The suddenness was probably more apparent than
real. A coral reef which just comes short of the ocean surface
is no more to the horizon than if it had never been begun, and
the mere finishing stroke is what often appears to create an
event which has long been potentially an accomplished thing.

He stood and meditated – a miserable man. Whither should
he go? 'He that is accursed, let him be accursed still,' was the
pitiless anathema written in this spoliated effort of his new-
born solicitousness. A man who has spent his primal strength
in journeying in one direction has not much spirit left for re-
versing his course. Troy had, since yesterday, faintly reversed
his; but the merest opposition had disheartened him. To turn
about would have been hard enough under the greatest
providential encouragement; but to find that Providence, far
from helping him into a new course, or showing any wish that
he might adopt one, actually jeered his first trembling and criti
cal attempt in that kind, was more than nature could bear.

He slowly withdrew from the grave. He did not attempt to
fill up the hole, replace the flowers, or do anything at all. He
simply threw up his cards and forswore his game for that time
and always. Going out of the churchyard silently and unobserved – none of the villagers having yet risen – he passed down
some fields at the back, and emerged just as secretly upon the
high road. Shortly afterwards he had gone from the village.

Meanwhile, Bathsheba remained a voluntary prisoner in the
attic. The door was kept locked, except during the entries and
exits of Liddy, for whom a bed had been arranged in a small
adjoining room. The light of Troy's lantern in the churchyard
was noticed about ten o'clock by the maid-servant, who
casually glanced from the window in that direction whilst taking
her supper, and she called Bathsheba's attention to it. They

looked curiously at the phenomenon for a time, until Liddy was sent to bed.

Bathsheba did not sleep very heavily that night. When her attendant was unconscious and softly breathing in the next room, the mistress of the house was still looking out of the window at the faint gleam spreading from among the trees – not in a steady shine, but blinking like a revolving coast-light, though this appearance failed to suggest to her that a person was passing and repassing in front of it. Bathsheba sat here till it began to rain, and the light vanished, when she withdrew to lie restlessly in her bed and re-enact in a worn mind the lurid scene of yesternight.

Almost before the first faint sign of dawn appeared she arose again, and opened the window to obtain a full breathing of the new morning air, the panes being now wet with trembling tears left by the night rain, each one rounded with a pale lustre caught from primrose-hued slashes through a cloud low down in the awakening sky. From the trees came the sound of steady dripping upon the drifted leaves under them, and from the direction of the church she could hear another noise – peculiar, and not intermittent like the rest, the purl of water falling into a pool.

Liddy knocked at eight o'clock, and Bathsheba unlocked the door.

'What a heavy rain we've had in the night, ma'am!' said Liddy, when her inquiries about breakfast had been made.

'Yes; very heavy.'

'Did you hear the strange noise from the churchyard?'

'I heard one strange noise. I've been thinking it must have been the water from the tower spouts.'

'Well, that's what the shepherd was saying, ma'am. He's now gone on to see.'

'Oh! Gabriel has been here this morning?'

'Only just looked in in passing – quite in his old way, which I thought he had left off lately. But the tower spouts used to spatter on the stones, and we are puzzled, for this was like the boiling of a pot.'

Not being able to read, think, or work, Bathsheba asked Liddy to stay and breakfast with her. The tongue of the more childish woman still ran upon recent events. 'Are you going across to the church, ma'am?' she asked.

'Not that I know of,' said Bathsheba.

'I thought you might like to go and see where they have put Fanny. The trees hide the place from your window.'

Bathsheba had all sorts of dreads about meeting her husband. 'Has Mr. Troy been in to-night?' she said.

'No, ma'am; I think he's gone to Budmouth.'

Budmouth! The sound of the word carried with it a much diminished perspective of him and his deeds; there were thirteen miles interval betwixt them now. She hated questioning Liddy about her husband's movements, and indeed had hitherto sedulously avoided doing so; but now all the house knew that there had been some dreadful disagreement between them, and it was futile to attempt disguise. Bathsheba had reached a stage at which people cease to have any appreciative regard for public opinion.

'What makes you think he has gone there?' she said.

'Laban Tall saw him on the Budmouth road this morning before breakfast.'

Bathsheba was momentarily relieved of that wayward heaviness of the past twenty-four hours which had quenched the vitality of youth in her without substituting the philosophy of maturer years, and she resolved to go out and walk a little way. So when breakfast was over she put on her bonnet, and took a direction towards the church. It was nine o'clock, and the men having returned to work again from their first meal, she was not likely to meet many of them in the road. Knowing that Fanny had been laid in the reprobates' quarter of the graveyard, called in the parish 'behind church,' which was invisible from the road, it was impossible to resist the impulse to enter and look upon a spot which, from nameless feelings, she at the same time dreaded to see. She had been unable to overcome an impression that some connection existed between her rival and the light through the trees.

Bathsheba skirted the buttress, and beheld the hole and the tomb, its delicately veined surface splashed and stained just as Troy had seen it and left it two hours earlier. On the other side of the scene stood Gabriel. His eyes, too, were fixed on the tomb, and her arrival having been noiseless, she had not as yet attracted his attention. Bathsheba did not at once perceive that the grand tomb and the disturbed grave were Fanny's, and she looked on both sides and around for some humbler mound, earthed up and clodded in the usual way. Then her eye followed Oak's, and she read the words with which the inscription opened: –

> 'Erected by Francis Troy in Beloved Memory
> of Fanny Robin.'

Oak saw her, and his first act was to gaze inquiringly and learn how she received this knowledge of the authorship of the work, which to himself had caused considerable astonishment. But such discoveries did not much affect her now. Emotional convulsions seemed to have become the commonplaces of her history, and she bade him good morning, and asked him to fill in the hole with the spade which was standing by. Whilst Oak was doing as she desired, Bathsheba collected the flowers, and began planting them with that sympathetic manipulation of roots and leaves which is so conspicuous in a woman's gardening, and which flowers seem to understand and thrive upon. She requested Oak to get the churchwardens to turn the leadwork at the mouth of the gurgoyle that hung gaping down upon them, that by this means the stream might be directed sideways, and a repetition of the accident prevented. Finally, with the superfluous magnanimity of a woman whose narrower instincts have brought down bitterness upon her instead of love, she wiped the mud spots from the tomb as if she rather liked its words than otherwise, and went again home.[1]

---

1 The local tower and churchyard do not answer precisely to the foregoing description.

CHAPTER XLVII

ADVENTURES BY THE SHORE

TROY wandered along towards the south. A composite feeling, made up of disgust with the, to him, humdrum tediousness of a farmer's life, gloomy images of her who lay in the church-yard, remorse, and a general averseness to his wife's society, impelled him to seek a home in any place on earth save Weatherbury. The sad accessories of Fanny's end confronted him as vivid pictures which threatened to be indelible, and made life in Bathsheba's house intolerable. At three in the afternoon he found himself at the foot of a slope more than a mile in length, which ran to the ridge of a range of hills lying parallel with the shore, and formed a monotonous barrier between the basin of cultivated country inland and the wilder scenery of the coast. Up the hill stretched a road nearly straight and perfectly white, the two sides approaching each other in a gradual taper till they met the sky at the top about two miles off. Throughout the length of this narrow and irksome inclined plane not a sign of life was visible on this garish afternoon. Troy toiled up the road with a languor and depression greater than any he had experienced for many a day and year before. The air was warm and muggy, and the top seemed to recede as he approached.

At last he reached the summit, and a wide and novel prospect burst upon him with an effect almost like that of the Pacific upon Balboa's gaze. The broad steely sea, marked only by faint lines, which had a semblance of being etched thereon to a degree not deep enough to disturb its general evenness, stretched the whole width of his front and round to the right, where, near the town and port of Budmouth, the sun bristled

347

down upon it, and banished all colour, to substitute in its place a clear oily polish. Nothing moved in sky, land, or sea, except a frill of milkwhite foam along the nearer angles of the shore, shreds of which licked the contiguous stones like tongues.

He descended and came to a small basin of sea enclosed by the cliffs. Troy's nature freshened within him; he thought he would rest and bathe here before going further. He undressed and plunged in. Inside the cove the water was uninteresting to a swimmer, being smooth as a pond, and to get a little of the ocean swell Troy presently swam between the two projecting spurs of rock which formed the pillars of Hercules to this mini-ature Mediterranean. Unfortunately for Troy a current un-known to him existed outside, which, unimportant to craft of any burden, was awkward for a swimmer who might be taken in it unawares. Troy found himself carried to the left and then round in a swoop out to sea.

He now recollected the place and its sinister character. Many bathers had there prayed for a dry death from time to time, and, like Gonzalo also, had been unanswered; and Troy began to deem it possible that he might be added to their number. Not a boat of any kind was at present within sight, but far in the distance Budmouth lay upon the sea, as it were quietly regarding his efforts, and beside the town the harbour showed its position by a dim meshwork of ropes and spars. After well-nigh exhausting himself in attempts to get back to the mouth of the cove, in his weakness swimming several inches deeper than was his wont, keeping up his breathing entirely by his nostrils, turning upon his back a dozen times over, swim-ming *en papillon*, and so on, Troy resolved as a last resource to tread water at a slight incline, and so endeavour to reach the shore at any point, merely giving himself a gentle impetus in-wards whilst carried on in the general direction of the tide. This, necessarily a slow process, he found to be not altogether so difficult, and though there was no choice of a landing-place – the objects on shore passing by him in a sad and slow proces-sion – he perceptibly approached the extremity of a spit of land yet further to the right, now well defined against the sunny portion of the horizon. While the swimmer's eyes were fixed upon the spit as his only means of salvation on this side of the Unknown, a moving object broke the outline of the extremity, and immediately a ship's boat appeared, manned with several sailor lads, her bows towards the sea.

All Troy's vigour spasmodically revived to prolong the struggle yet a little further. Swimming with his right arm, he held up his left to hail them, splashing upon the waves, and shouting with all his might. From the position of the setting sun his white form was distinctly visible upon the now deep-hued bosom of the sea to the east of the boat, and the men saw him at once. Backing their oars and putting the boat about, they pulled towards him with a will, and in five or six minutes from the time of his first halloo, two of the sailors hauled him in over the stern.

They formed part of a brig's crew, and had come ashore for sand. Lending him what little clothing they could spare among them as a slight protection against the rapidly cooling air, they agreed to land him in the morning; and without further delay, for it was growing late, they made again towards the roadstead where their vessel lay.

And now night drooped slowly upon the wide watery levels in front; and at no great distance from them, where the shore-line curved round, and formed a long riband of shade upon the horizon, a series of points of yellow light began to start into existence, denoting the spot to be the site of Budmouth, where the lamps were being lighted along the parade. The cluck of their oars was the only sound of any distinctness upon the sea, and as they laboured amid the thickening shades the lamp-lights grew larger, each appearing to send a flaming sword deep down into the waves before it, until there arose, among other dim shapes of the kind, the form of the vessel for which they were bound.

CHAPTER XLVIII

DOUBTS ARISE – DOUBTS LINGER

BATHSHEBA underwent the enlargement of her husband's absence from hours to days with a slight feeling of surprise, and a slight feeling of relief; yet neither sensation rose at any time far above the level commonly designated as indifference. She belonged to him: the certainties of that position were so well defined, and the reasonable probabilities of its issue so bounded, that she could not speculate on contingencies. Taking no further interest in herself as a splendid woman, she acquired the indifferent feelings of an outsider in contemplating her probable fate as a singular wretch; for Bathsheba drew herself and her future in colours that no reality could exceed for darkness. Her original vigorous pride of youth had sickened, and with it had declined all her anxieties about coming years, since anxiety recognizes a better and a worse alternative, and Bathsheba had made up her mind that alternatives on any noteworthy scale had ceased for her. Soon, or later – and that not very late – her husband would be home again. And then the days of their tenancy of the Upper Farm would be numbered. There had originally been shown by the agent to the estate some distrust of Bathsheba's tenure as James Everdene's successor, on the score of her sex, and her youth, and her beauty; but the peculiar nature of her uncle's will, his own frequent testimony before his death to her cleverness in such a pursuit, and her vigorous marshalling of the numerous flocks and herds which came suddenly into her hands before negotiations were concluded, had won confidence in her powers, and no further objections had been raised. She had latterly been in great doubt as to what the legal effects of her marriage would be upon her position; but no notice had been taken as yet of her change of name, and only one point was clear – that in the event of her own or her husband's inability to meet the agent at the forthcoming January rent-day, very little consideration would be shown, and, for that matter, very little would be deserved. Once out of the farm the approach of poverty would be sure.

Hence Bathsheba lived in a perception that her purposes were broken off. She was not a woman who could hope on without good materials for the process, differing thus from the less far-sighted and energetic, though more petted ones of the sex, with whom hope goes on as a sort of clockwork which the merest food and shelter are sufficient to wind up; and perceiving clearly that her mistake had been a fatal one, she accepted her position, and waited coldly for the end.

The first Saturday after Troy's departure she went to Casterbridge alone, a journey she had not before taken since her marriage. On this Saturday Bathsheba was passing slowly on foot through the crowd of rural business-men gathered as usual in front of the market-house, who were as usual gazed upon by the burghers with feelings that those healthy lives were dearly paid for by exclusion from possible aldermanship, when a man, who had apparently been following her, said some words to another on her left hand. Bathsheba's ears were keen as those of any wild animal, and she distinctly heard what the speaker said, though her back was towards him.

'I am looking for Mrs. Troy. Is that she there?'

'Yes; that's the young lady, I believe,' said the person addressed.

'I have some awkward news to break to her. Her husband is drowned.'

As if endowed with the spirit of prophecy, Bathsheba gasped out, 'No, it is not true; it cannot be true!' Then she said and heard no more. The ice of self-command which had latterly gathered over her was broken, and the currents burst forth again, and overwhelmed her. A darkness came into her eyes, and she fell.

But not to the ground. A gloomy man, who had been observing her from under the portico of the old corn-exchange when she passed through the group without, stepped quickly to her side at the moment of her exclamation, and caught her in his arms as she sank down.

'What is it?' said Boldwood, looking up at the bringer of the big news, as he supported her.

'Her husband was drowned this week while bathing in Lulwind Cove. A coastguardsman found his clothes, and brought them into Budmouth yesterday.'

Thereupon a strange fire lighted up Boldwood's eye, and his face flushed with the suppressed excitement of an unutterable thought. Everybody's glance was now centred upon him and the unconscious Bathsheba. He lifted her bodily off the ground, and smoothed down the folds of her dress as a child might have taken a storm-beaten bird and arranged its ruffled plumes, and bore her along the pavement to the King's Arms Inn. Here he passed with her under the archway into a private room; and by the time he had deposited – so lothly – the precious burden upon the sofa, Bathsheba had opened her eyes. Remembering all that had occurred, she murmured, 'I want to go home!'

Boldwood left the room. He stood for a moment in the passage to recover his senses. The experience had been too much for his consciousness to keep up with, and now that he had grasped it it had gone again. For those few heavenly, golden moments she had been in his arms. What did it matter about her not knowing it? She had been close to his breast; he had been close to hers.

He started onward again, and sending a woman to her, went out to ascertain all the facts of the case. These appeared to be limited to what he had already heard. He then ordered her horse to be put into the gig, and when all was ready returned to inform her. He found that, though still pale and unwell, she had in the meantime sent for the Budmouth man who brought the tidings, and learnt from him all there was to know.

Being hardly in a condition to drive home as she had driven to town, Boldwood, with every delicacy of manner and feeling, offered to get her a driver, or to give her a seat in his phaeton, which was more comfortable than her own conveyance. These proposals Bathsheba gently declined, and the farmer at once departed.

About half-an-hour later she invigorated herself by an effort, and took her seat and the reins as usual – in external appearance much as if nothing had happened. She went out of the town by a tortuous back street, and drove slowly along, unconscious of the road and the scene. The first shades of evening were showing themselves when Bathsheba reached home, where, silently alighting and leaving the horse in the hands of the boy, she proceeded at once upstairs. Liddy met her on the landing. The news had preceded Bathsheba to Weatherbury by half-an-hour, and Liddy looked inquiringly into her mistress's face. Bathsheba had nothing to say.

She entered her bedroom and sat by the window, and thought and thought till night enveloped her, and the extreme lines only of her shape were visible. Somebody came to the door, knocked, and opened it.

'Well, what is it, Liddy?' she said.

'I was thinking there must be something got for you to wear,' said Liddy, with hesitation.

'What do you mean?'

'Mourning.'

'No, no, no,' said Bathsheba hurriedly.

'But I suppose there must be something done for poor —'

'Not at present, I think. It is not necessary.'

'Why not, ma'am?'

'Because he's still alive.'

'How do you know that?' said Liddy, amazed.

'I don't know it. But wouldn't it have been different, or shouldn't I have heard more, or wouldn't they have found him, Liddy? – or – I don't know how it is, but death would have been different from how this is. I am perfectly convinced that he is still alive!'

Bathsheba remained firm in this opinion till Monday, when two circumstances conjoined to shake it. The first was a short paragraph in the local newspaper, which, beyond making by a methodizing pen formidable presumptive evidence of Troy's death by drowning, contained the important testimony of a young Mr. Barker, M.D., of Budmouth, who spoke to being an eyewitness of the accident, in a letter to the editor. In this he stated that he was passing over the cliff on the remoter side of the cove just as the sun was setting. At that time he saw a bather carried along in the current outside the mouth of the cove, and guessed in an instant that there was but a poor chance for him unless he should be possessed of unusual muscular powers. He drifted behind a projection of the coast, and Mr. Barker followed along the shore in the same direction. But by the time that he could reach an elevation sufficiently great to command a view of the sea beyond, dusk had set in, and nothing further was to be seen.

The other circumstance was the arrival of his clothes, when it became necessary for her to examine and identify them – though this had virtually been done long before by those who inspected the letters in his pockets. It was so evident to her in the midst of her agitation that Troy had undressed in the full conviction of dressing again almost immediately, that the notion that anything but death could have prevented him was a perverse one to entertain.

Then Bathsheba said to herself that others were assured in their opinion; strange that she should not be. A strange reflection occurred to her, causing her face to flush. Suppose that Troy had followed Fanny into another world. Had he done this intentionally, yet contrived to make his death appear like an accident? Nevertheless, this thought of how the apparent might differ from the real – made vivid by her bygone jealousy of Fanny, and the remorse he had shown that night – did not blind her to the perception of a likelier difference, less tragic, but to herself far more disastrous.

When alone late that evening beside a small fire, and much calmed down, Bathsheba took Troy's watch into her hand, which had been restored to her with the rest of the articles belonging to him. She opened the case as he had opened it before her a week ago. There was the little coil of pale hair which had been as the fuze to this great explosion.

'He was hers and she was his; they should be gone together,' she said. 'I am nothing to either of them, and why should I keep her hair?' She took it in her hand and held it over the fire. 'No – I'll not burn it – I'll keep it in memory of her, poor thing!' she added, snatching back her hand.

CHAPTER XLIX

OAK'S ADVANCEMENT – A GREAT HOPE

THE later autumn and the winter drew on apace, and the leaves lay thick upon the turf of the glades and the mosses of the woods. Bathsheba, having previously been living in a state of suspended feeling which was not suspense, now lived in a mood of quietude which was not precisely peacefulness. While she had known him to be alive she could have thought of his death with equanimity; but now that it might be she had lost him, she regretted that he was not hers still. She kept the farm going, raked in her profits without caring keenly about them, and expended money on ventures because she had done so in bygone days, which, though not long gone by, seemed infinitely removed from her present. She looked back upon that past over a great gulf, as if she were now a dead person, having the faculty of meditation still left in her, by means of which, like the mouldering gentlefolk of the poet's story, she could sit and ponder what a gift life used to be.

However, one excellent result of her general apathy was the long-delayed installation of Oak as bailiff; but he having virtually exercised that function for a long time already, the change, beyond the substantial increase of wages it brought, was little more than a nominal one addressed to the outside world.

Boldwood lived secluded and inactive. Much of his wheat and all his barley of that season had been spoilt by the rain. It sprouted, grew into intricate mats, and was ultimately thrown to the pigs in armfuls. The strange neglect which had produced this ruin and waste became the subject of whispered talk among all the people round; and it was elicited from one of

Boldwood's men that forgetfulness had nothing to do with it, for he had been reminded of the danger to his corn as many times and as persistently as inferiors dared to do. The sight of the pigs turning in disgust from the rotten ears seemed to arouse Boldwood, and he one evening sent for Oak. Whether it was suggested by Bathsheba's recent act of promotion or not, the farmer proposed at the interview that Gabriel should undertake the superintendence of the Lower Farm as well as of Bathsheba's, because of the necessity Boldwood felt for such aid, and the impossibility of discovering a more trustworthy man. Gabriel's malignant star was assuredly setting fast.

Bathsheba, when she learnt of this proposal – for Oak was obliged to consult her – at first languidly objected. She considered that the two farms together were too extensive for the observation of one man. Boldwood, who was apparently determined by personal rather than commercial reasons, suggested that Oak should be furnished with a horse for his sole use, when the plan would present no difficulty, the two farms lying side by side. Boldwood did not directly communicate with her during these negotiations, only speaking to Oak, who was the go-between throughout. All was harmoniously arranged at last, and we now see Oak mounted on a strong cob, and daily trotting the length and breadth of about two thousand acres in a cheerful spirit of surveillance, as if the crops all belonged to him – the actual mistress of the one-half, and the master of the other, sitting in their respective homes in gloomy and sad seclusion.

Out of this there arose, during the spring succeeding, a talk in the parish that Gabriel Oak was feathering his nest fast.

'Whatever d'ye think,' said Susan Tall, 'Gable Oak is coming it quite the dand. He now wears shining boots with hardly a hob in 'em, two or three times a-week, and a tall hat a-Sundays, and 'a hardly knows the name of smockfrock. When I see people strut enough to be cut up into bantam cocks, I stand dormant with wonder, and says no more!'

It was eventually known that Gabriel, though paid a fixed

wage by Bathsheba independent of the fluctuations of agricultural profits, had made an engagement with Boldwood by which Oak was to receive a share of the receipts – a small share certainly, yet it was money of a higher quality than mere wages, and capable of expansion in a way that wages were not. Some were beginning to consider Oak a 'near' man, for though his condition had thus far improved, he lived in no better style than before, occupying the same cottage, paring his own potatoes, mending his stockings, and sometimes even making his bed with his own hands. But as Oak was not only provokingly indifferent to public opinion, but a man who clung persistently to old habits and usages, simply because they were old, there was room for doubt as to his motives.

A great hope had latterly germinated in Boldwood, whose unreasoning devotion to Bathsheba could only be characterized as a fond madness which neither time nor circumstance, evil nor good report, could weaken or destroy. This fevered hope had grown up again like a grain of mustard-seed during the quiet which followed the hasty conjecture that Troy was drowned. He nourished it fearfully, and almost shunned the contemplation of it in earnest, lest facts should reveal the wildness of the dream. Bathsheba having at last been persuaded to wear mourning, her appearance as she entered the church in that guise was in itself a weekly addition to his faith that a time was coming – very far off perhaps, yet surely nearing – when his waiting on events should have its reward. How long he might have to wait he had not yet closely considered. What he would try to recognize was that the severe schooling she had been subjected to had made Bathsheba much more considerate than she had formerly been of the feelings of others, and he trusted that, should she be willing at any time in the future to marry any man at all, that man would be himself. There was a substratum of good feeling in her: her selfreproach for the injury she had thoughtlessly done him might be depended upon now to a much greater extent than before her infatuation and disappointment. It would be possible to approach her by the channel of her good nature, and to suggest a friendly business-like compact between them for fulfilment at some future day, keeping the passionate side of his desire entirely out of her sight. Such was Boldwood's hope.

To the eyes of the middle-aged, Bathsheba was perhaps additionally charming just now. Her exuberance of spirit was pruned down; the original phantom of delight had shown herself to be not too bright for human nature's daily food, and she had been able to enter this second poetical phase without losing much of the first in the process.

Bathsheba's return from a two months' visit to her old aunt at Norcombe afforded the impassioned and yearning farmer a pretext for inquiring directly after her – now possibly in the ninth month of her widowhood – and endeavouring to get a notion of her state of mind regarding him. This occurred in the middle of the haymaking, and Boldwood contrived to be near Liddy, who was assisting in the fields.

'I am glad to see you out of doors, Lydia,' he said pleasantly.

She simpered, and wondered in her heart why he should speak so frankly to her.

'I hope Mrs. Troy is quite well after her long absence,' he continued, in a manner expressing that the coldest-hearted neighbour could scarcely say less about her.

'She is quite well, sir.'

'And cheerful, I suppose.'

'Yes, cheerful.'

'Fearful, did you say?'

'O no. I merely said she was cheerful.'

'Tells you all her affairs?'

'No, sir.'

'Some of them?'

'Yes, sir.'

'Mrs. Troy puts much confidence in you, Lydia; and very wisely, perhaps.'

'She do, sir. I've been with her all through her troubles, and was with her at the time of Mr. Troy's going and all. And if she were to marry again I expect I should bide with her.'

'She promises that you shall – quite natural,' said the strategic lover, throbbing throughout him at the presumption which Liddy's words appeared to warrant – that his darling had thought of remarriage.

'No – she doesn't promise it exactly. I merely judge on my own account.'

'Yes, yes, I understand. When she alludes to the possibility of marrying again, you conclude —'

'She never do allude to it, sir,' said Liddy, thinking how very stupid Mr. Boldwood was getting.

'Of course not,' he returned hastily, his hope falling again. 'You needn't take quite such long reaches with your rake, Lydia – short and quick ones are best. Well, perhaps, as she is absolute mistress again now, it is wise of her to resolve never to give up her freedom.'

'My mistress did certainly once say, though not seriously, that she supposed she might marry again at the end of seven years from last year, if she cared to risk Mr. Troy's coming back and claiming her.'

'Ah, six years from the present time. Said that she might. She might marry at once in every reasonable person's opinion, whatever the lawyers may say to the contrary.'

'Have you been to ask them?' said Liddy innocently.

'Not I,' said Boldwood, growing red. 'Liddy, you needn't stay here a minute later than you wish, so Mr. Oak says. I am now going on a little further. Good-afternoon.'

He went away vexed with himself, and ashamed of having for this one time in his life done anything which could be called underhand. Poor Boldwood had no more skill in finesse than a battering-ram, and he was uneasy with a sense of having made himself to appear stupid and, what was worse, mean. But he had, after all, lighted upon one fact by way of repayment. It was a singularly fresh and fascinating fact, and though not without its sadness it was pertinent and real. In little more than six years from this time Bathsheba might certainly marry him. There was something definite in that hope, for admitting that there might have been no deep thought in her words to Liddy about marriage, they showed at least her creed on the matter.

This pleasant notion was now continually in his mind. Six years were a long time, but how much shorter than never, the idea he had for so long been obliged to endure! Jacob had served twice seven years for Rachel: what were six for such a woman as this? He tried to like the notion of waiting for her better than that of winning her at once. Boldwood felt his love to be so deep and strong and eternal, that it was possible she had never yet known its full volume, and this patience in delay would afford him an opportunity of giving sweet proof on the point. He would annihilate the six years of his life as if they were minutes — so little did he value his time on earth beside her love. He would let her see, all those six years of intangible ethereal courtship, how little care he had for anything but as it bore upon the consummation.

Meanwhile the early and the late summer brought round the week in which Greenhill Fair was held. This fair was frequently attended by the folk of Weatherbury.

CHAPTER L

THE SHEEP FAIR – TROY TOUCHES
HIS WIFE'S HAND

GREENHILL was the Nijni Novgorod of South Wessex; and the busiest, merriest, noisiest day of the whole statute number was the day of the sheep fair. This yearly gathering was upon the summit of a hill which retained in good preservation the remains of an ancient earthwork, consisting of a huge rampart and entrenchment of an oval form encircling the top of the hill, though somewhat broken down here and there. To each of the two chief openings on opposite sides a winding road ascended, and the level green space of ten or fifteen acres enclosed by the bank was the site of the fair. A few permanent erections dotted the spot, but the majority of visitors patronized canvas alone for resting and feeding under during the time of their sojourn here.

Shepherds who attended with their flocks from long distances started from home two or three days, or even a week, before the fair, driving their charges a few miles each day – not more than ten or twelve – and resting them at night in hired fields by the wayside at previously chosen points, where they fed, having fasted since morning. The shepherd of each flock marched behind, a bundle containing his kit for the week strapped upon his shoulders, and in his hand his crook, which he used as the staff of his pilgrimage. Several of the sheep would get worn and lame, and occasionally a lambing occurred on the road. To meet these contingencies, there was frequently provided, to accompany the flocks from the remoter points, a pony and waggon into which the weakly ones were taken for the remainder of the journey.

362

The Weatherbury Farms, however, were no such long distance from the hill, and those arrangements were not necessary in their case. But the large united flocks of Bathsheba and Farmer Boldwood formed a valuable and imposing multitude which demanded much attention, and on this account Gabriel, in addition to Boldwood's shepherd and Cain Ball, accompanied them along the way, through the decayed old town of Kingsbere, and upward to the plateau, – old George the dog of course behind them.

When the autumn sun slanted over Greenhill this morning and lighted the dewy flat upon its crest, nebulous clouds of dust were to be seen floating between the pairs of hedges which streaked the wide prospect around in all directions. These gradually converged upon the base of the hill, and the flocks became individually visible, climbing the serpentine ways which led to the top. Thus, in a slow procession, they entered the opening to which the roads tended, multitude after multitude, horned and hornless – blue flocks and red flocks, buff flocks and brown flocks, even green and salmon-tinted flocks, according to the fancy of the colourist and custom of the farm. Men were shouting, dogs were barking, with greatest animation, but the thronging travellers in so long a journey had grown nearly indifferent to such terrors, though they still bleated piteously at the unwontedness of their experiences, a tall shepherd rising here and there in the midst of them, like a gigantic idol amid a crowd of prostrate devotees.

The great mass of sheep in the fair consisted of South Downs and the old Wessex horned breeds; to the latter class Bathsheba's and Farmer Boldwood's mainly belonged. These filed in about nine o'clock, their vermiculated horns lopping gracefully on each side of their cheeks in geometrically perfect spirals, a small pink and white ear nestling under each horn. Before and behind came other varieties, perfect leopards as to the full rich substance of their coats, and only lacking the spots. There were also a few of the Oxfordshire breed, whose wool was beginning to curl like a child's flaxen hair, though surpassed in this respect by the effeminate Leicesters, which were in turn less curly than the Cotswolds. But the most picturesque by far was a small flock of Exmoors, which chanced to be there this year. Their pied faces and legs, dark and heavy horns, tresses of wool hanging round their swarthy foreheads, quite relieved the monotony of the flocks in that quarter.

All these bleating, panting, and weary thousands had entered and were penned before the morning had far advanced, the dog belonging to each flock being tied to the corner of the pen containing it. Alleys for pedestrians intersected the pens, which soon became crowded with buyers and sellers from far and near.

In another part of the hill an altogether different scene began to force itself upon the eye towards midday. A circular tent, of exceptional newness and size, was in course of erection here. As the day drew on, the flocks began to change hands, lightening the shepherds' responsibilities; and they turned their attention to this tent and inquired of a man at work there, whose soul seemed concentrated on tying a bothering knot in no time, what was going on.

'The Royal Hippodrome Performance of Turpin's Ride to York and the Death of Black Bess,' replied the man promptly, without turning his eyes or leaving off tying.

As soon as the tent was completed the band struck up highly stimulating harmonies, and the announcement was publicly made, Black Bess standing in a conspicuous position on the outside, as a living proof, if proof were wanted, of the truth of the oracular utterances from the stage over which the people were to enter. These were so convinced by such genuine appeals to heart and understanding both that they soon began to crowd in abundantly, among the foremost being visible Jan Coggan and Joseph Poorgrass, who were holiday keeping here to-day.

'That's the great ruffen pushing me!' screamed a woman in front of Jan over her shoulder at him when the rush was at its fiercest.

'How can I help pushing ye when the folk behind push me?' said Coggan, in a deprecating tone, turning his head towards the aforesaid folk as far as he could without turning his body, which was jammed as in a vice.

There was a silence; then the drums and trumpets again sent forth their echoing notes. The crowd was again ecstasied, and gave another lurch in which Coggan and Poorgrass were again thrust by those behind upon the women in front.

'O that helpless feymels should be at the mercy of such ruffens!' exclaimed one of these ladies again, as she swayed like a reed shaken by the wind.

'Now,' said Coggan, appealing in an earnest voice to the public at large as it stood clustered about his shoulder-blades, 'did ye ever hear such a onreasonable woman as that? Upon my carcase, neighbours, if I could only get out of this cheese-wring, the damn women might eat the show for me!'

'Don't ye lose yer temper, Jan!' implored Joseph Poorgrass, in a whisper. 'They might get their men to murder us, for I think by the shine of their eyes that they be a sinful form of womankind.'

Jan held his tongue, as if he had no objection to be pacified to please a friend, and they gradually reached the foot of the ladder, Poorgrass being flattened like a jumping-jack, and the sixpence, for admission, which he had got ready half-an-hour earlier, having become so reeking hot in the tight squeeze of his excited hand that the woman in spangles, brazen rings set with glass diamonds, and with chalked face and shoulders, who took the money of him, hastily dropped it again from a fear that some trick had been played to burn her fingers. So they all entered, and the cloth of the tent, to the eyes of an observer on the outside, became bulged into innumerable pimples such as we observe on a sack of potatoes, caused by the various human heads, backs, and elbows at high pressure within.

At the rear of the large tent there were two small dressing-tents. One of these, allotted to the male performers, was partitioned into halves by a cloth; and in one of the divisions there was sitting on the grass, pulling on a pair of jack-boots, a young man whom we instantly recognize as Sergeant Troy.

Troy's appearance in this position may be briefly accounted for. The brig aboard which he was taken in Budmouth Roads was about to start on a voyage, though somewhat short of hands. Troy read the articles and joined, but before they sailed a boat was despatched across the bay to Lulwind Cove; as he had half expected, his clothes were gone. He ultimately worked his passage to the United States, where he made a precarious living in various towns as Professor of Gymnastics, Sword Exercise, Fencing, and Pugilism. A few months were sufficient to give him a distaste for this kind of life. There was a certain animal form of refinement in his nature; and however pleasant a strange condition might be whilst privations were easily warded off, it was disadvantageously coarse when money was short. There was ever present, too, the idea that he could claim a home and its comforts did he but choose to return to England and Weatherbury Farm. Whether Bathsheba thought him dead was a frequent subject of curious conjecture. To England he did return at last; but the fact of drawing nearer to Weatherbury abstracted its fascinations, and his intention to enter his old groove at that place became modified. It was with gloom he considered on landing at Liverpool that if he were to go home his reception would be of a kind very unpleasant to contemplate; for what Troy had in the way of emotion was an occasional fitful sentiment which sometimes caused him as much inconvenience as emotion of a strong and healthy kind. Bathsheba was not a woman to be made a fool of, or a woman to suffer in silence; and how could he endure existence with a spirited wife to whom at first entering he would be beholden for food and lodging? Moreover, it was not at all unlikely that his wife would fail at her farming, if she had not already done so; and he would then become liable for her maintenance: and what a life such a future of poverty with her would be, the spectre of Fanny constantly between them, harrowing his temper and embittering her words! Thus, for reasons touching on distaste, regret, and shame commingled, he put off his return from day to day, and would have decided to put it off altogether if he could have found anywhere else the ready-made establishment which existed for him there.

At this time – the July preceding the September in which we find him at Greenhill Fair – he fell in with a travelling circus which was performing in the outskirts of a northern town. Troy introduced himself to the manager by taming a restive horse of the troupe, hitting a suspended apple with a pistol-bullet fired from the animal's back when in full gallop, and other feats. For his merits in these – all more or less based upon his experiences as a dragoon-guardsman – Troy was taken into the company, and the play of Turpin was prepared with a view to his persona-tion of the chief character. Troy was not greatly elated by the appreciative spirit in which he was undoubtedly treated, but he thought the engagement might afford him a few weeks for consideration. It was thus carelessly, and without having formed any definite plan for the future, that Troy found himself at Greenhill Fair with the rest of the company on this day.

And now the mild autumn sun got lower, and in front of the pavilion the following incident had taken place. Bathsheba – who was driven to the fair that day by her odd man Poorgrass – had, like every one else, read or heard the announcement that Mr. Francis, the Great Cosmopolitan Equestrian and Rough-rider, would enact the part of Turpin, and she was not yet too old and careworn to be without a little curiosity to see him. This particular show was by far the largest and grandest in the fair, a horde of little shows grouping themselves under its shade like chickens around a hen. The crowd had passed in, and Boldwood, who had been watching all the day for an oppor-tunity of speaking to her, seeing her comparatively isolated, came up to her side.

'I hope the sheep have done well to-day, Mrs. Troy?' he said nervously.

'O yes, thank you,' said Bathsheba, colour springing up in

the centre of her cheeks. 'I was fortunate enough to sell them all just as we got upon the hill, so we hadn't to pen at all.'

'And now you are entirely at leisure?'

'Yes, except that I have to see one more dealer in two hours' time: otherwise I should be going home. I was looking at this large tent and the announcement. Have you ever seen the play of "Turpin's Ride to York"? Turpin was a real man, was he not?'

'O yes, perfectly true – all of it. Indeed, I think I've heard Jan Coggan say that a relation of his knew Tom King, Turpin's friend, quite well.'

'Coggan is rather given to strange stories connected with his relations, we must remember. I hope they can all be believed.'

'Yes, yes; we know Coggan. But Turpin is true enough. You have never seen it played, I suppose?'

'Never. I was not allowed to go into these places when I was young. Hark! What's that prancing? How they shout!'

'Black Bess just started off, I suppose. Am I right in supposing you would like to see the performance, Mrs. Troy? Please excuse my mistake, if it is one; but if you would like to, I'll get a seat for you with pleasure.' Perceiving that she hesitated, he added, 'I myself shall not stay to see it: I've seen it before.'

Now Bathsheba did care a little to see the show, and had only withheld her feet from the ladder because she feared to go in alone. She had been hoping that Oak might appear, whose assistance in such cases was always accepted as an inalienable right, but Oak was nowhere to be seen; and hence it was that she said, 'Then if you will just look in first, to see if there's room, I think I will go in for a minute or two.'

And so a short time after this Bathsheba appeared in the tent with Boldwood at her elbow, who, taking her to a 'reserved' seat, again withdrew.

This feature consisted of one raised bench in a very conspicuous part of the circle, covered with red cloth, and floored with a piece of carpet, and Bathsheba immediately found, to her confusion, that she was the single reserved individual in the tent, the rest of the crowded spectators, one and all, standing on their legs on the borders of the arena, where they got twice as good a view of the performance for half the money. Hence as many eyes were turned upon her, enthroned alone in this place of honour, against a scarlet background, as upon the ponies and clown who were engaged in preliminary exploits in the centre, Turpin not having yet appeared. Once there, Bathsheba was forced to make the best of it and remain: she sat down, spreading her skirts with some dignity over the unoccupied space on each side of her, and giving a new and feminine aspect to the pavilion. In a few minutes she noticed the fat red nape of Coggan's neck among those standing just below her, and Joseph Poorgrass's saintly profile a little further on.

The interior was shadowy with a peculiar shade. The strange luminous semi-opacities of fine autumn afternoons and eves intensified into Rembrandt effects the few yellow sunbeams which came through holes and divisions in the canvas, and spirted like jets of gold-dust across the dusky blue atmosphere of haze pervading the tent, until they alighted on inner surfaces of cloth opposite, and shone like little lamps suspended there.

Troy, on peeping from his dressing-tent through a slit for a reconnoitre before entering, saw his unconscious wife on high before him as described, sitting as queen of the tournament. He started back in utter confusion, for although his disguise effectually concealed his personality, he instantly felt that she would be sure to recognize his voice. He had several times during the day thought of the possibility of some Weatherbury person or other appearing and recognizing him; but he had taken the risk carelessly. If they see me, let them, he had said. But here was Bathsheba in her own person; and the reality of the scene was so much intenser than any of his prefigurings that he felt he had not half enough considered the point.

She looked so charming and fair that his cool mood about Weatherbury people was changed. He had not expected her to exercise this power over him in the twinkling of an eye. Should he go on, and care nothing? He could not bring himself to do that. Beyond a politic wish to remain unknown, there suddenly arose in him now a sense of shame at the possibility that his attractive young wife, who already despised him, should despise him more by discovering him in so mean a condition after so long a time. He actually blushed at the thought, and was vexed beyond measure that his sentiments of dislike towards Weatherbury should have led him to dally about the country in this way.

But Troy was never more clever than when absolutely at his wits' end. He hastily thrust aside the curtain dividing his own little dressing space from that of the manager and proprietor, who now appeared as the individual called Tom King as far down as his waist, and as the aforesaid respectable manager thence to his toes.

'Here's the devil to pay!' said Troy.

'How's that?'

'Why, there's a blackguard creditor in the tent I don't want to see, who'll discover me and nab me as sure as Satan if I open my mouth. What's to be done?'

'You must appear now, I think.'

'I can't.'

'But the play must proceed.'

'Do you give out that Turpin has got a bad cold, and can't speak his part, but that he'll perform it just the same without speaking.'

The proprietor shook his head.

'Anyhow, play or no play, I won't open my mouth,' said Troy firmly.

'Very well, then let me see. I tell you how we'll manage,' said the other, who perhaps felt it would be extremely awkward to offend his leading man just at this time. 'I won't tell 'em anything about your keeping silence; go on with the piece and say nothing, doing what you can by a judicious wink now and then, and a few indomitable nods in the heroic places, you know. They'll never find out that the speeches are omitted.'

This seemed feasible enough, for Turpin's speeches were not many or long, the fascination of the piece lying entirely in the action; and accordingly the play began, and at the appointed time Black Bess leapt into the grassy circle amid the plaudits of the spectators. At the turnpike scene, where Bess and Turpin are hotly pursued at midnight by the officers, and the half-awake gatekeeper in his tasselled nightcap denies that any horse-man has passed, Coggan uttered a broad-chested 'Well done!' which could be heard all over the fair above the bleating, and Poorgrass smiled delightedly with a nice sense of dramatic con-trast between our hero, who coolly leaps the gate, and halting justice in the form of his enemies, who must needs pull up cumbersomely and wait to be let through. At the death of Tom King, he could not refrain from seizing Coggan by the hand, and whispering, with tears in his eyes, 'Of course he's not really shot, Jan – only seemingly!' And when the last sad scene came on, and the body of the gallant and faithful Bess had to be carried out on a shutter by twelve volunteers from among the spectators, nothing could restrain Poorgrass from lending a hand, exclaiming, as he asked Jan to join him, "Twill be some-thing to tell of at Warren's in future years, Jan, and hand down to our children.' For many a year in Weatherbury, Joseph told, with the air of a man who had had experiences in his time, that he touched with his own hand the hoof of Bess as she lay upon the board upon his shoulder. If, as some thinkers hold, immortality consists in being enshrined in others' memories, then did Black Bess become immortal that day if she never had done so before.

Meanwhile Troy had added a few touches to his ordinary make-up for the character, the more effectually to disguise him-self, and though he had felt faint qualms on first entering, the metamorphosis effected by judiciously 'lining' his face with a wire rendered him safe from the eyes of Bathsheba and her men. Nevertheless, he was relieved when it was got through.

There was a second performance in the evening, and the tent was lighted up. Troy had taken his part very quietly this time, venturing to introduce a few speeches on occasion; and was just concluding it when, whilst standing at the edge of the circle contiguous to the first row of spectators, he observed within a yard of him the eye of a man darted keenly into his side features. Troy hastily shifted his position, after having recognized in the scrutineer the knavish bailiff Pennyways, his wife's sworn enemy, who still hung about the outskirts of Weatherbury.

At first Troy resolved to take no notice and abide by circumstances. That he had been recognized by this man was highly probable; yet there was room for a doubt. Then the great objection he had felt to allowing news of his proximity to precede him to Weatherbury in the event of his return, based on a feeling that knowledge of his present occupation would discredit him still further in his wife's eyes, returned in full force. Moreover, should he resolve not to return at all, a tale of his being alive and being in the neighbourhood would be awkward; and he was anxious to acquire a knowledge of his wife's temporal affairs before deciding which to do.

In this dilemma Troy at once went out to reconnoitre. It occurred to him that to find Pennyways, and make a friend of him if possible, would be a very wise act. He had put on a thick beard borrowed from the establishment, and in this he wandered about the fair-field. It was now almost dark, and respectable people were getting their carts and gigs ready to go home.

The largest refreshment booth in the fair was provided by an innkeeper from a neighbouring town. This was considered an unexceptionable place for obtaining the necessary food and rest: Host Trencher (as he was jauntily called by the local newspaper) being a substantial man of high repute for catering through all the country round. The tent was divided into first and second-class compartments, and at the end of the first-class division was a yet further enclosure for the most exclusive, fenced off from the body of the tent by a luncheon-bar, behind which the host himself stood, bustling about in white apron and shirt-sleeves, and looking as if he had never lived anywhere but under canvas all his life. In these penetralia were chairs and a table, which, on candles being lighted, made quite a cosy and luxurious show, with an urn, plated tea and coffee pots, china teacups, and plum cakes.

Troy stood at the entrance to the booth, where a gipsy-woman was frying pancakes over a little fire of sticks and selling them at a penny a-piece, and looked over the heads of the people within. He could see nothing of Pennyways, but he soon discerned Bathsheba through an opening into the reserved space at the further end. Troy thereupon retreated, went round the tent into the darkness, and listened. He could hear Bathsheba's voice immediately inside the canvas; she was conversing with a man. A warmth overspread his face: surely she was not so unprincipled as to flirt in a fair! He wondered if, then, she reckoned upon his death as an absolute certainty. To get at the root of the matter, Troy took a penknife from his pocket and softly made two little cuts crosswise in the cloth, which, by folding back the corners, left a hole the size of a wafer. Close to this he placed his face, withdrawing it again in a movement of surprise; for his eye had been within twelve inches of the top of Bathsheba's head. It was too near to be convenient. He made another hole a little to one side and lower down, in a shaded place beside her chair, from which it was easy and safe to survey her by looking horizontally.

Troy took in the scene completely now. She was leaning back, sipping a cup of tea that she held in her hand, and the owner of the male voice was Boldwood, who had apparently just brought the cup to her. Bathsheba, being in a negligent mood, leant so idly against the canvas that it was pressed to the shape of her shoulder, and she was, in fact, as good as in Troy's arms; and he was obliged to keep his breast carefully backward that she might not feel its warmth through the cloth as he gazed in.

Troy found unexpected chords of feeling to be stirred again within him as they had been stirred earlier in the day. She was handsome as ever, and she was his. It was some minutes before he could counteract his sudden wish to go in, and claim her. Then he thought how the proud girl who had always looked down upon him even whilst it was to love him, would hate him on discovering him to be a strolling player. Were he to make himself known, that chapter of his life must at all risks be kept for ever from her and from the Weatherbury people, or his name would be a byword throughout the parish. He would be nicknamed 'Turpin' as long as he lived. Assuredly before he could claim her these few past months of his existence must be entirely blotted out.

'Shall I get you another cup before you start, ma'am?' said Farmer Boldwood.

'Thank you,' said Bathsheba. 'But I must be going at once. It was great neglect in that man to keep me waiting here till so late. I should have gone two hours ago, if it had not been for him. I had no idea of coming in here; but there's nothing so refreshing as a cup of tea, though I should never have got one if you hadn't helped me.'

Troy scrutinized her cheek as lit by the candles, and watched each varying shade thereon, and the white shell-like sinuosities of her little ear. She took out her purse and was insisting to Boldwood on paying for her tea for herself, when at this moment Pennyways entered the tent. Troy trembled: here was his scheme for respectability endangered at once. He was about to leave his hole of espial, attempt to follow Pennyways, and find out if the ex-bailiff had recognized him, when he was arrested by the conversation, and found he was too late.

'Excuse me, ma'am,' said Pennyways; 'I've some private information for your ear alone.'

'I cannot hear it now,' she said coldly. That Bathsheba could not endure this man was evident; in fact, he was continually coming to her with some tale or other, by which he might creep into favour at the expense of persons maligned.

'I'll write it down,' said Pennyways confidently. He stooped over the table, pulled a leaf from a warped pocket-book, and wrote upon the paper, in a round hand —

'*Your husband is here. I've seen him. Who's the fool now?*'

This he folded small, and handed towards her. Bathsheba would not read it; she would not even put out her hand to take it. Pennyways, then, with a laugh of derision, tossed it into her lap, and, turning away, left her.

From the words and action of Pennyways, Troy, though he had not been able to see what the ex-bailiff wrote, had not a moment's doubt that the note referred to him. Nothing that he could think of could be done to check the exposure. 'Curse my luck!' he whispered, and added imprecations which rustled in the gloom like a pestilent wind. Meanwhile Boldwood said, taking up the note from her lap —

'Don't you wish to read it, Mrs. Troy? If not, I'll destroy it.'

'Oh, well,' said Bathsheba carelessly, 'perhaps it is unjust not to read it; but I can guess what it is about. He wants me to recommend him, or it is to tell me of some little scandal or another connected with my work-people. He's always doing that.'

Bathsheba held the note in her right hand. Boldwood handed towards her a plate of cut bread-and-butter; when, in order to take a slice, she put the note into her left hand, where she was still holding the purse, and then allowed her hand to drop beside her close to the canvas. The moment had come for saving his game, and Troy impulsively felt that he would play the card. For yet another time he looked at the fair hand, and saw the pink finger-tips, and the blue veins of the wrist, encircled by a bracelet of coral chippings which she wore: how familiar it all was to him! Then, with the lightning action in which he was such an adept, he noiselessly slipped his hand under the bottom of the tent-cloth, which was far from being pinned tightly down, lifted it a little way, keeping his eye to the hole, snatched the note from her fingers, dropped the canvas, and ran away in the gloom towards the bank and ditch, smiling at the scream of astonishment which burst from her. Troy then slid down on the outside of the rampart, hastened round in the bottom of the entrenchment to a distance of a hundred yards, ascended again, and crossed boldly in a slow walk towards the front entrance of the tent. His object was now to get to Pennyways, and prevent a repetition of the announcement until such time as he should choose.

Troy reached the tent door, and standing among the groups there gathered, looked anxiously for Pennyways, evidently not wishing to make himself prominent by inquiring for him. One or two men were speaking of a daring attempt that had just been made to rob a young lady by lifting the canvas of the tent beside her. It was supposed that the rogue had imagined a slip of paper which she held in her hand to be a bank note, for he had seized it, and made off with it, leaving her purse behind. His chagrin and disappointment at discovering its worthlessness would be a good joke, it was said. However, the occurrence seemed to have become known to few, for it had not interrupted a fiddler, who had lately begun playing by the door of the tent, nor the four bowed old men with grim countenances and walking-sticks in hand, who were dancing 'Major Malley's Reel' to the tune. Behind these stood Pennyways. Troy glided up to him, beckoned, and whispered a few words; and with a mutual glance of concurrence the two men went into the night together.

CHAPTER LI

BATHSHEBA TALKS WITH HER OUTRIDER

THE arrangement for getting back again to Weatherbury had been that Oak should take the place of Poorgrass in Bathsheba's conveyance and drive her home, it being discovered late in the afternoon that Joseph was suffering from his old complaint, a multiplying eye, and was, therefore, hardly trustworthy as coachman and protector to a woman. But Oak had found himself so occupied, and was full of so many cares relative to those portions of Boldwood's flocks that were not disposed of, that Bathsheba, without telling Oak or anybody, resolved to drive home herself, as she had many times done from Casterbridge Market, and trust to her good angel for performing the journey unmolested. But having fallen in with Farmer Boldwood accidentally (on her part at least) at the refreshment-tent, she found it impossible to refuse his offer to ride on horseback beside her as escort. It had grown twilight before she was aware, but Boldwood assured her that there was no cause for uneasiness, as the moon would be up in half-an-hour.

Immediately after the incident in the tent she had risen to go – now absolutely alarmed and really grateful for her old lover's protection – though regretting Gabriel's absence, whose company she would have much preferred, as being more proper as well as more pleasant, since he was her own managing-man and servant. This, however, could not be helped; she would not, on any consideration, treat Boldwood harshly, having once already ill-used him, and the moon having risen, and the gig being ready, she drove across the hill-top in the wending ways which led downwards – to oblivious obscurity, as it seemed, for the moon and the hill it flooded with light were in appearance on a level, the rest of the world lying as a vast shady concave between them. Boldwood mounted his horse, and followed in close attendance behind. Thus they descended into the lowlands, and the sounds of those left on the hill came like voices from the sky, and the lights were as those of a camp in heaven. They soon passed the merry stragglers in the immediate vicinity of the hill, traversed Kingsbere, and got upon the high road.

The keen instincts of Bathsheba had perceived that the farmer's staunch devotion to herself was still undiminished, and she sympathized deeply. The sight had quite depressed her this evening; had reminded her of her folly; she wished anew, as she had wished many months ago, for some means of making reparation for her fault. Hence her pity for the man who so persistently loved on to his own injury and permanent gloom had betrayed Bathsheba into an injudicious considerateness of manner, which appeared almost like tenderness, and gave new vigour to the exquisite dream of a Jacob's seven years' service in poor Boldwood's mind.

He soon found an excuse for advancing from his position in the rear, and rode close by her side. They had gone two or three miles in the moonlight, speaking desultorily across the wheel of her gig concerning the fair, farming, Oak's usefulness to them both, and other indifferent subjects, when Boldwood said suddenly and simply —

'Mrs. Troy, you will marry again some day?'

This point-blank query unmistakably confused her, and it was not till a minute or more had elapsed that she said, 'I have not seriously thought of any such subject.'

'I quite understand that. Yet your late husband has been dead nearly one year, and —'

'You forget that his death was never absolutely proved, and may not have taken place; so that I may not be really a widow,' she said, catching at the straw of escape that the fact afforded.

'Not absolutely proved, perhaps, but it was proved circumstantially. A man saw him drowning, too. No reasonable person has any doubt of his death; nor have you, ma'am, I should imagine.'

'O yes I have, or I should have acted differently,' she said, gently. 'From the first I have had a strange unaccountable feeling that he could not have perished. But I have been able to explain that in several ways since. Even were I half persuaded that I shall see him no more, I am far from thinking of marriage with another. I should be very contemptible to indulge in such a thought.'

They were silent now awhile, and having struck into an unfrequented track across a common, the creaks of Boldwood's saddle and her gig springs were all the sounds to be heard. Boldwood ended the pause.

'Do you remember when I carried you fainting in my arms into the King's Arms, in Casterbridge? Every dog has his day: that was mine.'

'I know – I know it all,' she said, hurriedly.

'I, for one, shall never cease regretting that events so fell out as to deny you to me.'

'I, too, am very sorry,' she said, and then checked herself. 'I mean, you know, I am sorry you thought I —'

'I have always this dreary pleasure in thinking over those past times with you – that I was something to you before *he* was anything, and that you belonged *almost* to me. But, of course, that's nothing. You never liked me.'

'I did; and respected you, too.'

'Do you now?'

'Yes.'

'Which?'

'How do you mean which?'

'Do you like me, or do you respect me?'

'I don't know – at least, I cannot tell you. It is difficult for a woman to define her feelings in language which is chiefly made by men to express theirs. My treatment of you was thoughtless, inexcusable, wicked! I shall eternally regret it. If there had been anything I could have done to make amends I would most gladly have done it – there was nothing on earth I so longed to do as to repair the error. But that was not possible.'

'Don't blame yourself – you were not so far in the wrong as you suppose. Bathsheba, suppose you had real complete proof that you are what, in fact, you are – a widow – would you repair the old wrong to me by marrying me?'

'I cannot say. I shouldn't yet, at any rate.'

'But you might at some future time of your life?'

'O yes, I might at some time.'

'Well, then, do you know that without further proof of any kind you may marry again in about six years from the present – subject to nobody's objection or blame?'

'O yes,' she said, quickly. 'I know all that. But don't talk of it – seven or six years – where may we all be by that time?'

'They will soon glide by, and it will seem an astonishingly short time to look back upon when they are past – much less than to look forward to now.'

'Yes, yes; I have found that in my own experience.'

'Now, listen once more,' Boldwood pleaded. 'If I wait that time, will you marry me? You own that you owe me amends – let that be your way of making them.'

'But, Mr. Boldwood – six years —'

'Do you want to be the wife of any other man?'

'No indeed! I mean, that I don't like to talk about this matter now. Perhaps it is not proper, and I ought not to allow it. My husband may be living, as I said. Let us drop it for the present, please do!'

'Of course, I'll drop the subject if you wish. But propriety has nothing to do with reasons. I am a middle-aged man, willing to protect you for the remainder of our lives. On your side, at least, there is no passion or blamable haste – on mine, perhaps, there is. But I can't help seeing that if you choose from a feeling of pity, and, as you say, a wish to make amends, to make a bargain with me for a far-ahead time – an agreement which will set all things right and make me happy, late though it may be – there is no fault to be found with you as a woman. Hadn't I the first place beside you? Haven't you been almost mine once already? Surely you can say to me as much as this, you will have me back again should circumstances permit? Now, pray speak! O Bathsheba, promise – it is only a little promise – that if you marry again, you will marry me!'

His tone was so excited that she almost feared him at this moment, even whilst she sympathized. It was a simple physical fear – the weak of the strong; there was no emotional aversion or inner repugnance. She said, with some distress in her voice, for she remembered vividly his outburst on the Yalbury Road, and shrank from a repetition of his anger: –

'I will never marry another man whilst you wish me to be your wife, whatever comes – but to say more – you have taken me so by surprise —'

'But let it stand in these simple words – that in six years' time you will be my wife? Unexpected accidents we'll not mention, because those, of course, must be given way to. Now, this time I know you will keep your word.'

'That's why I hesitate to give it.'

'But do give it! Remember the past, and be kind.'

She breathed; and then said mournfully: 'O what shall I do? I don't love you, and I much fear that I never shall love you as much as a woman ought to love a husband. If you, sir, know that, and I can yet give you happiness by a mere promise to marry at the end of six years, if my husband should not come back, it is a great honour to me. And if you value such an act of friendship from a woman who doesn't esteem herself as she did, and has little love left, why I – I will —'

'Promise!'

'– Consider, if I cannot promise soon.'

'But soon is perhaps never?'

'O no, it is not! I mean soon. Christmas, we'll say.'

'Christmas!' He said nothing further till he added: 'Well, I'll say no more to you about it till that time.'

Bathsheba was in a very peculiar state of mind, which

showed how entirely the soul is the slave of the body, the ethereal spirit dependent for its quality upon the tangible flesh and blood. It is hardly too much to say that she felt coerced by a force stronger than her own will, not only into the act of promising upon this singularly remote and vague matter, but into the emotion of fancying that she ought to promise. When the weeks intervening between the night of this conversation and Christmas day began perceptibly to diminish, her anxiety and perplexity increased.

One day she was led by accident into an oddly confidential dialogue with Gabriel about her difficulty. It afforded her a little relief – of a dull and cheerless kind. They were auditing accounts, and something occurred in the course of their labours which led Oak to say, speaking of Boldwood, 'He'll never forget you, ma'am, never.'

Then out came her trouble before she was aware; and she told him how she had again got into the toils; what Boldwood had asked her, and how he was expecting her assent. 'The most mournful reason of all for my agreeing to it,' she said sadly, 'and the true reason why I think to do so for good or for evil, is this – it is a thing I have not breathed to a living soul as yet – I believe that if I don't give my word, he'll go out of his mind.'

'Really, do ye?' said Gabriel, gravely.

'I believe this,' she continued, with reckless frankness; 'and Heaven knows I say it in a spirit the very reverse of vain, for I am grieved and troubled to my soul about it – I believe I hold that man's future in my hand. His career depends entirely upon my treatment of him. O Gabriel, I tremble at my responsibility, for it is terrible!'

'Well, I think this much, ma'am, as I told you years ago,' said Oak, 'that his life is a total blank whenever he isn't hoping for 'ee; but I can't suppose – I hope that nothing so dreadful hangs on to it as you fancy. His natural manner has always been dark and strange, you know. But since the case is so sad and odd-like, why don't ye give the conditional promise? I think I would.'

'But is it right? Some rash acts of my past life have taught me that a watched woman must have very much circumspection to retain only a very little credit, and I do want and long to be discreet in this! And six years – why we may all be in our graves by that time, even if Mr. Troy does not come back again, which he may not impossibly do! Such thoughts give a sort of absurdity to the scheme. Now, isn't it preposterous, Gabriel? However he came to dream of it, I cannot think. But is it wrong? You know – you are older than I.'

'Eight years older, ma'am.'

'Yes, eight years – and is it wrong?'

'Perhaps it would be an uncommon agreement for a man and woman to make: I don't see anything really wrong about it,' said Oak, slowly. 'In fact the very thing that makes it doubtful if you ought to marry en under any condition, that is, your not caring about him – for I may suppose —'

'Yes, you may suppose that love is wanting,' she said shortly. 'Love is an utterly bygone, sorry, worn-out, miserable thing with me – for him or any one else.'

'Well, your want of love seems to me the one thing that takes away harm from such an agreement with him. If wild heat had to do wi' it, making ye long to overcome the awkwardness about your husband's vanishing, it mid be wrong; but a cold-hearted agreement to oblige a man seems different, somehow. The real sin, ma'am, in my mind, lies in thinking of ever wedding wi' a man you don't love honest and true.'

'That I'm willing to pay the penalty of,' said Bathsheba, firmly. 'You know, Gabriel, this is what I cannot get off my conscience – that I once seriously injured him in sheer idleness. If I had never played a trick upon him, he would never have wanted to marry me. O if I could only pay some heavy damages in money to him for the harm I did, and so get the sin off my soul that way! . . . Well, there's the debt, which can only be discharged in one way, and I believe I am bound to do it if it honestly lies in my power, without any consideration of my own future at all. When a rake gambles away his expectations, the fact that it is an inconvenient debt doesn't make him the less liable. I've been a rake, and the single point I ask you is, considering that my own scruples, and the fact that in the eye of the law my husband is only missing, will keep any man from marrying me until seven years have passed – am I free to entertain such an idea, even though 'tis a sort of penance – for it will be that? I *hate* the act of marriage under such circumstances, and the class of women I should seem to belong to by doing it!'

'It seems to me that all depends upon whe'r you think, as everybody else do, that your husband is dead.'

'I shall get to, I suppose, because I cannot help feeling what would have brought him back long before this time if he had lived.'

'Well, then, in a religious sense you will be as free to *think* o' marrying again as any real widow of one year's standing. But why don't ye ask Mr. Thirdly's advice on how to treat Mr. Boldwood?'

'No. When I want a broad-minded opinion for general enlightenment, distinct from special advice, I never go to a man who deals in the subject professionally. So I like the parson's opinion on law, the lawyer's on doctoring, the doctor's on business, and my business-man's – that is, yours – on morals.'

'And on love —'

'My own.'

'I'm afraid there's a hitch in that argument,' said Oak, with a grave smile.

She did not reply at once, and then saying, 'Good evening, Mr. Oak,' went away.

She had spoken frankly, and neither asked nor expected any reply from Gabriel more satisfactory than that she had obtained. Yet in the centremost parts of her complicated heart there existed at this minute a little pang of disappointment, for a reason she would not allow herself to recognize. Oak had not once wished her free that he might marry her himself – had not once said, 'I could wait for you as well as he.' That was the insect sting. Not that she would have listened to any such hypothesis. O no – for wasn't she saying all the time that such thoughts of the future were improper, and wasn't Gabriel far too poor a man to speak sentiment to her? Yet he might have just hinted about that old love of his, and asked, in a playful off-hand way, if he might speak of it. It would have seemed pretty and sweet, if no more; and then she would have shown how kind and inoffensive a woman's 'No' can sometimes be. But to give such cool advice – the very advice she had asked for – it ruffled our heroine all the afternoon.

CHAPTER LII

CONVERGING COURSES

I

CHRISTMAS-EVE came, and a party that Boldwood was to give in the evening was the great subject of talk in Weatherbury. It was not that the rarity of Christmas parties in the parish made this one a wonder, but that Boldwood should be the giver. The announcement had had an abnormal and incongruous sound, as if one should hear of croquet-playing in a cathedral aisle, or that some much-respected judge was going upon the stage. That the party was intended to be a truly jovial one there was no room for doubt. A large bough of mistletoe had been brought from the woods that day, and suspended in the hall of the bachelor's home. Holly and ivy had followed in armfuls. From six that morning till past noon the huge wood fire in the kitchen roared and sparkled at its highest, the kettle, the saucepan, and the three-legged pot appearing in the midst of the flames like Shadrach, Meshach, and Abednego; moreover, roasting and basting operations were continually carried on in front of the genial blaze.

As it grew later the fire was made up in the large long hall into which the staircase descended, and all encumbrances were cleared out for dancing. The log which was to form the back-brand of the evening fire was the uncleft trunk of a tree, so unwieldy that it could be neither brought nor rolled to its place; and accordingly two men were to be observed dragging and heaving it in by chains and levers as the hour of assembly drew near.

In spite of all this, the spirit of revelry was wanting in the atmosphere of the house. Such a thing had never been attempted before by its owner, and it was now done as by a wrench. Intended gaieties would insist upon appearing like solemn grandeurs, the organization of the whole effort was carried out coldly by hirelings, and a shadow seemed to move about the rooms, saying that the proceedings were unnatural to the place and the lone man who lived therein, and hence not good.

II

Bathsheba was at this time in her room, dressing for the event. She had called for candles, and Liddy entered and placed one on each side of her mistress's glass.

'Don't go away, Liddy,' said Bathsheba, almost timidly. 'I am foolishly agitated – I cannot tell why. I wish I had not been obliged to go to this dance; but there's no escaping now. I have not spoken to Mr. Boldwood since the autumn, when I promised to see him at Christmas on business, but I had no idea there was to be anything of this kind.'

'But I would go now,' said Liddy, who was going with her; for Boldwood had been indiscriminate in his invitations.

'Yes, I shall make my appearance, of course,' said Bathsheba. 'But I am *the cause* of the party, and that upsets me! – Don't tell, Liddy.'

'O no, ma'am. You the cause of it, ma'am?'

'Yes. I am the reason of the party – I. If it had not been for me, there would never have been one. I can't explain any more – there's no more to be explained. I wish I had never seen Weatherbury.'

'That's wicked of you – to wish to be worse off than you are.'

'No, Liddy. I have never been free from trouble since I have lived here, and this party is likely to bring me more. Now, fetch my black silk dress, and see how it sits upon me.'

'But you will leave off that, surely, ma'am? You have been a widow-lady fourteen months, and ought to brighten up a little on such a night as this.'

'Is it necessary? No; I will appear as usual, for if I were to wear any light dress people would say things about me, and I should seem to be rejoicing when I am solemn all the time. The party doesn't suit me a bit; but never mind, stay and help to finish me off.'

III

Boldwood was dressing also at this hour. A tailor from Casterbridge was with him, assisting him in the operation of trying on a new coat that had just been brought home.

Never had Boldwood been so fastidious, unreasonable about the fit, and generally difficult to please. The tailor walked round and round him, tugged at the waist, pulled the sleeve, pressed out the collar, and for the first time in his experience Boldwood was not bored. Times had been when the farmer had exclaimed against all such niceties as childish, but now no philosophic or hasty rebuke whatever was provoked by this man for attaching as much importance to a crease in the coat as to an earthquake in South America. Boldwood at last expressed himself nearly satisfied, and paid the bill, the tailor passing out of the door just as Oak came in to report progress for the day.

'Oh, Oak,' said Boldwood. 'I shall of course see you here to-night. Make yourself merry. I am determined that neither expense nor trouble shall be spared.'

'I'll try to be here, sir, though perhaps it may not be very early,' said Gabriel, quietly. 'I am glad indeed to see such a change in 'ee from what it used to be.'

'Yes – I must own it – I am bright to-night: cheerful and more than cheerful – so much so that I am almost sad again with the sense that all of it is passing away. And sometimes, when I am excessively hopeful and blithe, a trouble is looming in the distance: so that I often get to look upon gloom in me with content, and to fear a happy mood. Still this may be absurd – I feel that it is absurd. Perhaps my day is dawning at last.'

'I hope it 'ill be a long and a fair one.'

'Thank you – thank you. Yet perhaps my cheerfulness rests

on a slender hope. And yet I trust my hope. It is faith, not hope. I think this time I reckon with my host. – Oak, my hands are a little shaky, or something: I can't tie this neckerchief properly. Perhaps you will tie it for me. The fact is, I have not been well lately, you know.'

'I am sorry to hear that, sir.'

'Oh, it's nothing. I want it done as well as you can, please. Is there any late knot in fashion, Oak?'

'I don't know, sir,' said Oak. His tone had sunk to sadness.

Boldwood approached Gabriel, and as Oak tied the neckerchief the farmer went on feverishly —

'Does a woman keep her promise, Gabriel?'

'If it is not inconvenient to her she may.'

'– Or rather an implied promise.'

'I won't answer for her implying,' said Oak, with faint bitterness. 'That's a word as full o' holes as a sieve with them.'

'Oak, don't talk like that. You have got quite cynical lately – how is it? We seem to have shifted our positions: I have become the young and hopeful man, and you the old and unbelieving one. However, does a woman keep a promise, not to marry, but to enter on an engagement to marry at some time? Now you know women better than I – tell me.'

'I am afeard you honour my understanding too much. However, she may keep such a promise, if it is made with an honest meaning to repair a wrong.'

'It has not gone far yet, but I think it will soon – yes, I know it will,' he said, in an impulsive whisper. 'I have pressed her upon the subject, and she inclines to be kind to me, and to think of me as a husband at a long future time, and that's enough for me. How can I expect more? She has a notion that a woman should not marry within seven years of her husband's disappearance – that her own self shouldn't, I mean – because his body was not found. It may be merely this legal reason which influences her, or it may be a religious one, but she is reluctant to talk on the point. Yet she has promised – implied – that she will ratify an engagement to-night.'

'Seven years,' murmured Oak.

'No, no – it's no such thing!' he said, with impatience. 'Five years, nine months, and a few days. Fifteen months nearly have passed since he vanished, and is there anything so wonderful in an engagement of little more than five years?'

'It seems long in a forward view. Don't build too much upon such promises, sir. Remember, you have once be'n deceived. Her meaning may be good; but there – she's young yet.'

'Deceived? Never!' said Boldwood, vehemently. 'She never promised me at that first time, and hence she did not break her promise! If she promises me, she'll marry me. Bathsheba is a woman to her word.'

IV

Troy was sitting in a corner of The White Hart tavern at Casterbridge, smoking and drinking a steaming mixture from a glass. A knock was given at the door, and Pennyways entered.

'Well, have you seen him?' Troy inquired, pointing to a chair.

'Boldwood?'

'No – Lawyer Long.'

'He wadn't at home. I went there first, too.'

'That's a nuisance.'

''Tis rather, I suppose.'

'Yet I don't see that, because a man appears to be drowned and was not, he should be liable for anything. I shan't ask any lawyer – not I.'

'But that's not it, exactly. If a man changes his name and so forth, and takes steps to deceive the world and his own wife, he's a cheat, and that in the eye of the law is ayless a rogue, and that is ayless a lammocken vagabond; and that's a punishable situation.'

'Ha-ha! Well done, Pennyways.' Troy had laughed, but it was with some anxiety that he said, 'Now, what I want to know is this, do you think there's really anything going on between her and Boldwood? Upon my soul, I should never have believed it! How she must detest me! Have you found out whether she has encouraged him?'

'I haen't been able to learn. There's a deal of feeling on his side seemingly, but I don't answer for her. I didn't know a word about any such thing till yesterday, and all I heard then was that she was gwine to the party at his house to-night. This is the first time she has ever gone there, they say. And they say that she've not so much as spoke to him since they were at Greenhill Fair: but what can folk believe o't? However, she's not fond of him – quite offish and quite careless, I know.'

'I'm not so sure of that. . . . She's a handsome woman, Penny-ways, is she not? Own that you never saw a finer or more splendid creature in your life. Upon my honour, when I set eyes upon her that day I wondered what I could have been made of to be able to leave her by herself so long. And then I was hampered with that bothering show, which I'm free of at last, thank the stars.' He smoked on awhile, and then added, 'How did she look when you passed by yesterday?'

'Oh, she took no great heed of me, ye may well fancy; but she looked well enough, far's I know. Just flashed her haughty eyes upon my poor scram body, and then let them go past me to what was yond, much as if I'd been no more than a leafless tree. She had just got off her mare to look at the last wring-down of cider for the year; she had been riding, and so her colours were up and her breath rather quick, so that her bosom plimmed and fell – plimmed and fell – every time plain to my eye. Ay, and there were the fellers round her wringing down the cheese and bustling about and saying, "Ware o' the pommy, ma'am: 'twill spoil yer gown." "Never mind me," says she. Then Gabe brought her some of the new cider, and she must needs go drinking it through a strawmote, and not in a nateral way at all. "Liddy," says she, "bring indoors a few gallons, and I'll make some cider-wine." Sergeant, I was no more to her than a morsel of scroff in the fuel-house!'

'I must go and find her out at once – O yes, I see that – I must go. Oak is head man still, isn't he?'

'Yes, 'a b'lieve. And at Little Weatherbury Farm too. He manages everything.'

"Twill puzzle him to manage her, or any other man of his compass!'

'I don't know about that. She can't do without him, and knowing it well he's pretty independent. And she've a few soft corners to her mind, though I've never been able to get into one, the devil's in't!'

'Ah, baily, she's a notch above you, and you must own it: a higher class of animal – a finer tissue. However, stick to me, and neither this haughty goddess, dashing piece of womanhood, Juno-wife of mine (Juno was a goddess, you know), nor anybody else shall hurt you. But all this wants looking into, I perceive. What with one thing and another, I see that my work is well cut out for me.'

V

'How do I look to-night, Liddy?' said Bathsheba, giving a final adjustment to her dress before leaving the glass.

'I never saw you look so well before. Yes – I'll tell you when you looked like it – that night, a year and a half ago, when you came in so wild-like, and scolded us for making remarks about you and Mr. Troy.'

'Everybody will think that I am setting myself to captivate Mr. Boldwood, I suppose,' she murmured. 'At least they'll say so. Can't my hair be brushed down a little flatter? I dread going – yet I dread the risk of wounding him by staying away.'

'Anyhow, ma'am, you can't well be dressed plainer than you are, unless you go in sackcloth at once. 'Tis your excitement is what makes you look so noticeable to-night.'

'I don't know what's the matter, I feel wretched at one time, and buoyant at another. I wish I could have continued quite alone as I have been for the last year or so, with no hopes and no fears, and no pleasure and no grief.'

'Now just suppose Mr. Boldwood should ask you – only just

suppose it – to run away with him, what would you do, ma'am?'

'Liddy – none of that,' said Bathsheba, gravely. 'Mind, I won't hear joking on any such matter. Do you hear?'

'I beg pardon, ma'am. But knowing what rum things we women be, I just said – however, I won't speak of it again.'

'No marrying for me yet for many a year; if ever, 'twill be for reasons very, very different from those you think, or others will believe! Now get my cloak, for it is time to go.'

VI

'Oak,' said Boldwood, 'before you go I want to mention what has been passing in my mind lately – that little arrangement we made about your share in the farm I mean. That share is small, too small, considering how little I attend to business now, and how much time and thought you give to it. Well, since the world is brightening for me, I want to show my sense of it by increasing your proportion in the partnership. I'll make a memorandum of the arrangement which struck me as likely to be convenient, for I haven't time to talk about it now; and then we'll discuss it at our leisure. My intention is ultimately to retire from the management altogether, and until you can take all the expenditure upon your shoulders, I'll be a sleeping partner in the stock. Then, if I marry her – and I hope – I feel I shall, why —'

'Pray don't speak of it, sir,' said Oak, hastily. 'We don't know what may happen. So many upsets may befall 'ee. There's many a slip, as they say – and I would advise you – I know you'll pardon me this once – not to be *too sure*.'

'I know, I know. But the feeling I have about increasing your share is on account of what I know of you. Oak, I have learnt a little about your secret: your interest in her is more than that of bailiff for an employer. But you have behaved like a man, and I, as a sort of successful rival – successful partly through your goodness of heart – should like definitely to show my sense of your friendship under what must have been a great pain to you.'

'O that's not necessary, thank 'ee,' said Oak, hurriedly. 'I must get used to such as that; other men have, and so shall I.'

Oak then left him. He was uneasy on Boldwood's account, for he saw anew that this constant passion of the farmer made him not the man he once had been.

As Boldwood continued awhile in his room alone – ready and dressed to receive his company – the mood of anxiety about his appearance seemed to pass away, and to be succeeded by a deep solemnity. He looked out of the window, and regarded the dim outline of the trees upon the sky, and the twilight deepening to darkness.

Then he went to a locked closet, and took from a locked drawer therein a small circular case the size of a pill-box, and was about to put it into his pocket. But he lingered to open the cover and take a momentary glance inside. It contained a woman's finger-ring, set all the way round with small diamonds, and from its appearance had evidently been recently purchased. Boldwood's eyes dwelt upon its many sparkles a long time, though that its material aspect concerned him little was plain from his manner and mien, which were those of a mind following out the presumed thread of that jewel's future history.

The noise of wheels at the front of the house became audible. Boldwood closed the box, stowed it away carefully in his pocket, and went out upon the landing. The old man who was his indoor factotum came at the same moment to the foot of the stairs.

'They be coming, sir – lots of 'em – a-foot and a-driving!'

'I was coming down this moment. Those wheels I heard – is it Mrs. Troy?'

'No, sir – 'tis not she yet.'

A reserved and sombre expression had returned to Boldwood's face again, but it poorly cloaked his feelings when he pronounced Bathsheba's name; and his feverish anxiety continued to show its existence by a galloping motion of his fingers upon the side of his thigh as he went down the stairs.

VII

'How does this cover me?' said Troy to Pennyways. 'Nobody would recognize me now, I'm sure.'

He was buttoning on a heavy grey overcoat of Noachian cut, with cape and high collar, the latter being erect and rigid, like a girdling wall, and nearly reaching to the verge of a travelling cap which was pulled down over his ears.

Pennyways snuffed the candle, and then looked up and deliberately inspected Troy.

'You've made up your mind to go then?' he said.

'Made up my mind? Yes; of course I have.'

'Why not write to her? 'Tis a very queer corner that you have got into, sergeant. You see all these things will come to light if you go back, and they won't sound well at all. Faith, if I was you I'd even bide as you be – a single man of the name of Francis. A good wife is good, but the best wife is not so good as no wife at all. Now that's my outspoke mind, and I've been called a long-headed feller here and there.'

'All nonsense!' said Troy, angrily. 'There she is with plenty of money, and a house and farm, and horses, and comfort, and here am I living from hand to mouth – a needy adventurer. Besides, it is no use talking now; it is too late, and I am glad of it; I've been seen and recognized here this very afternoon. I should have gone back to her the day after the fair, if it hadn't been for you talking about the law, and rubbish about getting a separation; and I don't put it off any longer. What the deuce put it into my head to run away at all, I can't think! Humbugging sentiment – that's what it was. But what man on earth was to know that his wife would be in such a hurry to get rid of his name!'

'I should have known it. She's bad enough for anything.'

'Pennyways, mind who you are talking to.'

'Well, sergeant, all I say is this, that if I were you I'd go abroad again where I came from – 'tisn't too late to do it now. I wouldn't stir up the business and get a bad name for the sake of living with her – for all that about your play-acting is sure to come out, you know, although you think otherwise. My eyes and limbs, there'll be a racket if you go back just now – in the middle of Boldwood's Christmasing!'

'H'm, yes. I expect I shall not be a very welcome guest if he has her there,' said the sergeant, with a slight laugh. 'A sort of Alonzo the Brave; and when I go in the guests will sit in silence and fear, and all laughter and pleasure will be hushed, and the lights in the chamber burn blue, and the worms – Ugh, horrible! – Ring for some more brandy, Pennyways, I felt an awful shudder just then! Well, what is there besides? A stick – I must have a walking-stick.'

Pennyways now felt himself to be in something of a difficulty, for should Bathsheba and Troy become reconciled it would be necessary to regain her good opinion if he would secure the patronage of her husband. 'I sometimes think she likes you yet, and is a good woman at bottom,' he said, as a saving sentence. 'But there's no telling to a certainty from a body's outside. Well, you'll do as you like about going, of course, sergeant, and as for me, I'll do as you tell me.'

'Now, let me see what the time is,' said Troy, after emptying his glass in one draught as he stood. 'Half-past six o'clock. I shall not hurry along the road, and shall be there then before nine.'

CHAPTER LIII

CONCURRITUR – HORÆ MOMENTO

OUTSIDE the front of Boldwood's house a group of men stood in the dark, with their faces towards the door, which occasionally opened and closed for the passage of some guest or servant, when a golden rod of light would stripe the ground for the moment and vanish again, leaving nothing outside but the glowworm shine of the pale lamp amid the evergreens over the door.

'He was seen in Casterbridge this afternoon – so the boy said,' one of them remarked in a whisper.

'And I for one believe it. His body was never found, you know.'

''Tis a strange story,' said the next. 'You may depend upon't that she knows nothing about it.'

'Not a word.'

'Perhaps he don't mean that she shall,' said another man.

'If he's alive and here in the neighbourhood, he means mischief,' said the first. 'Poor young thing: I do pity her, if 'tis true. He'll drag her to the dogs.'

'O no; he'll settle down quiet enough,' said one disposed to take a more hopeful view of the case.

'What a fool she must have been ever to have had anything to do with the man! She is so self-willed and independent too, that one is more minded to say it serves her right than pity her.'

'No, no! I don't hold with 'ee there. She was no otherwise than a girl mind, and how could she tell what the man was made of? If 'tis really true, 'tis too hard a punishment, and more than she ought to hae. – Hullo, who's that?' This was to some footsteps that were heard approaching.

'William Smallbury,' said a dim figure in the shades, coming up and joining them. 'Dark as a hedge to-night, isn't it? I all but missed the plank over the river ath'art there in the bottom – never did such a thing before in my life. Be ye any of Bold-wood's work-folk?' He peered into their faces.

'Yes – all o' us. We met here a few minutes ago.'

'Oh, I hear now – that's Sam Samway: thought I knowed the voice, too. Going in?'

'Presently. But I say, William,' Samway whispered, 'have ye heard this strange tale?'

'What – that about Sergeant Troy being seen, d'ye mean, souls?' said Smallbury, also lowering his voice.

'Ay: in Casterbridge.'

'Yes, I have. Laban Tall named a hint of it to me but now – but I don't think it. Hark, here Laban comes himself, 'a b'lieve.' A footstep drew near.

'Laban?'

'Yes, 'tis I,' said Tall.

'Have ye heard any more about that?'

'No,' said Tall, joining the group. 'And I'm inclined to think we'd better keep quiet. If so be 'tis not true, 'twill flurry her, and do her much harm to repeat it; and if so be 'tis true, 'twill do no good to forestall her time o' trouble. God send that it mid be a lie, for though Henery Fray and some of 'em do speak against her, she's never been anything but fair to me. She's hot and hasty, but she's a brave girl who'll never tell a lie however much the truth may harm her, and I've no cause to wish her evil.'

'She never do tell women's little lies, that's true; and 'tis a thing that can be said of very few. Ay, all the harm she thinks she says to yer face: there's nothing underhand wi' her.'

They stood silent then, every man busied with his own thoughts, during which interval sounds of merriment could be heard within. Then the front door again opened, the rays streamed out, the well-known form of Boldwood was seen in the rectangular area of light, the door closed, and Boldwood walked slowly down the path.

'Tis master,' one of the men whispered, as he neared them. 'We'd better stand quiet – he'll go in again directly. He would think it unseemly o' us to be loitering here.'

Boldwood came on, and passed by the men without seeing them, they being under the bushes on the grass. He paused, leant over the gate, and breathed a long breath. They heard low words come from him.

'I hope to God she'll come, or this night will be nothing but misery to me! O my darling, my darling, why do you keep me in suspense like this?'

He said this to himself, and they all distinctly heard it. Boldwood remained silent after that, and the noise from indoors was again just audible, until, a few minutes later, light wheels could be distinguished coming down the hill. They drew nearer, and ceased at the gate. Boldwood hastened back to the door, and opened it; and the light shone upon Bathsheba coming up the path.

Boldwood compressed his emotion to mere welcome: the men marked her light laugh and apology as she met him: he took her into the house; and the door closed again.

'Gracious heaven, I didn't know it was like that with him!' said one of the men. 'I thought that fancy of his was over long ago.'

'You don't know much of master, if you thought that,' said Samway.

'I wouldn't he should know we heard what 'a said for the world,' remarked a third.

'I wish we had told of the report at once,' the first uneasily continued. 'More harm may come of this than we know of. Poor Mr. Boldwood, it will be hard upon en. I wish Troy was in — Well, God forgive me for such a wish! A scoundrel to play a poor wife such tricks. Nothing has prospered in Weatherbury since he came here. And now I've no heart to go in. Let's look into Warren's for a few minutes first, shall us, neighbours?'

Samway, Tall, and Smallbury agreed to go to Warren's, and went out at the gate, the remaining ones entering the house.

The three soon drew near the malt-house, approaching it from the adjoining orchard, and not by way of the street. The pane of glass was illuminated as usual. Smallbury was a little in advance of the rest, when, pausing, he turned suddenly to his companions and said, 'Hist! See there.'

The light from the pane was now perceived to be shining not upon the ivied wall as usual, but upon some object close to the glass. It was a human face.

'Let's come closer,' whispered Samway; and they approached on tiptoe. There was no disbelieving the report any longer. Troy's face was almost close to the pane, and he was looking in. Not only was he looking in, but he appeared to have been arrested by a conversation which was in progress in the malt-house, the voices of the interlocutors being those of Oak and the maltster.

'The spree is all in her honour, isn't it – hey?' said the old man. 'Although he made believe 'tis only keeping up o' Christmas?'

'I cannot say,' replied Oak.

'O 'tis true enough, faith. I cannot understand Farmer Boldwood being such a fool at his time of life as to ho and hanker after thik woman in the way 'a do, and she not care a bit about en.'

The men, after recognizing Troy's features, withdrew across the orchard as quietly as they had come. The air was big with Bathsheba's fortunes to-night: every word everywhere concerned her. When they were quite out of earshot all by one instinct paused.

'It gave me quite a turn – his face,' said Tall, breathing.

'And so it did me,' said Samway. 'What's to be done?'

'I don't see that 'tis any business of ours,' Smallbury murmured dubiously.

'But it is! 'Tis a thing which is everybody's business,' said Samway. 'We know very well that master's on a wrong tack, and that she's quite in the dark, and we should let 'em know at once. Laban, you know her best – you'd better go and ask to speak to her.'

'I bain't fit for any such thing,' said Laban, nervously. 'I should think William ought to do it if anybody. He's oldest.'

'I shall have nothing to do with it,' said Smallbury. ''Tis a ticklish business altogether. Why, he'll go on to her himself in a few minutes, ye'll see.'

'We don't know that he will. Come, Laban.'

'Very well, if I must I must, I suppose,' Tall reluctantly answered. 'What must I say?'

'Just ask to see master.'

'O no; I shan't speak to Mr. Boldwood. If I tell anybody, 'twill be mistress.'

'Very well,' said Samway.

Laban then went to the door. When he opened it the hum of bustle rolled out as a wave upon a still strand – the assemblage being immediately inside the hall – and was deadened to a murmur as he closed it again. Each man waited intently, and looked around at the dark tree tops gently rocking against the sky and occasionally shivering in a slight wind, as if he took interest in the scene, which neither did. One of them began walking up and down, and then came to where he started from and stopped again, with a sense that walking was a thing not worth doing now.

'I should think Laban must have seen mistress by this time,' said Smallbury, breaking the silence. 'Perhaps she won't come and speak to him.'

The door opened. Tall appeared, and joined them.

'Well?' said both.

'I didn't like to ask for her after all,' Laban faltered out. 'They were all in such a stir, trying to put a little spirit into the party. Somehow the fun seems to hang fire, though everything's there that a heart can desire, and I couldn't for my soul interfere and throw damp upon it – if 'twas to save my life, I couldn't!'

'I suppose we had better all go in together,' said Samway, gloomily. 'Perhaps I may have a chance of saying a word to master.'

So the men entered the hall, which was the room selected and arranged for the gathering because of its size. The younger men and maids were at last just beginning a dance. Bathsheba had been perplexed how to act, for she was not much more than a slim young maid herself, and the weight of stateliness sat heavy upon her. Sometimes she thought she ought not to have come under any circumstances; then she considered what cold unkindness that would have been, and finally resolved upon the middle course of staying for about an hour only, and gliding off unobserved, having from the first made up her mind that she could on no account dance, sing, or take any active part in the proceedings.

Her allotted hour having been passed in chatting and looking on, Bathsheba told Liddy not to hurry herself, and went to the small parlour to prepare for departure, which, like the hall, was decorated with holly and ivy, and well lighted up.

Nobody was in the room, but she had hardly been there a moment when the master of the house entered.

'Mrs. Troy – you are not going?' he said. 'We've hardly begun!'

'If you'll excuse me, I should like to go now.' Her manner was restive, for she remembered her promise, and imagined what he was about to say. 'But as it is not late,' she added, 'I can walk home, and leave my man and Liddy to come when they choose.'

'I've been trying to get an opportunity of speaking to you,' said Boldwood. 'You know perhaps what I long to say?'

Bathsheba silently looked on the floor.

'You do give it?' he said, eagerly.

'What?' she whispered.

'Now, that's evasion! Why, the promise. I don't want to intrude upon you at all, or to let it become known to anybody. But do give your word! A mere business compact, you know, between two people who are beyond the influence of passion.' Boldwood knew how false this picture was as regarded himself;

but he had proved that it was the only tone in which she would allow him to approach her. 'A promise to marry me at the end of five years and three-quarters. You owe it to me!'

'I feel that I do,' said Bathsheba; 'that is, if you demand it. But I am a changed woman – an unhappy woman – and not – not —'

'You are still a very beautiful woman,' said Boldwood. Honesty and pure conviction suggested the remark, unaccompanied by any perception that it might have been adopted by blunt flattery to soothe and win her.

However, it had not much effect now, for she said, in a passionless murmur which was in itself a proof of her words: 'I have no feeling in the matter at all. And I don't at all know what is right to do in my difficult position, and I have nobody to advise me. But I give my promise, if I must. I give it as the rendering of a debt, conditionally, of course, on my being a widow.'

'You'll marry me between five and six years hence?'

'Don't press me too hard. I'll marry nobody else.'

'But surely you will name the time, or there's nothing in the promise at all?'

'O, I don't know, pray let me go!' she said, her bosom beginning to rise. 'I am afraid what to do! I want to be just to you, and to be that seems to be wronging myself, and perhaps it is breaking the commandments. There is considerable doubt of his death, and then it is dreadful; let me ask a solicitor, Mr. Boldwood, if I ought or no!'

'Say the words, dear one, and the subject shall be dismissed; a blissful loving intimacy of six years, and then marriage – O Bathsheba, say them!' he begged in a husky voice, unable to sustain the forms of mere friendship any longer. 'Promise yourself to me; I deserve it, indeed I do, for I have loved you more than anybody in the world! And if I said hasty words and showed uncalled-for heat of manner towards you, believe me, dear, I did not mean to distress you; I was in agony, Bathsheba, and I did not know what I said. You wouldn't let a dog suffer what I have suffered, could you but know it! Sometimes I shrink from your knowing what I have felt for you, and sometimes I am distressed that all of it you never will know. Be gracious, and give up a little to me, when I would give up my life for you!'

The trimmings of her dress, as they quivered against the light, showed how agitated she was, and at last she burst out crying. 'And you'll not – press me – about anything more – if I say in five or six years?' she sobbed, when she had power to frame the words.

'Yes, then I'll leave it to time.'

'Very well. If he does not return, I'll marry you in six years from this day, if we both live,' she said solemnly.

'And you'll take this as a token from me.'

Boldwood had come close to her side, and now he clasped one of her hands in both his own, and lifted it to his breast.

'What is it? Oh, I cannot wear a ring!' she exclaimed, on seeing what he held; 'besides, I wouldn't have a soul know that it's an engagement! Perhaps it is improper? Besides, we are not engaged in the usual sense, are we? Don't insist, Mr. Boldwood – don't!' In her trouble at not being able to get her hand away from him at once, she stamped passionately on the floor with one foot, and tears crowded to her eyes again.

'It means simply a pledge – no sentiment – the seal of a practical compact,' he said more quietly, but still retaining her hand in his firm grasp. 'Come, now!' And Boldwood slipped the ring on her finger.

'I cannot wear it,' she said, weeping as if her heart would break. 'You frighten me, almost. So wild a scheme! Please let me go home!'

'Only to-night: wear it just to-night, to please me!'

Bathsheba sat down in a chair, and buried her face in her handkerchief, though Boldwood kept her hand yet. At length she said, in a sort of hopeless whisper —

'Very well, then, I will to-night, if you wish it so earnestly. Now loosen my hand; I will, indeed I will wear it to-night.'

'And it shall be the beginning of a pleasant secret courtship of six years, with a wedding at the end?'

'It must be, I suppose, since you will have it so!' she said, fairly beaten into non-resistance.

Boldwood pressed her hand, and allowed it to drop in her lap. 'I am happy now,' he said. 'God bless you!'

He left the room, and when he thought she might be sufficiently composed sent one of the maids to her. Bathsheba cloaked the effects of the late scene as she best could, followed the girl, and in a few moments came downstairs with her hat and cloak on, ready to go. To get to the door it was necessary to pass through the hall, and before doing so she paused on the bottom of the staircase which descended into one corner, to take a last look at the gathering.

There was no music or dancing in progress just now. At the lower end, which had been arranged for the work-folk specially, a group conversed in whispers, and with clouded looks. Boldwood was standing by the fireplace, and he, too, though so absorbed in visions arising from her promise that he scarcely saw anything, seemed at that moment to have observed their peculiar manner, and their looks askance.

' What is it you are in doubt about, men?' he said.

One of them turned and replied uneasily: 'It was something Laban heard of, that's all, sir.'

'News? Anybody married or engaged, born or dead?' inquired the farmer, gaily. 'Tell it to us, Tall. One would think from your looks and mysterious ways that it was something very dreadful indeed.'

'O no, sir, nobody is dead,' said Tall.

'I wish somebody was,' said Samway, in a whisper.

'What do you say, Samway?' asked Boldwood, somewhat sharply. 'If you have anything to say, speak out; if not, get up another dance.'

'Mrs. Troy has come downstairs,' said Samway to Tall. 'If you want to tell her, you had better do it now.'

'Do you know what they mean?' the farmer asked Bathsheba, across the room.

'I don't in the least,' said Bathsheba.

There was a smart rapping at the door. One of the men opened it instantly, and went outside.

'Mrs. Troy is wanted,' he said, on returning.

'Quite ready,' said Bathsheba. 'Though I didn't tell them to send.'

'It is a stranger, ma'am,' said the man by the door.

'A stranger?' she said.

'Ask him to come in,' said Boldwood.

The message was given, and Troy, wrapped up to his eyes as we have seen him, stood in the doorway.

There was an unearthly silence, all looking towards the newcomer. Those who had just learnt that he was in the neighbourhood recognized him instantly; those who did not were perplexed. Nobody noted Bathsheba. She was leaning on the stairs. Her brow had heavily contracted; her whole face was pallid, her lips apart, her eyes rigidly staring at their visitor.

Boldwood was among those who did not notice that he was Troy. 'Come in, come in!' he repeated, cheerfully, 'and drain a Christmas beaker with us, stranger!'

Troy next advanced into the middle of the room, took off his cap, turned down his coat-collar, and looked Boldwood in the face. Even then Boldwood did not recognize that the impersonator of Heaven's persistent irony towards him, who had once before broken in upon his bliss, scourged him, and snatched his delight away, had come to do these things a second time. Troy began to laugh a mechanical laugh: Boldwood recognized him now.

Troy turned to Bathsheba. The poor girl's wretchedness at this time was beyond all fancy or narration. She had sunk down on the lowest stair; and there she sat, her mouth blue and dry, and her dark eyes fixed vacantly upon him, as if she wondered whether it were not all a terrible illusion.

Then Troy spoke. 'Bathsheba, I come here for you!'

She made no reply.

'Come home with me: come!'

Bathsheba moved her feet a little, but did not rise.

Troy went across to her.

'Come, madam, do you hear what I say?' he said, peremptorily.

A strange voice came from the fireplace – a voice sounding far off and confined, as if from a dungeon. Hardly a soul in the assembly recognized the thin tones to be those of Boldwood. Sudden despair had transformed him.

'Bathsheba, go with your husband!'

Nevertheless, she did not move. The truth was that Bathsheba was beyond the pale of activity – and yet not in a swoon. She was in a state of mental *gutta serena*; her mind was for the minute totally deprived of light at the same time that no obscuration was apparent from without.

Troy stretched out his hand to pull her towards him, when she quickly shrank back. This visible dread of him seemed to irritate Troy, and he seized her arm and pulled it sharply. Whether his grasp pinched her, or whether his mere touch was the cause, was never known, but at the moment of his seizure she writhed, and gave a quick, low scream.

The scream had been heard but a few seconds when it was followed by a sudden deafening report that echoed through the room and stupefied them all. The oak partition shook with the concussion, and the place was filled with grey smoke.

In bewilderment they turned their eyes to Boldwood. At his back, as he stood before the fireplace, was a gun-rack, as is usual in farmhouses, constructed to hold two guns. When Bathsheba had cried out in her husband's grasp, Boldwood's face of gnashing despair had changed. The veins had swollen, and a frenzied look had gleamed in his eye. He had turned quickly, taken one of the guns, cocked it, and at once discharged it at Troy.

Troy fell. The distance apart of the two men was so small that the charge of shot did not spread in the least, but passed like a bullet into his body. He uttered a long guttural sigh – there was a contraction – an extension – then his muscles relaxed, and he lay still.

Boldwood was seen through the smoke to be now again engaged with the gun. It was double-barrelled, and he had, meanwhile, in some way fastened his handkerchief to the trigger, and with his foot on the other end was in the act of turning the second barrel upon himself. Samway his man was the first to see this, and in the midst of the general horror darted up to him. Boldwood had already twitched the handkerchief, and the gun exploded a second time, sending its contents, by a timely blow from Samway, into the beam which crossed the ceiling.

'Well, it makes no difference!' Boldwood gasped. 'There is another way for me to die.'

Then he broke from Samway, crossed the room to Bathsheba, and kissed her hand. He put on his hat, opened the door, and went into the darkness, nobody thinking of preventing him.

CHAPTER LIV

AFTER THE SHOCK

BOLDWOOD passed into the high road, and turned in the direction of Casterbridge. Here he walked at an even, steady pace over Yalbury Hill, along the dead level beyond, mounted Mellstock Hill, and between eleven and twelve o'clock crossed the Moor into the town. The streets were nearly deserted now, and the waving lamp-flames only lighted up rows of grey shop-shutters, and strips of white paving upon which his step echoed as he passed along. He turned to the right, and halted before an archway of heavy stonework, which was closed by an iron-studded pair of doors. This was the entrance to the gaol, and over it a lamp was fixed, the light enabling the wretched traveller to find a bell-pull.

The small wicket at last opened, and a porter appeared. Boldwood stepped forward, and said something in a low tone, when, after a delay, another man came. Boldwood entered, and the door was closed behind him, and he walked the world no more.

Long before this time Weatherbury had been thoroughly aroused, and the wild deed which had terminated Boldwood's merrymaking became known to all. Of those out of the house Oak was one of the first to hear of the catastrophe, and when he entered the room, which was about five minutes after Bold-wood's exit, the scene was terrible. All the female guests were huddled aghast against the walls like sheep in a storm, and the men were bewildered as to what to do. As for Bathsheba, she had changed. She was sitting on the floor beside the body of Troy, his head pillowed in her lap, where she had herself lifted it. With one hand she held her handkerchief to his breast and covered the wound, though scarcely a single drop of blood had flowed, and with the other she tightly clasped one of his. The household convulsion had made her herself again. The temporary coma had ceased, and activity had come with the necessity for it. Deeds of endurance which seem ordinary in philosophy are rare in conduct, and Bathsheba was astonishing all around her now, for her philosophy was her conduct, and she seldom thought practicable what she did not practise. She was of the stuff of which great men's mothers are made. She was indispensable to high generation, hated at tea parties, feared in shops, and loved at crises. Troy recumbent in his wife's lap formed now the sole spectacle in the middle of the spacious room.

'Gabriel,' she said, automatically, when he entered, turning up a face of which only the well-known lines remained to tell him it was hers, all else in the picture having faded quite. 'Ride to Casterbridge instantly for a surgeon. It is, I believe, useless, but go. Mr. Boldwood has shot my husband.'

Her statement of the fact in such quiet and simple words came with more force than a tragic declamation, and had somewhat the effect of setting the distorted images in each mind present into proper focus. Oak, almost before he had comprehended anything beyond the briefest abstract of the event, hurried out of the room, saddled a horse and rode away. Not till he had ridden more than a mile did it occur to him that he would have done better by sending some other man on this errand, remaining himself in the house. What had become of Boldwood? He should have been looked after. Was he mad – had there been a quarrel? Then how had Troy got there? Where had he come from? How did this remarkable reappearance effect itself when he was supposed by many to be at the bottom of the sea? Oak had in some measure been prepared for the presence of Troy by hearing a rumour of his return just before entering Boldwood's house; but before he had weighed that information, this fatal event had been superimposed. However, it was too late now to think of sending another messenger, and he rode on, in the excitement of these self-inquiries not discerning, when about three miles from Casterbridge, a square-figured pedestrian passing along under the dark hedge in the same direction as his own.

The miles necessary to be traversed, and other hindrances incidental to the lateness of the hour and the darkness of the night, delayed the arrival of Mr. Aldritch, the surgeon; and more than three hours passed between the time at which the shot was fired and that of his entering the house. Oak was additionally detained in Casterbridge through having to give notice to the authorities of what had happened; and he then found that Boldwood had also entered the town, and delivered himself up.

In the meantime the surgeon, having hastened into the hall at Boldwood's, found it in darkness and quite deserted. He went on to the back of the house, where he discovered in the kitchen an old man, of whom he made inquiries.

'She's had him took away to her own house, sir,' said his informant.

'Who has?' said the doctor.

'Mrs. Troy. 'A was quite dead, sir.'

This was astonishing information. 'She had no right to do that,' said the doctor. 'There will have to be an inquest, and she should have waited to know what to do.'

'Yes, sir; it was hinted to her that she had better wait till the law was known. But she said law was nothing to her, and she wouldn't let her dear husband's corpse bide neglected for folks to stare at for all the crowners in England.'

Mr. Aldritch drove at once back again up the hill to Bathsheba's. The first person he met was poor Liddy, who seemed literally to have dwindled smaller in these few latter hours. 'What has been done?' he said.

'I don't know, sir,' said Liddy, with suspended breath. 'My mistress has done it all.'

'Where is she?'

'Upstairs with him, sir. When he was brought home and taken upstairs, she said she wanted no further help from the men. And then she called me, and made me fill the bath, and after that told me I had better go and lie down because I looked so ill. Then she locked herself into the room alone with him, and would not let a nurse come in, or anybody at all. But I thought I'd wait in the next room in case she should want me. I heard her moving about inside for more than an hour, but she only came out once, and that was for more candles, because hers had burnt down into the socket. She said we were to let her know when you or Mr. Thirdly came, sir.'

Oak entered with the parson at this moment, and they all went upstairs together, preceded by Liddy Smallbury. Everything was silent as the grave when they paused on the landing. Liddy knocked, and Bathsheba's dress was heard rustling across the room: the key turned in the lock, and she opened the door. Her looks were calm and nearly rigid, like a slightly animated bust of Melpomene.

'Oh, Mr. Aldritch, you have come at last,' she murmured from her lips merely, and threw back the door. 'Ah, and Mr. Thirdly. Well, all is done, and anybody in the world may see him now.' She then passed by him, crossed the landing, and entered another room.

Looking into the chamber of death she had vacated they saw by the light of the candles which were on the drawers a tall straight shape lying at the further end of the bedroom, wrapped in white. Everything around was quite orderly. The doctor went in, and after a few minutes returned to the landing again, where Oak and the parson still waited.

'It is all done, indeed, as she says,' remarked Mr. Aldritch, in a subdued voice. 'The body has been undressed and properly laid out in grave clothes. Gracious Heaven – this mere girl! She must have the nerve of a stoic!'

'The heart of a wife merely,' floated in a whisper about the ears of the three, and turning they saw Bathsheba in the midst of them. Then, as if at that instant to prove that her fortitude had been more of will than of spontaneity, she silently sank down between them and was a shapeless heap of drapery on the floor. The simple consciousness that superhuman strain was no longer required had at once put a period to her power to continue it.

They took her away into a further room, and the medical attendance which had been useless in Troy's case was invaluable in Bathsheba's, who fell into a series of fainting-fits that had a serious aspect for a time. The sufferer was got to bed, and Oak, finding from the bulletins that nothing really dreadful was to be apprehended on her score, left the house. Liddy kept watch in Bathsheba's chamber, where she heard her mistress moaning in whispers through the dull slow hours of that wretched night: 'O it is my fault – how can I live! O Heaven, how can I live!'

CHAPTER LV

THE MARCH FOLLOWING – 'BATHSHEBA
BOLDWOOD'

WE pass rapidly on into the month of March, to a breezy day without sunshine, frost, or dew. On Yalbury Hill, about midway between Weatherbury and Casterbridge, where the turnpike road passes over the crest, a numerous concourse of people had gathered, the eyes of the greater number being frequently stretched afar in a northerly direction. The groups consisted of a throng of idlers, a party of javelin-men, and two trumpeters, and in the midst were carriages, one of which contained the high sheriff. With the idlers, many of whom had mounted to the top of a cutting formed for the road, were several Weatherbury men and boys – among others Poorgrass, Coggan, and Cain Ball.

At the end of half-an-hour a faint dust was seen in the expected quarter, and shortly after a travelling-carriage, bringing one of the two judges on the Western Circuit, came up the hill and halted on the top. The judge changed carriages whilst a flourish was blown by the big-cheeked trumpeters, and a procession being formed of the vehicles and javelin-men, they all proceeded towards the town, excepting the Weatherbury men, who as soon as they had seen the judge move off returned home again to their work.

'Joseph, I zeed you squeezing close to the carriage,' said Coggan, as they walked. 'Did ye notice my lord judge's face?'

'I did,' said Poorgrass. 'I looked hard at en, as if I would read his very soul; and there was mercy in his eyes – or to speak with the exact truth required of us at this solemn time, in the eye that was towards me.'

'Well, I hope for the best,' said Coggan, 'though bad that must be. However, I shan't go to the trial, and I'd advise the rest of ye that bain't wanted to bide away. 'Twill disturb his mind more than anything to see us there staring at him as if he were a show.'

'The very thing I said this morning,' observed Joseph. ' "Justice is come to weigh him in the balances," I said in my reflectious way, "and if he's found wanting, so be it unto him," and a bystander said "Hear, hear! A man who can talk like that ought to be heard." But I don't like dwelling upon it, for my few words are my few words, and not much; though the speech of some men is rumoured abroad as though by nature formed for such.'

'So 'tis, Joseph. And now, neighbours, as I said, every man bide at home.'

The resolution was adhered to; and all waited anxiously for the news next day. Their suspense was diverted, however, by a discovery which was made in the afternoon, throwing more light on Boldwood's conduct and condition than any details which had preceded it.

That he had been from the time of Greenhill Fair until the fatal Christmas Eve in excited and unusual moods was known to those who had been intimate with him; but nobody imagined that there had shown in him unequivocal symptoms of the mental derangement which Bathsheba and Oak, alone of all others and at different times, had momentarily suspected. In a locked closet was now discovered an extraordinary collection of articles. There were several sets of ladies' dresses in the piece, of sundry expensive materials; silks and satins, poplins and velvets, all of colours which from Bathsheba's style of dress might have been judged to be her favourites. There were two muffs, sable and ermine. Above all there was a case of jewellery, containing four heavy gold bracelets and several lockets and rings, all of fine quality and manufacture. These things had been bought in Bath and other towns from time to time, and brought home by stealth. They were all carefully packed in paper, and each package was labelled 'Bathsheba Boldwood,' a date being subjoined six years in advance in every instance.

These somewhat pathetic evidences of a mind crazed with care and love were the subject of discourse in Warren's malthouse when Oak entered from Casterbridge with tidings of the sentence. He came in the afternoon, and his face, as the kiln glow shone upon it, told the tale sufficiently well. Boldwood, as every one supposed he would do, had pleaded guilty, and had been sentenced to death.

The conviction that Boldwood had not been morally responsible for his later acts now became general. Facts elicited previous to the trial had pointed strongly in the same direction, but they had not been of sufficient weight to lead to an order for an examination into the state of Boldwood's mind. It was astonishing, now that a presumption of insanity was raised, how many collateral circumstances were remembered to which a condition of mental disease seemed to afford the only explanation – among others, the unprecedented neglect of his corn stacks in the previous summer.

A petition was addressed to the Home Secretary, advancing the circumstances which appeared to justify a request for a reconsideration of the sentence. It was not 'numerously signed' by the inhabitants of Casterbridge, as is usual in such cases, for Boldwood had never made many friends over the counter. The shops thought it very natural that a man who, by importing direct from the producer, had daringly set aside the first great principle of provincial existence, namely, that God made country villages to supply customers to country towns, should have confused ideas about the Decalogue. The prompters were a few merciful men who had perhaps too feelingly considered the facts latterly unearthed, and the result was that evidence was taken which it was hoped might remove the crime, in a moral point of view, out of the category of wilful murder, and lead it to be regarded as a sheer outcome of madness.

The upshot of the petition was waited for in Weatherbury with solicitous interest. The execution had been fixed for eight o'clock on a Saturday morning about a fortnight after the sentence was passed, and up to Friday afternoon no answer had been received. At that time Gabriel came from Casterbridge Gaol, whither he had been to wish Boldwood good-bye, and turned down a by-street to avoid the town. When past the last house he heard a hammering, and lifting his bowed head he looked back for a moment. Over the chimneys he could see the upper part of the gaol entrance, rich and glowing in the afternoon sun, and some moving figures were there. They were carpenters lifting a post into a vertical position within the parapet. He withdrew his eyes quickly and hastened on.

It was dark when he reached home, and half the village was out to meet him.

'No tidings,' Gabriel said, wearily: 'And I'm afraid there's no hope. I've been with him more than two hours.'

'Do ye think he *really* was out of his mind when he did it?' said Smallbury.

'I can't honestly say that I do,' Oak replied. 'However, that we can talk of another time. Has there been any change in mistress this afternoon?'

'None at all.'

'Is she downstairs?'

'No. And getting on so nicely as she was too. She's but very little better now again than she was at Christmas. She keeps on asking if you be come, and if there's news, till one's wearied out wi' answering her. Shall I go and say you've come?'

'No,' said Oak. 'There's a chance yet; but I couldn't stay in town any longer – after seeing him too. So Laban – Laban is here, isn't he?'

'Yes,' said Tall.

'What I've arranged is, that you shall ride to town the last thing to-night; leave here about nine, and wait a while there, getting home about twelve. If nothing has been received by eleven to-night, they say there's no chance at all.'

'I do so hope his life will be spared,' said Liddy. 'If it is not, she'll go out of her mind too. Poor thing; her sufferings have been dreadful; she deserves anybody's pity.'

'Is she altered much?' said Coggan.

'If you haven't seen poor mistress since Christmas, you wouldn't know her,' said Liddy. 'Her eyes are so miserable that she's not the same woman. Only two years ago she was a romping girl, and now she's this!'

Laban departed as directed, and at eleven o'clock that night several of the villagers strolled along the road to Casterbridge and awaited his arrival – among them Oak, and nearly all the rest of Bathsheba's men. Gabriel's anxiety was great that Boldwood might be saved, even though in his conscience he felt that he ought to die; for there had been qualities in the farmer which Oak loved. At last, when they all were weary the tramp of a horse was heard in the distance –

> First dead, as if on turf it trode,
> Then, clattering, on the village road
> In other pace than forth he yode.

'We shall soon know now, one way or other,' said Coggan, and they all stepped down from the bank on which they had been standing into the road, and the rider pranced into the midst of them.

'Is that you, Laban?' said Gabriel.

'Yes – 'tis come. He's not to die. 'Tis confinement during Her Majesty's pleasure.'

'Hurrah!' said Coggan, with a swelling heart. 'God's above the devil yet!'

CHAPTER LVI

BEAUTY IN LONELINESS – AFTER ALL

BATHSHEBA revived with the spring. The utter prostration that had followed the low fever from which she had suffered diminished perceptibly when all uncertainty upon every subject had come to an end.

But she remained alone now for the greater part of her time, and stayed in the house, or at furthest went into the garden. She shunned every one, even Liddy, and could be brought to make no confidences, and to ask for no sympathy.

As the summer drew on she passed more of her time in the open air, and began to examine into farming matters from sheer necessity, though she never rode out or personally superintended as at former times. One Friday evening in August she walked a little way along the road and entered the village for the first time since the sombre event of the preceding Christmas. None of the old colour had as yet come to her cheek, and its absolute paleness was heightened by the jet black of her gown, till it appeared preternatural. When she reached a little shop at the other end of the place, which stood nearly opposite to the churchyard, Bathsheba heard singing inside the church, and she knew that the singers were practising. She crossed the road, opened the gate, and entered the graveyard, the high sills of the church windows effectually screening her from the eyes of those gathered within. Her stealthy walk was to the nook wherein Troy had worked at planting flowers upon Fanny Robin's grave, and she came to the marble tombstone.

A motion of satisfaction enlivened her face as she read the complete inscription. First came the words of Troy himself: –

> ERECTED BY FRANCIS TROY
> IN BELOVED MEMORY OF
> FANNY ROBIN,
> WHO DIED OCTOBER 9, 18–,
> AGED 20 YEARS.

Underneath this was now inscribed in new letters: –

> IN THE SAME GRAVE LIE
> THE REMAINS OF THE AFORESAID
> FRANCIS TROY,
> WHO DIED DECEMBER 24TH, 18–,
> AGED 26 YEARS.

Whilst she stood and read and meditated the tones of the organ began again in the church, and she went with the same light step round to the porch and listened. The door was closed, and the choir was learning a new hymn. Bathsheba was stirred by emotions which latterly she had assumed to be altogether dead within her. The little attenuated voices of the children brought to her ear in distinct utterance the words they sang without thought or comprehension –

> Lead, kindly Light, amid the encircling gloom,
> Lead Thou me on.

Bathsheba's feeling was always to some extent dependent upon her whim, as is the case with many other women. Something big came into her throat and an uprising to her eyes – and she thought that she would allow the imminent tears to flow if they wished. They did flow and plenteously, and one fell upon the stone bench beside her. Once that she had begun to cry for she hardly knew what, she could not leave off for crowding thoughts she knew too well. She would have given anything in the world to be, as those children were, unconcerned at the meaning of their words, because too innocent to feel the necessity for any such expression. All the impassioned scenes of her brief experience seemed to revive with added emotion at that moment, and those scenes which had been without emotion during enactment had emotion then. Yet grief came to her rather as a luxury than as the scourge of former times.

Owing to Bathsheba's face being buried in her hands she did not notice a form which came quietly into the porch, and on seeing her, first moved as if to retreat, then paused and regarded her. Bathsheba did not raise her head for some time, and when she looked round her face was wet, and her eyes drowned and dim. 'Mr. Oak,' exclaimed she, disconcerted, 'how long have you been here?'

'A few minutes, ma'am,' said Oak, respectfully.

'Are you going in?' said Bathsheba; and there came from within the church as from a prompter –

> I loved the garish day, and, spite of fears,
> Pride ruled my will: remember not past years.

'I was,' said Gabriel. 'I am one of the bass singers, you know. I have sung bass for several months.'

'Indeed: I wasn't aware of that. I'll leave you, then.'

> Which I have loved long since, and lost awhile,

sang the children.

'Don't let me drive you away, mistress. I think I won't go in to-night.'

'O no – you don't drive me away.'

Then they stood in a state of some embarrassment, Bathsheba trying to wipe her dreadfully drenched and inflamed face without his noticing her. At length Oak said, 'I've not seen you – I mean spoken to you – since ever so long, have I?' But he feared to bring distressing memories back, and interrupted himself with: 'Were you going into church?'

'No,' she said. 'I came to see the tombstone privately – to see if they had cut the inscription as I wished. Mr. Oak, you needn't mind speaking to me, if you wish to, on the matter which is in both our minds at this moment.'

'And have they done it as you wished?' said Oak.

'Yes. Come and see it, if you have not already.'

So together they went and read the tomb. 'Eight months ago!' Gabriel murmured when he saw the date. 'It seems like yesterday to me.'

'And to me as if it were years ago – long years, and I had been dead between. And now I am going home, Mr. Oak.'

Oak walked after her. 'I wanted to name a small matter to you as soon as I could,' he said with hesitation. 'Merely about business, and I think I may just mention it now, if you'll allow me.'

'O yes, certainly.'

'It is that I may soon have to give up the management of your farm, Mrs. Troy. The fact is, I am thinking of leaving England – not yet, you know – next spring.'

'Leaving England!' she said, in surprise and genuine disappointment. 'Why, Gabriel, what are you going to do that for?'

'Well, I've thought it best,' Oak stammered out. 'California is the spot I've had in my mind to try.'

'But it is understood everywhere that you are going to take poor Mr. Boldwood's farm on your own account?'

'I've had the refusal o' it 'tis true; but nothing is settled yet, and I have reasons for gieing up. I shall finish out my year there as manager for the trustees, but no more.'

'And what shall I do without you? Oh, Gabriel, I don't think you ought to go away. You've been with me so long – through bright times and dark times – such old friends as we are – that it seems unkind almost. I had fancied that if you leased the other farm as master, you might still give a helping look across at mine. And now going away!'

'I would have willingly.'

'Yet now that I am more helpless than ever you go away!'

'Yes, that's the ill fortune o' it,' said Gabriel, in a distressed tone. 'And it is because of that very helplessness that I feel bound to go. Good afternoon, ma'am,' he concluded, in evident anxiety to get away, and at once went out of the church-yard by a path she could follow on no pretence whatever.

Bathsheba went home, her mind occupied with a new trouble, which being rather harassing than deadly was calculated to do good by diverting her from the chronic gloom of her life. She was set thinking a great deal about Oak and of his wish to shun her; and there occurred to Bathsheba several incidents of her latter intercourse with him, which, trivial when singly viewed, amounted together to a perceptible disinclination for her society. It broke upon her at length as a great pain that her last old disciple was about to forsake her and flee. He who had believed in her and argued on her side when all the rest of the world was against her, had at last like the others become weary and neglectful of the old cause, and was leaving her to fight her battles alone.

Three weeks went on, and more evidence of his want of interest in her was forthcoming. She noticed that instead of entering the small parlour or office where the farm accounts were kept, and waiting, or leaving a memorandum as he had hitherto done during her seclusion, Oak never came at all when she was likely to be there, only entering at unseasonable hours when her presence in that part of the house was least to be expected. Whenever he wanted directions he sent a message, or note with neither heading nor signature, to which she was obliged to reply in the same offhand style. Poor Bathsheba began to suffer now from the most torturing sting of all – a sensation that she was despised.

The autumn wore away gloomily enough amid these melancholy conjectures, and Christmas-day came, completing a year of her legal widowhood, and two years and a quarter of her life alone. On examining her heart it appeared beyond measure strange that the subject of which the season might have been supposed suggestive – the event in the hall at Boldwood's – was not agitating her at all; but instead, an agonizing conviction that everybody abjured her – for what she could not tell – and that Oak was the ringleader of the recusants. Coming out of church that day she looked round in hope that Oak, whose bass voice she had heard rolling out from the gallery overhead in a most unconcerned manner, might chance to linger in her path in the old way. There he was, as usual, coming down the path behind her. But on seeing Bathsheba turn, he looked aside, and as soon as he got beyond the gate, and there was the barest excuse for a divergence, he made one, and vanished.

The next morning brought the culminating stroke; she had been expecting it long. It was a formal notice by letter from him that he should not renew his engagement with her for the following Lady-day.

Bathsheba actually sat and cried over this letter most bitterly. She was aggrieved and wounded that the possession of hopeless love from Gabriel, which she had grown to regard as her inalienable right for life, should have been withdrawn just at his own pleasure in this way. She was bewildered too by the prospect of having to rely on her own resources again: it seemed to herself that she never could again acquire energy sufficient to go to market, barter, and sell. Since Troy's death Oak had attended all sales and fairs for her, transacting her business at the same time with his own. What should she do now? Her life was becoming a desolation.

So desolate was Bathsheba this evening, that in an absolute hunger for pity and sympathy, and miserable in that she appeared to have outlived the only true friendship she had ever owned, she put on her bonnet and cloak and went down to Oak's house just after sunset, guided on her way by the pale primrose rays of a crescent moon a few days old.

A lively firelight shone from the window, but nobody was visible in the room. She tapped nervously, and then thought it doubtful if it were right for a single woman to call upon a bachelor who lived alone, although he was her manager, and she might be supposed to call on business without any real impropriety. Gabriel opened the door, and the moon shone upon his forehead.

'Mr. Oak,' said Bathsheba, faintly.

'Yes; I am Mr. Oak,' said Gabriel. 'Who have I the honour – O how stupid of me, not to know you, mistress!'

'I shall not be your mistress much longer, shall I, Gabriel?' she said in pathetic tones.

'Well, no. I suppose – But come in, ma'am. Oh – and I'll get a light,' Oak replied, with some awkwardness.

'No; not on my account.'

'It is so seldom that I get a lady visitor that I'm afraid I haven't proper accommodation. Will you sit down, please? Here's a chair, and there's one, too. I am sorry that my chairs all have wood seats, and are rather hard, but I – was thinking of getting some new ones.' Oak placed two or three for her.

'They are quite easy enough for me.'

So down she sat, and down sat he, the fire dancing in their faces, and upon the old furniture,

> all a-sheenen
> Wi' long years o' handlen,[1]

that formed Oak's array of household possessions, which sent back a dancing reflection in reply. It was very odd to these two persons, who knew each other passing well, that the mere circumstance of their meeting in a new place and in a new way should make them so awkward and constrained. In the fields, or at her house, there had never been any embarrassment; but now that Oak had become the entertainer their lives seemed to be moved back again to the days when they were strangers.

'You'll think it strange that I have come, but —'

'O no; not at all.'

'But I thought – Gabriel, I have been uneasy in the belief that I have offended you, and that you are going away on that account. It grieved me very much, and I couldn't help coming.'

'Offended me! As if you could do that, Bathsheba!'

'Haven't I?' she asked, gladly. 'But, what are you going away for else?'

1. W. Barnes.

'I am not going to emigrate, you know; I wasn't aware that you would wish me not to when I told 'ee, or I shouldn't have thought of doing it,' he said, simply. 'I have arranged for Little Weatherbury Farm, and shall have it in my own hands at Lady-day. You know I've had a share in it for some time. Still, that wouldn't prevent my attending to your business as before, hadn't it been that things have been said about us.'

'What?' said Bathsheba in surprise. 'Things said about you and me! What are they?'

'I cannot tell you.'

'It would be wiser if you were to, I think. You have played the part of mentor to me many times, and I don't see why you should fear to do it now.'

'It is nothing that you have done, this time. The top and tail o't is this – that I'm sniffing about here, and waiting for poor Boldwood's farm, with a thought of getting you some day.'

'Getting me! What does that mean?'

'Marrying of 'ee, in plain British. You asked me to tell, so you mustn't blame me.'

Bathsheba did not look quite so alarmed as if a cannon had been discharged by her ear, which was what Oak had expected. 'Marrying me! I didn't know it was that you meant,' she said, quietly. 'Such a thing as that is too absurd – too soon – to think of, by far!'

'Yes; of course, it is too absurd. I don't desire any such thing; I should think that was plain enough by this time. Surely, surely you be the last person in the world I think of marrying. It is too absurd, as you say.'

' "Too – s-s-soon" were the words I used.'

'I must beg your pardon for correcting you, but you said, "too absurd," and so do I.'

'I beg your pardon too!' she returned, with tears in her eyes. ' "Too soon" was what I said. But it doesn't matter a bit – not at all – but I only meant, "too soon." Indeed, I didn't, Mr. Oak, and you must believe me!'

Gabriel looked her long in the face, but the firelight being

faint there was not much to be seen. 'Bathsheba,' he said, tenderly
and in surprise, and coming closer: 'If I only knew one thing –
whether you would allow me to love you and win you, and marry
you after all – If I only knew that!'

'But you never will know,' she murmured.

'Why?'

'Because you never ask.'

'Oh – Oh!' said Gabriel, with a low laugh of joyousness.
'My own dear —'

'You ought not to have sent me that harsh letter this morning,' she interrupted. 'It shows you didn't care a bit about me,
and were ready to desert me like all the rest of them! It was
very cruel of you, considering I was the first sweetheart that
you ever had, and you were the first I ever had; and I shall not
forget it!'

'Now, Bathsheba, was ever anybody so provoking?' he said,
laughing. 'You know it was purely that I, as an unmarried man,
carrying on a business for you as a very taking young woman,
had a proper hard part to play – more particular that people
knew I had a sort of feeling for 'ee; and I fancied, from the way
we were mentioned together, that it might injure your good
name. Nobody knows the heat and fret I have been caused
by it.'

'And was that all?'

'All.'

'O, how glad I am I came!' she exclaimed, thankfully, as she
rose from her seat. 'I have thought so much more of you since
I fancied you did not want even to see me again. But I must
be going now, or I shall be missed. Why, Gabriel,' she said,
with a slight laugh, as they went to the door, 'it seems exactly
as if I had come courting you – how dreadful!'

'And quite right, too,' said Oak. 'I've danced at your skittish
heels, my beautiful Bathsheba, for many a long mile, and many
a long day; and it is hard to begrudge me this one visit.'

He accompanied her up the hill, explaining to her the details of his forthcoming tenure of the other farm. They spoke

very little of their mutual feelings; pretty phrases and warm expressions being probably unnecessary between such tried friends. Theirs was that substantial affection which arises (if any arises at all) when the two who are thrown together begin first by knowing the rougher sides of each other's character, and not the best till further on, the romance growing up in the interstices of a mass of hard prosaic reality. This good-fellowship – *camaraderie* – usually occurring through similarity of pursuits, is unfortunately seldom superadded to love between the sexes, because men and women associate, not in their labours, but in their pleasures merely. Where, however, happy circumstance permits its development, the compounded feeling proves itself to be the only love which is strong as death – that love which many waters cannot quench, nor the floods drown, beside which the passion usually called by the name is evanescent as steam.

CHAPTER LVII

A FOGGY NIGHT AND MORNING – CONCLUSION

'THE most private, secret, plainest wedding that it is possible to have.'

Those had been Bathsheba's words to Oak one evening, some time after the event of the preceding chapter, and he meditated a full hour by the clock upon how to carry out her wishes to the letter.

'A license – O yes, it must be a license,' he said to himself at last. 'Very well, then; first, a license.'

On a dark night, a few days later, Oak came with mysterious steps from the surrogate's door in Casterbridge. On the way home he heard a heavy tread in front of him, and, overtaking the man, found him to be Coggan. They walked together into the village until they came to a little lane behind the church, leading down to the cottage of Laban Tall, who had lately been installed as clerk of the parish, and was yet in mortal terror at church on Sundays when he heard his lone voice among certain hard words of the Psalms, whither no man ventured to follow him.

'Well, good-night, Coggan,' said Oak, 'I'm going down this way.'

'Oh!' said Coggan, surprised; 'what's going on to-night then, make so bold, Mr. Oak?'

It seemed rather ungenerous not to tell Coggan, under the circumstances, for Coggan had been true as steel all through the time of Gabriel's unhappiness about Bathsheba, and Gabriel said, 'You can keep a secret, Coggan?'

'You've proved me, and you know.'

'Yes, I have, and I do know. Well, then, mistress and I mean to get married to-morrow morning.'

'Heaven's high tower! And yet I've thought of such a thing from time to time; true, I have. But keeping it so close! Well, there, 'tis no consarn of mine, and I wish 'ee joy o' her.'

'Thank you, Coggan. But I assure 'ee that this great hush is not what I wished for at all, or what either of us would have wished if it hadn't been for certain things that would make a gay wedding seem hardly the thing. Bathsheba has a great wish that all the parish shall not be in church, looking at her – she's shy-like and nervous about it, in fact – so I be doing this to humour her.'

'Ay, I see: quite right, too, I suppose I must say. And you be now going down to the clerk.'

'Yes; you may as well come with me.'

'I am afeard your labour in keeping it close will be throwed away,' said Coggan, as they walked along. 'Labe Tall's old woman will horn it all over parish in half-an-hour.'

'So she will, upon my life; I never thought of that,' said Oak, pausing. 'Yet I must tell him to-night, I suppose, for he's working so far off, and leaves early.'

'I'll tell 'ee how we could tackle her,' said Coggan. 'I'll knock and ask to speak to Laban outside the door, you standing in the background. Then he'll come out, and you can tell yer tale. She'll never guess what I want en for; and I'll make up a few words about the farm-work, as a blind.'

This scheme was considered feasible; and Coggan advanced boldly, and rapped at Mrs. Tall's door. Mrs. Tall herself opened it.

'I wanted to have a word with Laban.'

'He's not at home, and won't be this side of eleven o'clock. He've been forced to go over to Yalbury since shutting out work. I shall do quite as well.'

'I hardly think you will. Stop a moment' and Coggan stepped round the corner of the porch to consult Oak.

'Who's t'other man, then?' said Mrs. Tall.

'Only a friend,' said Coggan.

'Say he's wanted to meet mistress near church-hatch

to-morrow morning at ten,' said Oak, in a whisper. 'That he must come without fail, and wear his best clothes.'

'The clothes will floor us as safe as houses!' said Coggan.

'It can't be helped,' said Oak. 'Tell her.'

So Coggan delivered the message. 'Mind, het or wet, blow or snow, he must come,' added Jan. ''Tis very particular, indeed. The fact is, 'tis to witness her sign some law-work about taking shares wi' another farmer for a long span o' years. There, that's what 'tis, and now I've told 'ee, Mother Tall, in a way I shouldn't ha' done if I hadn't loved 'ee so hopeless well.'

Coggan retired before she could ask any further; and next they called at the vicar's in a manner which excited no curiosity at all. Then Gabriel went home, and prepared for the morrow.

'Liddy,' said Bathsheba, on going to bed that night, 'I want you to call me at seven o'clock to-morrow, in case I shouldn't wake.'

'But you always do wake afore then, ma'am.'

'Yes, but I have something important to do, which I'll tell you of when the time comes, and it's best to make sure.'

Bathsheba, however, awoke voluntarily at four, nor could she by any contrivance get to sleep again. About six, being quite positive that her watch had stopped during the night, she could wait no longer. She went and tapped at Liddy's door, and after some labour awoke her.

'But I thought it was I who had to call you?' said the bewildered Liddy. 'And it isn't six yet.'

'Indeed it is; how can you tell such a story, Liddy! I know it must be ever so much past seven. Come to my room as soon as you can; I want you to give my hair a good brushing.'

When Liddy came to Bathsheba's room her mistress was already waiting. Liddy could not understand this extraordinary promptness. 'Whatever *is* going on, ma'am?' she said.

'Well, I'll tell you,' said Bathsheba, with a mischievous smile in her bright eyes. 'Farmer Oak is coming here to dine with me to-day!'

'Farmer Oak – and nobody else? – you two alone?'

'Yes.'

'But is it safe, ma'am, after what's been said?' asked her companion, dubiously. 'A woman's good name is such a perishable article that —'

Bathsheba laughed with a flushed cheek, and whispered in Liddy's ear, although there was nobody present. Then Liddy stared and exclaimed, 'Souls alive, what news! It makes my heart go quite bumpity-bump!'

'It makes mine rather furious, too,' said Bathsheba. 'However, there's no getting out of it now!'

It was a damp disagreeable morning. Nevertheless, at twenty minutes to ten o'clock, Oak came out of his house, and

> Went up the hill side
> With that sort of stride
> A man puts out when walking in search of a bride,

and knocked at Bathsheba's door. Ten minutes later a large and a smaller umbrella might have been seen moving from the same door, and through the mist along the road to the church. The distance was not more than a quarter of a mile, and these two sensible persons deemed it unnecessary to drive. An observer must have been very close indeed to discover that the forms under the umbrellas were those of Oak and Bathsheba, arm-in-arm for the first time in their lives, Oak in a greatcoat extending to his knees, and Bathsheba in a cloak that reached her clogs. Yet, though so plainly dressed, there was a certain rejuvenated appearance about her: –

> As though a rose should shut and be a bud again.

Repose had again incarnadined her cheeks; and having, at Gabriel's request, arranged her hair this morning as she had worn it years ago on Norcombe Hill, she seemed in his eyes remarkably like the girl of that fascinating dream, which, considering that she was now only three or four-and-twenty, was perhaps not very wonderful. In the church were Tall, Liddy, and the parson, and in a remarkably short space of time the deed was done.

The two sat down very quietly to tea in Bathsheba's parlour in the evening of the same day, for it had been arranged that Farmer Oak should go there to live, since he had as yet neither money, house, nor furniture worthy of the name, though he was on a sure way towards them, whilst Bathsheba was, comparatively, in a plethora of all three.

Just as Bathsheba was pouring out a cup of tea, their ears were greeted by the firing of a cannon, followed by what seemed like a tremendous blowing of trumpets, in the front of the house.

'There!' said Oak, laughing, 'I knew those fellows were up to something, by the look on their faces.'

Oak took up the light and went into the porch, followed by Bathsheba with a shawl over her head. The rays fell upon a group of male figures gathered upon the gravel in front, who, when they saw the newly-married couple in the porch, set up a loud 'Hurrah!' and at the same moment bang again went the cannon in the background, followed by a hideous clang of music from a drum, tambourine, clarionet, serpent, hautboy, tenor-viol, and double-bass – the only remaining relics of the true and original Weatherbury band – venerable worm-eaten instruments, which had celebrated in their own persons the victories of Marlborough, under the fingers of the forefathers of those who played them now. The performers came forward, and marched up to the front.

'Those bright boys, Mark Clark and Jan, are at the bottom of all this,' said Oak. 'Come in, souls, and have something to eat and drink wi' me and my wife.'

'Not to-night,' said Mr. Clark, with evident self-denial. 'Thank ye all the same; but we'll call at a more seemly time. However, we couldn't think of letting the day pass without a note of admiration of some sort. If ye could send a drop of som'at down to Warren's, why so it is. Here's long life and happiness to neighbour Oak and his comely bride!'

'Thank ye; thank ye all,' said Gabriel. 'A bit and a drop shall be sent to Warren's for ye at once. I had a thought that we might very likely get a salute of some sort from our old friends, and I was saying so to my wife but now.'

'Faith,' said Coggan, in a critical tone, turning to his companions, 'the man hev learnt to say "my wife" in a wonderful naterel way, considering how very youthful he is in wedlock as yet – hey, neighbours all?'

'I never heerd a skilful old married feller of twenty years' standing pipe "my wife" in a more used note than 'a did,' said Jacob Smallbury. 'It might have been a little more true to nater if't had been spoke a little chillier, but that wasn't to be expected just now.'

'That improvement will come wi' time,' said Jan, twirling his eye.

Then Oak laughed, and Bathsheba smiled (for she never laughed readily now), and their friends turned to go.

'Yes; I suppose that's the size o't,' said Joseph Poorgrass with a cheerful sigh as they moved away; 'and I wish him joy o' her; though I were once or twice upon saying to-day with holy Hosea, in my scripture manner, which is my second nature, "Ephraim is joined to idols: let him alone." But since 'tis as 'tis, why, it might have been worse, and I feel my thanks accordingly.'

THE END

To my mother, who knew how to love. And had a
weakness for troublemakers with hearts of gold.

To my father, who has always loved and admired strong women.

And to Georgia Funsten and Patricia Young,
the smartest and strongest women I know.

Chapter One

I've been summoned to see the Nowhere Man.

He's at his desk when I step inside the gray cave of his office, his back turned.

"Uh, Pop?"

He holds up his hand, keeps scribbling on a blue-lined pad.

Standard operating procedure.

I flick my eyes around the room: the mantel, the carpet, the bookshelves, the window; try to find a comfortable place to land.

No dice.

Ma's fond of "cute" – teddy bears in seasonal outfits and pillows with little sayings and shit she gets on QVC. They're everywhere. Except here, a room spliced out of John Grisham, all leather-bound, only muted light through the shades. August heat outdoors, but no hint of that allowed here. I face the rear of Pop's neck, hunch further into the gray, granite-hard sofa, rub my eyes, sink back on my elbows.

On his desk, three pictures of Nan, my twin, at various ages – poofy red curls, missing teeth, then baring them in braces. Always worried eyes. Two more of her on the wall, straightened hair, expensive white smile, plus a framed newspaper clipping of her after delivering a speech at this summer's Stony Bay Fourth of July thing.

No pics of me.

Were there ever? Can't remember. In the bad old days, I always got high before a father/son office visit.

Clear my throat.

Crack my knuckles.

"Pop? You asked to see me?"

He actually startles. "Tim?"

"Yep."

Swiveling the chair, he looks at me. His eyes, like Nan's and my own, are gray. Match his hair. Match his office.

"So," he says.

I wait. Try not to scope out the bottle of Macallan on the . . . what do you call it. Sidebar? Sideboard? Generally, Ma brings in the ice in the little silver bucket thing ten minutes after he gets home from work, six p.m., synched up like those weird-ass cuckoo clock people who pop out of their tiny wooden doors, dead on schedule when the clock strikes, so Pop can have the first of his two scotches ready to go.

Today must be special. It's only three o'clock and there's the bucket, oozing cool sweat like I am. Even when I was little I knew he'd leave the second drink half-finished. So I

could slurp down the last of the scotchy ice water without him knowing while he was washing his hands before dinner. Can't remember when I started doing that, but it was well before my balls dropped.

"Ma said you wanted to talk."

He brushes some invisible whatever from his knee, like his attention's already gone. "Did she say why?"

I clear my throat again. "Because I'm moving out? Planning to do that. Today." Ten minutes ago, ideally.

His eyes return to mine. "Do you think this is the best choice for you?"

Classic Nowhere Man. Moving out was hardly my choice. His ultimatum, in fact. The only "best choice" I've made lately was to stop drinking. Etc.

But Pop likes to tack and turn, and no matter that this was his order, he can shove that rudder over without even looking and make me feel like shit.

"I asked you a question, Tim."

"It's fine. It's a good idea."

Pop steeples his fingers, sets his chin on them, my chin, cleft and all. "How long has it been since you got kicked out of Ellery Prep?"

"Uh. Eight months." Early December. Hadn't even unpacked my suitcase from Thanksgiving break.

"Since then you've had how many jobs?"

Maybe he doesn't remember. I fudge it. "Um. Three."

"Seven," Pop corrects.

3

Damn.

"How many of those were you fired from?"

"I still have the one at –"

He pivots in his chair, halfway back to his desk, frowns down at his cell phone. "How many?"

"Well, I quit the senator's office, so really only five."

Pop twists back around, lowers the phone, studies me over his reading glasses. "I'm very clear on the fact that you left that job. You say 'only' like it's something to brag about. Fired from five out of seven jobs since February. Kicked out of three schools . . . do you know that I've never been let go from a job in my life? Never gotten a bad performance review? A grade lower than a B? Neither has your sister."

Right. Perfect old Nano. "My grades were always good," I say. My eyes stray again to the Macallan. Need something to do with my hands. Rolling a joint would be good.

"Exactly," Pop says. He jerks from the chair, nearly as angular and almost as tall as me, drops his glasses on the desk with a clatter, runs his hands quickly through his short hair, then focuses on scooping out ice and measuring scotch.

I catch a musky, iodine-y whiff of it, and man, it smells good.

"You're not stupid, Tim. But you sure act that way."

Yo-kay . . . he's barely spoken to me all summer. *Now* he's on my nuts? But I should try. I drag my eyes off the

4

caramel-colored liquid in his glass and back to his face.

"Pop. Dad. I know I'm not the son you would have . . . special ordered –"

"Would you like a drink?"

He sloshes more scotch into another glass, uncharacteristically careless, sets it out on the Columbia University coaster on the side table next to the couch, slides it toward me. He tips his own glass to his lips, then places it neatly on his coaster, almost completely chugged.

Well, this is fucked up.

"Uh, look." My throat's so tight, my voice comes out weird – husky, then high-pitched. "I haven't had a drink or anything like that since the end of June, so that's, uh, fifty-nine days, but who's counting. I'm doing my best. And I'll –"

Pop has steepled his hands and is scrutinizing the fish tank against the wall.

I'm boring him.

"And I'll keep doin' it . . . ." I trail off.

There's a long pause. During which I have no idea what he's thinking. Only that my best friend is on his way over, and my Jetta in the driveway is seeming more and more like a getaway car.

"Four months," Pop says, in this, like, flat voice, like he's reading it off a piece of paper. Since he's turned back to look down at his desk, it's possible.

"Um . . . yes . . . What?"

5

"I'm giving you four months from today to pull your life together. You'll be eighteen in December. A man. After that, unless I see you acting like one – in every way – I'm cutting off your allowance, I'll no longer pay your health and car insurance, and I'll transfer your college fund into your sister's."

Not as though there was ever a welcome mat under me, but whatever the fuck was there has been yanked out and I'm slammed down hard on my ass.

Wait . . . what?

A man by December. Like, poof, snap, shazam. Like there's some expiration date on . . . where I am now.

"But –" I start.

He checks his Seiko, hitting a button, maybe starting the countdown. "Today is August twenty-fourth. That gives you until just before Christmas."

"But –"

He holds up his hand, like he's slapping the off button on my words. It's ultimatum number two or nothing.

No clue what to say anyway, but it doesn't matter, because the conversation is over.

We're done here.

Unfold my legs, yank myself to my feet, and I head for the door on autopilot.

Can't get out of the room fast enough.

For either of us, apparently.

Ho, ho, ho to you too, Pop.

Chapter Two

"You're really doing this?"

I'm shoving the last of my clothes into a cardboard box when my ma comes in, without knocking, because she never does. Risky as hell when you have a horny seventeen-year-old son. She hovers in the doorway, wearing a pink shirt and this denim skirt with – what are those? Crabs? – sewn all over it.

"Just following orders, Ma." I cram flip-flops into the stuffed box, push down on them hard. "Pop's wish is my command."

She takes a step back like I've slapped her. I guess it's my tone. I've been sober nearly two months, but I have yet to go cold turkey on assholicism. Ha.

"You had so much I never had, Timothy . . ."

Away we go.

". . . private school, swimming lessons, tennis camp . . ."

Yep, I'm an alcoholic high school dropout, but check out my backhand!

She shakes out the wrinkles in a blue blazer, one quick

motion, flapping it into the air with an abrasive crack. "What are you going to do – keep working at that hardware store? Going to those meetings?"

She says "hardware store" like "strip club" and "going to those meetings" like "making those sex tapes."

"It's a good job. And I need those meetings."

Ma's hands start smoothing my stack of folded clothes. Blue veins stand out on her freckled, pale arms. "I don't see what strangers can do for you that your own family can't."

I open my mouth to say: "I know you don't. That's why I need the strangers." Or: "Uncle Sean sure could have used those strangers." But we don't talk about that, or him.

I shove a pair of possibly too-small loafers in the box and go over to give her a hug.

She pats my back, quick and sharp, and pulls away.

"Cheer up, Ma. Nan'll definitely get into Columbia. Only one of your children is a fuck-up."

"Language, Tim."

"Sorry. My bad. Cock-up."

"That," she says, "is even worse."

Okeydokey. Whatever.

My bedroom door flies open – *again* no knock.

"Some girl who sounds like she has laryngitis is on the phone for you, Tim," Nan says, eyeing my packing job. "God, everything's going to be all wrinkly."

"I don't care –" But she's already dumped the cardboard

box onto my bed.

"Where's your suitcase?" She starts dividing stuff into piles. "The blue plaid one with your monogram?"

"No clue."

"I'll check the basement," Ma says, looking relieved to have a reason to head for the door. "This girl, Timothy? Should I bring you the phone?"

I can't think of any girl I have a thing to say to. Except Alice Garrett. Who definitely would not be calling me.

"Tell her I'm not home."

Permanently.

Nan's folding things rapidly, piling up my shirts in order of style. I reach out to still her hands. "Forget it. Not important."

She looks up. Shit, she's crying.

We Masons cry easily. Curse of the Irish (one of 'em). I loop one elbow around her neck, thump her on the back a little too hard. She starts coughing, chokes, gives a weak laugh.

"You can come visit me, Nano. Any time you need to . . . escape . . . or whatever."

"Please. It won't be the same," Nan says, then blows her nose on the hem of my shirt.

It won't. No more staying up till nearly dawn, watching old Steve McQueen movies because I think he's badass and Nan thinks he's hot. No Twizzlers and Twix and shit appearing in my room like magic because Nan

knows massive sugar infusions are the only sure cure for drug addiction.

"Lucky for you. No more covering my lame ass when I stay out all night, no more getting creative with excuses when I don't show for something, no more me bumming money off you constantly."

Now she's wiping her eyes with my shirt. I haul it off, hand it to her. "Something to remember me by."

She actually folds *that,* then stares at the neat little square, all sad-faced. "Sometimes it's like I'm missing everyone I ever met. I actually even miss Daniel. I miss Samantha."

"Daniel was a pompous prickface and a crap boyfriend. Samantha, your actual best friend, is ten blocks and ten minutes away – shorter if you text her."

She blows that off, hunkers down, pulling knobbly knees to her chest and lowering her forehead so her hair sweeps forward to cover her blotchy face. Nan and I are both ginger, but she got all the freckles, everywhere, while mine are only across my nose. She looks up at me with that face she does, all pathetic and quivery. I hate that face. It always wins.

"You'll be fine, Nan." I tap my temple. "You're just as smart as me. Much less messed up. At least as far as most people know."

Nan twitches back. We lock eyes. The elephant in the room lies bleeding out on the floor between us. Then she looks away, gets busy picking up another T-shirt to fold expertly, like the only thing that matters in the world is for

the sleeves to align.

"Not really," she says in a subdued voice. Not taking the bait there either, I guess.

I grope around the quilt on my bed, locate my cigs, light one, and take a deep drag. I know it's all kinds of bad for me, but *God*, how does anyone get through the day without smoking? Setting the smoldering butt down in the ashtray, I tap her on the back again, gently this time.

"Hey now. Don't stress. You know Pop. He wants to add it up and get a positive bottom line. Job. High school diploma. College-bound. Check, check, check. It only has to *look* good. I can pull that off."

Don't know if this is cheering my sister up, but as I talk, the squirming fireball in my stomach cools and settles. Fake it. That I can do.

Mom pops her head into the room. "That Garrett boy's here. Heavens, put on a shirt, Tim." She digs in a bureau drawer and thrusts a Camp Wyoda T-shirt I thought I'd ditched years ago at me. Nan leaps up, knuckling away her tears, pulling at her own shirt, wiping her palms on her shorts. She has a zillion twitchy habits – biting her nails, twisting her hair, tapping her pencils. I could always get by on a fake ID, a calm face, and a smile. My sister could look guilty saying her prayers. Feet on the stairs, staccato knock on the door – the one person who knocks! – and Jase comes in, swipes back his damp hair with the heel of one hand.

"Shit, man. We haven't even started loading and you're already sweating?"

"Ran here," he says, hands planted hard his on kneecaps. He glances up. "Hey, Nan."

Nan, who has turned her back, gives a quick, jerky nod. When she twists around to tumble more neatly balled socks into my cardboard box, her eyes stray to Jase, up, slowly down. He's the guy girls always look at twice.

"You ran here? It's like five miles from your house! Are you nuts?"

"Three, and nah." Jase braces his forearm against the wall, bending his leg, holding his ankle, stretching out. "Seriously out of shape after sitting around the store all summer. Even after three weeks of training camp, I'm nowhere near up to speed."

"You don't *seem* out of shape," Nan says, then shakes her head so her hair slips forward over her face. "Don't leave without telling me, Tim." She scoots out the door.

"You set?" Jase looks around the room, oblivious to my sister's hormone spike.

"Uh . . . I guess." I look around too, frickin' blank. All I can think to take is my clamshell ashtray. "The clothes, anyway. I suck at packing."

"Toothbrush?" Jase suggests mildly. "Razor. Books, maybe? Sports stuff."

"My lacrosse stick from Ellery Prep? Don't think I'll need it." I tap out another cigarette.

"Bike? Skateboard? Swim gear?" Jase glances over at me, smile flashing in the flare of my lighter.

Mom barges back in so fast, the door knocks against the wall. An umbrella and a huge yellow slicker are draped over one arm, an iron in one hand. "You'll want these. Should I pack you blankets? What happened to that nice boy you were going to move in with, anyway?"

"Didn't work out." As in: that nice boy, my AA buddy Connell, relapsed on both booze and crack, called me all slurry and screwed up, full of blurry suck-ass excuses, so he's obviously out. The garage apartment is my best option.

"Is there even any heat in that ratty place?"

"Jesus God, Ma. You haven't even seen the frickin' —"

"It's pretty reliable," Jase says, not even wincing. "It was my brother's, and Joel likes his comforts."

"All right. I'll . . . leave you two boys to — carry on." She pauses, runs her hand through her hair, showing half an inch of gray roots beneath the red. "Don't forget to take the stenciled paper Aunt Nancy sent in case you need to write thank-you notes."

"Wouldn't dream of it, Ma. Uh, forgetting, I mean."

Jase bows his head, smiling, then shoulders the cardboard box.

"What about pillows?" she says. "You can tuck those right under the other arm, can't you, a big strapping boy like you?"

Christ.

He obediently raises an elbow and she rams two pillows into his armpit.

"I'll throw all this in the Jetta. Take your time, Tim."

I scan the room one last time. Tacked to the corkboard over my desk is a sheet of paper with the words *THE BOY MOST LIKELY TO* scrawled in red marker at the top. One of the few days last fall I remember clearly – hanging with a bunch of my (loser) friends at Ellery out by the boathouse where they stowed the kayaks (and the stoners). We came up with our antidote to those stupid yearbook lists: *Most likely to be a millionaire by twenty-five. Most likely to star in her own reality show. Most likely to get an NFL contract.* Don't know why I kept the thing.

I pop the list off the wall, fold it carefully, jam it into my back pocket.

Nan emerges as soon as Jase, who's been waiting for me in the foyer, opens the creaky front door to head out.

"Tim," she whispers, cool hand wrapping around my forearm. "Don't vanish." As if when I leave our house I'll evaporate like fog rising off the river.

Maybe I will.

By the time we pull into the Garretts' driveway, I've burned through three cigarettes, hitting up the car lighter for the next before I've chucked the last. If I could have smoked all of them at once, I would've.

"You should kick those," Jase says, looking out the window, not pinning me with some accusatory face.

I make to hurl the final butt, then stop myself.

Yeah, toss it next to little Patsy's Cozy Coupe and four-year-old George's midget baby blue bike with training wheels. Plus, George thinks I've quit.

"Can't," I tell him. "Tried. Besides, I've already given up drinking, drugs, and sex. Gotta have a few vices or I'd be too perfect."

Jase snorts. "Sex? Don't think you have to give *that* up." He opens the passenger-side door, starts to slide out.

"The way I did it, I do. Gotta stop messing with any chick with a pulse."

Now *Jase* looks uncomfortable. "That was an addiction too?" he asks, half in, half out the door, nudging the pile of old newspapers on the passenger side with the toe of one Converse.

"Not in the sense that I, like, had to have it, or whatever. It was just . . another way to blow stuff off. Numb out."

He nods like he gets it, but I'm pretty sure he doesn't. Gotta explain. "I'd get wasted at parties. Hook up with girls I didn't like or even know. It was never all that great."

"Guess not" – he slides out completely – "if you're with someone you don't even like or know. Might be different if you were sober and actually cared."

"Yeah, well." I light up one last cigarette. "Don't hold your breath."

Chapter Three

"There is," I say through my teeth, "an owl in the freezer. Can any of you guys explain this to me?"

Three of my younger brothers stare back at me. Blank walls. My younger sister doesn't look up from texting.

I repeat the question.

"Harry put it there," Duff says.

"Duff told me to," Harry says.

George, my youngest brother, cranes his neck. "What kind of owl? Is it dead? Is it white like Hedwig?"

I poke at the rock-solid owl, which is wrapped in a frosty freezer bag. "Very dead. Not white. And someone ate all the frozen waffles and put the box back in empty again."

They all shrug, as if this is as much of an unsolvable mystery as the owl.

"Let's try again. *Why* is this owl in the freezer?"

"Harry's going to bring it in for show-and-tell when school starts," Duff says.

"Sanjay Sapati brought in a seal skull last year. This is way better. You can still see its eyeballs. They're only a

little rotted." Harry stirs his oatmeal, frowning down at what I've tried to pass off as a fun "breakfast for lunch" occasion. He upturns the spoon, shakes it, but the glob of cereal sticks, thick as paste, stubborn as my brother. Harry holds the spoon out toward me, accusingly.

"You get what you get and you don't get upset," I say to him.

"But I do. I do get upset. This is nasty, Alice."

"Just eat it," I say, clinging to patience with all my fingernails. This is all temporary. Just until Dad gets a bit better, until Mom doesn't have to be in three places at once. "It's healthy," I add, but I have to agree with my seven-year-old brother. We're way overdue for a grocery run. The fridge has nothing but eggs, applesauce, and ketchup, the cabinet is bare of anything but Joel's protein-enhanced oatmeal. And the only thing in the freezer is . . . a dead bird.

"We can't have an owl in here, guys." I scramble for Mom's reasonable tone. "It'll make the ice cream taste bad."

"Can we have ice cream instead of this?" Harry pushes, sticking his spoon into the oatmeal, where it pokes out like a gravestone on a gray hill.

I try to sell it as "the kind of porridge the Three Bears ate," but George and Harry are skeptical, Duff, at eleven, is too old for all that, and Andy wrinkles her nose and says, "I'll eat later. I'm too nervous now anyway."

"It's lame to be nervous about Kyle Comstock," Duff says. "He's a boob."

"*Boooooob,*" Patsy repeats from her high chair, the eighteen-month-old copycat.

"You don't understand anything," Andy says, leaving the kitchen, no doubt to try on yet another outfit before sailing camp awards. Six hours away from now.

"Who cares what she wears? It's the stupid sailing awards," Duff grumbles. "This stuff is vomitous, Alice. It's like gruel. Like what they make Oliver Twist eat."

"*He* wanted more," I point out.

"He was *starving,*" Duff counters.

"Look, stop arguing and eat the damn stuff."

George's eyes go big. "Mommy doesn't say that word. Daddy says not to."

"Well, they aren't here, are they?"

George looks mournfully down at his oatmeal, poking at it with his spoon like he might find Mom and Dad in there.

"Sorry, Georgie," I say repentantly. "How about some eggs, guys?"

"No!" they all say at once. They've had my eggs before. Since Mom has been spending a lot of time at either doctors' appointments for herself or doctor and physical therapy consults for Dad, they've suffered through the full range of my limited culinary talents.

"I'll get rid of the owl if you give us money to eat

breakfast in town," Duff says.

"Alice, look!" Andy says despairingly, "I knew this wouldn't fit." She hovers in the doorway in the sundress I loaned her, the front sagging. "When do I get off the itty-bitty-titty committee? You did before you were even thirteen." She sounds accusatory, like I used up the last available bigger chest size in the family.

"Titty committee?" Duff starts laughing. "Who's on that? I bet Joel is. And Tim."

"You are *so* immature that listening to you actually makes *me* younger," Andy tells him. "Alice, help! I love this dress. You never lend it to me. I'm going to die if I can't wear it." She looks wildly around the kitchen. "Do I stuff it? With what?"

"Breadcrumbs?" Duff is still cracking up. "Oatmeal? Owl feathers?"

I point the oatmeal spoon at her. "Never stuff. Own your size."

"I want to wear this dress." Andy scowls at me. "It's perfect. Except it doesn't fit. There. Do you have anything else? That's flatter?"

"Did you ask Samantha?" I glare at Duff, who is shoving several kitchen sponges down his shirt. Harry, who doesn't get what's going on – I hope – but is happy to join in on tormenting Andy, is wadding up some diapers from Patsy's clean stack and following suit. My brother's girlfriend has much more patience than I do. Maybe because Samantha

only has one sibling to deal with.

"She's helping her mom take her sister to college – she probably won't be back till tonight. Alice! What do I do?"

My jaw clenches at the mere mention of Grace Reed, Sam's mom, the closest thing our family has to a nemesis. Or maybe it's the owl. *God. Get me out of here.*

"I'm hungry," Harry says. "I'm starving here. I'll be dead by night."

"It takes three weeks to starve," George tells him, his air of authority undermined by his hot cocoa mustache.

"Ughhh. No one cares!" Andy storms away.

"She's got the hormones going on," Duff confides to Harry. Ever since hearing it from my mother, my little brothers treat "hormones" like a contagious disease.

My cell phone vibrates on the cluttered counter. Brad again. I ignore it, start banging open cabinets. "Look, guys, we're out of everything, got it? We can't go shopping until we get this week's take-home from the store, and no one has time to go anyway. I'm not giving you money. So it's oatmeal or empty stomachs. Unless you want peanut butter on toast."

"Not again," Duff groans, shoving away from the table and stalking out of the kitchen.

"Gross," Harry says, doing the same, after accidentally knocking over his orange juice – and ignoring it.

How does Mom stand this? I pinch the muscles at the base of my neck, hard, close my eyes. Push away the most

treacherous thought of all: *Why* does Mom stand this?

George is still doggedly trying to eat a spoonful of oatmeal, one rolled oat at a time.

"Don't bother, G. You still like peanut butter, right?"

Breathing out a long sigh, world-weary at four, George rests his freckled cheek against his hand, watching me with a focus that reminds me of Jase. "You can make diamonds out of peanut butter. I readed about it."

"Read," I say automatically, replenishing the raisins I'd sprinkled on the tray of Patsy's high chair.

"Yucks a dis," she says, picking each raisin up with a delicate pincer grip and dropping it off the side of the high chair.

"Do you think we could make diamonds out of this peanut butter?" George asks hopefully as I open the jar of Jif.

"I wish, Georgie," I say, looking at the empty cabinet over the window, and then noticing a dark blue Jetta pull into our driveway, the door kick open, a tall figure climb out, the sun hitting his rusty hair, lighting it like a match.

Fabulous. Exactly what we need for the flammable family mix. Tim Mason. The human equivalent of C-4.

∘ • ∘ •

We walk up the creaky garage stairs and Jase hauls a key out of his pocket, unlocks the door, flips on the lights. I

brush past him and drop my cardboard box on the ground. Joel's old apartment is low-ceilinged and decorated with milk crate bookcases, ugly couch, mini-fridge, microwave, denim beanbag chair with Sox logo, walls covered in *Sports Illustrated* swimsuit issue and all that − tits everywhere − and a gigantic iron weight rack with a shit-ton of weights.

"*This* is where Joel took all those au pairs? I thought he had better game than this massive cliché."

Jase grimaces. "Welcome to Bootytown. Supposedly the nannies never minded because they expected it of *American boys*. Want me to help yank 'em down?"

"Nah, I can always count body parts if I have trouble sleeping."

After a brief scope-out of the apartment, during which he makes a face and empties a few trash cans, he asks, "This gonna work for you?"

"Absolutely." I reach into my pocket, pull out the lined paper list I snatched off my bulletin board, and slap it on the refrigerator, *adios*-ing a babe in hot pink spandex.

Jase scans my sign, shakes his head. "Mase . . . you know you can come on over anytime."

"I've been to boarding school, Garrett. Not like I'm afraid of the dark."

"Don't be a dick," he says mildly. He points in the direction of the bathroom. "The plumbing backs up sometimes. If the plunger doesn't work, text, I can fix it. I repeat, you're always welcome to head to our house. Or

join me on the pre-dawn job. I gotta pick up Samantha now. She ended up not going to Vermont. Ride along?"

"With the perfect high school sweethearts? Nah. I think I'll stay and see if I can break the plunger. *Then* I'll text you."

He flips me off, grins, and leaves.

Time to get my ass to a meeting. Better that than alone with a ton of airbrushed boobs and my unfiltered thoughts.

Chapter Four

When I walk up the Garretts' overgrown lawn after the meeting – which only partially took the edge off – the first thing I see is Jase's older sister, Alice, tanning in the front yard.

In a bikini.

Shockwave scarlet.

Straps untied.

Olive skin.

Toenails painted the color of fireballs.

Can I say there are few things on earth that cheer me up more than Alice Garrett in a bikini?

Except Alice without a bikini. Which I've never seen, but I've a hell of an imagination.

She's almost asleep, in a tiny blue-and-green lawn chair, her head and her long, always-morphing hair (brown with blond streaks right now) flopping heavily to one side, curling shorter in the late-summer heat. Because I'm unscrupulous, I flop down on the grass next to her and take a good long look.

Oh, Alice.

After a few seconds, she opens her eyes, squints, flips her hand to her forehead to block the sun, stares at me.

"Now," I tell her, "would be an excellent time to avoid unsightly tan lines. I stand ready to assist."

"Now," she says, with that killer smile, "would be an even *better* time to avoid lame come-ons."

"Aw, Alice, I swear I'll be there to soothe your regret for wasting time once you realize I've been right for you all along."

"Tim, I'd chew you up and spit you out." She slants forward, yanks the straps of her bikini behind her neck, ties them, and settles back. *God.* I almost can't breathe.

But I can talk.

I can always talk.

"We could progress to that, Alice. But maybe we start with some gentle nibbling?"

Alice shuts her eyes, opens them again, and gives me an indecipherable look.

"Why don't I scare you?" she asks.

"You do. You're scary as hell," I assure her. "But that works for me. Completely."

She's about to say something, but the family van pulls in just then, even more battered than usual. The right front fender has flaking paint. They've tried to put some rust primer around the sliding back door. The side looks like it's been keyed. Both hubcap covers on this side are missing.

Alice starts to get up, but I rest my hand on a smooth, brown shoulder, press her down.

"On it."

She squints up at me, head cocked to the side, rubs her bottom lip with her finger. Then settles back in the chair. "Thanks."

Mrs. Garrett, wearing a bright blue beach cover-up type thing and a wigged-out face, climbs out of the van.

"Everything okay?" I ask, sort of a joke since there's nothing but ear-melting screeching when I slide open the side door. Patsy, George, and Harry are all red-faced and sweaty. Patsy's mouth is open in a huge O and she's a sobbing mess. George also looks teary-eyed. Harry's more like pissed off.

"I'm not a baby," he announces to me.

"Clear on that, man." Though he's wearing bathing trunks with little red fire hats on them.

"*She*" − he jabs a sandy finger at his mom − "made us leave the beach."

"Patsy's naptime, Harry. You know this. You can swim in the big pool for a while. Maybe we can get a cone at Castle's after the sailing awards."

"Pools aren't cool," Harry moans. "We left before the ice-cream truck, Mommy. They have Spider-Man Bomb Pops." He stalks up the steps, his angry scrawny back all hunched over his skinny, little-dude legs. The screen door slams behind him.

"Whoa," I say. "Child abuse."

Mrs. Garrett laughs. "I'm the meanest mom in the world. I have it on good authority." Then she glances at George and leans into me, smelling like coconut sunscreen. At first I think she's sniff-checking my breath, because that's why adults ever get this close. Instead she whispers, "Don't mention asteroids."

Not my go-to conversation starter, so all good there.

But George is clutching a copy of *Newsweek*, his shoulders heaving. Patsy's still shrieking. Mrs. Garrett looks back and forth between them, like, who to triage first.

"I'll take Screaming Mimi here," I offer. Mrs. Garrett shoots me a grateful smile and flicks open Patsy's car seat. Good thing, since I know dick about car seats.

As soon as she's freed, Patsy looks up at me and her sobs dry up, like that. She still does that hic-hic-hic thing, but reaches out both hands for me.

"Hon," she says. *Hic-hic-hic.*

I don't get why, but this kid loves me crazy much. I pick her up and her sweaty little hands settle on my cheeks, patting them gently, never mind the stubble.

"Oh Hon," she says, all loving and shit, giving me her cute/scary grin with her pointy incisors, like a baby vampire.

Mrs. Garrett smiles, swinging George out of the car onto her hip. He snuggles his head into her neck, magazine still rumpled in his clammy fingers.

"You'll make a good dad, Tim. Someday in the far distant future."

To cover a sudden embarrassing rush of . . . whatever . . . from the consoling weight of her hand on my back, I answer, "You better believe it. No the hell way am I adding knocking up some girl to my list of crimes and misdemeanors."

The minute it's out of my mouth I get that I'm an ass. Mrs. Garrett still looks pretty frickin' young and her oldest kid is twenty-two. Could be *she* got knocked up and had to get married.

Also, probably? *Knocking up?* Not a phrase you should use with parents.

"Always good to have a plan," she answers, unfazed.

She carries George into the house, leaving me with Patsy, who tips her teary, soft cheek against my own, nuzzling. Alice still has her eyes closed and is evidently removing herself from this scene every way but physically.

"Hon," Patsy says again, slanting back to plant a sloppy kiss on my shoulder, checking me out from under her dew-droppy eyelashes. "Boob?"

"Sorry, kid, can't help you there."

I avoid looking at Alice, who has again untied the top strings of her bikini. She yawns, stretches. The top edges down a little lower. No tan lines. I close my eyes for a second.

Pats grabs my ear, as if that's a cool substitute for a boob.

Could be. What do I know about babies? Or toddlers, or whatever you are when you're one and a half. Could be it's all about holding on to something and doesn't matter much what you grab. I, of all people, get that.

Chapter Five

"Alice?"

"Dad?"

"Recognized your Gators," he says.

"Crocs, Dad."

"Those. Come on in."

I brush aside the stiff hospital curtain. Even nearly a month after the car accident, I still have to struggle to pull on the "all is well" nurse face I never dreamed I'd need with my own father. He looks a lot better. Fewer tubes, color better, bruises faded away. But Dad in a hospital bed still makes my stomach crimp and my lungs too heavy to pull in air. Before all this, I'd almost never seen him lying down, not in motion. Now the only thing that moves is one hand, stroking Mom's hair. She's asleep, nestled tight against him in the tiny, cramped bed.

"Shh," Dad says. "She's beat."

She's totally out, for sure. One arm hooked behind his neck, one wrapped around his waist.

"You too, hmm?" His voice is still faintly slurry, but

gentle, the same steadying sound that got me through kid-nightmares, mean teachers, and Sophie McCade in eighth grade spreading rumors I'd had boob implants during the summer.

"I could ask you the same, Dad."

He makes a scoffing sound. "I lounge around all day."

"You have a broken pelvis. Not to mention lung damage from a pulmonary embolism. You're not exactly eating bonbons."

He peers at me, shifting aside Mom's hair so he can look me more clearly in the eye. "What *are* bonbons? I've heard it and I've never known."

"I have no idea, actually. But if I figure it out and bring you some, *will* you eat them?"

"I will if you will. We could make a contest of it. 'My boy says he can eat fifty eggs . . .'"

"No, God. No *Cool Hand Luke*. What it is with that movie? Every male I know has, like, a thing with it."

"We all like to believe we have a winning hand, Alice," he says, dragging up the pillow behind him one-handed and giving it a hard punch to fluff it up.

"Say no more." I reach for the cards in their familiar, worn box, next to the pink hospital-issue carafe of water, the kidney-shaped trough to spit into after tooth brushing, the clutter of empty, one-ounce pill cups, and the roll of medical tape to re-bandage his IV shunt. Nothing like home, his nightstand piled with wobbly, homemade, clay

penholders and mugs, heaps of sci-fi books, the picture of him and Mom in high school, big curly hair on her, leather jacket on him.

"I haven't the heart to break your streak," he says with that grin that crinkles the corners of his eyes before overtaking his entire face. "The painkillers gave you an unfair advantage."

"I'm six for seven, Dad. Is it your painkillers or my raw talent?" I smile.

"Well, I'm off 'em now. So we'll see." He edges to one side a bit and his face goes sheet-white. He looks up at the ceiling, his lips moving, counting away the pain, taking deep breaths.

"Pant, pant, blow," I murmur. Labor breathing. Everyone in our family knows it.

"Whoo, who, hee." Dad's voice is tight. "God knows I should have that one down."

"And yet Mom says you still don't." I try for another smile but it slips a little, so I focus on the cards, shuffling them once, twice, three times. "Do you want me to call your nurse?"

He reaches out for the cards, takes them, and does his famous one-handed shuffle.

"Only if she's got bonbons. Look, they're kicking me out of here soon," he says abruptly. "Not enough beds, I've outstayed my welcome, I'm all fixed now. Not sure what the latest explanation is."

"And then –?"

"Home," he says on a sigh. "Or a rehab facility. They've left it up to us." He glances down at Mom, smiles, the same grin as in the SBH photo, tucks the hanging-out tag of her dress under the neckline. She nestles closer.

"Rehab's covered by our deal with the devil," I point out. Our devil may be a tall, blond, conservative state senator, but facts are facts.

"You can't think of it that way, Alice." He shakes his head, winces.

Still in pain, no matter how often he says it's not a problem. The last of his summer tan is fading, the line of his jaw cuts sharper, his shoulders locked in rigid lines. He looks at least four years older than he did four weeks ago and it's all that woman's fault. However often she sends fancy dinner salads and gourmet casseroles over with Samantha, I can't forget. I can't drive past reality without even stopping, the way she did.

"Grace Reed did this, Dad. She wrecked us. She –"

"Look at me," he says. I do, trying not to flinch at the shaved part of his scalp where they drilled the hole to relieve pressure from his head injury. Duff, Harry, and George just call it "Dad's weird haircut."

"A little battered maybe. But definitely not wrecked. Accepting rehab, on top of all the hospital bills – charity."

"Not charity, Dad. Justice."

"You know as well as I do that it's time to get on with

33

things, Alice. Suck it up and get on home. I'm needed there."

I want him there. I want everything back the way it was. Coming in late at night from a date or whatever to find him watching random History Channel or National Geographic documentaries, baby after baby, Duff, Harry, then George, then Patsy conked out against his shoulder, clicker poised in his hand, nearly dozing himself, but awake enough to rouse and say, "Do you know the plane Lindbergh flew to Paris was only made of fabric? A little glue brushed over it. Amazing what people can do." But I'm enough of a professional to look at his vital signs and translate his medical chart by heart. No matter how amazing it is what people can do, bodies have their limits.

"You know better," I say, "about what's needed. What you have to do."

A muscle in Dad's jaw jumps.

How much pain is he in? He should still be on those pills.

I wipe my expression clean, rubbing the back of my neck with one hand. Game face.

The things Mom and I traded off doing, today alone. I did breakfast, while she did morning sickness and talked on the phone setting up everyone's back to school doctor appointments. I drove Duff to the eye doctor, she took Andy to the orthodontist, then the little guys to the beach. Then we all went to the sailing awards. Mom cheered up Andy

in the bathroom after Jade Whelan said something stupid to her, then took her to get frozen yogurt. I hauled the little kids to Castle's for hot dogs. Mom ferried the gang to Jase's practice, then dropped them off and came to visit Dad – and dozed off. I stayed home until everyone crashed except Andy, then came here, chugging a venti Starbucks on the way. And I'm only Mom's stunt double. I'm not Dad.

"If you leave here for home, you'll be picking up George and Patsy, toting them to the car. You'll be driving Harry and Duff to soccer. Taking Andy to middle school dances. Relieving Jase at the store. You'll be *on*, all the time, Dad. You can't do that yet. It'll only set you back and make things worse. For all of us."

He scrubs his hand over his forehead. Sighs.

"Aren't you supposed to be the child I'm imparting all my hard-earned wisdom to, Alice?"

Mom shifts in her sleep, pulling her arm from his waist to rest on her stomach.

The new baby. Right. I almost always forget about that. Her. Him.

Dad reaches his good hand down to cover hers. *He* never forgets.

○ ○ ○ ●

I rest against the windowsill, put my head down on my crossed arms. Cloudless night with, I don't know, crickets,

locusts, whatever, making sounds in the high grass the Garretts wait too long to cut. You can even hear the river if you listen hard enough.

When my eyes adjust to the dark, I see her.

Alice is tipped back against the hood of the Bug, looking up. Not at me. At the sky. Full moon, a few clouds. Stars. She's darkly silhouetted against the white car, all curves, one foot on the bumper, moonlight shining off a knee.

Jesus.

A *knee*.

Oh, Alice.

Chapter Six

Early the next morning, I jolt out of bed so fast my brain practically sloshes against my skull. Where am I? The familiar feeling – the burning, dizzy *oh shit* of it – makes my temples crash and bang.

I got drunk last night.

Or something.

Because, if not, why am I so freaking disoriented?

Then I remember, assisted by the twelve girls in twelve different improbable contortions staring at me. I rub sweat off my forehead, fall back on the hard-as-hell couch I crashed on after too much quality time with the Xbox, and listen to the emptiness.

I never realized how freaking *quiet* it is when you're all alone in a building.

Then I'm up, yanking one poster off the wall, then the next, then the next, until the walls are bare and I'm breathing hard.

Running – isn't that what Jase does when he doesn't want to think? I rummage around in my cardboard box

for gym shorts I can't find. Just lame gray slacks. Who packed those? And my Asics – nowhere to be found. I pull on the only workout option, a faded pair of swim trunks, and head for Stony Bay Beach. I read once that Navy Seals train by running on sand. Barefoot. It's harder, a better workout.

I'll jog to the pier. Gotta be like a mile or something. Good start, right?

It would be, except that a mile's a hell of a long way. The pier's still as distant as a mirage and I'm gasping for breath, wanting to collapse in the sand.

I'm seven-fuckin'-teen, for God's sake. The prime of my life. The height of my physical prowess. The golden age I look back on one day when I'm boring my own kids. But I can't run like the wind. I can't run like the *breeze*. Patsy could run faster, without needing an oxygen tank afterward. I slump down in the sand, falling first to my knees, then rolling to collapse onto my back, hand over my eyes against the early morning light, sucking in air like it's filtered through nicotine.

Gotta lose the cigarettes.

"Need mouth to mouth?" asks a female voice.

Damn, I didn't know there was anyone on the beach, much less someone close . . . Alice. How long has she been watching me? I edge my hand away from my eyes.

Ah, another bikini. Thank you, Jesus. If I'm gonna die of shame, at least I'll die happy. This is one of those

Bond-girl types, dark green with a lime green zipper down the front, a little belt cinching in the bottom, about three fingers below where her waist swoops in before her hips fan out. My fingers twitch, will of their own. I shove my fists in my pockets. "Definitely," I gasp. "I need mouth to mouth. Right now."

"If you can talk, I think you'll survive."

I lick my dry lips. "Don't think I'm ready for the triathlon, Alice."

She does an unexpected thing, lying down next to me on her side, tilting toward me, sudden smile, curvy as the rest of her.

"At least you've got your running shoes on." She looks down at my feet. "No, you don't even, do you? Who jogs barefoot?" Her toes tangle with mine for a second, then move away. She looks down at the sand, not at me, draws a squiggly line between us.

"It matters?"

"Traction, honey," Alice says.

"I thought that was only when you'd broken a leg. Navy Seals do it. So I've heard."

I wait for her to make fun of that, but instead she smiles a little more, almost undetectably, unless you're looking hard at her lips, which I may be doing – says, "Maybe put off the BUDs challenge until you've built up more . . . stamina."

There are so many ways I could answer that.

She moves closer; smells like I've always thought Hawaii would, green and sweet, earthy, sun and sea mixed together, smoky warm. Her greenish gray eyes, flecks of gold too –

"You've only got one dimple," she says.

"That a drawback? I had two, but I misplaced one after a particularly hard night."

She gives my shoulder a shove. "You joke about everything."

"Everything *is* pretty funny," I say, trying to sit up but sinking back, my back groaning. "If you look at it the right way."

"How do you know you're looking at it the right way?" Alice's head's lowered, she's still circling an index finger in the sand, only inches from brushing her knuckles past my stomach. The morning air is still and calm – no sound of the waves, even.

"If it's funny," I wheeze, "you're looking at it the right way."

"Yo, Aleece!" I look up and there's that douche-canoe, her boyfriend, Brad, looming large, big shoulders muscling out the sun.

"Brad." She's up, brushing sand from her swimsuit. He pats her on the butt, looking at me in this *my territory* way.

Dick.

"You're late. Brad, Tim. Tim, Brad."

"Yo, Tim." Brad, man of few, and strictly one-syllable, words. One of those guys built like a linebacker but

with a little kid face, all rosy cheeks and twinkly eyes. To compensate, I guess, he has a scruffy, barely there beard.

"So, Ally-pals," he says to Alice.

Ally-pals?

"Ready?"

"I've been ready for a while. You're the one who's late," Alice says, sharply.

Atta girl.

She turns to me, running her hands through her hair, flipping it back from her face. "I'm training for the five K – Brad's timing me."

"You're a runner? How did I not know that?"

She opens her mouth, like why on earth would I know anything whatsoever about her, but then looks down, tightens the notch on the belt of her bikini bottom. Which brings my attention back to her stomach, the belly ring, and I . . .

Roll over onto my stomach.

Brad clears his throat, arms folded, chin jutting. Got it, caveman.

"I won't hold you up," I add. Alice shoots Brad an unreadable look, drops down on her knees, bending over me again, her breath biting sweet as peppermint candy. "Sneakers next time, Tim."

I'm panting, hands on knees, at the end of my first sprint.

Sweat slides into my eyes, and I brush my hair back, try to corral what isn't in my ponytail behind my ears.

Brad uncaps the water bottle, hands it to me, stooping low to squint at my face. Then he says in a low voice, "You wanna tell me what that was about?" He jerks his thumb toward the distant figure of Tim, still collapsed on the sand, head on his folded arms.

"What? Tim? He's my kid brother's friend. We were talking."

He rubs his chin. "I dunno, Ally. That's all it was?"

Two more sips of water, then I pour some into my hand, rub it over my face.

Tim's standing up now, shielding his eyes, looking toward us – then the other way down the beach. Now he's sprinting in that direction, no stretching out, no slow jog to start, right into a flat-out run. Gah.

"Ally?"

"Of course that's all it was."

Chapter Seven

Sam's Club is no stranger to Garrett family meltdowns. Harry always loses it in the toy aisle, George is extremely sensitive about our ice cream choices, Patsy gets overtired and screeches. This time, though, the meltdown is all mine.

"I think you're taking this waaay too seriously," Joel says, holding up both palms in that *whoa, you overemotional woman* way that makes me furious.

I shake the papers at him. "It says two red, one-inch binders. Red. One-inch. I send you off to do that one simple thing. These are blue. Two-inch."

"So what?" Joel scratches the back of his neck, checking out a girl who's smiling at him while daintily placing huge packs of glitter glue in her cart.

"*So*, the school list says red. We get red. That's what lists are for. So people get things right."

"Al, I don't think this is about school supplies. You're scaring Patsy. You're scaring *me*."

"Good," I snap.

Patsy points at me. "Bad." She's scowling from her

perch in the shopping cart.

"Not you, honey. *You,* Joel. Maybe you *need* scaring, or some reminder of what's really going on. Because you're not around – not all the time. You don't see how close everything is to – to –"

"*That's* what this is about." My brother settles back against a wall of paper towels, tilts his chin. "Me not being around all the time. That you are."

"No," I say. "Not that at all. What do I care if you're moving in with your girlfriend and starting your training at the police academy when everything is up in the air? So what? Whatever."

Joel sighs, reaches over, and plucks a handful of chocolate chip cookies off a free sample tray. "Al, I'm twenty-two. Out of college. I need to get on with it. Gisele and I have been seeing each other for a while. I want to find out where that goes. I don't want to be living above our garage for the rest of my life. Not too functional."

"Since when has that mattered?" I say, moving away from Patsy, who's trying to yank down the top of my shirt, still scowling.

"Uh, since I spent my twenty-second birthday at the *hospital* the night Dad was hit. I love our family, Al. I'd do anything for any of us, even you. But everything – my life – it can't stop."

Everything has done anything but *stop* – as Joel should know. It's accelerated to warp speed. Before that, this

summer, for me, there were a few classes, a few hours of work at the hospital rehab center, maybe covering at the store, but other than that it was the beach and Brad and my favorite time of year. Sand and salt and ice-cream cones.

Now it's almost Labor Day and things – classes, sports, afterschool stuff – will be picking up – for everyone. Dad will be recovering for who knows how much longer, Mom pregnant, Jase's football schedule, band for Andy and Duff – we'll need to figure out more babysitting and my actual own life is –

Deep breath. I lower my shoulders, which are practically grazing my earlobes.

Joel tosses a 500-pack box of Slim Jims into the cart. I snatch them out and shove them back on the shelf. "Do you even know what's *in* those?"

"Is this about you not liking Gisele?"

"I like Gisele fine," I say.

Can't stand Gisele.

Last time she came by, she had Joel pumping up her bicycle tires while she stood there looking all Parisian in a striped blue-and-white dress and a red scarf, fluttering her hands. But I know better than to say that. He's moving in with her. *That* should be the kiss of death for both of them.

"Sure you do. Brad's no prize, you know." Joel hands Patsy a chocolate chip cookie, which she immediately smooshes all over her face and into her hair, wiping the last of the chocolate across her pink shirt for good measure.

45

"Brad's on his way out," I say, leafing through the school supply lists, mentally crossing things off. Harry – still needs twelve-count colored pencils, one "quality" pack of erasers, whatever that is. Duff – no, I am *not* getting materials for the solar system project yet – otherwise he's set, Andy can get her own supplies, for God's sake, she's fourteen. "Too time-consuming." As if to confirm this, my phone vibrates with what turns out to be another selfie of Brad at the gym.

"Alice," Joel says, giving yet another girl the once-over (Gisele, you are toast!). "That's what I mean. You're *supposed* to have your time consumed by that sort of thing." He flicks the school supplies list. "Not this."

"That baby is too young for chocolate," says a grouchy-looking woman who has her own baby in one of those weird sling things.

"Nobody asked you," I snap. Her brows draw together. Joel gives her his most charming smile, drawing me away by the elbow.

"But we're grateful for your advice. Who knew? Thank you."

She smoothes her shirt and actually smiles back at him. *Honestly.*

Here's Brad sitting on our steps when we get home, texting – probably me – with a frown. "Allykins," he says, coming to his feet for a hug.

Joel raises an eyebrow at me with a smirk, mutters, "I'm off to see Dad." And leaves.

Without carrying in any of the school supplies.

In the kitchen, Jase, obviously fresh from practice, sweaty and with grass stains on his jersey, is plowing through a huge bowl of chicken and brown rice. Tim's planted on our counter like he belongs there, scarfing down something with melted cheese all over it, hot enough to be steaming. Duff, Harry, and George are eating blueberry pie with melting vanilla ice cream. Dirty plates everywhere. The kitchen smells like boy and feet.

And . . . Tim again.

All relaxed and at home, wearing the swimsuit he was jogging in this morning and a Hodges Heroes baseball shirt that's slightly too tight even on him. He grins at me, lopsided dimple and all.

Hot mess inside and out, that boy, probably hasn't even showered. Certainly hasn't shaved carefully, since he's got a little cut near his chin. Yet another person who needs a mother, a maid, a manager –

I set Patsy down, grab her pink princess sippy cup, slosh milk into it, screw on the top, shove it at him. "Slow down. I'm not driving you to the hospital when you get second-degree tongue burn."

Tim takes a defiant bite of scalding cheese. Another. Then slowly raises the sippy cup, salutes me, and, watching me with serious eyes, gulps it down.

"Pie," Brad says happily. "I love pie." He pulls out a chair, flips it around, straddles it, and says, "Cut my slice *extra*-big, Allosaurus."

George cocks his head, wrinkling his nose. "Allosauruses were some of the biggest dinosaurs of all. They ate Stegosauruses. Alice isn't very big. And she's a vegetarian."

Brad can get his own damn pie.

"Get your own damn pie," Tim mumbles between more mouthfuls of volcanic cheese.

"Hey, Alice, Joel's completely out of the garage – he's not coming back for anything, right?" Jase slosh-pours himself a huge glass of milk, drains half of it, refills. Finally got groceries, and at this rate they'll be gone tomorrow.

"Thank God, yes," I say.

"Great," he says. "I told Tim he could take it. He moved in last night."

"No escaping me now," Tim tells me cheerfully.

"Boy, Alice. Your face is really red," George says after a second.

"Al –" Jase starts, then falters.

Tim takes one look at me and jolts off the counter, hand outstretched. "Whoa. What – hell – what did I – ?"

I hold up my own hand. "Don't say another word . . . There are groceries and school supplies in the Bug. Deal with them." Then I practically drag Brad out by his hair.

*

48

"I screwed up again, yeah?" I say to Jase as the door slams behind Alice and ol' Brad.

Jase rubs a hand down his face. "I'll talk to her."

"What, was she, like, going to move in there – with *that* guy? 'I love pie'? What is he, five?"

"Alice never said a thing to me, Tim." Jase picks up a forkful of chicken, puts it back down.

George says philosophically, "Pie *is* good. Except the kind with four and twenty blackbirds baked in it, prolly. You know, like, sing a songofsixpence, pockafullarye?" he warbles in this high voice that sort of slays me. "That sounds yuck."

"No way would they sing when they opened it," Harry says, with his mouth full of crust. "Because they'd all be cooked and dead."

George's eyes get big. "Would they?" he asks, looking back and forth between me and Jase. *"Cooked?"*

"No way," Jase says firmly, "because . . ." He hesitates a second, and George's eyes start filling.

"Because, dude, it wouldn't be an *eating* pie," I say. "It would be a *performance* pie. Like something to make the king laugh because he was all stressed from –"

"Counting out his money," Jase finishes, nodding, all confident. "Right, G-man? Isn't that what he was doing – 'in the countinghouse, counting out his money'?"

George nods, soberly. "He'd be all upset like Daddy at work, so they'd make him a performance pie? Like,

like a play?"

"Exactly," I say. "They'd make this, uh, fake pie —"

"To make him laugh. Like Mommy does." George is nodding, like the whole thing makes total sense now.

"But where would they get the *blackbirds*?" Harry asks. "Who has blackbirds lying around?"

"They'd probably have them in the barn or something," Duff says, all fake-casual. "Like, kind of tame ones. Maybe the king was, uh, into birds."

This story is getting away from us. But George is down with it. "We could look them up in my *Big Birds of the World* book. See if you can tame blackbirds." He slides off the kitchen chair and trots off, Harry at his heels.

"Nice job, Duffy," Jase says. "Thanks for chiming in."

"I was sort of lame," Duff admits, scraping up the last of his pie. "'The king was into birds'? But I tried. It's just hard sometimes to see what's gonna scare George."

"Dead, baked birds? It'd give *me* nightmares." I shudder.

That or that asskite Brad, and what Alice might be getting up to with him right this very minute.

"Do we have to?"

Brad may be upward of 225 pounds and over six feet tall, but he sounds like my little brothers when I drag them shoe shopping. "Yup," I say.

He weaves hesitantly through traffic — he drives like

he's in one of his video games on slo-mo, sudden spurts of speed and then well below the limit. Staring out the car window, I don't see the blur of the maple trees that line the turnpike but the garage apartment reinvented, the way *I* was going to do it.

All of Joel's heinous furniture piled into the attic. My great-aunt Alice's brass bed down from there. Along with her big wardrobe that Jase and I were always trying to find Narnia in. The walls painted a deep burnt-orange color, October Sky, a paint we got in at Garrett's Hardware last week – so not the dingy white that's in there now – far from the "bridal pink" in the room Andy and I share. I saw something in a magazine last month – this tulle canopy that goes over your bed, making it into your own cocoon. Splurge on those billion-thread-count sheets that are so soft you barely notice them at all. Stereo speakers for my iPod and a reading corner full of books that aren't textbooks, with big puffy floor pillows and –

"C'mon, Ally-pally. Let's hit Pizza Palace and you can bash my butt at Slimin' Sumos." Brad elbows me, giving me his best smile.

"I don't feel like eating bad pizza while we play videogames, Brad."

Now I sound whiny too. I dig my fingernails into my palm and kick my feet up onto the dashboard. *Let it go. It's just an apartment.* Just a space of my own, for the first time ever, and for the last time for a while too, assuming I

can still accept the transfer to Nightingale Nursing in the spring, assuming things at home are running smoothly, assuming I can get student housing and –

Sharp inhale. Another.

Brad squeezes the back of my neck. "Yowch, you're tense, Allo. Don't do that funky breathing thing. It freaks me out. How 'bout we go back to my place? I'll send Wally out for decent pizza. Like all the way to Ilario's or something. That would give us at least half an hour. I could . . . relax you." Now he's rubbing my shoulder, giving me a sunny, hopeful grin. No stormy weather with Brad. All one mood, like the easy listening music they play at the dentist.

"I see a smile, Als. You want to, don't you? C'mon. Let's book it home. I'll boot the Walster for the whole night if you want. Bummer for sure about the apartment – that would have been sweet – but it's not like I don't have my own place."

Brad's "place" is a three-story house in White Bay. His parents live on the first two floors, Brad and Wally in the basement, his grandmother, who I'm pretty sure refers to me as That Whore, on the top.

He reaches over and gives my knee a squeeze, while passing a camper on the right and leaning on the horn.

I sigh.

"Is that a yes? C'mon, Aliwishous. We could take a shower or something. My dad fixed the hot water tank."

"Let's go to the batting cages. I need to hit something."

"Works for me. Whatever floats your boat."

He's nothing if not steady. Which is good when you're a little bit shipwrecked. He's now singing along to the radio – a commercial for river cruises. Steady is solid ground under your feet. Even if the planks are a little thick.

But the garage apartment? I'm not letting that go down without a fight.

Chapter Eight

"You're actually knocking, sis?" I open the door to find Nan, one arm balancing sheets and towels, the other extended to knock again.

"I always knock," she says, swatting my nose instead. "*I* respect your privacy, unlike you, reading my diary."

I kick the door open wider. "C'mon, get my towels out of the rain, assuming those are for me and you're not dropping off laundry. And really? The diary again? Jesus. It was once, it was four years ago, and I had insomnia. Your diary was like a sleeping pill. 'Dear Diary, I –'" I start, all sugary. But I cut myself off. I'm being a jackass.

You want the truth, that diary about broke my damn heart. It was full of these letters from Nan to God. I knew she'd gotten the idea from this Judy Blume book she loved crazy much, because I'd read part of it when I was ten and someone told me it was all about tits. It was, but not in the way I was hoping. Anyway, Nan's diary entries were just sad – like, she was begging God as if he was Santa, the jolly old elf who could give you good grades and parents

who were always proud of you, and a brother who wasn't a fuck-up and get Mark Winthrop to love you forever and ever, amen.

Nan dumps the sheets and towels on the Sox beanbag chair and looks around, pulling off her windbreaker and wrinkling her nose. "Since when are you the big sports fan? What's with the weights? Where'd you get all this stuff, anyway?"

"I robbed Dick's. What do you care? What's with all that?"

"Mom wanted me to bring it and to —" She stops dead.

"Spy on me, right? Make sure I wasn't up to no good?"

"Are you?" Her voice is sharp. "Are you in trouble again or something?"

"Wha-at? No. Not more than usual. Why?"

"Some woman, or girl, or whatever — keeps calling, asking for you. Do you owe anyone money? I — know what Dad said to you. If you need money, I have —"

"Nan, kid, I'm fine. I don't owe anyone anything but a shitload of apologies. Don't stress. It'll affect your grade point average."

Her cheeks flame at that last and she says, "I . . . I've been doing my college applications. Starting them. So maybe I can be early-decision, I won't have to freak out all year. And —"

"Nano —"

"It comes easy to you, Tim, but it's really hard for me

55

to concentrate –" Her voice breaks a little. She's blinking rapidly, shoulders hunched, giving me the face.

But I shake my head. "Just no, okay. No."

Her expression goes blank for a second, then she says, "That's that, then. So . . . so . . . where do you sleep?"

I point to the bedroom door. "Be my guest. The drunk, naked babes are all in the shower right now, so no worries."

"You're such a jerk. I thought I'd make the bed, because I doubt you have any idea whatsoever how to do that. You can come watch and –"

"What, you'll quiz me on it later? I'll pass. I'm gonna get in the shower."

"Fine," she says. "Watch out for the naked girls. Word is they're slippery when wet."

I start laughing. She's a pain in my ass, Nano. But I'm a dick to her ninety percent of the time and she loves me anyhow. She went all uptight right when I went all crazy and I wish to hell there was an AA for perfectionism, because I'd haul her ass there in a heartbeat.

She's smiling back at me now, because I laughed, and she was the one who made it happen, because, as she said in that goddamn diary, "Dear God, make me funny like Tim, because people like funny people and maybe then Mark Winthrop would . . ."

Love her.

"Nano – the school shit," I say, then swallow. "I can't

56

help you that way anymore. You get that, right?"

She nods, staring fixedly at the beanbag chair. "Look, about the college money, Tim – Dad said I'd probably get it for Columbia because you –" She stops, and I can hear the gears turning as she tries to figure out how to put it. *Because you* –

Are the boy most likely to.

Fail.

Everyone and everything.

° · ° •

There it is again, its silver top gleaming under the light of the Schmidts' fake streetlamp, glossy from the rain. The car pauses at the end of our block, as it has three times since Brad dropped me off. Then, as I watch, it signals the turn, though our street is completely deserted. I edge down the steps, arms folded against the wet, silty breeze blown over from the river.

Looking up at the shaded windows of the garage apartment, I see Tim's rangy figure pass by, then someone else, a girl, hair in a ponytail, gesturing with both hands.

As I'm watching this, the car pulls slowly into our driveway at a bad parking angle, sharply slanted behind my Bug and Tim's Jetta.

The headlights snap off.

Enough. Who's *this* weird about pulling into a driveway?

Who cases the street beforehand? I can't see through the tinted windows.

Dealers?

Maybe the garage apartment's new tenant has brought his sketchy past with him.

Or hired a hooker to join the party.

I stalk down the steps to the car.

Rap sharply on the window.

Right as it occurs to me what a stupid thing this is to do.

No weapon. No Mace. Unless they're vulnerable to the power of Harry's authentic Nerfblaster Lightsaber with glow-in-the-dark detailing, lying in the grass nearby.

The car turns back on, window slowly rolling down, and I'm staring at a girl, my own age or younger, with long brown hair and huge, thickly lashed blue eyes, wide and unblinking in the throw-back glow of her headlights.

"Looking for someone?"

She edges back at the sound of my voice. Her fingers, with chipped dark pink polish, clenched at the ten-and-two position on the wheel, tighten even more.

"Yes. No. I mean . . . I . . ." she stammers. "I . . . I —"

"Are you lost?"

She gives a quick, unsteady laugh, and then says, "You got that right. Sorry — don't worry about it. I'll find my way." Then she rolls the window up and backs out as slowly as she drove in.

Chapter Nine

"I'm coming in, we need to talk," I say before the door's even half-open.

Tim blinks at me, takes a step back, then peers over my head as though expecting a lynch mob.

"The scariest phrase in the universe." He's wearing baggy striped pajama bottoms, with a toothbrush in one hand, Crest poised in the other.

"Let me in," I repeat, louder.

"Not by the hair on my chinny-chin-chin. You're looking predatory." He stares down at my shirt, slightly damp with rain. "And your – uh – chest is heaving. Is that you huffing and puffing?"

"Tim. Now." I'm not here to be disarmed.

Raising his hands holding the toothbrush and Crest, he steps aside. I brush past him, into the center of the room. *My* room. Which he's completely marked as his territory. Open Grape-Nuts cereal box and an empty carton of orange juice on the counter next to a worn leather wallet and a handful of crumpled bills. Socks and a sweatshirt

balled up in a corner. More clothes piled on the couch. Dishes in the sink. An iPod with a tangled wad of chargers and an Xbox next to the TV.

A lavender windbreaker tossed on the bean bag chair.

"Look, for starters, where's the girl?"

Except when he's loaded, I've never seen Tim so slow on the uptake. Now he's blinking again. "Um – you mean . . . ? What girl?"

"You've got more than one? Look – you can't do this – I need to be here, and I'm sorry if you were planning to use this place for your hookups and booty calls or whatever. I don't care what you told Jase you'd pay, he had no right to go ahead and hand this over to you."

Tim tosses the toothbrush and toothpaste on the counter, grabs a pack of Marlboros, whips out a lighter, shakes out a cigarette, and lights up, all in about two seconds.

I scowl at him. Smoking in *my* apartment.

"Sorry – where are my manners? Want one?" he asks around the cigarette trapped between his lips.

The bedroom door opens and out comes . . .

Nan, Tim's nervous as a cat on a hot tin roof twin sister.

"So, yeah," she says, twisting a coil of hair around a finger and reaching back to flip off the light, "I'll reassure Mom I did my duty. Think she wanted me to tuck you in too? I forgot to bring Pierre the Bear, but I can . . ." She stumbles to a halt. "Oh – hi, Alice."

"Hey, Nan." I give her a brief, but actually genuine

smile, which she returns hesitantly. This girl, she's like one of Jase's animals that was badly treated by its previous owner.

"We can skip the tucking in," Tim tells her. "Sending over sheets and towels, that was – uh, nice. Tell Ma thanks. Not when Pop's around, though. Pretty sure I'm supposed to be sleeping under some newspaper on a sidewalk grate somewhere."

Nan bites her pinkie nail, tearing at the cuticle so savagely, mine nearly bleeds in sympathy. Studying me with a vertical line between her eyebrows, identical to Tim's, she picks up the windbreaker, looks back and forth between us, then doesn't budge – until Tim sets his hand in the middle of her back, steering her toward the door.

"Good deed done, Two-Shoes. You'd better beat it. I don't think Alice here wants any witnesses to the homicide."

When the door closes behind her, he gestures at me, like, *bring it on*. Then, before I can say a word, "You want me to get lost, right, Alice? Spreading like a virus, that. Schools, jobs, my folks – should I start a running tally? We can put a list on the fridge."

No flirty flippancy. Hard, sarcastic – like a shove. I haven't heard him like this since he first stopped drinking. Then he studies me, eyes drifting from my face down to my clenched fists, back to my face again.

He turns away. "Shit, I'm sorry, Alice. I was gonna go to my friend Connell's, but he relapsed, so that was a no-go.

Jase said . . . I didn't know this place was supposed to be yours. Shoulda guessed. No worries. I'm one hell of a fast packer." He tosses me the kind of smile one of my little brothers would after skinning his knee. *See, I'm fine. It doesn't hurt at all.*

Then he starts skimming the crumpled bills off the counter, shoving them in the wallet, concentrating harder on it than the job requires.

"Where will you go? Back home?"

"Not your problem, Hot Alice."

I examine his downturned face, but the parts I can see reveal nothing. He finishes with the wallet, tries to shove it in his back pocket, then seems to realize his pajama bottoms have no such thing.

"Wait. Why exactly *are* you here, Tim?"

Shrugging, he steps around me to pick up an empty cardboard box from the floor, tosses the wallet, then the sweatshirt and socks into it. Automatically assuming I'm kicking him to the curb right this second, late on a windy, rainy night.

Even I am not that cold.

Then I get it, sharp as a slap.

His parents were on that get-lost list. His own mom and dad kicked him out.

When Tim glances at me, he goes suddenly, stunningly red, wraps both arms around his middle. "What?"

"How . . ." I start; I'm not sure how to finish. I can't

even imagine. "Never mind. I'm making you tea and you're going to tell me what happened," I say.

"Or what? I might like my other options better. Spanking? Water torture? I can get the shower going in no time."

Amazingly, there *is* tea. But of course no kettle. I fill a saucepan with water and cross my fingers that there are mugs. Ah yes, ugly black-and-yellow ones from Fitness Planet. Joel's such a class act. I turn to the fridge to see if there's actually milk too, and there, tacked to it, is a list. A long one, in various different colors of messy, boy-handwriting scrawls.

Tim Mason: The Boy Most Likely To . . .
Need a liver transplant
Find the liquor cabinet blindfolded
Drive his car into a house
I scan down the paper.

"Find the sugar," I say to him. "Then tell me the rest."

"I doubt there's sugar," he says, "but I see resistance is futile. Hey – it's not a big deal. Turns out . . . I guess . . . my parents, my pop . . . quitting the senator gig? Final straw. Embarrassing, see – Grace Reed is a family friend, yada, yada – he's done with me. I'm out the door – no need to turn up for Sunday dinner. Small upside, that. And I've got four months to turn it all around until I'm out a college fund, and probably stricken from the family Bible. End of story."

Now I feel sick. "He couldn't have been serious – I

mean . . . he's your dad."

Tim looks down at his fingers, raising his eyebrows as though surprised not to find the cigarette still there. "He's a serious guy, Pop." His voice deepens. "*Time to be a man, Tim.* Maybe I should have read the fine print on ditching ol' Gracie. That it meant" – he indicates the apartment – "this. But, I mean – he didn't repo my car and yank my allowance or anything." The smile that follows is tight, not his open, wicked one. "In his defense? He did offer me a scotch for the road."

I inhale sharply and he reddens again, rubs his hands through his hair so some parts are sticking straight up. I turn to the cabinet again, searching for sugar, but no such luck. "You're going to have to go without sugar."

He nods. "Here's where I tell you you're sweet enough, right?"

"It's definitely not. Move, so I can pour this without burning you." I slosh the boiling liquid into one cup, then the other, nod toward the couch. "Keep talking."

"While the Ilsa-the-She-Wolf-of-the-SS act is hot as hell, Alice, there's really nothing more to say. It's probably temporary anyway. If me not being office boy for Senator Grace is embarrassing for Pop, you can only imagine how he'd feel about me hanging around the steps of the building and loan with a tin cup." Tim collapses onto the couch anyway, without bringing the mug along. "Can we talk about something else? You? Your endless collection of

bikinis? Your tan lines? I notice you don't have any. Wanna show and tell?"

I carry both mugs from the kitchen, set his down in front of him.

"Look. Stay. I mean . . . I can wait. It's only fair. Jase didn't know I wanted it anyway. Four months is nothing. You can be here for four months and then . . ." I trail off.

Then what?

Troubled gray eyes search my face for a long time. Finally, he sighs, shakes his head. "Nah. I'll find somewhere else. You deserve it. You've earned it."

Like a home's something you have to earn when you're seventeen.

He's a kid. Not a man, not on some deadline. But with his jaw set and raised – I know that face. The *I'm going to push on through, no problem, I'll deal. Moving right along. Nothing to see here* face. Know it as well as my own. It is my own. And I picture the rest of the lines on that paper.

Tim Mason: The Boy Most Likely To . . .
Forget his own name even before we do
Turn down the hottest girl in the world for the coldest beer
Be six feet under by our fifth reunion

Don't go that way, Tim. Such a stupid, stupid waste. "I mean it," I say aloud. "Stay."

Pause.

"I want you here," I add, my cheeks flaring. He shifts on the couch and I'm hyper-aware of him next to me, the smell

of soap and shampoo, the heat of him, the alive of him.

"Please, stay."

My words fall into the silence, and something changes. Tim's shoulders straighten. He stills, but not frozen, more like . . . more like . . . alert.

"Yeah? Then . . . I'll be here," he says quietly. "Since you asked so . . . nicely."

"Look – if you stick around, there'll be rules."

"Always are," Tim says immediately. "Helps if they're clear."

Like, posted on the refrigerator? But I don't say it.

"Not that I'll necessarily follow them, but –"

"The cigarettes go," I say. "This place is not going to be a refuge if you burn it to the ground, and if I ever *do* get it to myself, I don't want it smelling like an old-man bar."

Unfolding himself from the couch, he brushes past me, wings the pack of Marlboros into the trash can under the sink, knots the bag tight, sets it next to the door. Collapses back down on the couch next to me, laces his hands behind his head, stretches.

"Sorry – again. Trying to kick 'em. I tossed a whole carton but . . . that pack was an impulse buy. Trying to control that, because my impulses suck."

His eyes flick to my face, my lips, lower, back to my eyes.

Outside, it's gone on raining, slashing sideways against the windows, the wind loud and constant. It's warm in here. Overheated even.

Even though I'm laying out rules, Tim is not one of my brothers.

He glances at my lips again, and there's the sound of a sharp inhale. His or mine?

I jolt up. "I have to get home."

"I'm walking you out." Tim gets quickly to his feet, grabs the green plastic garbage bag, steps in front of me. "Dangerous neighborhood and all that. There's a raccoon under the woodshed the size of a puma."

We keep our trash cans in a low shed near the stairs. When we reach it, Tim bends over to jettison the bag. "Don't tell Jase about, about . . . the whole thing with my parents, 'kay?" His voice is muffled. "A man has his pride."

I'm walking backward up the driveway, forcing a light laugh. "Of course not. I never kiss and –"

"I *missed* the part where we kissed? Wait, let's rewind. I promise not to put up a fight." He dodges in front of me, smiling, holding up his hands in surrender. "You'd take me, anyway. And I'd let you."

I shake my head, laughing, then shield my eyes as headlights flare, backlighting Tim, and a car backs slowly out of our driveway.

Chapter Ten

"I'm two seconds from utter and total collapse!" Andy calls from her handstand position, her legs, kicked up against the fence by the side of our driveway, swaying wildly.

"You can do this," Samantha says, slightly breathless, in the same position. "It's really great for your form, trust me. If you can get the handstand down, you're golden – right, Alice?"

"It's the core gymnastics move," I call. Andy and I share a bedroom, a bathroom, and half my clothes. I love my sister. But I thank God Sam's helping her practice for gymnastics tryouts.

Jase is fiddling with his Mustang. Mom's supervising Duff and Harry, who are mostly spraying each other and throwing sponges and sometimes washing the van. George is drawing on the blacktop, standing back, then jumping on his drawing, over and over again. Patsy waves at me from the kiddie pool. "Ayiss! A me, Ayiss!"

As usual, our driveway and lawn are completely overpopulated. Perfect. Easier with a crowd.

Brad has pulled gingerly in next to the Mustang, glancing around with an anxious look. He's terrified of our driveway. I think he worries about running over one of my siblings, but it might also be the damage Patsy's Cozy Coupe could do to his beloved Taurus. I slide into the passenger seat and Brad gives me a damp cheek smack and a thigh squeeze.

Beyond my open window, Harry swings the hose toward Brad's car, but, quick as lightning, Mom swoops down and puts a kink in it. "No spraying people unless they say yes, Harry. George, lovie, I think that only works when Mary Poppins is there."

George leaps again onto a chalk painting of, I think, a palm tree and a turtle. "Text her, then, Mommy."

"Mary Poppins doesn't believe in cell phones."

"So, Ally. Want to come over? We can hang with Wally, you can cook us up some mac and cheese. I scored the last copy of *Annihilation 7: The Grizzlies' Revenge*. I'm going to whip Wally's ass at it and wipe the floor with him."

I pause, turn to him. "Here's the thing, Brad. I've been thinking . . ."

Jase's gaze lights on me for a moment, eyebrows lifting. He's seen these dominos fall before.

"Mommy!" Harry bellows, "Patsy's getting bitey!"

"She walked on my island picture. It's wrecked now!" George adds, pointing accusingly at Patsy, who is chasing Harry, top-knot of hair bobbing, tiny teeth bared.

Mom scoops up Patsy, who squirms in her arms. "I tiger, Mama," then "Grrr" to Harry.

"You're a friendly tiger," Mom suggests. "George, actually, the wave part looks more watery now. It's good. Step back and take another look."

Patsy's still glaring at Harry. "I bite," she says ominously. "Mom!"

"A sleepy tiger." Mom strokes Patsy's back. "All cozy. With her jungle friends. Harry, you're the elephant. The hose is your trunk. You missed a spot on the back window."

Brad chuckles. "Your mom's awesome."

And then he says things like that, which make this harder. Tim's car eases in behind Jase's Mustang, hanging half out in the street so as not to cover George's drawings. Sam waves him over, but he calls distractedly, "Late for a meeting! Been running. Gotta shower and book it."

He heads past the Taurus, pauses. "Hey Alice."

"What did you have on your feet this time?" I ask.

"Toes," he replies easily, and grins at me, lifting one long foot to put it on the sill of the car, wiggling his toes for emphasis. There's a jagged open cut near his big toenail. "Well, toes and blood. Cut it on a shell. But I made it all the way to the pier this time. Very Navy Seal, huh? Ran right through the pain, because I am just that full of testosterone."

I try hard not to laugh, looking away, straight at Samantha, who's descended from her handstand position, watching us

with a very slight smile. Jase, who has a smudge of dirt on his nose, is frowning over something to do with the windshield wipers. Or something.

"Clean that up," I say to Tim. "And put something on it to *keep* it clean. Toes are seriously prone to infection because the bacteria can get trapped in your shoes."

"I love it when you talk dirty," Tim says, then, seeming to notice him for the first time, "Hey, Brad."

"Yo bro, do you mind?" Brad asks. "We're talking here."

Tim backs away, raising his hands in exactly the same gesture he used in the rain the other night. This flicker of – something – licks up my spine.

As he's climbing the steps, Andy comes over and calls, "Tim! You're a guy, right?"

"Last time I checked."

"Can I ask you a question I can't ask my brothers?"

"No," Jase calls.

"Uh – Andy – sorry, I really have to get to a meeting," Tim says, glancing at Jase before the garage apartment door slams behind him.

"What were you saying, Ally-baba?"

Bite the bullet.

"Look, Brad."

Obediently, Brad looks me in the eye. He's taken a bite of one of the zillion protein bars overflowing his glove compartment, and he's chewing, cheeks bulging. Harry and George have started playing Limbo with the water

from the hose, Mom's pulling out the back of Patsy's swim diaper to check its contents, Jase has jerked his head up quickly and banged it on the hood, so Samantha, who's come up beside him, is rubbing the spot, saying something under her breath. Andy's doing a back walkover – without having stretched out enough first.

With the usual chaos and color, my chilly tone is suddenly so off.

Cold, really.

"Your family is a riot," Brad says. "Crazy as anything, but ya know . . ." He trails off.

More than one boyfriend has said to me that breaking up meant breaking up with my family too, and that was the hardest.

But I have to push on here. No point dragging things out. Maybe *I'm* hard, the hardest.

Brad swallows, gnaws off another chunk, and says, mouth full, "What is it, Ally?"

"Brad. Here's the thing."

Jase winces. "Hey, Sam, can you hold the hood open for me? The prop rod keeps giving out."

"Let's all go inside, guys," Mom says. "Duff, Harry, George – time to wash up and get something to eat. Andy, you too." Everyone but George, who's now jumping into the puddles left by the hose, follows. Jase keeps working on his car.

"We've come to the end of the road," I say quickly.

"We've gone as far as we can go."

Brad looks puzzled. "It's a driveway."

"I mean us. As a couple . . . It's not working out."

"What?" Brad says frowning. "That . . . that's not possible."

"Can you hand me that Sharpie while still holding the hood?" Jase calls to Sam.

"We always knew it was temporary." I've said these lines so many times. It's possible that I am a complete bitch.

"We did? Why?" Brad, forehead squinched, says in a faint voice. "What was missing, Ally-baby? We hung out, we made out, we worked out. All the good stuff. I don't get it."

His brown eyes are pleading. Jase frowns over something on the inside of the hood. Samantha is also apparently very absorbed in the whole process.

"Brad, we never *talked*. We didn't –" *laugh*. Tears are starting to run down his cheeks. Oh God.

"Talked?" he repeats, sounding confused. "About what?"

This is going nowhere. Wrap it up. I set my hand on his knee, squeeze. "You're a good guy."

"Oh, no," he says, suddenly loud. "Don't do that. Don't 'good guy' me. I'm better than that. I'm a great guy. I've stuck by you. I've been there for you."

He has. He's put up with my crazy hours, all the homework and housework and babysitting I've had to do. On the other hand, I've put up with his roommate – the missing link – his CrossFit obsession, the wicked

73

Grandmother of the West, and all those nicknames.

"You have, Brad. Which is what makes this so hard." My voice is gentle, but it doesn't make any difference. Now he's actually sobbing, giant shoulders heaving, tears streaming down his face, his nose running. I flick my gaze to the garage apartment. "Brad . . ." I say helplessly. How can he have felt this deeply without me realizing it?

Now he's buried his face in his hands. I try to rub his shoulder but he shakes me off. "Just go. Go away, Alice."

More tears.

"Brad –" I say helplessly. "I feel –"

"You feel nothing," he says. "You don't even know how to feel. Get out of my car."

My feet have barely hit the driveway when he yanks the door shut, then peels out with a screech of tires, zooms down the road, totally unlike himself. He usually drives like a little old lady.

I'm staring after him, biting my thumbnail, which I haven't done in years. Jase slams the hood closed, wipes his greasy hands on some rag. After the roar of the car fades away, the silence is particularly loud.

"Well . . . that could have gone better," Jase says. "Don't you ever get tired of this, Al?"

"Do you want to talk about it?" Samantha asks at nearly the same time.

I shake my head. Should I have known how he felt? Where were the signs? "I didn't . . ." Wait. Is that the same

74

silver car, idling across the road?

"He's wrong. About the feelings thing. He was just pissed. Guys are dicks when their pride gets hurt," Jase offers.

"My fault," I say absently. "He was never a dick before."

"Want me to beat him up for you?" he asks. "He's big, but I could hire henchmen. George would go for it if there was a cool uniform."

"Tim would help," adds Samantha.

The stalker car jerks into reverse, then forward, like a replay of Brad. One of Joel's castoffs? Tim's drug connection? Whatever. The least of my problems.

Speak of the devil. I turn at the sound of Tim's feet banging down the garage steps. He's whistling, head bent, counting change. "I'll be back around seven, guys, do you wanna –"

The tension in the air is practically solid. He looks back and forth between us. "Alice? Sam? What'd I do?"

After they all leave, I plop down on the steps next to George. He looks at me, head cocked. "He cried."

Sighing, I tug him onto my lap, resting my chin on the top of his head. His fly-away hair tickles my nose as I inhale his scent – chalk and grass and hose water. "Yup, I know."

"I've never seen someone so big cry like that. It was kind of like when the Cowardly Lion cries."

It sure was.

Guess that makes me Tin Alice.

Chapter Eleven

Today's meeting is at the hospital, the same one Mr. Garrett
is at. I come late, and my AA sponsor, Dominic, scowls at
me when I slouch into the chair next to him.

"Unavoidably delayed," I mutter.

"Avoid it next time," he mutters back.

This is how Dominic got to be my sponsor: he copped
on to me fast. Almost as fast as Mr. Garrett, who had the
advantage of being my Cub Scout troop leader long ago. It
was Mr. G. who told me to go to AA, and Mr. G. I went with,
at first. But some days he couldn't, was working or doing
something with the kids. Those days I would still go, but I
would sit – or stand – near the door. Then I'd leave early.
Never when Mr. Garrett was there, but when he wasn't,
every time. Earlier and earlier. After I did this four or five
times, Dominic grabbed me by the side of my T-shirt as
he was walking in the door, towed me over to the seat next
to him, and pulled me down. We were way in the back of
the room, as far from the door as could be. He's this boxy-
shouldered guy, young, huge hands, skinny but strong, deep

tan skin with one of those permanent five-o'clock-shadow types. When I started to get up ten minutes before the end of the meeting, he stuck his foot out in front of mine, like he was going to trip me. "What is this, kindergarten?" I hissed out of the corner of my mouth. He mouthed, "Later." The minute the meeting ended I said, "I didn't know there was assigned seating at these things. You want to see my ID now? You're an asshole."

He stared at me, no expression. "No. No. You found me out. Don't leave early. Asshole."

No messing around with Dom.

Later I found out other stuff. That he was twenty-two. That he got married right out of SBH because he got his girlfriend pregnant on prom night. "In the car, on the way there," he always adds. "I didn't even buy her a corsage." That his wife left and took the baby when they'd been married a year. That he spent the next six months so smashed, he still doesn't remember if he went to work or not. That now he's been clean for three years.

So, here we all are, at the end of the meeting, all holding hands like it really is kindergarten. A few months ago, that would have seemed lame as hell; something you do all the time when you're little, crossing the street with your mom and all that. But after you're, say, ten, who does it? But I actually kind of like it, here, sandwiched between Tough Guy Dominic and Mr. Smooth Jake, who I formerly knew as Coach Somers, my gym teacher from Hodges. He

smiles at me, which trust me, he never did when I was at Hodges on his team. He was more given, back then, to asking me to drop and give him fifty for my lousy attitude. Back then, I thought he was a bitter-ass old guy who didn't get teenagers. He's maybe in his late twenties.

Now, as I head out to get coffee with Dominic, Jake tosses me a salute. Feels good.

∘ • ∘ •

Dom and I are at Cuppa Joe and Piece-a Pie – sucky coffee, awesome pie – talking about whether he should buy this old junker truck with 100,000 miles on it – when he suddenly looks up, eyebrows raised, then smirks at me. "Some guy hates one of us. My bet's on you. Because if looks could incinerate, you'd be a smoking pile of ashes."

"It's usually the girls I piss off – my money's on you. Where is he?"

"Riiight, I forgot you were the big Casanova. Third table from the left. I'm pretty sure that one-fingered salute was all yours. He has good aim. If he had a gun –"

"No man detests me like that except my pop." I pretend to be cracking my neck to get a glimpse of the guy.

Yeah, he looks like he hates my ass, all right. It's Alice's Brad.

"Need to go make amends?" Dominic asks. "I'm sure he'd be happy to accept it. If not, he only outweighs you

by, maybe ninety to a hundred pounds. Might show some mercy and leave you *almost* dead instead of a bloody smear on the floor."

"You seem to like imagining different ways for me to bite it, Dom. Way to be supportive."

"What did you do, sleep with his girlfriend?"

"Uh – what? No!" My voice goes a little loud on that one. "No," I repeat more quietly.

"You blushing?" Dominic asks, amused.

"No. So . . . tell me more about this truck thing – how does it, uh, handle?"

Dominic looks down, lips compressing to hide his smile. "Yeah, like *that's* what you care about handling." He sips his coffee. "Speaking of, what happened with the GED thing?"

Turns out that in Connecticut, you can't apply for a GED unless you're at least nineteen, or if you get a letter from your school saying you "withdrew." Not precisely how it went down at Ellery.

I rub my thumb into a glob of cherry pie, lick it off. "Um, yeah. I took care of it. Not exactly sure it was . . . kosher, twelve-step-wise."

"You didn't forge anything, did you, Tim? Because –"

"No! I, um, relied on something I sort of maybe shouldn't have. With the school secretary."

Dominic cocks an eyebrow. "And that would be?"

"My charm."

Dom snorts. "Had that one fooled too, huh? She should have talked to Smiley over there."

Christ. Brad's still glaring at me like I stole his favorite pacifier.

"Ms. Iszkiewicz – she always" – I hunch a little lower in my seat – "thought I was cute or something. She said she'd type up a letter and get the headmaster to sign off on it. Dobson never paid attention to shit he was signing unless it was a donation check."

"Tim," Dominic says. "C'mon."

"Did I cross the line?"

Dom takes another sip of coffee. "What do you think?"

"But if I don't lie, how can I get what I need?"

"Did you just hear yourself?" He relaxes back in his chair, watching my face.

I curse.

"I know," Dom says. "But part of this whole thing is not being a manipulative bastard anymore, remember?"

Brad's leaving. As he walks by our table, he accidentally on purpose bangs into the back of my chair with his giant thigh.

What, no wedgie? What the hell does Alice get from this douchewit?

Chapter Twelve

Alice's hands are behind her back, her beat-up purse hanging off her elbow. Green scrubs, circles under her eyes, smells like anti-bacterial gel . . . and she still kicks my pulse into high gear.

"I've got something for you," she says, brushing past me.

"Is it kinky? Does it involve you, me, some body oil?"

She snorts. "In your dreams, junior."

"Just the really good ones. But we could totally make those a reality."

"Here." She holds out what she's had hidden behind her. A package wrapped in bright blue tissue. She shoves the box at me so fast, I have to snatch at it before it drops to the ground.

"You got me a housewarming present, Alice?"

"Unwrap it already." She walks over to the sink, full of two days' worth of dishes. Most with Grape-Nuts laminated to the sides.

I open it to find a box with the Nike swoosh on it.

"If I wear these, does it mean we're going steady?"

"If you wear these while you're running, it means you won't wind up in a cast."

I examine the sneakers. They'll fit. Perfectly.

"You know my size?" I check the tiny tag. Yup, thirteens.

"You've left your disgusting Sasquatch shoes by our pool often enough. Your feet are like, freaks of nature."

"You know what they say about large feet."

"Uh-huh. Big smelly socks. Stop it, Tim. I just thought if you were even remotely interested in being healthy, you should have the right equipment."

"Trust me, Alice. I have the right equipment."

She starts to laugh. "Please. You're like one of those overgrown puppies who can't stop humping everything."

My smile fades. But Alice has turned away, hands on hips, to survey the room. "You're a bigger slob than Brad," she says. "Impressive."

This means that she's been in lame-ass Brad's room – quick one-two punch to the gut, even though, Christ, *of course*. I mean, she's nineteen.

She squints at the apartment some more, walks around. Which is, ya know, embarrassing in the daylight. It was pretty dim when she was last here. In addition to the sink pileup, I have a small mountain of used boxers and shorts in one corner and the sweatpants I slept in last night draped over the couch.

"Hey. Uh . . ." I indicate the box of Grape-Nuts

before she can notice the raised toilet seat and wad of wet towels on the floor of the bathroom. "I'd offer you cereal, but I only have one spoon. I know how anal you are about germs."

"I'm *educated* about germ transfer. You drink out of the orange juice carton. I've *seen* you. Why do guys do that? Foul."

"Because when we want things, we want them now. We're thirsty, we need a drink – we take a drink. Finding a clean glass, washing out a dirty one and all that crap – nah. We're just basic. We want what we want right this minute . . . or maybe that's just me."

"Tim, cut it out. Now. Please." Her face is as expressionless as her voice. But of course, I keep going.

"Like that old song: *Antici-pay-ay-shun is making me way-yay – yait.* That could only be written by a chick. Guys hate anticipation. That's why we all write about satisfaction. Why we never wrap presents. I notice you wrapped mine."

"I thought it was because you're all too cheap to buy wrapping paper. Or too clueless to find it in the store."

"There's that. But honestly, you go to the trouble of getting someone a present, something you think they'd like – why hide it and make them work for it? It's coy."

Alice laughs, shifting aside my sweatpants and dropping down on the couch. "It's not coy. It . . . it shows you care." She gathers her hair up in a knot, showing off her long neck.

"The *present* shows you care. The wrapping paper shows you aren't as concerned about the environment as you should be. Like showering alone. A needless waste of resources."

"Are we ever going to have a conversation without you coming onto me, Tim Mason?"

"I doubt it. We want what we want, right? Basic, babe."

"Please. No 'babe.' No 'chick.'"

"You prefer Allykins? Ally-o? Ally-ums? Noted."

"Tim. Don't." Her voice sounds a little funny. Damn. Is she that sold on Brad?

She roots through her purse, pulls something out. "I have another present for you, actually. I didn't wrap this one." Holding up a small clinical-looking square box, she wags it at me without looking at my face.

"Nicotine patches, Alice – seriously?"

"I told you you can't smoke here."

"And I told you I'm trying to kick it."

"I know." She waves me over, clasping the box between her knees, and flips it open with her other hand. When I plunk down next to her, she slides the rolled-up sleeve of my shirt higher, cool fingers on my skin. "You need to put these on parts of your body that aren't hairy. Not that you're very hairy. Only a bit on your chest." Her fingers freeze for a second before she continues. "Stick it on your shoulder or your back. Or your ribs. But rotate the spot, because the nicotine irritates your skin."

She's touching my upper arm, totally professional, like the nurse she's training to be, and hell if I'm not reacting like she's unzipping my jeans.

I edge away, scratch the back of my neck, which doesn't itch, a little dizzy.

She pulls my arm to her stomach, holds it steady, and plasters on the patch. "Change it once a day. Different location. Six to eight weeks."

"Did you have a secret vice, Alice? You sound so knowledgeable."

"I read directions. Another thing guys rarely do." Patting my arm, she flips my sleeve back down, hesitates a second before meeting my eyes. "What you're doing is tough, Tim. Not drinking, no drugs. Living on your own. Add quitting smoking. I admire you for it."

I stare at her. "For real?"

"Of course. I'm nineteen and still at home. This is no easy thing" – she reaches out and taps where the patch is under my shirtsleeve – "but you don't always *have* to take the hard way. Not when there are easier ways."

My throat tightens. Of all people I expected to . . . whatever, Alice might be dead last. I swallow. Her green-brown eyes are sincere. I lift my hand a few inches toward her cheek. Then drop it, shove it in my pocket as I stand, jingle the loose coins in there.

Alice inspects me sharply for a sec, school-marm-over-her-glasses-style, then licks her lips and looks away, wiping

her palms on her scrubs. She stands up. "What's it with you and the Grape-Nuts? Besides pizza, it's almost all I ever see you eat."

"I like Grape-Nuts."

"You *live* on Grape-Nuts. That's more than liking. It's obsession."

"You sure are getting worked up about this." To keep my dangerous hands occupied, I pour myself a bowl, get milk out of the fridge, sniff at it.

"Well, it isn't rational."

Her tone is mad huffy. Why? What'd I miss?

"All this emotion over cereal? What do you care what I eat?"

"You're all thin and pale, Tim. You look like you're not sleeping. People worry about you." She lobs her droopy, too-big purse back over her shoulder. "I should get going. I'm on babysitting call tonight."

I move between her and the door before I can think. "Okay, Alice. I'll grant that worrying people has always been a talent of mine. But my family's pretty much given up. You're the one who came all the way over here to save my ankles and so on. Are we talking worrying *people* . . . or are we talking worrying *you?*" The words rush out, hover in the air. I'm noticing again how little Alice is, aside from those curves, barely coming up to my shoulders. Five two? Five four?

She yanks her purse onto her shoulder again, looks

down. Her cheeks go pink.

"Well?" I ask, because I've pushed it this far already.

One finger after another, she ticks things off. "You're my little brother's best friend. Though sometimes I have no idea how or why he puts up with you. You're a minor. You're a potential, if not an ongoing, disaster. You –" Then she sighs, shuts her eyes. "Listen, I have a long day tomorrow. Three classes, a clinical. When I get through it" – her voice drops to a low mutter, like even she doesn't want to hear what she's saying – "could we just meet for dinner? Like a . . . sample date?"

This goes through me like an electric shock.

A date.

With Alice Garrett?

Wait.

A *sample* date?

"What would we be sampling?"

She looks like she might laugh. Doesn't. "Not *that*. I don't do hookups."

"I didn't mean that. I never thought that for a second."

She gives my shoulder a shove. "Of course not."

"Okay. But it was like a millisecond, a nanosecond. Then I remembered how much I respected you and that I would never –"

Alice puts her hand, her fingertips, over my mouth. "Tim. Stop talking now."

I snap my mouth shut.

87

"We'd be sampling *dinner*."

Then I remember a certain two-hundred-and-fifty-pound boyfriend. Who apparently already hates my ass. "Wait. Is this a setup? Are you trying to get my ass kicked by ol' Brad?"

She shakes her head quickly, pulling her hand away from my face and burying it in the pocket of her scrubs. Her purse strap falls down again. My hand goes to slip it back up, but then no, I shove it back in my pocket.

Alice hesitates for a second, then: "This has nothing to do with Brad. He wouldn't mind, anyway."

"Then he's even more of a putz than I thought. Hard to believe."

Her eyes flick to mine, then away. "It's not like that."

It's not? Okay. So that makes me . . .

Dinner.

"Meet me at Gary's Grill in Barnet. Six thirty. Tomorrow night."

Barnet is three towns away. Apparently Alice isn't prepared to be seen in the immediate vicinity with her underage, recovering alcoholic sample date.

I say I'll meet her there. She nods, gives me a subdued version of her sexy, crooked, smile, then her lips brush my cheek. That Hawaii smell. *Oh, Alice.*

"See you then."

I nod, speechless, and shy-Alice morphs back into take-charge-Alice, jabbing a finger at me. "Don't you dare be

late. I hate it when guys pull that, like my time doesn't matter. Like they're all casual and time is a relative thing while I'm sitting there with the waiter pitying me."

"Should we synchronize our watches?"

"Just don't let me down."

Chapter Thirteen

Waiting out in front of Hodges, school number one of my three, is bizarre. I've been back for Nan's this-or-that achievement awards, but my neck still starts to itch as I stand there, like I'm stuck in the old uniform, gray flannel pants and stiff white shirt.

Here to pick up Samantha, offered to walk with her to the condo she and her mom moved into a week ago – ol' Gracie's brilliant plan to get her away from Jase and the Garretts next door, by relocating crosstown. Out of sight, etc.

She comes out of the big-ass oak doors, down the steps with the stone lions, spots me, waves, then halfway down the path, gets called over by this cluster of girls. They're laughing and gesturing, and in their matching outfits, long straight hair, prep-clean looks, Hodges could slap 'em right on the cover of the school catalog.

Sam's not like that, but she blends.

Then I see something else. My sister, walking with her head down, rooting through her bag like she'll find the Ark

of the Covenant in there. She's so preoccupied, I think she's gonna crash right into the girls, but she makes a wide, careful path around them. So I get it. She sees them, but doesn't want them to see her.

Sam does, though, raises one hand, hello. But Nan keeps walking, rummaging away, because that treasure in her bag must and shall be found.

She's not short, Nan, five seven or so, but from here she looks it.

Text her: **You okay?**

I think she's gonna look around and spot me, propped against the magnolia tree only a few yards from the brick pathway, but she doesn't.

Nan: **Why wouldn't I be?**

Chew my lip, try to figure out whether to say I'm right here or not. Nan would be . . . not happy with the Sam pickup – I mean, she knows we're still friends. But . . .

I settle for: **Just checking in.**

Nan: **That's out of character.**

She's stopped on the path and is making this phony face like she's oh so excited about whoever's texting her. It's a "for the benefit of others" face.

Me: **Yeah, well, I'm all about turning over the new leaf. So . . . you know where I am if you need me, K?**

Nan: **Who are you and what have you done with my brother?**

Me: **Ha.**

Nan: **Look, I've got a thing. Gotta go.**

Right, the infamous "thing" we all have. Jesus, Nan.

As I'm trying to figure out whether to call her out on it in person, Sam strides up next to me, cups one of her ears, then the other with a few swift taps. "Water in my ear. Forgot my earplugs, and I'm going crazy trying to up my time before tryouts next week. So, you're actually asking me for advice, Tim? The apocalypse, much?"

Her tone is light, but the look she shoots me isn't.

"The apocalypse? Come on. I ask for stuff."

"Tim, I've known you since we were five. Cash, yes. Excuses, totally. But not this."

"Well, I'll take whatever you've got."

I haul her bag off her shoulder onto my own, hunting around for Nan, but she's blended somewhere into the girl herd.

We walk. "It's left up here." Sam points to the road up the hill, the summit of Stony Bay, fanciest, richest part of town. "So, this is an actual date you're going on."

"Just – just something I'd rather not screw up. So – hit me with your best. Like, for starters, what the hell do I even wear?"

Samantha grins.

"Don't," I say. "I know exactly how lame I sound."

"Start by passing the sniff test," she says, smelling the air exaggeratedly, like some crazy bloodhound or whatever. "Which that shirt doesn't, by the way. And" – she smacks

me on the shoulder – "if she's older than you, like you said, no shirts with school insignias. No point in rubbing it in that she's a cougar."

"She's not a cougar. Jesus God."

We're a little over one year apart, me and Alice. It's nothing.

Samantha studies me for a sec, then continues lightly. "Shower. Take her someplace low-key. Listen when she talks. Ask questions but only if you actually care about the answers. Don't keep trying to interrupt with stories about the last time you got drunk."

"Believe me, I'm not gonna touch that."

Besides, Alice has been there. I puked all over her and she took off her shirt, calm as moon-low tide, *owning* this black lace bra with this tiny red ribbon and . . . it's the one thing I remember perfectly about that night.

"You'd be surprised at how many guys do."

Samantha's shoulders stoop a little as we hit a bend in the road, cut off by huge black iron gates, tacked all over with signs: PRIVATE COMMUNITY, NO TRESPASSING, you are not welcome here. "Here we go, home sweet home as of last week. The code is 1776."

"Sorry, kid. Should have given you a housewarming present. A casserole, at least."

"Believe me, nothing could warm this place up. The condo makes our old house look festive. We're right up by the clubhouse." She gestures to this low building with a Swiss-

chalet-looking roof, surrounded by a golf course spattered with dudes in pastel, knocking away at tiny white balls. It all looks like a retirement village.

"Wow," I say. I got nothin' else.

"I know." Samantha shakes her head. "I haven't even let Jase see it yet. I mean, did you notice the streets? General Dwight D. Eisenhower Drive, Lady of the Lake Lane, Pettipaug Peak? The names aren't even consistent! And check out the houses. You could walk into the wrong one and suddenly find yourself living someone else's life." She waves her hand at row after row of identical houses.

"What time do all the handsome husbands pop out of their doors with their matching briefcases?"

"Leaving their blond wives to take their Valium, at the same second, elbows bent just so? Not sure. We've only been here a week. Give me time. It's over here, Wolverine Wood Road."

I squint. "Are there any actual woods? Or wolverines?" The landscape is green and grassy and flat, except for an unnatural-looking lake.

"Right? No, they took down all the trees to build this. I'll keep you posted on the wolverines. We're here." She points past a narrow row of hedges. "By the statue of the non-specified Revolutionary War soldier."

"Do I need to lay a wreath?" I ask as we head past the scarily smiling iron statue. "Or salute?"

"Why couldn't we have stayed put?" She sighs.

Samantha knows the obvious answer to that, so all I say is, "Cheer up, kid. College next year. '

Gracie, Sam's mom, is out on the porch of Clairemont Cottage, planting some brassy orange flowers in big stone urns. She jolts to her knees when we turn the corner, trowel in hand, then, seeing it's me with Sam, beams, waves, settles back down on her heels again. For reasons known only to her and God, Grace persists in thinking Jase is the delinquent and I'm the upstanding citizen.

Samantha studies me for a sec, then says, "One more thing. The most important. On this date? Just be, you know, smart and funny and sweet. Like you are."

"Pretty sure that's not actually me."

"It is." She flips her hair out of its braid, sliding her fingers through to shake it out. "If she's going on a date with you, she probably thinks so too. Do I know her?"

"Not really."

"Tim, c'mon."

"It's not a big deal. It's just a" – I have no idea what it is – "thing."

Not buying it. All over her face.

But Samantha smiles, tugs her bag off my shoulder, puts her hand in its place. "Two more things, actually – but they're crucial. Don't wear that stupid Axe stuff clueless guys think is sexy. It reeks of desperation."

I fake scribble on an imaginary pad. "Noted."

"And don't let her break your heart, okay?"

"Sammy-Sam, I think that's already a given."

"I get to ride on the feet!" George squeals.

"Bro. You can't ride on the wheelchair feet. I'd lose my job," Brad says, maneuvering Dad out of the hospital room, skillful and grounded in his transporter role. We're a parade to help move Dad to the rehab part of Maplewood. Joel's got the duffel full of the clothes we brought so Dad would feel semi-normal. Mom's arms are bundled full of his books. Andy's carrying a stack of artwork the little guys made, carefully detached from the Scotch tape on the wall. Duff has the Xbox and the videogames. Harry, the old deck of cards, the pick-up sticks, the dominoes, the old-fashioned games we rediscovered to make time pass.

I have all the paperwork, most of which my parents don't know about.

It *would* be Brad they sent to do the transfer, of all the 'porters in all of Maplewood Memorial. He's ignoring me. I'm ignoring him. This is fun. At least he's been decent to the kids, even though George keeps giving him sidelong glances, no doubt worried the tears will start again.

I check my watch – plenty of time to do what I need to do, get home, and get ready to go out with Tim, as long as this all goes quickly.

Two and a half hours later – twice as long as it was

supposed to take – Dad's in his room, everything (more or less) sorted out.

Mom leaves with the kids, Joel heads to cop class, I linger. Sticking the pictures up on the wall, stacking the games in piles, making the bare room a little like home. Dad shut his eyes the instant they all left, "just for a moment." But he immediately dropped off to sleep.

I sit down on the side of the bed. Really, I want to lie down too, put my head on his shoulder. I was up late last night studying, and George had a wake-up-screaming nightmare, something about a supervolcano under Yellowstone Park. After I convinced him it was absolutely nothing to worry about and he finally fell asleep in my lap and I carried him back to bed, I googled it.

There is one.

Looking at my father's face, worry lines smoothed out, faint smile, his big hands brown against the white hospital sheet, air siphons out of my lungs for an instant. Black spots collect at the corners of my vision.

Deep breath.

Deep breath.

The spots scatter and fade.

On to the next thing, because what else can I do?

I brought a change of clothes for tonight along with me, just in case.

I mean, I'm not dressing up. Not for Tim, for God's sake. But, I've been wearing this black V-neck and skirt all

day long, and Harry squeezed his juice box too hard and –

Anyway.

I shower in the bathroom off Dad's new room, crowded in by the walker, the quad cane, and the commode chair. Tiny hospital-issue soap and body wash and shampoo, because I forgot to bring my own. Hospital towels are rough and tiny, it takes two to dry off, and still my dark blue sundress clings in a few wet patches. No blow dryer, so my hair will dry curly. So be it. When I look in the mirror, I recognize myself again.

There's a sharp sound from the other room, like air through teeth.

Sweat stands out on his forehead and his face is chalky white.

"Dad?"

"Al," Dad says gently, "come back a little later, okay?"

"Not happening. What do you need?"

My hand is poised over the call button. He sets his on top of it. "They'll only dope me up. Not what I want."

Dad shifts in the bed with a crackle of plastic hospital mattress pad. He sucks his breath in hard, again blows it out. My own breath snags.

"Scale of one to ten," I say, groping to find the professional in me.

"I'm not your patient, tiger," Dad says. "Luckily for both of us."

Without warning, my eyes fill. I don't cry. I never cry.

Which Dad knows. His hand shoots out, squeezes my shoulder. "You know I didn't mean it like that. You know that." Now he's batting at the box of tissues at the side of his bed, which is slightly out of reach, and something about that, my dad, who can do *anything*, who can fix everything –

"You look gorgeous, Alice," Dad says. "Hot date?"

"Just a thing," I say, my face going hot.

He studies me, saying nothing, waiting for information to come to him. Mom and Dad have that one down to an art.

"How's Tim these days?"

These two questions are not connected. He's making conversation. Distracting me from calling the nurse and another debate about pain medication. "How Mom and Dad Met" is a family fairy tale – Mom's told us the story so often, we can all fill in words when she pauses. But there's a part she leaves out when we're younger . . . that charming, perceptive Jack Garrett had a dark side back then. He was, as he tells it, "mad at the whole live world" because his mother had died the year before, and his little sister and brother, my aunt Caroline and my uncle Jason, had stayed behind in Virginia with their grandparents, while his father had taken my father, alone, since he was sixteen and old enough to bring in a paycheck, up to Connecticut. Dad had a drinking problem, which got worse until his twenties, when he realized he could go that route, or have a life with Mom, and turned his around.

I have never seen my father drink alcohol. He doesn't

99

even have soda, although he'll be the first to tell you that entire coffee plantations are supported by his caffeine habit.

It could go that way for Tim. Or it could go the other way.

"Oh . . . you know. The usual."

Dad laughs. "That kid has no 'usual.'"

Out in the hallway again, I rub the back of my neck, close my eyes, flip back my hair. I'm looking forward to Tim – Tim! – like a steaming hot bath after a long, cold day.

Still, I pull Dad's chart from the plastic holder outside the door, page through it. Standard entry, expected procedure, the usual blah, blah, blah.

But then . . .

Holy.

Holy Mother of God.

Chapter Fourteen

I'm doing pushups as a healthier alternative to a pack of Marlboros, wondering when the hell the magic powers of the nic patch will kick in, when I hear the knock at my door – so faint, it's not really a knock, more like a scratch or a tap. I'm at that top-of-the-pushup, arms-shaking point, right before I exhale –

Collapse.

Wipe my arm across my sweaty forehead. I'm wearing Ellery gym shorts and a sweaty black polo. Not exactly poised to receive company. But I've still got time to get it together for Alice.

Whatever it is we're sampling on this date, the thought of it has me grinning as I open the door.

But when I do, the face I see is so out of context, it takes me a few seconds.

Big blue eyes, small pointed chin, tidy ponytail. One seat to the left of me in English Writers of the Western World. I used to borrow her perfectly sharpened pencils. Never gave 'em back.

"Tim?" she says, like I might be Tim's evil twin.

"Hi. Uh . . . Heather." How I scrounge that name from my subconscious, I have no idea.

"It's Hester. Can I come in?"

What? I think, at the same time I say, "Sure," and open the door wider for her. She brushes past me, sits down on the couch, and looks at her shoes. Hester was a Brain and a Good Girl. So we had nothing in common. What's she doing here? She smoothes down her khaki skirt, readjusts her white shirt. Prep wear. *Clothing as birth control,* my douchey friends and I used to joke. All those fuckin' buttons. Little gold hoop earrings, neat part in her brown hair. Shit, is she, like, a Jehovah's Witness or something? I don't have time for this. But now she's weaving her fingers together, studying them. "So, Tim . . . you left Ellery early this year."

"Yeah, left, as in got booted."

I look at the clock on the stove right as it flips from 5:58 to 59. Less than half an hour to meet Alice, and it takes fifteen minutes to drive. If you don't run the lights or speed.

Hester lifts her face and looks at me squarely. "Before that, you went to Ward Akins pool party."

I did? Geez, I was so messed up back then, worst of my worst. I can hardly remember those last months of school. Little flashes. Ward Akins? Asskite guy on my tennis team. Pool party? Would I have gone to one of those? Who'm I kidding? I would have gone to *anyone*'s party.

But also? Who the eff cares what party I did or didn't go to.

"Uh. Look, can we catch up some other time? Sorry – I mean . . . not to be a dick, but . . . why are you here?"

"Ward is my godmother's stepson," Hester says, like family history answers the question. "Even though he's an abject loser, I went to this party because . . . well, never mind." Her voice, which is husky, throaty, stalls out for a sec. Then she braids her fingers together even more tightly, swallows. "Big house – very modern, glass windows . . . the pool's indoors, heated. They have a tiki bar . . . do you remember any of this?"

Not even the tiki bar. "No. Sorry. I got nothing."

Her face shuffles through a boatload of emotions in, like, seconds – there and gone. Then her features smooth, totally composed. She looks dead on at me, blue eyes crystal clear, focused, narrowing, like she's aiming a gun. "You don't have 'nothing.' You have a son."

Chapter Fifteen

I do the most wrong thing I could possibly do.

Laugh.

Looking Hester straight in the eye, I slump down on the couch next to her.

And laugh.

It's like I can't stop. I'm holding up one hand, holding the other to my stomach, and she's staring at me like I'm dog shit she's stepped in, except that her eyes are filling with tears.

So I try to get a hold of myself, say something.

And again, straight to the worst thing.

"You're fucking kidding me, right?"

She's standing up now, slowly, in this rickety way, like she's aged fifty years at my response.

Brushes her hands on her skirt again. Tucks some stray hair behind her ears.

"No joke. Sorry."

She's halfway to the door before I stop her, hand on her shoulder. "Hester. That's not possible . . . I'm not *that* stupid."

Yeah, hack off foot and shove it permanently in mouth.

Her eyes flash. "You were. Sorry again. You were a bit drunk. For a change. Never mind."

"Never *mind?*" I repeat incredulously.

Hester reaches into her purse, foraging around, all anxious. Then smacks her forehead with the heel of her hand, stuffs it into the front pocket of her skirt, pulls something out, and hands it to me. "It's an awful picture. I didn't know that hospital pictures are a scam. They get you while you're groggy and suddenly you have all these wallet-sized photos and a mouse pad for, like, eighty bucks . . . he looks better now." She hands me this little snapshot. Of this baby with his eyes squinted shut like he's pissed off. And a fluff of red hair. My hair. When I was little it always stuck straight up exactly like that.

"His name's Calvin."

Really? What a sucky name.

I stare at the picture, the closed eyes, the defiant face. Scrabble for something . . . anything . . . to say.

Fuck.

"Where is he now?"

"In my car." Hester takes the picture back, tucking it into her wallet, carefully closing the purse back up, all focused. "He was sleeping and I thought it'd be better if I —"

"You serious? It's eighty-five degrees!" I hurtle down the garage steps.

"The windows are all open!" Hester calls after me.

The windows may be open, but the baby in the car is soaked with sweat, dark red hair plastered to his forehead, hunched down in one of those backward bucket baby-type seats, boneless and kinda bowlegged. He's wearing a blue undershirt, a diaper, and a weird-ass sailor hat. His eyes, with these little spiky eyelashes, dark like mine, oh hell, are shut tight, his mouth puckered like he's dreaming about kissing.

I bend in, try to unlock the car seat, sweating like a mother myself. There are these two thick red buttons on either side and I press them hard, jiggle harder. Nothing happens. Hester moves forward. I think she's gonna unlatch things, but instead, she takes off his hat.

"Here he is," she says, like, *ta-da*. "This is Calvin."

"Yeah, can we save the introductions?" I'm punching and jiggling the buttons. "This kid really needs air."

Actually, I don't know this. Just guessing. If he were a dog in the car, he'd need air. I sure need air. I'm breathing so hard, I'm pretty much panting when I finally hear the click of the car seat disengage and drag it out. Look at the kid.

My kid.

Wait, wait. No. This isn't. This isn't real and I'll wake up and see that this is some crazy dream test. At least I'm not naked. Except that I feel it, more naked than actual naked because –

He stares at me, blue eyes, confused face, and I might as well be looking at one of the baby pics on our living

room wall. The world is sucked silent, just a faint hum. I'm gonna puke.

Because –

At the same time that I'm thinking *no, no, no way,* some other part of me is not surprised. Not at all. Of course. Of course I would do this. Of course.

Through the buzzing in my ears, Hester's talking again. "I want to go to college next spring. Taking a gap now. Because of Calvin. Obviously. I'm already in at Bryn Mawr. It's where my favorite teacher went, where I've always wanted to go. I took this time off so I could . . . deal."

I'm still looking at the kid, whose little dark eyelashes are fluttering, sinking closed again.

"My grandfather – I live with him – said you deserved to be told," she adds, in a voice so low, it's almost a whisper. "He said you deserved a chance to be a man."

A man. Shit. Not again. I don't want to be a man. I'm not even good at being a boy.

His eyes open again – blue as . . . blue stuff.

He stares, unfocused, for a second, then waves a fist at me.

"Hold out one finger," Hester says, and I do. Calvin knocks his fist against it, prizefighter-style, then opens up his little starfish hand and clenches onto my index finger. His clutch is hot and sticky. He stares at me, eyes crossing.

"Do you want to . . ." Hester clears her throat. "Hold him?"

Hell no. He looks completely breakable. But I *should* want to, right? "Uh, sure. Yeah. I do. Absolutely."

Hester peers at me. Like she's wondering if she can trust me not to break her baby. She shouldn't. I break everything.

She unlatches the little belt, scoops her hand behind Calvin's head and under his butt, straightens up and passes him to me.

My hand covers his entire backside. He's wet with – I hope – sweat, and has this weird milky smell.

I wait for him to start screaming because, Christ knows, *I* want to, but he doesn't. He simply gazes, all fathomless navy blue eyes.

"Serious little guy," I say, finally, because I should say *something.*

I'm holding the kid, my kid, for the first time and no natural instincts are kicking in. Except the "flee" one.

"They don't smile when they're this little," Hester says softly as I focus on pulling up the sock that's about to slide off Calvin's midget foot, the size of my goddamn thumb. "They learn in a month or two."

Hope so. On the other hand, this kid might not have much to smile about.

We stand there for a second next to the car – me awkwardly balancing the baby, Hester flicking her gaze between us. All I can think is, *What now? What does she really want?*

108

"What, uh . . . what can I do for you, Hes?" I'm startled to hear that abbreviation coming from my lips, like they know her better than the rest of me. She looks down at the tar of the driveway. The silent stillness is halted by a gentle rumbling noise. Her stomach.

Her fair skin flushes and she puts her hand there, like she can hush it that way. Or like there's still something – someone – in there.

"Can I start by giving you a sandwich?" I vaguely remember that you're supposed to eat a lot after you have a baby. Or is that before? Is she, like, nursing this kid?

Yikes. I steal a look at her tits. They look pretty much as I dimly recall. Small.

"I'd love that," she says, apparently not noticing the direction of my gaze. "He's probably hungry too."

I check Calvin's face, still waiting for the screaming to begin, but he's watching me, hanging tightly on to my finger.

Hester grabs what looks like a small suitcase – *Oh God* – from the backseat of the car and walks up the steps, leaving me to follow. With Calvin. And what may be the lead-up to a coronary squeezing my chest.

Is she here to – uh – stay? Please tell me I don't have to *marry* this girl. The bag doesn't look big enough to hold her stuff *and* his. But his things are probably pretty tiny. Maybe she's a really efficient packer. She *looks* like an efficient packer.

She holds the door open, as if she's inviting me into her own home. But, given that my hands are occupied with the kid, it's possible she's just being helpful.

As soon as we get in, I give him back to her, after carefully unpeeling his clingy, sweaty little paw from my finger.

Which is when the crying I've been waiting for gets going.

Hester hoists the small but solid weight of the baby against her shoulder, tipping her chin to hold him more firmly against her, and rummages the suitcase, pulling something out.

A bottle.

That answers the breastfeeding question. Thank Christ. I don't think I could deal with her exposed boob at the moment.

Then a can of formula, which she unseals with a *shhhzz*. Which sounds eerily like the beer I wish I were cracking open. "Just pour it in this and zap it for thirty seconds." She gestures at the microwave.

"Uh. Right. Sure." I take the bottle and the can, fill the bottle, then stare as it revolves in the microwave.

A wave of dizziness crashes over my head and I clutch the side of the counter.

An hour ago I was worrying about practice dating.

Now I'm heating formula for my baby. Alice is . . . *fuck* . . .

I glance over at Hester, her pink lip stuff and her neat,

if slightly rumpled and a size too tight, white shirt. *She's not even my type, for God's sake.* Delicate. Fragile. These big Bambi eyes. Someone I could do serious damage to.

Make *that* mission accomplished.

The microwave beeps. My hand is actually shaking as I crack it open. The kid's still wailing, cranking it up a notch or two every second.

When I hand the bottle to Hester, she whips me a quick look of gratitude, and then stuffs the nipple in Calvin's wide-open mouth. He hesitates, catching his breath, as if considering whether to continue with the misery or go for liquid comfort. He picks comfort.

Of course he does. My kid, after all.

My kid.

I shut my eyes, and, because I might possibly black out right now, I crouch next to Hester, putting a hand on her knee.

She looks down at it, and I get a sharp shock of weird. Wrong. Although I've clearly done a lot more than casually touch this girl. How is that even possible? I remember her from class. From *class*. Eyes forward, neat little notes, never even catching my eye, even when she loaned me pencils. Now that I'm up close, I see there are dark smudges under her eyes, and that her hair in its ponytail is sorta messy. The Hester I recall (vaguely) was one of those chicks who always looked perfect. At the moment her stomach is kind of puffy, squishy. The shoulder of her white shirt has some

yellowish stain on it.

I did that. I, like, *marked* this girl, changed her. And I don't even remember holding her hand.

Clawing for air in my own personal mineshaft now.

Okay.

She's here.

With this baby.

Why *now* and, Christ, what next?

"Hester." My voice cracks a little, like I'm still thirteen. "Look, I've got some leftover pizza. Orange juice. Milk. Some cheese that's not that old. Grape-Nuts. You can have any or all of that. But you gotta tell me why exactly you're here. What are you looking for from me?"

She looks up at me, her eyes vast, blue, and totally unreadable.

"Aside from the life-changing complication I've already provided," I add.

To my surprise, she gives a quick huff of laughter. "Poor Tim. You look terrified."

Now I'm ashamed, at least more familiar and comfortable than flat-out panic.

"Sorry," I say, approximately nine months too late. Calvin is glugging away again, his clenched fists waving in the air like he's fighting some invisible but formidable opponent.

"I'd love some pizza," Hester tells me, with a little smile.

I get a sudden surge of liking for her. She does seem to

be able to handle this whole hundred-shades-of-awkward meeting practically, without, say, sobbing uncontrollably or pointing an accusing finger at me. Jesus. What a year she must have had. Ellery would not have been an easy place to be a pregnant teenager. Anorexic, sure. Addicted to cocaine – totally. But pregnant? Hell, no – that's for public school girls.

I stand up slowly, check out Calvin's face. His eyelids are so thin, you can see little blue veins. On his temples too, near the tips of his ears.

"Yeah, sure. Pizza. Coming up."

The pizza's several days old and pretty disgusting. I have to peel it off the bottom of the cardboard box. I slap two rubbery, congealed pieces into the microwave and pour orange juice into one of Joel's Fitness Galaxy coffee mugs.

No napkins. No paper towels even. Offering her toilet paper would not be okay, right?

Hester somehow interprets my frantic hunt around the kitchen.

"I have baby wipes," she calls.

I go rigid. Somehow this just drives home the whole *I have a baby* thing.

I set the plate down in front of her. The kid's urgent gulping has emptied most of the bottle. He's bending his skinny, half-triangle legs up and down in time to his swallowing. Every time I look at him, I get a cold shockwave, like I have the flu. I know dick about babies. Patsy's cool,

but she's a real person already, not, like, an amoeba.

"Hey, I know this is a surprise," Hester says, after swallowing a tiny bite of sucky pizza. "I've had months to take it in. You've had twenty minutes. I appreciate you" – she pauses, then finally continues – "not yelling or saying he's not yours or any of that."

I look at his wavy hair, dry now and as rusty red as my own. "I'm not that guy."

As I say it I realize that this is the first time in years, maybe in my whole life, that I've said what I was and had it mean anything good. Hester nods. "I know. I mean – I hoped not. That's . . . um . . . why I'm here." She tilts the bottle so Calvin has better access to the last bit.

I rest my hands on the countertop, try to beat back visions of this future where I'm suddenly married to her – this girl I don't know – with a child I have no memory of making, and we're living in the Garretts' garage apartment. Forever. I'm this old man hobbling out to my job at, I dunno, Hot Dog Haven again or Gas and Go, trying to convince myself my life hasn't been a complete waste.

As if she's reading my thoughts, Hester glances around the room. "So . . . do you have a roommate? A . . . girlfriend?"

"Why?" My voice comes out like a bark. Hester flinches. Calvin pauses for a second in his glugging, but then speeds up again, his eyes practically lolling back in his head in ecstasy.

She shifts the baby so she can wave her hand around the

apartment. "Just wondering why this is where you live now. You left Ellery and . . . you're . . . here?"

"It belongs to friends of mine. I, uh, needed a place away from home, so I . . ."

Can't even finish a sentence.

Hester nods, sharp dip of her chin. "It's" – she looks around at the bare white walls with their thumbtack holes, the milk-crate bookcase, the dead plant next to the bathroom door, the basketball hoop above the trash can in the corner of the living room – "roomy." I get this sense that Hester's a nice girl who's used to saying nice things about things that aren't nice.

"Look . . . *please*. I gotta know. What *do* you want from me?"

She squirms in her seat, chips a hardened piece of pepperoni off the crappy pizza. "After Calvin was born, when I first saw his face – his hair – I knew I had to talk to you. So, as soon as I was, you know –"

"Back on your feet?"

"They put you on your feet right after you give birth, Tim," she says. "Practically as soon as the umbilical cord gets cut."

Gross. I flinch, yeah, I'm a dick. She had a baby, labor and all that, which probably involved some serious mess, and I can't even handle vaguely hearing about the minor details.

"So. When I saw his . . . when I knew, I was trying to

figure out how to find you. I asked around and . . . heard that you were, well, better —"

"Sober," I clarify.

Hester turns pink again. "Yes. Like I said, Grand told me that you deserved a chance. So . . . here I am."

My temples are throbbing.

I need a smoke. Or a drink. Or a handy firing squad to end me.

"Right. Sure. What does 'a chance' look like to you?"

Her voice drops low and she adjusts Calvin's little sweaty shirt. "I'm hoping — I want — to go back to work next week. This school-slash-camp place where I've worked summers and vacations for the last few years. They know me, and they were happy to have me back. Even before he was born. But the daycare doesn't have a space for him yet. Like I said, I put off college, but I can't just . . . tread water. This baby . . . derailed me. Grand could watch him some. He said he would, just so I know about the choices I'm making. But —" Her eyes are pleading, big and blue.

Fuckity fuck.

"He can't do it all the time, he has to be with my grandmother — she's got Alzheimer's, she's at a home, but she needs him — and he's got his hospital work, and I *have* to get back to normal. I thought if you knew and all, you might want to take him for an afternoon or a day or, even, more than that. Get to know your son. See if you're all fine with him. I mean, obviously I'm planning on giving him away."

Christ. Wait? What? To me? I *can't* do this.

"You mean, like, getting adopted?" Please almighty God, mean that.

"Of course," Hester says, in that calm, smart-girl voice I dimly remember from class, like there's only one right answer and she's got it. She's concentrating on detaching another bit of pepperoni from her slice, not even eating any of it, just making a dried-out stack on one side of the plate. Something about the tidy little pile just pisses me off.

"Why am I in here, Hes, if that's the choice you've already made?" The kid's turned his head to the side, eyelids drooping, but still looking as if he's watching me. I lower my voice, like he already knows how to listen to things he should never hear. "Are you some kind of sadist? Why should I even have to know about this if it's all decided?"

"My grandfather told me you should," she repeats again. "That it's the right thing to do."

Right. *Be a man.* "Sure. No problem. I'll do it." Accept the things you cannot change, right? Damn it.

She grins suddenly, and I get what I hadn't seen before. Rumpled, stained clothes, extra ten pounds, milk-pale skin aside, she's really pretty when she smiles.

"You will? That's great, Tim." She holds her hand out, bargain-style, and I reach out over the kid, grabe hold, and shake it. "I was thinking – maybe – we could meet – for lunch tomorrow? That way you'll have time to let this – sink in."

Sure, I'll absolutely have my head wrapped around it by then.

"Okay. That'd be . . . . good. Fine. Yeah. Fine."

She looks grateful, the way she's been thankful for the crappy pizza and the fact that I didn't yell at her.

"Is there any place you'd like to go?" she asks, as if this is a date.

I try to think of a good meeting place. I never took girls anywhere, other than, say, whatever room was unoccupied at whichever party. Sweat beads on my forehead.

"There's this restaurant, Chez Nous, in Riverton," Hester continues. "It's really little and nice. They have great tarte tatin. We can meet there and go over all the details."

Details? I can't even wrap myself around the big picture.

I swallow, nod.

Then, total autopilot, I open the door, gesture for her to go out first, lock up, trail her down to the car, watch Hester strap Calvin into the car seat, shove the diaper bag into the front passenger seat, smile and nod and knock once against the top of the car to say good-bye, because my voice has completely failed me.

I climb the steps, collapse on the top one, dig the heels of my hands into my eye sockets, like it'll relieve the pressure detonating in my brain.

Through the fog of panic and nausea, two things are crystal clear. I've found my way into a nightmare.

Also?

I've just stood up my dream girl.

Chapter Sixteen

First thing I see when I pull in is Tim leaning in the driver's-side window of a little silver sedan. So much for my theory/excuse/delusion that he didn't meet me because he was run over by a truck or called away to the zombie apocalypse or some awful, urgent, no-way-around-it disaster.

I could strangle the part of me that's relieved he's here, with his baggy school shorts and hair that needs cutting, flopping over his ears and forehead. But apparently just fine. The asshole.

He straightens up to give the top of the car a fist-knock, all calm, pulled-together, holding up a hand in a casual farewell as it backs down the driveway.

That same car. That same girl.

The moment the car jerks back onto the main road, he folds down on the steps, pats his chest where a pocket would be if his shirt had one. Then he rubs the shoulder where I put the nic patch, drops his head, and spreads one palm across his forehead as if he's taking his own temperature.

I slam the door of the Bug hard and it pops right back

open, because it's ancient and doesn't latch unless you prop it while closing. Slam again, louder this time.

Tim doesn't react at all, just keeps rubbing the patch.

"Just rip it off," I say, walking close, jangling my car keys in one palm. "Might as well admit it's no use."

Now he looks up, but almost through me, his eyes hazy and confused. Sighs. Doesn't say anything for a second, then, "Huh?"

"Tim. Where were you?"

He shudders like he has a fever, and he's staring into the distance, two streaks of color high on his cheekbones, the rest of his face pale.

"Tim."

Nothing.

As if he doesn't even know I'm here.

"You're drunk? Perfect. Good job, Tim."

He shakes his head, hunches his shoulders, doesn't look at me. Unbelievable.

I stand over him, for once taller. "Or is it weed? Or pills? God. Who was the girl? Your dealer? She was essential enough to blow me off? Fine."

I start to leave, brush past him, but he puts his hand on my leg, right above my knee. "It – it's not like that. I swear."

Clench my thumbs inside my curled fingers. "How many times have you 'sworn' about that one?"

"I didn't . . . bag on you on purpose, I mean.

Something . . . came up."

I stare pointedly down at his hand until he curses under his breath, tucks it under him, then pulls it back out, picking at a hole in his shorts instead.

"So what made you do it? What was *that* bad? You were doing better!"

"Yeah, well, now I've done worse." He has the hoarse, smothered voice boys get when they're trying not to be emotional, eyes fixed unblinking on the end of the driveway, like if he looks any nearer, he'll cry. He looks younger than usual, keeps picking at that tear near his pocket, and I find myself wrapping my hand around his wrist, giving it a little shake.

"Just as expected, right, Alice? I wanted to be better than that." He glances at me for a moment. "You look incredible. God."

Obviously something serious has happened, but I'm not getting what it is, and he's not giving it to me.

But I've got my whole family. He has a lot less than that.

Ugh, the little guys have left the sidewalk chalk all over the grass near the steps for the millionth time. I start scooping them up and shoving them into the bucket. "Look. Relapses happen. People come back from them. You can get back from this."

His laugh doesn't sound like a laugh at all. "That's what you think."

"It's true. Ask Dad. He never relapsed, but he knows

plenty of people who have. It happens."

"Alice. I'm not hammered. I'm stone-cold sober, though I wish to hell I —" He reaches into his pocket and pulls out car keys, flips them at me. "Here. Take these. Don't give them back until tomorrow. Even if I beg."

I snag the keys, move closer. He smells like sweat, but nothing criminal. Reaching up, I take his chin in my hand, turn his face to mine. The whites of his eyes are clear, his pupils look normal, his eyes aren't glassy. He's pale, not so flushed anymore.

But as I look, his eyebrows draw together. "Gonna breathalyze me now, Alice? Have me walk a straight line? Frisk me?"

I drop my hand. "You do *not* get to be sarcastic with me. You lost that right while I was waiting forever for you."

"I lost a lot of things, then," Tim mutters.

I open my mouth to ask, but he sets his hands on my shoulders, looks me full in the face.

"Alice. Please."

"Okay. Okay. I believe you. But I'm keeping your keys for now."

"Swell," Tim says, standing up in one swift fluid motion. No swaying.

"You're in trouble somehow then?"

"You could sure as hell say that. Or you could just say I'm wicked good at getting other people into it."

"Tell me."

"I can't, Alice. I can't now. I just –" He waves his hand. "I'm sorry. Leave it at that. And keep the goddamn keys for all I care. I'm going nowhere. Trust me."

Chapter Seventeen

It's been in my wallet like a dirty little secret all this time.

You're only as sick as your secrets – that's the word in AA, and I've held on to this one.

My fake ID, a fifteenth-birthday present from my dealer's big brother. He was good at his job. I've never even gotten a suspicious glance when I handed it over. It helps that I'm so tall.

No car keys. Good. That's good.

Start to walk to a meeting, then don't trust my feet. Dominic didn't pick up on his shitty-service cell phone, so I end up hanging a left to town, down to the marina, looking for his battered old motorboat. I find the Cuddy, sure enough, tied up, bumping hard against the worn wooden dock. No sign of Dom, though. Although I do find his cell tossed on the yellow slicker that I bunch up to rest my head on.

He'll come.

I'll wait.

Simple.

I fall asleep so fast and hard, it's more like a pass-out. When I open my sandy eyes, sticky from the river mist, it's after ten. The liquor stores are closed. I'm safe.

But this feeling, this jangling itch to tear out of my own skin – it doesn't want to be safe, not anywhere near it.

I let Alice down, gave her my keys – and I am so pissed with her for thinking I'd go get spun – but at the same time I'm nearly dying for exactly that.

That blue dress. She was gorgeous.

Here's what I should do: go to an online meeting since there aren't any this late. Go find safe people to be with. Mr. Garrett, for God's sake. It's after visiting hours at the hospital, but I could talk my way in somehow. Steal scrubs or something.

Here's what I actually do: shuffle through my wallet for my fake ID, get forty bucks at the ATM of Dad's bank, head uptown to the Dark and Stormy, the only bar on the main drag. Stand staring at the ugly-ass wooden figurehead of a female pirate jutting out over the door of the bar.

It's late, but the D & S is hopping. Tourists love this place and Stony Bay gets 'em by the boatload, end of summer, Stony Bay sidewalk sale season and all that. The bartenders are all female and dressed like buccaneers with a lot of cleavage, and the poor bastards who happen to be waiters dress like French sailors in striped shirts and berets. Guess who gets more tips.

Stride on in.

Two minutes later, I've shoved my way through a crowd of yacht guys still wearing their goddamn captain hats, propped myself up against the thick-planked, dark pine wall, am staring at all the colors on the well-lit glass shelves – the deep amber of whiskey and the sunny yellow of white wine and the Hawaiian surf blue of curacao. Pretty. All that trouble wrapped up in beauty. Inhaling the must of sawdust, the musk of closely packed bodies, the sharp chemical scent of all that booze. I tell myself this is all I'll do and then I'll go. That'll work. Or maybe I'll have to sit at the bar and order something . . . I won't drink it . . . only get a whiff of it. Then I'll go. Safe and sound.

Simple.

Because – because the fact that I am a goddamn *father* does not mean I'm stupid enough to blow more than two months of sobriety, piss away my thirty-day chip, my two-month-er, the single solitary smart thing I've done this year.

Heaving myself off the wall, I sink onto one of the bar stools.

"Ahoy there, hottie," says a cheerful voice, and a waitress plunks the fake pirate's map that's the drinks menu down on the counter and gives me a jolly smile.

Jesus. The waitress is Ms. Sobieski, who was my sixth-grade math teacher. Also my Sunday school teacher. Now wearing a puffy white top that makes the most of the reasons I remember her so well.

Open my mouth to blurt out some excuse, tell her I'm waiting for a friend – *like, say, Jack Daniels?*

"Want the fancy stuff or something straight up?" She slides a wicker basket of unshelled peanuts in front of me, and gives a cheerful wink, and I get it. She has no clue who I am. Or used to be.

Still, she's gotta know I'm underage. But no ID request. Maybe she just figures I'll order a Coke or something.

Maybe I will do only that.

The responsible thing.

But the part of me that wants and needs to do the right thing has been avalanched and I can't dig far enough down to reach it.

Wet my lips. "I –" Before I can say more, she comes forward, giving me an up-close-and-personal with her great rack, and asks, "You've been away at school, right? I see your mom and dad at church. Surprised to see *you* here, though."

Me too.

Pop wouldn't be.

Wouldn't even raise an eyebrow if he walked in right now and saw me.

I edge off the stool. "Be right back."

Walking quickly – walking at all – toward the exit is not easy. I stall out at the ancient cigarette machine. Then I do more than that, put in a ton of change and pull the lever. But there aren't any Marlboros left; just Kool Menthol

and I hate menthol even more than I crave nicotine. So I get outside, stumbling like I actually *had* taken a few drinks, prop myself against the brick wall, gasping, almost gagging, black spots flicking in front of my eyes.

Get some air. Don't, for Chrissake, go back in.

No sense of how long I stand there.

"Mase?" calls a voice, like it's been calling for a while, and there's Jase climbing off Joel's motorcycle. "You okay?" He walks closer, eyes moving from to the door of the D & S and then back to me.

"Kinda," I say, still breathing hard, like I'm trying to outrun something.

He settles in next to me, stretches back against the wall like I am. Like this is no big deal. For a few minutes he's quiet. My raspy inhales and exhales are the only sound in the night air, except the clattering and laughter, the rumble of loud conversation from inside.

"You okay?" he asks again.

I nod, but don't move. "What the hell are *you* doing out so late?"

He looks at his watch. "It's only ten thirty-seven." Jase has a digital watch and always tells the time to the exact minute. "I went for a run on the beach."

"Are you nuts? In the dark? Haven't you seen what happened to the chick in the opener of *Jaws*?"

"She swam. I was on the sand. The big mechanical shark can't jump that far," Jase says. "C'mon, Tim." He reaches

for the extra helmet, looped around that steel thing at the end of the seat, unbuckles it, and tosses it at me.

I catch it automatically. "You kidding? I can't ride on that."

"I ride. You're the passenger," he says patiently, like he's explaining to George.

"No the hell way, man. I'll walk."

"Will you?" Jase asks. His tone gives nothing away, but his eyes steal back to the lit windows of the D & S.

"I didn't do anything," I say. "I didn't." I put my hands in my hair and pull, like I can tear out my thoughts.

"No? Good. Let's get out of here."

"On that? With you?"

"Jesus, Tim. Yeah. You need to leave this place. I have a fast exit. Put the helmet on. Get on the bike. You can hold on to the handle in back."

"You bet I will. You can save the reach-around for Samantha."

"Bite me," Jase says, knocking back the kickstand.

Chapter Eighteen

Jase comes slamming in the kitchen door, bringing with him a whiff of the night air in town, silt of the river, wet grass, mud from his sneakers. He stomps a few times, leaving diamond-shaped pieces of dirt on the tile floor, then looks up. "Al – wow."

"Samantha did it for me. What do you think?"

He studies my newly re-dyed hair, the first time in years it's been nothing but plain brown, my real color. "Job interview?" he asks finally. "That supervisor at work giving you attitude?"

I ruffle my hands through the still-damp waves. "Just seemed pointless to keep doing something I started to do to bug Mom when I was fifteen. Does it look bad?"

He shakes his head. "Where's Sam?"

"Curfew." I point to the clock. "Everything all right there?"

Samantha was quiet and a little edgy, I thought. Only really relaxed with my siblings, where she's always in her element. The things that throw me, make me want to

run screaming, never bother her. Not Harry insisting on sleeping with his soccer guards on, not Patsy calling Sam back to her crib twenty times in the usual way, by running her sippy cup back and forth across the crib slats like a prisoner summoning the jail warden, nothing. Except a call from her mother, which had her tossing on her hoodie and leaving almost without a word, nothing but a quick, embarrassed glance in my direction.

"Mmm," Jase says, opening the refrigerator and staring into it in that guy way. Like all the answers to any question I'd ask him are in the crisper or pasted onto the label of the orange juice.

"J., talk," I say, looking down at the ledger I'm balancing, my phone set to calculator, the red pen I'm using much more often than the black one. "You and Sam on the outs?"

"Mmm. What? No. Far from it, I think. Did you see Tim today?"

"God. Boys. Why do you have to be so inscrutable all the time? What do you mean 'I think'? Aren't you in this relationship? Wouldn't you actually know what's going on?"

Jase finally shuts the refrigerator door with a thunk, frowns at it, opens it again, reshuts it. "I think the seal is going here. But I can probably fix it."

"Forget the fridge. Did you and Samantha fight or something?"

He pulls out the orange juice, sloshes some into a cup. "No. It's just . . ."

"Does Tim have something to do with it?"

"What? No. Why?" Jase takes a long swallow of orange juice, his mouth twisting as though it's gone bad.

"You just asked about him," I prompt.

"Did I?" He's pulled his cell phone out of his pocket now and is studying it.

I angle my hip on the counter, reach over and give his chest a little shove. "You're being spacey and weird. Tim was – off – tonight. What gives?"

"Nothing," my brother says absently. He's dropped his phone now and is staring at the figures on the ledger. He swears under his breath. "Mom and Dad know?"

I swallow. "I've been doing the books. Said I'd do it for a little while. They know that, but not how bad it is. It keeps getting funkier and – I – but – Dad gets headaches every time he tries to look at numbers."

"Since when?"

"Since the accident. Apparently. He's got double vision. Periodically."

"The hell? No one told me that."

"No one told me either. I read it on his chart this afternoon. Mom knows. They didn't want to worry us."

Jase curses again, a long creative string. He never swears, and some of these I've barely ever heard, which makes it extra jarring. God, everything is off today.

"Temporary, right?" he asks.

"They hope. It's from the head injury. Some weakness

in an eye muscle. Probably temporary. There might need to be surgery, though. They just called in a specialist this week."

He turns his back, walks over to the sink, braces his hands on either side, stares out the window into the dark. Then he's kicking at the baseboard below the sink, swearing again. "How's Dad going to get back to the store if he can't see straight? Drive? How's he even going to get through rehab?"

"He can do physical therapy without having to see perfectly. As for the store – looking at the numbers? That may not be a concern anyway."

Jase curses again, polishes off the orange juice, drops the plastic carton to the ground and steps on it harder than necessary. "We can't just let it die, Alice. What then? Goddammit."

I swallow. I know what I have to say, to do. The math all those columns add up to. "I have to leave school. It's the only way. Until Dad's better. Mom can't do it. Which was a huge battle to convince her of in the first place. She has to be the one handling all the hands-on stuff with him."

He argues, of course. "I'll do it."

"And lose your scholarship shot? You've never been in better shape in your life. You can't."

"Joel –" he starts, talking over me. Then we both fall silent. Not Joel. He's given his summers and plenty of nights and weekends to Garrett's Hardware. He's finally

133

finding his feet in the police academy. We can't let – we can't allow – Grace Reed to plow us *all* down. And I'm the expendable one here. It's not like I'm at some turning point. I've already delayed my transfer. What's a little more time?

"It's got to be me, J."

"I won't let you do it. Why should it be you? Because you're the girl? That's just stupid," he says. "There's got to be someone else who can pinch-hit. Someone it won't derail."

The door kicks open and Tim's standing there, river breeze ruffling his hair. "Came for my car keys."

"Get them tomorrow," Jase says, slice of a hard edge in his voice.

"You said not even if you begged," I remind him.

"My apartment keys are on the chain too. I locked up – wasn't thinking. You want me on my knees, Alice?"

"Jesus, shut up, Tim." My brother's voice turns steely. Tim takes a step back.

"You're pissed at me now? How did our relationship status change in five minutes when I wasn't even here to eff it up?"

"Hon!" says a cheerful voice behind me. Tim glances over at the doorway to the living room. His eyes widen.

"A me! Hon!" Patsy is at her most imperious, her baby voice nearly a growl, stomping into the room, all proud for being the Houdini of crib breaks.

She wavers her way across the kitchen, surer of her purpose than her feet, arms raised to Tim. "Upsi. Now."

Not only has the baby escaped her crib, she's also peeled off her clothes, and her diaper. She must have gone looking for me in my room, opened my closet to find the overflowing wicker basket I keep there. Stark naked, except for one of my black thongs dangling from her neck, a flowered push-up bra draped across her pale little chest like a Miss America sash, and a bright red lacy garter belt perched in her fluffy hair like a tiara, hanging across one big brown eye.

Both Jase and Tim are openly laughing, like a relief valve has opened.

Tim scoops her up. "You, Patricia Garrett, are my kind of girl."

"I'll let Tim back in. You deal with Pats," Alice says.

Jase hesitates.

"You're better at getting her down, J.," Alice adds. "She gets all ornery with me."

Still the hesitation. Then, after one swift look at me, Jase hooks his hand around Patsy's waist, lifts her out of my arms, and sets her on his hip. She smooshes his cheeks between her hands, rubs her nose against his.

Alice gives me a tight smile, opens the screen door, strides out in front of me.

She always does that, walks ahead, like she expects people to fall in line after her like ducklings or something. She's wearing these yoga pants with a bleach stain on the back of the knee, another near the waistband. Probably supposed to be some comfortable, *I don't give a damn* outfit. But I spend the whole too-short walk up the steps trying to locate the thong lines under them.

Shoves the key in the lock, bumps open the door with her hip. Then she looks at me and everything goes quiet except for a car swishing by.

Crazy long eyelashes on this girl. Sparkling eye stuff on her lids, partially worn off − a little glint of it near the corner of her eye. Silver hoop earrings with these little bells hanging from them, which explains the faint jingling I hear when she tosses her hair back to look me in the eye. Then the clink of keys as her fingers tighten on them.

"You gonna hand those over or do I really have to beg?" I ask.

She doesn't say anything. Reaches out and takes my hand, flips it palm up. "I can rely on you with these, right?"

Her dark green-brown eyes probe mine, like they could zero in and lock on to any lie I'd tell.

"I'm reliable."

Even after the keys, warm from her hand, drop into my palm, she keeps looking. If there's still darkness closing in on me, like earlier, she's sure to spot it.

"Scout's honor," I say, finally.

"That won't work," Alice says. "My father was your Cub master. I know all about your scouting career."

"What, you picked *that* as a bedtime story, Alice?"

"We have a picture. You're in the back row. You're holding the tie of the guy standing next to you and flicking a lighter underneath it. You were, what, nine? Ten? Worth a thousand words."

No defense there.

The breeze blows in through the maple trees, one hard gust up from the river, smelling like mud and sea grass. Alice's hair blows across her face, her mouth.

"That's your real hair color, huh?" Without the distraction of the extra chunks of different colors in her hair, she looks younger, eyes duskier, lips redder.

"Yes, dark brown. More like Joel than Jase and Andy. My dark secret."

"One of many, I'm sure." But not as dark as mine.

Alice shrugs, looking down at her bare feet. When she glances up, she's smiling, unexpectedly. That crooked smile of hers. "No secrets about my lingerie anymore, though."

"And that was the best one." For a second, "back to normal" hovers between us . . . whatever our normal was.

But she's still watching me, seeing me a bit too well, even in the dark. "I want to believe you, Tim. That you're trustworthy right now. But you have to admit, this hasn't been your most reliable day."

Nope.

"Do you want to keep the keys, Alice?" I ask, and I can hear the completely illegitimate anger in my voice.

"Not exactly the point, Tim. Is there anything you want to tell me?"

Delay the inevitable, a tried and true habit that I thought I'd left in the rearview mirror.

Pull out my old smartass smile. "Only that you're more than welcome to store your lingerie collection here at my apartment. How extensive is it, anyway?"

Her lips flatten out and she shrugs, already turning away. "Guess you'll never know."

I watch her dark figure, only bright with the bleach stains, disappear into the night.

Chapter Nineteen

When Hester walks into the restaurant the next day and sees me, she does that thing where about six different emotions cross her face. Pissed, sad, relieved that I actually showed, hormonal, who the hell knows. I hop up to pull out her chair. I might have done a hump and dump, but what a gentleman, yeah?

"Wait just a minute," she says. "I left something in the car. I wanted to make sure you were here, first."

"Something" turns out to be the sleeping baby, huddled in his car seat – so frickin' puny – wearing this frilly bonnet-type thing.

"Hester – you gotta stop ditching the kid in the car," I say, watching her rest the car seat precariously on one of the chairs. It tips to one side. "Wouldn't he be better off on the floor?"

Listen to me, acting like I know anything at all.

Probably thinking the same thing, Hester says, "He's fine. This way we can keep an eye on him."

Like she was doing when she left him in the

backseat? Jesus.

I pull out her chair again, and she settles in, spreading her napkin in her lap. "Have you looked at the menu?"

I bite my lip so I won't snarl, *This is not a freakin' date.* Instead: "I need to understand more about how" – Calvin's eyelashes flutter and I lower my voice – "uh, how all this happened."

She nods, looking worried now. What'd she think we were going to talk about? The specials on the menu?

The waiter interrupts to plunk down bread, pour water, light the candle, and hover around until Hester sends him trotting off to get her a ginger ale.

"I just need . . ." What I need more than anything at the moment is something to do with my hands, so I pick up one of the books of matches with the restaurant logo from the little crystal bowl on the table, start methodically tearing them out one by one. "I need to know how we hooked up." *Why* too, but asking that? Dickish.

Hester blinks at me. "You honestly don't remember making love?"

"Nope." Wow, way to be an asshole. Apparently it's like riding a bicycle.

Her eyes well with tears. Jesus, no.

"Sorry, I . . . just don't get why you'd have anything to do with my drunken ass."

The waiter, who returned with the ginger ale just in time to hear "drunken ass" backs away, the glass still poised.

Her hand shoots out, rests on mine for an instant as I continue to mutilate the matchbook. Any time she touches me, or I touch her, it feels off, so . . . wrong. She's freaking *pure*-looking. A horrible thought occurs to me. "That wasn't, uh, it wasn't your, um, you'd had, um –"

Hester somehow makes sense of this.

"No. Oh no." She pats my hand reassuringly. "I'd had this boyfriend, Alex. Alex Robinson. Remember him?"

Total void there too.

"Head of the school newspaper? Tall? Student council? Class secretary?

I fumble through my unreliable memory bank. Alex Robinson . . . Dark-haired officious-type dude? Yeah . . . On my tennis team, major tool. Senior when I was a sophomore. And Hester was a junior.

"Riiiight," I say.

"The night before the party, Alex . . ." Hester pauses, clears her throat. Not that it makes any difference. She has one of those throaty, raspy voices that *should* be sexy. "He's doing a post-grad year at Choate. He called up and said we should admit the long-distance thing was hopeless." The waiter's crept back, sets down the ginger ale, then flees as though it might detonate. "I mean – come on! – it's still in the same state! Not even an hour away! We'd been going out since freshman spring! He was my first –" She stops dead. "Anyway. That's why I went to that party. I didn't want to think or remember; I wanted to have fun."

Having torn all the matches out of two different packs, I go to work on the bread basket, ripping off pieces, tearing them into smaller pieces, shoveling them in my mouth. Calvin — I freaking hate that name — stirs a little, frowns, but dozes on.

"Anyway . . . you were there and . . . kind of sad too."

I plunge another chunk of bread into the butter, ignoring the butter knife, take a bite, and then pause. "Please tell me this wasn't a mercy f— I mean, that you didn't have sex with me out of some kind of *pity*, Hester. Tell me you didn't screw up your life — and mine — and frickin' create his — because you *felt sorry* for me."

She twists at this little ring on her pinkie. "No. It wasn't like that. We talked. A lot. We went to Ward's room and we talked for, like, hours. You were charming and goofy and, yes, sad, but that's not why I . . . why we . . ."

Again with the waiter, who recites a long list of incomprehensible appetizers. Hester orders and I mutter, "I'll have what she's having."

"I didn't really notice how much you'd had to drink. You acted . . . great. I was upset. I wanted to be — not me. I just . . . kissed you. It went from there. It was stupid. I was stupid."

This little tear slides out of her eye, snakes down the side of her nose. She swats at it, hard enough to make a little *slap* sound. I wince.

"But, I mean, Hester. Didn't I even use anything? I can't

believe I was that out of it." However badly I've generally messed up, this is a new low. I thought I'd stuck to being Thoughtless Bastard, rather than Complete Sack of Shit. I mean – I have a sister, after all.

"Oh, you did. You were very insistent on it. Made sure I got your . . . your wallet and all that," she assures me, turning red. "It's just that, afterward, you sort of, well, fell asleep without –" She makes this indecipherable waving gesture with her hand.

I decipher it well enough, though. I passed out without . . . removing, disposing of the condom. Which obviously leaked. Or broke. I'm a prince.

"I'm a catastrophe, Hester," I point out glumly. "You're too smart for that."

"Guess not, right?" She takes a gulp of soda like she's slinging back a shot of tequila. Now the glitter in her eyes comes off more like anger than tears. "I wasn't smart and you weren't sober. We made love . . ." She trails off as I cringe.

We made Calvin, not love.

"Then you got kicked out." She spreads her hands helplessly. "And here we all are."

"Not quite. Why the hell didn't you . . . find me, or contact me before things – when you first figured out what was doing. Or why didn't you ever once – *once*, Hester – think, maybe you should tell *the father?* Like, right away?" The waiter, who is approaching with more Perrier, once

143

again scuttles off to a less emotionally volatile table.

"I didn't know how to get in touch with you."

"You found me now. You could have found me then. Instead you just went on ahead and had this baby on your own. Decided to keep him long enough to show him to me so now I'm guilty for the rest of my life." The words are spewing out. "You didn't give me any choices here." I almost can't see Hester, it's like the whole world is red and swirling, tight and hot as the feeling in my gut.

"Well, I didn't have a whole lot myself, Tim." She's definitely angry now. "You were a mess, like you said. Was I supposed to hunt you down and say, hey, mind putting down that liter of rum and the joint so we can have a rational discussion about *our baby?*"

I try to imagine what I would have done if she had. Got no clue. The Tim Mason I was back then is like some loser roommate I had years ago. Except that that guy came over last night and nearly moved back in. The waiter plops down our appetizers, flees without a backward glance.

"Besides," Hester adds. "I . . ." She circles her index finger around the rim of her water glass. "I –"

I look down at the appetizers. Uh . . . what are they? Never mind.

"What?" I ask, poking with my fork.

"It's kind of personal."

I just stare at her. Though I barely know her, we are way past personal.

"I know. Silly, at this point. I have these irregular periods, and I didn't have any, well, morning sickness, so it took me a long time to figure out."

"How long?" She can't have been one of those chicks you hear about who thinks she's maybe gotten kinda chubby and then gets a stomachache and pops out a baby.

"Ten weeks. Then I went and had a sonogram. He was sucking his thumb . . . he was . . . I couldn't make any choice except to have him."

"Oh, Hester. Jesus Christ." My appetite is gone but I eat a bite of whatever just to do something other than puke or say *I'm sorry I'm sorry I'm sorry* over and over and over again.

"This tastes better with lemon." She hands me a dish of lemons. Like what I'm really concerned about here is the right seasoning. "It wasn't that bad. Really."

"You can't tell me it didn't suck ass being a pregnant senior at Ellery."

"Well, good news." She raises her glass of ginger ale as if she's toasting me. "It took a long time to be obvious. Of course, a ton of *Scarlet Letter* jokes after that, but . . . my real friends, they stuck by me. So did Grand, of course."

"Yeah, and I've heard actually delivering a baby is a blast," I mutter.

"I went for drugs." Hester actually smiles. "Too bad you never got into epidurals recreationally. They're the best."

"I can't believe you're joking about this."

"Well . . . here we are, Tim. Things could be a lot worse."

How? Searching . . . searching . . .

The waiter comes back, practically on tiptoe. I decide to change the subject for a while.

"So, uh, how, uh, old is the kid?" The words sound twisted, bizarre, like I'm some stranger in a checkout line inquiring about a random baby, instead of the one plopped right in front of us, ours, fidgeting slightly in his sleep. "I mean, him, Calvin."

"He was three weeks early, I think, so now he's almost five and a half weeks. Beyond his birth weight by two whole pounds."

"Oh. That's nice. Uh . . ." I eat more whatever these round things are. They taste chewy and weird. The waiter advances with the wine list. Can't he tell we're frickin' underage? I wave him away with a scowl. Hester toys with her fork.

"So," she continues in nearly a whisper, "he was born and . . . I ended up finding your address in the yearbook."

"Wait – did you go to my parents' house first? With the kid, I mean?"

"No! I called, and I got this girl? She gave me your new address." The waiter whisks away our appetizer plates, replacing them with yet another plateful of unidentifiable stuff.

I sniff at it suspiciously. *This girl.* Nan, obviously. She could have given me a heads-up. But then, even though my

twin usually fears the worst, how could she guess that some random girl on the other end of the phone would chuck my life into a wood chipper like this?

"So," Hester says, all businesslike suddenly. "We should talk about the details." She swishes whatever the hell she's eating around in whatever that gloppy white sauce is, takes a tiny nibble, sets it back down.

"Yeah, that . . . how exactly do we work this?" *And how long do we have to?* I gulp more water, draining the glass. At this point, the waiter is totally MIA, avoiding eye contact, standing with his arms folded, eyes cast to the ceiling. "I mean, I'm pretty booked – I have a job, and I'm getting my GED . . . and . . ."

Don't have time for you, kid. Calvin gives this little flicker of a frown.

Hester looks down at her plate. "We can figure it out. We can get the adoption thing rolling right away," she says quickly. "But before that's taken care of, it's not all on you. I mean, I'll help, and Grand can too. He wants to meet you, by the way."

Yeah, I'll bet.

Wait, did she say she'd *help?* Am I supposed to be the primary parent here? Hell, no. The baby stirs again, kicking a foot, and then quiets down. Fuck. He's so small. His hand is, like, the size of one of the cherry tomatoes in my salad.

"Don't think I'm a bad person," Hester warns. "But I

147

can't just drop my whole life till I fix things."

"Obvious who the bad guy is here, Hester. Hey, I'll work around my schedule. I mean, I'll babysit, of course, because, because" – I swallow, set my jaw – "he's my son, after all."

She nods, blinking rapidly. "He is. Yours."

Undeniable. I might not get the fatherly bond, but the facts are the facts: I was wasted. I didn't use a condom right. There's a baby. Health class 101.

Suddenly, her shoulders start quivering and there's a complete tsunami of tears, ragged sobs that get louder and louder with each one. Her voice rises and she points a finger at me, jabbing in the air. "I know you don't want this. But you can't possibly know what it's like for me . . . he's tiny – he was born early and he's eating all the time to catch up and . . . and . . . he never ever sleeps. He's always pooping and crying and I have no idea why, what's wrong. Why can't he just be quiet? Isn't it all enough without that? For *days* after he was born my breasts were swollen and leaking and I had to have stitches because of vaginal tearing. I'm eighteen years old . . . It's just *wrong*."

Jesus God. Kill me fast. All these other people are staring at us.

"All *you* did was get your rocks off! You don't even re-re-member it. And I'm fat now – aren't I?"

This seems the slightest of her problems but at least I know the answer to that one. "No! No. Of course not. Not

at all. You look just the same."

As the girl I can't remember.

Sweat rolling down my forehead. "Better! You look better!"

She gulps, looks around for her napkin, which she must have dropped. I start to hand her mine, and then remember that I spat one of the scallops out into it.

"Better . . . really?"

"Totally." The waiter is in the corner, examining the ceiling some more. The bunch of women drinking cosmos at the next table look like they want to shoot me in the nuts, chop me up with dull knives, and throw my body in a sinkhole. Go right ahead, ladies, please.

I shove my chair back, come around next to her, pat her on the shoulders. "*Shh,* Hes. It's no problem. I got this. I don't sleep all that well myself, so that's probably my fault too. I'll just . . . I'll just deal. I mean, uh, do you want me to take him – uh – tonight?"

What am I saying? I can't have a baby at the garage apartment. Overnight? Next to the Garretts? To Alice? This is like a car pileup that keeps rolling on and on, like some replay Satan shows on a panoramic screen when you get to hell.

"I'll make sure he has everything he needs, don't worry," Hester assures me, her voice even lower and raspier than normal.

That kid is entire universes away from having everything

149

he needs.

Somehow Calvin has managed to sleep through all of this. He stays conked out when we head to Hester's car, me lugging the car seat, Hester paving the way, somehow having recovered from total breakdown. If these are hormones, they suck.

The entire backseat of Hester's car, and her whole trunk, are jammed with baby stuff. How can he need so much? He's the size of a tennis racket.

First she hands me that big-ass diaper bag. Then this straw-basket-looking thing that looks like a supersized version of something Goldilocks would use.

Am I supposed to . . . take the kid on a picnic or something?

"I just washed the sheepskin," she adds.

"Uh?"

Hester rustles in the backseat, and comes out with an actual sheepskin, some blankets, and this sock monkey. The kind with the red butt. I'm still standing there with the picnic basket and the diaper bag, which is getting heavier by the second. My heart is cramping, squeezing tighter and tighter like my hand that's fisted around the handle of the basket.

"So you put this in the bottom, and then make sure Calvin's always on his back." She slides the sheepskin into the basket, then sets the monkey on top. He seems

to be glaring at me with these evil little eyes. Those things have always creeped me the hell out. "Only a few more things, and then the baby and you can get going on your day together."

Yay.

Now she's back with a blanket, this little mirror, and what looks like a parachute pack.

The basket is a bed, then, but apparently I'm taking Calvin skydiving.

"I should have had this better organized. It's hard to get it together."

Having trouble getting *myself* together, so I head out to my own car, flip the hatch, shove aside my sleeping bag, a container of tennis balls, a jumbo pack of Dr Pepper, and a pillowcase full of laundry and put it all in the back. I leave the hatch open, because there may be more to come. Like a pup tent and a croquet set.

Starting to think she's giving me the kid permanently. She's here now, with him in her arms, bonnet on.

"Want me to help you with the car seat?"

"Nah. I'm good," I say. "No problem."

It takes an insane amount of time to get it in. I can't reach my fingers far enough under it to snag it, and when I do, the belt keeps snapping back out from the bottom, hitting my knuckles. Ow.

I pull back; sucking my knuckles, hit my head on the top of the open door.

"Here he is. You put that mirror right at his feet so you can see him while you're driving." Holding Calvin, she hands me the bucket part of the car seat. Awake now, he stares at me. I stare back. I have to watch him *while* I'm driving? How's that going to work?

"Uh. Hi there, Calvin." My voice starts out squeaky, then goes game-show-host-hearty. He gets that worried pucker between his eyes again, screws up his mouth a little, and his lower lip trembles.

Hester scoops him into my arms so quickly. No warning. Just boom, I'm holding this warm squirming thing. Wearing a bonnet. The back of his undershirt is damp. *He's* sweating too.

I pat him on his midget shoulder. "We're good," I tell him. Serious eyes, anxious expression. It's the Nan face, version 2.0.

Once he's all buckled in, Hester hands me this thick bunch of papers covered with round, loopy writing, torn from a loose-leaf notebook, stapled together. Like the first draft of an English paper in 1986. "Just because I'm anal, I wrote everything down." Then she keeps talking and talking and talking: *Make sure you do this, and never do that and I know you'd probably figure all this out, but just in case . . .*

Hell, no, I would not have figured it all out. How could I? Sure, I would have magically guessed which side of the diaper was the front and how to put him in that parachute thing, which turns out to be this weird little kangaroo

pouch that you wear him in like a fanny pack for your chest, and that you need to hold his head at all times since it'll, like, snap off otherwise, because all that jazz is just instinctive, right?

Simple.

Finally, ten fucking thousand years later, we're on the road. I almost have an accident because when we hit the first stoplight, I worry that I braked too hard, reach back to check him, and this anger-management asshole with a beer gut and an attitude nearly hits us with a motorcycle, giving me the bird, and calling, "Go screw yourself, kid."

Done, dude.

Calvin starts making little squeaky sounds as we head onto Route 7, and I realize I've left the window open and he's probably getting a blast of exhaust in his face. The first exit leads to Brinkley Bay, a private beach area with those huge signs that make it sound like you'll be shot by a firing squad if you go anywhere close to the water.

I pull into the parking lot anyway.

Open the back door and crouch next to the car, reach under his chin, tuck my fingers into this fold of skin, so soft, it's not even like skin. Like . . . like silk. Only drooly. Untie the bonnet thing, and toss it to the car floor. His lips give a little twitch, not a full-on smile, but better than that worried trembly jazz.

"Yeah, you won't be wearing ruffles. No son of mine,

and all that shit − sorry, stuff − right? *That* goes." The wrinkle's back between his eyebrows. Automatically, I stick my fingertip there, smoothing it away the way Ma always used to do with me when she saw me do the same, back when I was a kid. *You'll give yourself wrinkles before you're nine!*

Ma. She's gonna kill me.

But first she'll cry.

Pop −

Shit.

Calvin can't even focus, really; his eyes keep looking like they're almost crossing. Is that normal? Is *he* normal? I hadn't even thought of that. I've done a hell of a lot of everything bad. God knows what funky stuff there could have been in anything that came from me. Maybe I've already messed him up without even knowing I made him.

I reach out a finger, bump it against his small soft fist, clamped so tightly shut. Probably a bit young to get the whole fist bump thing, so I uncurl his damp fingers, slide my index finger into this sweaty starfish hand. So small it curls around the top joint of my finger with room to spare.

"It'll be okay, Cal. You're okay," I say, patting his stomach under the straps, in what I hope is a reassuring way. Because that's what parents do, right? Lie their asses off.

Chapter Twenty

A corner of something peeks out of the mailbox, some bright flyer. Harry must have forgotten his mail-boy duties yesterday. I scoop out the envelopes, flip through: some letter with lipstick kisses on it for Joel – really? *Justine* magazine for Andy, a box from Mustard of the Month Club for Mom (Christmas gift from Mr. Methuan from down the street – Mom drives him to doctors' appointment's sometimes), electric bill, flyer about the SBH homecoming dance, letter from the bank. Shove the others under my armpit, flip that one open.

Read once.

Read twice.

My lungs lock shut, like a window slamming.

Who took all the oxygen out of the bright September air?

"I don't like this place," George says. "It makes my stomach hurt."

"Just a few minutes, G. Then we'll go to the bookstore. A book and a magazine." Bribery: My new middle name.

Patsy's silent, fingering the Pooh Bear Band-Aid from her polio vaccine. She fixes me with an unforgiving glare. I hold up my index finger, where she bit me during the shot, and glare back.

Yes, I am nineteen years old, but waiting on the hard bench at Stony Bay Building and Loan makes my stomach hurt too. It doesn't help that I'm wearing a button-down shirt and my navy-blue interview skirt, control-top tights digging into my waist.

"How many more minutes?" George asks.

"Not sure, Georgie." I try to distract him with "I spy," but there's very little to see in the bank's main room, which looks like the "after" photo of a Suck the Personality out of a Room challenge. Beige carpet. Beige walls. One of those white noise machines whirring. Hushed voices.

"How many more minutes now?"

"Not long."

"Ice cream after?"

"It's not even noon, G."

Six more "How many more minutes?" before the door to the bank manager's office opens at last.

There's only one chair and George immediately claims it, sliding his butt back, his legs swinging high, kicking the metal chair legs. The man behind the desk doesn't look up despite the loud clanging.

"Hey!" George says loudly.

The man glances up briefly, raises a warning finger,

keeps writing something, then, finally, sets down his pen with a heavy sigh. I expect him to look me in the eye at this point, but his gaze is fastened just beyond my shoulder.

"There was an urgent matter?"

"Yes. This." I set the letter from the bank on his desk. "We've been receiving money from a trust here. This says that won't be continuing. That's impossible, Mr." – I check out the brown placard with his name – "Mason."

Holy . . .

Tim's dad?

Yes, it's obvious somehow, although he looks like part of the Vacuum Out the Personality contest. Same thick hair with a slight wave as Tim's – but ash-gray instead of flame – same high cheekbones, but less prominent without a smile – same long, thin body, but it comes off gaunt instead of lean.

He's holding the paper up, reading through it. "Yes, I sent this, as instructed by the donor of the trust account. All further transactions are to cease."

"Did you kill that deer?" George asks, staring in horrified fascination at a moth-eaten deer head mounted on the wall.

Mr. Mason is wearing a similar expression, looking back at George. "It was here when I inherited the office."

"They can't *cease*," I say. "There was an agreement. As long as bills come in, they're supposed to be paid."

My voice is rising. George chews his lip. Patsy shoves

her sturdy body closer to mine, hard enough to knock my breath out.

"I sent the letter as instructed by my client," Mr. Mason says. "I don't know the details, except that, as you say, the expenses sent to this address were to be covered as some sort of scholarship donation – political in nature, perhaps? Perhaps the monetary cap for such donations has been reached and so . . ."

He's still not meeting my eyes. It's weirdly disorienting, especially since his eyes are the same color as Tim's. But Tim's tilt up slightly at the corners, perpetual smile almost always lurking. Nothing like that going on here. Mr. Mason doesn't look mad or sad. Just . . . gone.

"No cap. There was no limit. The bills were just supposed to be –"

My voice is full-on loud, and now there's a flicker of expression, but indecipherable. Alarm, annoyance – I can't tell. He glances at the screen of his cell phone, as though he might have an app to summon some armed guards to escort the crazy girl from the room.

"If you'll just give me the legal document stating the terms of the agreement, I'm sure we can settle this. It's notarized, of course."

It's nonexistent, of course. My parents would never have thought to get the arrangement with Grace Reed in writing. Half the agreements Dad does with suppliers at Garrett's are handshake deals – and I'm sure Senator

Grace would have flat-out refused to put this in writing anyway. What if it leaked to the press? No. There was no notarized anything. But we should've at least gotten a damn lawyer.

I put my head in my hands, look up. "It was a debt of honor. There isn't any –"

Honor here.

"Proof," Mr. Mason says, sounding faintly – very faintly – sympathetic. "I'm afraid I have no authorization to do anything without documentation."

"You have to – we're depending on this – we can't do without it. It pays my father's hospital bills and –"

He shakes his head. "My hands are tied, Ms." – he glances down at the paper – "Garrett. I'm sympathetic, of course, but I'm afraid the bank requires more than that."

I open my mouth to argue again, but there's no point. For the first time, I can translate the expression in his eyes. Dead end.

Chapter Twenty-one

When I set the car seat down on the church basement floor with a semi-defiant clunk, the conversations going on all around me shut right down. Dominic, who I finally got on the phone last night – he'd been out night-fishing on some friend's boat and left it behind – mutters a quick, "Whoa," before turning away and keeping on talking to my old coach Jake. But before another minute passes, everyone is crowding up, jostling, freaking out over Cal.

They're all flipping out and all I can think is: *You take him. Or you. Or you. Please.*

I've had him for half an hour. Already I'm wiped out. I've got this kid for hell knows how long, and it's only 3:00 and what do you *do* with babies, for God's sake? Take 'em to the playground? Obviously I'm not going to whip him down the slide or put him on a swing. He can't even hold up his head. He's like one of those bobblehead dolls. When I went to pull him out of the car seat, he just stared at me, like, *Oh hey. Yeah, I'm trusting you with this dad stuff, because, face it,*

I'm completely at your mercy. Please don't screw up. I'm gonna fall asleep again now.

He makes it about halfway through the hour before starting to twist from side to side, opening and closing his mouth. I drag myself outside, pop the top of a can of formula, offer him the bottle. He receives it with tremendous enthusiasm. Occasionally he turns his head toward me, in what I can tell is a gesture of Supreme Will. *Look. Although all I want is to keep drinking, I'm acknowledging your existence. Get it? Good. 'Cause I'm really, really thirsty.*

I'm sitting, bending over him, watching his face carefully, when a hand descends lightly on my back, someone slides into place next to me.

Coach Somers – Jake – dark blond hair all rumpled, Hodges Soccer sweatshirt with the sleeves cut off. He reaches out to straighten the kid's wrinkled undershirt, brushes his hair back from his forehead.

"No one thought for a second I was just babysitting, did they?"

"Well, he's a really cute kid," he tells me, "who looks a lot like you, newborn-style."

"I've only got one chin," I point out.

"True – but look – his top one has a little cleft, just like yours." Jake puts his index finger in the appropriate spot on Cal's midget face.

"I'm not denying paternity," I say, though that sounds awesome right about now. Jake rests back on his elbows

and grins at me. I catch a faint whiff of cigarette smoke. One sharp inhale and I'm dying to bum one off him. But what am I gonna do, blow smoke in this baby's face while he chows down? No. I'm no textbook dad, but still. I balance him carefully on my knees, touch the nic patch Alice gave me.

There's the snick of the big wooden door closing, and Dominic's standing behind us. Looking down at Cal. His thick brows pulled together. Can't tell what he's thinking. Sometimes he cries in meetings when he talks about his daughter. This tough-skinned guy, all angles and attitude, sobbing.

Jake himself has gotten emotional lately because he and his partner have been trying to have a baby through a surrogate and things keep falling through. He's trying to quit smoking for the sake of the baby and then can't keep it going because there *is* no baby – shit's fallen through twice in the three months I've been around. I'm surrounded by men who want to be in my shoes.

Fuck, welcome to 'em.

I'm cradling the kid's head in one hand and tilting the bottle into his mouth. Little milky dribbles of formula keep escaping out the corners, running down his chin, and he suddenly stops, sneezes. Then looks really upset, brow all squinchy, like, *Fix me, Dad*. "Dad" is hard enough to wrap my head around, let alone *do something about it*.

"Try burping him," Dom suggests.

"How?"

Hester's printed instructions are crumpled in my glove compartment, but I don't remember her covering burping. Yeah, I skimmed.

"Pat him on the back – real soft," Dominic says. "They like that." Amazing he's not grabbing the baby out of my hands and doing it himself.

I tip him cautiously forward and tap him between his little sharp shoulder blades with three fingers of my hand, then with my whole palm. So freakin' fragile.

And . . . nothing. Now he's whimpering, and I have no tools whatsoever to solve this.

I shoot a pleading look at Dom, my own version of *Fix me*, but he just smiles.

"Sometimes you have to do it a few times."

More tapping. More whimpering and squirming.

"Try putting him on your shoulder," Jake says. "Up high."

I hoist him there, so his head is dangling over my shoulder and give a few more taps. Then he lets out this huge belch, like someone's fat old uncle. This warm spurt of liquid dribbles down the back of my shirt.

"Holy shit," I say. "That is . . ."

Gross. Surreal. Everything I'm thinking is wrong.

"Real. Right?" Jake pulls a crumpled Kleenex out of his pocket, tosses it my way as I settle the kid back down on my legs. Cal looks at me urgently, smacking his lips, then

making a feeble swipe at the bottle, fingers splayed.

"I think he's still thirsty," I tell them, settling the bottle back into his mouth.

"Who isn't?" Dominic asks, with a short laugh.

"Don't drink over this, Tim," Jake adds.

I know, I know, I know.

The bottle slips out for a sec and the kid gives this high-pitched, desperate squeak, like a baby mouse. That sound, helpless and mine to fix – it's like someone heated up a knife and jabbed it hard in my stomach, then twisted. I actually put my hand there, where it grips and burns. Goddamn Jake and his surrogates and Dominic, who misses his kid like a lost leg, and Hester and her effin' endless-care essay and this guy I see walking by just now with a kid on his shoulders, knobbly kid-knees kicking out, heels back against his dad's chest, giggling. Goddamn everyone else in the world who had kids or wants kids and knows what the eff to do with them. I try to cram this fury far down or take it out somewhere safe and contained, kicking my loafer against the wrought iron fence, but that jiggles Cal. His half-closed eyes fly open and he looks at me in alarm, like, *Are you having a tantrum, Dad?*

After the meeting, I shove the baby in his backpack and just walk on the beach, on and on and on, like some endless Bataan march. Then he needs a new diaper, which I don't have on me, and I've walked from Stony Creek past the

breakwater practically to Maplecrest. When I look at my watch it's nearing six. So I turn around, slog back to my car, and change the kid. Four hours with him and he's not dead yet. But now I have to go home.

The Garretts.

Alice.

When there are no cars in the Garretts' driveway as I pull in, I'm not sure whether I've dodged a bullet or my parachute hasn't opened.

Between the baby, the car seat, and the shit-ton of stuff Hester unloaded all over me, I need a Sherpa trailing behind to get all this in at once. Obviously, since I've been über-self-righteous to Hester about leaving him in the car, the first thing to do is to move him in. But the moment we get in the door, he starts screaming like a mother. He's turning purple, his fists are clenched, his knees are pulled up to his stomach, he's a banshee. I try to jam the bottle in his mouth and he pretty much punts it away. I consider the burping thing again but I'm afraid to pick him up. He's frickin' possessed. No wonder Hester was losing it after five and a half weeks of this. Screw adoption. Can we just do the leaving on the doorstep thing?

I left the trunk open with all the incriminating baby crap inside, visible to every Garrett eye. But it's not as if I can leave this kid behind to close it. He's obviously about to pop an aneurysm. How come he was so Zen at the restaurant?

There's nothing to do but carry him with me and lug the stuff in piece by piece. Any minute the van or the Bug or the Mustang will pull in and the jig will be up.

The pauses between eardrum-exploding shrieks are getting longer and longer. The kid probably has no air left in his lungs. I'm the same, worse off than the other day when I ran all the way to the pier and had to lie on my back in the sand for half an hour before slogging back. Now he's limp over my shoulder, asleep. I stagger back upstairs, put him back in the car seat, lock him in, and trudge back down to the car.

I'm just about done carrying up way more than I packed even for my own move, am shouldering the heavy suitcase, aka diaper bag, when someone taps me on the back.

"Tim?"

It's Andy. She's dragging off her bike helmet, pitching it next to her bike, which is already cast aside in the grass, whisking back her wavy light brown hair.

She studies me, silent.

Uh-oh.

Quick scan of the exterior of the diaper bag reveals no obvious "baby" signs – it's not, like, covered with yellow ducks or anything. Just navy blue. Butch enough. Except for the spare bottle peeking out of one side. I shove it further down.

"'S'up, Ands?"

"Remember I said I had a question for you? That I

really needed to ask *you*?"

"Andy, if this is about hooking you up with drugs or something, I don't —"

She starts giggling, mouth full of braces, and pretty soon I'm smiling too.

"Seriously, Tim. Please?"

"Uh, whatever it is, just say no?"

She tilts her head, shakes back her hair, then stills, squinting a little.

Is that Cal cranking up again? "Hit me, Andy. I'm kinda in a hurry."

"Okay." Then she says in a rush, "Whenyouarekissingsomeonelikereallykissingthemwheredoyouputyourhands?"

Christ.

"Uh. Well. Uh." She nods, encouraging me, all hopeful hazel eyes. "Shoulders are a good start." That seems safe. Nothing Jase is going to whale on me for.

"What about after that?"

"Stick with shoulders for at least a year."

"C'mon, Tim."

That's definitely Cal.

"Waist. I guess. Or back. I don't know. Don't ask me, Andy. Whatever I'd tell you, do the goddamn opposite. Take it slow, is all I can say."

She takes a step back, shaking her head. "You're so mean to yourself. It makes me sad. What's that sound?"

"Uh — teakettle." I start to book it up the stairs, then

167

remember something, stop. Andy's heading toward the house, her shoulders sort of drooping

"Andrea! Wait. Who's the dude?"

"Kyle Comstock."

"You mean the putz who ditched you by Post-it note?"

Squalling's getting louder.

"He said he wanted to go with Jade Whelan because I was a bad kisser. I thought –"

"Stay miles away from that douchewit. I mean it, Andy. Like, frickin' oceans away. Or I'll tell Jase, Joel, *and* Alice."

"Not Alice!" She gives a shiver, smiles at me, and says, "That's kind of what I thought. I just wanted to ask someone who might . . ." Her voice gets all quiet, so I bend closer to hear her. Or maybe it's the kid's roar amping up even louder.

"Know how a sleazehead thinks?"

Swift, embarrassed, smile.

"'S'all good, Andy. I'm glad my shady, manipulative past is of use to someone."

"Hey, Tim? Tim!"

I'm leaning back on the couch with Cal on my shoulder. He finally fell asleep and I'm just lying there, staring into space, dying for a smoke, running the whole thing in my head, the crackle of plastic, the light, smooth weight of the cigarette between my fingers, the molasses-y smell of unburnt tobacco, the first drag, inhale, brain unclogged.

Why am I so freaking tired? It's not like Cal's all physically demanding. He can barely do a thing. Thank Christ we won't have to worry about him when he's Patsy's age and trying to eat rocks and drink shit from under the sink.

"Mase!" I hear again. It's been noisy out my window on the Garretts' lawn, but this is nothing new, so I've ignored it, trying to get Cal to crash. Now I open the casement and peer out, easing Cal onto his back, flush against the couch cushion. There's a crew of people in the driveway, a bunch of Jase's football buddies, Mac Johnson and Ben Rylance, kids from Samantha's swim team, maybe, that prepster Hodges crowd. Jase and Sam are standing at the bottom of the garage apartment steps.

"We're going to Sandy Claw Beach for a bonfire," Samantha calls up. She's in a blue sarong thing, towel around her neck, arm around Jase's waist. "Come with?"

Jase jerks his head in the direction of the Mustang. "Yeah, come on."

Everyone's already crowding into various vehicles, laughing and shoving, little squeals from girls climbing on guys' laps, low laughter from the dudes.

It looks like fun. The kind of fun I haven't had in a while.

"Can't." It's not like I can drag the kid along to a beach party. *Toss me a Coke without braining the infant?* Besides, he's already asleep . . . for a while.

"C'mon, Tim. You can't just lurk in there like a troll

169

under a bridge," Sam calls. "Throw on your trunks. We're going to have a swim to the breakwater challenge. We need your speed."

Cal stirs, makes this strange face, and I hear a gurgling sound.

Crap. Literally.

"I can't, got it? Not right now."

Sam starts to protest and Jase puts his hand on her arm. He shoots me a look. "Hey, we can blow this off, snag a pizza and hang out."

He thinks it's about getting spun. And I let him. "Nah. I'm just gonna study" – maybe Hester's baby instructions – "and crash. I'm good."

Samantha shields her eyes. "We'll stay." She puts her hand on the railing, all set to climb the steps and charge into the middle of my current nightmare.

Cal's squirming around and kicking off to cry.

"No!" I say. "Take no for an answer, will you?"

"Oh!" she says. "Got it. Okay."

She obviously thinks I've got some chick up here. Jase thinks I'm stressing about booze.

I'm lying to both of them.

Thought I was done with that garbage.

Feels as shitty as Cal's diaper.

Well, almost.

Chapter Twenty-two

"You're not taking the Mustang? Reliving your lost youth on the school bus, J.?"

"Ha-ha. My youth isn't lost, Al. Still around here somewhere. But nah. Too much hassle for parking spots on the first day. Just ends in aggravation and dings on the 5.0."

"You certainly wouldn't want dings on perfection," I say, eying Jase's battered car, which he spent half the summer rehabbing and tinkering over, after buying it with a chunk of his college savings.

He grins, sliding his palm along the side. He's repainted only the hood so far, a deep, rich, sparkling dark green. The rest of the paint job is a jumble of dark red-orange primer and the original color, a metallic '70s-style lime. "Some respect. She's a work in progress."

He's been up for hours now − for his paper route, the second job he insists on having, despite the fact that he's either too old or way too young to be delivering *The Stony Bay Sentinel* before dawn's early light. Then for a run on the beach. Now it's barely six thirty and he's showered and

plowed his way through a virtual coop full of eggs and is already waiting at our mailbox, the bus stop. In a decent mood.

I can't bring myself to drag him into the hospital bill mess, the bank – he was already offering to quit school over Garrett's – let alone tell Mom and Dad. I picture Mr. Mason at his desk, feel my breath come short, my throat shrink. I close my eyes. Open them. Deep breath. I'll figure something out. I just need a little time.

"Andeeeee," I call back to the house. First day of ninth grade and she's, of course, running late.

"You'd be better off texting her," Jase advises. "She's been in the upstairs bathroom for nearly an hour."

On cue, Andy comes hurtling down the front steps, heels in one hand, hair straightened, tank top and bright red mini on.

"Go change," I say flatly. "You look like the poster girl for freshman fresh meat."

"No time," Andy says breathlessly. "Besides, you're one to talk. This is *your* skirt. It's in your first-day-of-high-school picture. I can't believe Mom's not awake to take one for us today."

It's my skirt. Of course it is. Though Mom and I had plenty of debates about my clothing choices, I don't sound like her now; I sound like some bitchy Puritan. Some days I don't even recognize myself anymore.

"She's exhausted, Ands. And trust me, those pics are

hard to live down if the bus comes while she's still lining up the shot," Jase says. "But Alice is right about the outfit."

"Again, let me repeat: you guys are *not* Mom and Dad," Andy says. "I have a hoodie, anyway." She wags her backpack in our direction with one hand, tugging a shoe on with the other.

"I need evidence." I reach for the backpack.

"Al-ice. God. It's like you two have been replaced by pod people."

Of course there's no hoodie in there ("I swear I put it in"), so I'm about to head for the house to get some Amish cover-up when Jase pulls a T-shirt out of his backpack.

"Wear this." He tosses it to her. It's one of our Garrett's Hardware "WE NAIL IT" shirts, which we just had done up for the Fourth of July sale. God, how much did those set us back? "Promotion and protection in one handy package."

Andy regards him dubiously. I can read her thoughts. *A T-shirt? Big-brother sized? On the first day of high school? Might as well just commit social hari-kari during first assembly.*

"Okaaaay," she says finally, dragging it on over the tank top. Andy is a nicer person than I am. Or more devious. As she stretches to pull it over her head, I realize my little sister is taller than me. No wonder that skirt looks so short.

"Twenty bucks says that lives in her locker all day. Maybe all year."

Jase shrugs. "Not taking that one, Alice. You were young once too."

"Of course, I also have my period," Andy adds, looking back and forth between us as though we both, definitely, need to hear this. "Naturally. Because why *wouldn't* I be breaking out on the first day of school? Does being on the Pill really help with that, or is that just something people say because they need to use it for other reasons?"

"Don't look at *me*," Jase says.

"Why not? Sam's on it, right? And she never has pimples – ever."

"Andy. None of your business."

"Alice? Come on, *you* know, right?"

"Talk to Mom," I mutter. Wait – I've been taking mine, right? I can't remember punching the little vacuum pack, holding the pink tablet in my hand, washing it down. But I wouldn't forget. I never forget. Besides, Brad's gone.

Or not. My cell phone dings. Brad. Early-morning at the gym probably. It's a picture of a puppy begging, "I may not be Red Rover, but can I come over?"

What happened to *we're* over?

I put my head in my hands.

"Alice!" shouts Duff from the house steps. "I can't find my glasses anywhere! Or my summer reading book."

"Alice!" yells Harry from the screen door, "Whatja do with my owl? Someone moved it!"

"Alice!" George calls from Jase's window upstairs. "That lady who lived in the shoe – what kind of shoe was it? I hafta draw a picture."

"Alice," Jase says, bending to pick up his backpack, "Go for a long run on the beach as soon as we get on the bus. I grabbed a three-pack of spearmint Mentos for you at Gas and Go this morning – it's hidden behind the box of that oatmeal stuff so no one else gets to it first. There's an everything bagel too."

The school bus screeches, hitting the top of the hill. As it comes down the street, the brakes shrill out a long, groaning sigh, almost exactly like the sound I'm trying hard to repress.

I'm a hundred and ten.

I'm the old woman who lives in the shoe.

"Hang in there," Jase calls, turning back with one foot on the bus stairs. "You're only temping as Mom."

"Thank God for that," I call. "I'm selling these kids on eBay and never having any of my own."

Andy scrambles up the steps, the door slams shut, there's more squealing from the brakes, a puff of gray exhaust rising into the bright blue sky.

A whistle and an "Al-eece!" from some guy in the back of the bus. Jimmy Pieretti. Dated his brother Tom three years ago. Under normal circumstances, the whistle would make me roll my eyes. Jim's, what, Jase's age?

Oh.

Right.

So's Tim.

But Tom was fun, Jim's a sweetheart, and I'm grateful

175

for any evidence that I'm not as ancient as I feel, so I shoot a smile at the window.

Scattered whistles.

There's almost a spring in my step as I turn away from the bus.

Total blur. All of it.

Cal's sleeping, he's crying, he's drinking, he's lying on my stomach while I lie on the floor of the apartment or the grass at Dominic's waiting for the fever to break or the buzz to go away so everything goes back to normal.

But it doesn't, because neither of those things is real. Cal is real. When he sleeps for a while, I jolt up sweaty because I'm afraid he's dead. When he only sleeps for a short time, I walk around sweaty because I'm so bushed and what's *wrong* with this kid anyway? He doesn't have any rhythm or I can't find one. He drinks the whole bottle and then screams for an hour like he's starving. He drinks nothing and falls asleep fast. I don't know if this is because he's a baby or because he's mine and therefore terminally unreliable. Either way, it blows. I can't believe I ever felt sorry for myself about anything ever before because I should have saved it all up for this. This tops anything Pop could have devised – I mean, he could have sectioned me, for Chrissake, locked me away to recover in rehab for as long as he wanted. Because *this*? It's been three whole days and it's honestly lasted longer than

the entire seventeen years of my life.

Not to mention: it was cake to pull crap over on my parents because *they didn't want to know,* so sucky excuses and lame explanations played fine.

But with the Garretts, I don't have that home-field advantage. Too many sharp eyes, too many working brains. Not to mention the fact that I'm not trying to smuggle Bacardi into a movie theater in an antibacterial gel container, but an actual human in and out of my apartment and their yard with his diaper bag and all his other crap. I actually do drive-bys to make sure there are no cars in the driveway or the lights are off or whatever before I skulk into or out of the apartment. Then I haul ass faster than Christmas. So Cal and I are spending a lot of time hanging at Dominic's, since he's in between fishing gigs. I sit on his steps, throw sticks for Dom's massive German shepherd Sarge, and hold the kid while Cal sleeps or drinks or stares, and Dom power washes the hull of his boat or chops firewood or repaves the driveway.

"Could you maybe, like, bake cupcakes or sew an apron or something?" I ask, after watching him clean out the storm drains.

"You have messed-up ideas about manhood. I bake awesome cakes, by the way. What's losing you *cojones* points is that you're holing up here."

I know, I know, I know.

Me on the phone with Hester, way the eff early in the morning on day three: "Look, I've got – stuff – to do. I've got an econ class online that I'm behind in and a civics test and a physics one I need to get in by the end of the week. Not to mention a couple days on at the hardware store." With Alice there too, during at least one of them. God. "When can I drop off Cal?"

Hester: (long pause) "This morning. We need to talk anyway."

Do we hafta? The thought does not fill me with joyous anticipation.

First off, I smuggle Cal into the car as the school bus pulls away and the screen door flaps shut behind Alice. Hester and I have set up a Cal swap in Willoughby Park, where I used to buy weed. She didn't want me to come to her house, but all she'd say when I pushed for an explanation was, "It's not a good time."

When I get to the park, I try to give back all the baby crap, but about all Hester'll take is the actual child. I half expect her to hand me a dime bag in exchange.

Right away she's rooting through the big-ass diaper bag, like she's counting stuff in there, like maybe I stole some of the formula and fenced it on the street or something, and my jaw clenches so tight, my neck muscles start throbbing. I never used to get angry, and now it's like I'm a goddamn volcano set on "continuous erupt."

I look away, kicking the dust with the toe of my flip-flops. Willoughby is not one of those nice parks with tons of green grass and leafy trees and all that jazz. It's more on the scraggly, sad side. The better to do the drug deals. In fact, I see one going on as we speak. Over in the far corner, near the stone wall that marks the end of the park, there's Troy Rhodes, the guy every school has at least one of, the guy who can set you up with whatever you want or need, any day, any night, any second, as long as you can pay.

My dealer, in other words.

Until a few months ago, probably the person I knew best in town

He's doing the old hand-shake pass-off with some middle school type. The guy's little-kid skinny, his chest practically concave, pants hanging low, wearing a Pokémon shirt that he probably doesn't know yet is uncool.

When I refocus, Hester's passing her hand back and forth in front of my face. I grab her wrist and she does this cringe thing like I'm going to snap it.

Christ, I was annoyed, but I'm not a psychopath.

"I know you're not, Tim."

Whoops, said that out loud.

"You looked glazed. I know what that can mean. But you're just tired, right? And trust me, you look way better than I usually do after time with him. It's like your worst nightmare ever, isn't it? Like hell."

I've spent the past days thinking that 345,678,900 times,

but when she says it, it sounds almost criminal, like there's something really wrong with *her*.

Seeing me blink, she focuses on packing things back into the bag. "I don't have any brothers or sisters, and I do the older kids at camp and I just" – she shrugs – "thought they were like babies in commercials, somehow."

"Like, as long as you gave 'em" – I pull out my Moviefone voice – "Sleepy Hollow Brand Formula, your little one will sleep like Rip Van Winkle."

She laughs, the first one I've heard from her since that first day, then covers her mouth like she's let something shameful escape. When her fingers move away, there's still a smile.

"That," she says, "is how Calvin happened." Her voice is accusing.

"Uh –"

"You made me laugh."

"Luckily, I don't need a rubber for that. When do I have to get him back again?" That sounds even worse than what she said, so I'm not surprised that she looks like she wants to deck me with the diaper bag. "I mean –"

"You don't. Never mind. Here's the thing, Tim. I thought about what you said – that I was being a sadist by bringing you into the picture at all."

I can barely remember using those words, even though *of course* I did. I'm such an asshole. "Forget about it, I shouldn't –"

"No, I can't. It makes sense. I was the one who got in trouble."

"Fuck that, Hester. This is not actually *The Scarlet Letter.* I don't have a problem with babysitting."

She purses her lips, looks down at Cal, away into the distance, narrowing her eyes in the bright sunlight.

"It's not babysitting if it's your own child. What I'm saying is that you don't have to be involved. It can just end here."

Cal's punted off a sock. He loves to do that, like it's some personal baby challenge. I bend over and pick it up, pulling it up his squirmy pink foot. He watches me somberly. Probably can hardly see me at this distance yet, according to the baby facts I've googled. I could be gone before he can. Say *yeah, sure, I'm done,* and putting his sock on could be the last thing I ever do for him, other than, presumably, sign off on some paperwork. *A baby? Right, I had one for a day or two. It didn't work out. End of story.* He'd never remember I existed and I could try to forget he ever had. I can see the tape rewinding, me walking backward through the past few days, up the steps to the apartment, lying back down after push-ups, the only thing on my mind meeting Alice in forty-five minutes. Poof. Erased.

But.

Hester's still staring out at the river, so I turn her chin toward me. She sort of freezes at my touch, wash of pink under her pale skin. "Hes. He happened. You let me know.

We can't time-travel and un-happen it any more than I can go further back and unscrew you."

That was beautiful, I hear Dominic say in my head.

She looks like I've smacked her. Of course. "You – I –" Tears come to her eyes.

Can't go back and unsay it either, so I bumble onward:

"What I mean is – I'm in this. He's not, like, a movie I checked out the preview of and decided not to watch. He's my kid. So, let's just get on with it. What happens next?"

She blinks, her face smoothes. Totally back to prissy-tone: "I'm doing a follow-up with the adoption agency this morning – that should help us figure out the timetable."

She looks even more rumpled today than the first time I saw her. Her dark hair's in this twisted knot-thing that looks like a squirrel's nest, she's got khakis on, but they're tight – and not in a good way – and her shirt is buttoned wrong. She's going somewhere like this?

"So when's your appointment?"

She brushes some flyaway hair out of her eyes. "It doesn't matter. You don't need to come. I wasn't asking you to. Your name isn't on the birth certificate anyway."

I hadn't given one second of thought to the birth certificate, but, "Uh, shouldn't it be?"

Hester explains, in this elaborately patient tone, that she wasn't sure I would "acknowledge paternity."

"And yet here I am, acknowledging," I say, my voice, like hers, sounding like someone is chopping each word off

from the one next to it. She pulls out her phone and scrolls through it, the text-check blow-off move. Usually I have to know someone better for them to piss me off this much.

The kid who was over in the bushes buying is now riding down the street toward us on his bike. He's got the backward hat thing going on and kind of a freak-out face – because he sees us, or because he hasn't done this before, or because he somehow knows he's taken a giant step down the Road to Stupid.

He can't be more than twelve.

Almost as much of a baby as Cal.

He speeds on by; his eyes dead ahead, jaw set, legs a blur.

Takes just about all I have not to step out into the street in front of him like the goddamn Ghost of Christmas Future.

I come into the kitchen after the school bus trundles away to find Duff and Harry dueling with Popsicles. It's seven o'clock in the morning.

"I am not left-handed," Duff says triumphantly as I walk in, swapping his Popsicle to the other hand and smashing it into Harry's, shattering sugary purple shards of ice all over the floor.

Harry leaps onto Duff's back, all ready for hand-to-hand combat. I grab both the backs of their pajamas, twist, and pull them apart. "Knock it off or you're both

going to the fire swamp."

I serve breakfast, helped by the presence of actual food in our cabinets and fridge.

I even find both Duff's glasses and his summer reading book hidden in and under Harry's LEGO castle, as part of a complicated revenge plot, the details of which I'd rather not know. "You have a lot to learn about revenge," I say, drowning out Harry's outraged, "No fair no fair no fair." "Never hide things in the most obvious place, for starters."

"Don't give him *tips*, Alice!" Duff says. "Whose side are you on?"

"Whichever pays better. Get dressed."

I have this down. I can hear water running, so Mom's up, but the least I can do is give her time for a shower. Assuming Andy left any hot water.

Patsy has escaped from her crib, of course, but she's no match for me. Although my diapering while she's trying to run away skills really aren't up to Dad's.

I tell George to draw eight kids for the Old Woman's shoe, and negotiate a discussion of what kind of shoe it would be, which turns ugly.

"It wouldn't be a high heel, duh," Duff says. "They'd all escape."

Or she would. But I don't even say that out loud. I'm a goddess.

Except I forgot about the owl.

"Where is it?" Harry asks, tears streaming down his

freckled cheeks, searching frantically through our kitchen junk drawer, scattering pizza delivery menus and pencils all over the floor.

"Do you have something to do with this?" I ask Duff.

He gives me an actually innocent look, instead of the super-wide-eyed one that is always suspect. "I was the one who found it for him in the first place!"

Text Jase: **Where is effin owl?**

But he doesn't answer because no cell phones at school, duh.

Harry's now on his hands and knees, rummaging through the drawer where all the Tupperware is, tossing it all out on the floor, sobbing. His skinny little shoulders . . . he sounds so lost – and I could be right there on the floor with him in a heartbeat, kicking and screaming. I put my arms around him, try to pull him onto my lap, the way I would George (who is hunting for the owl in the broom closet, judging by the crashes) but he looks at me like I'm a demon from the pits of hell. "You took him. I know you did, Alice. You never wanted me to have him in the first place. I hate you."

"Jesus God," I say loudly, sounding like Tim. "Shut up."

Beat of silence.

"We're not supposed to say that," Duff says righteously.

Patsy is now crunching something that looks a lot like it came from the cat dish.

I can't do this. I don't want to do this. I never, ever, signed on for this.

185

Now my chest is seizing up and I really can't breathe, and . . .

Mom comes in, slightly green, and solves it all. She might as well have a wand. The owl turns out to have mysteriously disappeared, but there are many photographs of it, from every disgusting angle. "This is better," she tells Harry firmly. "I'm fairly sure Mrs. Costa is allergic to feathers. Besides, it would've been hard to carry in your backpack."

"I could have put him in my lunch box," Harry says sulkily, but the fight's gone out of him, even as he still has almost as many tears on his face as freckles.

She admires George's picture, while scooping the cat food (yes it was) out of Patsy's mouth, saying, "Jase needs to keep this in his own room."

Sends Duff off to reorganize the broom closet, because he loves to do stuff like that, and I'm glad someone does.

Then looks up at me, shielding her eyes from the light streaming in from the window over the sink. "Go for a run, Alice. I'm on this."

I practically beat my best time just getting to the hallway, then turn back. "Mom . . ." *Why the hell would you ever do this? Why?* "How do you do this?"

"I have access to the Dark Arts. Run, Alice."

So I do.

Chapter Twenty-three

From hell to heaven, the minute I get back to the Garretts'.

Alice is in the driveway, washing the Bug. White halter bikini top, cutoffs. Man, will it suck when the cold weather comes. Right now, this can make up for everything – GEDs, global warming, even the last few days of my life.

Alice swipes her forehead with the back of her hand, which aims the hose directly at me.

"Hey!"

She jumps, whips around. Sees me soaking. Smiles so wide, I think I might die right there. Happy. She covers the end of the hose with her thumb and slowly flicks the spray up and down, so now I'm drenched. I look around for another weapon – tossing the entire water bucket over her seems brutal. But before I can seize the Super Soaker from the lawn, she lifts her hands in surrender, which, since she's still holding the hose, does the job for me, getting her totally wet.

"Always asking for trouble, Tim."

"You started it. Trouble pretty much finds me without

having to ask directions."

We stand there dripping. Droplets on her long eyelashes and this fine mist in her hair.

It's crazy quiet, except for the *shhh* of the water still draining from the hose.

"Where the hell is everyone?"

"First day of school," Alice says.

The bus earlier. Right. *First day of school.*

I swallow. Not for me. For the first September since I turned five, I'm not walking through any school doors.

"So, you're saying that as of today, I'm *officially* a high school dropout."

Alice wipes her wet hands on a towel, hoops it around her neck, scans me over, lingering on my eyes. She pulls her lower lip between her teeth, and squints at me, then nods like she's come to some decision. "Change clothes and meet me here in five, okay?"

When I do, she's now in a yellow bikini top and this orange skirt that technically covers her ass. But I can trace the outline of the rest of the bikini through it. As if she's reading those thoughts, she almost touches the nic patch, now on my side, a square bump under my T-shirt. "How're you doing with everything, Tim?"

Yeah, about that everything. Got some news. I open my mouth, but only a slice of the truth comes out. "Well, shitty. Basically."

She studies me for a sec, then turns and walks toward

the Bug. "Come on. Let's just . . . go."

Anywhere.

I slide into the passenger seat. Those cars? Your legs are, like, right there. So I accidentally brush against Alice's smooth, tan thigh with the back of my knuckles as I'm fastening the seat belt. Drum my fingers on my knee. Close my eyes. Deep gulp of air. Salt, sea, sun, sand.

Alice.

The Bug has shrunk. Tim seems to be taking up more space – more air – than his fair share. He adjusts his long legs, knees bumping the dash, hand grazing my leg. I grind the gears as I shift into reverse. Look over quickly to see if he's giving me that annoying cocky smile, but he's tipped his head partly out the window, resting his chin on the heel of the hand propped on the sill, eyes closed, hair whipping around like a dark red hurricane.

The only other time we've been in this car together he was passed out cold in the backseat after a suicidal joy-ride with Samantha and his jumpy sister. We had to carry him into his house, he was so wasted. That was barely three months ago.

No time at all, really.

I open my mouth to say *let's go back*, *not a good idea*, but then the breeze shifts, I smell the tarry open road and the sparkling clean air and Tim's shampoo.

We've passed the Reeds' old house, wind through downtown, past the building and loan, away from everything.

Just for right now. This once.

We hit the intersection of Old Town Road and Route 17. I smooth my thumbs against the worn plastic of the steering wheel, hesitate over the turn signal.

Tim angles his hip, pulls something out of his pocket. "Let's play Flip It," he says, and hands me a quarter. "Every time we get to an intersection, we flip the coin. Heads are right, tails are left."

I toss the coin to him and he whips it out of the air, quick as a seagull, and slaps onto the back of his hand, then points left, leans over, flicks the turn signal.

"Let's wait a few exits to flip it again. Not much adventure in Stony Bay."

"So it's adventure you're looking for today, Alice?"

I shrug. Tim resettles his legs again, rubs the side of one thigh, makes a face.

"Leg cramp? Navy Seal workout getting to you?"

"Pain is weakness leaving the body," Tim says solemnly. "Also nicotine. The coin says take this right."

Right, and flip left, and finally we wind up at McNair Beach, three towns away, but still a destination beach because it's a lot less rocky than the ones close by.

"Just so you know," Tim says as I park in the empty lot, "I cheated. I wanted the beach. Shame not to get that

bikini wet."

He grins at me, unabashedly checking me out. I straighten, pull my shoulders back, smile sideways at him. Then freeze. I've made those moves a thousand times and can translate them, even if Tim can't. *Go ahead. Look. I want you to.* What the hell am I thinking, pulling this with him? There should be sky-writing, a billboard, a Jumbotron: *You know better.* And I do. And still.

Alice flicks off her flip-flops, tosses them into the backseat without saying a word. Then strides off like she's leading a charge. I trail after her, hands crammed in my pockets.

Still without talking, we walk down the path lined with sea grass, onto the wide beach, the ragged, stony breakwater, toward the boarded-up hot dog and burger stand. She's still a length ahead and it occurs to me that I'm trailing after her like Brad or any of her lame-ass boy-toys.

I catch up to her easy – longer legs and all that. "I'm not some lapdog, like your Cro-Magnons," I tell her. "You don't get to call all the shots."

She stops, shading her eyes to look up at me. "No, you're not a lapdog, Tim. I know that."

"Just so we're clear," I say, my eyes straying to her belly ring, which is winking in the late morning sun.

"You're too big to be a lapdog. An Irish setter maybe."

Then she turns and starts to run down the beach.

I laugh. So I'm, like, the sample workout buddy in this scenario? Cramping quad muscle and all, it takes me a minute to catch up to her this time. At least I'm not gasping like a landed trout. I tag her on the shoulder.

She whips around but doesn't realize how near I am, so she winds up smack against me. Smile fading, she steps back, folds her arms tight against the bare brown skin of her stomach, exactly where I want to reach out and set my fingers, nudge my thumb against that little silver belly ring.

"Let's . . . let's . . ."

"Yeah?" I say, and step closer. Because Alice, fierce Alice, who always meets my eyes square on, doesn't seem to know where to look.

"Let's just . . ."

I close my eyes, blood pounding in my ears.

Let's just lie down in the sand.

Please.

Let me just . . .

Have this.

She looks up at me through her lashes for a second, lips parted just a little.

Then . . . "God." She shields her eyes, staring out at the tossing waves, then down the beach. "It's really over. Summer. So fast."

"Naaah." I point. "The Shore Shack cart's still here. Always summer in the land of frozen dairy products in

colors not seen in nature. C'mon. I'll buy you something."
I shove my hand back into my pocket, jingle the change
and crumpled bills I stuffed in there on my way out the
door. "As long as it doesn't cost me more than four bucks
and twenty-seven cents."

"Big spender."

"Hey, eternal youth doesn't come cheap." I start to set
my hand on her back to steer her toward the cart but can't
because there's no end to what I want to touch when it
comes to Alice. I'm almost as wheredoyouputyourhands
as Andy.

We have a brief argument over which flavors are the
most immature. "Neapolitan," Alice insists. "Vanilla,
chocolate, strawberry. The basics. It's the first ice cream
babies get to eat."

Cal.

Don't think about it. I just want to pull this day out of
time and space the way a magician snatches a quarter
from thin air.

"That's just a sneaky way of using up all that strawberry,"
I argue, "because who the hell likes that shit?"

"You're overthinking this."

"I specialize in that."

"Live in the moment, Tim." Her tone's cheerful, even a
little goofy, and hell yeah.

In the end she gets Cake Batter, which is pink and has
little strips of frosting mixed into it. I get electric-blue

Bubble Bum, complete with waxy little gumballs. Watching Alice lick her cone makes me happy in all sorts of non-little-kid ways. I bite the bottom of my cone off.

"I *knew* you'd be that guy," she says, polishing off her own.

"What guy?" I slurp down the last bits of ice cream, discarding one of the hard, stale-tasting gumballs, a perfect basket into the rusting iron trash barrel.

"The one who just has to do it the wrong way."

The fact of Calvin, successfully shoved out of my head for a good two minutes, smacks me in the face again like a cold wave.

But.

I take a breath.

Live in the moment.

Cal's not here at *this* moment, and I am, and Alice is.

Nobody looks mature eating ice cream, and Tim, with a streak of blue on his right cheekbone, is no exception.

He would be in *high school* right now if he hadn't taken the wrong exit.

I'm only one year out, it's true, but it feels longer. So much longer. Field hockey and band and Spirit Day and dances . . . some other girl's life.

Tim lobs the last of his cone toward the trash, grabs the back of his shirt and pulls it off, wipes his face.

There's suddenly a lot of bare skin in front of me.

I point at the sand. "Lie down."

His mouth drops open for a second. "Uh . . . what?"

"Lie down," I repeat.

"Do I get a biscuit if I obey?" But he does, he lies down, falling on his back in the sand as I drop to my knees next to his hip. I start scooping sand onto him, beginning with his chest.

"Only if you're very good. Stop moving, Tim, I can't cover you up if you keep moving."

His hand shoots out, grabs my wrist. "You'll leave a hole for oxygen, right?"

"I – I –" His thumb presses in a little harder, right where my pulse jumps. I yank my hand away, keep piling on the sand. "When I did this to Andy, I always sculpted a mermaid tail out of sand over her legs."

"Yeah, and you won't be doing that this time."

I'm just starting to smooth down around his thighs when he erupts out, scattering sand, in my hair, down my suit, everywhere.

He shakes his head, whipping more sand onto me. Then crouches, hands on his knees, breathing like he's been sprinting – barefoot – instead of lying flat under my moving hands.

Cold water.

Now.

"Now we *have* to swim," Alice says to me, like she's reading my mind. Or, you know, body.

"Race you to the buoy line?"

"*Pffft,*" I say. "Kid's stuff. Gotta head for the breakwater, if you're going for a challenge."

"Isn't kid's stuff what we're doing? Besides, the breakwater is out of bounds for swimmers."

I point to the empty lifeguard chairs. "Come on. Take a chance, Alice."

"Stretch out that right leg first," she advises.

"You forgot to say 'Simon says.'"

She flushes, looks down and readjusts her halter strap. "What's that supposed to mean?"

"Just that you don't get to be the boss of me."

She shakes her head. Like she wants my words and this weird push-pull between us to flip away with the breeze.

"I wasn't saying that. I wasn't doing that."

"No?"

"No." All brisk and practical now. "You're still favoring one leg when you run. That's probably why the other one is cramping up. I do that when I don't pay attention, because of this broken ankle I had a few years ago. Ever break anything?"

"Other than curfew and the speed limit? A few hearts here and there."

Total bullshit, the last. I wait for her to call me on it, to know that no one ever got that close. Instead she squares

her shoulders, widens her stance, hands on hips. Like a dare.

"No worries. I'm pretty heartless."

That's bullshit too, but I don't say so. "So how do I fix it? The favoring the leg thing?"

"Try a few lunges." She demonstrates, one toned, tanned thigh balanced, bending smoothly at the knee, jaw fixed, looking out over the water, strong chin, full lips, these two little dimples inset neatly at the base of her spine.

Oh Alice.

Trying *not* to lunge, thank you very much.

No sign of Tim anywhere. I'm bobbing in the cool water beyond the slimy swim line that connects the buoys and he was *right there*, yards ahead of me, and now there's nothing. No splash, no streak of arms against the waves, nothing but a seagull shrilling and plunging in the air overhead.

Nothing at all.

Panic flickers at the edge of my vision, almost visibly, like someone flipping white lights on and off in a dark room. A wave slaps me in the face. I can't catch my breath.

Not one of these.

Not here.

Not now.

And not him. *Where is he?*

I shield my eyes, sweep a look one direction, the other.

A head, rusty hair nearly the same color as the buoys, bobs up.

Laughing, damn it.

"Where the hell were you?"

"To the breakwater – and back. Underwater. I win."

"I thought you'd drowned."

He cocks his head at me. "Seriously? I was on the swim team."

"How would I know that? I thought you'd gone under." My voice is trembling, "Which is the last thing I need, I mean, we need – I mean, what would happen if you drowned? If you got hurt or *died* while I was watching you?"

"*Watching* me? You're not *babysitting* me," he says, then flushes.

"I didn't mean that. I just meant – you could have hit your head on a rock or come across a riptide or –"

"The really bad riptide is at Stony Bay Beach," he interrupts. "Not here. Besides, I know how to get out of it. I'm a big boy, Alice. And not your problem."

"I didn't mean that. But you –" I stop, not even sure what I'm so angry about.

He purses his lips, studying me, moving up and down in the waves, so close, his feet whirl the water around me as he treads, red hair dark and glinting. "I don't fuck up *everything*, Alice."

The sound is that clear, sea-glass green it often turns in the fall, though it's still summer-warm. His eyes are also

clear, grayish blue, nothing shielded.

"I know that." Some things you say automatically and then, inside, feel a quiet little nod. The hitch in my breath, the knot in my chest, they untangle and wash away as I look back at him, waves slapping around us.

"Hot fake leather! Hot fake leather! I forgot to leave a towel on the seat," Alice says after sliding into the driver's side. "Holy crap! I never forget to do that."

"You were probably distracted by my hard, manly body." I stretch into the backseat for a towel and toss it to her. She misses the catch, fumbles for it, crams it beneath her. Then turns to face me. Presses her lips together, sets her jaw, bracing herself. I wait for her to blast me for something – scaring her in the water, that she already knows about the kid, that she can read my mind and knows every little nook and cranny it's gone to in the last two hours.

"What?"

Pucker between her brows now. Her eyes move over my face.

"What?" I ask again, reaching up to rub my chin self-consciously. I haven't shaved.

Still frowning, she rests her index finger between my eyebrows, brushes away the worry lines.

Then she wraps one arm around my waist, sets her fingers at the back of my neck to pull my head down. She

touches her tongue to my bottom lip, and then opens her mouth. Tastes like salty ocean and sweet birthday cake and everything I've ever blown out candles and wished for.

I kiss her back, skim one thumb slowly down her spine, the other hand hesitating at her waist for only one inhale before I press my palm hard against her soft skin, turn her to face me more fully, pull her all the way into my lap, bend all I have into all of her.

We're in a Volkswagen and I'm six three. The fine German engineering of the People's Car was *not* engineered for this. Still, there's no freaking way I'm gonna stop and request a more comfortable situation. Even if my legs are wedged under the glove compartment and my rib cage is about to be cracked by the gearshift.

"What am I doing with you?" Alice whispers, sliding her hands up my back. "This is crazy," she says, shifting her hips to accommodate me. "You're a kid."

"I'm no kid. And you know it." I move my lips behind her ear, along her throat, her neck, lower. Then slip one hand very slowly, tips of my fingers, edge of my thumb under the triangle of her suit.

God, God, God.

There we are in a tiny car with the windows down in a public parking lot and you'd think sanity would stop us, but nothing does.

I pluck the strap of her halter top to the side.

Drop my mouth to her collarbone where the strap has

left a small red indentation.

Her hands on me, my lips on her, her fingers tightening, my breath catching.

Hers coming in these little puffs of air, hot against me.

I edge one hand down to touch the lever to recline the seat back and instead it folds around this thing, this loop of plastic and squish of rubber that I don't immediately identify until I get it − a pacifier. For a baby.

In this case, Patsy, but . . .

Alice will hate herself, and me. Why did this have to happen now?

"This is . . . probably not a good idea."

"Hmm?" She's kissing my collarbone, her palm flat against my chest, over my heart.

"Alice."

She looks up.

"We need to cool off here," I tell her. *Now* I have to discover my inner maturity?

Her eyes are hazy. "We do?"

No. "Yeah."

"Right, you're right," she says, sliding off my lap back into the driver's seat. I'm abruptly cold without her heat. Her head's bowed and I bend over to kiss her forehead.

"In case it wasn't obvious, I didn't want to stop."

"Uh-huh," she says, still looking down.

"Alice. Look at me."

She slowly raises her head and swallows. All shimmery

eyes and wild hair and every kind of gorgeous. Then holds up a hand, stopping anything I might say.

"Give me a second."

Reaches into the back of the car for a sweatshirt, pulls it on like armor, rests the flat of her hand over her eyes for a beat of my heart. Then another.

Then she turns her keys in the ignition, looks over her shoulder, and peels out of the parking lot so fast, rubber would burn if the drive weren't made of broken clamshells. As it is, shells fly.

We don't say a word the entire ride back. Tim opens his window all the way, tips his head out, drums his fingers on the dashboard. I can only see his profile, and not much of that.

My legs are shaking, like I've run miles, breath hard to scrape out of my lungs, my toes tingling as if coming back from numbness. Probably true, they were so tightly curled before. When I reach over to shift gears, my hand trembles a little. I stop to get gas and he pulls up the parking brake, his thumb slipping along my calf as he does so.

He looks down at my leg for a moment, swallows, his Adam's apple visibly bobbing.

"There's something I think – I know – I should tell you. But first, I've got to know. What *was* that?" he asks, in a low voice.

"What was what?" I scribble my name on the receipt and hand the card back to the gas station guy.

Tim jerks his thumb over his shoulder, indicating the beach we've driven away from. "You know. Are you, like, toying with me, Alice? Just be straight up, if that's what this is."

I hate that he's so much taller than I am, the top of his head brushing the roof of the car.

"I'm not toying with you," I say, pulling up to a red light. "God. Like I do that."

Tim meets my eyes.

"Fine. I do that. But I'm not doing that now. At least" – I put my head in my hands – "I don't know what I'm doing. But it's not toying, like a cat with a mouse. Or whatever."

"So this is . . . what? Sample dating? Even though I screwed up our first? Temporary insanity? I don't know what this *is*."

"I don't know either," I say, looking at him. "Besides . . . you're the one who got smart and put the brakes on." My voice sounds hurt, and I hate that.

"I didn't want to. You had to know that. It couldn't have been more obvious. But . . ."

I wave one hand at him, brushing it off, him away. "Whatever. It doesn't matter."

"Alice."

I flick my hand at him again, trying to regain myself, shift back into Tin Alice, the girl with no heart.

"Alice. Don't *whatever* me. It matters. Could you look at me, for Chrissake?"

"I'm driving. Have to focus."

He sighs.

I drive down the main street of Stony Bay, around the roundabout shaped like a lighthouse, then out onto the straightaway without looking at him again. But, just as we get to our road, I reach out one hand, palm up, and after a pause, he slides his big warm hand into mine, squeezes. Holds on.

When I pull into the driveway and finally sneak a look, he's drumming on the other leg with one thumb. I turn to him.

"Look, Tim. What if we just try −"

"Alice. There's something important I've got to tell you −"

He breaks off, stares over at the garage apartment.

"Oh, fuck me."

"What?" I follow the direction of his gaze. A girl is sitting on the steps. Silver car girl. With a huge bag slung over her shoulder. And a baby in a car seat beside her.

Chapter Twenty-four

Hester waves, all welcoming and chipper, like I've popped by to see her at *her* house with some flowers and a meatloaf.

"My car was acting crazy – making all these strange noises, like *Eeeeeeee*," she calls, walking over, leaving the baby behind, "so I left it at that garage on North Street. They gave me a lift over here. It's good you're back. Cal's all fussy, and he probably shouldn't be out in the sun too long."

Alice is a statue, hand frozen on the gearshift. Hester's smiling. Cal's asleep. I, at this moment, would sell my soul for any number of things, but first and foremost that stupid sailor hat. Or the lame-ass bonnet. Because there's nothing covering Cal's head but his shiny, incriminating red hair.

Hester processes the fact that I'm in the car with this dazzling girl in a bikini at exactly the same second that Alice takes in the whole picture. Hester's smile dims. Alice squares her shoulders. "Sounds like the fan belt needs replacing," she says flatly. "Yeah, you should probably get that baby out of the sun."

"Alice . . ." I say. "It's not . . ." *What, not what it looks like? It's exactly what it looks like.* "I can . . ." *Explain? Not really.* "I —"

"It's most likely a good idea if you don't say anything right now," she says, kicking open the car door.

"But —" I slide out of my seat, start to circle around the Bug.

"Don't. Talk." She slams the door, then shoves it shut after it pops open again. Cal startles and begins to cry. Alice casts one incredulous look at me, then strides toward the house.

"I thought you said you didn't have a girlfriend." Hester's voice lifts over the baby's shrill wails. She's scooped him into her arms and is jiggling him up and down. His eyes are saucers.

"I don't."

She stares after Alice's fine retreating ass. I punch the side of the Bug, hard, and then boot the tire for good measure.

"So who was that?"

"Hester." I'm gritting my teeth so hard, I expect shards of molars to fly out onto the tar of the driveway. "None of your business."

"If it would help to talk about it —" Her voice is all soothing, and where the hell does she get off with that? The baby, who has paused with the screeching, cranks it up again.

"No offense, but you don't know me at all."

More shrieking from Cal.

"Hell, give him to me, Hes."

Gnawing her lip with her teeth, she passes him over. "My car should be done soon. You could drop me off in town. Or . . ." Her shoulders slump. "I guess I could walk. How far do you think it is?"

Nail yourself to the freakin' cross, already. I hoist the baby on my shoulder, bury my nose in his neck. He makes this little wiggling movement, snuggling in safe. I don't feel safe, my gut tight, my intestines squirming like snakes, so I shut my eyes; try to recite the Serenity prayer or something in my head. The best I can do is take my mind back to the beach, cool water glistening silver on Alice's tanned shoulders, the flash of her ring in the sunlight, her smile.

"Sure she's not your girlfriend?" Hester asks. "Because she's looking out the window at us."

"It doesn't matter. Let's get Cal inside."

"His name is Calvin."

I'm spoiling for a fight, and I'll take one anywhere, on any grounds, no matter how much of an asshole that makes me.

"I'm calling him Cal. Calvin is a pussy name."

Hester flinches, blue eyes, pale face. I've sucker-punched a kitten. Muttering an apology, I head up the stairs, Hester following. Only one quick backward glance to see if Alice actually is watching.

She's not.

Inside, I fill a glass of water from the tap, guzzle it down, then set the glass on the counter and stick my face right under the faucet. Gulping, trying to cool down.

Hester's got Cal now, patting his back. She keeps trying to talk to me, going on and on, something about the adoption intake interview and my medical history and ethnic background and paperwork, paperwork, paperwork.

My temples are pounding and I'm hot, then cold, then hot again. "How long is your car going to take? I can't do this now," I say. "Call the garage and tell them it's the fan belt. Better yet, let's just go over there."

"It may not be the fan belt. Unless that girl is a car mechanic. She didn't look like a car mechanic. Is she –"

"Leave it alone," I say, picking my cell up off the counter. "Which garage is it?"

"Oh, no. This diaper is leaking. Here." She shoves the baby at me in this offhand way, like he's a pile of towels, then heads to the sink to wash her hands, adding over her shoulder, "Can you get this one? As I said, they need a medical history. Do you have any chronic diseases?"

"Nope," I snap, resting Cal against my chest, head on my shoulder, with one hand and bending over to rummage through all the crap in the bag for one of his postage-stamp-sized diapers.

"Unless you count my slight touch of alcoholism." And horniness. And douchebaggery.

Cal's little scratchy fingernails are digging into my chest

like Jase's cat's paws do, like milk's going to come spilling right on out. "Hang on," I mutter to him. "Cleanup first."

Something's warm and sticky on the hand that's holding him and I know before looking what it is.

"Jesus God, Hes. Why is it this color? What is *wrong* with this kid?"

"Nothing! He's just fine. Fine. Why would you even ask that?"

Shifting Calvin to the other side, I hold out my hand, the hand that was on Alice's back, her neck, her waist, less than an hour ago. "It's green. That can't be right."

"He's fine," she repeats, handing me a box of baby wipes and this folded plastic thing and, for some reason, this little wooly hat with a pompom. "Sorry about that. Change him on that so he doesn't leak on the couch."

"Do you think I give a damn about the couch? God knows what could be in those genes or chromosomes or whatever was my contribution to the party. I'm surprised my sperm could even swim straight, if you want the truth."

"He's perfectly healthy. Calm down. You're making him upset." She pauses. "Look, Tim." Her voice softens. "I know this is hard. For both of us. But we need to get along for the sake of the baby."

My hand jerks as I'm undoing the tape thing on the side of the diaper, and the plastic shreds, so more crap spills out, on the couch, on me. "We do not need to get along for the sake of the baby. We are not married. He's, like, an

amoeba." And he'll be gone as soon as I can possibly make that happen.

I drive her to Reynold's Garage, all but change the fan belt myself (yes, it's the fan belt). Guilty for comparing my son to a one-celled organism, and a major pussy, I agree to take Cal for another night. When I ditch her in town, it's like I'm scraping her off my shoe.

The house is dead quiet when I come storming in, sandy, and suit still damp with seawater. I chuck my wet towel in the corner of the kitchen, like I'm one of my messier brothers. Then I kick one of the stools near the island, which crashes to the ground. My repaired ankle is already killing me from my assault on the car door while making my mature exit.

I'm glad Mom's not here.

I wish Mom were here.

Just Mom, alone. Nobody else she had to pay attention to.

My throat feels as though I've swallowed clamshells from the beach parking lot. My eyes are hot sand.

I pick up my cell to call her, and then drop it with a clatter on the counter. What would I say? *Guess what, we'll need to be picking up a Father's Day card for Tim Mason next year. In other news, I kissed him and I didn't want to stop and now I have to because, well, obviously. And also, great news! Grace Reed stopped paying Dad's bills, so there's that to celebrate too.* The thought

brings a crush of guilt, heavy, like someone sitting on my chest, because my dad, my family, is screwed if I don't figure this out, and here I am thinking about *Tim Mason*.

I kick the stool again, harder, so it smashes into the trash can, which someone must have pulled out to empty and then forgot about. The can tips over, spilling orange rinds and a coffee can and some of Patsy's diapers out on the floor, which was already getting grimy.

I'll just let myself cry. Blast some music. Shower off. Shake it off.

He and that girl made a baby. Whatever.

That's his type?

God, I hate it when people even say there *are* types, like people come in flavors.

Was *that* why his parents kicked him out? He's been here for three weeks. That baby seems older than that. Was that why he got kicked out of prep school? Who *is* that girl? Is she going to move into my apartment with him? Sleep in his bed and eat Grape-Nuts with him and go to the beach and –

She's very pale. I bet she sunburns.

I am the worst person in the world.

I start to drag myself upstairs to my room, throw myself down on the bed, and cry myself to sleep. Trash the room. Something.

But I share my room with Andy, who, because she's now in high school, as of today, is already home. She's lying on

her back on my bed (because hers is covered with clean laundry she hasn't taken the time to put away yet) painting her fingernails, periodically pausing to eat a Nilla Wafer from the jumbo box propped against my Tardis pillow.

When I come in the door, she jolts up, guiltily. "I didn't get any crumbs on – What's wrong? Is it Dad? Mom? Oh, God, Alice, don't look like that." She's jumping up and putting her arms around me, getting pink nail polish in my hair as she brushes it back. "Oh honey," she says, in a quite good imitation of our mother.

"Everyone's fine," I choke out. Tears would be a relief at this point, my eyes sting so badly.

"But not you. You aren't fine," Andy says, pulling me over to my own bed and tapping the comforter (also getting nail polish on that, but what the hell at this point). "Talk to me. Alice, please."

"And what, you'll braid my hair and do *my* nails?"

She blinks for a moment. I'm Tin Alice once again. My little sister with her open heart and her open arms.

"If you want," she says after a minute. "I was thinking of just listening."

I swallow, can barely swallow. "It's . . ."

I can't. I can't get the words out, because then . . . then they'll be true. That he's a dad, and that I'm a mess. That he lied to me. With what he did, if not actually what he said, since I didn't happen to ask him if, by any chance, he'd recently fathered any children.

I was thinking . . . for just a moment, I was thinking we could – nothing serious – but we could –

Well, no we can't.

"It's a guy," my sister says. "Brad? No, it would never be Brad."

"Why not?" I ask immediately. It would be a natural assumption. I just broke up with Brad. Andy was a wreck for a month after Kyle Comstock broke up with her, the faithless twit.

"Flip?" she guesses again. "I liked Flip. He took me wakeboarding."

"That was two years ago. Not Flip. Why wouldn't it be Brad?"

"Brad couldn't get to you. Not the real you. He didn't have the –"

"Balls?"

"Gag." Andy makes a face. "No. The . . . I don't know, the strength or whatever . . . the depth. You didn't *need* Brad."

I'm brushing at my eyes, even though they're dry as driftwood. "What I don't need is *this*."

"No. You don't," Andy says with absolute certainty. "To hell with this. Whatever this is. You're too great and tough to let anything or anyone get to you."

Yeah, except unpaid bills and Dad and school and redheaded ex-junkie alcoholics with infants and my entire life.

Don't panic. Don't go there. I take a minute, focus on drawing a slow invisible circle on my thigh. Chase away all that. Andy would freak out.

"I'm not all that tough, Andy," I say on a slow exhalation. "Just so you know. I mean, don't do that to yourself. Think I'm the tough one so you have to be the not-tough one. It's just – I just –"

"Alice, c'mon. You can have a bad day. Without it being your period or you being a ball-buster – see, I said it – or a wimp or calling yourself names. Although, if it would help, we can call this guy names. I know a lot. Dip-twit. Tool. Douchemonkey. Eejit. Wenis. Sludgeball. Asskite. Showerfunk. Dirtbag. Ratfink. And those are just the nice ones. I've been collecting them."

She's still got her skinny arms around me, and my head is tipped against her shoulder. She smells like vanilla and nail polish remover and my gardenia perfume.

I'm laughing a little, and she does too, bumping her shoulder against mine. "Tim taught me most of them. Along with how to knee a guy in the crotch. He taught me lots more, but they might shock you."

"Not much can at this point," I say sadly. But that's not true. I am shocked. Well down the road beyond that, even; all the way to flabbergasted. Floored. But why? Isn't this the kind of thing everyone would expect to happen? The Boy Most Likely To strikes again?

Oh, Tim.

Just as expected, right, Alice? I wanted to be better than that.

I flop down on the bed, fold my arms, rest my head in them.

"Tim also taught me to hit someone in the nose, upward, with the heel of your hand" – Andy pulls on a lock of my hair, raising my face so she can demonstrate – "to break it."

"You're going to pull this move on some poor fourteen-year-old idiot?"

"Only if absolutely necessary. He gave me a whole lecture about that. Not to bust it out on some poor sucker who was just trying to cop a – anyway. He was awesome. Like a brother."

"You've already got more than your share of those, Ands."

"Joel and Jase would want to go beat the guy up *for* me. They're not going to teach me swears or kickass moves. I'd love to have Tim as a brother."

"I wouldn't," I say, which comes out a little louder than I'd like.

"You probably don't know him as well as I do," Andy points out. "Speaking of shock, would it shock you if I told you I needed a ride to Megan's? Or that you're late to pick up Jase from practice? And I could use some money for Starbucks."

"No. That wouldn't shock me at all."

"Alice. We all love you. If this guy doesn't, he's a rhino-

skinned, horse-faced baboon-butt."

"Tim again?"

"Duff and Harry," Andy says, smiling full-on, braces shining. "I have multiple sources."

Holy crap. Literally. On the short car ride back from the garage, despite the fact that you'd think there'd be nothing left in that tiny-ass body, Cal's managed to fill his diaper and the entire back of his shirt and part of his *hat*! How is this even possible?

I'm squatting in front of him as he stretches out on a blanket on the living room floor. I knew things were bad when I ejected him from the car seat, but . . . He looks back at me anxiously, little tears crystalized on his eyelashes.

"Don't worry. I'm on this. We'll handle it," I say in a manly, deeper-than-my-own-voice way, when in fact I'm not sure there are enough wipes to handle this. In all of Target. In all the Targets in all the world.

He keeps staring at my face. *So sorry, Dad. I seem to have lost control here.*

"No big deal, Cal. These things happen," I tell him, although I'm not sure they do. His hat?! Maybe my genes really did completely screw him over. All this can't have come from a body so small. There are only two thin wipes left. And no paper towels or anything like that.

The shower is the only answer. His clothes are already

off, in a hellish pile on the floor that I'll have to deal with later, so I shuck my own off quickly, kicking my loafers across the room, and carry him in to the shower stall. He goes rigid with shock at the blast of water.

Please don't scream again, Cal.

"'S fine. It's a shower. Us guys like 'em. Give it a chance."

He's clinging to my chest like a spider monkey. A messy redheaded spider monkey. I rub down his back under the water. His face crumples – yikes, the water *is* a little hot. I turn it down to nearly cold. Cal looks even more freaked out.

I scrub up and down his back with the soap again, then lift him up so we're face-to-face. "You're fine, Cal. It's all good," I say firmly. His round blue eyes stare into mine. He bobs his head forward, puts his mouth on my nose . . .

Begins to suck on it.

I can't help it, I start laughing. He keeps sucking away.

"You're not going to get what you need from my nose, kid," I tell him.

Probably not from the rest of me either. But here in the cold-as-hell shower, him slippery as a bar of Ivory soap, and both of us barely recovered from the diaper of doom, I'm happy. For the moment anyway, I can be what this baby needs.

Or at least my nose can.

Ten minutes later, I'm knocking on the Garretts' screen

door with my big secret in one arm.

"MOMMMMMY. Tim's brought us a baby. Can we keep him?"

Mrs. Garrett's washing dishes at the sink. She turns around, looks at me, Cal, back at me. "Oh . . . wow."

"George, this is Cal." I bend down to George's level. "He's, uh, mine. So you can't keep him."

Neither can I.

"Geez," says George. "He's got a lot of fur."

I laugh. It's true. Even damp, Cal's fluff of red hair sticks up like a rooster comb.

Mrs. Garrett has come over, kneeling next to me. "Oh my," she says, even more softly.

I can't tell what she's thinking, so I say, "Oops. Sorry, Mrs. G. You did say I'd make a good dad. My timing got a little screwed up. Alice home?"

She stands. "She went to pick up Jase. I'm sure there's quite a story here, Tim. Why don't you let me hold your baby, get yourself something to eat, and tell me about it."

I run through the story between bites as I engage in a feeding frenzy of epic proportions. No old pizza here. I eat three turkey sandwiches, two containers of Greek lemon yogurt, a bag of pretzels, and guzzle practically a gallon of chocolate milk.

Explaining Hester's part in the whole thing? Awkward. Especially with George (and soon Harry and Patsy too) sitting right there, round-eyed.

"So . . . I went to this party, last winter; there was this girl – I didn't know her very well – and, um, she got an extra prize in her goody bag, but I didn't hear until a few days ago that this prize was, uh, handed out."

Mrs. Garrett nods in comprehension.

"That must have been some party." George sighs. "All I ever get to take home is a bunch of gum and Super Balls and squirt guns and stuff."

"Tim might have been happy with that, George," Mrs. Garrett says.

She cradles Cal expertly over the small bump of her own stomach and reaches out to ruffle my hair. "You know you could have come straight to us. This is a lot to handle on your own."

"He's pretty teeny," George says. "*I* could handle him. He could sleep in my bed. I bet *he* pees too. Then I'd for sure have a baby brother, in case the new baby is another dopey girl."

"Hon!" Patsy commands, and stretches her arms up to me, elbowing my knee insistently, making it known she's my *real* baby. And no dopey girl.

I pick her up, put my face in her hair and without warning my eyes sear like they've taken a hit of Tabasco. *Fuck, no*.

Mrs. Garrett sighs. "He's a lovely baby, which of course you know. Looks healthy too."

I nod without looking up.

"But your plate was already full. I'm sorry, Tim."

"'S' okay." I say hastily, since sympathy is making it harder to ditch the dampness in my eyes. "I can handle full plates. Just power through 'em. You know that – I eat here all the time."

When I glance up, Mrs. Garrett looks unfooled by my bullshit.

"This girl," she asks carefully. "What's she like?"

"Is she hot?" asks Harry.

"Harry!"

"What?! Joel asks that all the time. So does Duff."

Mrs. Garrett rolls her eyes. "Duff too, now?" Joel has always been a walking hormone, but Duff's only eleven.

Patsy is stroking my arm lovingly, sighing "Hon" periodically.

"I don't even *know* what she's like. She's very, uh, clean. Got straight A's in the classes we were in together. Always did the extra credit work too. She writes her baby care notes in outline form."

"Doesn't *sound* hot," Harry mutters.

"Harry, be still. Eat something." Mrs. Garrett reaches into the fruit bowl, hands him an apple. "So . . . you'll be getting to know her at the same time you get to know your son."

"Yup. Like I say, my timing has always su–" I glance at George and Patsy. "Stunk."

Mrs. Garrett's eyes are sad, but her voice is brisk and

practical. "I bet you need supplies – clothes and things. Joel's *Animal House* bachelor pad doesn't come equipped with baby gear. We have lots. Let's go look in the basement."

Downstairs, Mrs. Garrett is opening up big plastic bins marked BOY and GIRL and GEAR and making little stacks of stuff. Because none of the kids have followed us down here, wanting to stay upstairs and make faces at Cal, I can say what I couldn't before.

"I don't need much. She gave me a ton of crap. It's all temporary anyway; Hester's plan is to get him adopted quickly." By this morning would have been perfect.

She pauses in the act of folding some fluffy blue blanket, face neutral, and then starts folding it again, without looking at me. "How do you feel about that?"

"I got nothin', Mrs. G." Then I flinch, remembering the last time I used that phrase.

She reaches out for a second and rubs my cheek with the back of her hand. Doesn't say a thing. Then she hands me a stack of blankets, little undershirts folded on top. One of the blankets has DUFFY sewn onto it in wobbly red yarn letters.

"Won't you need this shit yourself? Stuff, I mean."

"I'm not going to wash your mouth out with soap, Tim. I've heard the word. Used it, even. Recently. And, not for another six months or so. By that time your Cal will be bigger, or he'll be gone. Take it for now."

"But, the thing is, for now?" I add. "Don't know my ass

from my elbow here." I explain about the in-the-hat thing. And the green thing.

She laughs. "Normal. As long as you have a handle on which is *Cal's* elbow, you'll be fine. None of us knows what to do, to start, Tim. You and the baby will figure it out together."

I trudge upstairs with a ton of things – including a baby gym, whatever the fuck that is (*Oh good, I've noticed that my abs lack definition, Dad*) and a windup stuffed bear that plays "Twinkle, Twinkle Little Star," and a stack of what looks like fuzzy long underwear.

When I get to the top, there, standing in the kitchen, is Alice, still in her yellow bikini and cover-up, hair ruffled, face flushed, eyes boring into mine. With Jase and Sam right next to her. And my kid in her arms.

Shit? Meet Fan.

Chapter Twenty-five

Tim peers at me around a huge pile of baby supplies, then drops it all at his feet, cocks his head at me, complete with smirk. "I see you've met Calvin. Guess the cat's out of the bag that I'm no virgin."

"Tim –" Samantha starts.

"What's a virgin?" Harry asks loudly.

"Something about a forest," George whisper-yells back.

"This" – I joggle the baby, and Mom, who's come up the stairs behind Tim, makes a concerned sound – "is no joke. This could only happen to you!"

"Technically," he drawls, sloping back against the wall, "it could happen to any guy with a working –"

"What the hell is wrong with you? You're seventeen years old!"

Tim pats the pocket of his shirt, looks down at his feet. "Eighteen in December. You're fuckin' nineteen, in case you've forgotten. Not nearly old enough be my mom, babe, so you can ditch *that* line of bullshit right now. Besides, you didn't mind –"

The kitchen is dead quiet.

Jase was bending over to unlace his Converse, and his fingers go motionless.

Sam has her hand to her mouth.

Even the baby looks stunned.

Then Harry says cheerfully, "Tim swore. Twice. The bad ones."

Tim looks over at George, who's watching us with a scared expression, nearly in tears. Tim brushes his hand over his face, lets out a short, shaky laugh. "Uh. Sorry, guys."

I cradle the baby's head in my hand, look from him to Tim, back again. "Even though I saw . . . I knew . . . it had to be . . . Unbelievable."

"And yet true. Exactly why are you so ballistic? It doesn't eff up *your* life. You don't have to babysit. That one's on me, babe."

"How about you reserve the 'babe' for your actual *baby*? And, newsflash, it's not called babysitting when it's your own child."

Jase and Samantha are exchanging glances like crazy. Jase clears his throat. "Guys . . ."

"George, Harry," Mom cuts in, gathering up Patsy, who kicks her feet ferociously, twisting and reaching out for Tim. "Let's go get some of your stuffed animals to loan the baby. Something soft you don't play with anymore."

The boys trail toward the stairs. "He can't have Happy,"

George says belligerently.

"Who is that girl? Apparently *not* your dealer. That's one whopper of a secret you've been keeping for nine months. Not to mention –"

"I didn't know! I just found out, like, days ago. I didn't know," Tim repeats. "I don't even remember doing her. Like, total blank."

"Jesus," Jase mutters.

"Is that supposed to make it better? You ruined her life, but that's all good, *babe*, it was in a blackout? *That's* your get-out-of-jail-free card?" The baby starts to fuss and I rest him against my shoulder, rub his back, sway from side to side, automatically. Baby on board, activate Garrett instincts.

"Let me have him," Samantha suggests, when the whimpering continues.

"Nah, he's probably hungry. Again," Tim mutters. "My job. Hand him over." He reaches for the baby, lifting him out of my arms, setting his palm against the soft folds at the back of the baby's neck. "I'll come back for that stuff later." He heads for the screen door, kicks it open with his bare foot, and lets it slam behind him.

Jase gives a long, low whistle under his breath.

Samantha bends to scoop up the clothes and blankets. "Wow," she says. "His parents must – I can't even imagine."

Yup. The Boy Most Likely To has really outdone himself this time. If the Masons kicked him out of the house for

225

job stuff, what now? Get him deported?

"It is honestly like the guy makes a profession of messing up. As if he wakes up and the first thing he does, before he even showers – *if* he even showers – is write a punch list of all the many creative and moronic ways he can be more of a disaster."

I'm yanking open the screen door as I speak, and when Jase puts his hand on my shoulder, saying, "Al, this is not your fight," I just yank away.

"Let me talk to him," Samantha says, almost, but not quite, blocking my path. "He –"

"No way. You'll both be too nice."

∘ ∘ ∘

"What now?" Tim says when I catch up to him at the threshold of the apartment, which he's pushing open with his elbow. "A little busy here, Alice. Hands full and all that."

"In." I shove the door open, set my hand on his back, and follow him. The room now has an open diaper bag, a bouncy seat, a few bottles soaking in the sink, and a Moses basket, in addition to the usual piles of dirty clothes and Grape-Nuts-encrusted bowls.

Tim looks back at me, straightening his spine like *hit me*. Waiting for it, like all the ugly things I want to say are already out there, hanging in the air like toxic smoke. I press my lips together as if that will keep the words sealed up.

He brushes past me, taking up more space than he needs to, cracks open a formula can, sloshes a bottle full to the top and puts it in the microwave, whistling under his breath. Cal's head bobs up and down over his shoulder, round blue eyes staring at me.

"How is it that all you do is screw up?"

He caps the bottle, shakes it, collapses back down on the couch, kicking his legs out onto the scarred coffee table, resting the baby's head on his thigh. "Sometimes I screw around. Clearly."

"Don't you dare do that." The baby sneezes and formula sprays. Tim cleans his little face with the bottom of his T-shirt. "Don't pull your la-la-la *everything's funny if you look at it the right way* act."

"What else am I supposed to do?" he asks, suddenly heated.

"Gosh, I don't know, Tim. What's your plan?"

"I don't have a fucking plan, Alice. It's been less than a week."

"You're going to have to do better than that. I can't fix this for you."

"Sorry – did I forget when I even *asked* you to?"

I'm pacing. Cal sneezes again, this time gushing Tim's face.

"Could be – sounds like you have a talent for forgetting key moments in your –"

"What's with the sneezing?" he interrupts, wiping his

face. "D'you think he's sick?"

"No, I think you have him too flat. You've got to prop up his head more."

Tim edges his knee up a little.

"Like this." I take his arm and move it so Cal's resting in the crook of his elbow. "And tilt the bottle like this or he gets too much air."

"You're good at this." His voice is resigned.

"I would be, wouldn't I?" I step back. The baby wriggles, and one hand smacks Tim in the eye. He raises his hand to cup it and Calvin – Calvin, right? – evidently thinks Tim is letting go of him, because he does that startle-reflex motion, neck stiffening, hands flying out to his sides, eyes wide and shocked.

"Let me have him," I say, practically dragging him out of Tim's arms.

His face has gone whiter. "What the hell was that? Why'd he do that? Was that, like, a fit or something? Did I hurt him?"

I'm pulling a blanket from the side of the couch, a red one with scary sock monkey heads all over it, turning it, folding the bottom, one arm down, fold, the other arm up, wrap around. Basic baby burrito. A life skill, by now.

"You wrap him like this," I say wearily. "Makes him feel safe. And, for God's sake wash your hands."

I survey the apartment. "When was the last time you did laundry? I'll bring you over two baskets – one for

him and one for you and – do you have a pad of paper? I'll make a list. You can probably get everything at Target, but –"

Tim's studying me. "I hate this," he says quietly.

"Too bad," I say shortly. "He's all yours. Congratulations."

He does look all Tim's. The red hair, the stormy eyes, bluer than Tim's, the long string-bean skinny body. I don't see much of that girl in him, but he's a baby, still a blank canvas. Besides, I barely looked at her.

"Not him," Tim says. "This. I don't want this."

"Sorry, stud. You don't wrap it before you tap it" – air quotes – "*this* is what you get."

He winces, opens his mouth as if to argue, then says quietly, "I don't need baby tips from you, Alice." He swallows, and then looks at me squarely. "That's not what I want. With us."

"Us?" I say, and sigh. "There isn't an us. There's a you and a me."

"And baby makes three?" he suggests.

"You're hilarious. I'll take your laundry back for now and throw it in with ours, but I'll be damned if I'm folding it for you."

"Cut it out. I'm not one of your brothers. No way are you washing my boxers."

I continue as if he hadn't spoken. "Have you worked out a schedule with this –"

"Can you keep holding him for a sec? I gotta hit the

head. Or puke. Something."

He unfolds himself from the couch, slowly, as if the movement hurts his stomach.

Calvin stares at me, his barely there reddish eyebrows pulling together, half worried, half cross. All Tim. I pull one miniscule hand out of the blanket, set my finger in his palm.

"Boy. The stork really dropped *you* off on the wrong doorstep," I tell him.

In six months, I'll have another sister. Or brother. Nine of us. Patsy's not even two. Where's the new baby even going to sleep? Patsy's still in Mom and Dad's room. Do Andy and I get him or her bunking with us, while Tim and Calvin occupy the apartment that was going to be my getaway?

Damn it.

"The last thing we need around here is another kid to worry about," I say out loud.

I don't notice that Tim has returned until I hear his quiet question. "Are you talking Cal, or me?"

I hand over the baby.

"Figure it out. Babe."

Chapter Twenty-six

Can't face Jase, my best friend. Can't face Samantha, my oldest friend. Can't face me.

Tell Nan? My folks? Right.

Can barely look at Cal. Do all the tending-to-him stuff without meeting his eyes. It helps that he can't focus his.

Dom's out on his ten-day shtick with the fishing fleet, so I call Jake. He's at work, staying late at Hodges with the soccer team. First day of school. First day of practice. He lets me in the back door of the gym. A door I used to walk through all the time, two schools ago. Before I snuck a joint in the music closet, left in a panic, didn't notice the spark that had jumped from my sputtering lighter to the cheap-ass choir robe fabric – and nearly burned down Hodges, crenelated buttresses and all.

"Signed you in for backboard time," he says. "You can use my racquet."

He doesn't even wait for me to say anything, just takes the handle of the car seat out of my hands and winks at me. "I'll handle this guy. Go get your head on straight.

Head to my office when you've blown off enough steam. I *know* you know the way there. Right near detention."

∘ ∘ ∘ •

Text from Brad: **Ally-baby. Got carried away the other week. No hard feelings? Come for a run? I can at least train you. I will talk! LOL.**

Attached is a shot of him doing burpees at CrossFit.

Dad has this saying: "Sometimes the best solution is no solution."

He means: Don't rush into decisions you're not ready to make.

Not: Decide not to decide.

I text back. **Nice shirt. It looks better on the floor. :)**

Brad. No big surprises. No dark corners.

Another of Dad's sayings: Less drama, more dishes.

My fingers move before I think. Brad doesn't care if I think. *What* I think. **Will you be too beat for the beach?**

He answers with a picture of a Scottie begging.

I'm not a lapdog, like your Cro-Magnons.

My thumb freezes over the phone for only an instant. Then I send him a thumbs-up emoji.

When I reach Brad on the beach, his face breaks into a big smile, then he shuffles his feet in the sand. "I didn't think you'd really show. I was a moron the other day, right?"

"You were." I flop on my back, start stretching out my hamstring. Brad wraps his hand around my ankle, inclines in a little, lengthening the stretch.

"I thought," he starts, then shakes his head, "you were ditching me for some other guy. Like that bud of your brother's who's always around now. Jealous, y'know? But I thought about it, talked to the Wall-man. Realized that wasn't it. I mean, you barely have time for me. When would you be hanging with anyone else?"

It's a windy day, whitecaps curling on the water, distant buoys rocking wildly, rose hip bushes blowing in the dunes. The ocean is dark green gray. The sky dull. A puff of wind gusts sand into my face, into my mouth, and I cough.

Brad uncaps a bottle of orange-flavored Gatorade and hands it to me with the swift efficiency of a nurse passing a scalpel.

After a few deep swallows, I look him in the eye. "I meant it. We can't date anymore. We are not on a break, or whatever. We're done, that way."

"I heard you," he says, after a second. "But I think you'll change your mind."

"I won't."

"You're stubborn, Alice." He takes a swig of Gatorade. "But you're wrong here. I can wait until you figure it out."

"Look, I'm not going to lead you on —"

"We'll just see who's doing the leading. I'm gonna give you a head start on the run, 'kay?"

I squint at him, my jaw tight. "Don't baby me."

Babe. Baby.

I shake my head to let everything – boys and babies – blow out to sea in the cold, sandy wind.

"I don't need a head start." I skip the rest of the stretching, use pure annoyance to power my steps and am a good distance away before I realize he gave me a head start anyhow.

Because he thinks he knows what I need better than I do.

Chapter Twenty-seven

Knock. Knock. Knockknockknockknock.

Barely light out. Before I even open the door, I know it's Jase. Who else is up this early but enterprising teen dads like me and guys with a crazy-ass training schedule – and/or a paper route. When I whip open the door, he's resting his forearm against the jamb, rubbing his hip.

I'm holding a kid against my shoulder.

One of those moments that *has* to be a dream because this is *not* my life and I want a rewind and a refund. Then Cal squirms and Jase reaches out to steady him, hand on back, eyes meeting mine.

"Ride along?"

This is how he knows I'm probably awake. After his dad had the accident, when Samantha broke things off for a while, we got into a habit. Once or twice a week, he'd show up early outside my parents' house and I'd do the paper route thing with him. Toss the papers that were on my side. Half the time we didn't even talk. When we did, it was about George's fear of tsunamis, or the new

235

shipment of paint at the hardware store, or how to get rid of athlete's foot.

He has the car seat out of my car, buckled into his in nothing flat. Pulls into Gas and Go and orders two large black coffees for me without having to ask what I want. Tosses me a sleeve of Drake's cakes and an apple.

"Mom worries you're not eating enough."

"Yeah, gotta keep my energy up now that I'm breastfeeding."

He grins, turning right out of the gas station. "Jesus, Tim. Were you planning on mentioning this any time before I – or the baby – went to college?"

We pull onto Caldicott Street and he inclines his head toward my window – my turn to throw. I wing the paper at the stoop and it skids and nearly falls off the side.

"I was working up to it. Not because I thought you'd ream me, just –" So tired of being the fuckup.

He's squinting, lining up the perfect shot out the other side, a much farther toss than mine. And yes, *smack,* centered on the mat.

"I could do that if you'd let me use a tennis racket, you know."

I hit against the backboard at Hodges last night until my arm ached so bad, the racquet was too heavy to lift. Trailed after Jake to a meeting, then went to his house and ate about ten bowls of pasta and meatballs while Jake and his partner traded Cal back and forth between them

like the world's most coveted baseball card (a 1909 Honus Wagner, apparently – Jake is a baseball fanatic).

"No doubt." Jase pulls the car forward to the next house, which is one Samantha, Nan, and I used to call The White Witch's House when we were little, because the whole front yard is cluttered with statues of lions and rearing horses and dudes on horseback and this fountain with a kid peeing water into it.

We're quiet for the next four houses. He pops some cinnamon gum. I pound the first cup of coffee in three scalding gulps, scarf one of the coffee cakes, fiddle with the radio, flipping channels until he reaches over and punches the off button. Our little ritual.

Jase doesn't have a lot of nervous habits. But now he's biting his lip, edging around in his seat like the peeling leather's stuffed with barbed wire and hot rocks.

"What's doing?" I ask, staring straight ahead.

"Wishing life were more like football." He tosses another paper.

"But then *I'd* suck at it even worse."

"Yeah, but . . . you know, the rules are defined." He lets out an unconvincing laugh. "Chaos, but controlled chaos. You have some discipline, you use your head, you put the team first – it works." He sighs. "Everything's such a mess since Dad got hurt."

I grope for something wise to say.

"Yeah, it blows."

Fail miserably.

"But," I add, "still seems like it's working. I mean – you're training, in the game, still showing up for stuff. The rest of the family – it's working. Right?"

Christ, now *I'm* asking *him* to tell *me* stuff is okay.

"Dad and Mom say just to keep doing what we're all doing. Every day I wake up and try to figure out what matters most." He's pushed the gas pedal a little too hard and we've gone past the right house. Jase reverses, moves back, and lobs the paper onto the stoop.

Another genius throw.

"Getting a scholarship? Samantha? The store? Grades? Trying to help keep things sane at home? What about next year – assuming I can go to college – are things gonna be on an even keel with my family by then? And if not, can I really just take off?"

"Have you talked to your dad about this?"

Jase hands me two copies of the paper and indicates the house nearest me. "They fight over the newspaper, the couple who lives there. Used to stand on the stoop and practically engage in hand-to-hand combat. Now I just give 'em an extra for free. Dad and Mom say to focus on school and ball. But, the store is . . ."

Out it comes in a rush – Garrett's Hardware is circling the drain, fast. Bank loans coming due. Not enough income. Not enough to hire anyone to cover. Where Joel is. Mr. Garrett's medical crap. Jase's football stuff. Alice,

what Alice plans to do.

I hold up a hand halfway through this last, halting part, which Jase doesn't even see, because he's pulled over; talking with his head tipped back against the seat, eyes shut, like saying this all is shitty-tasting medicine he has to force down his throat.

"I got this, Jase. I can cover the store. No problem. I mean – what the hell else do I have going on?"

He starts laughing. "Sure. Life's just one big party for you. Except for, oh, him." He points a thumb toward the backseat.

"Well, isn't there a 'take your kid to work' day? He's portable. Weighs less than your gym bag. Besides – it's only a few weeks with him. A month, maybe. Then he's history." As I say this, I hear this little snuffle from the back, Cal moving around, making himself known.

Jase studies me for a second. "A month, huh? Why wait that long? Doorsteps all over the place around here."

I laugh. "You'd have to do the toss – no way would I get the landing right."

Glance to the backseat myself. Kid's kicked that blanket off his feet. Doesn't like the covered-up thing. The socks will be next.

Jase ticks off the other things I'm supposed to be doing too, meetings, GED, and I shoot them down like we're playing that videogame Andy and Duff are so crazy about, *Allied Aces* or whatever the hell it's called. "And you don't

need to pay me. I've still got my allowance, and I've cut waaaaaay down on expenses, if you know what I mean."

Got my allowance through December, anyway. Well before the new year, Cal'll be gone and I can forget this whole chapter. Maybe Pop will be impressed with my initiative here anyway. Singlehandedly saved struggling store – that's got to look better to him than Stayed Sober. Or Sired Son.

"What about the other night?" Jase asks, bending down to my feet, where another stack of papers is tied up, pulling a Swiss army knife to cut the rope.

Yeah. That.

"I fucked up," I say. "But not all the way."

He presses his lips together, looks weirdly like Alice for a second, puts the car into gear, and rolls forward a few houses. I try to read his profile, but get served a helping of Jase Blank Face, his bland, *I'm just a jock* look. He throws yet another newspaper, another flawless-without-even-trying toss and, hell knows why but there's that rage, white-bright as lightning.

I slouch down in my seat and mutter, "Hard to explain this crap to someone who never makes mistakes. The guy who fixes everything. *Text me if the plunger breaks.*"

Jase balls up one hand on the steering wheel, sets his jaw. Stares straight ahead for a second, and then finally starts in on me, his voice low and furious. "Stop it. I can't even talk to you when you pull *this* crap. It's like you climb

into a time-out corner, with the *I'm some poor misbegotten creature you can't possibly understand* garbage. You know me better than that. Like everything I touch turns to gold? Jesus, Tim, I wish."

My face heats. "I'm sorry, I —"

"Don't be sorry. Be — here. Instead of in some swamp in your head." He rubs a hand over his face. "You want mistakes? I got plenty." Turns to me, props his elbow next to the headrest. "Apparently I should have made a collage video of my game highlights and uploaded it to YouTube *months* ago, so coaches could review it for the scholarship thing. Didn't. No one told me to, and I was too dumb or preoccupied or whatever to think ahead and come up with it myself. I mean, all the colleges that might work for me aren't going to be sending scouts to Stony Bay, Connecticut. But I didn't plan ahead. Speaking of which, Sam and I nearly — um —" His face turns this deep dull red color. "We were at the bonfire and — I didn't have —"

"Oh," I say. "Yikes, man."

"Sam's mom would love that, right? If I couldn't get to college and the baby in the car seat was mine next time? Just what she expects from me. To stupidly blow away my future and Samantha's too." His voice is bitter.

Exactly what she probably expects. He's one of "those Garretts" to Samantha's mom, like I'm "What now Tim" with my folks.

Silence while I try to figure out how to say I'm sorry

241

in a way that actually means something and Jase rolls up about ten more newspapers, snapping rubber bands around them.

"I'm right, aren't I?" he says finally. "I mean, you know her better than I do, but —"

"You're right. It's prolly what she expects," I admit. "My advice: If you're going to mess up, score points for creativity. Do it in a way ol' Gracie would never imagine. Don't give her the satisfaction."

He grins, anger gone like it was never there. How does he *do* that?

"This *was* bad. I feel guilty, Sam feels guilty. It's been a lousy week. Plus her mom's doing something, putting pressure on her, and I don't know how or where or why. Every time I ask, she just changes the subject."

"I'm sure you have ways of getting her to talk," I say mildly.

Jase jiggles his leg, and then winces. "I haven't even told her what I've told you. She's got swim tryouts this week —"

"Garrett, the spare-the-girlfriend-spare-the-boyfriend junk never works out for you two. Come on."

He passes me a paper and I toss it haphazardly, so it lands in a bush. I have to get out and retrieve it. The slamming car door wakes up Cal, who starts bawling.

Jase pulls over and I drag the kid out and do the patting-the-back thing. He'd better not be hungry, because I forgot to bring a bottle or the diaper bag or anything. I put my

knuckle in his mouth and he sucks on it, loud slurpy sounds.

"All that with Dad was probably what was going on when Alice jumped all over you the other day," Jase says, slanting me a look. Cal's clenching and unclenching his fists in my shirt and I concentrate on unbending his little fingers and freeing myself, heat rushing to my face so fast, my ears burn.

"Uh – what?" Alice wouldn't have said anything about the beach to Jase – would she?

Fuck, should *I*? But there's nothing to say. Me and Alice = nowhere now.

I get Cal buckled back in and slide into the passenger seat.

"Getting on your back about Cal." Jase shifts gears as we head onto Shore Road, looping around by the river. "It's not like her to play the blame game like that. Things are getting under her skin these days."

Not the moment to think about Alice's skin. Anything of hers.

He's focused hard on the road, even though it's pin-straight and we're clocking two miles an hour. He clears his throat. "Maybe not the best time to – uh – start something with Alice."

"What, you don't think my plan to sex it up with your sister, make another baby, and move us all into the garage apartment is flawless?"

"Dial down the default-dick mode, Mase. I know Al

well enough to know no one gets close without permission. It's just – forget it. I don't know why I brought it up."

"Hey, not a big deal. But Jase, Jesus, tell Samantha what's up. Saying nothing about real shit – that's the Mason family way, which, trust me, is a one-way ticket through the Looking Glass to the land of up is down, wrong is right."

And like a show-and-tell of what I just said, I spot a figure standing on the sidewalk three houses away from us, windbreaker hood up, shoulders hunched against the river breeze, one hand twisting a lock of her hair, just a little lighter, but unmistakably similar to Cal's. Nano. Right in front of her, slouched casually against the bed of a beat-up old dune buggy, longish hair blowing back, good old Troy Rhodes.

I watch him tap her on the back with the hand nearer me, and I can't see – is he slipping something into her windbreaker pocket with the other hand? Fuckity fuck fuck.

I duck down.

Jase looks at me quizzically. "You planning on lying on the floorboards and asking me to gun the car? What happened to getting things out in the open?"

"Do as I say, not as I do. Now drive."

Chapter Twenty-eight

For the next week, I manage to avoid Alice, except in the most extreme, strangers-passing-in-the-night way, like when my car has hers blocked in, or I come out to help her unload groceries, which I do even though she tells me she can do it all herself. On one of my non-Cal days, I'm jogging on the beach, and there she is in the distance, cooling down. I play through this whole lame-ass movie in my head where she hurts herself and I have to carry her to her car and – there my imagination stalls out because the minute I make it to the Bug in my mind, I rewind and replay that day at the beach and think of all the things I might have done – or even said – if I'd known for sure that was my one shot.

For the next week, I almost never bump into Tim. Evasive maneuvers – my new favorite pastime. Forget schoolwork, and rotation at the hospital, the forty-thousand pounds of paperwork that go with moving Dad to the rehab, the

unpaid hospital bills piling up. There's running as though I'm being chased by cheetahs, going to the batting cage with the baffled Brad as though I'm training for the majors, and taking care of my brothers and sisters like Mary Poppins on amphetamines. I keep waiting for Tim to show up with Cal and ask for help, but he doesn't. I keep waiting to get used to seeing him climbing the steps of the garage apartment with the car seat, but I don't. When I look out the kitchen window while I'm doing dishes, I think I see him on the steps, but he never snaps the outdoor light on, and without the glow of a cigarette to place him in space, he could be only a shadow. It's a rainy, cloudy September too, cool for Connecticut, and there are times when I think the last time the sun shone was with him on McNair Beach.

"Al," Andy says, her voice drifting through the dark in our bedroom, scantily lit by the blue lava lamp night-light, one of the few things we agreed on when we redid the room two years ago.

"Mmm."

"When I see Kyle in the hallway –"

"Ugh, Ands, not Kyle again."

"When I see Kyle in the hallway," she perseveres, "should I ignore him? Like, obviously? Look away or make a face or glare at him?"

I honestly can't remember where the Kyle saga left off – just that he's either playing games or is oblivious. Either

way, he's no good for Andy.

"Just live your life. Don't glare, because then he'll think it matters too much to you."

Sigh from my sister. "It kind of does matter."

"Don't give him that power. Really. It won't be worth it."

And what, exactly, am I doing with Tim, while handing out this sage advice to my sister?

It kind of does matter.

o ₒ o

"Honey, I'm home."

I've wanted it, dreaded it, known it can't be avoided, and here it is: Tim and me, working together at Garrett's Hardware.

Here *he* is, striding into the back office, carrying a large cup of coffee with a blueberry muffin balanced precariously on top, assorted baby paraphernalia, including Cal in his car seat, and a greasy-looking brown paper bag. He hands me the last, drops everything else down on the counter. (Except Cal.)

And I make no sense because the moment I see him, a wave of sheer happiness rolls in, swamps me completely. His hair's shorter, freshly trimmed, He's wearing an olive-green T-shirt that brings out the fire in his hair, and worn-in jeans. Somehow, he looks less lost, there's something competent and confident in the way he sets Cal in the car seat down.

I fumble for Dad's reading glasses, which I've been using as I sit at his desk, crunching numbers, making lists. When I shove them onto my nose, Tim goes blurry, except for his wicked smile.

"Hullo, Alice."

The wave rolls on, snatching my breath too, because I don't, can't, say anything. I look down. Scribble *Make appt. at eye doctor* on the to-do list unfurling in front of me.

"Vegan breakfast burrito from Doane's. I had no idea they made those. They acted kinda surprised too."

I write the date at the top of the list. Don't look up because I'm just so busy.

"Here I am to save the day. You're free to go." He studies me, head tilted, grin broadening as he takes in the glasses. "Ah, the librarian look. A classic for a reason."

Now the wave sucks right back out, leaves behind a jumble of anger and sadness – because once again, one small turn of events – a car crash, a baby – and the whole landscape has changed. I keep tripping over things that just aren't where I expect them to be.

I look at him over the glasses. "We're playing it this way, are we?"

He passes me the coffee, which turns out to be an extra-large cinnamon mocha cappuccino, my favorite. "The Doane's barista guy knew this about you, for some reason. I assumed you'd want the biggest size."

"Don't pull the evasive maneuver. I'm immune."

Hypocritical to the max. But I can't seem to stop it. I ball my hands into fists under the desk.

Tim sighs, wedges his hip against the edge of the desk, then says in an overly patient voice, "Playing it what way, Alice?"

"Like everything's carrying on the way it was before. Like – Calvin – didn't exist."

"That would be hard, even with my well-honed denial skills, since Cal is right here in front of us. Got a better plan? Hit me."

The truth comes crashing out. "I'd love to."

"Yeah, got that down last time we actually spoke. I'm sure you would. Get in fucking line." Still the relaxed lean against the desk, but his voice has roughened.

I take off the glasses, rub my eyes, stare down at the list in front of me like that's the only thing that matters in my world.

"I'm not disappearing in a puff of smoke if you shut your eyes, Alice, if that's what you're hoping. I'm here. He's here. But you don't need to be here. Go – study. Administer CPR. Stick pins in a voodoo doll of me. Whatever you need to do. You're free. I'm on for today."

"So am I."

"Alice," he says. "It doesn't have to be both of us."

"But here we are. So let's just keep this civilized, shall we?" I thrust the glasses onto my nose again, tilt my chin up so they don't slide right off.

He bursts out laughing. Then salutes me. "Whatever you say, Professor."

I ignore that, even though my cheeks heat, even though my hand is suddenly tingling with the urge to slap him. Something I've never done to anyone. Not even Joel.

"You're right, though," I manage. "At this point, the store really doesn't need two people manning it. So from here on we should come up with a schedule, some rules."

"Again with the rules. You're so rule-based. Is that a nurse thing or an oldest daughter thing?"

"It's a practical thing," I say. "I'm assuming you've worked out some kind of a schedule with Hester?"

"Does 'you get the baby when I'm about to lose my mind' count as a schedule?"

"If that's all you've got."

He spreads his hands.

I outline a plan, working around classes and clinicals – maybe I can have someone take notes for me – I can keep it all going if I do that. Then we sketch out his work days. "So basically, four days a week, alternating mornings and afternoons," I finish. "Stock delivery is Monday and Friday, so if you can manage not to have Cal with you then –"

"No overlap with me and you, Alice?"

"Not much need for it, is there?"

"That would depend on what need we're talking about." He does that stupid smirk thing.

"Professional. You asshole."

"Alice said a bad word." Singsong.

I drop my pen, bend forward, planting my hands flat on the desk – the better not to slap him. "Tell me something, Boy Most Likely To. Why is it you are the biggest sarcastic idiot when you are entirely and deeply in the wrong?"

The second the words are out, I know I've gone too far.

Tim opens his mouth, shuts it, looks up at the ceiling, turns to go. Stops, comes back, bends over the desk, landing hard on his elbows. "I did something I'm not proud of. Yep. But you are not my judge or my sponsor or my pop. You want to keep things professional? Fine. I'm not even sure what that means in your dictionary, but in mine, it doesn't mean making judgey personal jabs. I did not do this to you. I did not even do it to me. I did it to Hester and this kid. Especially to him. So my penance, or punishment – if that's what you're looking for – is to take care of him. Which I am now going to do. Out front. Where you will find me if you want to continue our *professional* discussion about when stock deliveries are. Which I already know, because I've been working here all summer long – and I only black things out when I'm wasted. Which I do not happen to be at the moment. Although, if you'd like to take my car keys, be my guest."

He scoops up the car seat and stalks to the door.

"You *gave* me your car keys!" I call after him.

∘ • ∘ •

Three hours later, the store's still dead. As is the air between us. You wouldn't think you could completely avoid each other in an eight-hundred-square-foot space, but we succeed. I rip open the boxes full of new deliveries out back, wielding the box cutter, waving Tim off.

He backs away, stone-faced.

As I restock, he sits behind the counter, studying trigonometry, feeding Cal, drumming the callused fingers of one hand on his thigh, changing Cal's diaper, biting his thumbnail, rocking the car seat with one foot – in the shoes I gave him – while frowning over a textbook, jumping up every once in a while to refill his coffee cup.

I arrange and rearrange a short and simple string of words in my head, but they never make it all the way to my lips. Five words. "I was wrong. I'm sorry." Every time I head toward Tim, he busies himself with something else. There's just not that much to do around here, trust me.

Coming back from a totally unnecessary mail run, I find him trying to wedge open the bottom of our broken cash register with a screwdriver – pointless. "Don't bother with that."

He mutters under his breath, "At least I can fix this."

In goes the screwdriver once again. He's trying. Cal squawks a little and Tim again rocks the seat distractedly, still wrestling with the cash register.

He's trying.

"Look," I start. "I was –"

He looks up at me, then away, doing the whole muscle-twitching-in-jaw thing so beloved of angry boys. Then turns his back — actually physically turns his back — on me and keeps on jamming the screwdriver into the bottom of the register. At least it's not into my head.

"Tim," I start again.

More screwdriver action. Back turned.

"Never mind."

Brad stops in for last-minute tips on his way to an interview for a part-time training job at the gym. Tim scowls at him over the top of his civics textbook, highlighting away in multiple colors, while I hand Brad a comb, get a stain off his sleeve, etc. Tim's hunched so far down in the seat, feet kicked up on the counter, that Brad doesn't even notice him.

"Kiss for luck, Liss?" he says, popping the collar of his shirt.

I fold it back down. "Remember to call your boss by his name, not 'Big Mac' during the interview."

"You forgot to put a note with a smiley face in his lunch box," Tim says, without looking up from his civics book as the door closes behind Brad.

"Nans, I need you," I mutter into my cell, on break out behind Garrett's, slouching on the back stoop.

My twin's voice goes instantly high-pitched. "Why? Do you need bail money?"

"Jesus Christ, Nan. When have I ever needed *bail* money?"

"Well, I don't know. You've been gone for weeks and I've hardly heard anything from you. I just thought . . . I don't know." She sighs.

"Well, I've missed you too. Jesus. Can I see you —" Uh, where? *Not* ready to spring *Mason Family: A New Generation* on the parents. So I say, "What are Ma and Pop up to these days?"

"Who knows? She's doing all that Garden Club fall planting stuff. He's . . . just busy all the time. Till six when he heads for the 'home office,' then goes comatose in his recliner. So it's safe to come here, unless you want to meet in an underground garage or something."

I laugh. "Not only do I not need bail money, kid, but I haven't become a government mole. Can I come over in a little while, during lunch?"

"Why? I've got Key Club this afternoon, and I was going to go to the library and —" The twin-psychic connection thing is bullshit, but her voice is high-pitched again, nervous. Guilty conscience much?

"Blow off Key Club. This is important."

"I'm home," she says simply, after this pause where I can hear her breathing a little fast. "Come anytime."

I don't even hear the bell ring when Tim's Hester comes

in, as though she materialized in the room, hovering near the garden tools.

When I do look up and see her, she's watching me, her dark eyebrows drawn together.

"Oh. It's you. I didn't recognize you without your bikini."

We're studying each other like there's going to be a midterm. She's tall with longish, straight brown hair, wearing sort of plain, old-fashioned clothes, blue skirt, white long-sleeved T-shirt, pale blue sweater. Almost like a uniform. She has one of those old-fashioned faces, too, heart-shaped, sweet, like something you'd see inside a locket. I try to picture her with Tim and I can't bring that into focus at all and *why* am I even doing that.

Stranger still is that she's chewing her lip and looking me up and down and maybe sort of doing the same thing.

Pause.

"Where's Tim? Where's the baby?" she looks around a little wildly, like I've maybe done away with both of them.

"Cal's right here."

"It's Calvin," she corrects. "That's the name I gave him. After Calvin O'Keefe."

"*A Wrinkle in Time*," I say. "My first book boyfriend."

"I loved him too," Hester says. "Obviously. He was so smart. And he liked the awkward girl. And –"

"He had red hair," I finish.

Oh God. Is she in love with Tim?

255

Her hand moves to her neckline, and she pulls on her necklace, a plain gold chain with a single pearl. "Are you – you and Tim –"

"I'm a friend of his." Not sure if that's strictly true at the moment. "That's all."

"I'm –" She falters. Understandably. "Calvin's mother. Obviously. I mean, of course you know that. I thought Tim was expecting me. I'm only half an hour late."

We both check the clock, which at least breaks up our staring contest.

"He's late himself, actually." A lash of worry whips up my spine. It doesn't seem like Tim, who is apparently making a mission out of not asking for baby help, to abandon Cal for long. Or at all. I had to kind of insist on him leaving the sleeping Cal behind when he went to get lunch.

Even then, he actually started to tell me what to do if he wakes up, more talkative than he'd been all day. "Look, I'll be fast with the pickup. I've got an errand to run afterward, but it won't take me long. And Hester should be here any minute. He always gets a little freaked out when he first opens his eyes, if he doesn't see anyone there, you have to pick him up right away, or he gets cranking and –" He stopped himself. "I'm sure you've got this."

Do I tell Hester to wake Cal up and get going? Pour her a cup of coffee and talk books with her?

"So – have you known Tim a long time?" She's toying with her necklace again.

Now, as Hester pauses mid-sentence, there's a gasping, indrawn breath from behind the counter, then a piercing scream. She practically rockets to the ceiling and back.

I hurry to scoop up Cal, already blotchy, teary, legs rigid. "*Shh. Shh.* Got you," I whisper into his ear. He snuffles, bumping his head into my cheek for a second, then resting against it, fisting a hand in my hair. I'm holding him, swaying back and forth and he's giving those shivery little baby sobs. Hester stares at us for a moment. "It's so constant. He cries *all the time*."

He seems pretty mellow to me, but I'm not with him 24/7.

She takes him, with a sigh, and is fumbling in the diaper bag one-handed when Tim returns, whistling, with a white cardboard box of takeout from Esquidero's, splotched with grease, the peppery-spice smell of their signature curly fries heavy in the air.

Hester hands me Cal.

I'm holding him reflexively, stunned, to tell the truth. She just passed him on over, like he was Hot Potato and her turn was up.

Now she's pouring out the words on Tim.

"Thank you so much for holding on to him for so long. You honestly saved my life. My sanity anyway."

Tim nods, without saying anything, looks over at me, face unreadable.

"Have you ever had any STDs? I forgot to ask the other day," Hester continues.

My eyebrows hit my hairline. Tim, who has scarfed a French fry out of the bag, coughs.

"Um. No?" Then he clears his throat and repeats, not as a question this time, "No."

"Did you finish filling out the medical history? We need to get that in as soon as possible."

"E-mailed it to you last night. That's everything from me, so we should be able to really get a move on this, right?"

"Oh. Good. That's good. Yes."

They sound like polite strangers on an elevator. But here's Cal, with his Mason hair and his wide, innocent Hester eyes.

"Put him in the basket. Thanks, Alice," she says briskly. She has a raspy voice, almost as though she's been a pack-a-day smoker for a long time, which I somehow doubt is the case.

Then there's a weird pass-off thing, where Tim, with an exasperated glance from Hester to me, takes Cal out of my arms, hands him to Hester, and she puts him in the Moses basket, straightens up, looks back and forth between us, then focuses on Tim again.

"My grandfather really wants to meet you. Do you want to come over for dinner – tomorrow night? Or the night after? Or do you . . . have plans with . . . someone?"

Her voice goes higher on the last part, the words running together fast.

"I've got nothing going on. Nothing at all."

"That's good. My grandfather's a great cook. So . . ." She hesitates, as though she's waiting for Tim to fill in, make this any less awkward.

But he only adjusts the blanket around Cal, skims a tear away from the baby's cheek, nudges it with a knuckle, gives him a little smile.

Hester half waves to me, scoots toward the door, bending to pick up the car seat. Then she tries to open the door with her foot, with the basket in one hand and the seat in the other, bumps both against the wall. Cal lets out a thin wail that gets louder.

"Oh for Chrissake," Tim mutters, striding over to take the basket, open the door with his hip, and usher her out.

The outside of my parents' house is "cheery." Not a word I usually use, but there really is no other. Ma's got yellow flowers blooming along the walkway. There's this little statue of a girl in a polka-dotted dress bending over with a watering can, and then another kid, in overalls, flopped back against our lamppost, blowing a horn for some weird-ass reason. They've been there as long as I can remember, but their paint's still shiny. Does Ma repaint them? Freakin' depressing thought.

I push open the front door. "Kid?"

My sister bursts out of the living room.

Unlike the house, Nan is totally different from just a few days ago. She never even wears makeup, and now she's got dark eyeliner, bloodred lipstick, a black T-shirt, and white jeans. Her hair is chopped short just below her chin.

"Nans. You look different."

"Different, like, better, right? As in incredibly chic and urbane and not like I'm from some dinky Connecticut town?"

"Right. Like that. You look . . ." Guilty, honestly. But it's Nan's curse that she constantly looks that way. The girl could tell the stone-cold truth and come off guilty as hell. The house smells the same, like musty stuff covered by Tropical Breeze Febreze. Same old Thomas Kinkade crap paintings lining the wall. She leads me into the living room, like I'm a guest.

Here it's all Tim and Nan Are Twins shots, each one worse than the last.

"Because that's the idea – new Nan, new leaf, moving on." She's chattering. Also plumping the pillows and straightening coasters and all busy-busy-busy.

I'm barely listening, because what I'm mostly thinking is that I'm a stranger in my own home. Like my life has already left all this behind, and it's some museum I'm visiting, trying not to disturb the velvet ropes, the Hummel stuff everywhere, the window seat with a tiny village on it

and a mirror that's supposed to be a lake, and a bunch of houses with windows Ma plugs in so they light up at night. She puts cotton on the roofs in the winter to look like snow. Now there's some miniature pumpkins scattered around and a tiny bale or two of hay. It's possible that my ma, like me, like Nano, does not have enough to do with her hands.

"What's wrong?" Nan asks.

I collapse onto the couch, plop my feet on the coffee table, knocking to the ground a pile of books like *Chicken Soup for the Whatever* and *Who Moved My Cheese?*

"Well, yeah, here's the deal." As I give her the details, quick and dirty, she methodically chomps her fingernails down. When I wind up, Nan gusts a long, exhausted sigh, like she's been doing all the talking and is just. So. Tired.

"Say something. What? You'd rather you had to post bail than find out you're an aunt to a son of mine?"

She steeples her fingers, lowers her forehead onto them.

Shades of Pop.

When she finally says something, it's the last thing I expect.

"How are you sure he's yours?"

Chapter Twenty-nine

"Wha-at?"

"Tim," Nan says, all exasperated. "You can't possibly have been the only ginger guy at Ellery Prep. What about that Mike McClasky guy you roomed with fall semester? The one with the pierced eyebrow? Why not him? How do you know this Hester is telling the truth?"

"What . . . you think she's come up with some con because I'm, like, such a great candidate for fatherhood? Ha."

"Well, I don't know." Nan plunks down on the sofa and reaches for the cut glass bowl Ma always keeps full of gumdrops and Swedish fish and begins pulling out a school of the suckers, holding up one after another as she counts off. "You have no recall of the party. You only remember seeing her in classes. You didn't hear anything about this pregnancy, which had to have been major gossip."

"I was booted. How the hell would I hear?"

"You're not in touch with *anyone?* Not one single solitary person passing on the latest Ellery drama?"

"Nah. The crowd I hung with? I barely remember them, and I'm sure likewise. It's not like we're all pal-sy online."

Nan's troubled expression lasts only a second before it's traded for deep suspicion.

"I'm trying to protect you here, Tim. This girl . . . I don't know what she's up to, but it doesn't sound right to me."

She scarfs down a few fish, then offers me the candy bowl.

I shake my head, shuddering. Gummy crap – give me stale Peeps or Pixy Stix any day.

"How can you be sure?" she presses. "That this girl wasn't involved with some other guy who wouldn't take responsibility, and then decided to use you?"

"Because she's not that kind of girl? Because that's freakin' psychotic? Because I'm hardly known for taking responsibility?" I look around the room like one of the Hummel figurines has the key to convincing my surprisingly cynical sister that I'm Cal's dad. Even though by all rights I should be jumping at the idea that I might not be.

My eyes light on the bookshelf by the mantel where, sure enough, there's a baby picture of Nan and me – our first Christmas – propped against each other in a puffy pink armchair with a stuffed Rudolph at our feet. I'm dressed in a Santa suit, Nan as Mrs. Santa (nice, Ma – incestuous baby outfits). Of course, I've got the Santa hat on so no hair's visible, but still, there's that little chin cleft Dominic pointed out on Cal.

"He looks like me," I say finally.

I still don't have this "blood bond" thing with the kid, but after you've slept next to someone (me on the couch, Cal in the basket, my hand on his stomach half the night) and cleaned up after them and fed them and frickin' *worn* them, you're kinda tight with them.

"All babies pretty much look alike, Timmy."

All Patient Tone.

Patient gives me a rash. Subtext: *I know what's really going on here while you're wandering around in the dark.*

"Since when do you know shit about babies? '*Babies pretty much look alike, Tim,*'" I say, high and squeaky. "Right, Captain Infant Expert. The last time you were around one for any amount of time was *me*."

I expect her to get pissed and yell back. I *want* her to get as angry as I am, chuck it right back in my face. Instead, she hooks an arm around my waist. The sharp point of her chin digs into my collarbone. Nan never eats enough. That *I'm too fat* crap girls do.

Or is it actually drugs now?

I sigh. Release my fingers from fists. "He's my kid. I mean . . . it's not like I want this. Since when did you get all cynical? That's supposed to be my deal, Nano."

"You were always faking that," Nan says.

"BullSHIT," I say, on a startled laugh.

She picks up the Easter picture of us posed next to a chick the size of Godzilla in comparison. She's screaming

in it; I look zoned out. Now Nan wrinkles her freckled nose as she traces a finger over our bunny-ear hats, first mine, then hers. "How old were we when Mommy stopped with the dress-ups?"

"Fifteen or so. Kid, you're not four. Lay off the 'Mommy' jazz. That's not going to play with the sophisticated set. Makes you sound ridiculous, trust me."

She starts to laugh, tightens her arm around my waist. "You have no idea how much of a difference it makes not having you home." She lifts her face and, hell, I should've guessed it from the sound of her voice. She's crying.

"Hey." I tap her back awkwardly, drumming my fingers. "I know I'm a ray of happy sunshine, but how different can it really be?"

"There's no one to make me laugh. No spare change to scrounge out of the swear box without you being a supplier. There's no one to rearrange the Hummels in compromising positions." She sniffs and wipes her face with a swat of her wrist.

"Well, I grant you that was an important service I provided."

She looks up at me, all gray eyes spilling over, cheeks wet, lower lip quivering. The Fix Me face. Doesn't work as well as it used to, not since Cal. Who has no one else to fix him and honestly can't do it himself.

"Speaking of services, wanna itemize the ones ol' Troy Rhodes is providing for you?"

Nan jerks away like I'm a downed wire.

"Who told you? Samantha?"

"Nooo. Why would she know? I was under the impression you two weren't speaking."

Nan grabs a handful of Swedish fish and shovels them into her mouth. "Then who?"

"I spied you with my own little eye. What gives, Nan?"

She's still chewing the fish, points to her mouth like "I can't talk."

Once she finishes, and swallows, she folds her arms, and stares me down. "So, when do I get to meet Cal?"

"Don't pull this crap with me, Nan. You don't get to change the subject here."

That angry, hard voice? Dead ringer for Pop's.

"Why are we talking about me? You're the one with a *baby!*"

"What's going on in here?" asks an even voice from the door.

I don't have time to arrange my face, so Nan and I probably both look equally guilty as we turn to face Pop.

Hell, I forgot the time – nearly six. His tie's loosened, jacket still on. Thank God no scotch yet. But then, Ma isn't home to bring him the ice bucket. Don't think I've ever seen him get it himself.

"Hi, Daddy. Dad," Nan says, flicking me a glance.

"What's doin', Pop?"

He looks back and forth between us the way he did

when we were little and up to no good.

"We haven't seen you lately, Tim. In some kind of trouble?"

"Nope, all good. Just, you know, don't live here anymore. Checking in with Nano."

"Asking her for money?"

"No, Dad," from Nan, just as I say, "Nah, Pop." Then add, "The drug-running gig is really working out for me. Add in the pimping and I'm golden."

"Is that a joke? Is he joking?" Pop addresses Nan, who's fidgeting and turning red at the drug reference. Then to me: "Not seeing the humor."

"Not all that funny," I say. "Look, I'd better beat it. I have a − thing." I jerk my chin at my sister. "We'll talk about this new little project of yours later. Count on it."

Nan starts twisting at a hunk of her hair. I notice that she's twirled one on the other side so much that she's got this Rasta thing going on. Not the best look with the new do. She doesn't answer.

Pop claps me on the back, gives me a very small shove in the direction of the door. I'm half expecting him to pick me up by the collar and toss me out on the lawn. Instead he says, "I'll walk you to your car."

"What, to make sure I really leave?"

He actually steers me down the driveway. It's half prison march and half one of those scenes in some old flick where the dad dispenses fatherly advice. But ten will

get you twenty he's not slipping me some cash so I can take Mary Lou to the soda fountain for a milkshake.

We reach the Jetta. He stands there for a sec, his eyes darting around the street. I kinda expect cops to leap out of the Crosbys' bushes, clap cuffs on me, and shove me into the backseat of my own car.

Nothing but silence.

Pop, looking anywhere but at me.

Me, waiting for whatever he has to say.

We're not in his office, though, and I'm not under his roof. I prop my back against the car, cross my arms. If he can wait, I can wait.

And wait.

Pop edges his cell phone out of his pocket, glances at it, shoves it back in, more like a reflex than like he's actually checking. I scrape at a callus on my hand with a thumbnail. Some dry leaves blow across the street. The grass grows. Somewhere, a star is born.

Again with the cell phone check. How many important calls can the manager of the Stony Bay Building and Loan get?

"Pop. I've gotta head back to work. I took an hour off to come see Nan. Time's up now. Are we done?"

His lips compress and he looks at me, but doesn't say anything. Then, finally, "I've never understood you, Tim. Not one single day of your life."

What is there to say to that? *Ever try?*

"We're done," I say, and get into the driver's seat, shift into first, and pull away.

"So – just friends," Andy says, leaning her elbows on the counter next to the scattered pieces of the cash register. "Does that mean *anything*? Or is it some kind of code? Does it ever mean what it says?"

"I need context," I say, looking up from reorganizing the paint chips.

"It's a kiss-off." Tim flips a page in his chem book, without looking up.

"Really? Like, not even a second place ribbon thing? An actual 'get lost'?" Andy sounds crushed. Tim looks up, checks her face, and says, "Wait. No. Not always. Uh – context is right. Need that. Could have it all wrong."

"Suppose there's this guy –" Andy says.

"Kyle. Ditch him," I interrupt.

"Whoever. That's not the point. When he's around his friends, he doesn't even talk to me. But whenever he sees me on my own, he's all nice and talky and jokey and says he wants to be friends."

"Loser. Ditch him," I repeat. "He's just hoping for benefits."

"We weren't doing that," Andy says. "We were nowhere near that. We were just barely beyond hanging out. Like

at – hanging out with potential. And some kissing. With definite potential."

Tim's all about the cash register once again, trying to reattach the type transfer wheel to the spindle, brow furrowed. He flashes me a quick look midway through Andy's explanation, then hunkers back down, wipes grease off on his jeans, refocuses on the scattered parts.

"If he acts differently in front of his friends, forget him. Hypocrite *and* player. Ditch him."

"He's not mine to ditch," Andy says. "We aren't dating and we weren't even friends before we went out. Up till then, we'd said, maybe, three sentences to each other? Or, actually, he'd said them all to me, because I was always speechless. He has this really great smile – you just want to lick his cheek when he does it. And the first month of sailing camp three years ago, he said. 'Will you untie the jib sheet?' and then last year, he told me to haul down the clew lines while slacking away on the halyard and –"

"So, you weren't friends," I sum up. "Before the potential kicked in."

"Exactly. We were basically strangers. With magnetism. Or not. I mean, I thought there was. And obviously he did for at least a moment or two – because he asked me on a date. And, you know, kissed me? Some. But then that didn't work out. Although I thought it was working, but obviously I was wrong, which is why I doubt my own instincts now."

"Bottom line," I translate, "you didn't know each other."

"Yes. So there's no context . . . to translate him. Which is why I need you guys. Together you've probably dated, like, fifty people, right?"

"I didn't date," Tim says flatly.

"Far fewer than fifty," I tell her.

Andy rolls her eyes. "You're missing the point. I need experienced perspective. Because I. Know. Nothing. Does he want us to be something we weren't before – like now that we aren't . . . possible . . . now that there's no potential, does he want to get to know me?"

"Probably not," I say.

Andy's lip quivers a little. "So it's all bullshit?"

"Not necessarily," Tim says.

"Oh come on. Give me a break, Tim."

"Give *someone* a break, Alice. Maybe he's genuinely sorry. Maybe he really thinks he blew it. Maybe he's one of those poor bastards who doesn't know what he has until it's gone. Maybe he sees what a great girl Andy is and wants to honestly, actually get to know her. Everyone who makes a mistake isn't doomed to be an asshole forever." He waves one hand for emphasis, and the counting arm, which he'd been trying to reattach, goes flying, tinkling on the tile floor and disappearing somewhere near a tub of asphalt sealant.

"This guy is," I say. "He's just playing games."

"So, basically, let's be friends is at best an insult and at worst completely meaningless," Andy says. "Great. That's

wonderful. Thanks, you two have been a huge help. Self-esteem at an all-time high now."

"It isn't you," I say. "Some guy being a loser takes nothing away from you."

"It takes away potential," Andy says, raising her eyebrows, widening her eyes as if the answer's so completely obvious. "Which is another word for hope."

"Ands —" both Tim and I say at the same time, each of us starting forward. He reaches her first, circling around the counter, arm around her shoulders.

"Maybe we're wrong, maybe —"

Tim should be trying to fix the bell over the door because, again, it makes no sound as the door swings open, but Tim's dad's footsteps are loud enough to stop Tim mid-sentence

"I'll cut to the chase," he says abruptly, his face thunderous. "Your sister spoke with me. We have a few things to talk about."

"We were just headed out back," I say, motioning urgently to Andy, who mouths "Why?" at me, then takes one look at Mr. Mason's face and follows me out.

Pop barely registers that two people have fled the room. His eyes are, for once, locked on mine, not on his desk or his phone.

"As I said, Nan and I talked. I've heard about

your latest –"

Ah, Nano. Always so forthcoming with my sins.

"Escapade?"

Long sigh from Pop. "Issue. I know about this girl, and this child. I'm not happy, but that's beside the point."

So used to having my hands full of the kid. Pull on my ear, weave them through my hair, thrust 'em in my pockets. Look down the long back hall to the open office door. Alice has her legs propped up on Mr. Garrett's desk. Tour my gaze slowly from her crossed ankles to the fall of her skirt above her knees, the long line of her body, her face, with those crazy glasses on. With luck not overhearing any of this crap. The back door slammed a minute or two ago, so Andy's gone, at least.

"This is the last thing you should be tangled up in," Pop continues, pointing his cell at me like he can Tase me with it.

"Obviously too late for that, Pop."

"I'd appreciate it if you could try not to automatically make a smart-ass response so we can have a reasonable conversation."

"I'm not expecting you to fix this for me." Alice crosses and recrosses her ankles, fidgeting. Listening?

"I won't. But that's also beside the point." He drops the phone back into his pocket. "You have enough going on without this added complication."

"And yet it exists. Whoops."

"Goddamnit, Timothy." My head snaps up. Not a cusser, Pop. Not with me, anyway.

"What I'm saying is that this is not something you should waste time on."

"He's my son. What happened to manning up?"

Again with the cell phone. He should get a holster.

"You need to focus on getting yourself and your own life together. That's the bottom line. Unless your plan is to marry the girl, which –"

Jesus. He doesn't *want* me to do that, does he? Talk about the ultimate ultimatum.

"No. We're – he's going to be adopted as soon as Hester and I figure that out."

"That's the first smart plan you've had in years. The girl is on board?"

Hate that corporate-speak shit. "Yeah, the girl and I are looking at the big picture, thinking outside the box, we're going to do some team-building, deliverable by leveraging –" But he's talking over me.

". . . extricate yourself," he finishes, annoyed.

"It's all on me. My problem to solve. Understood. Anything else I need to know?"

My hands in my pockets, jingling my keys.

Pop digs in his jacket pocket, pulls out his wallet, where the bills are crisp and tidy, no doubt lined up correctly. He edges out a fifty. "Get out of this mess. Here."

"Thanks, but no thanks. Buy Ma a milkshake."

He studies me for a sec, then turns to go. Stops at the door.

"Tim."

Christ. Enough already.

"This changes nothing about December."

"Hey," I say quietly, coming up behind Tim.

He's pouring himself another cup of coffee, doesn't turn around. The only way I know he's heard me is the slight stiffening of his shoulders. He's looking down and something about the back of his neck, slumped, a little defeated-looking, makes me almost reach out to hug him. But we're barely even on speaking terms. I wrap my arms tight around my own ribs instead.

His *father*. This is the man he grew up knowing best. At the bank, he came off sort of awkward and bureaucratic. But this?

"Tim."

"If you've come to point out that you were right about my chances of fixing the cash register –"

"'This changes nothing about December'? What the hell, Tim?"

"Yeah, I know." He finally turns around with a smile that doesn't reach his eyes. "I'm shocked too. I was *sure* this would totally wipe me off the naughty list."

"I'm sorry —"

"Don't," he cuts in. "I don't want — that. The pity thing. Which I —" He runs his hand through the hair at the nape of his neck. When he speaks again, it's in an embarrassed voice. "Which I've been known to go for, I think. I mean, I see how my sister kinda makes a play for it. Hester too. It's . . . I don't know. I just don't — want that. Okay? So if that's all you've got? Don't bother." He turns his back again, gathers up the guts of the cash register and dumps them into the trash can.

There is some perfect thing to say or do here, and I can't get hold of it.

"Where's the extra garage apartment key again, Mom?" I ask, wiping my feet and pulling off my raincoat.

Mom, who's sitting at the kitchen table with Duff, Harry, and a large assortment of balls of various sizes, barely looks up. "Should be right on the hook."

"It's not there. Are there any others?"

"Duff, I don't think you can sew the fishing line on the foam. Andy tried that and it broke off really easily."

"God, Mom, not the solar system project again. Duffy, try wrapping Saran Wrap around the ball. Then you can sew through that. Where could the key be? Do you think Jase has it?"

"Try Patsy's purse."

"The old crib is still in the basement, right?"

"Yes, over against the far wall. Duff, tie the fishing line to the hanger *after* you put the planet on it. Harry, you have three more spelling-word sentences to write. Then you can help make the rings for Saturn."

"I hate this stupid project," Duff says savagely. "Why can't *we* decide what we want to make a scale model of? Why does our project have to be just exactly like everyone else's in the class?"

"And the class the year before and the class the year before that, and on and on into the distant mists of history. We should have just saved Joel's," Mom says wearily.

The missing keys are indeed in Patsy's Elmo purse. Opening it is like cutting open the stomach of a great white shark, except instead of seal bones and partially digested life rafts, Patsy's purse has matchbox cars, LEGOs, credit cards, spoons, crumbled graham crackers, etc.

Mom watches, bemused, as I clunk up from the basement with the various crib parts, the bag full of nuts and bolts, sheets under my arm.

"I'm assuming that's for Calvin. Tim going to help you put it together?"

"This one's on me," I grunt, moving one of the crib's unassembled sides out the door. Move them across to the garage apartment. Looking back through the screen, I can see Duff hold up the biggest planet. It all looks near normal, the typical chaos. The little things that once were a big deal. For the first time in a while, we're maybe, finally,

putting the shipwreck behind us.

Except that I'm totally ignoring a looming iceberg.

The bills.

It takes me forty-five minutes to put together the crib . . . a job that still defeats Dad, in spite of all his experience. After snapping the fitted bottom sheet into place, I go the kitchen to wash my hands, passing the refrigerator. The list on the door –

The Boy Most Likely To . . . self-destruct in various ways.

I used that against him. Those very words. Tin Alice.

I pick up a pen. Stare at the paper. Not quite brave enough to cross it all out, I scrawl on the bottom:

. . . have more formula than food in his fridge

. . . keep trying to fix things

I chew my lip, then scribble the last.

. . . deserve a . . . My pen wavers. Second chance? As many chances as it takes? Different dad? Apology?

I let myself in just as the dark clouds overhead break and the rain comes sheeting down.

The garage apartment has a tin roof and the sound is pure music. Which I'm too wiped out to appreciate. I kick off my pants, toss 'em with my T-shirt to the side of the room.

In serious need of oblivion. Too beat to shower, my

legs nearly boneless as I tug off my boxers and dive onto the bed.

Crash right into a warm, soft, very female form.

"What the hell?" she snaps, rocketing upright so fast and hard that her forehead smacks into mine and I see flashes of light even in the darkness just as her knee comes in hard right where it counts.

Feel no pain.

No pain.

But I know this freaking pause and then . . .

"Ow." I hunch to my side on the end of the bed, eyes watering.

"What are you doing here?" Alice asks, bewildered but feisty-sounding.

"Nothing for a long, long time, that's for sure. Where's a pillow? Gimme a pillow."

"Oh. God. I'm sorry. Let me turn on the light." Alice is evidently swinging her arm at the bedside table, because I hear a pile of books cascade to the floor.

"No! Just get me a pillow. And an icepack. And . . . last rites or something."

She shoves several pillows in my direction, then starts giggling.

"Yeah, yeah. Hilarious," I mutter, trying not to whimper. Or puke. "Maybe now you can take my appendix out with a fork or something."

"Icepack?" she asks. "Does that actually help?"

I groan. "Let me die in peace. After you tell me what you were doing between my sheets. And maybe if you're wearing anything, 'cause that might give me something to live for."

She flips over on her stomach, I guess, because her face is suddenly right against mine. "Fully clothed. Sorry. I was just closing my eyes for a sec. I didn't mean to sleep."

I try to answer but it's sort of a moan. The bed shakes with her suppressed laughter. I swat at her feebly, jam the pillow more firmly in front of me.

Ow.

"I'm truly, truly sorry," Alice says. "It was instinct. Well, that and self-defense classes."

"Can you get me a —" I'm buck naked here, but I can't stand the thought of any cloth brushing over me. Not that I have a robe or anything. I shift the other pillow over my bare ass. Just that movement makes me grit my teeth.

"Be right back."

I hear the door outside open, the louder whoosh of rain and wind, and then it slams shut. Commando-crawl slowly up to the top of my bed, lie down on my stomach, swear. Try my back, which is no better. Roll over. Rest my weight on my knees and elbows, head on pillow. No improvement. Collapse. Pull up the sheets, which feel like roof tiles weighed down with lead. Everything is throbbing, honestly.

Since I'm alone, I can swear out loud, and I do, but then time passes and there's nothing but the sound of the wind

and the too-quiet of the apartment.

Would she leave me like this?

Door slamming again. Alice, carrying the rain smell with her. "I have ice," she whispers. "And Motrin. Still alive? Can I turn on the light now?"

The dark, her figure-eight shadow against the dim light from the living room, the sense of Alice bringing all the outside world, its damp-leaf smells and its whooshing-wind and river sounds, with her into this stuffy silent bedroom.

"No. Let's just . . . keep it like this."

The mattress dips as she settles down next to me. I suppress any sound of agony by grabbing the pillow and biting it.

"Here," she says, reaching out for my hand, flipping it palm up and dropping tablets into it, then placing a cool bottle of water next to me. I swallow and chug, let my head fall back again.

"Can I –" I bite down on my lip. The pain seems to be moving off. Sort of.

She leans closer. Nope, still hurts like a mother.

"Am I allowed to ask what you were doing in my apartment, much less my bed, Goldilocks?"

Silence. A sigh. Then:

"I was . . . wrong. You were right to call me on it, Tim. I don't – apologize often. Or well. So . . . So . . . I thought . . . deeds speak louder than words and all that." Hers are coming out in a rush and she's so close I can feel

her breath on my cheek. "I put together a crib. For Cal. It took forever. You'd think I could do it in the dark with my eyes closed, but no. I had class tonight and — it was a long emotional day at the store — and I thought I'd take a power nap."

"You definitely regained your power. No worries there."

"No, listen. Don't joke. Listen. Really. I'm sorry."

"You're forgiven. Don't do it again. Either thing."

"I promise," she says, her voice solemn and serious in the darkness, so near that if I turned, I'd be brushing right up against the length of her.

Except that rolling to my side might kill me.

"This is so not how I imagined getting you into my bed."

"So not how I imagined being in it."

"You've —" I start to sit up. *Ow.*

"*Shh,*" Alice says, and lies down next to me, on her back, on top of the sheet I'm under. Wrapping her fingers around mine, she edges my hand over to the icepack.

"Hush," she says again, but somehow it's not like she's calming down some fussy kid. It's more like the dark makes things clearer. Cleaner. Sharper. No blurry lines.

She turns her nose to my shoulder, breathes in. Her hair's wet. She shivers a little. The rain is pinging against the roof, and suddenly the wind gusts loud, spattering drops hard against the window, like someone throwing pebbles to get attention. I start to sidle my arm around Alice, but that simple movement jars me and aches like holy hell. So I

don't move, Alice doesn't either, except to burrow closer, as her shivers die down.

Her fingers are still laced in mine, warm against the melting ice. The tension in my muscles — everywhere — is slowly easing too, undone by her small, solid weight against me.

"Tim?"

"Mmmm."

She props herself up on an elbow, barely visible except the glimmer of her wide eyes, the slight sheen of her hair in the distant light from the streetlamp.

"When I was twelve . . ." She stops.

"Go on," I whisper.

"I came back after the summer and I had" — she looks down at her chest, then sweeps her hands across — "this." She moves the hand that's holding mine, presses it against her chest, so her breast . . . God . . . fills my palm, no doubt freezing cold from the ice pack. My fingers tighten. Then I pull my hand away — sheer force of will.

"I was basically the first girl in my class with boobs. It was like — overnight — and suddenly all these people — these kids I'd known forever were calling me names. Some of these girls hated me — again, overnight. Guys were always asking stuff about whether I'd gotten implants, and whether Dad had to take a loan out to pay for them." She looks up at me again. "Joel had just moved on to high school, so he didn't know about the teasing. Jase was still in

283

elementary. I didn't want to tell my parents, because Mom was pregnant with Harry, and Dad's dad was really sick. I have no idea why I'm telling you this," she says.

Alice's eyes meet mine, searching for something. Even in the dim light, she must find whatever it is, because she continues. "So I just decided to flip it. If people were going to take how I looked and figure out how I was, I was going to . . . I don't know . . . take charge of it. So I wore things that showed off my body, and I picked boys I was stronger than, and . . . that's the way I handled it."

I have to admit I've never thought of Alice as "managing her image," as the politicians would call it. I've always thought she knew she had a great body and felt fine about showing it off. I pull her even tighter against me, bury my lips near the pale gleam of the part in her hair. Her body goes rigid, then relaxes against me. She mutters something, too soft for me to hear.

"That's what you do. With your father. You flip it. Just sort of own whatever it is. Not just with him. You do it a lot. 'Everything's funny if you look at it the right way.'"

"Um." I squint against the prickle of dampness in my eyes. "Right? It is."

Her only answer is to press closer. "You can get under the covers, you know," I whisper.

"Better not." Her voice is low.

I smile. "You've never been safer with me than you are now."

Her quiet laugh shakes the bed, but not painfully anymore. Alice shifts, her wavy hair tickling my cheek. Warm skin, soap, damp hair that smells like rain and leaves.

The branch of the tree outside scratches against the window, moving with the wind. All the rain sheeting down . . . it's like we're in a cocoon, wrapped up, falling into sleep.

"Mmmm," Tim murmurs, then yawns into the pillow, stretches his arms over his head, then yawns again.

"I've got to go. Will you be able to crash again?"

"Incredibly."

I tug the sheet and the blanket up to his neck. Pat him quickly on the back, bend to put my lips there, just where his hair curls down, before I even think, then pull back before I make contact.

"I'll lock the door."

I scribble one more note. *The Boy Most Likely To . . . need a little recovery time.* Call "Sweet dreams." But there's no answer.

He's already asleep.

I could have kissed him after all.

° ° ° •

I'd have said there was no way in hell I could sleep with

Alice sitting there beside me, one hand on my back and the other brushing my hair away from my forehead. But when I wake up, it's morning – the rain long gone and the sun slanting through the window, so I must have done just exactly that.

It's only later, when I'm in the kitchen, slurping coffee, unknotting George's shoelaces, Krazy Gluing the broken nose pad back onto Duff's glasses, quizzing Harry on his spelling words, and I stand up to stretch, sore from Tim's hard mattress, that I know what happened here.

Lying next to him, breathing in the rhythm of his breaths. Watching dreams chase across his no-defenses face. Having him tuck me closer, head under his chin, anchored against his heart and heat . . .

Out the kitchen window, I watch Tim plunge down the garage steps, long legs, hands shoved in pockets. He hits the grass, headed for his car, washed clean and sparkling by last night's rain, windshield plastered with stuck-on leaves, then shields his eyes and looks toward our house. His face blazes, happiness purer and more unfiltered than I've ever seen from him.

Like the whole wide world is dazzling with potential.

Another word for hope.

Chapter Thirty

The guy who opens the door at Hester's three days later looks like a skinny Jerry Garcia. He wears a faded, tie-dyed T-shirt and baggy corduroy cargo pants. He's barefoot, balding, and bearded.

"You must be Tim," he says.

You can't *be Hester's grandfather,* I think. Lousy casting. They'd never even be in the same movie.

"Yep," I say. "That's me."

"Waldo Connolly. Come on in. Like Thai food?"

I haul in Cal and all his crap, looking around. *Not* what I expected for Hester's backdrop. Shitloads of big, bright abstract oil paintings, one glass wall that juts out back, turning into a greenhouse-type room, plants everywhere, big braided rugs, loads of furniture that looks like it's been carved out of trees, sometimes with the bark still on. A hobbit would be right at home.

I'm definitely not.

Waldo Connolly's just standing there, smiling at me, thumbs hooked into his belt loops. I finally remember that

he asked me a question. "Oh, uh, yes, uh, sir. Thai food. Love it. Probably. I've never had it."

"Hester, he's here," he calls up the stairs.

I guess no court-martial.

I look around at the tables and bookcases. Lots of pictures of Hester with friends, Hester alone, Hester with Waldo, Hester with Waldo and some old lady – her grandmother, maybe. No pictures of the kid.

Speaking of, he's chomping on my finger ferociously with his gummy little mouth. I scrounge out his bottle.

"Come on into the kitchen. You can heat it up in there," Waldo says, walking through a brick-lined archway into another room.

The kitchen too is decorated in early Middle Earth. Copper kettle, huge black iron stove, lots of woven rug things on the walls and glass witch's balls hanging in front of the windows, big puffy red armchair, big table that looks like it was hewn from a hundred-year-old redwood by John Henry or whatever.

"Microwave's right there." Waldo waves to a corner of the counter.

I'm actually surprised there's a microwave and not a huge iron kettle over the fireplace.

The air smells spicy and thick. Waldo picks up a gigantic machete-type knife and stands looking at me as Cal's bottle revolves. I resist the urge to protect my privates. But then Waldo pivots and starts whacking away at some big green

288

vegetable-type thing on the counter.

"You like green papaya salad?" he calls over his shoulder.

"Love it." I push the nipple into Cal's mouth and his head immediately lolls back against my forearm, eyelids half-lowered in ecstasy. This kid sure does love to drink. Can only hope he's equally stoked about the solid stuff.

"That's what we got going for dinner tonight. That and tom yum goong."

"Great." Whatever.

"Take a load off. Tell me about yourself." Waldo aims the machete toward the big red armchair.

"I'm Tim and I'm an alcoholic" would not be the appropriate response. *I'm a Sagittarius? I'm generally much more reliable with birth control than you might think? Not that I've had sex in a while. Like forever. Like since I had it with your granddaughter. Not that I remember that.*

"Hi Tim. Hi Grand." Hester bounces into the room at this point, wearing a surprisingly clingy blue dress – with cleave, even. Her hair's wet and not in a ponytail, just down. Lipstick, eye stuff, the works.

"You look good," I say, rising to my feet.

"Thanks. Um, thanks, Tim. Grand, did you give him a drink?"

I glance at Waldo, who's looking a hell of a lot less friendly than he was a second ago. Oh, right, dumbass. He'll think you just want in her pants again.

Screw being charming. I'm not good at that anyway

when I'm not buzzed.

"Sir, I know what you must think of me . . . well, no, I don't really, but I want to apologize. The year must have sucked for you too. I mean, that is, it must not have been easy for you either. So –" I cross the kitchen and extend the hand that's not cradling Cal, which means I let go of his bottle. Cal lets out an angry squawk. I check on Hester, figuring she'll reach for him, but she doesn't.

Her fingers don't even twitch like she's restraining herself. Instead, she keeps her eyes steady on me.

"That's mature of you, Tim," Waldo says, pointedly not taking my hand. "I think Hester's the one who deserves the apology. All *I* had to do was watch her suffer."

Oh, just use the damn machete.

"He did. He did apologize to me, Grand. I told you that," she says quickly.

Cal wriggles around in my arm, trying to latch back onto the bottle.

Dad? Dad! Help me. It's right there. *Dad!*

I drop my hand and reposition the thing. At least I can make *him* happy.

"Would you like some nam dang-mu pan?" Waldo asks pleasantly, as though he hadn't just left me hanging and made me feel like shit. Which is, I know, appropriate under the circumstances.

Still.

"It's like a watermelon cooler," Hester translates for

me. "You'll like it. Really delicious. Grand was a chaplain in Vietnam during the war, then he and Gran lived in Thailand for a few years after that."

A chaplain. Like a minister. That explains the lack of soldja vibe.

"I'll have that, then. Sir." I'm standing straight and stiff in front of him, practically saluting. Or genuflecting.

"Tim, relax!" Hester pulls this big rocking chair that's over in the corner of the room toward me, tips it so it rocks a little, pats the seat. Her grandfather gives her a sharp look over his granny glasses, then goes back to mashing something up in a big wooden bowl with this mallet-type thing.

Cal's nearly fast asleep, his lips still twitching.

Waldo plunks a large hand-blown glassful of orange-red liquid next to me. "Here's your drink."

"It's not alcoholic, is it?" I eye the glass, praying for a "no," because right now I'm not sure I wouldn't pound it even if it is.

"Just watermelon and ice. I know you're in the program now. I respect that."

Hester, who I didn't notice had left the room, returns with a picture. "That's my gran," she tells me, her raggedly trimmed index finger tapping the face of a gorgeous brunette laughing, her head thrown back. "There's Waldo. And here's my mom."

Ah. Hester's missing mother. I've wondered what her

story was, how she died, all that. I squint at the photo. Uh, she looks quite a lot like Madonna in her *Like a Virgin* phase. Fake pearls, crazy hair, shiny bustier displaying a shit-ton of tit. This is Hester's mom?

"When did your mom, uh" – not *croak* – "pass away?" I ask.

Hester and Waldo both laugh.

"She's alive and well," Hester assures me.

"Lives in Vegas. She can still kick it as a showgirl," Waldo says, with a trace of pride. "Got her mother's legs and her sense of rhythm. Not a damn thing of mine, lucky girl."

Not the background I would have pictured, if I even imagined one for Hester. More like the double strand of pearls and the blue blazers. No showgirls. No Vegas. I glance at Hester for a sec. She's so orderly, controlled-looking. Well, no wonder, I guess. Her grandfather is the lead guitarist of the Grateful Dead, her mother, Madonna. How else could she rebel but to be Nancy Drew?

I sip the watermelon thing cautiously, trying not to jiggle Cal awake. "I should probably put him to bed."

"It's this way." Hester stands up and leads me upstairs . . . to her room.

Which kinda breaks my heart.

It's a kid's room, that's all I can say. Pink flowy curtains, flowered bedspread, concert stubs and movie stubs and those pics in vertical rows of four you get at booths in the mall – Hester and some girls – all shoved into the corners

of a mirror. Worn, well-loved-looking teddy bear on the yellow pillow. Lots of chick-type books – *Jane Eyre* and *Twilight* – all that.

"Calvin's crib's in here."

Not in her room. *Through* her room in a hallway. Plus it's one of those port-a-crib type things, not like some ancestral cradle carved from ancient oak. Plain sheet, plain blue blanket, no stuffed animals – not even a sock monkey. I mean, it's not like Cal lives the life of luxury at the garage apartment. But, ya know, he's got his plastic keys, and this stuffed duck I found, and the weird blanket with bears Mrs. G. loaned me that he likes best – he always sucks on a corner of it. This is like the baby equivalent of a Motel 6. It screams "just passing through." I ease Cal onto his back. He waves his arms, screws up his face like he's ready to blast us, but gives in to sleep faster than I could snap my fingers.

We tiptoe out, back through Hester's room. She's walking in front of me. I touch her on the shoulder.

"I know I apologized before. But I am sorry. I'm so fucking sorry I screwed up your life."

Hester drops down on her bed. "Tim." She blows out a long sigh. "I don't know how different forgiving you would be from now. I don't blame you for what happened. It was just as much my fault."

"I was the one who was plastered, Hes."

Her eyes fill with tears.

"Oh shit. Don't do that." I look wildly around the room for

tissues or whatever. "Don't cry on me. Hes . . . stop it. Please stop it."

"It's just weird. That's what you called me that night. You kept calling me 'Hes.'" Her chin wobbles. "I liked it. Hester's so formal. It's odd to me that you don't remember anything else, but that nickname keeps slipping out. I keep thinking maybe you're lying and you do remember."

Not even a sliver of light in that blackout. Sometimes I get little flares of lost days or nights, but that one – tiki bar, her –

"There's nothing there," I say, as gently as possible.

She sniffs and wipes her eyes with the back of her hand briskly, then sniffs again. "Not one thing? Not even the color of my bra? You didn't have any trouble getting it off. Do you remember that at least?"

"Uh . . . pink?"

"It. Was. Navy blue." She pounds the heel of her hand against her forehead.

I rub my own through the hair at the back of my neck, look out the window at my car.

"I don't know why it matters to me. It's just . . . right before we, you know . . ."

There's a pause, and I feel like a bastard, and also totally pissed off. *You know?* Can't you even say *sex*, Hester? You have a baby. We all know how it got here.

"I kind of realized how drunk you were, and I said we shouldn't . . . because you wouldn't remember. And you

294

said, you said" – she stops to grab a Kleenex by the side of the bed and blow her nose – "'Of course I'll remember. Why wouldn't I? How couldn't I?' Like I was so special, I'd be unforgettable. And . . . I believed you. And . . . and . . . you just *didn't*."

Now she's sobbing away, and it's starting to get loud and either she'll wake up Cal, or Waldo will come charging up with his handy dandy machete. No idea what else to do but sink down on the flowery bedspread next to her. Not too close.

"It had nothing to do with you, Hester. That's just . . . not the way it works. I'm an alcoholic and I was an active one then and I just blacked the fuck out because of how I am – was – not because of anything about you. You could have been . . . Marilyn Monroe. . . and it wouldn't have made one bit of difference."

Her sobs quiet down. She looks up at me through her damp lashes, and then lowers her eyes. Edges a little closer. Flips back the dark hair that's fallen over one side of her face.

Her eyes shift to my mouth.

I've kissed a ton of girls. They didn't matter to me. I didn't matter to them. *I* didn't even matter to me.

I know what Hester's going for here . . . some way to think of what happened with us as not just random. Believe there was actual feeling going on, not just biology. And Bacardi. But . . . I can't. I'm a dick, but not that much

of a dick. Not anymore, anyway.

I jerk my hand away from her back, shove it through my hair, jolt to my feet. "Man, I'm starving. Is your grandfather as good a cook as it smells?"

Hester's head remains lowered, her hair parting to show the nape of her pale neck. I suddenly remember George Garrett telling me that showing your neck or your stomach were "the most vun-rable thing" animals could do, their softest, most easily destroyed parts exposed. I hate myself more than usual.

"Hester!" Waldo shouts up the stairs. "You two come on down. Dinner!"

"He's great. A great cook."

Waldo looks at us from under bristly brows as we enter the room. "Baby take a while settling down?"

"Not at all," Hester says, just as I say, "Uh, yeah. Sort of."

"Hmmph." He pulls this wooden tray over and starts whacking at the round pieces of bread on it. *Thwack.* "About Calvin." *Thwack.* "How much nuts-and-bolts talking have you two done?" He points the knife at me, then Hester.

"We've talked . . ." she says slowly.

"More about how he got here than what to do with him now that he is," I blurt. Waldo's face darkens. Hester turns red.

He ladles out a stew thing that includes shrimp with

their tails still on, poking freakishly out of the broth, slides the wooden bowl toward me. "You two are on the threshold. This is the space between the questions. How are you going to walk through and come out enlightened?" He gives both me and Hester this hardcore stare, like he can pull the enlightenment out of us and slap it on the table next to the stew.

Uh . . . I dip a spoonful of steaming rice into the bowl and slurp it down, buying time. Hester sighs, shoulders slumping.

Minutes pass and we're all staring down at our plates. Waldo starts eating, and then looks up through that forest of eyebrows at each of us again. "Well?"

"I just want to get back on track," Hester says.

"I'm just hoping to come out of this sober," I add.

"On track. Sober." Waldo takes a mouthful of stew. "Those are destinations, for sure. But for now, there are doors known and unknown."

Hester drops her spoon with a clatter. "Grand. So help me God, if you quote Jim Morrison at me one more time – I don't want to hear it. He was as big a mess as Tim."

Her voice is low, shaking. Waldo's eyes widen for a second and he stops chewing.

"Bigger, even," I say. "I wouldn't be caught dead in leather pants."

Waldo chuckles. Hester picks up her soup spoon again.

"Sooo. Where are we with the adoption agency?" I ask.

She's right back to straight-A student, like her outburst never happened. "Obviously we're not going to have any trouble placing him. The adoptive parents have to prove themselves to us more than we ever do to them – home studies, health tests, all that. That's their job." She's scooping up broth with her bread. It's hot as hell. I took one sip, my eyes watered, and I pounded back my entire glass of watermelon stuff. She doesn't even blink. Waldo has actually picked up his bowl now and is drinking from it.

"So the question is the next step," Waldo says. "The way through the woods."

"We're taking our time," Hester assures him.

We are? There's a "we"? My temples are starting to pulse.

"I'm all for doing this fast, like right away," I say. "I mean, take the bull by the horns, bite the bullet."

I have never used either of those expressions in my life.

"This is why it's good that Tim's involved," Hester tells Waldo. "We're on the same page here, as a couple."

Waldo looks at me; back at her. "You're both very young for this, Hester. And you two are not exactly a couple." He smiles at me, but it's a little like baring his teeth.

"Exactly," I say. "We're not."

"You're his father," Hester says, looking down at her bowl like she's reading tea leaves. "I'm his mother."

"Yeah, but –"

"Our baby. Our decision. Do you understand, Grand?"
Again, she's looking at him, not me. "It has to be between
Tim and me."

He nods, weaves his fingers behind his neck, tilts it
to one side, then the other, cracking it. "Which is why I
thought you should bring him in in the first place."

"And here he is," Hester tells him.

Sometimes I really think I broke my brain, messing with
it the way I did. I'm hearing what they're saying, but it's
like I can't make sense of it. What *are* they saying? I may be
here, but am I really? Because I *feel* like the sperm donor.
Which, I guess, is pretty close to the truth.

"We'll figure it out. Together. Right, Tim?"

"Sure," I say, staring at the clock. There's a quiet wail
getting louder and louder.

Thanks, Cal. I half rise from my chair. Hester heaves a
heavy sigh. "No . . . I've got this. My turn, after all." She
straightens her back like she's facing enemy gunfire and
not a seven-week-old baby. Takes a slug of watermelon
drink. Squares her shoulders.

For God's sake. "Lemme see what's going on," I say,
moving in front of her toward the stairs. Not hard, since
she's walking like her feet are encased in lead boots. "I'll
take him again tonight," I tell her. "No big deal. What's
another night?" *Of no sleep.* And probably no late-night visit
from Alice. Man – my own place, no parents, no house-
parents, no hall monitors, but now I have a baby monitor.

Cal's soggy and has leaked onto his long-underwear-type thing.

"I have a fresh sleeper he can wear," Hester says from behind me. I nearly jump out of my skin. She has this ultra-silent way of moving — like her feet make no impression on the ground. She'd be an awesome assassin.

"Thanks," I say, swabbing at him. I'm fumbling the diaper back on, clumsier than usual because Hester's watching, then he pees. In my eye.

Blech. He's my kid and by now I actually think he's, you know, semi-cute and all that, but he frickin' *peed* in my *eye*.

Hester starts laughing.

"Not funny," I snap, swabbing my face with a baby wipe. Which makes my eye sting and water. She's giggling more, laughing outright now, practically holding her stomach.

"Sorry. Sorry. I'll be serious." She makes an elaborate attempt to keep a straight face and hands me this fuzzy thing that looks like a pillowcase with arms.

"What's that?"

"It's a sleeper. You just zip him into it."

I zip up Cal, who has stopped bawling and is looking at me nervously. Then I put him against my shoulder and pick up the diaper bag. Just a few weeks ago, I never needed to carry anything, just shove my license and my ATM card in my back pocket. Now I'm a pack mule.

After a shit-ton of *that dinner was awesome* and *thank you so*

much, I stick one hand out to Waldo, ready to say good bye. He clasps it between both of his hairy hands and kind of wags our hands back and forth while staring me in the eye like he's reading my aura or seeing through to my soul or making sure my pupils aren't dilated.

My voice, which has been going on and on with the *this was great*'s, falters and grinds to a halt.

"You're connected to Calvin," he says, not like it's a question.

"Uh," I say. "Not really." Cal wriggles, and I boost him back up, hand on his butt. He smells like diaper rash cream and laundry detergent. "I don't know what that means," I add. "Sir."

"That's the question, isn't it?" Waldo says, lowering his chin and looking at me over his granny glasses, bushy gray brows drawn together. He finally gives me back my hand and says, "Anon, then, Timothy."

"Right on," I say, fisting and unfisting my hand. He'd held on to it kind of tight.

Right on? Jesus.

Just as I'm about to shift into drive, Hester taps on the window. When I open it, she rests her elbows on the sill. "Have you done that with anyone else?" she whispers.

"Uh, you mean sex?" *How bad* was *I?*

"No – the forgetting. All of it."

"What do you want me to say, Hester?"

301

Yep, you're the only one I totally forgot. Nope, you're one of many. The truth is the first, as far as I know. Then the thought sinks in. The gear knob slips through my fingers as I imagine a tangle of girls I've left behind in guest bedrooms, backseats, empty classrooms, hair rumpled, shirts askew, faces accusing, all trooping my way with redheaded babies in their extended arms.

Takes me three more tries to get my shaky hands to shift from park.

"Never mind," she says.

Waldo's watching me, a thick-set statue in the doorframe, when I surge forward out of his driveway.

"See," I say, crashing on my back on the couch with Cal on my chest, "this is why you never hook up with some random person for some random reason at some random place. Sure, she could have an STD, she could get pregnant. No picnic. But really, you find yourself *in* the life of someone you don't know and don't get and they're in yours too and there's no fucking way out."

Cal bobs his head against my collarbone.

My phone vibrates with a text. Hester again. If she asks me what color the nail polish on her toes was, I am going to lose my mind.

Again, don't know how to thank you.

Thank me by getting the adoption ball rolling ASAP, I am dead serious, I text back, holding the phone up over

Cal's back. Vaguely guilty typing this, with his fluffy hair brushing my chin. But he *has* to be a blip in the rearview mirror before Dad does my year-end performance review.

Sleep well, she responds.

Ironically, I have to assume.

A car wheels into the Garretts' driveway and, after a second, I peer out my window to see Sam and Jase standing by Jase's Mustang, which I know he's been giving her driving lessons in. He's got his hands in her hair and she has her arms around his waist, her head on his chest, and I just want that.

I'm like some weird voyeur, but . . . it's all quiet, peaceful. No big rush to make the moves, just easy, natural. As much of a creep as I am for watching, for not making any noise, not clearing my throat to let them know I'm there, I'm even worse for this, like, *wanting*. Like a vise grip on my shoulder, I feel it harder than any craving for booze or that kind of oblivion. It's something that actually . . . aches . . . instead of nagging like a mosquito I can't manage to swat. Jase says something, and Samantha laughs, buries her head against him, fits right into him even though she's almost as short as Alice and he's almost as tall as me.

I'm a douche wanting what my best friend has. He loves her, she loves him . . . the rest can wait. There are no crazy complications, no classmate you can't imagine screwing, no baby you don't remember making.

I want the best for Jase – and Sam – who deserve all

that. But at the same time, I wish my missteps could be canceled out by the times I did the right thing. Which I can probably count on one hand.

Finger?

Less than a week ago I had Alice here in my bed, and now I've got the baby from the pits of hell.

Blue eyes so red, he looks like he needs an exorcism, deep painful breaths, knees yanked hard up to his chest. It's bum-crack of morning, Cal's miserable, and I have no clue how to fix him. He wants nothing to do with my nose, but whenever I put him down to try to get a bottle or something, he screams even louder. My ears hurt so bad and I want so damn much to put him down and go into another room, shut the door. Go outside, onto the lawn, down the street, to the beach. I mean – no one's ever died from crying, right? Maybe he'll just wear himself out?

So. I don't leave. The least I can do. I just keep on holding him while he thrashes around like a hammerhead on a line.

And cries. Endless. And wicked loud.

"Cal. I don't know what the f– I don't get what you want. What you need. I wanna help you here, kid. Help me understand." He pauses for a second, like he's thinking my words over, then starts screeching yet again, desperate.

I'm asking for direction from someone who has had less time on the planet than I've had in recovery. Pick him up

and put him on my stomach, hold tight to his tense, flailing body. He collapses, sweaty, all his damp red waves flopped down, instead of sticking straight up as usual. After a long while, as though it's taken time to collect his strength, he raises his big heavy head back up and looks me straight in the eyes.

Smiles.

This goofy, toothless smile, his head bobbling back and forth like it weighs extra to show emotion. It completely changes his whole face – from worried crinkle dude to jolly Buddha guy. *Hi, Cal. Hey, kid.* I grin back at him.

Dad. Hi, Dad.

That whatever, that blood bond, that "Luke, I am your father" thing . . . I don't know, but maybe I get it. A little.

Then, like his smile has taken all his energy, he slumps his head to the side, grabs a handful of my chest hair, snorts loudly, and tumbles off to sleep.

My left hand still covers his whole butt. The other hand is bigger than the side of Cal's head. I can hardly breathe, but I'm damn sure not gonna move and wake him up. So I just stay there, listening to his snuffly breaths, almost counting them, breathing in that same slow rhythm. He's partly me. Because of me. I did this.

For the first time, that idea doesn't make me sick, or guilty, or wrong. For the first time, I really know he's mine.

Chapter Thirty-one

"Mom always lets me sit in the front," Harry tells me, wedging his skinny, seven-year-old ass into that very seat as I sweat to install Cal's car seat in the middle of the Garretts' van. Cal's wiggling and trying to whack me with his stuffed duck. George is cracking up over it.

I smell Alice's salt-air scent before I see her standing next to me like a mirage. All the craziness around me and in me shuts down. Catch a whiff of peppermint – minty soap, or candy she's sucked on just now.

"Better?" she asks. "No permanent side effects?"

"Mom does not *ever* let you sit in front," Duff says from the way back. "That's bull, Harry."

"Tim, tell him he can't say that. It's bad," George says.

"Watch your mouth," I call over my shoulder. *Hypocrites are us.* I expect Duff to call me on this, but instead he just kicks his shoes against the back of George's seat.

"Completely recovered," I answer Alice. "All systems go." I concentrate on polishing off my water bottle. Alice doesn't need to know she was in the shower with me

this morning.

But she flashes her killer grin and says nothing.

"Do you have class tonight?" I ask as Andy hurtles out of the house.

"Whew, thanks for waiting, Tim! Can you speed? I'm late for band and I swore to Alyssa I'd bring her Munchkins before the game – you don't mind stopping at Dunkin', do you? Do you have any cash? Is my hair a mess? Did I put on too much mascara?"

"You're fine," Alice says firmly. "Tim is not your ATM." She turns back to me. "No – I had night duty, but that's done for now. Come by after the game?"

I cough, nearly spitting out the water. "Um. Do we have a plan?" Why am I asking? Who cares?

She stretches. Air's crisp. Sun's out. She sweeps her hair off her neck. "We can improvise."

"Can we get going, plleeeease?" Andy groans from the front seat. Harry's now in back.

"Harry burped in my face on purpose!" Duff says. "That's rank."

"After the game? You'll be here? I'll . . . be here too."

Christ.

"Sounds good." Alice looks down, pushes her toe into the soft tar of the driveway.

"Tim! Come *on*! I know you two are all busy, but have some mercy here."

Check the rearview mirror of the van, because this

307

thing is humongous.

Cal, who had zonked out, now pops his eyes open, so wide-awake in the back-facing mirror thing. He goggles at Alice, and then gives his biggest, goofiest smile.

"Wow," she says. "Look at that." She sets her finger in the corner of Cal's mouth. They look at each other for a second, as if they're adding each other up. Then his smile gets wider.

"Yeah, he just started doing it."

She bends closer, brushes his hair back. "There you go, Tim."

"Huh?"

"There's your missing dimple. Cal's got the other one." She touches her finger into the little crease on his cheek.

God, I hadn't noticed, but it's true.

Alice backs off, drags her heavy purse up her arm, and heads toward the house, giving me one quick grin over her shoulder.

"Fi-nal-ly," Andy says as I climb in.

"*Buuull,*" Patsy yells now, experimentally. I shake my head at her. She leans back, looking like I've offended her deeply.

"Why don't guys ever put emojis in their texts? How are we supposed to have any idea how they're feeling!"

"Most of the time we have no clue ourselves, Andy," I mutter.

I love the Garrett kids, but my mind is definitely in

another place now. Plus, they're all fighting like fisher cats the entire drive. By the time we get to the crowded SBH parking lot, vans and SUVs parked everywhere, I have a headache like a frickin' ice pick, sharp between my eyes.

HESTER – PLS. NEED YOU TO TAKE HIM TONIGHT. PICK HIM UP FROM SB HIGH. TEXT IF NEED DIRECTIONS. YOUR SO-CALLED COPARENT.

The last was dick mode, I know, but c'mon. Alice aside, I could fall asleep right here. The twenty-four-ouncer with an espresso shot didn't make a dent.

"Whassup," asks a familiar voice as the little guys and I are wedging our asses into the second row of bleachers. "Long time no see, Tim Mason."

"What are you doing with my sister?" I ask immediately.

Troy cups a hand behind his ear, shrugging helplessly. Word is his hearing's shot on one side because his dad whaled on him a bit too hard a bit too often.

Then he moves in, arms outstretched, lurching in for an actual hug, not noticing that I have a person strapped to my chest. When he encounters the front pack and the feathery back of Cal's head, he edges back, then just readjusts his reach and loops his arms around my neck. "Missed you, man! What the hell? You're a manny now?"

"What? No," I say, before I realize that I sort of am.

"Hi!" George says cheerfully. "You're Tim's friend?" He sticks out a hand. "Name of George. That's me."

Troy fist-bumps George's outstretched palm, which is

309

just messed up, then checks out Harry and Patsy, who are watching this exchange curiously. Cal's sucking his hand with these loud slurpy sounds.

"Don't talk to him. He's a stranger," Harry stage-whispers to George, suddenly Mr. Play By the Rules despite his totally illegit bid for the front seat.

"Naaah. Tim here, he and I go way back," Troy says easily, flipping his too-long hair out of his eyes. He looks, as always, like Hollywood's idea of a teenage drug dealer. I've never been able to figure out if this is irony on his part or pure stupidity. I'm thinking Door Number Two.

"Need anything to take the edge off, Mason? You look tense as hell," Troy says. "No wonder, am I right? Hear you're home for the duration now."

"I'm fine," I snap. Troy backs up, palms extended.

"No big," he assures me. "'S all cool. Priorities change and all that."

"This is Tim's baby," George tells him chattily. "Name of Cal. He got him at a party."

"Geez," Troy says profoundly, shifting his glance between Cal's head with its telltale red hair, and me. "I heard rumors, but whoa. Talk about your misspent youth coming back to haunt you."

"My misspent youth funded yours, Rhodes."

"True," Troy says, looking unaccountably stung. "But I get to go to college baggage free. Sucks to be you, I guess."

"Wait here, guys," I tell the Garretts, then give Troy's

forearm a shove in the direction of the back of the bleachers.

"Ha. I knew you'd go for it, Mason," he says smugly. "Phonying up for the kiddos, huh? What can I getcha?"

"The truth. What are you selling my sister? She's screwed up enough."

"Your sister?" he says thoughtfully, with the wide-eyed, *I'm so wrongly accused* look that hasn't gotten him out of detention since middle school. "You mean Nan?"

"Cut the bullshit, Troy. Yes. Her. What's going on?"

His slow, faux-surfer voice goes hard as physics. "I don't mess with family drama. You want to know what's going down with the girl, ask her."

George scoots around from the front of the bleachers, extending Cal's bottle and then yanking on my sleeve. "Hurry up! The team's coming out now! Hurry!" He pulls on Troy's army jacket. "You can come too. Are you a soldier?"

"Kind of," Troy answers cheerfully.

"A freedom fighter against the war on drugs?" I ask, and he laughs, pointing his finger at me like a gun.

"Ex-act-ly. Lead on, midget."

"More civilians than soldiers get killded during any war," George tells him. "Look – there's the team!"

At this point, the Stony Bay and Maplecrest teams jog, two by three, onto the field, round into a circle.

"*Raah!*" Cal says, shifting angrily in the front pack.

"*Raah. Raah. Raahaaah.*"

"He cwying, Hon. Do somfin. Cal cwying." Patsy sounds like a pissed-off truck driver, at odds with her little sprouty ponytails.

"There's my brother!" George says to Troy. "He's number twenty-two. Right over there. The one who just stopped that big running guy in the orange shirt."

George, Harry, and Duff all have their eyes riveted to the field.

"Nice tackle for a loss," Duff calls. "Take that, Maplecrest High – you stink."

"Duff said another bad word," George singsongs.

I'm thinking of a few that would put him to shame.

Patsy watches me try to feed Cal, and then looks at me with this betrayed expression, lower lip trembling. "Hon . . ." she says, like it's my funeral.

"Maybe I could, like, walk her around," Troy suggests. "I've got this half sister. She's an infant. I mean, being on the move helps, man, I know that."

"Are you jacked?" I ask.

His face twitches, miffed. "I, like, deal it, man. I don't, like, do it."

Yep, you're a real man of principle, Troy. I assess his clear eyes, his healthy color. Messed up that I never asked or wondered about this before. But then, first things first. "Back and forth, then, in front of the bleachers where I can see you," I order.

So here, in Surrealland, my friendly neighborhood drug dealer soothes a kid I'm babysitting, while I try to change my own kid's diaper on my lap – not a brilliant idea, that – and Harry, Duff, and George cheer Jase on like this is all totally normal and fine.

"Hoo boy," Duff says under his breath. "Jase got burned deep on that pass."

Cal yanks his mouth away from the bottle like this knowledge personally pains him. I shove it back in. "Just chug it, kid."

Troy has Patsy up on his shoulders and is hovering near us, pointing out Jase on the field. "Check it out, little babe. See how he was smart and stayed in his lane on the punt return so the returner couldn't get outside of him?"

"No," George says solemnly, edging closer to Troy. "But is that good?"

"It rocks, little dude. It, like, so rules."

The game's winding down when Hester taps me on the shoulder. I unsnap the BabyBjörn thing and haul Cal out, pushing him unceremoniously into her arms so fast, she nearly drops him. He looks back at me, lower lip wobbly, gives this tentative version of his smile. *Dad?*

I take him back, hold him against my shoulder. "Sorry, sorry, sorry, kid." Low in his ear.

She's studying me, squinting, hand to her mouth, chewing a thumbnail. "Ready to let him go now?"

I stand still for a minute, put my hand on the back of his head, the little folds of skin there, like extra skin he's waiting to grow into. Kills me a little bit.

"Keep him safe, 'kay?"

Chapter Thirty-two

I'm up to the door, in what, three steps, standing there in the shoes Alice gave me, hand upraised to rattle the screen, when she opens it before I can.

My brain freezes, because she's in nothing but a short dark green towel, hair dripping, fresh out of the shower. She smells like baby shampoo and damp skin. Tan and clean and wet.

As the silence lengthens, she stares back at me, eyebrows slowly climbing.

A trickle of water slides slowly down from her collarbone, disappearing into the cleavage just barely covered by the green terry cloth, which she adjusts, pulling the towel higher in the front but making it dip on the side.

Having trouble thinking in words.

"I just . . ."

"Happened to be in the neighborhood?"

"That's it."

"Come in."

*

In our kitchen now, dark except for the electric light above the stove and what spills in from the street. Quiet except for my music from the other room and a semi-insistent complaint from Jase's cat, Mazda, because something must be done about that empty food dish.

Tim bends down to pet her and she batters herself against his calf, gets up immediately on her hind legs and begins kneading his thigh, butting against it. His hand looks big against her fur, and Mazda is not a small cat.

She attempts to clamber into his lap, but she's too fat, so she does the disdainful-tail, *you're beneath me anyway* cat thing and wanders off.

Tim looks up and smiles at me.

That same dazzled smile from the other day.

The glow from the streetlamp far down our driveway throws everything in the room into sharp relief, lighting Tim's red hair and bringing out deeper, warmer tones.

He rubs a hand over his face. Yawns, says, "Sorry," blinks, smiles again.

"Look . . . do you want to . . . take a walk? I'll throw on some clothes."

Not go out in this towel, in case you were assuming that.

"Damn," Tim says, but it sounds almost automatic, a reflex, like that's what he thinks he'll say, all I expect from him.

"I'll just . . . get dressed."

He nods, standing up. Walking to the table aimlessly.

316

Picking up my tea mug, a smudge of red on the side, turning it around in his hands, setting it down. Selecting one of Joel's left-behind drumsticks, tapping it against the corner of the table, setting it down.

When he opens the refrigerator, stares into it, shuts it again, I repeat, "I'll put some clothes on . . . my body."

"Sounds like a plan," Tim says absently.

When I come back, having thrown on my favorite jeans and Jase's football jersey, he's at the kitchen table with his head down on his folded arms.

I touch his back and he startles, rubs his eyes, blinks up at me.

"I wasn't gone that long," I say, amused. "Sure you're up for – anything?"

"Yeah. Hold on." He turns on the tap, splashes water on his face, frowns at the coffeemaker, which still has about two inches of cold coffee in it from this morning, then actually tips the carafe to his lips and downs about half of it.

"No mug?"

"We want what we want when we want it, Alice, remember?" He wipes his lips with the back of his hand, smiles a little, the one dimple making a brief appearance. "So, where to?"

His car has mine boxed in, so we take that, drive along some bumpy unpaved roads in Maplewood to the Hollister

Fairgrounds, all set up for the annual Fall Fair this weekend, but for now dark except for the parking lot floodlights.

The Ferris wheel is a ghostly-looking hoop against the sky, the Funhouse and the Balloon Burst and the Tilt-A-Whirl and Teacup still and mute.

"I haven't been to this thing in years," Tim says, sliding out of the car and peering up at the Ferris wheel. "Ma always does that jam contest. Ol' Gracie Reed wins it every time. Drives Ma ballistic."

"Grace probably pays off the judges."

But not the bills. Tomorrow, I promise myself. Tomorrow I will find a way to fix this. Her. Two more fat bills in the mail today, stamped all over with TIME SENSITIVE *and* URGENT.

Tim shoots me a sharp look, but says a noncommittal, "Mmm." I know he's known Samantha's mom all his life, but can he really have any sympathy for her now?

We've gotten close to the Ferris wheel, and one of the passenger cars is docked right next to the metal platform. I climb in. "C'mon."

Tim reaches for my hand, his grip tightening as he slips into the car beside me. Then he doesn't let go, looking down, his thumb pressing over my knuckles.

The night air wraps around us, dry leaves, someone's smoky wood fire.

I break the silence. Poetically.

"Andy throws up on this thing. Every time. It's a tradition."

"Nan too," he says. "Scared of heights. I used to bribe the operator to stop it when she was at the top, just to make it extra-humiliating for her. Of course, I usually barfed too, but that was too much beer or whatever."

I kick my feet against the footrest and the car rocks slightly, a creak of metal.

"Since you were how old?"

He shrugs. "Twelve?"

A year older than Duff – whose idea of getting high is, literally, hitting the top of the Ferris wheel.

"Hey, Tim?"

"Uh-huh." He's got his head tipped back against the cracked plastic seat-back now, looking at the moon, an almost invisible horseshoe of silver. He stretches and the bottom of his T-shirt rides up to expose navy-blue boxers with little white anchor crests peeking out from his jeans.

He looks up after a moment, finds me staring, fixedly, at the elastic banding.

"Nice shorts," I offer.

"Hot, right?" He pulls the waistband farther out, snaps it. "Complete with the Ellery Prep motto: 'Live purely, seek righteousness.'"

I snicker and he grins at me, runs his hand over his face like earlier, yawns, then drapes his arm over my shoulder, warm fingers landing lightly near my elbow.

"There's an innovative move," I say.

"Again, a classic for a reason. Besides, we're on a Ferris

319

wheel. It's like a reflex – practically Pavlovian."

"You simply can't help yourself," I say. "The motto on your shorts, no deterrent."

"Maybe you should take them off," Tim suggests. "Since they're obviously ineffective."

I elbow him.

The car rocks back and forth with a loud squawk, finally settling, tilted back in an unnatural position, so our legs are raised.

"I wish this wheel were running," Tim says. "Or we were at a drive-in movie. That would be a better atmosphere."

"Than this, which is kind of like being in a dentist chair?" I tilt back, close my eyes, his arm solid behind me, his index finger moving slowly up, down, around the bend of my elbow. Should be lulling, relaxing. But my skin's electrified. It's a cloudless night with a bite of chill in the air, sharp-sweet as an apple. The moon's just a slice and the stars look like a handful of glitter tossed across the black. I'm far away, floating in space, distant from everything and everyone except Tim.

His shoulders shift. His other hand reaches out, palm grazing across the back of my hand, fingers interlacing from above. Squeeze. Then nothing.

Just us.

His hand, my hand.

Should be innocent. Middle school moves.

But isn't.

Here in the dark where I can see clearer . . . if it isn't innocent, it *is* simple.

"The next move?" I say, a few minutes later. "I think it's this one." I pretend-shiver, press closer to his side. He makes a soft sound of surprise deep in his throat, then gathers me tighter.

I trace one finger lightly up and down his jeans, circle it around his kneecap, feel him shudder. He shuts his eyes, a wince, like it's the last thing he wants to do but he can't help it.

"Cold?"

"Anything but. You?"

Shake my head as he drops his hand, so his knuckles graze my side, up-down, past the side seam of my bra, trailing over my rib cage, slow, slow, slow.

There's a flash of light, sweeping past us, then back, pinning us both, a brusque voice. "Who is that? Who's there?"

Tim swears under his breath, is up and out of the car, tugging me along before I've even inhaled, then we're stumbling across the hilly grass, huddling behind a huge billboard advertising Hyman Orchards, The Apple of Connecticut's Eye. I look back, see the flash of a white car with a blue stripe, lights twirling, turning the fairgrounds ruby-red, lightning-bright.

"The police?" I say incredulously. "No way."

"*Shhhh.*" Tim plants two fingers on my lips.

"There weren't any keep-out signs. We weren't even doing anything!"

"If we'd had five more minutes we could have been."

"Who the dickens is that?" bellows the voice, closer now.

"We can get arrested for this? Seriously?"

"*Shhh,*" he says again, holding up a hand. "Let's not find out. The Stony Bay po-po are bored out of their skulls. They leap on this kind of shit. Trust me."

"I know you're out there," the voice says implacably. "State your name and come out."

Still pulling my hand, Tim crouches down and runs from behind the billboard into a patch of bushes. The flashlight beam zooms around wildly. Fizz of a walkie-talkie. "ATL suspect and/or suspects for trespass. Copy."

Loud crackle of unintelligible response.

I start to stand up, brushing off my shirt, prepared to argue. Tim yanks me back to the scrubby grass.

"Let go. This is ridiculous." I'm struggling against him, wriggling away. "Who do these guys think they are?"

"Alice," he hisses. "Nothing else is going on here tonight, unless they need to rescue a cat in a tree. They will bring us in, for real. That would suck for Joel."

For that I fall silent, stop moving. My police academy brother.

More crackling from the walkie-talkie. "UTL, repeat, UTL. Over."

Slow loop of the light all around. I press my head to Tim's chest, wriggle up to ensure my feet aren't poking out of the bush like the dead Witch of the East's, and then freeze, listening.

The shaft of light moves slowly, outlining the side of the billboard, up across the top, back down the side. What does this guy expect – that we're scaling the Hyman Orchards sign? To do what? Hang from our knees and graffiti it upside down?

Crackle-crackle. "No sign of the perp. Repeat, negative as of this time. Over."

"Perp? We didn't perp anything!" I whisper. "There was no caution tape, there was no no-trespassing sign."

"Alice. Be. Quiet."

Finally, the crunch of footsteps moving away. I begin to slide off Tim and he traps my hips between his palms.

"Don't move."

"What? Is he still there? Is he trying to fake us out? Do you *know* this cop?"

"I know almost all of 'em. No, he's gone. Don't move. Except the wiggling. That was good." Lips drag along my ear, his voice lowers, close to a whisper. "Alice. Kiss me."

"Tim . . ."

"I'm right here."

Me too, no honest way to pretend I'm not.

I squirm as if to roll off, but I have his sleeve, pulling him over with me until his face is above mine, the sliver of

moon behind it.

I move my hands up slowly, inching, brush one dark eyebrow, then the other with the tip of my index finger. Along one high cheekbone, the dip in the middle of his top lip, the bottom line of the lower one.

See the gleam of his eyes in the dim light. Watching. His skin, warm in the cool night air.

I twist a little underneath the length of his body, look away.

Try to laugh but there's hardly any air to breathe, he's so firmly against me, so it comes out as a gasp. He smiles, lifts to plant his elbows on either side of my head, nudging my cheek lightly with the left one so I have to turn my own head, look him full in the face.

"Alice."

Close my eyes. "You're totally taking advantage of this situation."

"Hell, yeah. You're free to return the favor." The tone is light, but his eyes are serious.

His hand slides across my neck, up behind my ear, thumb moving to the hollow of my throat where my pulse is knocking hard. I expect his lips, but instead I get his cheek, so lightly rested, it's almost not touching.

Rise and fall of his chest against me, leg edging between mine. Then stillness.

For a breath.

One more.

When our mouths meet there's a suspended instant when Tim freezes, total tension in his shoulder and neck muscles, but then he dives into me.

I hear myself make this noise in my throat and I'm pulling him tighter against me, sinking into him. I'm shivering, actually shaking and making sounds . . . I don't know . . . they'd embarrass me if I could stop. But I can't.

We pull apart for a moment, breathing hard.

"This could be a big mistake." I slide my hands down to his hips and lock them closer, hard against my own.

"Nope. I've made mistakes. They don't feel like this."

"Gotcha," says a loud voice. We both jerk our heads up, blinded by a flashlight. Tim swears under his breath. I hold my hands up to shield my eyes. Tim flips over to the side, in front of me, blocking me from the light.

"Stand up slowly," calls a voice. "Palms to your sides. No sudden moves. Step apart."

"Shhh," Tim whispers, moving a foot away from me. "It'll be fine. Just don't say *anything*."

"This is ridiculous," I say. The two policemen are talking to each other, all low official tones, walkie-talkies still crackling away, so I don't think they'll hear, but one of them freezes, shields his eyes, and flicks his flashlight back up.

"Oh, hell. That's my sister."

*

In the end they have nothing to bring us in for, although Alice manages to make it a very close call.

"Since when have you been skulking around checking out bushes like the pervert security guard at SB High, Joel?"

"This is part of my ride-along, Al. Since when have *you* been rolling around in the bushes with random dudes?" Joel flicks his flashlight up. "Oh. Hi, Tim."

I raise one hand. "Uh – hey, man."

"What I do is none of your business," Alice hisses. "And he's not a random dude, so –"

"Okey-doke," says Joel's superior officer. "Save that for the playground, kids. Speaking of which, you two" – again with the flashlight flicking from Alice to me, in case he'll need to ID us later in a lineup – "not smart to be around all that heavy equipment when the fair's closed. Easy to get hurt. But we can't arrest you for bad judgment."

"Lucky for you, Alice."

"Shut up, Joel," Alice says. "You hardly know him."

"Compared to you, guess not. He's what, Jase's age? When I said to relax and kick back, I didn't mean by hooking up with Holden Caulfield."

I shrug. Meh. Could be worse.

Alice, though, I expect her to flush, move away, put some distance between us. But instead, she edges closer, takes my hand. Moves a little bit in front, partially blocking me from Joel's amused grin, my shield.

"You hardly know him," she says again.

She stays close on the drive home too, scooching far over in the seat and up against me like she's still making some kind of stand, a statement, even though there's no one here but us. After I pull the car into the driveway, park it, I don't know what to do with my hands.

The fairgrounds, what we did there came naturally. Now it's like some movie moment, the motionless car, the cool dark around us, the streetlight picking up the shine of her hair. I've *seen* this in movies. I'm looking at us from a distance – waiting for some sort of cue: *Here is where you brush the hair away from her face, then you bend close and she makes that little sound of hers, halfway between a gasp and a hum of satisfaction. Then you kiss her and* –

Yup, I'm thinking in the second person.

Alice is looking at me, head tilted. I wait for her to look annoyed or puzzled, but she doesn't. I wait for her to take charge, climb into my lap, face me square on, lift the decision out of my hands and into her own. She doesn't. She studies me for a second more, then drops her head onto my shoulder, rests it, breathes in sync with me, but not like she's trying to. Just that she is.

No impatience rising off her, no confusion. It's like this is all good, just as it's meant to be. For some reason, I remember standing in the shower, the water streaming down – but not the times I've conjured up Alice there. Of

being under the spray with Cal, him sucking on my nose. Me thinking that right in that moment, I had everything he needed, and he was giving me everything I needed right back, simply by being there.

Resting my head against his shoulder. Something I've done without a second thought with my brothers. But never with any other guy. Tim would have no way of knowing that. But I do. When he tucks me nearer to his side, wraps a few strands of my hair around his fingers, lets them go, wraps them again, as though he can't help but keep touching me once he starts, it's then that I let it in. I'm most likely in love with him.

∘ ₒ ∘ •

"This is the first time I've ever done this," I say, a few minutes later.

Alice rests back against the door, her shoulders flat against the screen.

"This?"

She knows what I mean, but I say it anyway. "Walked someone to their door."

Alice left the porch light on, but the kitchen's dark. The house is quiet in a way the Garrett house is never quiet.

To my right there's the long fence that separates the Garretts' yard from what used to be the Reeds'.

Big maple tree, tossing boughs in the blowing air, with that *shhh* sound leaves start to make when they're beginning to dry out. Clouds coming across the moon, wind swept in from down by the river, smells like riverweeds, mud, leaves, and drying grass, the kickoff of fall.

It's all quieter than anything in my world has ever been. Peaceful.

Almost don't know what to do with peaceful.

Alice lowers her head, looks up through her crazy-long lashes. I brace one hand on the door, to the side, well above her head.

"I should have won you a big-ass stuffed teddy bear and one of those huge lollipops."

"At the Coconut Shy? I'll take a rain check."

"What about Joel?"

"More a High Striker kind of guy — always loved swinging that mallet."

"You know what I mean, Alice."

"Is he going to come looking for your blood because you had your hand up my shirt? I'm not thirteen. He'll show *me* no mercy, though."

She smiles, shivers a little.

"You should get inside." My voice comes out husky halfway, then breaks on the last word. The whole sentence is the opposite of everything I want to say, but that's probably a pretty good guideline still.

I lean down just as she moves up, on her tiptoes, one

hand flat against my chest.

Her lips just touch against my mouth, then the cleft of my chin, back to my lips.

"Good night, Tim."

My lips on her forehead.

"Good night, Alice."

I can't remember ever having something and not reaching for more.

But I back away from her, hands in my pockets.

Enough.

"Are you with *him* now?" The kitchen's dark, but the tone of Brad's voice is darker, one I've never heard from him. "Is that what's going on?"

"Where are you?" I'm flicking on the kitchen lights, all of them, one after another, waiting for the answer. Cell phones, God. Andy's been known to call the kitchen from the living room on hers. But Brad calling me from inside my own house is way too babysitter-slasher-horror movie.

"I was driving by to give you a printout of that new warm-up. The one with the trunk rotations? Cyn at CrossFit swears it cut her time by a solid five minutes. And there you are, with that redheaded kid."

"Where are you?" I repeat, walking through the living room, opening the bathroom door, back to the kitchen, the basement door.

"You can't be with that guy." Brad's voice is louder through the phone, and I think it's because I've found him, he's lurking in the basement just exactly like the movies, but no, he's just talking louder. "You're with me."

"We broke up," I say, sitting down abruptly against the wall by the basement door. "I told you that, Brad. We're not together."

"Alice. You. Can't. Be. With. That. Guy," Brad repeats. "He's a druggie with a kid. C'mon."

"He's in recovery and the baby is tempor—" I start, then stop. I don't need to defend Tim to Brad. "This is none of your business."

"You were the one who ended our break, Alice."

"It wasn't a break, it was—" I refuse to have this argument with a cell phone. "Where are you?"

"Nearby."

Now I'm outright scared. "Stop it! We are not dating anymore. Or working out anymore after this. We're done, Brad. This is not okay."

"That's exactly what I'm saying," Brad says.

And hangs up.

Chapter Thirty-three

It starts when I'm driving.

Just as I've always been afraid it would.

This car whips by, passing on the right, swerving around, too close to my side, too close in front. I smash down on my brakes but I'm on the bridge over the river, high up, and there's a strong wind whistling up from the bay, making the bridge cables overhead bounce and shake. The Bug fishtails a little, but I know I can correct it, happens all the time, not a big deal.

Until it is. Until the black sedan's weaving through cars far ahead of me, long past posing any danger, the Bug once again driving straight, nearly to the exit, but I'm chasing after something I can't catch.

My breath.

I'm only exhaling, no air coming in; almost right away my hands are tingling and seizing up because that's what happens, that's what bodies do, to get oxygen where it most needs to be, shut down the things that aren't as vital.

Except that my hands *are* vital because I have to hit the

turn signal and ease down the ramp or someone will bash into me from behind or I'll go spiraling into the guardrail or –

Going hot, then glacial under the sweat breaking out all over my skin.

Don't know how I make it off the highway, onto the smaller Route 7, then down a few miles, to the Stony Bay exit. Later, I won't even remember how I did that.

Exit.

Downhill.

Left turn.

Familiar enough to be automatic, but it's harder and harder to pull any air in at all, some trapdoor in my throat has slammed shut, sealed so tight I can't even swallow.

I should pull over.

Here, on the shoulder.

But the curve of the road near the roundabout at the top of Main Street *has* no shoulder, the street's too narrow, no side parking, so I keep going, trying to shake my fingers out so they work better. So they work at all. Flatten my tingling left hand on my thigh for a second, then my right. Drive too close to the roundabout, so that one back wheel bumps up over the raised base, then slams down. Some old lady about to cross at the crosswalk in front of the Dark and Stormy glares at me because I don't stop for her.

I can't stop for anything, just need to get home.

Now my toes are tingling, edging into numb as I shove

down on the brake to switch gears, fourth, third, second. Into the driveway, thank God, right behind Tim's car. Roll the window down, but even though air pours in, it's not enough. I'm trying to pull burning sandpaper into my lungs and it sears my throat all the way down.

Snatch at the door handle but it's not opening; it's locked and for some reason that's just it, too much. Bury my forehead in the crook of my arm, shoulders shaking, all of me shaking.

Then there are hands tight on my upper arms and Tim saying, "Alice. Alice!"

If this were another movie, I'd haul her into my arms and up the garage steps, kick open the door with one heel, muscle her over to the couch, all without breathing hard.

As it is, small as Alice is, she's so tense that I can't even bend her, much less scoop her up, so I half drag her out onto the driveway, back over onto the lawn, land on my ass with her held tight against me, rigid as a surfboard. She's, like, quivering, and I'm scared out of my mind.

So we're both gasping for breath. "Tell me what's going on!" I try for a calm, neutral tone. My voice cracks twice in the short sentence.

"P-panic attack." She's flicking her hand toward her face, the harsh breaths coming a little less close together.

"Do you have a —"

Something to fix this? What? An inhaler? It's not asthma. Brown paper bag to breathe into? Not on me, no.

"You're okay," I say finally. "Just breathe. You're okay."

Stroke her back in slow circles, like she's Cal.

"You're safe. You're okay." Her eyes are so wide, frantic. My chest clutches like I'm not getting enough air either.

"'S okay," I repeat. Her hand shoots out and grabs on to my wrist, tight. All sweaty. I rub my other palm against the back of it. Despite the sweat, her hand is icy. "It's fine. You're fine. It's all good."

o ● o ●

It takes about ten minutes, longer than I ever remember it taking. By the end, I'm lying across Tim's legs, my head in his lap, staring up at the wedge of his chin, the pale blue sky, the scarlet leaves of our maple tree filtering the light.

It'sokayit'sokayit'sokay. He keeps saying it over and over and finally the air comes all the way into my lungs and hangs around long enough to fill them. Still I don't move, and he keeps on massaging his palm over my back, my neck, my upper arms.

In.

Out.

In.

Out.

No idea how long we stay like that.

"Are you back?" Tim asks, in a hushed voice.

I nod. "I think so." My voice is squeaky and breathless but at least I can talk.

So, progress.

"Can you walk?"

I shake my head.

"Do you want water?"

Shake my head again.

"Does it help if I hold you? No funny business."

"Funny business?" I say.

"I have no idea where that came from. Please forget I said it. What happened here? Can you tell me?"

Shake my head. My breath starts to clutch up again.

○ ● ○ ●

Five minutes later I'm flopped back on Tim's couch and he's pacing around the kitchen, waiting for water to boil. He keeps checking on me.

"Still okay?"

"Stop asking that. Makes me tense."

He runs his hands through his hair, short, sharp nod. "Of course. Sorry."

In. Out. I'm tracing slow circles on my thigh, concentrating hard on that. When I first had these, back in middle school, that's what the school counselor, Mrs. Garafalo, had me do. Circle, bigger circle, bigger circle.

She also had music – a CD she gave me – lutes or sitars or gongs or something slow and rhythmic with no words.

"Have any music? Just, like, instrumental?"

He looks around the room, his fingers scrubbing at his hair, then reaches down and scoops something out of the basket, twists something, and sets it next to me. It's a small lavender stuffed elephant, evidently with a music box inside, because it's playing a song that takes me a moment to identify.

"'I Am the Walrus'?"

"I know. And it's an elephant. Don't ask. Obviously a refugee from the Island of Misfit Toys. Just close your eyes and listen, Alice. Do the breathing thing."

I tip my head back against the couch, listen to him moving around the apartment. Then I feel him standing near me.

"It's happened before," Tim says. Not as a question.

I nod.

"A lot?"

My stupid throat is tightening again. "Years ago. When I was twelve."

"Ah. Before you 'flipped it.'"

"There were other things going on. But yeah. Not since then. Till a few weeks ago."

He shoves a hand into the breast pocket of his rumpled oxford shirt, in that "reaching for a cigarette" way, comes up empty, looks around helplessly for a moment, then

scoops up a fireball from a bowl on the table. Pops it through the plastic coating directly into his mouth.

"What happened a few weeks ago?" The fireball's scrunched in his cheek, so his words come out funny.

I start telling him. Only a few halting sentences in, Tim jumps up and starts pacing back and forth like a caged coyote. All the way through he keeps peppering me with questions:

"Did you go by the bank?"

"Did you talk to a lawyer?"

"Have you tried going through Samantha?"

"I've thought about it," I admit to him, "but I thought, first —"

"You know you have to talk to Gracie," he says, setting tea on the coffee table next to my feet. My hand goes toward my throat and he grabs it, holds on it, squeezes. "I know Grace Reed, Alice. She backs down. She's gotta know she's in the wrong all over the place here."

"You think she cares? This is the woman who was going to pretend nothing happened when she smashed her car into my family's life, Tim."

"Until Samantha called her on it. And your brother. She's a coward, really. Bullies usually are."

"These bills are going to collection. I got nowhere at the bank," I repeat, not telling him who I spoke with there, because why make things harder.

"So you have nothing to lose," Tim says. "Drink your

tea. Let's get there. I have to pick up Cal, but not until four – that gives us plenty of time."

"I don't need you to go with me."

"I'm driving you, in case you freeze up. I'll be in the car outside, in case shit gets weird. And I'll have my phone, in case you need me to go ninja and crash through the window or something."

"But –"

"*Shhh.*"

"Don't *shhhh* me!"

"Angry? Good. Now let's get you to Gracie."

Grace Reed is wearing overalls, but designer – definitely not Oshkosh – and holding a paint roller in one manicured hand. "Yes?"

She looks a lot like Samantha, except her hair is silvery blond and straight, while Sam's is tawny and wavy. But Samantha doesn't have anything close to her mother's smooth, expressionless face. Everything Sam thinks is right there, easy to read. If Grace had expressions, she might have wrinkles. Laugh lines, like Mom, who I'm pretty sure is younger.

Reaching into my backpack, I pull out the pile of envelopes secured with a rubber band. "These are for you."

She takes a step back, her eyes skating over the envelopes, back to me. Opens the door wider. "I think you'd better

come in. You can leave your shoes right outside."

Swallowing hard, I slip off my sneakers. She drops the paint roller into a paint pan, wipes her hands on her pants, and leads the way into the living room.

White on white on white, with a few splashes of black – the pillows, the frames of the muted photographs of Samantha and her sister, Tracy. The only color is a huge painting over the mantel of the white brick fireplace. Grace at a piano, with a preschool Tracy and toddler Sam at her feet, all of them wearing dark green dresses with pink satin sashes. Sam is all ringlets and big wide eyes. Tracy looks a tiny bit scornful – typical, from what I know.

Grace Reed points to the frost-white couch, looming like an iceberg off the snowy carpet. "Would you like some lemonade?"

Please. We are not making this into a social occasion. I shake my head. Hold out the envelopes again. Repeat, "These are yours."

"I think I'll have a glass of Pinot, myself," she says, giving me a conspiratorial smile. "I've always hired someone to do the work before. Never appreciated how tiring it is when you DIY!" She click-clicks her heeled sandals across the wooden floor into what I guess is the kitchen. The footsteps seem to go on forever. Huge, this place. High ceilings. So white. I'm small, hunched on this sofa, cushions so puffy, my feet barely reach the ground.

My chest cramps.

Deep calming breaths.

I fan the envelopes out on the coffee table. She returns with a large glass of white wine, sets it down on the table with a clink, crosses her ankles, and looks me, at last, in the eye.

"Which one are you?"

I'm torn between rolling my eyes – yeah, "those Garretts" are one big indistinguishable blob – and throwing the contents of her glass in her face. Does she even know *Jase's* name?

"Alice. Jase's older sister. I do the hospital bills." I tap the envelopes with a finger, settle back on the couch, lean forward to touch them again. Grace's brows edge together. "These are yours. They've gone to collection. That affects my parents' credit, since their names are on them. Your bank wrote and said you weren't paying anymore. When I spoke to them, they said those were your instructions."

Grace Reed used to be a politician, and that practiced poise shows in her face, if nothing else does. She gives me a pleasant, small smile, but her eyes trade nothing away. She takes a sip, waits for me to go on, looking, at best, mildly interested.

"You cover it. That was the deal," I say. "The one you made with my mother *and my father.*" I pick up one bill, hold it up like show-and-tell. "Dad's had a bunch of tests recently, and a few specialists in because of – well, because he needed them. The total so far is seventeen thousand

dollars. I'll accept a check."

"I had no idea it would be this expensive," she says, bending forward to set down the glass, thinking better of it and taking a quick sip. "Fortunately your father is relatively young. He should make a fine recovery. I'm sure the doctors have told you that." Her tone's still light. She sounds like someone I'd run into at the post office, like it all has nothing to do with her, like *Wish you the best, buh-bye.*

"If he gets good care, he will. But if the rehab has to toss him out on his ass because he can't pay the bills, what then?"

"I don't believe they can legally do that," she says, and takes another sip, leaving a touch of coral lipstick behind. "In fact, I supported a bill that –"

"You're not the state senator now. You're the person who caused all of this."

The hand that lifts the wineglass is just a bit shaky; some sloshes over onto the coffee table. Grace takes a measured sip, sets the glass down, reaches out and touches my knee, confidingly. "Listen now, I know this has been an ordeal for your family. Make no mistake, it's been one for mine. It's affected everything. My relationship with my daughters. My romantic connection. Up in smoke. It'll follow me for the rest of my life. I may never be able to serve the people of Connecticut in any official capacity again. This may even rebound on Tracy and Samantha. Don't you think we've been punished enough for a mistake anyone could

342

have made?"

"My parents wouldn't have made this 'mistake.' My brothers and I – who never swore on a Bible to uphold the law – wouldn't have either. My four-year-old kid brother would know better."

"Alison, you need to understand my position. The bulk of my money comes from a family trust. I do get generous dividends every quarter. Generous for my purposes. But not when one adds in astronomical medical bills. After this latest round of your family's, I barely have enough to pay Tracy's fall fees at Middlebury."

"Senator Reed. I don't give a damn. Sell stock. Sell paintings. Sell your Manolos. Use whatever extra you've put away in your sock drawer or stuffed in your bra. Pay the bills so my father can get the care he needs and we don't have creditors after us."

I start toward the door and her voice stops me. "I'm not even able to come up with Samantha's semester fee for Hodges." She stands up. "We can see the main school building from here. How will Samantha feel if she can look at it but not attend anymore? It's her senior year. She stands a solid chance at any one of the Ivies she chooses. That's her future. Is your brother planning to go to college? Or straight into the workforce?"

Being outright rude to this woman will only make her think she's more right and I'm more wrong. But –

"Jase has been in the 'workforce' since he was fourteen

– working at my dad's store. Like my brother Joel and me. And yes, he'll go to college. If he gets a scholarship. Or some loans. If we come through this without going bankrupt. My parents went to college. My brother Joel went to college. I'm at nursing school at Middlesex College in White Bay."

"I had a fund-raiser there. Lovely campus. So rural. Is that a community college? I can't remember."

As if community colleges and public schools are some inferior species – unless, of course, you need votes.

"Yes, it is. And – and – I applied to transfer to Nightingale Nursing School – in Manhattan – for this fall. I got in. Off the waiting list, at the end of the summer. But because of what happened to Dad, I deferred. I'm not sure I'll ever get there now."

I haven't told anyone but Joel about those two things. Not even my parents. They would have argued. Another thing to add into Grace Reed's tally. Turning us into a family of secret-keepers. Something we've never been. Something that makes me a little sick.

"That is truly unfortunate," Grace Reed says, her voice sincere. "That's a wonderful school. I'm a huge believer in the value of a good education."

Yes, I'm sure you've made a speech about it.

She looks me directly in the eye now, her voice going quieter. "You're protective of your family. I'm the same about mine. I'm a single mom, Alison, and I've had to fill

the role of both parents since before Samantha was born. Hodges is the only school she's ever known – it's been stability for her, an extended family."

"Not my problem, Senator Reed."

"That's a pretty cold comment, Alison. How would your brother –"

The two-tone sound of the doorbell. She startles, and for a moment her eyes flick around the room, almost frantic, as though she's making sure no evidence – her fingerprints on the bills, a shattered headlight from her car – is in sight. But the only evidence is me, my red face, the angry tears building in my throat.

"Samantha must have forgotten her key. Again. Why don't you come with me and I can let you out when I let her in?"

There I am, trailing after her clacking heels down the long hallway. I haven't fixed a thing. The only thing that's changed is that I hate her more.

"Samantha, I've told you and told you to remember that I –"

"Yo, Gracie," Tim says cheerfully. "You're looking lovely as ever. Already whipping the house into shape."

Grace looks like she's trying to smile and frown at the same time, which even she can't pull off – she looks like someone's just goosed her. "Ah – um –"

"Tim," he says helpfully.

She laughs. "I wasn't expecting you, Timothy."

"You know me, I get around."

I'm glaring at him from behind Samantha's mom. He takes off a pair of sunglasses I've never seen him wear and polishes them on his shirttail, still smiling. "I'm still welcome, aren't I, Gracie?"

"Well . . . yes, though Samantha's not home yet, but – I thought you were her, actually, but – my guest was just –"

"Yes, I came for Alice. I'm her chauffeur today. One of my many jobs. I'm working for the Garretts now. In all kinds of ways."

Grace, like other women in Tim's life, obviously has no idea what to do with him. She settles for a faint "That's . . . enterprising."

"Isn't it? I try not to pass up any opportunity. Hey, speaking of that, Brendan, your campaign manager? I guess I should say 'former campaign manager' – he called me this week. On your behalf. Another volunteer opportunity."

She does that tilt of her chin, mildly interested thing.

Tim raises his eyebrows at her, smile broadening. "Thinking of throwing your hat in for treasurer?"

"Just a thought," Grace says. "Not a lot of opposition and – it's late in the game, so it's probably not likely, but –"

"But you like to gamble. Besides, it's been a couple of months since you retired. Practically a lifetime in politics."

Politics are not my thing. But I get the definite sense that more is being said here than has been spoken out loud.

346

"Yes, well . . ." Grace's gaze flits from Tim to me. All the discomfort I wanted for her? I see it on her face now.

"Ready, Alice?" He slips an arm around my shoulder, herds me out the door. "Sorry to cut things short. I know Alice will continue your conversation another time soon. And hey, thanks for giving Brendan the heads-up to call me. I'm glad all the stuff from your last campaign is behind you. Ancient history, right?"

She's still standing in the doorway as Tim the chauffeur ushers me across the well-tended lawn to his car.

Chapter Thirty-four

"Classic Grace," Tim says in the car, after I finish my description of the hellish visit. "Could have scripted it all."

"Why'd you tell me to talk to her if it wouldn't do any good? If you knew she was going to do all that – cry poor, and act like I was a big meanie and not budge an inch? And what were you doing, anyway? What was with the 'Yo, Gracie,' smooth campaign talk?"

"Trust me, Alice. It did some good. She's sweating right now. Count on it. Or perspiring, because sweating would be tacky. If nobody calls her on shit, Grace thinks no one sees it. Now she knows different. Me? I was just using what I knew and fucking with her."

All the anger that got lost under the white rug in the Reeds' hygienic little bubble buzzes around me now.

"It's not a game, Tim!"

He turns to me, face hard suddenly. For an instant, I can see how he'll look when he's older, when the sharp lines of his bones and the smoothness of his cheeks all come together to make a man's face. "I thought we'd been through this. I

am taking it seriously, Alice. I'm taking *everything* seriously. But, hey, thanks for the reminder that ultimately I'm a loser. Almost slipped my mind."

"No." I grab his sleeve as he reaches for the gearshift. "I don't look at you that way. At all. I – I –"

He puts a hand on my leg. "It's okay. You're okay. Breathe. Don't worry about it. But also, stop saying that shit to me. I don't care about Pop's naughty list, but hell if I'll be on yours. If this is going to work with us, I can't be auto-fuckup all the time."

His eyes widen, as though the words startle him as much as me. But then he adds, "I mean it."

This.

There's a "this" and an "us." And he's just laid that on the table.

"Unless it's just a hookup, Alice. Or not even that." His eyes search mine. When I don't say anything, his voice falters, drops lower. "Can you please talk?"

"No, it's not. And you're –"

My hands are around the back of his neck now, and I'm kissing him, kissing him, kissing him. His shoulders are vibrating because he's laughing now as I'm practically climbing into his lap.

"Whoa. We're in the Hodges school zone. If we get hauled in on public indecency charges, Joel will show no humanity this time."

He slides me off, carefully moving me almost to the

far side of the seat as though I'm magnetic or flammable, flashes a wink at me and turns around, elbow on armrest, to back up and pull out of the cramped parking space. I study him, sleeves rolled back, shoulders surprisingly broad beneath the rumpled striped shirt.

"When did you develop all this self-control?"

"You kidding? I have no self-control whatsoever. None." He sounds as though I've accused him of something shameful. "None."

"Every time we've kissed, you've stopped us."

He ticks things off on his fingers. "That night at the garage apartment when you agreed to let me stay there —"

"We didn't kiss then."

"I would have gone for it — you were the one who backed away. Also you were with Brad. The beach — too public. Also — other insane stuff going on. The Ferris wheel — that was the long arm of the law, also known as your big brother."

"And the house was empty."

"Sure. We could have used Jase's room. That would have been awesome." He punches in the cigarette lighter, blasts on the air-conditioning, readjusts the rearview mirror, concentrates hard on pulling out into traffic.

"Your apartment was empty too."

"Yeah, well. Man, this traffic better lighten up. I'm s'posed to pick up Nano before I get Cal, and Hester always freaks out if I'm late. God, that guy just went right

through the stoplight. You see that?"

"Tim, are you blushing?"

"No. I don't blush. Guys don't blush."

"I think you are."

"It's hot in here, Alice. Can you crack open your window?"

It is not, in fact, hot in here. It's actually sort of a chilly, cloudy fall afternoon. Plus, he has the air-conditioning cranked, which is completely unnecessary. I open my window anyway.

He rolls his down too, and sticks his head out when we get to a stoplight, cooling his face. Which is not blushing. Because guys don't blush.

Chapter Thirty-five

No matter where we do it – the store, Waldo's house, the garage, whatever, the Cal exchange has this weird, sketchy vibe. First off, Hester and I are so frickin' polite that you'd think we'd have to be speaking in code, because there are no conversations on earth so dull as this except the ones in introductory language courses. Instead of, "Where is the pen of my aunt?" we say, "They were all out of Huggies, so I bought blah blah blah," or, "He only slept four hours this morning, but he had a nap in the car." Plus which, you'd think that Hester was one badass spy because each time I get a different girl – sloppy sweats, jeans and T-shirt, dress. Cleavage, no cleavage, turtleneck. Sometimes she's all flustered and nervous, sometimes she's poised and composed. Sometimes she's got notes written out about when Cal did what, sometimes she looks startled when I ask and says, "He did all the usual things."

This afternoon is awkward times eight hundred billion because Nan's along for the ride. So she's running into both my one-night-stand and its byproduct at the same time.

We're at the damn park again, which Nan just cannot get over. "It's weird. Who does that?"

"Dunno, sis. All the *other* mothers of my bastard children meet me at the courthouse. Who cares?"

Now Hester (Model 2.0: jeans and a sweater, both clean-looking) holds out a hand, and Nan takes it, scanning her face. Hester just looks back like she's expected close scrutiny. Nan's eyes run from the tip of Hester's head to the toe of her Keds. Then she drops down on her knees to look at Cal.

"He's beautiful," she tells Hester, who stays impassive. "When did you say his birthday was?"

"July twenty-ninth. Tim, I'm almost out of formula. You'll have to pick up some to get him through the day. Sorry." She hands me a crumpled twenty-dollar bill.

I shove it back at her. What the fuck? She's never done that before. And indeed, Nan's looking at me with *you deadbeat dad* written all over her face.

I squat down to Cal's eye level, unbuckle him, remove his latest stupid hat, which has mouse ears, and ruffle his flyaway hair.

"Hey kid."

Hester says something about having to run because it's her day to do whatever at the place where she works. Once again I'm smacked by how little I know this girl. Do I owe her that, the way I owe it to Cal, before they're both gone? I'm having a harder time than usual listening because I'm

so focused on Nan's reactions. Also, Cal's grabbed my hair and is trying to stuff some in his mouth. And part of me is with Alice, wondering if she's okay, if she's worrying about Grace, starting to panic –

Squeal from the kid, another sharp tug on my hair, pulling me back.

"Yow, Cal." I disentangle his hand and he immediately grabs my ear and tries the same maneuver.

"Remember, adoption agency, you signing the birth certificate, next Thursday at three o'clock," Hester calls as we walk away. "Wear a tie."

Christ. "Right, sure," I call back curtly over Cal's slurping on my ear.

Nan says nothing as she watches me strap him in, let him gnaw on the knuckle of my index finger while I rummage in my pocket for car keys. When I finally locate them, Nan's still looking.

"Sooo . . . whad'you think?" I wipe drool off on the side of my jeans.

"Hunhn," Nan says, unhelpfully.

"*Hunhn,* what? Don't you think he looks like me?"

But Nan just cocks her head at me, then Cal. "Sort of . . . maybe."

"Nans, *look* at him." I reach under his first chin to indicate the cleft, wave my hand at his leggy little body. "Come *on.*"

"I thought maybe it would just be obvious. He'd have a completely identical birthmark or something. I guess, the thing is, Tim, I can't figure out what she's up to. Why keep quiet so long and then show up – *ta-da!* – with a baby. Why not put him up for adoption right from the delivery room?"

It's not like I don't get what Nan's saying. I've had that thought. If Hester had just, say, written me a letter with the facts and some papers to sign off on, if Cal had been abstract, would I have left it at that? So much easier than these uncomfortable swaps, and weird-ass waiting-for-Hester-to-get-the-kid-together conversations with Waldo. Last time, I asked where the bathroom was and he said, "The body tries to tell the truth." Not exactly directions to the john.

"Raaaaah. Rah. Rrraaaaaaaah!" Cal contributes at this point.

I locate the set of plastic keys Mrs. Garrett gave me and hand them to him.

"What, you think she's one of those crazy people who steals babies, and she decided to bring me into her little scam so she can get access to my millions?"

"Don't yell at me," Nan says, her calm voice cutting through my increasingly loud one. "Maybe she wants you . . . back?"

"That would imply that she *had* me, that we had a thing going, which we didn't. So in this scenario of yours, she

wants me, she decides to present me with a baby, because hell knows nothing turns on a seventeen-year-old guy like a *child*."

Cal hits himself in the eye with the keys, drops them, and starts screaming, pissed as hell. I grin, unbuckle him again, pick him up. He nudges his face into my biceps, stops screaming, and gives a long, shuddery sigh.

Nan closes her eyes, tips her head back against the car. "I'm tired of worrying about you, Tim."

"We could always swing by Troy Rhodes's house so you could get something to calm your nerves."

Nan repeats, as she has every single time I've brought this up, "It's not how it looks."

"Just so ya know, that's one of the least convincing of all bullshit lines. That one never even worked for *me*. What gives, Nan?"

"As if it's that easy," she says. "I'm finally not terrified you'll die of alcohol poisoning or in a car crash."

"Strange, I thought we were talking about you. Quit worrying then. Back to –"

"You're finally turning your life around, and now you have to get into *this* situation."

"You know what? You sound exactly like Pop. Situation. Circumstance. Issue. Try 'baby.' He's your . . . your nephew." The word tastes strange in my mouth. My sister's an aunt. Pop and Ma are grandparents. Why those should be so much harder to wrap my head around than the fact

that I'm a father, I don't know.

She's giving me that same old *Not Again, Tim* face. Anger swamps in like a hot red tide. I hate to even touch Cal when I'm like this. But he's chomping away on my shoulder, oblivious to whatever it is pulsing in my veins.

Nan, however, must sense it. She slides her back along the car, away from me, wary.

"See, here's what I don't get, sis. Maybe you can explain it to me. All the mistakes I've made, and you and Pop are still on my ass when I'm trying to do the *right* thing. Temporarily."

"That's just it, Tim. Temporarily." She indicates Cal, my hand on his back, his cheek against my shirt. "And here you are. Acting like a dad."

"I'm not really acting like a dad," I point out. "Just babysitting. What do you want from me, anyway, Nan? You want me to say I don't know what the fuck I'm doing? Consider it said."

"I'm not worried you don't know what you're doing, Tim. I'm worried you do. Look at you." She waves her hand at me and Cal. "*That's* what worries me."

Nan's phone and mine vibrate simultaneously as I pull onto the curb in front of our house, and I snatch hers before she can get to it. **WHAT WE TALKED ABOUT STILL A GO? GOT ALL THE SUPPLIES, SO YOU ARE SET! – T.**

"I don't even get how you can come down on me, Nano,

when you're the one getting 'supplies' from the candy man."

"You don't know what you're talking about," Nan says, all heated.

"I know *exactly* what I'm talking about. No one knows better. So don't even –"

I'm so busy arguing with my twin that I don't notice the car parked behind us. Don't take in a thing until I hear Nan say, "Uh-oh." And look back to see Ma's figure bent over the trunk of her car, hauling bags and bags onto the driveway.

"She can't be worse than Pop about this."

"You didn't hear him when he first found out," Nan offers grimly.

Ma turns around as I get out and wipes her forehead, squinting at the car. "Timothy?"

"Uh, yo, Ma." Nan's sunk down in her seat and put her head in her hands.

"Well!" Ma says. "I was beginning to wonder if we'd ever see you again! Goodness!"

I pick up a bag, then another. They're all from the Christmas Tree Shop, Ma's addiction.

"Nanette! What are you doing, lurking in the car? Come carry some of this in. I got the cutest rug for your room!"

Nan looks apprehensive as she climbs out. Christ knows what the "cutest" rug might be, but I'm betting it won't go with her new look. I'm guessing kittens in a basket. With hats.

"Look at this!" Ma says, pulling something out of a bag.

"Can you stand it?"

It's a four-foot-tall stuffed elf, in an apron that says THE HELP YOURSELF ELF, holding a bowl labeled SWEET TREATS. Piss-awful, but suddenly there's this this wave of – I dunno, sympathy, pity, love, whatever, and I start to give Ma a hug just as I hear a shrill *"Raaaaaaaa!"* from the car.

"Uh-oh," Nan repeats.

"What's that?" Ma cranes to see around me. "What's that sound?"

"Here, I'll get those." Nan grabs about seven of the bags and bounds up the steps into the house.

"Timothy?"

"Oh, yeah . . . um, it's uh . . ."

"RAAAAAAAA!" Cal sounds both loud and alarmed.

I hurry to open the back door and reach in for him.

Geez, Dad. I had no idea where you were! Don't do that again! It's scary. It makes me hungry! Raaaaaaa!

Ma has her hand to her mouth and her face, always rosy, is completely white.

"Timothy Joseph. How did this happen?"

Let's see. Possible answers:

Well, Ma, I had sex with a stranger. But don't worry, I don't remember a thing about it.

God, I have no idea. I knew I should've taken better notes in health class.

Well, it turns out they were wrong, and kissing does *make babies.*

359

I tell the truth. "Uh, accidentally, Ma."

She marches up to me. "Like everything else in your life, Timothy! Oh, sweet Lord, I cannot believe this! What will your father say!"

I jiggle Cal a little and he settles, slightly, then turns his head, with the expression he always wears when he does that, as though it's taking an enormous amount of energy and concentration, and focuses his blue eyes on Ma.

She looks back at him and I notice that her eyes are that same intense blue. Her red hair is fading into gray, but it has the same wave as my own. And Cal's.

Her voice is low. "How could you? We raised you better than this."

You guys raised me better, Ma. This was all on me.

The Jaguar reels into the driveway, as always reserved only for Pop's car. He's on his phone. Ma clucks her tongue. "I just can't imagine what he'll say. I'm afraid you're in for it, laddie."

But when he gets out, Pop barely looks our way. He lowers the phone, shields it with his hand, and says, "I'll see you in the office in a bit, Tim. I've made some calls about your situation with the child."

The shock, incredulity, and devastation show on Ma's face, plainer than the wrinkles and the makeup she hides them behind.

"I guess this is old news to everyone but me then." She turns and walks into the house, stumbles for a second on

the first step, leaves a bunch of Christmas Tree Shop bags in her wake.

I start to go after her – to apologize, hug her, to do some freaking – God, I don't know, whatever – thing. But the door closes behind her with a click. I stand there, look down at Cal. He gives me the calm face back, then the goofy grin, like he's all full of confidence that I'll figure this out.

And again, I'm looking for direction from an infant.

I bring the bags in one-handed, Cal propped in my other arm.

Inside, Ma's nowhere to be found. No Nan either. I'm about to knock on Pop's door when there's the familiar rhythm of footsteps on the stairs. Ma's face is blotchy, her eyes blue, blue against pink, puffy skin, and it near about breaks me. Sure, we Masons cry easily, but I don't get the idea there was anything easy about these tears.

"Well, then," Ma says, all hold-it-together smile and straight back, "now you'll be filling me in on the episodes everyone else has already seen."

Alice's "so we're playing it like this?" hits me. Mason family mode – moving right along, nothing to see here, folks.

From there, the conversation rolls pretty much as you'd expect.

Me: And then, blah-blah-blah.

Ma: Oh my sainted aunt!

Me: So she blah-blah-blah.

Ma: Stars above! This cannot be good for your father's blood pressure!

Me: Then I blah-blah-blah.

Ma: Sweet Mary and all that's holy!

Cal, finally fed up with the swaddling and maybe the exclamations: *Raaaaaaaa!*

Except for this part:

"He looks just exactly like you did," Ma says. "More like your twin than Nan ever was. Goodness!"

"Goodness had nothing to do with it, Ma." Ha-ha. I'm unsnapping the sleeper thing, getting ready for a diaper change.

To my surprise, she smiles, sets a hand lightly on my shoulder. "Let me do that. You're making a mess of it. Just like a man!"

On cue, the man of the house emerges from his gray cave, looks at us, says, "I got in touch with Gretchen Crawley, who runs that Crawley Center for Adoption Services in West Haven."

Cal, freed from his blanket, kicks his feet at me, his eyes shining. I cup my hand around his face, rest my fingers in those red curls.

"Excuse me? What happened to 'I won't fix this for you,' Pop?"

"This is strictly big picture. Not your strong suit."

"Maybe not, but I thought the deal was that you were

362

out of this particular picture. Like Ma was. Apparently."

"Tim," Ma interjects, "you don't need to –"

Without looking at her, Pop holds up a staying hand.

"So what happened to this 'changing nothing about December'?"

"What about December?" Ma asks, looking confused.

In the dark about that too, looks like.

"She'll be happy to meet with this girl to discuss placement."

I focus way harder than I need to on the task of diaper changing, something that's pretty automatic at this point, and I'm acting as if it requires incredible reflexes, split-second timing. Cal snags my fingers as I peel off the tape, yanks them to his mouth, watching me intently.

"And with me, right?"

What he says: "It's not necessary."

What I hear: "You're not necessary."

Why does it piss me off so much to be shoved out of a picture I don't even want to be in?

The meeting I flee to, right after this? It's a topic one – and the topic is "acceptance," which generally makes people either eloquent or pissed as hell. Vince, who lost a leg and an arm in Afghanistan, yells and throws his crutch across the room, "Accept this? No way. I didn't sign on for this!" This other guy talks about how his wife accepted him, despite all his drinking and cheating, for years, then when

he finally got sober, she got lung cancer and died before he could "give her all those good memories to replace the bad ones." Alyson, who lost custody of her kids to her ex when she was still drinking, says she tries to accept every day that she deserves this, but every morning when she eats breakfast alone she thinks about how her ex-husband is a workaholic stockbroker who's hired three nannies to watch the kids.

"Was I really so much worse? I speak English," she says, swiping tears away from her cheeks.

I talk about Ma, and her unexpected acceptance of Cal, and about the Garretts and how acceptance is a given there . . . then a word or two about Pop. After the meeting, Jake gives me this hug and starts, like, talking. "When my partner came out to his parents," he's telling me, "they called the pediatrician to see if he had some sort of shot that could fix him. The first time he came to our house for dinner, my folks called the week before to find out what foods he liked so they could serve them." He looks at me, sort of meaningfully. I look back, like *Whaa . . . ?* He sighs, smiles. "We don't all get the winning hand with the parent thing. If we're lucky, we can find family in unexpected places."

Oh.

"So this is what normal people do for fun, huh?" Tim asks, sticking his head out the passenger window of the Mustang

as it jounces over the dirt road.

"Who knows?" Samantha gathers her hair in a messy bun. "It just seemed like the thing to do. It's been all work and no play for most of us lately."

"*Ooooo,*" Cal contributes. He's in his seat between Sam and me, wide-awake at eleven o'clock at night, eyes shining, arms waving. I look at him, look at Tim. His dad.

His dad.

Roll that around my head for a little.

I'll get there.

"This on Joel's patrol route?" Tim asks, catching my eye in the rearview mirror.

I grin. He flashes the dimple back.

"I don't think Stony Bay's finest bother with the corn maze at Richardson's Farm," Jase says from the driver's seat. "Let's park here before the underbody gets destroyed."

Actually a bit spooky. Richardson's Farm has a huge amount of acreage right along the salt marshes off the coast of Seashell Island where the marshes run into the bay. Tonight it looks beautiful and desolate, completely abandoned except for us.

"If we don't see the Great Pumpkin, I want my money back," Sam says, clambering out of the backseat, throwing her arms around Jase, who's stretching, fingers laced, looking out at the water.

Automatically, I'm pulling Cal out, holding his wiggling body tightly to my chest, reaching for a blanket. Tim's

buckling on the Babybjörn, muttering "Don't start" in response to Jase's muffled laugh.

Then I'm tucking Cal into the front pack, adjusting his fiercely kicking legs, snapping him in. Tim's pulling Cal's fingers away from my ear, my upper lip, the front of my hoodie, all the things he's determined to grab. We're in sync in a surreal way that I've seen with my parents, anticipating each other, compensating, filling in.

Crazy.

I'm doing this. I'm with a boy who has a baby and I'm right here acting like a mom.

I stumble over a rock concealed in the high grass, whoosh of exhale loud in the still air.

Temporary. This is all temporary.

By this time next year – God, by springtime – Cal will be with another family, Tim's deadline will have come and gone, maybe I'll be in Manhattan.

I don't get the rush of comfort I expect. Instead, my breath snags harder, my lungs too small. My phone chooses that second to buzz and I don't even want to look at it.

Ally, please. I can't give up. I won't. Where are you? Out with that kid? Alice, we're not done.

"All good?" Tim asks, his hand on my elbow, looking into my face, glancing at my phone.

I nod. All good if I don't need to use any air to talk.

He stops on the path. "Alice."

Sam and Jase are farther down the hard-packed dirt

trail, almost to the maze, arms looped around each other's waists.

"What is it?"

I remember this from that seventh-grade year – one thing gets to you and then the others come in like a football pile-on. The good – Tim. The bad – this thing with Brad. The ugly – Grace Reed. In this moment, they're all stealing my breath.

Stay in the moment, stay in the moment, stick with what's happening.

Deep breath.

"She's really getting back into politics? Grace?" I ask. "They actually called you?"

"I see the romantic atmosphere is getting to you, you softie. Yeah, kiss-ass Brendan did. Not much time to assemble a team – since it's already October and elections are less than six weeks away. Don't worry, I'm not working for her again. Though it would certainly make Pop stand up and cheer if I did. Or at least give a faint smile."

"He'd honestly want you to do that?" Dumb question. I saw Tim's father in action.

"Baaa," from Cal. We've entered the maze now, with its high hay-bale walls closing us in, away from the sweep of field running down to the ocean.

"Shit. Forgot the pacifier thingie." Tim offers Cal his thumb, notes my expression, pulls his hand away. "You betcha Pop'd want that. He doesn't know the reasons Grace

367

pulled out of the race. Hardly anyone does. Your family. Me. Samantha, who was there when it went down. And Grace's boy-toy Clay Tucker, who has reasons of his own to keep his lip zipped. There's only one real witness."

And no notarized document. Grace Reed can, once again, get away with it all.

I swear under my breath.

"There's an answer. We'll find it. Grace has plenty of chinks in her armor."

"We?"

"We. You get my political savvy and my sleazy, manipulative mind along with all my other many irresistible charms."

Cal's started bumping his head against Tim's chest, rooting for food, whimpering a little. We make a left turn, then another. The wind is rising, the autumn chill deepening with the night. Another turn and we practically stumble over Jase and Sam, all wrapped up in each other against a prickly wall of straw.

"A roll in the hay is supposed to be a figure of speech, you two," Tim says, bumping his shoulder deliberately into them.

"Move on," Jase says, out of the corner of his mouth, barely taking his lips off Sam's.

Tim reaches for my hand, tight grip. Warm. Down a long corridor, past a few moth-eaten scarecrows pinned against the side, and a bedraggled Jack Sparrow propped

against a wooden stake. Two more turns and he backs me into a corner, rests his long fingers on either side of my face. "You asked for a kiss?"

"I didn't ask!"

"You're right. It was more like a demand. You wanted me to lose all self-control."

I hear Samantha's laugh, not far away.

"Not the ideal moment for that, Tim."

"Sometimes you just have to take the one you've got."

We're kissing in a corn maze twenty feet from my younger brother, with a baby wriggling between us.

And I wanted things simple.

"I think about sex too much," I tell Dominic, who's walking on the beach with me, exercising Sarge, his massive German shepherd. God forbid Dominic not have a dog as macho as he is. I've got Cal in the pussy front pack.

"There's a limit?" Dom picks up a piece of driftwood and tosses it with a neat flick of his wrist. Sarge catches it, shakes it ferociously, and then drops it at Dom's feet in a *killed it, next challenge?* way.

"Every second. Sometimes twice a second." I'm an asshole, because it's not sex I'm thinking about, it's Alice. All of Alice.

"Huh." Dom shoves his hand into the pocket of his jacket, yanks out a tennis ball, and hurls it. "Sounds

normal, Tim."

"Freakin' inconvenient. Not to mention scary as hell."

"Wanting sex – or wanting it with Cal's mom?"

"Nope. *God* no. Kinda general. Kinda specific. Just constant," I continue, picking up a flattish rock and winging it into the water. My skipped stones always sink like . . . uh . . . stones. "You know how they say you don't do anything when you're wasted that you wouldn't do sober?"

"Yeah, they say that. Think it's bullshit myself."

"Really?" I'm relieved. "Because my sister keeps telling me this is all some elaborate plot of Hester's. I get paranoid and I think maybe Nan's right, because when I see Hester, I can't imagine, like, jonesing for her. Ever."

My voice is rising, and Cal squirms, twisting his neck as if to face check and make sure I'm cool.

"This while thinking about sex every second," Dom mutters. "Here. Can I hold him for a sec? It's been . . . a while since I held a kid."

"Sometimes twice a second. Yep."

I unsnap the harness thing and Dom moves his hands around in this awkward way, like he's trying to figure out where to pick up something hot so it won't burn him. Then he finally settles them under Cal's armpits and lifts him up, looking him in the eye. And Goddamnit, he's got tears in his own eyes.

I reach down for a stone, even though this one's not nearly flat enough, rub my thumb against the mica, focus

on the little flakes that flicker in the sunlight, not the wetness on Dom's cheeks.

"So damn small. You just forget," he says finally, and wipes his face on the shoulder of his jacket. He clears his throat, once, twice, this hollow, hacking sound, looks out at the water, adjusts Cal's collar, swipes the back of his hand over his eyes again. Finally, "Why scary?" He reaches into his apparently bottomless pocket and places a flat stone in my hand. "It's all in the wrist."

"I dunno. Don't want anyone hurt."

"You want to bag that chance, stick to celibacy."

"Yeah, and just keep beating my dick like it owes me money."

"That's beautiful, man." Dom shakes his head. "So – sex but not specific, huh? That even possible?"

"What about, uh, someone I've known for a while?" I ask, in this fake casual voice.

"Like . . . ?" Dom says.

"No one in particular," I mutter.

He gives me a *yeah right* look, sighs heavily. "Take it easy, Tim. Work on self-control. You're just beginning to think straight."

Here's the thing, though . . .

I am, I *am* thinking straight – about Alice. For, like, the first time, about her, about anyone. But I'm . . .

"Skip the stone, man," Dom says. "That you can control."

371

"I'm no good at that."

"Do it anyway."

"I feel like the frickin' Karate Kid. Are you trying to give me some, like, lesson in letting go or something?"

"I'm Portugese – we like to keep busy. Wouldn't do you any harm either. So I'm trying to teach you to skip stones. It's a dying art, like whittling."

"No way am I learning to whittle."

"You're always saying you need stuff to do with your hands," he points out. "Aside from the one you're already doing. Unlike that, it's something you can teach your kids."

"He'll be someone else's kid by then."

"I didn't mean only Cal, Tim." He peers at my face. "How you doing with that? Him?" I'm kicking at the sand with one toe, holding the flat granite rock tightly enough that the sharp edge digs into my palm.

"Good. Fine. Whatever. I don't know."

"That's four different answers. Which one's the truth?"

I toss the stone, which sinks immediately.

"Do *you* feel like he's your son? Like he – belongs to you?"

Yes.

God, I do.

Um. Shit.

Blindsided, I bend over, hands on knees. I fuckin' care about this kid. Not just like I'm babysitting him and waiting for his goddamn parents to come home. Like he's home

when he's with me. Or fuckin' scarier still, I'm home when I'm with him. And Alice. And that's the thing . . . you let people in . . . they're there. They're goddamn part of you. Except that at any time – soon, in Cal's case – anytime, in Alice's – they could chip right off and float away.

"Tim?" Dom's voice floats in my head, a little distant. "Tim. Talk."

Okay, okay. That's okay that I do. Care about Cal. Good that I do. Less chance I'll screw up and leave him somewhere by accident. It's a good thing.

Right?

But, God, why bother with this? I had the dad who wasn't there. Now the kid who won't be there. Which makes me another dad who won't.

Dominic reaches over, puts a new stone in my hand, bending his elbow around my neck, giving me a whacking hard pat on the back.

"Is this the part where we hug?" I ask.

"Manly back-patting is plenty. Save the hugs for the kid and Ms. No One in Particular."

Chapter Thirty-six

Self-control. Alice called me on having it, using it too often, but pretty sure we both know that's not what's going on here.

Whatever it is, I'm so done using it with her.

I'm across the kitchen in two strides, too fast to even see what she's wearing or her expression or anything.

I reach out, very slowly, rub my thumb along Alice's soft deep-pink lower lip. No lipstick or that sticky gloss crap. Just her, just Alice. Her dark lashes lower and she takes a deep breath. My thumb trails to circle under her jawline, tilting it gently up as my head slopes down.

A calmer, more deliberate kiss than we've ever shared. Different from the times before when we locked together fast and hard as if drawn magnetically. This is intentional, like it's saying something. When her lips part, it's a declaration as much as an invitation.

When I inhale, I take in Alice, sunshine, salty-sweet, peppermint. Not losing myself. It's finding her.

Oh, Alice.

She makes her little hum in the back of her throat, curling in. I edge my hands down her back, to the tops of her thighs, pulling her closer, just as she does the reverse, slipping her palms up under my shirt to shove my shoulders down. She was standing in the light from the window. Her skin is sun-warm under my fingertips.

Our kisses are still calm, amazingly, since all of Alice is aligned against all of me. I fall back against the wall, scooping her even closer as my fingers move down her back, slide along the tops of her legs.

I should stop. I'll stop. I'll just take this last minute. And this one. And this next one and . . .

"Wow. *Mommy*. Alice and Tim are kissing in the kitchen."

Alice jerks back from me and both of us whirl to look at George, who's wearing an I MET SANTA ON THE ESSEX STEAM TRAIN shirt and for some reason, pink sweatpants. "You two were kissing," he tells us, in case we might have missed it the first time.

"George . . ." Alice waves her hand in a circle, looking like she's trying frantically to come up with an explanation.

"Kissinnnnnnng," George repeats as Mrs. Garrett comes in with some shopping bags, followed by Jase, Andy, Duff, Harry, and Patsy. What, no camera crew?

"Hi Tim." Mrs. Garrett sets her bags down on the kitchen table. "Are you hungry? We ran out of everything – it was Cheerios or nothing – but we're restocked now."

I look up and meet Jase's eyes. He gives me a quick, rueful smile, and then becomes preoccupied with emptying grocery bags. No chance in hell he didn't hear George.

Not surprisingly, Tim does not stick around. He says, "Thanks, Mrs. G. Gotta head out, I have a – thing. Catch you later, Jase. And, um, you too Alice." And leaves.

"Why were you kissing Tim, Alice?" Beating around the bush is not in George's bag of tricks. He pulls on the hem of my shirt. "The longest kiss was fifty-eight hours. Do you think they did that without drinking water? Wouldn't they die, Alice? How'd they pee?"

"I'm sure they . . . I don't – I was just, um . . . here, Mom, let me help you put those away."

Mom, because she's tactful or because she's trying to torture me, says nothing as we put things in cabinets. Jase, who usually helps, who *was* helping, has faded away. The others always vanish at chore time, so it's just me, Mom, George, and Patsy in the kitchen.

Patsy attaches herself to my leg like a limpet. "Where Hon?" she cries mournfully. "Why Hon go? I love on Hon."

I sneak a look at my mother, afraid she's going to ask exactly how much loving on Hon I've been doing, but she seems preoccupied with putting away the frozen food, jamming the extra-large Sam's Club containers into our crowded freezer.

I'm humming under my breath when Mom puts a hand on my arm, nods her head at the cabinet under the sink where I've just placed a container of ice cream, a jumbo package of pork chops, two cartons of eggs, and a can of shaving cream next to the dish soap and the glass cleaner.

"Um . . ."

In the end she must take pity on me, and tells me to go upstairs. I am a coward and do it, leaving her to unpack the last forty-five grocery bags alone, or with the dubious help of George, who just takes something out, says, "Oh good, we have Oreos," and opens up the package. And of Patsy, still mourning the disappearance of Tim. "Want my Hon . . ."

Oh Pats. Me too.

∘ ∘ ∘ ∘

I'm sitting on my bed a few minutes later, trying to resist the urge to march over to Tim's, when the door opens and Jase comes in with his corn snake entwined around his forearm.

"You've brought Voldemort to attack me?" I ask. Jase has always loved animals. His bedroom is like Petco.

"Nah. He escaped and made a break for Mom's shoe rack again." He sits down on the edge of Andy's bed, incongruously masculine against her lavender-and-purple tie-dyed bedspread. I've had years to get used to the fact

377

that my little brother is a hottie, but his looks still startle me sometimes. Jase takes a breath, puffs it out, resting back on his elbows, letting Voldemort the corn snake sashay slowly across his chest, kicks the rug with his shoe.

"Just say it."

He glides a finger along the length of Voldemort. "This is your business, Alice. Just . . ."

We Garretts are all about two or three years apart in age, and you'd think that we'd be equally close – but in real life, it doesn't work that way. Not all the time. Things shift. But Jase and I have been tight ever since Dad drove Joel and me to the hospital to pick up Mom and the newborn Jase for the first time. In an attempt to stave off jealousy, as the story goes, she put him in my arms and said, "Here's your baby."

I believed her.

I called him "my baby Jase" for the first three years of his life. I used to crawl into his crib and hold his hand at night, sure he'd sleep better, be safer if I were there.

Maybe he even *was*. Because that closeness never has left.

His green eyes meet mine, then shift downward. "Don't do your thing with him, Alice."

"My *thing*?"

Jase has never warned me off a guy. I've done it to him (with girls, obviously) – once when I heard rumors about his ex-girlfriend Lindy and again when he and Samantha

were briefly broken up last summer. I caught him by the sleeve as he was headed out to try to talk to her, get her back, told him to give it up, have some pride. As it turned out, I was wrong to do that, and they got back together.

So he has every right to advise me . . .

I warned Jase off Samantha because he was in too deep with her almost before they'd even spoken. I'd seen Jase catch sight of her walking up her driveway or looking out of her window and lose track of what he was saying. I wanted no part of that.

But this . . . is nothing like that. Not the same at all.

I fold my arms over my stomach, hunch forward against the inevitable real.

It's just like that. I'm just different now.

"Your thing," he says. "Your date 'em, dominate 'em, ditch 'em thing. Tim . . ." Voldemort slithers off his lap and starts to glide down Andy's bedspread in search of our closet, our shoes. Jase scoops the snake back around his wrist. He chews his lower lip, sighs.

"Tim what?"

"He's got enough going on. He doesn't need anything else messing with his head right now."

"Shouldn't you be off punching him because he's dishonored me?"

"You're completely capable of doing that on your own. If it were any other guy, I'd leave you to it −" A shadow crosses Jase's downturned face. He looks up at me. "What's

up with Brad anyway? I saw you two running last week."

"He's out. For keeps."

"He knows that for sure?" Jase asks carefully, looping Voldemort around his neck and catching him as he slithers down the front of his shirt.

"I'm not stringing anyone along, Jase. Or playing games. I've been up-front with him. He's not happy, but he's gone."

"Let me know if that changes." He stands up, wrapping the snake around his upper arm this time. "Or you need backup."

"J.?"

He pauses in the doorway.

"It's not my 'thing.' With Tim. Not anything I know. I don't *know* what I'm doing. But I'm not out to hurt him."

He nudges the corner of my rug up, then back down with the toe of his shoe. "Alice . . ."

"What?"

"Do better than that." He heads out of the room before I can answer or argue or defend. Or tell the truth.

Chapter Thirty-seven

"I just happened to be . . ."

"In the neighborhood?" Tim shoves the door open wider. He props one arm against the doorframe, shoves his hair out of his eyes, his smile shifting from sweet to wicked as he looks down at me. "You decided not to sneak in while I was out, play Goldilocks again?"

"That turned dangerous last time. I'm being civilized."

"Damn. Back to professionalism and rule-making. I thought we busted through that."

"You mean when we got busted? Jase told me to stay away. Not to do my 'date 'em, dominate 'em, ditch 'em thing.'"

"Yeah, I got a dose of that too. But here you are."

"Here I am. Come with me. Outside," I say.

He trails me down the steps, across our dew-wet grass to the purple-dark backyard, no questions asked, although they're radiating off him. I lead him back behind the pool fence, near the playhouse Dad started to build this summer, which still smells like fresh-cut pine.

"We're camping out?" Tim surveys the saggy, army-green canvas tent, flap open, electric lantern set on low, floor heaped with blankets, pillows, sleeping bags.

I shrug. "We don't have to . . . Duff was having a sleepover, but they got freaked out. They're asleep now. Everyone is. I thought . . ."

"Are we telling scary stories? Playing truth or dare?"

"This is as far as I got with the plan."

"Works for me." He drops to his hands and knees, ducks his way through the flaps, halts a moment, possibly sighting the box of condoms over on the side of the tent, on top of a stack of Duff's LEGO Mindstorm books. Then he keeps moving, readjusts two pillows so they're lined up close to each other, smoothes out the dark green nylon sleeping bags, turns over onto his back, and folds his arms behind his head.

Ruffled dark red hair, watchful eyes, at last a slow smile, vivid in the muted light.

He moves one hand down now, carefully, until it lies, palm up, flat on the blanket. Silent appeal. Eyes locked on mine.

"Do I have to dare you?" he asks quietly.

His hand, resting there. For a moment I stare at it, my stomach giving a small, jolting flip. Calluses. A little cut on the pad of the thumb. No Band-Aid, of course.

Something so Tim about that hand.

"No," I say. "This is more truth than dare."

I stretch out by his side, slide my own hand into his;

tighten my fingers on the fast-beating pulse in his wrist, know it picks up pace, although his face stays the same – thoughtful, focused, only the widening of his eyes showing any effect. My whole body is both loosening and tightening at the same time.

"Can I ask you something?" I rush on before he can say yes or no. "All the flirting you've done? Now when I'm – here – it's different. It's like you're holding back. What is that? It's not – about the chase, is it?"

His thumb swipes across my hand, bump-traces each knuckle. Then he slowly pulls it to his lips, kisses the back. Rests his mouth there for the space of one breath. Two.

Then he meets my eyes.

"*Hell* no. No. I guess . . . I . . . wanted . . . you to come to me. Be sure we're in this . . . uh . . . together?" His voice cracks a little on the last word, flush high on his cheekbones. "Besides, um . . ."

Say it.

"Ah, I've never . . ." My voice is hoarse again. Alice's eyes, fixed on me, pupils wide and dark in the pale light from the lantern. Circle of green, glints of gold. Steady.

Say it.

"I've never had sex sober. Never. I – might actually suck at it."

Her crooked smile dazzles me, then she looks away, face revealing nothing now, not soft and open the way it was

383

only a minute ago.

"Not that that's necessarily what's happening here," I add quickly. "Just – you know – fair warning –"

She's staring down at our hands wrapped up together. When she speaks, it's like she's addressing them. "I've always had to be in control. I've never –"

She flings the words out quickly, like she's being defiant. But there's her face and I can read it well enough, now.

Not defiance. Bravado. She's scared.

Yeah, me too.

I repeat, "I've never . . ." Never told anyone this. Not my best friends. Not my mother. Not the diary I don't keep.

"Not even, um, on your own?"

"Not even."

He looks a little staggered. Why did I let him know? Just more pressure. But Tim doesn't seem freaked out. Only surprised and a little sad.

I stumble to reassure him, piling on more hard-to-speak truth. "You've already made me feel things I didn't think I could feel. So, if we – when we –"

"We don't have to –" he says immediately.

"I know. I'm not saying anything has to be right here right now. Just that there are, um, things I haven't done. So, I might not be able to. It's not a big deal, so don't –"

"Truth, Alice?"

"Um –" That was about all the truth in me. What more?

"You won't fake it. Promise me."

This boy. Eyes on my face again, little smile lurking, just barely parenthesizing the corners of his lips. He lifts his eyebrows, waiting. And willing to. However long. At the sight of it, there's an ache in my chest, a flash of near pain, knife-swift, something letting go, slipping free.

"I do promise." The words come out in a whisper.

His fingers find me now, move to cover my heart, as though he knows.

I swallow.

"Also? If you have any, uh, suggestions for improvement along the way, you'll –"

"God, Tim. Is there nothing you won't say?"

"One or two things."

Now he's grinning again, the smile that goes all the way to his eyes, his entire face glowing. I shrug off my sweater. He flips onto his side, pulls me near.

Then he strokes up and down my arm, and as warm as his palm is, goose bumps scatter behind it.

Hand behind my knee now, pressing, the heel of his hand suddenly urgent, although his voice is lazy, almost drowsy, sharp contrast to the intensity of his eyes. "One more promise, Alice."

"Are you always this chatty?" My own voice, octaves higher than usual, gives me away.

"*Chatty*?" He starts to laugh.

I wince, look down. His hand is beneath my chin, lifting my eyes back to his face. "Sorry," he says. "Fair warning again. I'm gonna move your leg, like this, up over my hip. Promise not to kick me."

"Are you going to narrate this whole thing?"

"*Shh.*" A kiss, pressed against the corner of my mouth, the next word only a breath of air. "No."

Now my leg is looped over his hip, the side of my knee pressed against his waist. He's barely touching me – his hand hovering just above my skin – so close – the almost-graze of his fingers, along my thigh, down over my calf, to my heel, the arch of my foot. There he does touch, thumb pushing hard, then lighter, then outlining the whole shape of my foot, back up my leg, the lightest possible skim. His head bent to my shoulder now, not quite on it, but close enough to feel the uneven rise and fall of his breath, the rapid pounding of his heart.

"I'm gonna need to get that box over there. Soon. But not yet, because I have to –"

"You *are* going to narrate this, aren't you?"

"Not narrating. Appreciating. You have to give me time to let this – you – sink in." He pulls gently at my tank top, shifting it up over my stomach, peeling the straps down. His rough knuckles brush my skin and I inhale sharply. He does too. Then he sets his hand flat on my stomach, eyes serious, face wearing a look of concentration and determination.

He looks at me so long that I squirm, and he presses

lightly on my stomach. "Let me look. You're amazing, Alice." His thumb touches my belly ring.

His lashes lift and he studies my face again. "What's wrong?"

"I'm . . . I . . . I need to know what you're thinking." My own thoughts are scattered – firing off rapidly all over the place. The look in his eyes, the feel of him solid against me, the scrape of his voice, husky.

"I didn't think I'd be here. Have this . . . you. How did this actually happen? And . . . and . . . how beautiful you are. Mostly the last one."

I prop myself up on one elbow, yanking at my tank, which snags on my earring.

"Yow!" I clap a hand to my ear.

Suddenly exuberant, moving fast, he detangles the snag, tosses my top somewhere, kisses my ear, which tickles. I'm exposed, open to the cool air, to him, and he's still dressed. I start giggling, part nerves, part excitement, part a jumble of things I have no experience with and no name for.

Reaching forward, I catch my finger in the waistband of his jeans, the back of my hand skimming the skin just above.

I put my other hand on his shoulder to steady myself.

We're both shaking.

"Lights out? I vote no." Another dip of his thumb into my belly button, then a teasing nudge, before he gets to his feet.

"Yes. Please."

"As you wish, then. Stay there."

Tim snaps the light off, but not before swearing, evidence he burned his thumb on the heated metal. Then rustling sounds of him closing the tent flap, then hunting around for the box of condoms. I sweep my hand out, locate them before he does, wing them at him. "Suit up."

He chokes and starts laughing. "Suit up? Wha-at? So this is a professional sporting event?"

Now I'm too impatient even to be embarrassed. I laugh too.

"Forget I said that – just – hurry, okay?"

"Jesus, you're bossy. Hang on."

Sound of a zipper, Tim kicking away his jeans, more rustling.

"All right, I'm coming back. No ninja moves now either."

"Hurry," I say again as he falls down beside me, laughing so hard, I start laughing again too. Lips on my bare shoulder, then finding one breast, hand cupped beneath, bringing me closer – but only for an instant.

I hear myself make a sound in the back of my throat, unmistakable frustration.

"Hurry, huh? What's your rush?"

"We want what we want when I want it," I whisper.

"Ah, so you want something, Alice? A glass of water, maybe?"

His index finger glides down from my chin, down the

center line of my body.

"Grape-Nuts?" His breath stirs the hair curled around my ear. His mouth shifts down again.

I jerk against him, feeling too fast, too good.

"What is it you need? Ask me."

"Being – able to – breathe – would be good."

"Overrated." His mouth travels back to mine. "Close your eyes. Just feel, okay?"

Twenty minutes, hours, weeks later, I drop my head to the pillow. "Wow."

"I'll say." Tim touches his nose to mine. "The real thing, Alice? Don't lie. I know anyway." He sounds slightly triumphant, but that's okay.

"I . . ." I take a deep breath, then can't do more than exhale, overwhelmed. "That was . . ."

The real thing.

Wow.

Alice falls silent, and I am too. The hair at her temples, damp, sticks to her hot cheeks. Totally light-headed even though she was the one who . . . I'm almost afraid to exhale, shatter the spell, afraid even now that she'll stand up and walk away and I'll . . . I don't know what I'd do.

What she does is laugh, almost without making a sound, because she's totally winded. Her bare stomach

shakes against mine – and for a bad second I'm afraid she's crying, which would suck. But no, laughing. She lifts one long graceful arm, drapes it, boneless, over my waist. When she moves, it's only to get closer.

I try to shift my hips away, give her room, time to recover, but my body is having none of that shit.

Neither is Alice.

Thank God.

I'm pressing on both his shoulders, one knee against his thigh so he'll move onto his back and then Tim's grinning up at me, just as I realize my cheeks are hurting because I'm smiling so much, so hard.

"Tim?" My fingers trail over his chest, then the muscles of his legs, the developing lines of his abs, moving back to cup his jaw and kiss him speechless again.

"Mmmf."

"Want to cross off another 'I've never'?"

His hands are frozen in the air by my sides, hovering as though he can't decide what to do next. "Yeah. This one." An arm goes up to cover his eyes. Under my hands, tension ratchets up in his muscles. "I lo –"

"– ve you."

"Alice! You didn't let me finish saying it. And that was my first time."

"Mine too. Sorry. You needed to know. Or I had to tell

you. Tim, I –"

"Love you," he says. "Let me say it. Geez."

"Okay. If you – insist."

"I absolutely do. This is me, insisting."

He flips us and braces himself over me, on his elbows.

"I love you, Alice."

"Prove it."

"If you insist."

Making love. I've cringed every time Hester used those words. So off and awkward and unrelated to what actually goes on between two bodies. You make breakfast, you make time, you make the team. Love? Not so much. But I get it now. Like making fire. Not rubbing two sticks together to pull something out of thin air. More like finally being able, knowing enough, to warm your hands at something you built, stick by stick.

Chapter Thirty-eight

I'm whistling in the kitchen as I pour cereal for my brothers, and Duff's herd of nerds, Ricky McArthur, Jacob Cohen, Max Oliviera – the leftovers from last night's sleepover.

Harry's grouchy because they kept him awake most of the night. I was awake most of the night too, but I am definitely not grouchy. Joel, who came in bearing a huge box of donuts, a police cliché, smirks at me.

"What?"

"I dunno, Al. There are practically bluebirds and fluffy chicks fluttering around your head. Just enjoying the view."

"Chicks don't fly. Not even chickens fly," George says through a mouthful of Gorilla Munch. "You're silly, Joel."

"I'm serious. It's nice to see you so cheery. You look much less feral."

"Shut up, Joel." But I say it mildly, pouring myself coffee, and managing to ignore a barrage of fart jokes from Duff and company, Patsy's outraged screech because Harry's grabbed her sippy cup and is holding it just out of her reach, and George's lengthy explanation of the difference between

feral and just plain wild.

"Rainbows, unicorns, kittens," Joel continues, chuckling even more. "Awww, Al."

° ° ° °

I'm with Hester at Breakfast Ahoy. The far table on the left is full of swim team guys from Hodges, who I only dimly recognize. They're all carbo-loading like maniacs, shoving one another, laying stupid bets, arguing about who picks up the tab, dissing each other's form and time and attitude at the last meet, hitting on the waitress, doing stupid shit. My team from four years ago – I'd have been right there with them. Now they're like some tribe I'm observing from far, far away.

From everything, really. Any thoughts I have are back in the tent with Alice, breathing her in, watching her face. We never looked away from each other unless we had to close our eyes for a little.

"Uh . . . What?"

No idea how long Hester's been talking.

". . . why I didn't bring Cal along. Figured it would be easier to focus. Geez, Tim." Snap of fingers in my face. God, that's annoying. "You're not high, are you?"

"Nope. Focus on what?"

Hester scrabbles around in this tie-dyed backpack she brought, pulls out a sheaf of papers, shoves them toward

me. "This is the consent form for termination of your paternal rights – it's called relinquishment. All you have to do is sign right here." She taps the line with an *X*, then drops the pen on the paper in front of me.

The pen's dark brown, glossy, with copper trim and copper lettering stamped on it. I don't need to look any closer to know how it reads: WINSLOW S. MASON, BRANCH MANAGER, STONY BAY BUILDING AND LOAN, STONY BAY, CT.

"You met with my pop." No emotion in my voice at all. None in me anywhere, really. Guess I should be surprised, but I'm not. Big picture. "When?"

"Two days ago," she says without hesitation. "He came by in the evening and talked to me and Waldo. I figured you'd told him to come, take over, move things along faster."

My coma-calm recedes. "Did he order you around, Hes? Intimidate you?"

"No! He was friendly, really sure what to do." She gives a little laugh. "Not like you and me, without a single firm opinion between us. Besides, you know Grand – his advice is a little murky. Everything sounds like a Japanese koan." She smiles up at me and I find myself looking back, not sure what to do with my face. Pop, fuck, whatever. He does what he does. This is almost over. That's what counts, right?

"This is all I have to do?" I click the pen, flip over the

paper, and scribble a few circles to get the ink flowing.

"Yes. He had it all drawn up. All you need to do is sign it, then your father gets it presented to a judge, and once we find adoptive parents, we submit more paperwork and they approve it all as a 'good cause' termination. But you need to go first, because you aren't on the birth certificate and it has to be obvious to the court that you're surrendering all rights permanently."

I've flipped the papers over. A waitress blows through the swinging door from the kitchen and it flaps a little, making a crackling noise like something going up in flames.

Click the pen closed. Open again. Closed. Scratch my neck.

Relinquishing.

Surrendering.

All of this over, all of it.

All of it?

My head hurts like a mother, and suddenly I'm spent. Exhausted.

The nights of no sleeping, the diapers of doom, the freak-out moments when I'm afraid he's stopped breathing or that the car on the side street will keep going and T-bone mine directly into the baby's side. Having to take the kid with me everywhere like a squirmy twelve-pound ball and chain.

The sweaty fingers clutching my shirt. The cries I can't interpret.

Even the ones I can, when he stops in the middle of wailing and just stares at me – like he's saying, *That's right, here's what I was looking for.* The way that one smile made him look like a completely different kid. Not just a baby. Like mine.

Once again, don't tune in to Hester till she's halfway through whatever she's saying.

". . . your father's going to come by my house to pick it up so he can be sure to file it first thing in the morning. After that's official, your job is basically done."

"So this is my resignation notice? Or am I being fired?"

She laughs. "I never thought you'd show up for it the way you have. You've been . . . great. We do this, and then we have some interviews with prospective parents, choose, and get back to normal life. Chapter closed." She flips her dark hair back from her face.

We aren't ordering Chinese takeout here. "We don't agree on anything, Hester. How are we going to pick his new parents together?"

Hester sighs. "In this case, we both have the same goal. And Waldo and your father will be there to mediate. Along with the adoption counselor, I guess. But your signing off is just a technicality, your father said. If the birth father does nothing, he automatically loses all rights when the adoption goes through. So you don't even have to be involved, if you don't want to."

This again. "I wish everyone would stop acting like my

being 'involved' was some sort of choice. I mean, I – he's – I . . ." I push back my chair. "I need some air." Bump into the doorjamb, like I'm loaded, head out on the Breakfast Ahoy deck. The air's so thick with bacon grease and maple syrup that you could put in on a plate. There are seagulls diving and plunging around the Dumpster and the faint breeze from the river is sending up nothing but sludgy air. Brace my hands on the rail, but it's still like I'm falling.

Get it over with.

All of it.

Slide back into my seat. Hester's texting.

"Do you have any pictures of Cal on there?" I ask abruptly.

Her eyebrows lift. "No," she says carefully. "Do you have any on your phone?"

Nope, as a matter of fact. But I'm not much for taking pictures. Still, there's some point I'm making here, and I'm too slurry-headed to figure out exactly what it is. It has something to do with Cal's impersonal sleeping arrangement at Hester's house, something to do with the scratchy sock monkey with the chokeable beady eyes she gave him, something to do with how she scrubs up with antibacterial gel before she takes him from me and after she hands him back, like she's going to operate immediately. Like I have cooties. Or Cal does. Something about this new thing he does where he opens and closes his hands when I come close, like he just can't wait to grab on to me.

How he yells "Bah!" when no one has paid attention to him for a while. Something to do with "chapter closed," like he's some old textbook from sophomore year that I never have to look at again.

But I can't figure out what shape that kaleidoscope is supposed to click into.

Hester looks down at my hands. "What are you doing?"

I've taken the pen apart without even knowing I was doing it, and it's on the table in front of me – the push button, the clip, the thrust tube, the ink cartridge, the spring, the ballpoint itself, all scattered in separate pieces like I've dissected the thing for science class.

"*Now* how are you going to sign this?" She's half laughing, but exasperated, rooting in the diaper bag again.

"I'm not."

"Here's one." She waves another bank pen triumphantly. Then her hand freezes. "What?"

"Look . . . look, can't we do the open thing, adoption-wise? The one where the parents send you updates and pictures and shit? I mean, why not, that way we can just, you know, check up on him, whatever. Make sure it all works out?"

"No. I don't want that. Let's just let him go. Completely."

"No," I say.

What?

"What?"

"No." A little voice in my head is screaming at me to

shut up, waving me away from my next words like they're a pileup on Route 95. "I'm not doing it. I –"

Nearly every time words I can't stop have changed my life, it's been because I was being an immature, insufferable ass. Not this time. "He's mine, Hester. I'm not letting him go."

"You can't be serious."

"I can be." I swallow. "I am."

Do I mean that?

Yes.

I bend over the table, holding on to the edge, breathing like I've been sucker punched. Like Alice.

Jesus, Alice. What's she going to think if I –

"Tim?" Hester's voice floats in my head, distant. "What's going on?"

Okay, deep breaths. In. Out.

If I take Cal, if I have Cal, that's it for being seventeen. I will have to man up, be there, put myself second, take care of business, daycare and school and, hell, I don't even know . . . for years and years and years. Till I'm, like, old. Thirty-six or more. God.

"Tim. *Think*. That's crazy. You're in no position to take on a baby. You're living above a *garage*."

Of all the reasons why I'm in no position to deal with a baby, this has gotta be one of the less important.

"Your point?" I snap, lungs suddenly functional. "You're the one who's always calling me to come get him, or take

him for the night because you just can't deal."

"And I admit it. I don't want this. Him. Besides, sounds like you kind of resent me for all this responsibility," Hester bites out, "so I wonder why you'd want more of it."

She waves her hands. Our waitress mistakes this for a signal to pour more coffee. Hester waits until the cup is full and the waitress has retreated.

"You can't be serious about this. Calvin isn't even four months old! How are *you* going to take care of an infant? You're a high school dropout."

"I did *not* drop out. I got kicked out." Like it's so much better. "I don't know *how* I'll take care of him. I guess the same way I've been trying to since you showed up on my doorstep."

The waitress returns and sets down Hester's wheat toast and my scrambled eggs and home fries. Hester continues to stare incredulously at me before finally continuing. "You're crazy, Tim. Selfish. Cal could go to a family, a real family, with – parents who love each other and . . . and things . . . and security and good schools and . . . everything that matters. And you think he'd be better off with his seventeen-year-old dad who lives above a garage."

"Will you quit it with the frickin' garage? Don't try to make it out like I'm some blue-collar townie boy who got you pregnant, as if that even matters. But we were *both* at prep school when we did the deed, don't forget."

She glares. "*I* haven't forgotten a thing. What I'm saying is that Cal shouldn't suffer because he was a stupid mistake. I have plans."

"*You* planned every bit of this. I didn't plan a thing."

"Exactly," she says, pointing her butter knife at me. "Which doesn't give me much confidence in your ability to be a father. Not to mention the whole 'you're an alcoholic' thing."

"Recovering. Recovering alcoholic, Hester. And I *already am* a father."

I have, for once, no appetite, and watching Hester butter her toast pisses me off. She puts butter on one corner, takes a bite, puts it on another spot, takes another bite. Who eats like that? It's like she can't commit to an entire piece of toast. The waitress, who evidently finds angry recovering alcoholic teenage fathers of illegitimate babies who live above garages a turn-on, squeezes my shoulder as she refills my coffee cup.

Hester sighs and says in an elaborately patient tone, "I don't want to be fighting with you. If what it takes for you to realize you're wrong is a little time, take the papers home. Look them over. We can talk about it rationally next time."

"I won't change my mind," I tell her.

She stands up and shoves the sheaf of papers over the table at me. "Then you've lost your mind. I'll see you Tuesday. I'll call you about where to pick up Cal." She

reaches into the diaper bag and pulls out a crisp fifty. "Here, this should cover the meal."

"Keep it," I snap. Again with the fifty-dollar bill. What did Pop do, tip her?

"No. You keep it. You can put it toward Cal's college fund. Maybe he'll end up going, even though you never will." She tosses the bill on the table, turns, and marches away, her ponytail swinging behind her.

"For keeps? I mean . . . from now on? Forever?"

Tim, hands jammed in pockets, is looking out at the ocean, not at me. He's barely met my eyes since he caught me as I was stretching after this morning's run, and said, "We have to talk."

Alarm buzzer, sirens, whistles. That's my line. The warm-up to "this isn't working." But our *this* only just started. And it's working for me, more than working. I'm Brad now, blindsided in the driveway?

"Not here," he added as Patsy pressed her nose against the screen door, calling "Hon" imperiously.

Tim insisted we go to the beach. Then said we should walk out to the lighthouse. Went on ahead of me so I had to scramble over the jagged rocks to catch up with his rapid strides. When he finally turned to face me, his shoulders were hunched, his face closed-off, as though expecting anger or criticism. Then he told me what happened with

Hester. What he wanted with Cal.

His voice shook, he stumbled a little when he started off, but got calmer and calmer, quietly resolved, as he kept going.

"It's the only thing that makes sense. He needs me. I need to do this. I mean, I did this. And I can't – just – act as if I didn't and move on. Here's my chance to fix things, to get something right."

"For you or for Cal?"

Tim's eyes are practically blazing with determination. "See, that's the thing, there's no separating us. I'm what he has. He's what I have."

The craggy rock we're standing on, still wet from the last high tide, with a few globs of sea lettuce snagged on outcroppings, is not made for pacing around. I do it anyway, trying to jam this new fact into the picture I had of my life now.

My . . . boyfriend. My . . . Tim – not just a dad as a footnote in his life, a season. For keeps. Cal's father, for good, with all that means. No hand-offs to Hester. The crib a permanent fixture in the bedroom – until Cal's old enough for a big-boy bed. Tim needing to find daycare if he graduates from high school and goes to college (will he? How can he?). If he gets another job. Needing babysitters if we want to go out together at night. Responsible for immunizations and introducing Cal to solid food and potty-training and all the steps I know so well, all the duties and

chores and worries and things I thought were only part of my life for a little while longer – and simply because I was subbing for someone else.

Tim, a father by his eighteenth birthday.

Me.

And baby makes three. Ha.

I sit down abruptly on the rock, barely feeling the seawater seep slowly through the seat of my jeans.

He slides down near me, but not too close, his legs dangling over the edge, tracing the seam of his jeans.

"I know what you're thinking," he says, addressing his knee.

"I doubt that." Since I myself have no idea.

"I knew it as I was saying it – to Hester. It's too much. The last thing you need. Now what you signed on for – which was, of course, my striking good looks and massive amounts of testosterone, not the byproduct of those things. I get it. But, Alice – what else can I do?"

He's trying for a light tone, but it falls flat, and his eyes are shadowed.

I fold my legs up to my chest, wrap my arms around them, rest my chin there. Look at him.

The straight nose with a few freckles, his hair, slightly too long again, the dark eyelashes, downcast, the tall, rangy body . . . already older-looking than he was a month or two ago.

"I won't hold it against you – walking away. I hope we

can stay –"

"Don't you dare give me the 'friends' speech, Tim Mason."

"We're not even that? Shit, Alice. Okay. Okay. I get it."

"You can't get it. Because I haven't gotten it yet. You have to give me a little sink-in time."

His eyes, startled, move to mine.

"Another new ballgame. It's a lot. Give me time to get used to this." Another wave, another changed landscape.

"I'll give you anything it takes," he says. "All I've got."

"I know," I say somberly. Give his shoulder a small shove. "You had to do it, didn't you? Get all responsible on me."

"No one has ever said, least of all me, that my timing doesn't completely suck."

It's after eleven: everyone's asleep. Except me and George. He had a nightmare about clowns, and I've been going around and around in circles about bills and banks and Grace Reed. So we're huddled under Great Aunt Alice's big crocheted bedspread in the living room, and I'm reading George my favorite fairy tale, The Snow Queen. Gerda, the best fairy tale heroine. No sitting around waiting to try on slippers – nope, off to the coldest place on earth to rescue the hero.

Georgie likes Gerda too, that she and Kai, the hero, live next door to one another. "Like Jase and Sam did." He cozies closer just as there's a muffled knock at the door and

405

a rattle of the doorknob. It's got to be Tim – who else would show up at this hour?

But it's Samantha, bundled into a rumpled letter jacket I recognize as Jase's, her hair all windblown.

George throws his arms around her knees, tells her he loves her, and asks what she thinks of clowns. She doesn't even seem to hear him. She's red-faced and I can't tell if that's the cold or the wind until I look into her eyes, which are almost glimmering. Not with tears, though.

Anger.

George tugs on the bottom of her jacket. "Sailor Supergirl, Jase is sleeping. I checked on him because I had a bad dream but he wouldn't wake up. His mouth was a little open, but don't worry 'cause that thing that people tell you about how you swallow spiders when you sleep? That's made up. Like no bubblegum trees growing in your stomach if you swallow gum."

"George – that's good about the spiders. But I need to speak to Alice." She smiles at him but is talking so rapidly, her words run together as if she's out of breath. Her eyes focus on me.

My little brother agrees to go back to bed if I pinkie swear that he can watch two episodes of "Animal Odd Couples" tomorrow. And if I promise there will be no clowns involved. He backs upstairs slowly, adding new demands: "And ice cream after breakfast? No, *for* breakfast. Promise?"

The moment his footsteps fade away, Sam says, "My mom. I found out she's been filling out my college applications *herself*. All to colleges far, far away, of course."

Seems to me this newsflash could wait till morning, even though it just adds to the Ten Things I Hate About Grace Reed list.

"But that's not even it. It's another thing – she told me that you'd come over to talk about the bills, Alice. I checked with Tim and he said it was true, that she stonewalled, and I'm done letting that happen. It's not okay. I know what happened with your dad. I saw it. Well, I was asleep but I knew something was wrong – and I didn't – well, I came to say that I'll . . . go to the police or whatever. Whatever it takes."

Before she's halfway through this speech, I'm pacing around the kitchen table, putting my hands in my hair and pulling, picking up an abandoned paper towel and shredding it.

Sam watches me, suddenly amused. "You want a cigarette? You look exactly like Tim."

"Ha," I say.

"He says that one too."

"Sam, are you really willing to do that? This? The police, everything?"

"Yes," she says – no hesitation. "I've been thinking about it for weeks. Since the accident. It's . . . I can't stop thinking about it, Alice. And now this." She closes her eyes,

407

takes deep breath. "But Tim said that you guys should talk with her first. Because if . . . if things go bad, if there's a trial, big-time lawyer bills" – Sam winces, shakes her head – "your family bills will be put on the backburner. Maybe forever."

"Damn, he's good," I say.

Sam laughs, looking much more like herself. "He'd be the first to tell you that."

"Yeah, but the last to believe it," I say.

She tilts her head, serious again. "You get him, Alice. I'm glad."

∘ ∘ ∘ ∘

Like Tim with Cal, I see no other way. There *is* no other way. But instead of doing something out of a warm and open heart, I'm doing this because I am the only one cold enough. And it has to be just me – he's got Cal and Hester to handle.

When she opens the door, I brush past her, down the white hallway. I don't take off my shoes.

This time she doesn't offer a refreshing drink, small talk.

Nothing but her gaze, level on mine, moving to the stack of bills I set, yet again, on the glass-topped table. "These are copies. There are more than there were last time."

"I see that."

"I've seen this." I take the *Stony Bay Bugle* clipping off

the top of the stack and hold it out to her. "'Former State Senator Stirs Speculation About a Return to the Stage.'"

"Yes. I've been approached for that state treasurer position. I make a difference in politics, Alison. I help people. I don't believe it's right to turn my back on that." She walks over to the tall arched window that looks out on her green lawn, still emerald even though we're well into fall. Not a fallen leaf on it.

"I'm not asking you to understand. You're still very young. It takes more perspective than you have to see that the greater good –"

"Senator, I'm not here for a debate. Here are the bills. You want to be treasurer? This is the perfect place to start. I talked to Samantha. It turns out your daughter would feel worse about Jase's father not getting the care he needs than about her needing to change schools. So, she's fine with going to SBH."

Grace looks at me sharply. "Where my daughter goes to school is hardly your decision to make."

"I know. The decision is hers. So is the one to go to the police as a witness to the accident you were involved in that landed my dad in the hospital. She's fine with doing that too."

Grace Reed is already pale as the Snow Queen. You'd think she couldn't get any more parchment-white. But she manages.

"You had absolutely no right to get involved in this."

"I didn't!" I laugh. "You *stopped paying the bills*. If it wasn't me, it would be Jase himself. We're all involved. My whole family is. So I need your word, and, actually, more than that. I need your signature on a piece of paper that says you will pay these bills, and any more that come, as long as they come. If not, Samantha will be changing schools. It'll give her a lot more time with my brother."

The last was an impulse. I really am made of ice.

I have a check in my pocket, folded along with the paper with her signature, when she walks me to the door. As I turn to leave, she rests a hand on my shoulder, very briefly. To my horror, there is almost a look of admiration on her face.

"You'd make a good politician, Alison." She smiles at me, all charm. "You remind me of myself."

God forbid.

Chapter Thirty-nine

Waldo Connolly opens the door wearing a dress.

Not sure I can handle this.

On closer examination, it's like a really long shirt – goes past his knees, and is loose, with little mirrors around the neckline. Not a dress, but still.

"C'mon in. Hester should be back soon." He turns, shirt flapping behind him, exposing hairy-as-hell legs. If he weren't relatively tall, I'd think he really was a hobbit. I follow, lugging the car seat and Cal. Starting to feel like my left arm is longer than my right from carrying this thing.

Get used to it.

Alice isn't the only one who still needs sink-in time.

Pop will totally stroke out about this.

Nano is definitely getting my college fund.

I set the seat down and flop into the puffy chair next to it. A cloud of dust rises up, motes whirling in the air coming in from the high window, as crazy in motion as my thoughts.

Waldo puts on a kettle, hauls something that looks like

a palm frond out of the fridge, and picks up his trusty machete. *Chop. Chop.* "You want to serve as a father to this child."

"Yeah. Sir. I mean, I already am. But I mean – from now on. Yes. I just want a little time to know for sure."

Chop. "That sounds brave. Maybe it is brave. But how's it going to work? Are you going to open your world and rearrange it around this baby? Put Calvin between you and your horizon?" *Chop-chop.* "You ready to put your money where your love is?"

Could this guy sound a little less like a fortune cookie on acid?

My throat hurts. Also my stomach, which it pretty much has ever since I said no to Hester. And told Alice what's up. Maybe I'm getting an ulcer? Waldo sweeps the junk he's hacked up and puts it in the teakettle, turns the flame on with a quick twist of his wrist. Looks like lawn clippings.

"Look," I say. "I'm not exactly sure what you're saying here, but . . . you may think I just . . . do shit without thinking, but that's not it. Maybe Hester can move on and forget about it. But not me. I'm not that guy. Uh, now. I don't even need to see her. I'm only here to get the rest of Cal's stuff."

Waldo moves back against the counter and looks at me, his face impassive. He reaches behind his back with one hand, without taking his eyes off me. Is he going for the machete? But no, he's just got some kind of tea

strainer thing.

"You've bonded with this baby."

"Haven't you? You're the one who told Hester to keep him for a while."

"I'm sixty-four, Tim. I've learned that those irrevocable decisions deserve time. Michelle, Hester's mother, wasn't married when she had Hester. She regretted a lot about her choices. Hester's too young to start racking up more should-have's." He turns, pouring steamy hot water and lawn clippings into two gray-blue pottery mugs. He offers me one, hoists it like he's toasting me. "To the truth of our hearts, which can chain us down."

He puts his mug on the table, rests his chin on his palms, and does that intent-stare thing from under his bristly eyebrows. I stare back. *He* can blink first.

"Have you and Hester talked about Alex Robinson?"

Who? Oh, right, Hester's old boyfriend who did the long-distance-dump routine. Favorite tool of dickheads and douchebags everywhere.

"Sorta."

"Maybe you should explore that cave with a stronger light." Waldo reaches for a jar of honey and twist-pours some into his tea with this weird wooden spoon.

He sounds serious, his tone the way people's voices get when they're breaking bad news. I don't know why, but coldness crawls over me, icy-sharp, though the kitchen air is heavy with lemony steam.

"Could we cut the crap here?" I ask. "What exactly are you saying?"

Waldo scrubs his hand through his thatch of graying hair. "Alex and Hester were together for a long time." Now he's dropped his hand, paying unnecessarily careful attention to stirring his tea. Silence, except this thumping noise.

So?

What does that . . .

"I didn't hear any talk of you until the baby was a few weeks old."

Again, so?

"Until then, Hester was very insistent on him being Alex's." He stirs his tea some more, spoon clinking against the side of the mug. "She didn't bring you up to me until Calvin's hair started coming in."

The thumping is my heart.

"That's it, though – he's got my hair and . . ."

Waldo says nothing, heaving himself away from the counter as though he's suddenly gained mass. He pads out of the room, coming back a few minutes later with a picture in his hand. He passes it to me.

"I'll give you that the baby looks a hell of a lot more like you. Still, this is Hester's dad. Mike Pearson."

I check out the picture. In it, Hester's mother, still looking like *Madonna: The Early Years,* is laughing, one dimple grooving deep in her cheek, cleft cut hard in her

chin, her head with its teased, streaky brown-blond hair resting on the pale stomach of a guy with his shirt off. A guy with puffy hair nearly as long as hers. As red as my own.

"You want plain talk? A conversation needs to happen between you and Hester."

Got caught in a riptide once and this is just like that, if the water burned and clung like just-poured tar. Everything's hazy with heat.

He looks just like me.

His hair. His dimple. His chin.

Everyone says.

Everyone but Nan. But what does she know – she's probably high.

Waldo's taken his tea, gone upstairs, humming under his breath, like he hadn't just used that machete on me.

Fist my hands into my hair, pull hard, slump back in the chair, then jump back up and stare at the kid. Look and look and look some more. Watch this quick smile race across his face when I move one finger down his cheek, see how he curls closer, grabs tight to my thumb without waking – even though he's usually restless and quick to wake up – *like me, like me* – bending his head close to my forearm, so sure I'm there. Now I get it, the goddamn all of it, that he's mine, that I made him, that I love him.

Hell to the hell. I throw myself back on the chair, splay

415

my legs onto this bookend thing next it, not giving a damn that I knock over some weird-ass statue of a chick with too many arms.

Little click of the front door and Hester comes down the hall into the living room on her little cat feet, which I only hear because I'm listening for her and every sense is amped up.

She's sorting through some mail, she doesn't look up as I stalk toward her.

"We need to talk."

She jumps a little, does that hand to heart thing and the letters flutter to the ground.

"A-about the adoption? Have you changed your mind?"

"Let's start somewhere else," I suggest, in that cornering-with-a-whiplash voice I learned so well from Pop. "Say, oh, last fall. You're gonna have to help me out here."

Hester sits down on this footstool thing with a little jolt. She's staring at me with the Bambi eyes. Hasn't looked at Cal once.

"So . . . Alex Robinson. Did he happen to pay you a visit in, say, early November?"

Look baffled. Say you don't know why I'm asking.

But she doesn't look baffled. And she doesn't ask why.

"Calvin is yours. I think."

"You. Think."

Then a rush of words like a flood I'm drowning in, yes, Alex was home for a long weekend for Veteran's Day, but

416

he's conscientious, I thought it was his, *wanted* it to be his – of course – at first, but then the hair –

My stomach clasps hard and tight, like someone's punching it with a hot fist. "Did we ever have sex at all?"

"We did make love," she breathes. "I would never lie about that. You can ask my friend Michaela, and Jude, and Buck. I told all of them right after the party."

"That wasn't 'making love.' It was sperm meets egg. Or not. Tell. Me. The. Truth."

She grabs a floor pillow from the corner and hugs it to her, quivering with suppressed sobs. "The truth is I hope it's you. I thought . . . I thought all along it was Alex's. I mean, he and I had a relationship. So I wanted it to be his. But all he said when I told him was that he was sure I'd work it all out. Work it all out! Like it was a geometry problem or something. That whatever I did was fine. Fine! Nothing was fine, Tim. They wanted to kick me out of Ellery, did you know that? Waldo brought in his lawyer and told them they couldn't, but I had to go the rest of the year, through graduation, knowing that they all wanted me gone. Alex didn't need to do anything like that. You didn't need to do anything like that. All you had to do was screw me once."

I can actually feel my hands around her neck, gripping hard, tightening harder on pulse and tendon and skin. Jesus. Flex my fingers, tighten them, jam them against my thighs. "Yeah, well, now you've done it twice."

I'm backing away from her.

"Where are you going?"

"Someplace safe. I'm taking Cal."

"You don't have to." She's across the room, grabbing my arm.

"He's coming with me. I don't trust you."

She raises her chin, gives a little nod. "All right. I accept that. Maybe I deserve it. But I am his mother."

"Must be nice to know that for sure. Get away from me, Hester."

Chapter Forty

Tim's lying on his back on the grass outside the garage apartment, smoke curling in the air above him, cigarette in one hand, staring at the sky.

When I sit down on the bottom step near him, he doesn't even turn his head. The cigarette's nearly smoked all the way down. As I watch, he pulls another one out of the pack of Marlboros, lights it from the tip, drops the first butt into a foam coffee cup, where it hisses.

"Your mom tell you what's up?" His voice is idle, uncurious, like it doesn't much matter either way.

"Just now. Cal's fine. George was doing 'Itsy Bitsy Spider' for him. He's good. Where were you?"

Tim takes another drag. "Went to town. Out of diapers. And cigarettes."

"You probably shouldn't do that with the patch on."

He tips the foam cup at me. In the bottom, floating in an inch or so of coffee, along with six or seven cigarette butts, is the nicotine patch.

He blows a smoke ring.

Then, abruptly, he rolls over on his stomach, crushes out the cigarette, gray eyes sharp. "There are all these things, all these little pieces of him that are just like me. I keep telling myself that. But you probably have more medical – genetic – whatever – facts than I do."

Facts come easily to my lips, like I'm reading them off the whiteboard at school. "It's not all that straightforward with physical characteristics. They don't just get inherited as simply as dominant and recessive. So that cleft chin?"

He nods, his eyes still locked on mine.

"Maybe yes, maybe no. The red hair. Same story. There's more than one gene controlling each. Who knows? The dimple. That's rare."

"Hester's mom has that. So you're saying there's no real way to tell. What about a blood test?" He strips his shirt down to his elbow, like I can pull out a Vacutainer and do a venipuncture right here and now.

"That can only rule someone out, not in."

He digs the heels of his hands into his eye sockets, shakes his head, then drops his fists again. The look on his face. Lost, frightened, frustrated. Despite the stubble and the circles under his eyes, it reminds me of George's expression when I can't explain exactly, scientifically, why an asteroid won't hit the earth. Can't tell him that we know for certain there isn't one already headed straight for us.

Tim just keeps staring at me like he doesn't understand the instructions, or doesn't want to.

My cell sings out "Eye of the Tiger."

I start to mute it, but Tim's hand flashes out, yanks the phone away before my fingers close on it. "Back off," he snarls into it.

There's an angry rumble of sound.

"I *said* back the fuck off. Leave her the hell alone . . . Yeah, I'll make you."

He's practically baring his teeth at the phone and in an instant all my worry coalesces into fury. "Quit it!"

"*He* needs to quit it."

I jerk the phone out of his hand. "Cut it out, Brad. You're better than this. If you keep it up I'm filing a restraining order. Enough already." I hang up, hit the keys to block his number, my thumbs flying, then toss the phone on the stairs.

"There. Solved. I've got this handled. I don't need you —" *To fix it* is what I mean to say, but before I can, Tim puts both hands out, palms facing me.

"Gotcha. Not needed here either. That's great, Alice. Thanks. It must be terrific to have it all handled. Know how to handle it all."

"You know better than that. Quit acting as if you're the only one who ever feels anything. We can figure this out. We'll —"

"Except it's not your problem to solve, Alice, is it? I don't want to be handled. Just another item on your list of people to rescue, things to fix? I'll pass. How am I supposed

to handle this? My son may not – might not . . . shit . . . might not be my son."

His hand trembles as he grabs the lighter again, shakes more as he tries to flick it and the sparks won't ignite. I take it from him, flip it, hold the flame to the cigarette he's jammed between his lips.

I'm helping him hurt himself.

Then I do more.

"Lighting up won't help Cal, dad or no dad."

"Whoops, thanks. Forgot how much older and wiser you are. You're probably even 'mature' enough to be relieved about this. No need for *sink-in time*" – he makes air quotes – "right? Bye bye baby."

"You're the one acting like a kid here, Tim."

He laughs. "Sure. Got it. Thanks for the light."

Still laughing, he plunges down the driveway into the Jetta, out onto the road.

Going, going, gone.

I'll be just like him.

If Cal isn't mine, if I can't keep him, I'll be another Mason man with no photographs of his son on the walls.

My heart is doing this racing thing – maybe tension, maybe too much nicotine because I blew through a few butts before I remembered to adios the patch. Still, I fire up another, even though I feel more like yacking.

All the rules I broke, and it hasn't occurred to me for

422

years to enter Pop's sanctum when he wasn't here, much less make myself at home. Now I throw myself into his well-padded chair, spin it around, legs kicked out. Never even did this as a kid.

Another twist of the chair and back to the desk, which has a stack of his blue-lined pads on it, a silver pencil holder full of his brown-and-copper building and loan pens. Desk calendar with Nan's field hockey games penciled in. One note, near the end of the month: "Crawley Center for Adoption Services, 3:30 p.m. Bring health records, birth cert."

Only noise in the room is the gentle burbling of the fish tank. No fish in the tank, however. Pop likes aquatic snails. There they are, sliding up the wall and bobbing around on the lettuce leaves he feeds them every five days or so. Don't require a lot of upkeep, those guys. Not much attention paid. Not even to the big picture.

Twirl in the chair again, and this time my legs strafe the wedding photo – Ma with puffy sleeves, Pop with a shiny silk vest – the pen holder, and Nan's middle school graduation picture, Hodges beret and all. They tumble off the desk, land – a perfect basket into the leather trash can, as unerring as one of Jase's newspaper throws.

And I wasn't even trying.

I think I hear a door slam, but then all's quiet.

The little silver bucket is lined up; a good little accomplice, right next to the Macallan and the cut-crystal

highball glass. No need to wait to fill it with ice. We want what we want when we want it, right? Into the tumbler it goes. One finger, two fingers, three. It sloshes onto my hand and the desk calendar. Wipe my hand on my shirt, but the desk calendar can fend for itself.

You still might be his father.

Don't do anything you can't take back.

But Cal's not here right now, he's safe with the Garretts. Nothing to stop my hand from reaching for the glass, from picking it up, turning it around, and frowning into it.

A Pop habit.

Don't think there's quite enough scotch in this glass, since I spilled some and all. It smells like disinfectant or that red stuff Ma puts on cuts.

But I'm tipping the glass and parting my lips when the office door swings open.

Chapter Forty-one

"Oh, Tim."

Nan closes the door behind her, so gently that it barely makes a sound, not even the usual click of the latch. Then she stands against it, blinking at me in the sleepy, unfocused way she does when she first wakes up, waiting for the world to make sense.

Can't help her with that one.

"Cheers!"

Now she's standing next to me, fingertips pressed against her lips.

Another "Oh, Tim."

She doesn't even sound surprised.

The glass travels toward my mouth again. Now she's shaking her head, that look on her face, corners of her mouth turned down, spaniel eyes. *There you go again.*

I respond to the words she doesn't even need to say – they've been said so often in this very room that they're probably hovering in a cloud above us. But then I catch a whiff of what surrounds her like a burnt, grassy-sweet fog.

"Don't judge, Nano. You aren't exactly on the moral high ground here." I sniff in an exaggerated way.

She lifts her forearm and smells her pressed Hodges navy blue blazer. Her red eyebrows shoot up like she's shocked, *shocked*, at the scent. Then it's like she crumples, spaniel eyes even bigger, face a paler triangle. "It's not what you –"

I laugh. Harsh in the quiet room. She flushes. "You know what? Forget explaining to you. You're just trying to blow off what's really going on here. What the hell is that doing in your hand?"

"Taking *waaay* too long to get to my mouth."

Tip the glass again, still with it too far from my lips, so some sloshes onto my jeans. Whoops.

She reaches out and I think she's going for the glass, but instead she rests her hand on my shoulder, awkward. "That guy you were turning out to be? I liked him. I was proud of you. In two months, you've been ten times the father Dad was. Ever."

"Except I love my kid. I mean – that kid."

Now she takes the glass out of my hand, and I let her, my fingers going slack. She sets it on the desk calendar, centers it like she's gonna be judged on that, turns back to me.

"Probably he loves us. He just isn't good at it."

"It's not rocket science, Nan. You show someone they matter to you – do whatever it takes to show that."

She lowers the hand resting on my shoulder, slides it

to my own, and pulls, so we're both sitting on the couch, hand in hand like lost kids in a fairy tale.

"Drunk Dad will definitely hammer that home for Cal."

And then it's out, all of it, blurt it all out, all over her – Hester, Alex Robinson, Alice.

"What is it about those Garretts?" Nan's short, sharp laugh sounds like it was rabbit punched out of her. "First they get Samantha. Now you."

"What they get is how to show up. The stuff that you and me aren't so great at."

"*You* help," Nan says, unexpectedly. "You're good at it."

"Yeah, right."

She looks me in the eye. "I owe you my GPA. My good grades in English. That." She gestures at the framed newspaper photo of her at the Fourth of July parade.

I've waited fucking forever for her to say this, admit it, and now it's just some little nothing, one of those things you desperately want for Christmas that you've forgotten about by the time the wrapping's in the trash.

But she's looking at me, The Look, spaniel face, like she's dropped something at my feet and I owe it to her to say how special it is, how much it means that she brought it to me.

I sigh. "Sure, Nan. You plagiarized from my papers, and even when I knew, I didn't say a word. I'm a hero."

"You helped me, Tim. You let me keep on doing it, and you didn't tell anyone."

"Just like you didn't let on that I was full of more drugs than a Pfizer warehouse. Yay for us. I'll stand right next to you at the next Fourth of July parade. Masons rule."

I reach for the glass again and she smacks my knuckles like an old schoolteacher.

"You helped me," she repeats.

"Nan, me 'helping' that way? Made you think you were crap. Helped cost you Samantha, if I'm guessing right. Help isn't supposed to make you weaker and even more effing lost. I might as well have been old Troy, supplying you shit."

"Don't say that." Her voice rises, higher pitched.

Not sure who she's defending. Also if it matters. Close my eyes. I would reach for the scotch again, but it's impossibly far away. My head hurts.

"You helped me."

"Stop saying that. So fucking what, Nan. So maybe you'll get into Columbia. Maybe. Gonna be happy there? I wouldn't take a bet on that one."

Tears stream down her face now, big gaspy sobs. She sounds like Cal, lost and sad and sure there's no help in the world for that. I let go of her hand, put my arms around her, pat, pat, circle, circle. Do everything but burp her as the tears and the shuddering keep on and on and on, like she's waiting for the one magic word or gesture that I'm so not coming up with.

"You could have *asked*," I say finally. Total opposite

of reassurance. "I would have, I dunno, coached you or something without you ripping off shit behind my back."

Nan sighs. "Back then? You wouldn't have handed me a drink of water in the Gobi Desert. You wouldn't have shoved me out of the path of a meteor. You were gone, Tim. Don't you remember?"

I squeeze her hand, tug her a little closer so she's resting her cheek on my shoulder. "Not the way you do. That was sort of the point."

She shakes a little, but this time with the tiniest of laughs. "Guess so. Job well done."

I pull back, look at her. Her hair all over the place, except the pieces that are plastered around with snot, her "edgy" mascara making her eyes into a creepy clown portrait that only needs a black velvet background. God, what a mess. My stupid, crazy sister. I love her so much.

"Kid . . . Nan . . . I . . . I didn't screw myself to screw you up. I know that happened anyway. I'm sorry. I'm so sorry."

Pull off my long-sleeved shirt, pass her one sleeve, use the other myself.

"One, two, three, blow," Nan says, muffled by the shirt.

Ma always said that.

For a few minutes, we sniff and breathe at the same time, twins for the first time ever, probably.

"You weren't the only one to screw me up, so you don't get to take all the credit or the blame. I did a super job all by myself, but . . . but Tim. You and Sam were my

best friends. You left me behind one way. Then she left me behind another."

"Kiddo. You couldn't have rescued me from anything I did. But Samantha . . . she was just down the road. A phone call away, as they say. All you had to do was say I'm sorry."

"You don't even know what happened," Nan says, a trace of her old self-righteousness creeping back.

Hell with that.

"I do, though." I lean back so we're once again side by side. Her head on my shoulder, my hand on her hair. We could be posing for a really effed-up version of one of Ma's twin pictures. "She called you on your bullshit and you ditched her. It's not exactly an original story. I've starred in it a billion times."

"Samantha's not perfect . . ." Nan says, and then she yawns, like even she's too sick of this to go on.

"Despite that sandwich board she wears that says she is?"

Watery giggle. "I hate you."

"Yeah," I say, hauling myself to my feet, using her thin shoulder as leverage. She catches at my leg to stop me, until I reach for the scotch and her fingers let go, hover in the air. "I hate you right back, kid."

I pour the scotch into the snail tank.

Nan comes up next to me and we both stare down into the clear water with its bobbing lettuce leaves and their

little black passengers. I feel guilty.

"Did you just wipe out a squadron of snails?"

"Maybe. That was cold-blooded of me. Ha."

Nan looks over at Pop's desk. "Well . . . you come by it naturally."

I toast her with the empty glass. "Touché. Keep it up and there won't be any pictures of you in here either."

Chapter Forty-two

Nan brushes at the wet scotch stains on me, wrinkling her nose. "Yeech. You reek."

"You're one to talk, Bob Marley. Since we're spilling our guts: What the hell are you pulling, Nan? Truth, this go-around."

In the time it takes to brew a pot of coffee, we're chowing down in Nan's room, having dumped her top desk drawer out on the bed. It's much better stocked with candy than Doane's, Stony Bay's biggest dentist's nightmare.

"I'm seeing him, Troy, not for drugs," she tells me, all in a rush.

"Weed, then, obviously. Pills?"

She shakes her head. "It was for pills initially. My reliable supplier went and got himself clean."

I laugh obediently, thinking she's joking. For all my sins, I never dealt to my twin. But one look at her face and she's obviously drop-dead serious.

No.

I ignored her, I needled her, I didn't show up for her, but

I didn't, didn't, didn't mess up my own sister. Something I know for sure.

Or not. I couldn't have forgotten that too. Could I?

"Take that back," I say, like the goddamn school bully.

"It wasn't you! It wasn't your fault. Tim. This one's on me." She shuts her eyes, opens them.

"Nan. In God's name, why? Or, never mind that, what? Oxy? Percocet? Vicodin? Please, God, not E."

"None of those, Timmy. Ritalin. Remember when you went to that doctor who said you had ADHD because you couldn't focus?"

"The one who also thought I was bipolar? Because I was always showing up for appointments altered by a different substance? Yep. He was a genius."

"You didn't fill the prescription, but I did. I thought it would work miracles with my focus. And it did, I guess. I definitely concentrated on different ways to get my school-work done without actually having to do it."

"Aw, Nan."

"But then the prescription ran out. So I went to Troy."

"That bastard is –"

"He wouldn't sell to me. Or give it for free. Or write my papers, though one of his brothers does that on the side. His family is even worse than ours. But he did" – she looks down, then up at me, reddening – "ask me out. No judging. That Alice is a million times more of a badass than Troy will ever be."

"That I'll give you."

"My brother's in lo-ove."

"I sure am. And, as always, I've got better taste than you-oo."

There's a pounding on the door.

Nan jumps like an overbred Chihuahua.

Really got to knock it off with these dog comparisons.

"Bet that's your girl," Nan says, giving my shoulder a shove.

"Nan . . ." I look down at my scotch-y jeans, my black T-shirt that smells like cigarette smoke, my bitten nails. "The last time I saw her I was a total jackass."

More pounding on the door.

"Go down before she gets the battering ram." Nan opens the bedroom door, shooing me out.

But when I swing open the front door, with its wreath covered with smiling pumpkins, it isn't Alice after all.

It's Samantha, all flushed, hair messy, Hodges uniform with its little plaid skirt rumpled, beret caught in a tangle of her blond hair.

"Everyone said you wouldn't come here but I – oh, Tim. Alice told me. It'll be okay. Thank God you're all right."

She throws her arms around my neck, in what may be a hug but is more like a choke hold.

Then she steps back, holding my arms just above the elbows, scanning me over. "You *are* all right, aren't you? It's like everyone's gone crazy tonight. My mother's

freaking out –"

"About me?"

"No, because I did what you said, told Alice to go nuclear – but Alice is panicking about you –"

"Is she okay?"

"She started to really stress out. But she calmed down. She's out looking for you. We all are. I mean, Jase, Alice, me, Andy and a squadron of her friends. Mom's home with Cal and the phone. George is drawing up missing posters. He's scared. But you're okay. Jeez, Tim."

"Great, *George* knows?"

"You're not someone who can disappear without people taking notice."

"Neither are you," says a small voice from behind me, and Samantha's arms loosen; she moves aside to look past me, toward my sister, hesitating on the stairs.

"Nan." Sam sounds apprehensive, and damn right since Nan still looks like Pogo the Evil Clown.

Nan holds up a hand, silent, waves it a little, like she's returning the half wave Samantha gave her back at Hodges, weeks ago.

Sam's phone blasts "Life on Mars."

"God, it's Mom. No matter what's going on, her drama always has to be the biggest one."

Nan sort of snorts, but not rudely. "Remember what your sister always said? 'Grace Reed: the bride at every wedding, the corpse at every wake.'"

"I'd totally forgotten that," Sam says.

"I remember a lot of things," Nan offers.

"Can you two, like, hug or whatever? I have to get to Alice."

Halfway to the beach, there he is, loping along, hands in pockets, head down. I pull over, call his name. "Get in!"

Tim breaks into a smile when he sees me, but it leaves his face just as fast. He pulls at the collar of his sweatshirt, folds his arms.

"Are you okay?" I climb out of the car. He steps farther off, but I grab his sleeve. "Tim, talk. It's me. Everything all right?"

"Nope. Sorry I was such an asshole, Alice."

"No, I shouldn't have fallen back on facts and genetic explanations. I should have just done this." My hands are around his back, my face against his chest. There's a shuddering breath against my cheek, almost a sob. He bends down and I tip up, touch my lips to his, which open, warm and welcoming, tasting faintly of root beer. He rests one palm against the back of my head, the other skimming down to my waist.

It's only when I pull back for air that I detect it – this smoky, slightly medicinal odor –

I swallow hard.

Tim gives a rueful smile. "Yup. That's exactly what you think it is."

I absorb this; choke back anything I might say.

"I only applied it externally. You know what, though? I'm thinking it's not really the best signature scent for me. I need something more musky, with some notes of leather and saddle soap."

"You didn't drink."

"Got way closer than I had any business doing. But no."

I hesitate for a minute or two outside the church basement door. Not only do I reek of scotch, I no doubt look like a mess in every other way. I stand there, remembering how when I first started coming to meetings, back at the beginning with Mr. Garrett, I'd pause in the parking lot and straighten my shirt and comb my hair and shit, like my mom would have done if I really were heading to church. Like I had to look so pulled together outside because I was such a hot mess inside. After a couple viewings of this, Mr. Garrett laughed, took the comb out of my hands. "The official photographer isn't here today, Tim. AA is strictly come as you are."

Yeah, no judging here. As I told my ma – that's why I need the strangers.

Chapter Forty-three

The lights are all on in the Garrett house when I get home, and I can see Mrs. Garrett pacing back and forth in front of the kitchen window, baby in her arms. Cal. Joel's motorcycle slant-parked near the house. Jase's tall figure balancing a gallon of milk on his shoulder moving through the room. Duff and Harry and George sitting on the steps with ice-cream sandwiches.

And there's Alice. Cross-legged outside my door, waiting, with this little red-and-blue box in her hands, flipping it up in the air, catching it.

Then she catches my eye, stands up and comes down the steps.

I spread my hands, *here I am*, and she comes closer, takes one hand, folds my fingers around the box. E-Z-Gene at-home DNA testing.

"You don't have to do it," she says. "But it's one way to be sure. If you put a rush on it, it only takes two days."

"For our next anniversary, you can just get me a tie," I say, sitting down heavily on the steps, and flipping over the

box to read the instructions.

◦ ◦ ◦ ●

I mail the swabbed cell samples – scraped from the inside of my cheek, then Cal's, the next morning, expedited delivery, return receipt requested. Everything but accompanied by armed guards. After I hand it to the postal clerk, I have to fight every impulse I have not to snatch it back from him.

E-Z-Gene my ass. This is the hardest test I've ever taken.

"Bright side," Tim says, saluting me with his coffee cup as I polish off the last of my vegan burrito, bright and early at Garrett's Hardware the next day. He snags my hand just as I'm about to lick the last bit of guacamole off my index finger, and does it himself, looking at me underneath his eyelashes. "You wanted sink-in time. We've both got forty-eight hours. At least."

"Look, about that sink-in stuff," I say. "I never thought – ever – good riddance or bye bye baby or anything like that"

"Forget I said that. You were right anyway. Fuck the self-pity. I was just being a –"

"Whatever happens, Tim . . . it just . . . happens. I'll deal. We'll deal. As long as you don't go charging off to bathe in scotch."

"Deal. As long as you don't go facing down Grace without backup again. When I asked Sam if she'd be your ace in the hole, I didn't think you'd be going there without me."

"It had to be between me and Grace. You would just have been a distraction. I think she sort of has a thing for you."

"Christ, no. She just recognizes a fellow amoral person. One of her tribe."

"You remind me of myself." God. There aren't enough showers to wash that off me.

"We need to talk about choices, Alice," Dad says.

I look up sharply from the floor, where I'm once again packing things – Dad's about to be dismissed from rehab.

His tone is serious. I know what this is all about. Mom walked into Garrett's during lunch, catching Tim and me kissing, yet again. She didn't say anything, just offered to take Cal because she was headed to the playground with Patsy and George. But there's no doubt Dad heard about it.

"Look. I know what I'm up against here – I'm not flying blind. He's got a long road ahead of him and a lot of growing up to do – he's draped in red flags – I know that – and if he starts drinking or whatever again, all bets are off. I'm not walking that road. Well, not hand in hand with him. I'll be there, of course, because he's – he's worth

it, but I won't be moving into the garage apartment with a baby and a drunken teenage boy, if that's what you're afraid of. I can look out for myself, Dad, I do, first and foremost – you guys know that –"

"While reassuring, Alice, that's not what we need to talk about. We'll get to that later."

"Oh." *What else have I done?* "If it's about the –"

Dad holds up a hand. "About the what, Alice? The store? Your schoolwork? Taking care of your brothers and sisters? Holding the fort down? Going up against Grace Reed? All the battles you're fighting? On how many different fronts? That's without any personal life of your own, plus whatever is going on with –"

"The recovering alcoholic high school dropout teenage father I'm in love with?"

He smiles. "Let's just call him Tim. Yes, except for that and whatever comes or doesn't come of it – none of these battles are yours to fight."

I open my mouth to argue and he stares me down. "None of them," he repeats gently. "No exceptions."

"But that's ridiculous, Dad. I'm, I'm one of us – that's who I am. When something happens to my family –"

"Al – yes, you are. But that's not all you are. And it's time for you to be Alice, not the standard bearer for your family. You can give that job back to your mother and me."

I'm hovering on a tightrope, somewhere between a relief so great that my breath comes out in a whoosh, and

441

a totally lost feeling. This has been my fight. This is my job. Looking at Dad's steady green eyes, calm as they've always been, I shake my head.

"Dad – I have to do this. I'm supposed to do this."

"No, Alice. You're not. You didn't choose to have a large family. Your mother and I did. But this isn't the eighteenth century. We didn't decide to have you to be our workforce on the farm, or at the store."

"You didn't decide to get hit by a car –"

"And you weren't driving that car. This" – he moves one hand slowly down from his eyes, past his ribs, down the length of his body – "is a setback, and a pain in the ass. But it's all temporary. I'm a jock. I understand recovery time, when to push myself, when not to. You can let go of that."

Tears are jabbing at my eyes now, prickles of heat. I blink, swallow. "I know. I mean, I'm not giving up my life forever and ever. Just until things are on an even keel at home."

"When will that be, honey? When I'm all better? When the new baby is born? When Jase goes to college? When George and Patsy do? When the new baby is doing the solar system project? There's never going to be an even keel. It's a matter of constant adjustment. And that's just fine. I wouldn't recognize it any other way."

"But Dad –"

He puts his hand on my arm, shakes his head. "Speaking of balance, give me those." He indicates the

442

crutches, propped against the wheelchair with all the other apparatus of injury – the walker, the reacher, the quad cane. One tucked under an arm, he swings to a stand, grabs the other, walks a few steps, pivots, slide-walks back to the bed, sits down, looks at me, raising one eyebrow. He's whiter than my nurse shoes and sweating more than Jase during practice. And he's walking.

"Dad," I say, that word that means everything.

"Nothing to it," he says, completely out of breath. "By the time the new baby is walking, I'll be running wind sprints – if not well before. Pass me that reacher thing, if Harry hasn't broken it again."

I hand it to him, resolutely ignoring the fact that he's gasping for air. He hooks it into the handle of the bedside table drawer. Pulls. It clatters to the ground. I hand it back to him. This time, he pulls the drawer slowly out, then, winded, holds up a hand, breathing hard for a moment. Flash of Tim running on the beach at the end of the summer.

"Get me what's on top, 'kay?"

What's on top are two packages, both wrapped in construction paper, art by George. I recognize the troop of Garrett stick figures on one, accompanied by various pets, some of which we don't actually own, like a centaur and a whale shark. "The little one first."

The little one is covered with drawings too – a bucket, a broom –

I look up. "I never saw myself as Cinderella slaving away, Dad. I've done all this gladly —"

"And dutifully, and resentfully, and impatiently, and lovingly, and many other ways, Alice. I know. Open the little package."

Crackle of paper, and the Kleenex-wrapped contents drop into my hand — a cardboard heart with a gold star in the center, hanging from a twist of dark yellow pipe cleaner. Dad reaches for it and holds it up. "George does good work. Lean over."

"It's a —"

He attaches it to the front of my shirt, only pricking me with the safety pin once. "Your purple heart, Alice. Well done. You're discharged."

Tears hot on my face, so many, they're dripping off my chin. I put my hand over the heart, then my arms around Dad, my wet cheek against his sweaty, stubbly face. "I'm almost afraid to look in the second box."

His big hand comes up, rubs the back of my neck. "Oh, that? It's Godiva chocolates. The closest we could get to bonbons. Now go, lie back and eat them while everyone else is at the game and the house is quiet. As close to an even keel as we're going to get."

For the next two days — forty-eight hours — Cal gets a taste of what it's like to be a Garrett.

Mr. Garrett gets released from Maplewood, the deal being that he'll do daily physical rehab at Live Oaks Center for Living, the best PT place around, according to Alice the research queen.

"Doesn't that place cost an arm and a leg?" Joel asked as he, Jase, Samantha, Alice, and I pounded the last nails into the hastily constructed ramp for the Garretts' front steps – a bitch to build, but everyone but me got all stubborn about it and insisted it was a DIY project and not a call-in-a-professional one. Even when Joel put his foot through one of the floorboards.

"Not Dad's, in this case," Alice answers with a Cheshire Cat smile.

"Worth every penny," Sam agrees, sucking on her thumbnail, which she kept whacking with the hammer until Jase pried it out of her hands. "Every pound of flesh."

So the afternoon we bring him home, we've raked up all the leaves in the Garretts' yard, and the younger kids jump into them and make sure all that sweaty work is shot to hell. Joel lights up the coals in one of those copper fire-pit things. Mr. Garrett whistles for the kids and tells them all to find sticks. Everyone abandons the leaves, and piles sticks on sticks on sticks, so the coals get smothered and have to be relit.

"Do the honors, Duff?" Mr. Garrett calls. "Use the extra-long matches, you little firebug."

"He always gets to light the fire! I never do!" Harry groans.

"You're seven. You have years of pyromania ahead of you." Jase claps him on the back, pulling him farther away from the leaping flames.

Mrs. Garrett stretches out a blanket on the grass and Cal kicks the air and grins while we grill hot dogs and burgers and Patsy climbs into my lap with extreme firmness, planting her butt like she's hoping to grow roots. Every time I look at Cal, she claps her hands on my cheeks and turns my face away. Afterward, I put on the pussy front pack – Cal can look outward in it now – while everyone plays freeze tag. All these games I would have thought were completely lame – aren't. Patsy, however, hates the kid in the front pack thing a lot.

"No!" she bellows at me, pointing her finger accusingly. "No no no, Hon. Off boy!" She hisses at Cal. A sharp crease in my heart for a moment. Deep breath, it's gone. Thirty-six hours left still. Don't have to think about it now. Not yet.

If life is fair, Cal will get this. To be close to something like this. "You're not toasting," Alice says, sitting down thigh to thigh with me and indicating the packs of marsh-mallows, graham crackers, and Hershey's bars Sam just donated to the cause.

"Go. 'Way. Bye-bye, you," Patsy tells her, not willing to compete further for my affections. "Mines."

"No." Alice fixes her with her fiercest glare. "Mines."

Patsy looks disconcerted and begins to suck on her knuckles.

"No marshmallows?" Alice repeats to me, taking a bite of one, chewing.

"*This* is the moment where I say something about you being sweet enough?"

"This is the moment when I tell you that moment doesn't actually exist."

I check around, on the lookout for disapproving stares. None. Barely any attention at all, except from Patsy, dividing her glare between Alice and Cal.

So I bring Alice closer, kissing the corner of her lips, then her eyebrows, then returning to her mouth, holding on tight, until Cal gives a furious (and breathless) squawk from between us. Pulling away, I look over Alice's shoulder, catch Mr. Garrett's eye, feel the blood rush to my face. Mrs. G. is one thing, but him? But all he does is give me a quick smile, then turn his attention back to the fire.

"No shotgun, I guess," I say.

Alice rolls her eyes. "Dad won't be building an extension to the house just for us, but no, no shotgun."

"Hey, no problem. We've got the luxury apartment. The tent can be our summer home."

That night, the second we're inside the apartment, the sky outside opens up and there are torrents of hard rain, the

heavy-fall, near-nor'easter kind. The windows look like they're surrounded by gray curtains, the sheets of water are so thick. Thunder rumbles. Alice holds Cal against her shoulder while I slam windows shut.

"Looks as though I'm stuck here."

It's twenty feet to her house, but I agree, "It *is* coming down pretty hard."

She sits on the couch, kicking off her flats, pulling her knees up under the skirt of her dress, resting Cal against them.

The rain's like white noise in the background, occasional flashes of lightning and low growls of thunder.

"You never dated at all, Tim?" Alice asks, flexing her toes. She has a little silver ring on one with a turquoise stone. I slide my own foot against it.

"Nope. That would have taken too much focus."

She shakes her head, looking at me. She's got a fireball in her mouth and one cheek is bulging like a chipmunk's with a nut. "Mmm-hhh." She takes the fireball back out, holding it delicately between thumb and forefinger. "How can you stand these? My mouth is on fire."

I edge closer, bumping her thigh with my knee. "I like to play with fire."

Alice casts her eyes to the ceiling but then tips her forehead to mine. She smells like heat and cinnamon.

"They're showing all three *Evil Dead* movies back to back. Want to hang out and watch 'em?"

Her face lights up. "I love *The Evil Dead*! Got popcorn?"

No, I do not, since I'm shopping impaired. So Alice runs through the rain back to the Garretts', coming back with a few bags of Paul Newman's Best shielded under a yellow slicker.

She comes in, slamming the door loudly, waking up the kid. He squawks and Alice apologizes, but it's fine. I feed him his bottle while Alice heats popcorn in the microwave.

He finally crashes, resting against the crease of the couch to one side of me, and Alice puts her head in my lap, kicking out to the other side. Only a little while ago, none of this would have happened to me. I would never have spent time with a girl, much less one I was into, without doing more than curling my fingers in her hair. I wouldn't have known to keep one hand on a baby so he wouldn't roll over and fall off the couch. I wouldn't have felt content just listening to the rain and being there. I didn't even know what content was.

Chapter Forty-four

The next day's a school day for most of the Garretts; Mr. and Mrs. G. head off to Live Oaks for the first sessions, George and Patsy along for the ride. Cal and I have already been out with Jase, tossing papers. Alice has class all day, but comes up to say good-bye, stays so long she's almost late and has to scramble, rushing around the apartment trying to chug coffee, pull her sweater back on and rebrush her hair, which I've completely messed up. Cal belly-laughs at her from beneath his baby-gym thing and she tosses the dead duck toy at my head while I do bent rows with Joel's weights.

It's all good until things get quiet. Too quiet.

That's when you hit a meeting, and I do, then get coffee with Jake and walk on the beach. But it's cold and windy there, the sky harsh gray, this edge of winter in the air, even though it's only October. Where will Cal have Christmas?

Plus, I'm supposed to have my freaking life solved by then, according to Pop's line in the sand . . . this huge abyss at first – but nothing compared to now, to what I'm about

to find out "with just a few EZ clicks to access paternity results."

Make a list:

1. Deal with GED. I took the test last weekend, without taking a prep test online, but I figured the real thing would be a good warm-up. I think I'm still screwing up on the math portion, even though I've got language arts, science, and social studies nailed.

2. Check out local community colleges, course credits, and daycare. Maybe I can transfer from two-year to four-year when he's a little older. If that's the way it goes.

3. Talk to Ben Christopher. Grace Reed's opponent in the state senate election is a good guy. A shoo-in for the November election since she dropped out. And I actually liked politics before I realized I had to sell my soul if I was on board with Grace.

Oh, screw and all the numbers that follow. It's too quiet, except the noise in my head.

Even if he's not mine . . . maybe I could adopt him?

Yeah, because I look fantastic on paper.

Maybe my parents could . . .

Right. Give Cal a shot at being No One with the Nowhere Man. Not going to happen.

Maybe the Garretts could . . .

Then I'd get to see him all the time but have a safety net against screwing up.

Like they need a tenth kid.

∘ ₒ ∘ •

Lunchtime at Hodges. Maybe she'll have her phone on.

"Nan. Come over? I can't be alone."

"I only have PE this afternoon. I can skip it."

"Spoken like a good delinquent. Thanks."

"I'm trying to own it." My twin's voice is so loud in my ear, it's like she's already in the room. "Besides, I have something for you to take a look at."

"Something" turns out to be the *Ellery Epogee,* last year's yearbook, which Nan somehow unearthed from my room. Alex Robinson must have known someone on the staff and worked the connection, because he's freakin' everywhere, but mostly as another little, white, prepped-out face in an interchangeable crowd. In his best close-up, in the Ellery newspaper office, settling back in a chair, all chiseled jaw and incisive stare, Hester's standing next to him like she's his secretary or office page or something.

"I don't know," Nan says slowly, holding up the year-

book close to Cal's face.

"He's so little, Timmy. His features are so . . . soft. He could be anyone's baby. Yours, Alex's, Leonardo DiCaprio's . . ."

"I think we can safely eliminate the King of the World."

Cal makes one of his little spastic jerky movements with his hands, clenching and unclenching his fists, but staying asleep. "Can I hold him?" Nan whispers.

She drops the *Ellery Apogee* and curls the baby into her lap, awkwardly. I hover my hand nearby to fix the way she's holding him, then let it drop to my side. Not going to be one of those control-freak dads.

If I am a dad.

Nan whispers, "Dad won't help with Cal, you know. He just won't. Unless you do go for adoption. Mom . . . maybe. She said she might come by later. But, Tim? My heart hurts every time I think what you'll need to do to keep this baby. I know I couldn't do it. Wouldn't even *want* to."

"You'd feel different if he was yours," I say. Then get that twist, stab, burn in my stomach. Because who knows.

"Hellooo. Hell-ooo-oo," calls a voice.

No knock, still, for Ma. "Everyone decent?"

An odd question since I'm here with my twin sister, but trying to figure Ma out is like trying to read fortunes at the bottom of a beer can. "Door's open," I call. Ma bustles in with a cardboard box of stuff and several bags

from the Christmas Tree Shop. Oh help. "Here, let me get that." I take the box from her. It's got tons of baby stuff in it – books and stuffed animals and this seat with elastic attached at each sides. It's pink.

"I could only find Nan's bouncy swing," Ma tells me. "Now that I remember, I think you wrecked yours somehow. But I found some of your old things and washed them all – except the books, of course."

She reaches into the box and pulls out the bouncy thing, glancing around. "It has to hang in a doorway." She walks over to the bedroom door and reaches for the frame, bending apart this clamp to try to attach it. But she's way too short to reach, so I go over and take it from her.

"You have to latch it around the wood and make it really secure," she instructs. After a few minutes of wrestling, I get the clamp attached securely. Ma immediately grabs Cal and sits him in it. He looks stunned and instantly face-plants on the little tray in front.

"Ma, maybe he's a little young for that. And you know he might not be staying long."

Like the kid's a hotel guest with an undetermined check-out date.

"No, he's holding his head up fine now, aren't you?" she says in a high-pitched voice. His forehead scrunches up like he's trying to figure Ma out. Good luck with that, kid. Then he pushes his feet against the floor. The chair bobs up and down. He does it again and beams at us.

Ma smiles back at him. I wonder if she was like this with me and Nan when we were babies. She looks . . . relaxed. Calm, almost. Happy?

Because Dad's got the adoption under control and this is all short-term?

"Ma, I might not have him for much longer . . ." I say again.

Less than twenty-four hours now.

"We shall see what we shall see," she says enigmatically. "Look what else I brought. This was your favorite book when you were little. *Busy Timmy*." She hands me a little yellow book with a redheaded kid on the cover. Since he's like, three or something, I can only hope Timmy wasn't busy with the sorts of things I got busy with in later years.

Nan starts giggling. Cal's now actually bouncing, pushing his legs down and bobbing in the air higher and higher.

"I bought him some clothes too," Ma tells me. "Yours were pretty much all stained, so I don't have many hand-me-downs from you."

Yup, there's a theme here. I trashed my bouncy swing and my wardrobe. Soon she'll tell me I wrecked hotel rooms and smashed toy guitars.

"You could even coordinate your outfits."

Uh, hell no. "Thanks, Ma. This was . . . this was awesome of you to do."

She blinks at me for a second, her face startled, then

says briskly, "Well . . . naturally. He's just a baby. He can't help how he got here, can you, Calvin?" She has that sing-song voice. Cal's into it, though. He pauses in his bouncing and gives her his smile, then goes back to hopping up and down and up and down.

"He pretty much got here the usual way, Mommy," calls Nan from the kitchen.

"Nanette Bridget! We don't need to discuss that sort of thing. You both know what I mean. The sins of the fathers shouldn't be visited on the innocent."

As it turns out, Ma has also brought food, some big sticky-roll type things. They have about eight cups of sugar in a single bite, but they taste good with the coffee Nan's made. Cal bounces and beams at us, and we eat. It feels like we're family. Surreal.

Chapter Forty-five

Hester being Hester, she doesn't leave me be in my bubble-world with Cal and the good stuff. She texts:

NOT COMFORTABLE WITH THE WAY WE LEFT THINGS.

UNDERSTAND THAT YOU'RE ANGRY BUT THERE ARE TWO SIDES TO THIS.

WANT TO HAVE A CONVERSATION LIKE ADULTS.

After the last one, I text back, totally misspelling because I'm furious. **Is that what we air? Not seenin huge maternity level going on here.**

The phone immediately rings as Alice is coming in the door with Chinese food.

"I am his mother," Hester says in a low, trembling voice. "You don't have the right to act like you have all the power here. Maybe you don't have any at all."

I slam the phone down.

Call Hester back. Apologize. Alienating her is stupid.

Twelve hours or so left, if there wasn't some lab disaster or

it didn't get lost in the mail on the way.

° • ° •

Go to three meetings on Tuesday and that takes up four hours, when you count in travel time to and from (which I do).

Take Mr. Garrett to physical therapy and a meeting afterward. Five hours.

Alice catches me checking my computer and drags me into the shower. Don't know how much time that takes up because it's not long enough, even though the hot water comes to an end long before we do. We use up two bars of soap, though.

"You don't actually have to do this, you know. No one's making you," Nan offers. We're chowing down on ice cream at Doane's, downtown in Stony Bay. Nan's got some god-awfully large banana-split type thing, and I'm all about the chocolate and coffee double scoop.

"Good thing, right? If someone was trying to make me, I definitely wouldn't do it." I position Cal, who's slumped on my lap, away from Doane's biggest draw, Vargas, the candy-corn-attacking robot-chicken. He gave me nightmares when I was little, worse ones when I was tripping. Cal keeps peeping around my shoulder, letting

458

loose a blood-curdling yell, hiding, then peeping again.

Nan points with her spoon. "Seriously, no court is ordering a test. If you wind up keeping him, if you don't have to prove parentage for some adoption deal, what does it matter?"

"*Raaah!*"

"*Shh.* Just don't look, Cal. You were the freaking snake in the Garden of Eden about this, Nano. All 'he could be anyone's baby'. . . Now I'm not supposed to find out? Besides, it's too late. They'll send an email tonight. Or tomorrow."

She stirs her ice cream, reducing it to a mud-colored soup. "You could delete it. Without reading it."

But the thing is? I couldn't. The voices that have told me to make things easier on myself or avoid the truth – they've always lied to me.

"Congratulations! It's that E-Z! Double click on the link and follow our instructions to get the facts on your paternity relationship!!"

Two exclamation points, seriously? They're awfully cheery about this.

My mouse hovers over the link.

Then I push it away, off my mouse pad. Turn off the monitor.

I'm alone in the apartment, except for Cal, who's crashed at the moment.

Jase is at school. Nan too. I could text and ask either of them to ditch – but that seems like bad karma.

I could take it over to the Garretts', sit down with Mr. and Mrs. G.

I could even call Hester, since this involves her just as much as me. Maybe a whole lot more.

Meh. Or maybe not.

I move the mouse into position again. Move it down the screen. Click. Click again.

∘ ₀ ∘ ●

The apartment's dark and cold when I get in, at almost eleven o'clock at night. "Tim?"

No answer.

He's fast asleep, curled on his side, Cal tucked against him. Tim doesn't stir, but Cal's eyes open and he stares at me. I rest my hand on his red curls.

"Good news," Tim says, his voice thick with sleep. "He's yours."

I laugh quietly. "And?"

"Don't know yet." His hand catches mine. "I thought I might need a shoulder and his is not quite up to the job."

"Very broad shoulders here," I offer, sitting down on the bed beside him. "Freakishly, really. Joel used to tell me I'd make a great linebacker."

"But I *am* officially a high school graduate. Passed the

GED test . . . so there's that."

I'm kissing him and saying it's great − and it is − and he stops me, fingers on my lips. "I need to just do it, don't I, Alice?"

I nod.

"Just do this," he repeats, slides up to a sitting position next to me, pulling Cal with him, standing up, moving to the computer. "One click. Simple. E-Z."

He settles in the chair, shakes the mouse so the blue screen lights up.

His hands slide under the baby's armpits. Cal strains toward him. Tim rests his forehead against the baby's. Takes a breath. Hands Cal to me.

"Want me to do it? You can hold him and I'll −"

He shakes his head, clicks on the line, reads out loud: "E-Z Gene, the finest and least expensive OTC paternity kit offers you blah, blah, blah . . . the analysis seeks matches of the allele number values between the alleged father and child . . . you can be included as father with as few as one allele match . . . exclusion involves . . . Jesus Christ, where's the link?"

He clicks, shuts his eyes, opens them.

I close my own.

Silence.

"Did you look?"

Silence.

"Tim?"

461

Chapter Forty-six

It's not babysitting if it's your own child.

"I guess –" Swallow once. Again. "I was babysitting. After all."

I'm reaching for Cal, and Alice's eyes are all shiny with tears. Beautiful colors in those eyes. I'm wiping at them with the edge of Cal's blanket. He's grabbing at the other edge and trying to stick it in his mouth.

"Raaah?" Now he's reaching for my nose.

That little wrinkle between his eyebrows, those worried lines, just like mine.

But obviously not mine.

I put my thumb against them anyway, smooth them out.

"Shhh, Cal. You're good. I'm here."

More tears running down Alice's face, but at least she's not sobbing out loud. I keep mopping at them with the corner of this navy blanket, one of the few things I bought for him, along with the dead duck toy, to replace Hester's many modes of sock monkeys.

If Hester keeps Cal – which she has a right to do and

I . . . I . . . don't – I won't be able to protect him from the stupid monkeys anymore. I won't be able to protect him from anything

Alice hands me the baby, turns away for a minute, wiping her eyes. Cal wiggles closer and I hold him, maybe too firmly, judging by the angry squeak.

Then somehow I'm on the bed with Alice facing me, the kid in between, and her arms around both of us and it would be good to throw up or cry or do something now, but nothing's coming.

Grateful for Alice's silence. Glad she isn't saying she's sorry. That her arms around me are enough. Almost everyone I know would say something. I can hear all the voices.

Nan: Oh, Timmy. I knew there was something not right about this. But you don't have to tell anyone . . .

Jake: You find your family in unexpected places.

Ma: This little one can't help how he got here.

Pop: You're well out of that disaster. You couldn't have handled it anyway.

Jase, Samantha, Mr. and Mrs. Garrett: We're here.

Dominic: C'mon over. I'll teach you how to take apart the engine of a Harley and put it back together again. That you can control.

Waldo: Blowing in the wind through the long strange trip it's been.

Hester: I had no choice. Now we can both move on.

"So," I say.

Alice takes a deep breath, but stays quiet, tightening her arms around us.

"I can cross both 'Most likely to never graduate from high school' and 'Most likely to be a teen father' off the list. Efficient, right?"

"Leave room to write in 'Most likely to get it right in the end,'" Alice says.

So, *that's* when the goddamn tears kick in.

Chapter Forty-seven

Time, which was dragging its ass like hell when I waited for E-Z-Gene to come through, is now on fast-forward.

So, no, Hester's not going to keep the baby. Cal. Who I guess is Calvin from now on. Or whatever name his new parents come up with. Waldo, and this adoption lady Pop found, and Pop – who is no longer technically in a position of authority here, but who never lets that slow him down – big picture – are meeting in Waldo's living room, and Hester and I are ordered to get snacks or make tea or just stay out from underfoot. After all the "be a man" stuff, we're supposed to be good kids and do as we're told.

Old Alex Robinson has to sign off on the "Affidavit of Paternity" now that he's done his own E-Z test and found out all his alleles are where they should be in order to claim Cal as his kid. Which he has to do so he can go through more legal stuff to "Renounce Paternity" once the adoption is under way. Is it me or is this effed up? Like marrying someone so you can divorce them.

But Alex has no problem with all this, except that he has

some exams coming up and needs to get his wisdom teeth removed, so he's doing it all long-distance, since that works out better for his schedule.

Better for his health too, really.

Dick.

"I wish it had been you – if that helps," Hester says now.

I nod, say thanks, although it actually doesn't make much difference one way or another what she thinks or wishes or wants.

To the last, "I just don't get you," will be Hester's and my theme song.

Kind of like me and Pop.

As we were walking into Hester's this morning, he pulled me aside for a second. "Er . . . Tim."

Then, of course, the requisite cell phone check, looking off into the distance thing. Finally. "It's . . . good that you have the ability to admit that this is not your mess to clean up and to walk away. That shows maturity."

He looked me in the eye then, with this expression I don't think I've ever seen on his face, like he was actually waiting to hear what I had to say.

The weird thing? Got nothin'.

I've thought, all this time, that it would mean a lot if he could say he was proud of me. This was as close to that as it's probably going to get. But – it's like getting a prize in a contest you didn't enter. Because actually, Pop, what showed maturity was my *not* walking away.

"If I'd known what I know now," Hester says, "I would have had you with me in the delivery room."

There's an opportunity missed.

"I'm sorry you ended up getting hurt," she adds. "I never meant to do that. Even though having you around in this made me feel much less . . . alone, if I had it to do over again, I wouldn't have gotten you involved."

"I wouldn't want that," I say.

She's concentrating on making coffee, measuring out the grounds in this methodical, scientific way, but when I say this she looks up, studies my face. "You really wouldn't, would you? If I could go back in time, I couldn't say the same."

My automatic Hester-fury, that anger that comes out with her so damn easily, hovers, then recedes. For the first time, I think it's a damn good thing Cal is going to be adopted. Neither his mother nor his real father wants him. He'll never have to know that.

"So strange," she adds. "There were moments in this whole thing when I thought . . . it would make things better if you and I were a couple. That it wouldn't be this embarrassing 'teen mom' story if that happened. But you didn't fall in love with me. You fell in love with Cal. You really were . . . are . . . his father. In all the ways that mattered."

Here's where I should probably – hug her or something.

"Yeah, um, thanks. Hester. I know this – all of this – sucked ass for you. I'm –"

Sorry? That sticks in my throat. Fuckin' Alex Robinson should be the one spitting that out.

She's looking up at me with those big question-mark eyes, just like Cal's – she's *his* mother – and I lick my lips, swallow, find the words. "I wish things had gone the way you planned. I hope they do from now on."

For a second, my hands hover at her shoulders – my old problem: what do I do with my hands? A questions I didn't have to ask when they were full of Cal.

I didn't know what I was doing when I first got him. I didn't understand how he worked at all. By the time I handed him back, I knew. I knew what cry was hungry, angry, tired, lonely. I knew when he needed something to hold in his hand or to put in his mouth. I knew when to hold him and when to put him down. Maybe it isn't that Pop didn't try those things with me – maybe I was just always at some frequency he couldn't turn his dial to. Not his fault, and not my own. I'm lucky that wasn't me and Cal. I would have missed a lot. And I'll take missing him, for a long time or even forever, over having missed that.

"Hester, we need you in here," that Mrs. Crawley calls, poking her head into the kitchen. "Hello, Timothy. You're still here? We're all set – you're free to go."

Back to my normally scheduled life.

Epilogue

"Yours to command. Where's this mysterious place you wanted us to go?" Tim asks, rubbing his hands together because, of course, no gloves. The car heat's on, but the window's open, and he has to raise his voice to be heard over the swish of the tires.

"Would it be mysterious if I told you? Just go left when I say and right when I say."

"As you wish."

I planned this – rehearsed it – the way I used to do with my "It's been great fun but we're done" kiss-offs. But still. For most of the drive to McNair Beach, I look down at my gloves, pull them off, push at my cuticles, unzip and rezip my coat, fiddle with the heat. When I start drumming my fingers on my leg, Tim puts his hand over them. "Alice, what's going on?"

I swallow.

"Do I have to dare you? Say it."

I squint over at him, then back down at our hands, the knob of his wrist bone, his slightly chapped knuckles.

Finally: "I deferred Nightingale Nursing again. Take this right, here."

Tim glances at me, frowning. "But, but – you accepted. You were in, you were set –"

For the first time since I made the call, a stall, hitch of my breath.

But . . . Yes.

"Still set. I just told them I'd see them next fall."

"Are . . . are you doing this . . . Who are you doing this for, Alice?"

"For me. Look, it just makes sense. They can't promise housing, and that's a huge deal when it's New York City – and they can't positively guarantee my student loan anymore – and this way I'll have another semester at Middlesex Community to get more experience on the floor, I'll be around for the new baby, and Dad's great but, you know, he has a ways to go, and Garrett's isn't going to run itself, so it's simply –"

"Was I a factor in this decision?"

"You were in there. "

"I was *in* there? Was it good for you too?"

"Gah, Tim."

They've cordoned off the parking lot at McNair Beach, so we park in what's basically a snowdrift right outside. You can see a sliver of ocean – barely – through the path between two high dunes, snow piled on sand, looming like the Pyramids against the pewter sky. The low-hanging

clouds, snowfall over, are lifting, giving way to muted light slanting through.

We sit there. Tim's hand still around mine. He smoothes his thumb from my knuckle down to my wrist, head ducked, ginger hair flopping onto his forehead, curling a little at the back. His lips are slightly pursed, like he's about to whistle. But, silence, doubly quiet in the winter-still hush. Just the brush of his thumb. The crinkle of his parka as he shifts a little toward me. I lean back, smile, get an answering grin, dimple deep.

"You know we have to hit the beach," I say at last.

"We do, huh? You win the race to the breakwater. I'm forfeiting."

But he climbs out of the car anyway, comes round to open my door, which takes some doing – snowdrifts and all. The snow gets into the top of my boots as we trudge along, it's higher than my knees in some places, and the wind starts rising again, whipping our hair back. Tim holds up his hand – stop – then struggles through the drifts until he's standing in front of me, bends down, pats his shoulders with the palms of his – *still* ungloved, of course – hands. I wrap my arms around his neck – "No choosing this moment to throttle me, Alice" – my legs wrap around his waist, he scooches me up onto his back, and we head toward the bay.

For a few minutes all I hear is the rustle of our parkas, Tim breathing a little hard (I loosen my grip), but then as

we get farther up the path, the roar of waves, loud in my ears. High tide. But so different from the sparkling green-blue of the summer sea. We reach the top of the bluff, the angry ocean in front of us, waves beating hard, foam churning, deeper gray than the sky, pounding against the packed sand, then the *shhh* of water drawing out to sea, dragging stones, surging forward again.

I slip off his back, take a few steps forward, and Tim snags the hood of my parka and turns me around, flush up against his coat, wet with blown snow. I expect a kiss, but instead he puts his freezing cold palms against my face and says, "I haven't been here since I was here with you. That was a good day."

"It was." I search his face. His eyes are set on me, the same intense slate color of the sky today. I smile. "It was also exactly two and a half months ago. Give or take."

"Riiiiight . . . ?" He drags the word out. Shuts his eyes for a moment. Then says, "Um. Can you cut the mystery now? Historically, girls telling me about timing like this . . . makes me . . . nervous."

"No! Not that. God, Tim. We didn't have sex on the beach that day, for God's sake."

"Well, no, but –"

"Geez, it's not that. It's just, kinda, our anniversary. Sort of."

He starts to laugh, eyebrows raised. Then his face goes serious. "I think you're pushing it, date-wise, but I know

what a sentimental fool you are. Pussycat." His face cracks into another smile, lighting the whole damn sky.

"Cut it out. Here."

I slide my hands up his arms, press the back of his neck, warm over the chill of his coat, until he leans down, exhaling a sigh against my cheek, my lips catching his, his mouth drawing away for an instant, then a sharp tang, tart and sweet; his tongue tastes like lemon drops, his latest sugar fix.

"So . . ." I whisper, catching my breath.

"Yeah. So. You know I'm not patient." His hands tighten on my back, then slip down, low on my back, lifting me higher so our faces are level and our mouths align perfectly.

"So far, I've given you a nicotine patch, some sneakers, and a paternity test. You suggested a tie for our anniversary, but I . . . I figured I owed you something more romantic."

"Alice . . . I kind of thought the whole deferring thing was, like, all the gifts for all the Christmases forever. That was plenty. But I'll . . . um . . . cherish this. Whatever it is."

I pull away from him, step back, my boots crunching on a shell beneath the snow. "I've been back here since that day we were here. Once. A few weeks ago. Thinking. I walked all the way." I point far up the beach, to where the spit of land curves.

"Impressive."

"Anyway." I unzip my parka, ignoring his lifted eyebrows, take out the contents of the inside pocket, curl my fingers

around it. It's warm from my body heat. "Anyway. I found this." I drop it into his hands, a reddish slate stone, ocean-worn, shaped roughly like a heart. "It's got this little hollow, see, and you can rub it – kind of a calming thing – when you . . . need something to do with your hands. You say you still don't always know what to do with them. And I know you're definitely *not* taking up whittling."

I finally look at his face. His lips are a little parted – also faintly chapped – his eyes as calm and . . . tender . . . as I've ever seen them.

"Thank you," he says quietly, and puts it into his pocket at the same time he leans forward for another kiss, this one just a touch of lips, potential promised, bargain sealed.

"Although I notice you didn't wrap it."

"I'm too cheap to buy wrapping paper. Besides, why hide it and make you work for it? It's coy."

Hard to believe, but true: I actually marked it on my calendar. More what Alice would do than me, but yeah, X marks the spot in December when Pop's deadline is officially up.

X for expiration date.

Which would be today.

When I made those lines on the calendar, with the only pen I could find – running out of ink, all kinds of symbolic – that's what it was: The day the ticking stopped and the

bomb went off.

Standing here now, towel on, fresh out of the shower, I do this body-check thing – part of Alice's new skills for staving off panic attacks. No wetness from my eyes, though I've been pretty much a wuss lately. No strangling tangle of barbed wire in my throat. No bomb fragments tearing through me, cluster-exploding through tissue and bone. I feel those things, sure, but not like before, not usually – not anything Grape-Nuts and having had Alice in the shower with me wouldn't help. And except for the X, this space on the calendar looks just like the others.

Just another day.

Well, except it is Christmas Eve, so there's that.

And my first visit to Cal in his new digs, so there's also that.

I guess as adoption processes go, this one went fast. Didn't seem like it to me, or to anyone probably, except Alex Robinson. I knew right away that the choice of prospective parents was right, but Hester was . . . indecisive, Waldo a little inscrutable with his advice, and Pop, who had his fingerprints all over the thing when the ball started rolling, extricated himself when my "job was done."

The more things change . . . right?

After the day I handed Cal over – which I don't want to think about, thanks – I tried to give the new family of three time to settle in so they could bond and get comfortable together and be, you know . . . family.

Lasted three spaces on the calendar – or two and a half days if I'm being completely honest. So, I'm still working on the patience thing. But, as Dominic would remind me, aren't we all?

Visiting Cal someplace that isn't the garage apartment with people who aren't me in charge of him?

Yeah.

Well.

I change my shirt three times. Seriously. Like I'm going to a fucking job interview. This is a kid who's gotten just about every body fluid there is on my shirts – even blood, 'cause as I was suiting him up on Turnover Day, he bashed his nose hard into my collarbone and got this nosebleed and this tiny bruise – so I handed the kid over looking like a prize fighter who'd lost a round.

After the shirt dilemma, I actually make a goddamn list, partly because my brain keeps doing this blank-out thing. Maybe there is a little shrapnel in there from deadline day.

1. Drop off Christmas presents to Ma, Pop, Nan. This is the first year in who-the-hell-knows that I've actually done the present thing, so I figure whatever I give is a bonus. Picture of Cal in Santa outfit for Ma. Picture of Cal and me snapped in front of Vargas the candy-corn-attacking chicken for my sister – Cal's screaming and Nan's laughing

nervously. Picture of Cal, Nan, and Ma for Pop, with card telling him to put it in his office. Because I'm still an asshole.

2. Go to a meeting. Which I'll need after this visit to my parents' house.

3. See Cal at Jake and Nate's house. It'll be fine. I've been there before, for Chrissake.

4. Then home. Christmas Eve at the Garretts'. I don't know what that even means. With luck, Alice for a sleepover? That may be pushing it, the night before Christmas, but hey.

5. Then the next few squares of the calendar, then the next calendar, which will not be the babes on bikes one Joel left behind.

I'm sort of getting a rhythm going with the whole Christmas cookie production. Okay, we're out of some things – the semi-sweet chocolate chips I bought yesterday, for example, but flexibility is key and all that.

I'm working on it.

Harry comes up behind me, grabs the spoon out of the cookie batter, and slurp-licks it all over.

"Knock it off!" is barely out of my mouth before he's rushed to the sink, spat out the batter, and started spraying water from the sink nozzle over his tongue.

"It's not that bad. That's what you get for eating raw batter!"

"Oh barf. A hundred times barf," Harry gasps out, wiping his tongue on a dishcloth.

"I'm sure it's not that bad," Mom says from her seat at the kitchen table, where she's trying to sew cotton balls onto a flesh-colored leotard, size 2T, because Patsy's a sheep in this year's church Nativity play. We had them all glued on, but Pats kept finding the costume and plucking the balls off.

"Shorn Sheep Patsy," Dad said cheerfully, when Mom unexpectedly lost her cool about this. "It'll work."

Mom wiped her eyes with the heel of her hand. "We're just lucky if she's not Rabid Coyote Patsy."

"Grrr," Patsy contributed.

Now she's butting her head against my leg saying, "Hon where?" and my cell phone is ringing (Brad – not picking up), and Duff's tried the batter and is saying, "Is this chocolate . . . or is it *excrement*?" and Jase and Joel are coming in from some sort of brother-bonding workout session with that eau de sweaty boy with a splash of coffee and an undertone of bacon.

Joel picks up one of my early cookie attempts and tosses it Frisbee-style at Jase. "Think fast."

But Jase is checking his phone and it hits him in the chest and bounces off.

"Penalty! Now you have to eat it." That's Duff, singsong.

"Hysterical, all of you," I say. "I'm going for a run. Make your own damn cookies."

At Ma and Pop's front door, ever festively decked out for Christmas with a herd of stuffed reindeer heads. Just the heads, mind you, mounted on the door, with these shiny black eyes and stuffed white antlers. Like Rudolph's revenge: the Christmas all of the other reindeer finally got what was coming to them.

Crack my knuckles, knock, only a second before I'm swept in by Hurricane Ma.

"Goodness! Don't be shivering out there – but for heaven's sake use the mat and don't tramp snow all over the good carpet."

Awkward doesn't begin to cover the five minutes I'm there, in this room with its shiny-mirror lake, open-mouthed Christmas Chorus Dolls that actually look as though they're screaming, not singing. And more pinned all over the tree.

Ma shouts, "Nanette!" and Nan comes on in – with Troy – from the kitchen, where they were, apparently, baking brownies, because why the hell not.

"For non-pharmaceutical use only, man."

Shoulders braced, fire pit back in my stomach, waiting for Ma, for Nan, to ask, or say, anything about Cal or his new parents. But they don't. Nan's hug is a little on the Heimlich maneuver side, and Ma pretty much has an aneurysm about a rip on the shoulder of my parka, but other than that, no dramarama and I'm nearly out the friggin' door and –

"Your father wants you in his study."

Fuck.

The thing is, I can just . . . not go. *You can choose where your feet take you, man.* That's Dominic again, who's like my own little Jiminy Cricket, Portuguese fisherman style.

But I go. Because, whatever.

The more things change . . .

Pictures restored to the desk, (no snails in tank though!), Pop doing a cell-phone check. It's like that stopwatch he clicked on back in August, ticking to D-day, cryogenically froze the whole exhibit.

"Yo, Pop," I say, not sitting down on the couch. "Merry Christmas."

He puts down the phone, lowers his palm, the "sit" gesture for dogs.

Do I get a treat if I do? Can already feel Bastard Tim creeping in, running through my bloodstream.

For the first time, I notice that the size of his chair positions him automatically higher than anyone on the couch. Plant myself there anyway, arms outspread along

480

the top, ankle crossed over knee.

Fine. Pop can win the Great and Powerful contest.

He clears his throat.

I clear mine. Run my finger around the inside of my collar.

Neither of us says a thing for a sec. He picks up a pen, initials something, then drums the end of the pen against the chair arm.

Tap. Tap tap tap. Tap.

"You've done what you needed to do," he says after the requisite eon.

Pop has to be the one to mention Cal?

"The college fund stays in your name. I'll keep paying your health and car insurance. The allowance ends, because you're eighteen now, but the others are yours. To keep. Merry Christmas."

I'm rising before he's even finished, right when he says "ends," and step up close to the chair. A flash in his eyes – alarm, maybe.

"Thanks," I say.

That earns me a swivel of the chair to put the phone down.

"But, I'm set. Nano can have my share to help with Columbia, if she gets in. 'Roar, Lion, Roar.' Merry Christmas."

"I thought you were done making rash decisions, Tim."

Now I'm out the office door and he's trailing me, even after I call bye to Ma and Nan – and Troy – and hit the front steps.

Snow coming down, again, the wet kind that clings to your clothes and hardens, there's this whisk of wind, and flakes blow down my collar. The trees shake, and glops of snow splat onto the street. The piles on the sides of the road are already that dirty-brown-sugar shade.

I turn to face Pop just as he skids on a patch of ice. Grab his hand to balance him. His fingers splay out, like he's still falling instead of holding on. He gets his balance back, reaches into his blazer pocket. For the cell phone? Fifty bucks? But his hand comes out empty, and he looks at it for a second, while I slide into the car, buckle up.

"Buy Nan a college education, Pop. Buy Ma a milkshake."

So, yeah, we're being given our privacy, even though no one calls it that. Jake has to stir something on the stove and his partner, Nate, is on call and must return a message or two. So it's Cal and me, me and Cal, in the living room with the big-ass Christmas tree and the menorah and glass-fronted case in the corner full of worn baseballs and old-style gloves.

As Jake leaves the room, he glances at me, then puts Cal into this saucer-type thing instead of into my arms. Maybe giving Cal back after being on the other side of the hand-

off is also hard. Already hard.

Cal fists and unfists his hands, arms out, his "pick me up" thing, says, "Bob!"

"Already forgotten my name, huh?"

His nose looks better, bruise still there. He's wearing this new outfit, like jeans and a button-down shirt, which has this big drool-oval on it. No socks, though. They're lying like roadkill near the couch. Still likes to get as naked as possible, this kid.

Sure enough, now he's trying to stuff the collar of his shirt into his mouth. I pull it out and he clamps down on my thumb with his two sharp bottom teeth. When I pull it away, he goes for my nose, chomps. "*Yow*, Cal."

"Bob," he says, muffled, because his mouth is full of nose.

Maybe that's his new name.

None of my business.

Right?

I fucking hated the name Calvin from the get-go. Now I want to tattoo it on the kid's arm so it will stay, stay, stay.

Time to go.

So I call to Jake and he comes out of the kitchen looking disheveled and pissed off.

I automatically apologize for whatever the hell I've done. He shakes his head, smiling at the floor, then at me. "What, you think I'll make you run ten times around the track the way I did when you were a mouthy middle-schooler?"

That would be easier.

Turns out he's all bent out of shape because Nate baby-proofed the burners and Jake can't figure out how to turn them on.

I kiss Cal on top of his red, fluffy head, do a swift chin-swipe drool-off with the bottom of my shirt, and hand him over like Hester used to, all speedy like he's scorching my hands, and beat it out the door with Jake trailing behind like Pop, but not.

Say the Merry Christmas thing, thank-you-for-letting-me-visit, and don't ask what they're planning to call the kid.

And then Jake asks me that very question.

"I'm, uh, fine with Calvin. Actually."

Weird look from Jake, and it turns out that the question was what do I want Cal to call me.

"Uncle Tim? Just plain Tim?" he offers.

"Whatever works, as long as it's not Bad Example Don't-Be-Like-Tim."

"As long as it's not Wait, Who's Tim?" Jake corrects, and pulls me in for a half hug, and I let him.

"Waiting for someone?" I ask around a grape Tootsie Pop – my latest addiction.

Alice flushes, sweaty at the temples, hot as hell in black ski-type pants. "Just" – *pant* – "shoveling." Halfway up one side of the driveway, she's left a cleared path, although the Bug is a hump of snow, and the van has all its scrapes and

dings frosted away.

She bites the thumb of her mitten, pulling it off, wades through the snow and takes me around the elbows, looking me in the eye.

"So? Cal? You? Jake and Nate? How'd it go?"

Just shoveling, my ass.

I wonder how long she's been out here. Her eyelashes are frosted, her lips look chapped, and she's already cleared the path to the garage steps.

Oh, Alice.

I pop the pop out of my mouth. "Well, you know. It was touching. Poignant. We all wept. Cal had made me a homemade present, since Christmas was coming. It was a used diaper, but you know, it's the thought that counts. Jake and Nate and I all gathered around the booze-free Wassail Bowl and sang 'What Child is This?' or, no, '*Whose* Child is This?' And then –"

She puts two cold fingers over my lips. "Tim. C'mon."

I shrug. It's snowing kinda hard again, and snow's piling up on her white knit hat and the shoulders of her bright red parka, her nose a little pink. Alice in Wonderland, winter style. We should go inside and warm up – something to look forward to – but instead I shove my hands into my pockets, stamp snow off my boots, then try to wrestle her for the shovel –

"Tim!"

"Yeah, Cal has this awesome room – huge – and

Jake and Nate are all jazzed, and there are eight million presents under the tree, and since the last stuffed animal I bought for the kid turned out to be a dog toy, he's coming out way the hell ahead. The whole house is already kid-proofed and shit, and all's well that ends well or whatever." I bend, shovel some snow, manage to toss a few loads of it to the side before Alice puts one foot on it and slides her re-mittened hand up my shoulder to where my pulse jumps in my neck.

"That all sounds great. Can I have the no-bullshit translation now? Or do I need to get the talking stick?"

"Same moral. He's in a good place. It's the Right Thing."

"And?"

"And it's going to suck. For a while. I'll live. Got a lot to live for, Hot Alice."

• ○ ○

At some point, I'll need to tell Alice more. About the college money, and that I'm basically broke now. But of all the "challenges" we face, I don't think there being no chance of my being her sugar daddy is going to be one of them.

So, yeah, I trail after her toward the Garretts' house. I can see Patsy at the door, her breath making this little circle on the glass, her hands – bigger starfish than Cal's –

plastered against it.

Christmas Eve at the Garretts'. Like I said, I don't know what that means.

Not Ma's special whiskey-spiked eggnog, dinner at the club, that weird a cappela group that always sings there, Nan's tense white face, some chick in green velvet that I run into and try to charm out of her pants on my way to the punchbowl or the head.

And an evening I mostly don't remember.

Things will be different tonight.

Because of the previews I've already had this winter, I know about some things – the fire, well-built because Jase built it and he's like a freaking architect with the logs. That popping sound when sparks fly out. Hot cocoa and cider. Alice in blue pajamas and this fuzzy robe that manages to be just . . . lovely on her. Harry and Duff, who have gone around with their faces red and white and sticky for the last week, candy cane junkies on a bender. That wet-dog mitten smell from wool stuff drying in front of the fire. Mr. Garrett reading these stories and doing all the voices, even if he skips huge parts that might possibly scare George.

Those other times I've sat in front of the fire at the Garretts', I've had Cal, and spent most of my time negotiating lap space with Patsy, and trying to make sure the kid didn't eat a popcorn kernel or get too close to the fire. It'll be different tonight.

They have to have a double row of stockings to fit

everyone. There's one for me too. One for Cal. We weren't sure the adoption would come off before Christmas.

But I have a feeling there would have been one there for him anyway.

Yeah, so – nothing gets lost. Cal isn't, and not just because he'll still be a little part of my life. I get to carry him with me, the way you do all your memories and mistakes. He started out a mistake I had no memory of, and he wound up being, well, my kid.

Maybe thinking any one person can show up and give you all you need is as much of a delusion as thinking you can find truth in a bottle. Maybe you can just find what you need in little pieces, in people who show up for one crucial moment – or a whole chain of them – even if they can't solve it all. Maybe this is the secret of big families, like the Garretts . . . and like AA. People's strengths can take their turn. There can be more of us than there is trouble.

ACKNOWLEDGMENTS

Every day I find more people to thank in this writing life of mine. Every letter I get from a reader, notice from a blogger, comment or question from a librarian – my gratitude is boundless. There is no way I would be here, and enjoying it so much, without the time and effort and kindness of all of you.

All of you – starting with my erudite, extraordinary editor, Jessica Dandino Garrison, who always knows what I, or my characters, love scenes, and books themselves, need before I do, and stands ready with adjectives, plot ideas, exclamations, questions – and cupcakes. Her contributions go far beyond the call of duty – she's invaluable.

And Penguin Random House in general, a mighty army at my back – Lauri Hornik, Namrata Tripathi, Dana Chidiac, Jasmin Rubero, Maya Tatsukawa, Lily Malcom, Kristen Tozzo, the awesome Tara Shanahan, and truly everyone in Sales, Marketing, Design, Managing Editorial, Production, and Sub Rights who has a hand in the life of these books. The careful, cautious, and kind Regina Castillo. So many magicians behind the scene.

Christina Hogrebe – my agent/miracle worker/thought-

ful critic/judicious story and business advisor and friend of the bosom to both me and the books. You have been, from the start, one of the best and brightest and most amazing of all my lucky breaks. Thanks are inadequate. Gratitude = endless.

The rest of the JRA team – most especially Andrea Cirillo, Meg Ruley, Rebecca Sherer, Jessica Errera, and Jane Berkey.

A huge shout-out to all the friends of Tim, who believed in this story and this boy from the get-go – my peerless Plotmonkeys: Shaunee Cole, Jennifer Iszkiewicz, Karen Pinco, and Kristan Higgins. Yes, the fabulous KH, as remarkable a friend as she is a writer – generous beyond words with her time and kindness, ever willing to crawl into the trenches with me, Tim, and Alice, and drag the good stuff out.

Friends near and far who read, listened, and supplied car suggestions, medical details, "guy" translations – particularly Alicia Thomas, whose cut-to-the core critiques made this a better book. Huge thanks to Kim and Mark Smith, Paula and Roy Kuphal, the mighty awesome Apocalypsies, and the FTHRWA critique group, particularly Ana Morgan, Amy Villalba, and the late Ginny Lester.

Of course, always, my father, my brother Ted, Leslie and Grace Funsten. Colette Corry – who spent endless hours with me and Tim. Tina Squire, friend of a lifetime.

Brian Ford – once my teacher, now my friend and fellow writer, funny, acerbic, generous and wise with his comments, critiques and questions – who never failed to say "show it to me" when I struggled over a scene, and spent almost as much time in that tent as the characters and I.

Finally, the ones who fill my every day with laughter, love, laundry, and flat-out joy, my husband, John, and K, A, R, J, D, and bookworm C – you're everything to me.

Fall in love with more books by Huntley Fitzpatrick ...

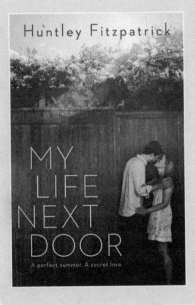

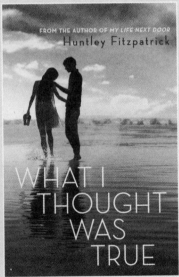